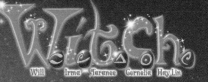

W.I.T.C.H.

Will Irma Tarance Cornelia Hay Lin

Part IX.
100% W.I.T.C.H.
Volume 1

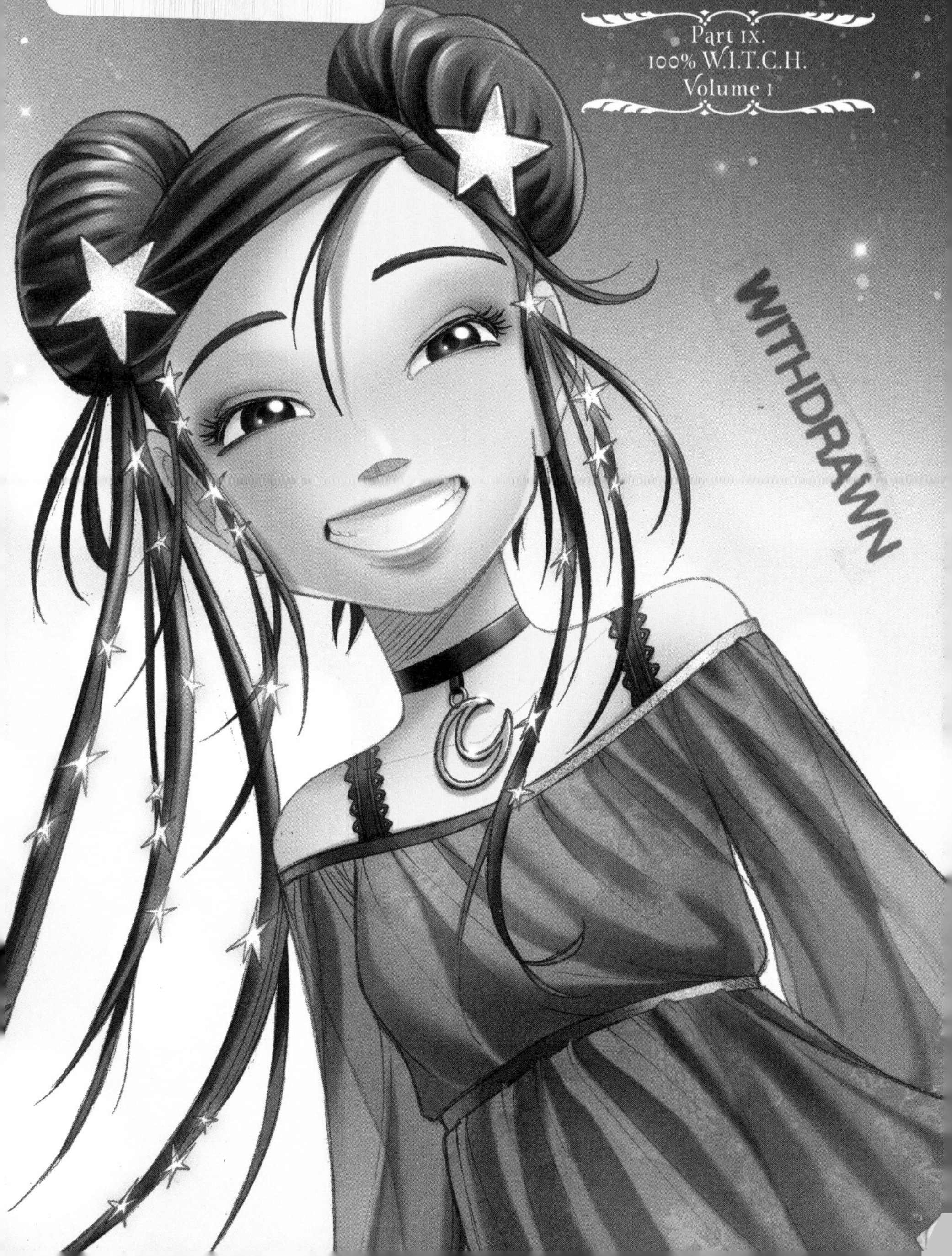

W.i.t.c.h

Will · Irma · Taranee · Cornelia · Hay Lin

Part IX.
100% W.I.T.C.H.
Volume I

CONTENTS

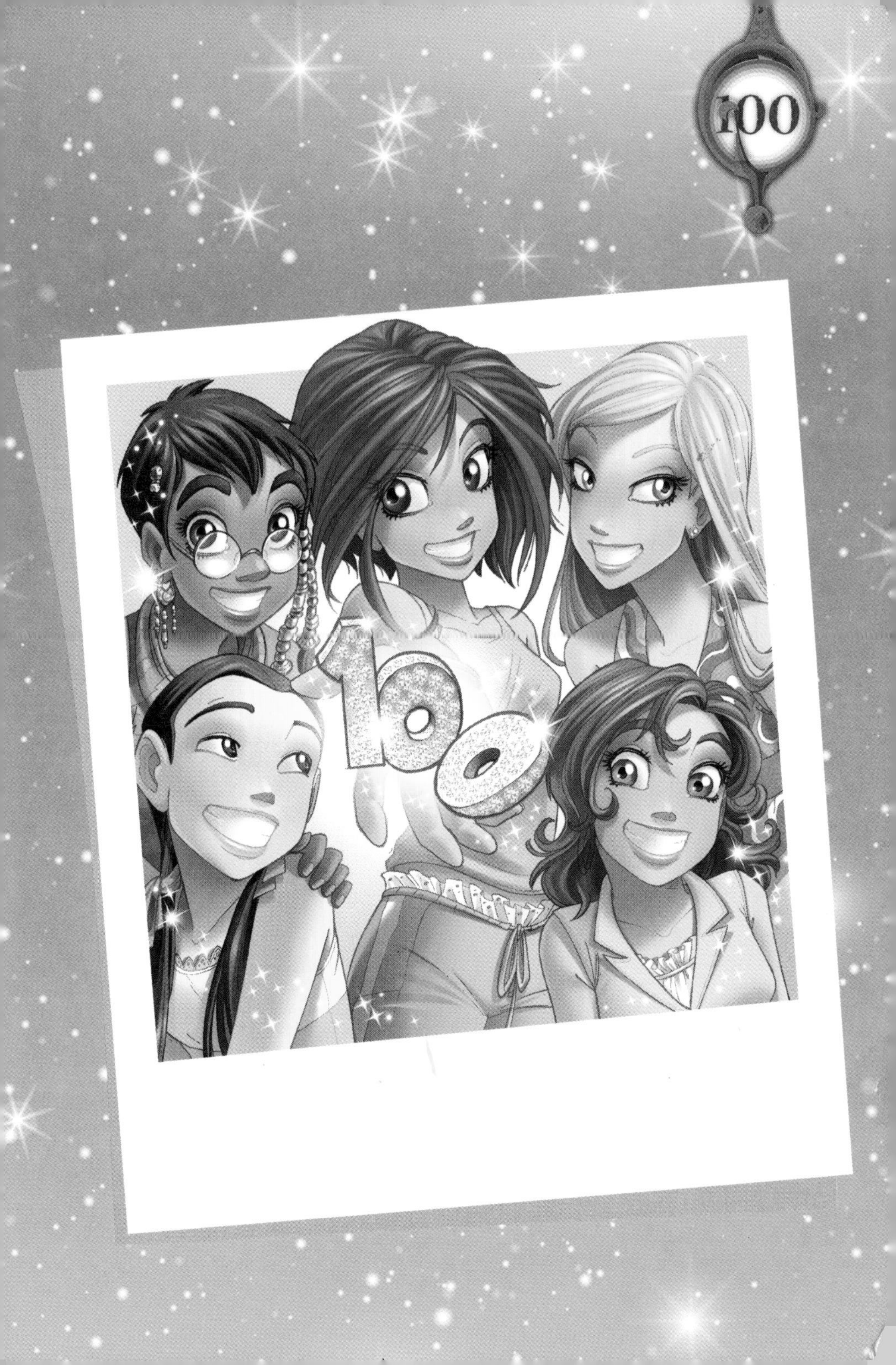
100
100

W.i.t.c.h.

Will   Irma   Taranee   Cornelia   Hay Lin

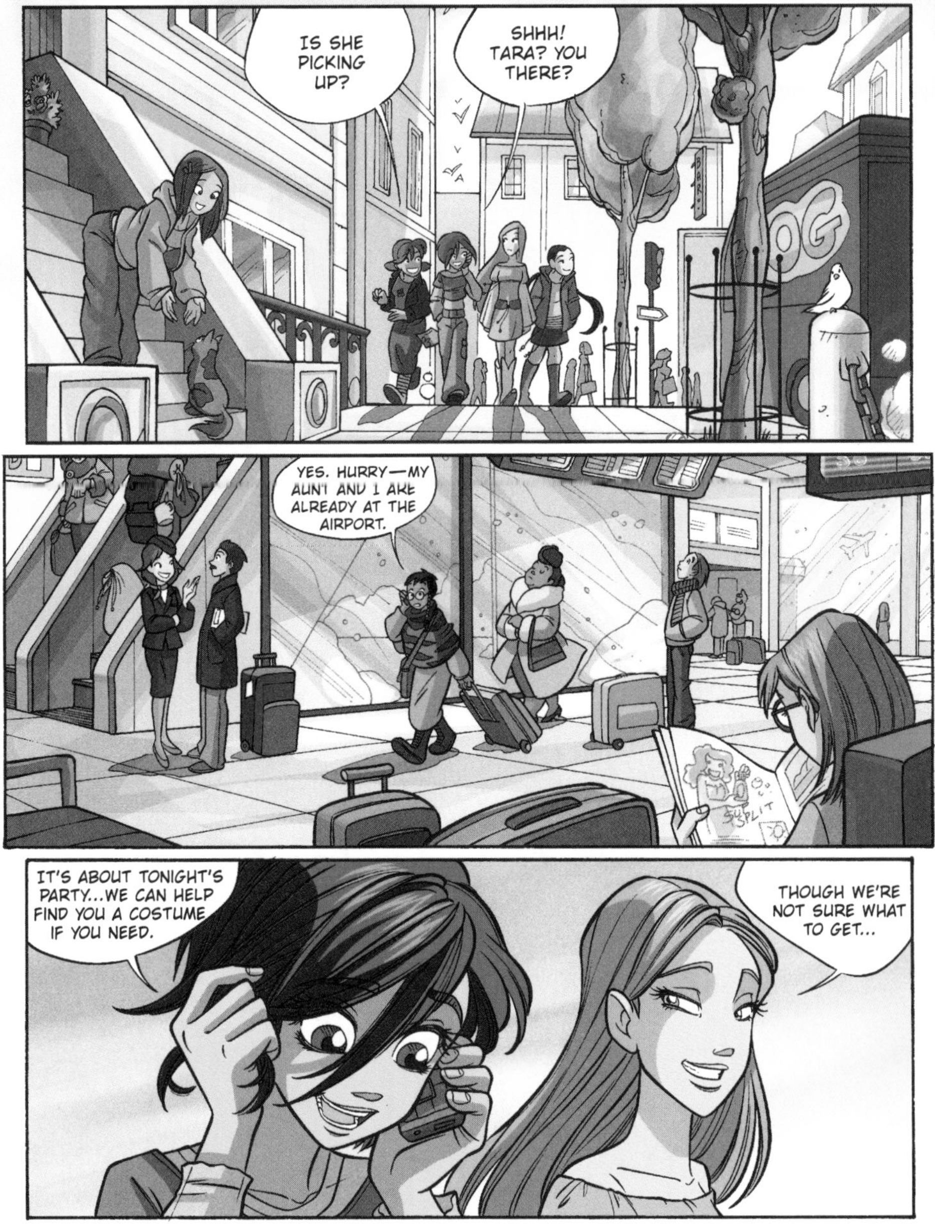
IS SHE PICKING UP?
SHHH! TARA? YOU THERE?
BAR
YES. HURRY—MY AUNT AND I ARE ALREADY AT THE AIRPORT.
SPLIT
IT'S ABOUT TONIGHT'S PARTY...WE CAN HELP FIND YOU A COSTUME IF YOU NEED.
THOUGH WE'RE NOT SURE WHAT TO GET...

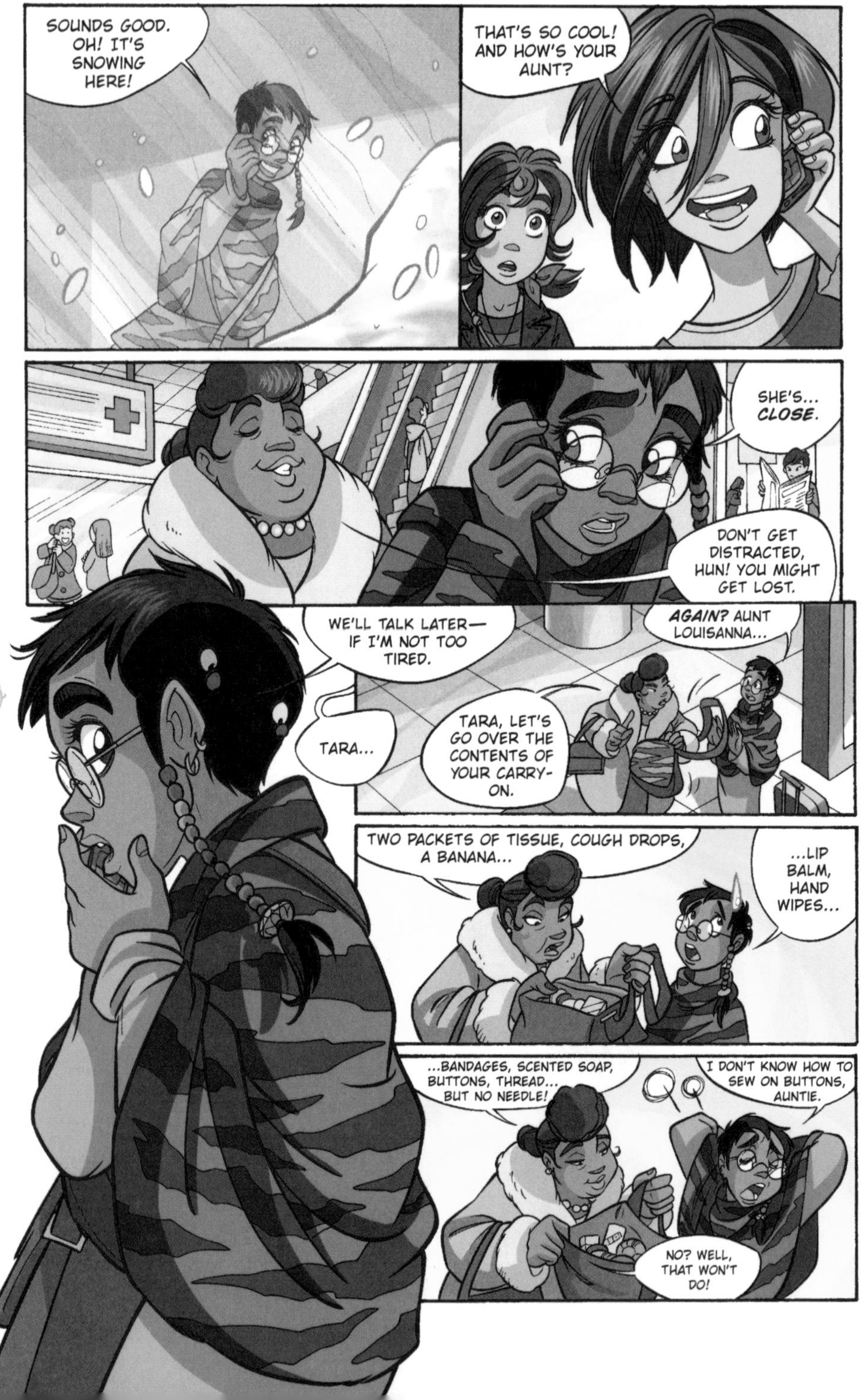
SOUNDS GOOD. OH! IT'S SNOWING HERE!
THAT'S SO COOL! AND HOW'S YOUR AUNT?
SHE'S... CLOSE.
DON'T GET DISTRACTED, HUN! YOU MIGHT GET LOST.
WE'LL TALK LATER—IF I'M NOT TOO TIRED.
TARA...
AGAIN? AUNT LOUISANNA...
TARA, LET'S GO OVER THE CONTENTS OF YOUR CARRY-ON.
TWO PACKETS OF TISSUE, COUGH DROPS, A BANANA...
...LIP BALM, HAND WIPES...
...BANDAGES, SCENTED SOAP, BUTTONS, THREAD... BUT NO NEEDLE!
I DON'T KNOW HOW TO SEW ON BUTTONS, AUNTIE.
NO? WELL, THAT WON'T DO!
6

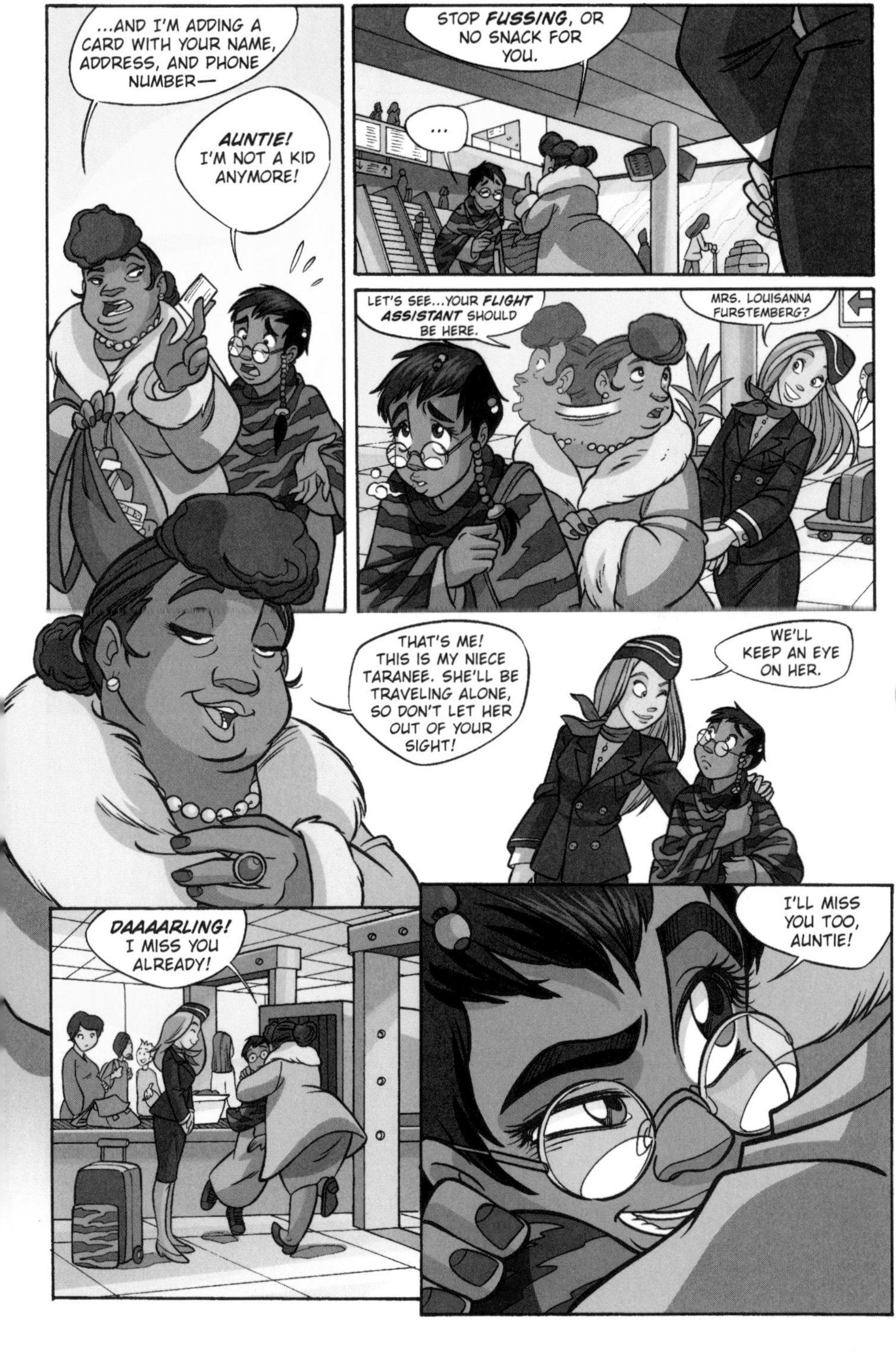

...AND I'M ADDING A CARD WITH YOUR NAME, ADDRESS, AND PHONE NUMBER—
AUNTIE! I'M NOT A KID ANYMORE!
STOP FUSSING, OR NO SNACK FOR YOU.
...
LET'S SEE...YOUR FLIGHT ASSISTANT SHOULD BE HERE.
MRS. LOUISANNA FURSTEMBERG?
THAT'S ME! THIS IS MY NIECE TARANEE. SHE'LL BE TRAVELING ALONE, SO DON'T LET HER OUT OF YOUR SIGHT!
WE'LL KEEP AN EYE ON HER.
DAAAARLING! I MISS YOU ALREADY!
I'LL MISS YOU TOO, AUNTIE!

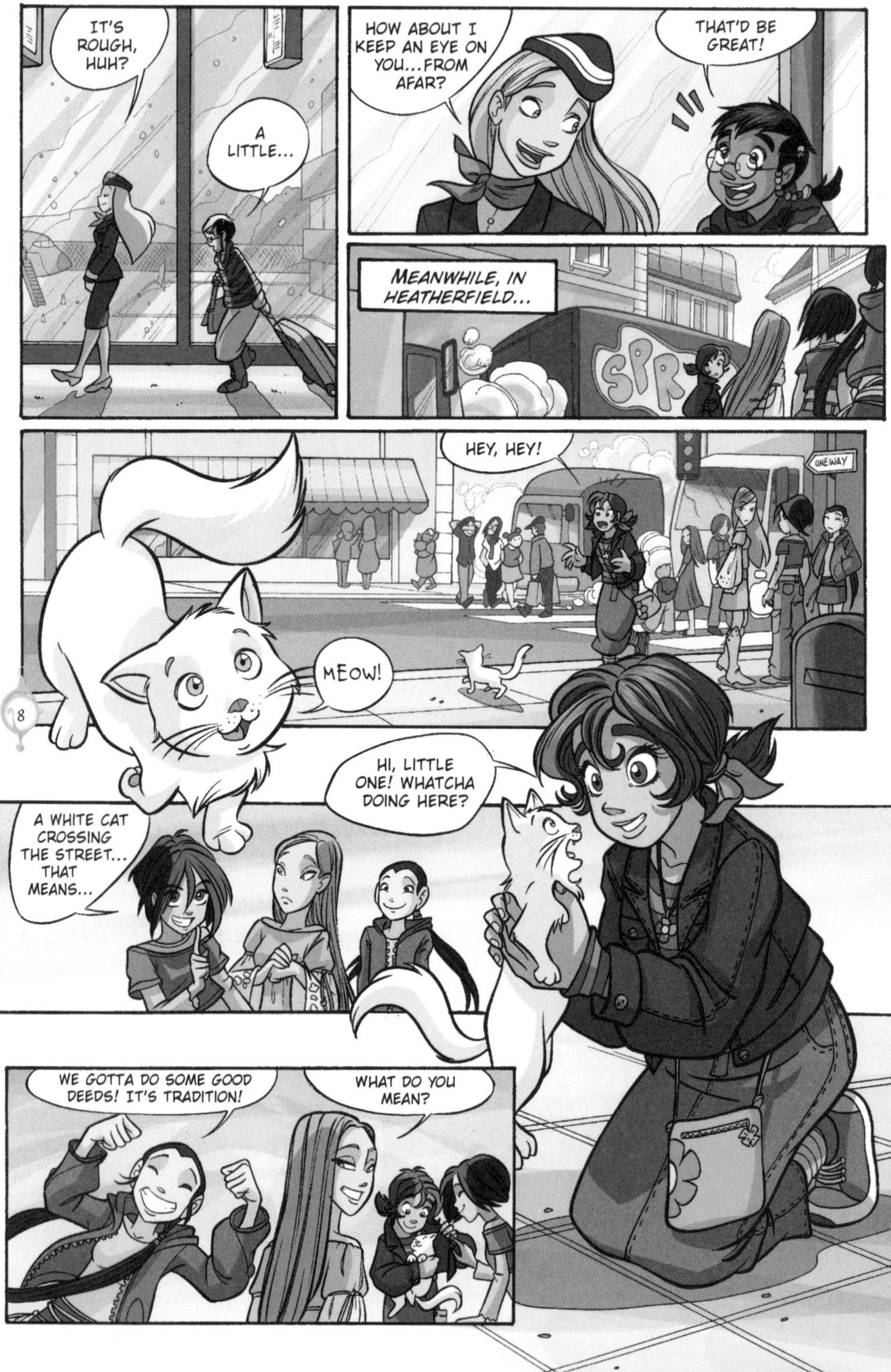
IT'S ROUGH, HUH?
A LITTLE...
HOW ABOUT I KEEP AN EYE ON YOU...FROM AFAR?
THAT'D BE GREAT!
MEANWHILE, IN HEATHERFIELD...
SPR
HEY, HEY!
ONE WAY
MEOW!
HI, LITTLE ONE! WHATCHA DOING HERE?
A WHITE CAT CROSSING THE STREET... THAT MEANS...
WE GOTTA DO SOME GOOD DEEDS! IT'S TRADITION!
WHAT DO YOU MEAN?

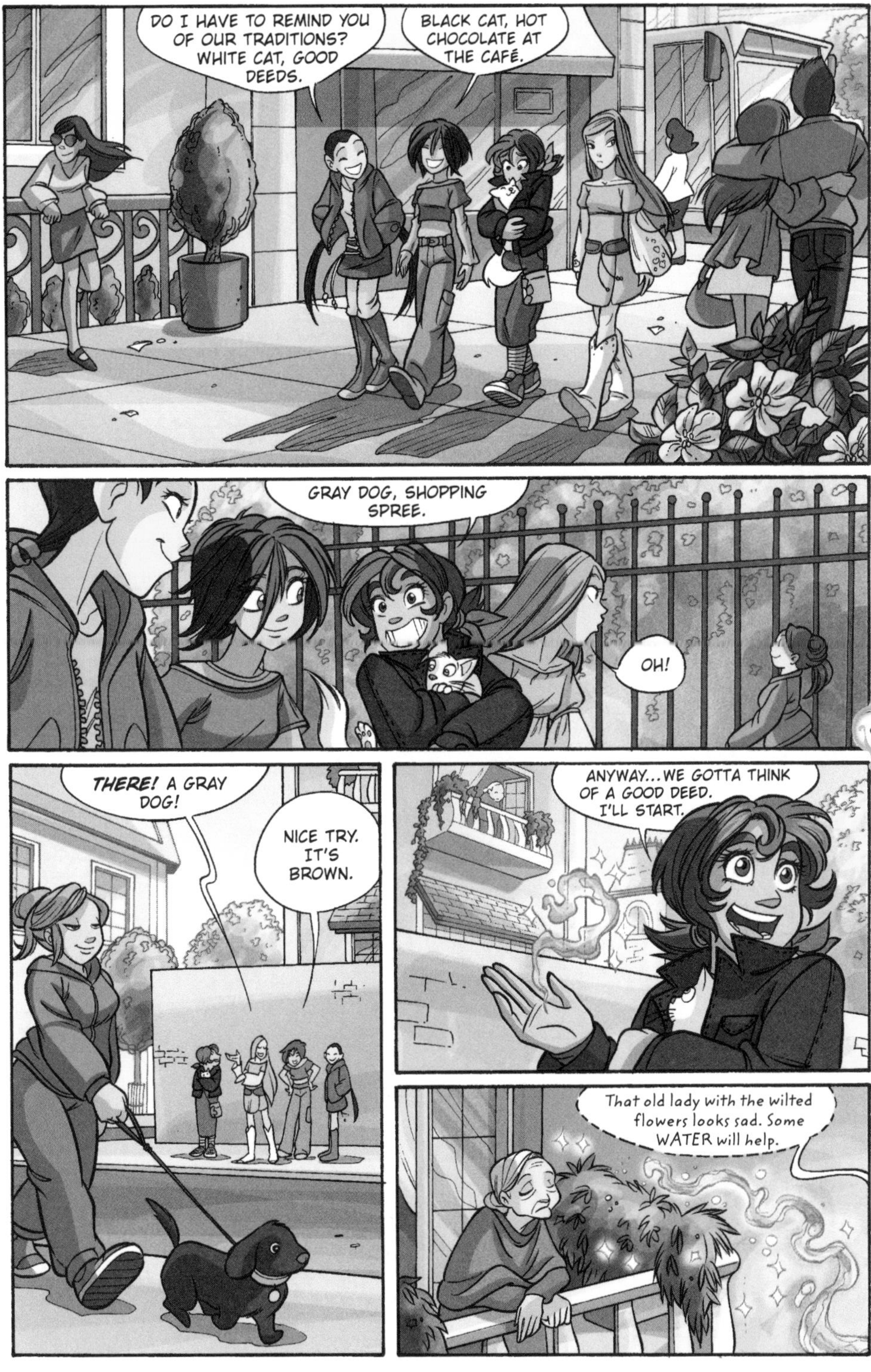
DO I HAVE TO REMIND YOU OF OUR TRADITIONS? WHITE CAT, GOOD DEEDS.
BLACK CAT, HOT CHOCOLATE AT THE CAFÉ.
GRAY DOG, SHOPPING SPREE.
OH!
THERE! A GRAY DOG!
NICE TRY. IT'S BROWN.
ANYWAY...WE GOTTA THINK OF A GOOD DEED. I'LL START.
That old lady with the wilted flowers looks sad. Some WATER will help.

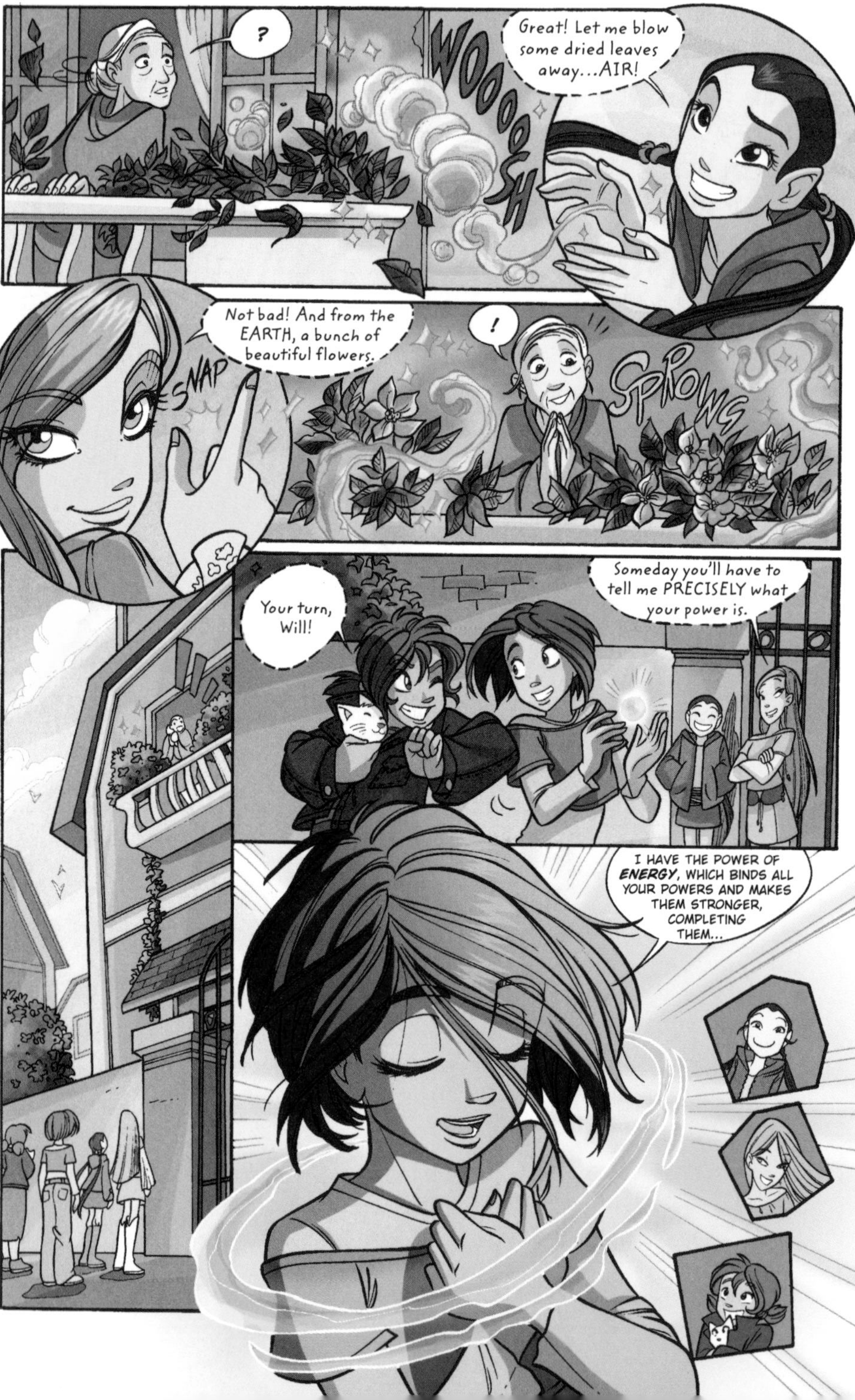
?
Great! Let me blow some dried leaves away...AIR!
WOOOOOSH
Not bad! And from the EARTH, a bunch of beautiful flowers.
SNAP
!
SPROWS
Your turn, Will!
Someday you'll have to tell me PRECISELY what your power is.
I HAVE THE POWER OF ENERGY, WHICH BINDS ALL YOUR POWERS AND MAKES THEM STRONGER, COMPLETING THEM...

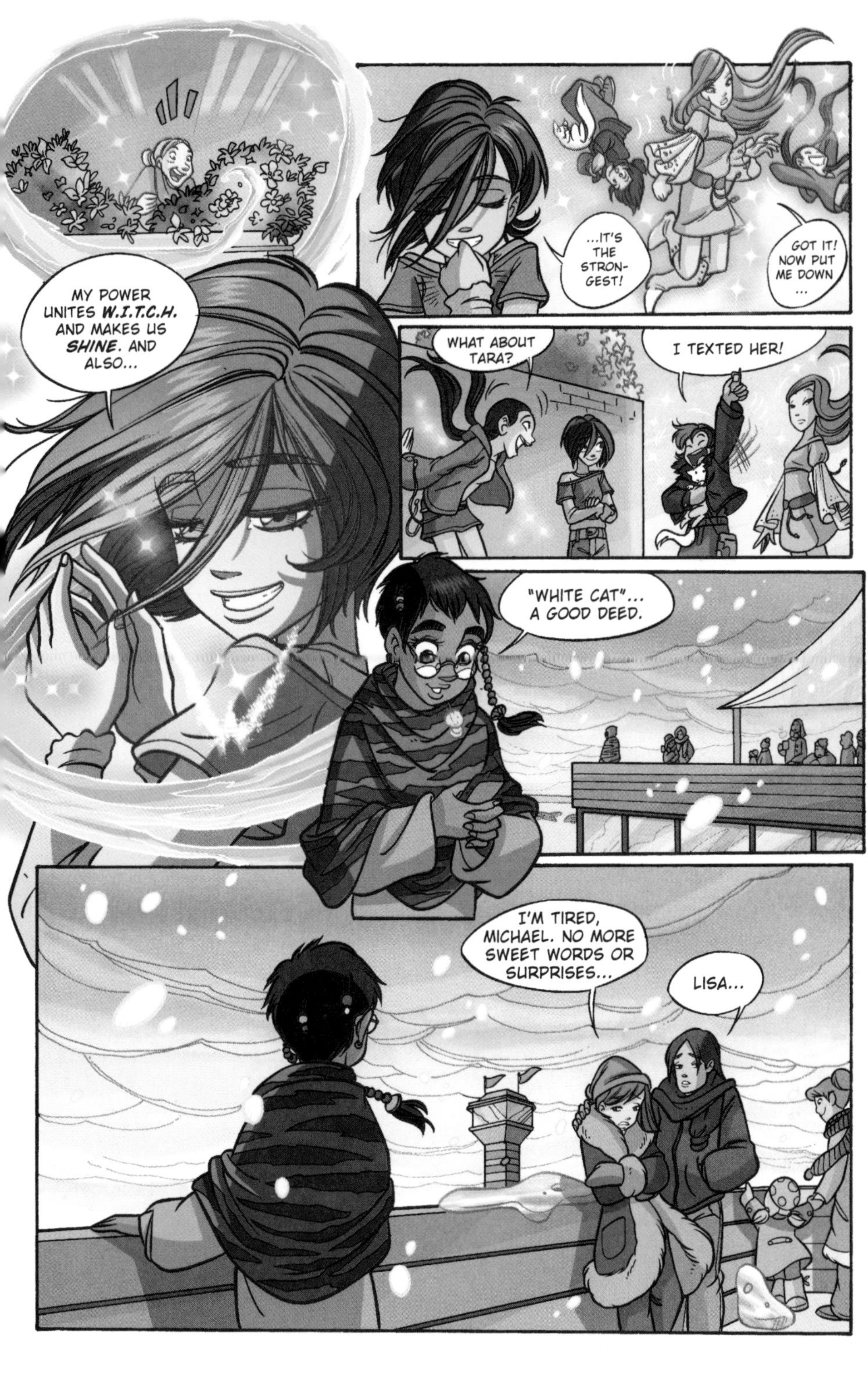
MY POWER UNITES W.I.T.C.H. AND MAKES US SHINE. AND ALSO...
...IT'S THE STRONGEST!
GOT IT! NOW PUT ME DOWN ...
WHAT ABOUT TARA?
I TEXTED HER!
"WHITE CAT"... A GOOD DEED.
I'M TIRED, MICHAEL. NO MORE SWEET WORDS OR SURPRISES...
LISA...

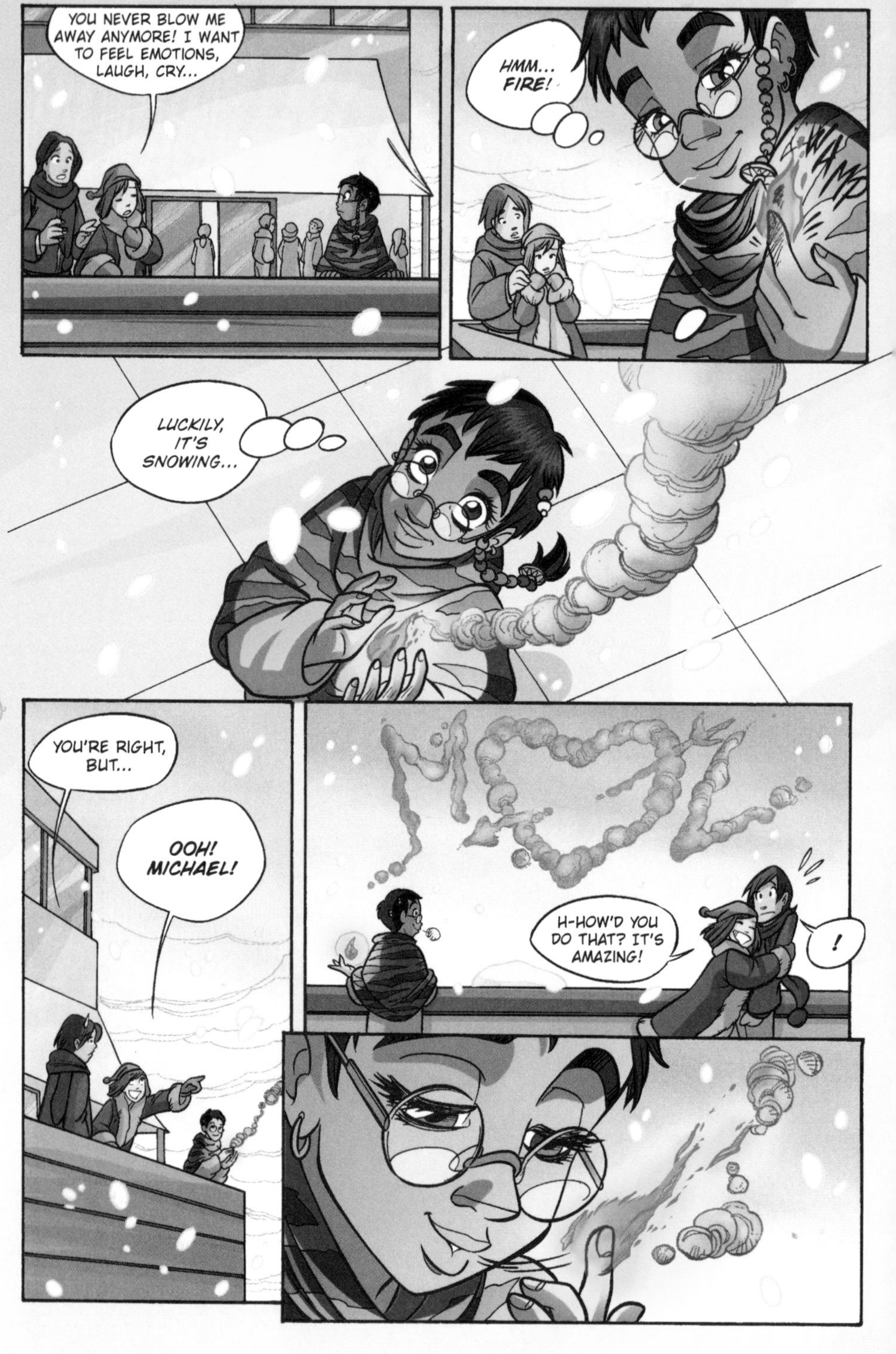
YOU NEVER BLOW ME AWAY ANYMORE! I WANT TO FEEL EMOTIONS, LAUGH, CRY...
HMM... FIRE!
LUCKILY, IT'S SNOWING...
YOU'RE RIGHT, BUT...
OOH! MICHAEL!
H-HOW'D YOU DO THAT? IT'S AMAZING!
!

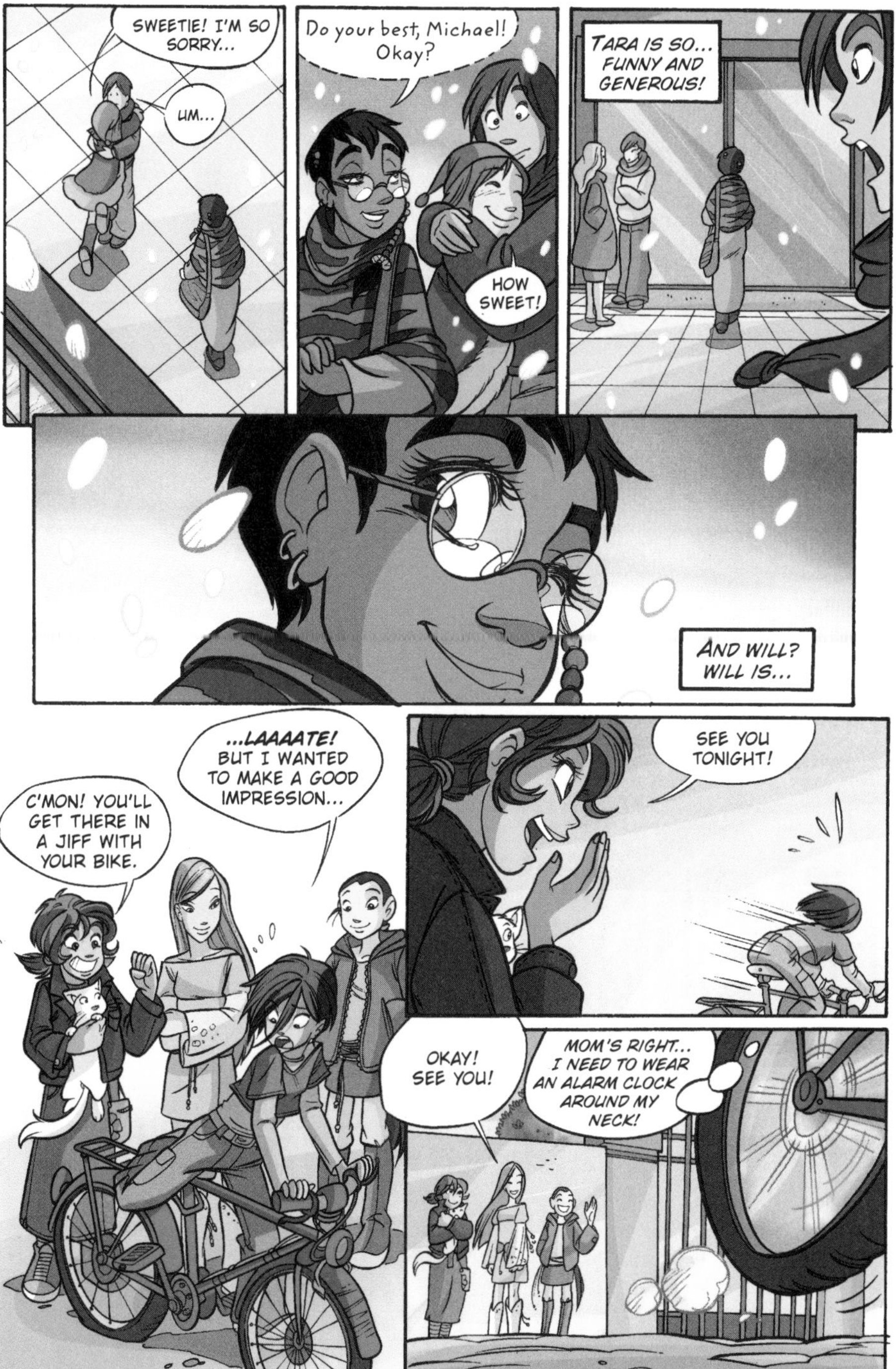
SWEETIE! I'M SO SORRY...
UM...
Do your best, Michael! Okay?
HOW SWEET!
TARA IS SO... FUNNY AND GENEROUS!
AND WILL? WILL IS...
C'MON! YOU'LL GET THERE IN A JIFF WITH YOUR BIKE.
...LAAAATE! BUT I WANTED TO MAKE A GOOD IMPRESSION...
SEE YOU TONIGHT!
OKAY! SEE YOU!
MOM'S RIGHT... I NEED TO WEAR AN ALARM CLOCK AROUND MY NECK!

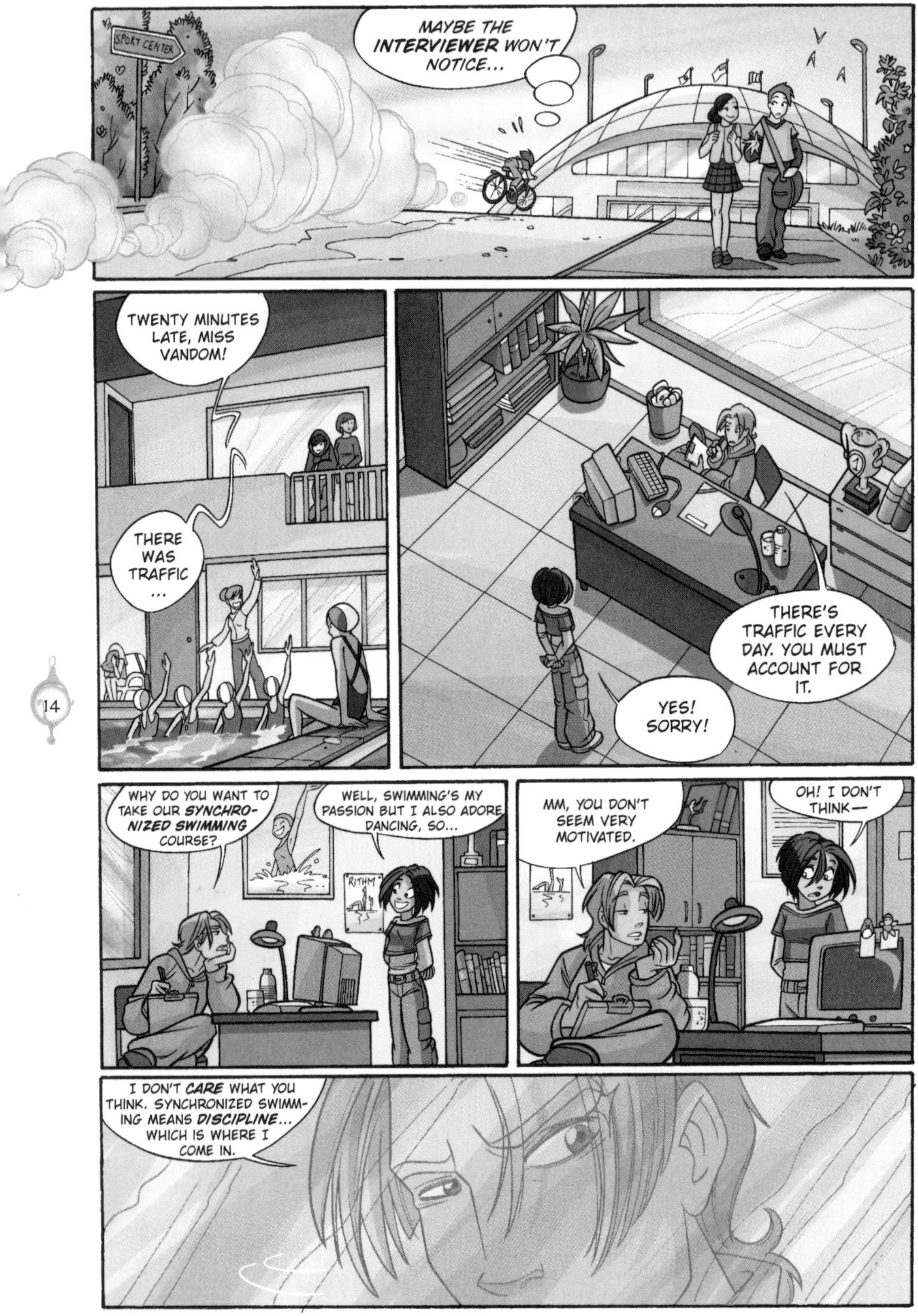
SPORT CENTER
MAYBE THE INTERVIEWER WON'T NOTICE...
TWENTY MINUTES LATE, MISS VANDOM!
THERE WAS TRAFFIC ...
THERE'S TRAFFIC EVERY DAY. YOU MUST ACCOUNT FOR IT.
YES! SORRY!
WHY DO YOU WANT TO TAKE OUR SYNCHRONIZED SWIMMING COURSE?
WELL, SWIMMING'S MY PASSION BUT I ALSO ADORE DANCING, SO...
RITHM
MM, YOU DON'T SEEM VERY MOTIVATED.
OH! I DON'T THINK—
I DON'T CARE WHAT YOU THINK. SYNCHRONIZED SWIMMING MEANS DISCIPLINE... WHICH IS WHERE I COME IN.

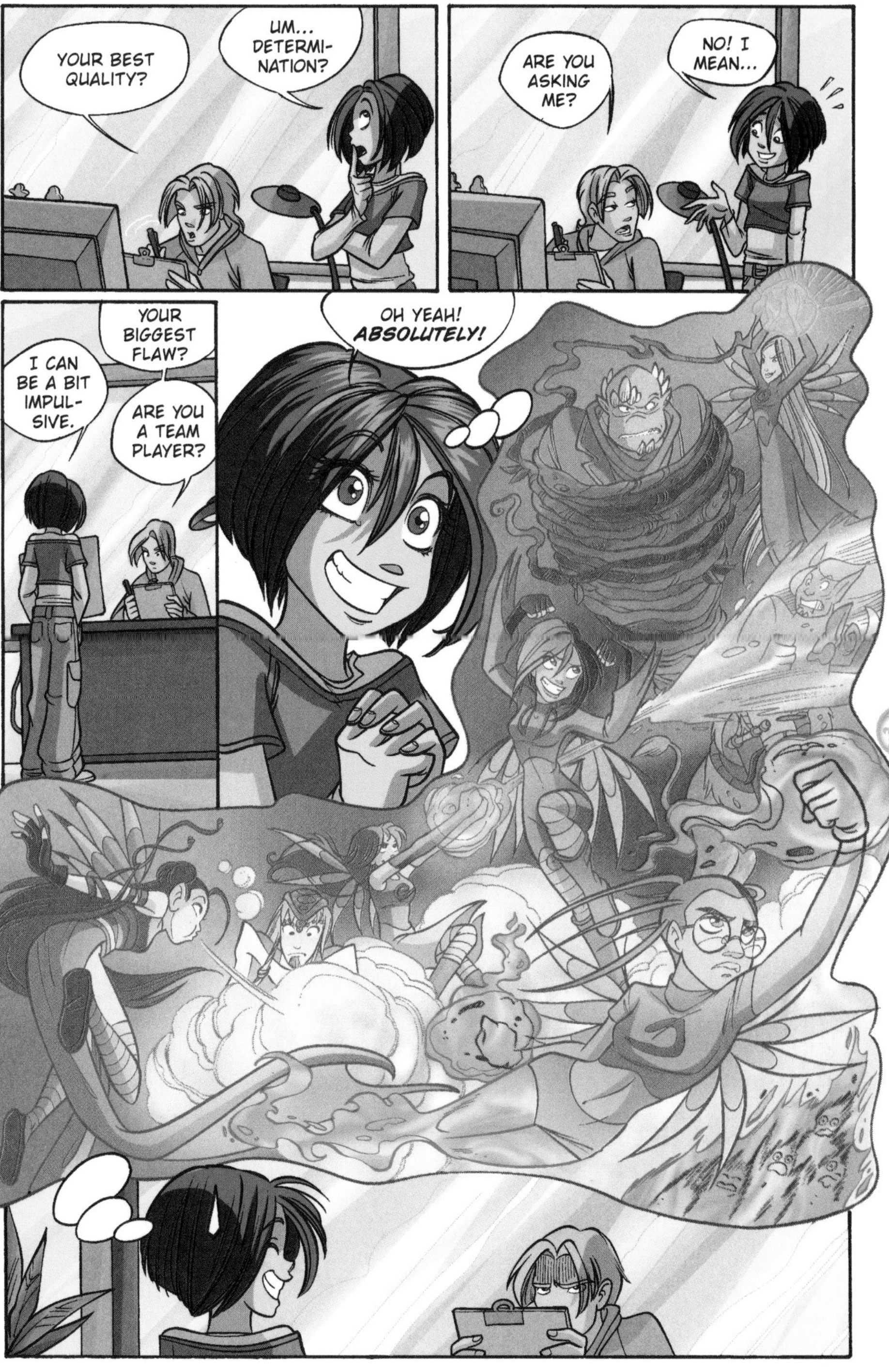
YOUR BEST QUALITY?
UM... DETERMINATION?
ARE YOU ASKING ME?
NO! I MEAN...
YOUR BIGGEST FLAW?
I CAN BE A BIT IMPULSIVE.
ARE YOU A TEAM PLAYER?
OH YEAH! ABSOLUTELY!

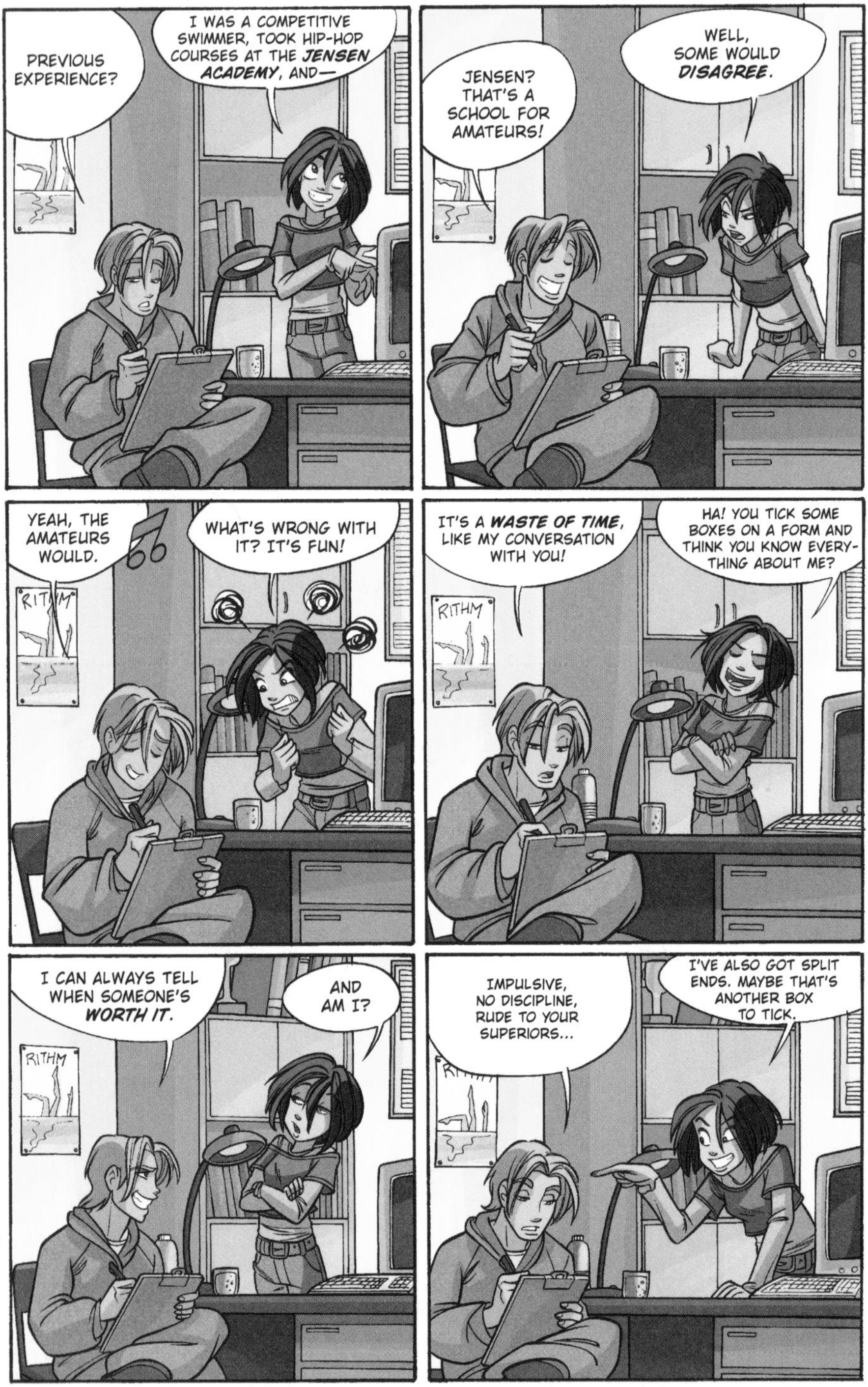
PREVIOUS EXPERIENCE?
I WAS A COMPETITIVE SWIMMER, TOOK HIP-HOP COURSES AT THE JENSEN ACADEMY, AND—
JENSEN? THAT'S A SCHOOL FOR AMATEURS!
WELL, SOME WOULD DISAGREE.
YEAH, THE AMATEURS WOULD.
WHAT'S WRONG WITH IT? IT'S FUN!
RITHM
IT'S A WASTE OF TIME, LIKE MY CONVERSATION WITH YOU!
HA! YOU TICK SOME BOXES ON A FORM AND THINK YOU KNOW EVERYTHING ABOUT ME?
RITHM
I CAN ALWAYS TELL WHEN SOMEONE'S WORTH IT.
AND AM I?
RITHM
IMPULSIVE, NO DISCIPLINE, RUDE TO YOUR SUPERIORS...
I'VE ALSO GOT SPLIT ENDS. MAYBE THAT'S ANOTHER BOX TO TICK.

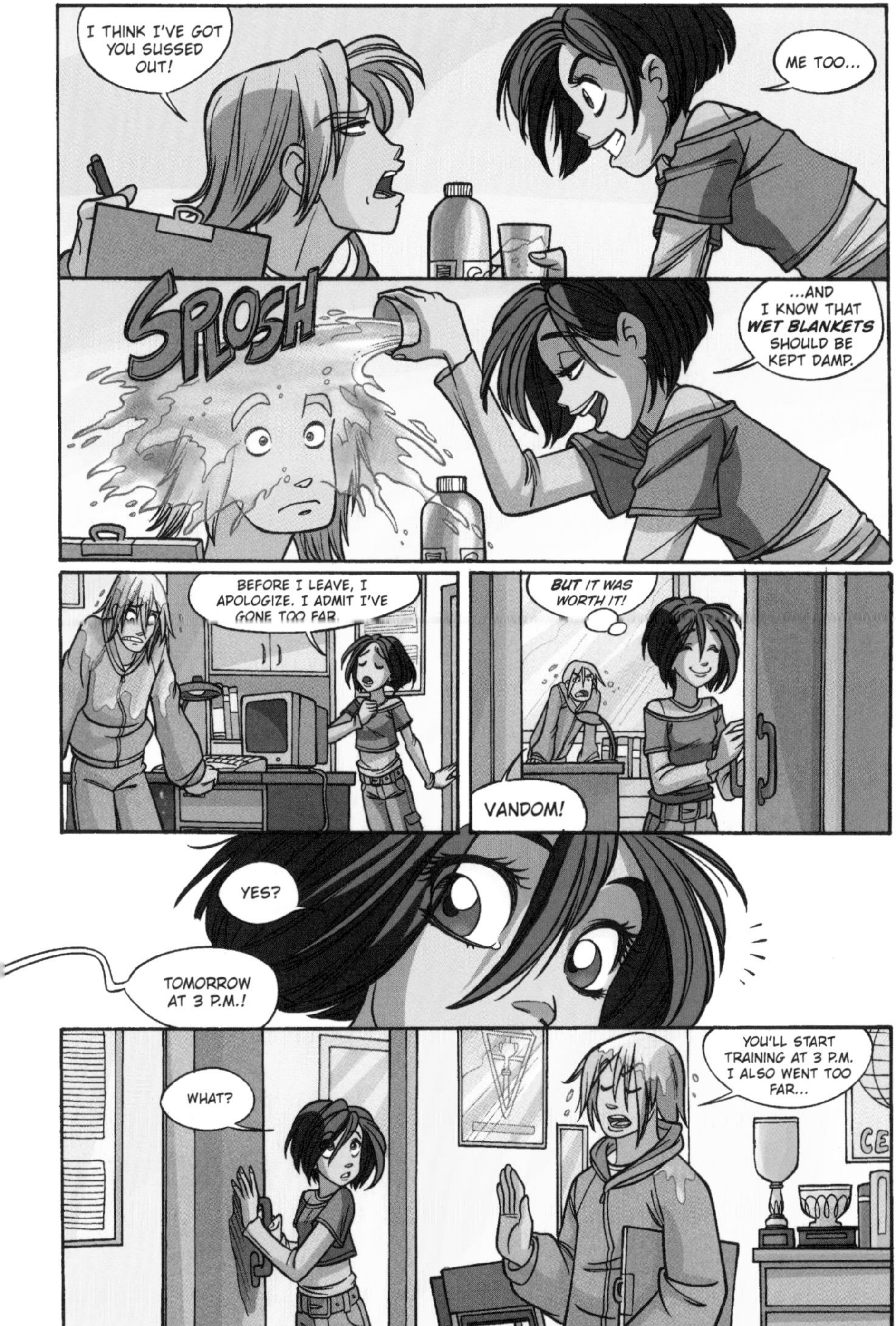
I THINK I'VE GOT YOU SUSSED OUT!
ME TOO...
SPLOSH
...AND I KNOW THAT WET BLANKETS SHOULD BE KEPT DAMP.
BEFORE I LEAVE, I APOLOGIZE. I ADMIT I'VE GONE TOO FAR.
BUT IT WAS WORTH IT!
VANDOM!
YES?
TOMORROW AT 3 P.M.!
WHAT?
YOU'LL START TRAINING AT 3 P.M. I ALSO WENT TOO FAR...

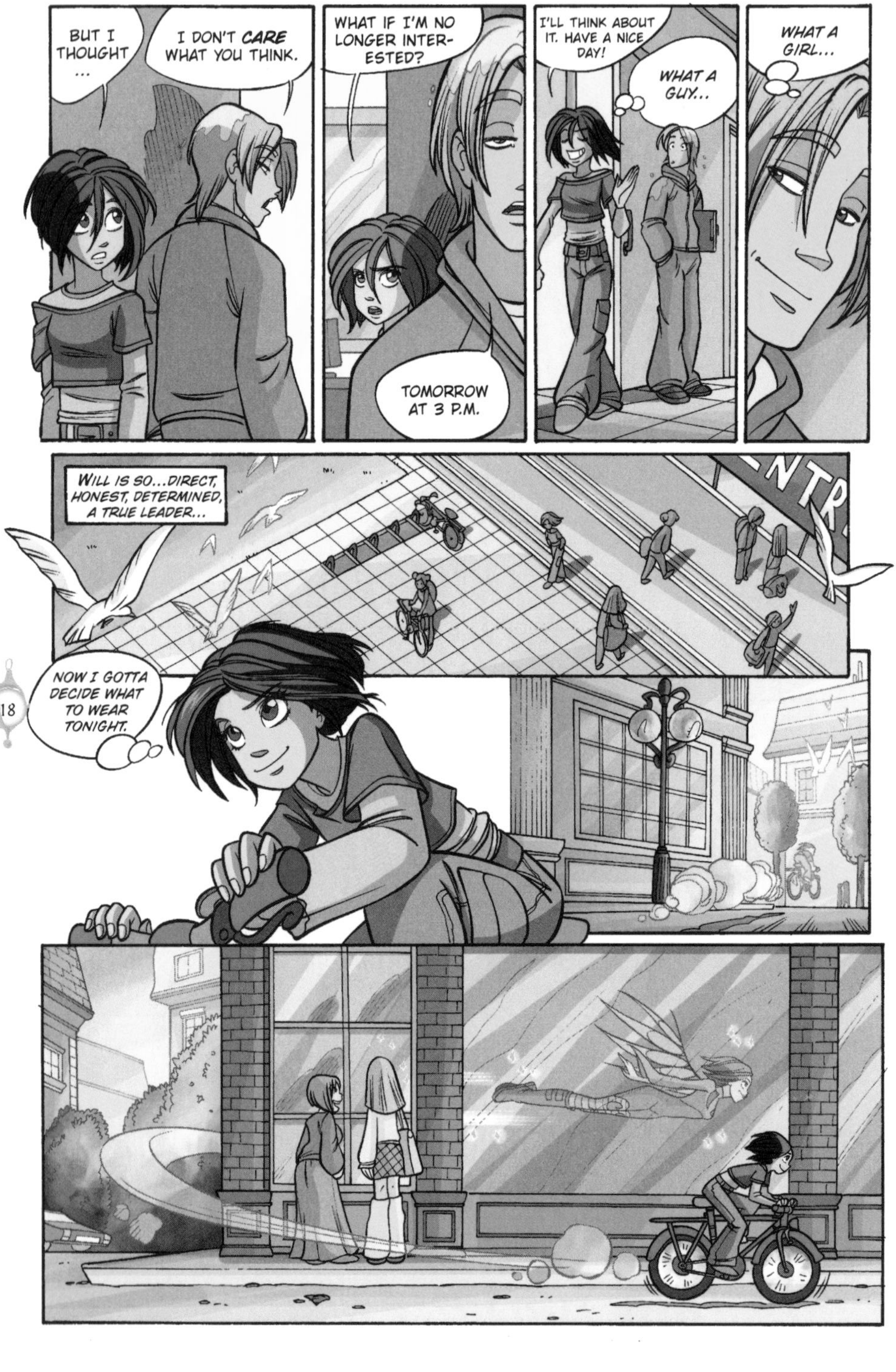

BUT I THOUGHT ...
I DON'T CARE WHAT YOU THINK.
WHAT IF I'M NO LONGER INTER-ESTED?
TOMORROW AT 3 P.M.
I'LL THINK ABOUT IT. HAVE A NICE DAY!
WHAT A GUY...
WHAT A GIRL...
WILL IS SO...DIRECT, HONEST, DETERMINED, A TRUE LEADER...
NOW I GOTTA DECIDE WHAT TO WEAR TONIGHT.

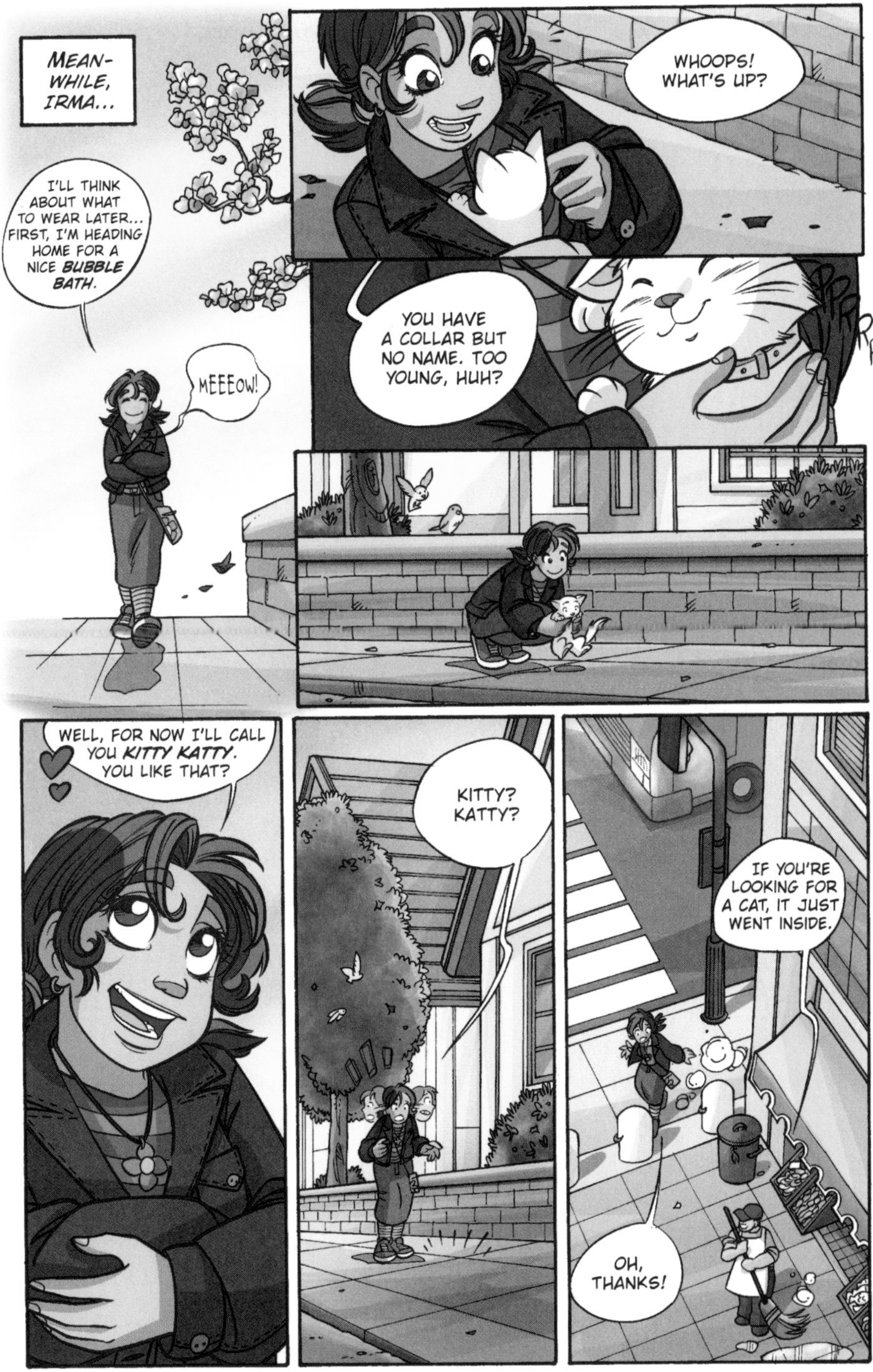
MEAN-WHILE, IRMA...
I'LL THINK ABOUT WHAT TO WEAR LATER... FIRST, I'M HEADING HOME FOR A NICE BUBBLE BATH.
MEEEOW!
WHOOPS! WHAT'S UP?
YOU HAVE A COLLAR BUT NO NAME. TOO YOUNG, HUH?
PRRRR
WELL, FOR NOW I'LL CALL YOU KITTY KATTY. YOU LIKE THAT?
KITTY? KATTY?
IF YOU'RE LOOKING FOR A CAT, IT JUST WENT INSIDE.
OH, THANKS!

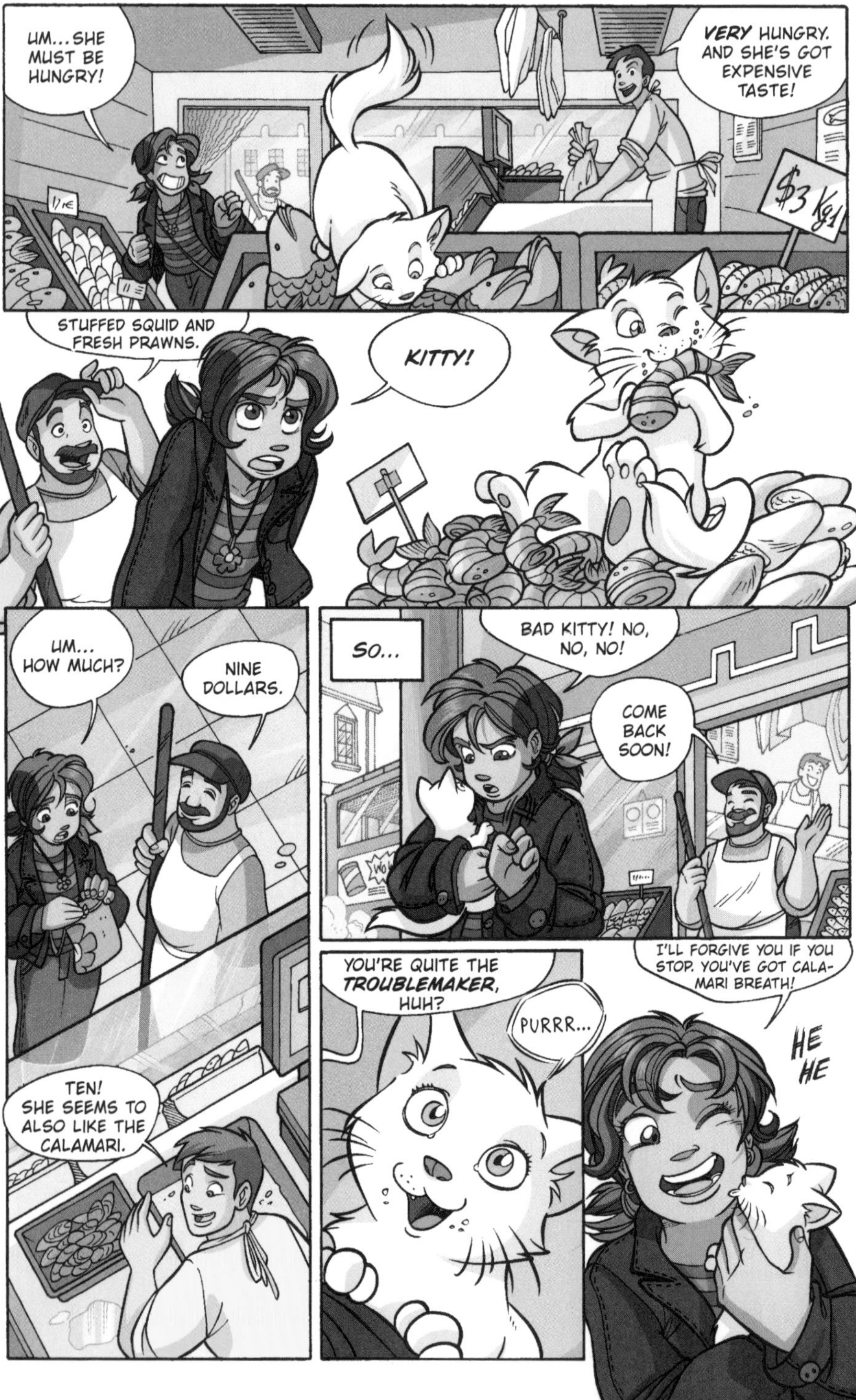

UM...SHE MUST BE HUNGRY!
VERY HUNGRY. AND SHE'S GOT EXPENSIVE TASTE!
$3 Kg1
STUFFED SQUID AND FRESH PRAWNS.
KITTY!
UM... HOW MUCH?
NINE DOLLARS.
SO...
BAD KITTY! NO, NO, NO!
COME BACK SOON!
TEN! SHE SEEMS TO ALSO LIKE THE CALAMARI.
YOU'RE QUITE THE **TROUBLEMAKER**, HUH?
PURRR...
I'LL FORGIVE YOU IF YOU STOP. YOU'VE GOT CALAMARI BREATH!
HE HE

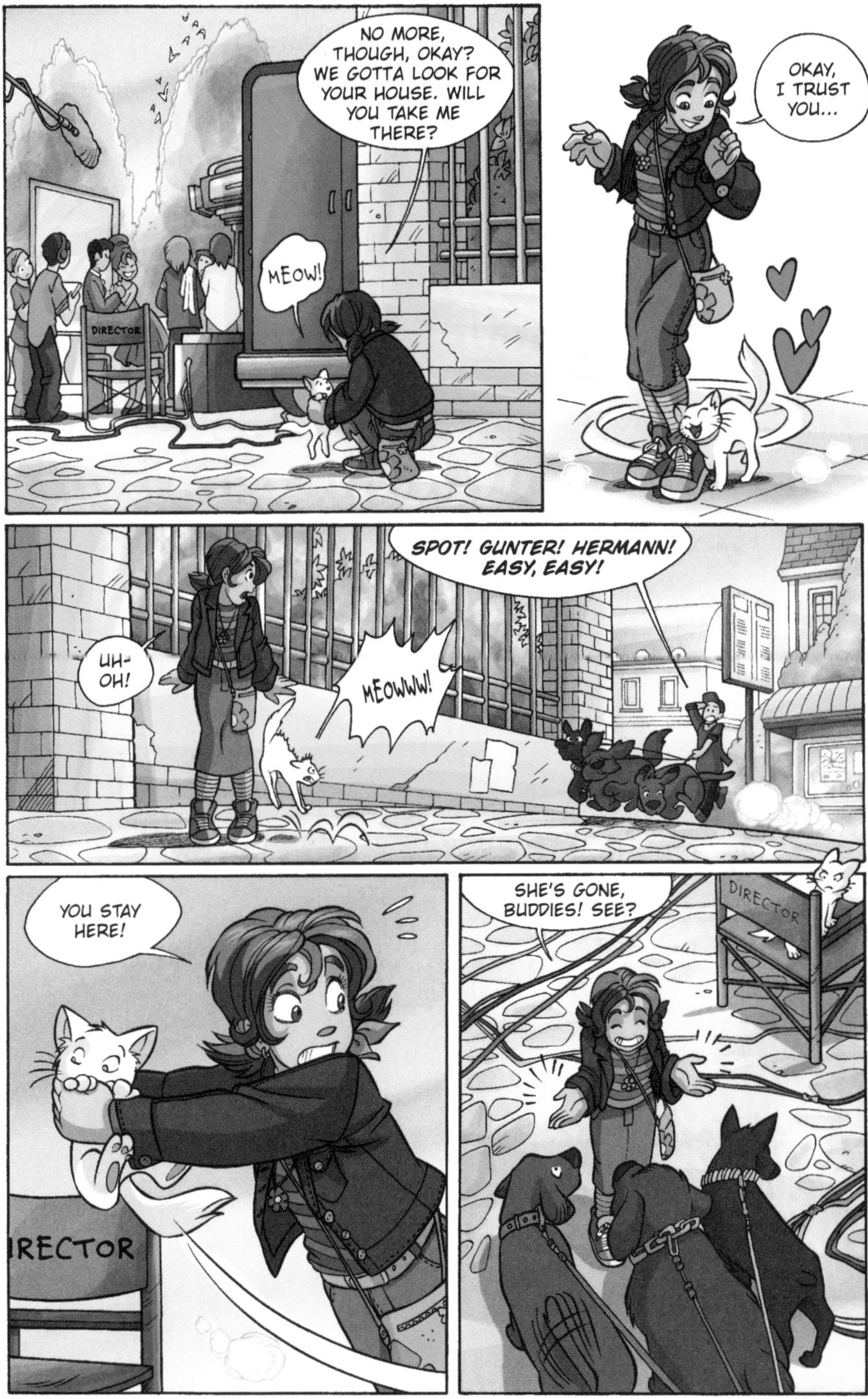
NO MORE, THOUGH, OKAY? WE GOTTA LOOK FOR YOUR HOUSE. WILL YOU TAKE ME THERE?
MEOW!
DIRECTOR
OKAY, I TRUST YOU...
SPOT! GUNTER! HERMANN! EASY, EASY!
UH-OH!
MEOWWW!
YOU STAY HERE!
IRECTOR
SHE'S GONE, BUDDIES! SEE?
DIRECTOR

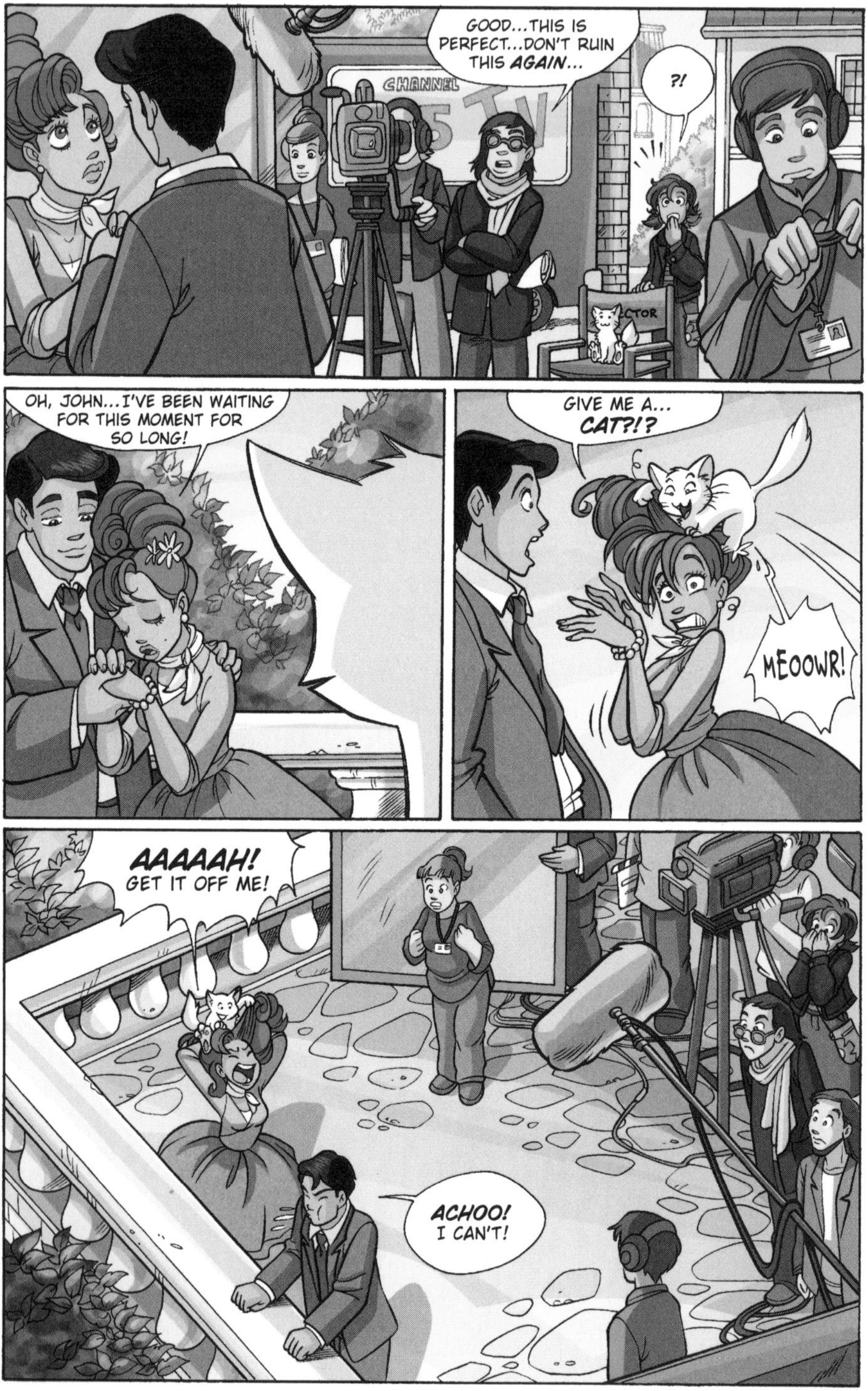
GOOD...THIS IS PERFECT...DON'T RUIN THIS AGAIN...
?!
OH, JOHN...I'VE BEEN WAITING FOR THIS MOMENT FOR SO LONG!
GIVE ME A... CAT?!?
MEOOWR!
AAAAAH! GET IT OFF ME!
ACHOO! I CAN'T!

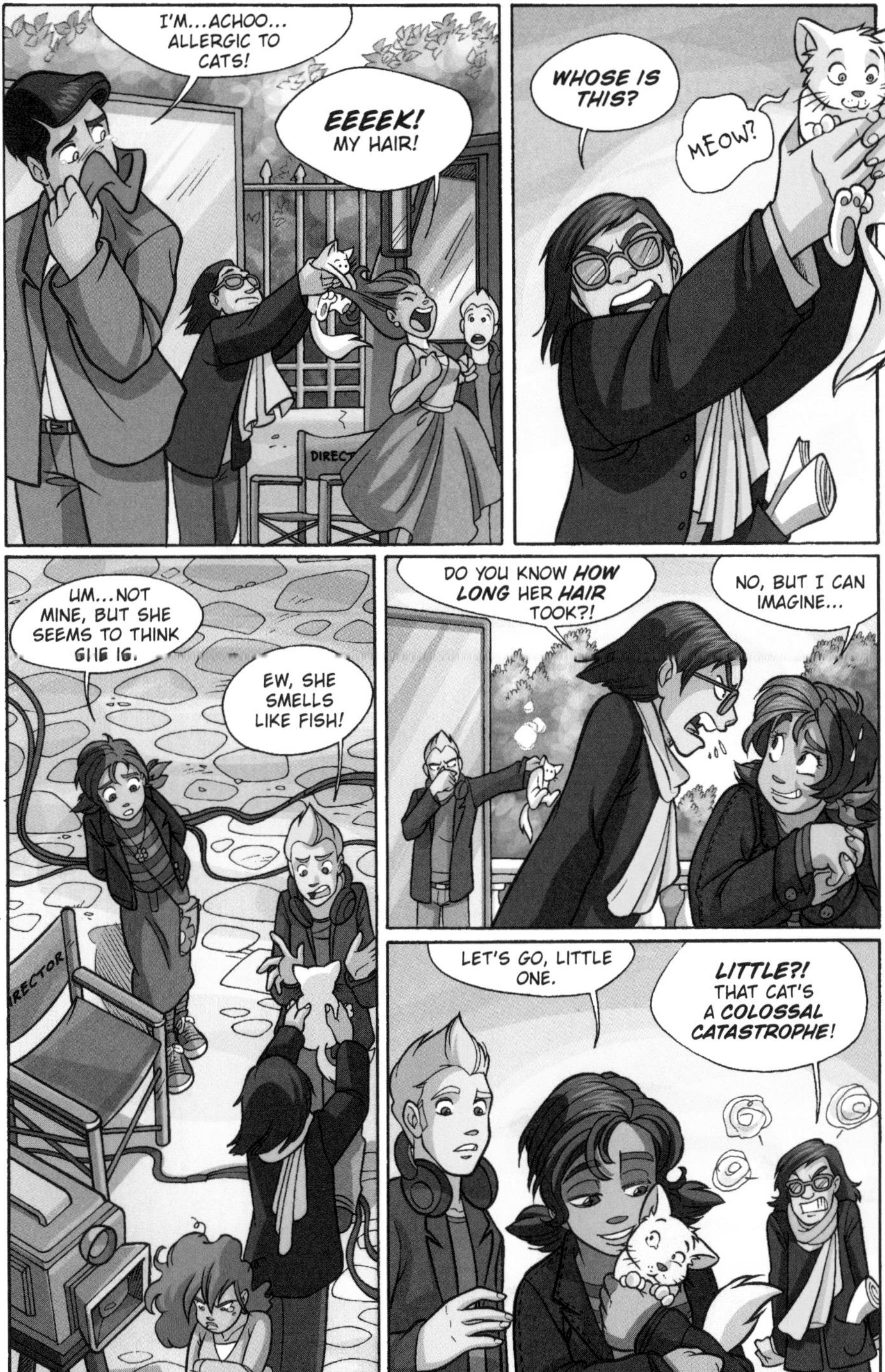

I'M...ACHOO... ALLERGIC TO CATS!
EEEEK! MY HAIR!
DIRECTOR
WHOSE IS THIS?
MEOW?
UM...NOT MINE, BUT SHE SEEMS TO THINK SHE IS.
EW, SHE SMELLS LIKE FISH!
DIRECTOR
DO YOU KNOW HOW LONG HER HAIR TOOK?!
NO, BUT I CAN IMAGINE...
LET'S GO, LITTLE ONE.
LITTLE?! THAT CAT'S A COLOSSAL CATASTROPHE!

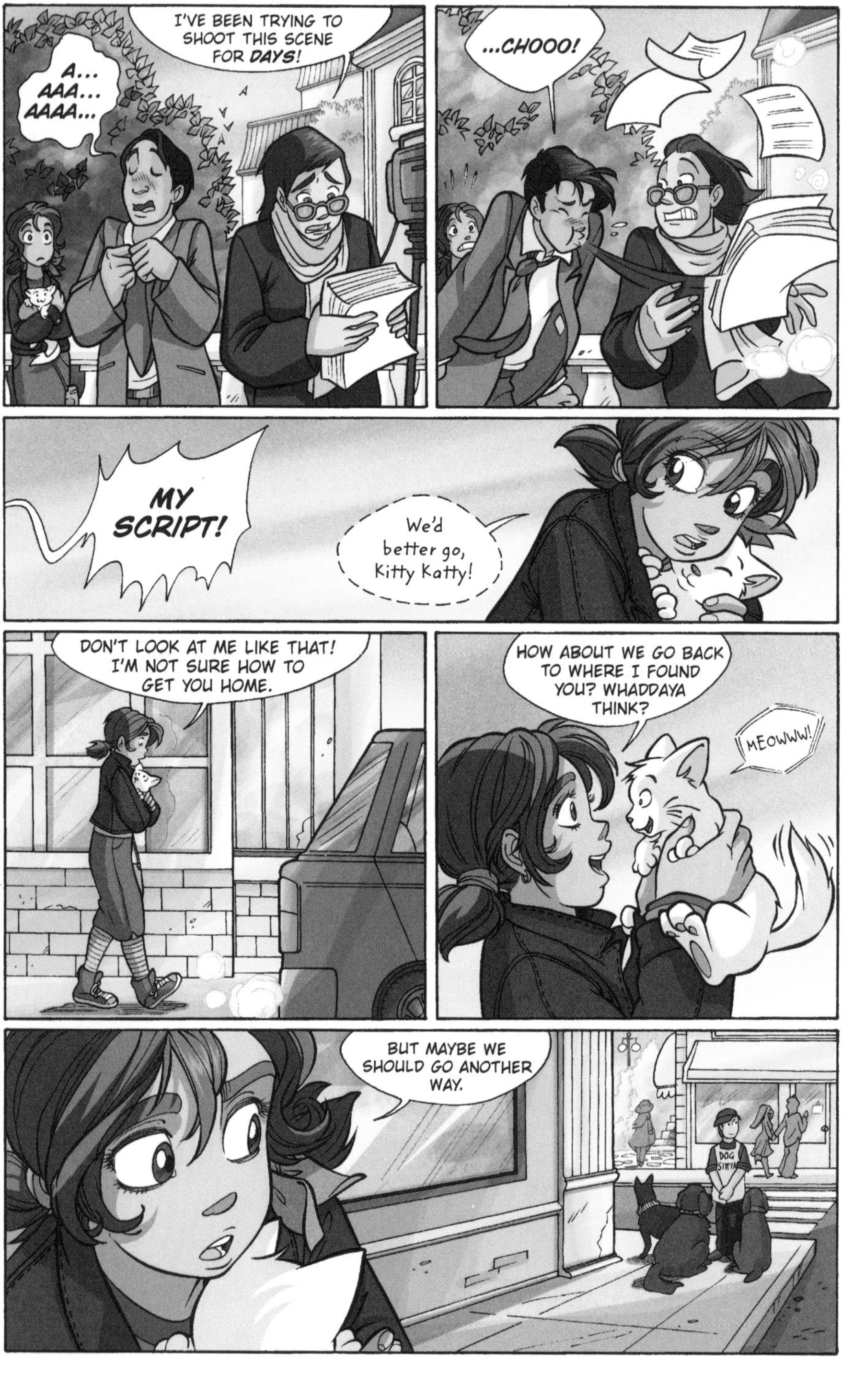
A... AAA... AAAA...
I'VE BEEN TRYING TO SHOOT THIS SCENE FOR DAYS!
...CHOOO!
MY SCRIPT!
We'd better go, Kitty Katty!
DON'T LOOK AT ME LIKE THAT! I'M NOT SURE HOW TO GET YOU HOME.
HOW ABOUT WE GO BACK TO WHERE I FOUND YOU? WHADDAYA THINK?
MEOWWW!
BUT MAYBE WE SHOULD GO ANOTHER WAY.
DOG SITTIN

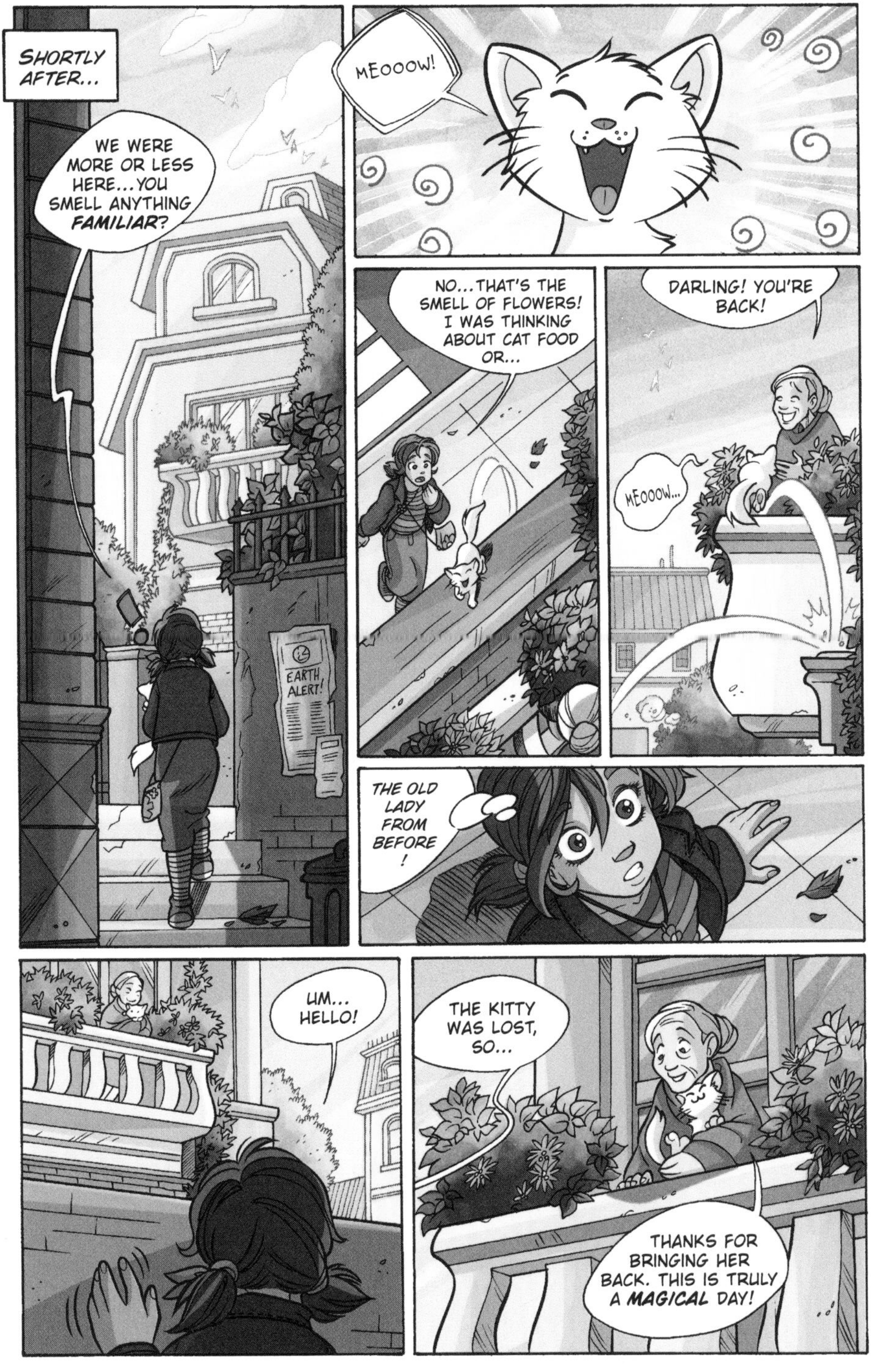
SHORTLY AFTER...
WE WERE MORE OR LESS HERE...YOU SMELL ANYTHING *FAMILIAR*?
EARTH ALERT!
MEOOOW!
NO...THAT'S THE SMELL OF FLOWERS! I WAS THINKING ABOUT CAT FOOD OR...
DARLING! YOU'RE BACK!
MEOOOW...
THE OLD LADY FROM BEFORE!
UM... HELLO!
THE KITTY WAS LOST, SO...
THANKS FOR BRINGING HER BACK. THIS IS TRULY A *MAGICAL* DAY!

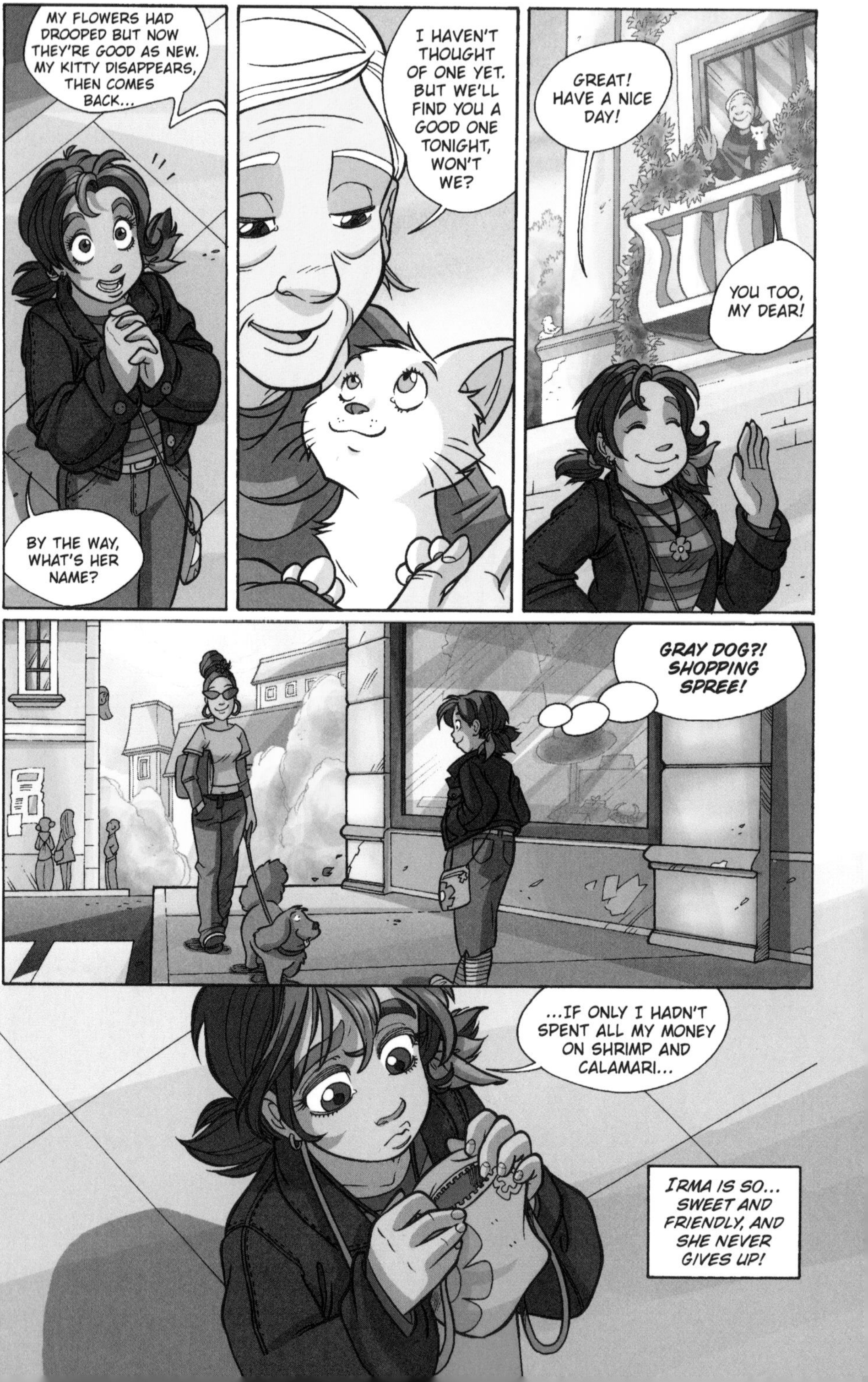
MY FLOWERS HAD DROOPED BUT NOW THEY'RE GOOD AS NEW. MY KITTY DISAPPEARS, THEN COMES BACK...
BY THE WAY, WHAT'S HER NAME?
I HAVEN'T THOUGHT OF ONE YET. BUT WE'LL FIND YOU A GOOD ONE TONIGHT, WON'T WE?
GREAT! HAVE A NICE DAY!
YOU TOO, MY DEAR!
GRAY DOG?! SHOPPING SPREE!
...IF ONLY I HADN'T SPENT ALL MY MONEY ON SHRIMP AND CALAMARI...
IRMA IS SO... SWEET AND FRIENDLY, AND SHE NEVER GIVES UP!

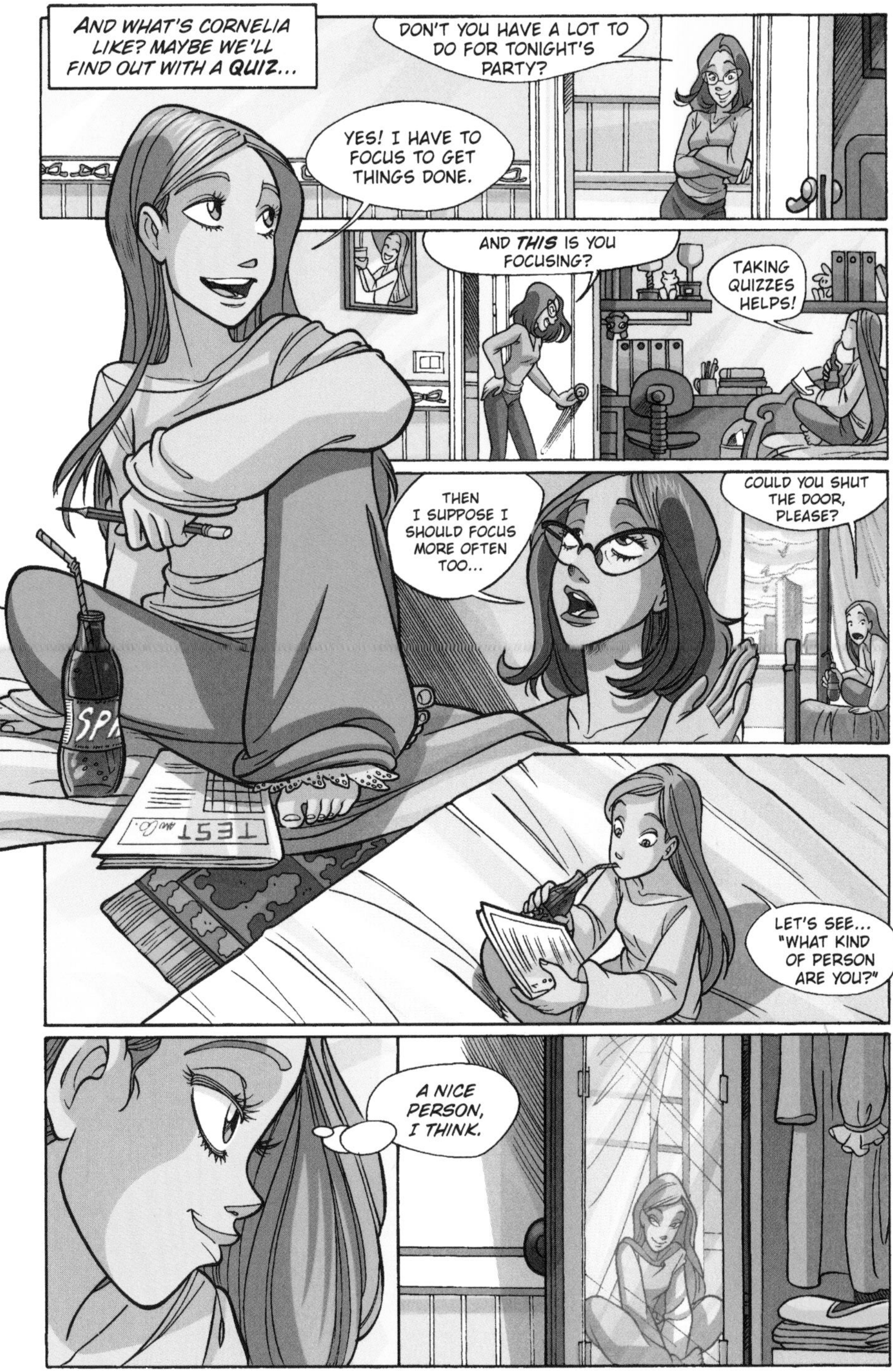
AND WHAT'S CORNELIA LIKE? MAYBE WE'LL FIND OUT WITH A QUIZ...
DON'T YOU HAVE A LOT TO DO FOR TONIGHT'S PARTY?
YES! I HAVE TO FOCUS TO GET THINGS DONE.
AND THIS IS YOU FOCUSING?
TAKING QUIZZES HELPS!
THEN I SUPPOSE I SHOULD FOCUS MORE OFTEN TOO...
COULD YOU SHUT THE DOOR, PLEASE?
TEST
LET'S SEE... "WHAT KIND OF PERSON ARE YOU?"
A NICE PERSON, I THINK.

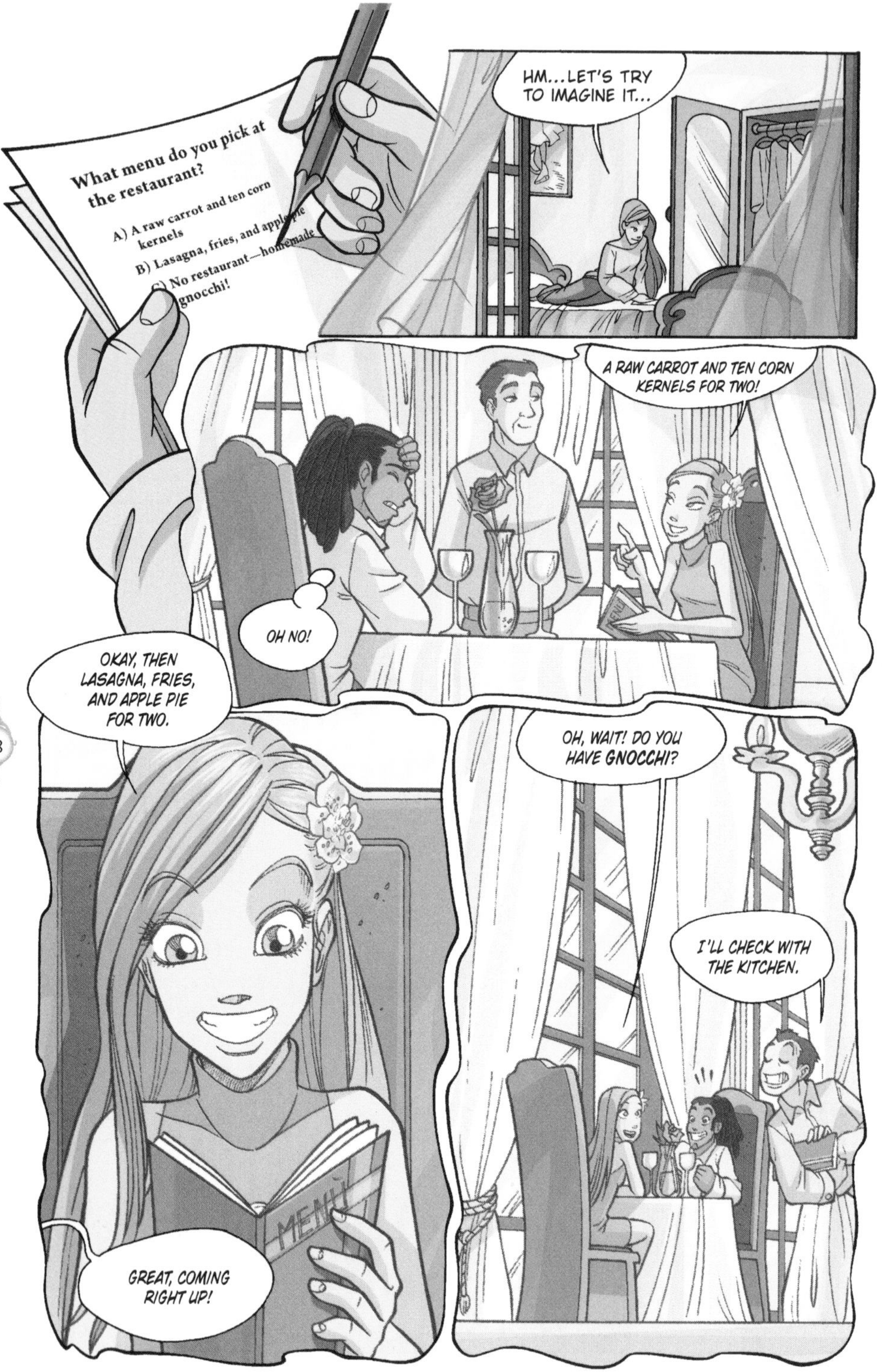
What menu do you pick at the restaurant?
A) A raw carrot and ten corn kernels
B) Lasagna, fries, and apple pie
C) No restaurant—homemade gnocchi!
HM...LET'S TRY TO IMAGINE IT...
A RAW CARROT AND TEN CORN KERNELS FOR TWO!
OH NO!
OKAY, THEN LASAGNA, FRIES, AND APPLE PIE FOR TWO.
GREAT, COMING RIGHT UP!
MENU
OH, WAIT! DO YOU HAVE GNOCCHI?
I'LL CHECK WITH THE KITCHEN.

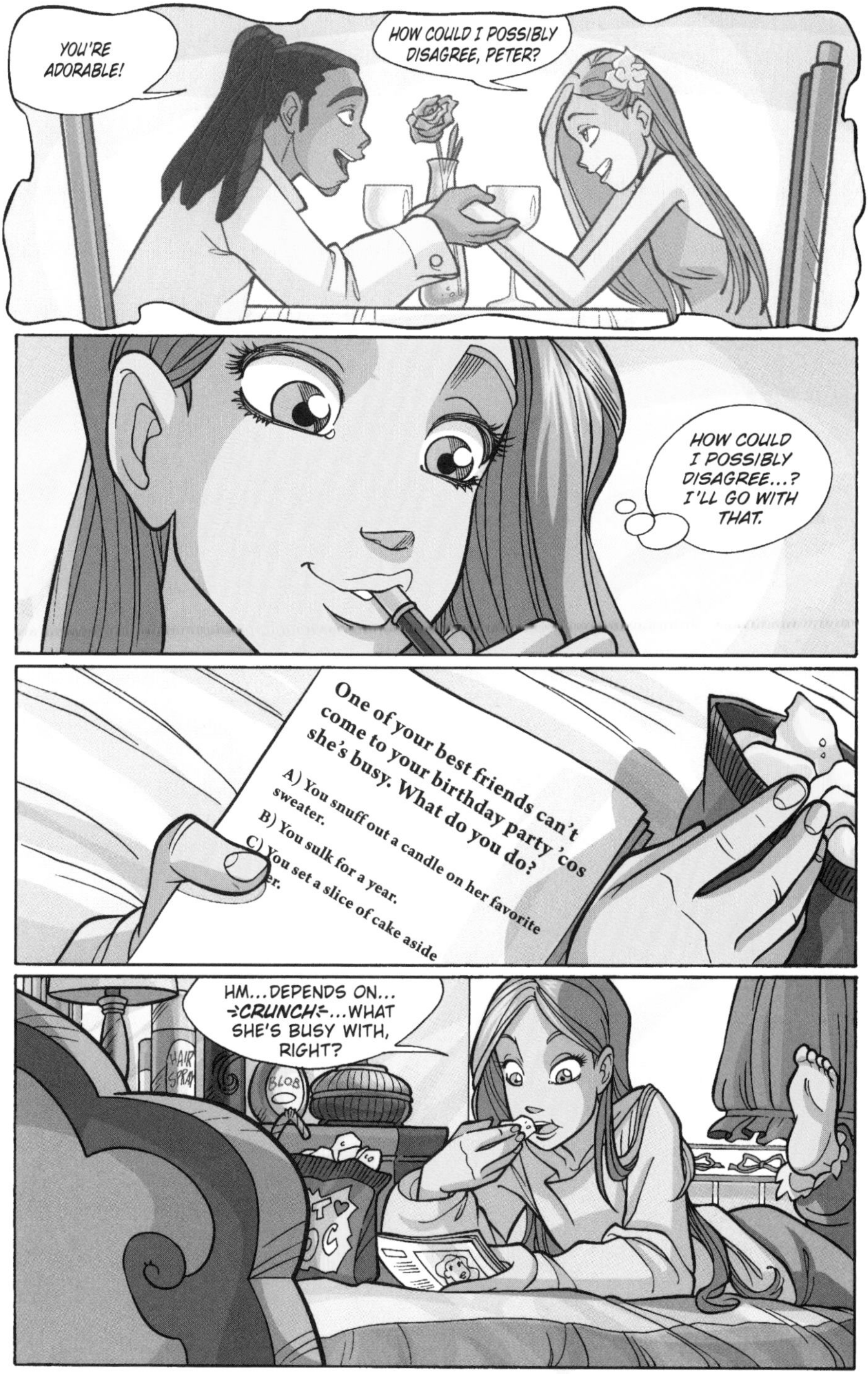

YOU'RE ADORABLE!
HOW COULD I POSSIBLY DISAGREE, PETER?
HOW COULD I POSSIBLY DISAGREE...? I'LL GO WITH THAT.
One of your best friends can't come to your birthday party 'cos she's busy. What do you do?
A) You snuff out a candle on her favorite sweater.
B) You sulk for a year.
C) You set a slice of cake aside
HM...DEPENDS ON... =CRUNCH=...WHAT SHE'S BUSY WITH, RIGHT?
HAIR SPRAY
BLOB

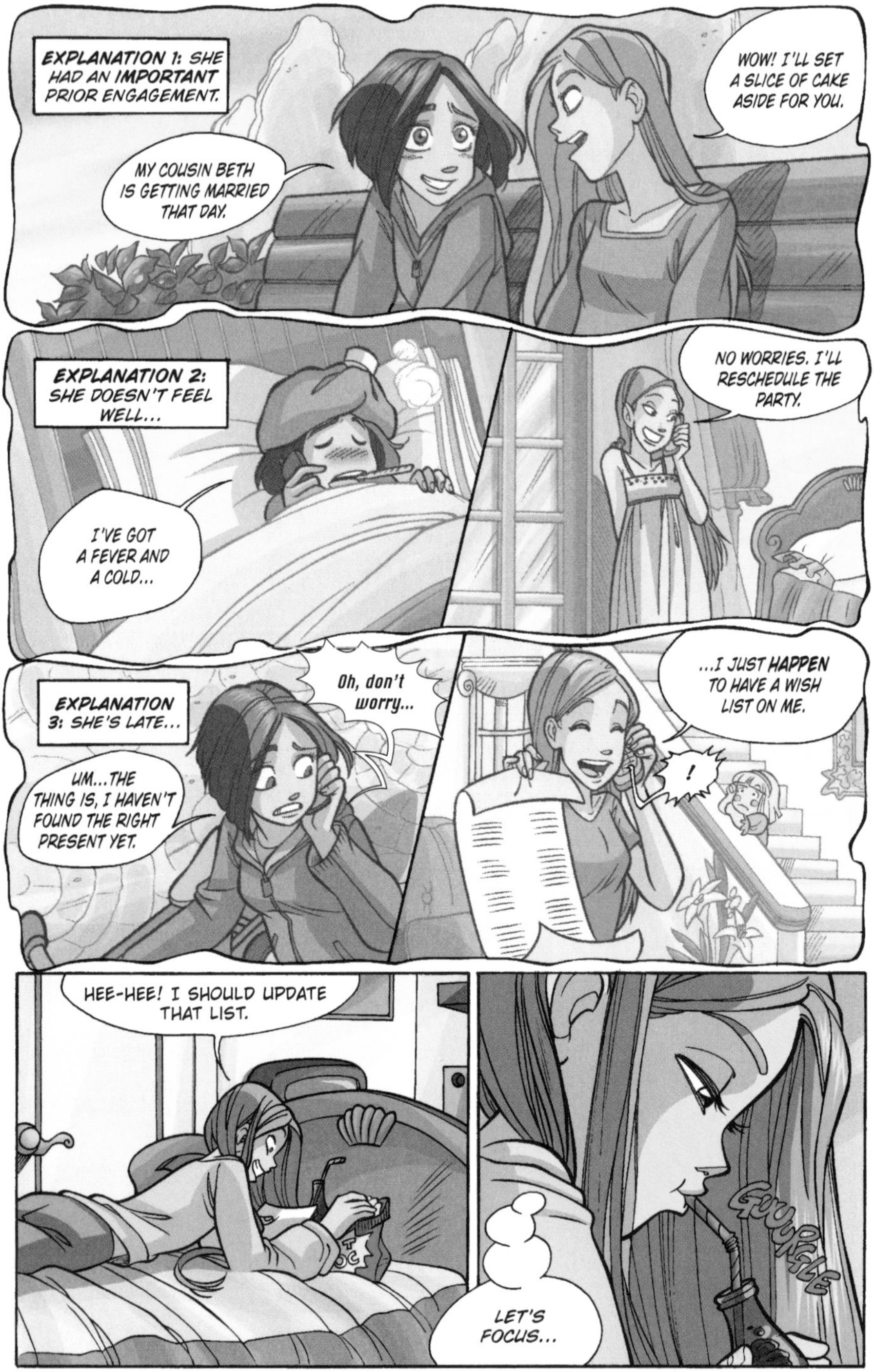
EXPLANATION 1: SHE HAD AN IMPORTANT PRIOR ENGAGEMENT.
MY COUSIN BETH IS GETTING MARRIED THAT DAY.
WOW! I'LL SET A SLICE OF CAKE ASIDE FOR YOU.
EXPLANATION 2: SHE DOESN'T FEEL WELL...
I'VE GOT A FEVER AND A COLD...
NO WORRIES. I'LL RESCHEDULE THE PARTY.
EXPLANATION 3: SHE'S LATE...
UM...THE THING IS, I HAVEN'T FOUND THE RIGHT PRESENT YET.
Oh, don't worry...
...I JUST HAPPEN TO HAVE A WISH LIST ON ME.
!
HEE-HEE! I SHOULD UPDATE THAT LIST.
GUUURGLE
LET'S FOCUS...

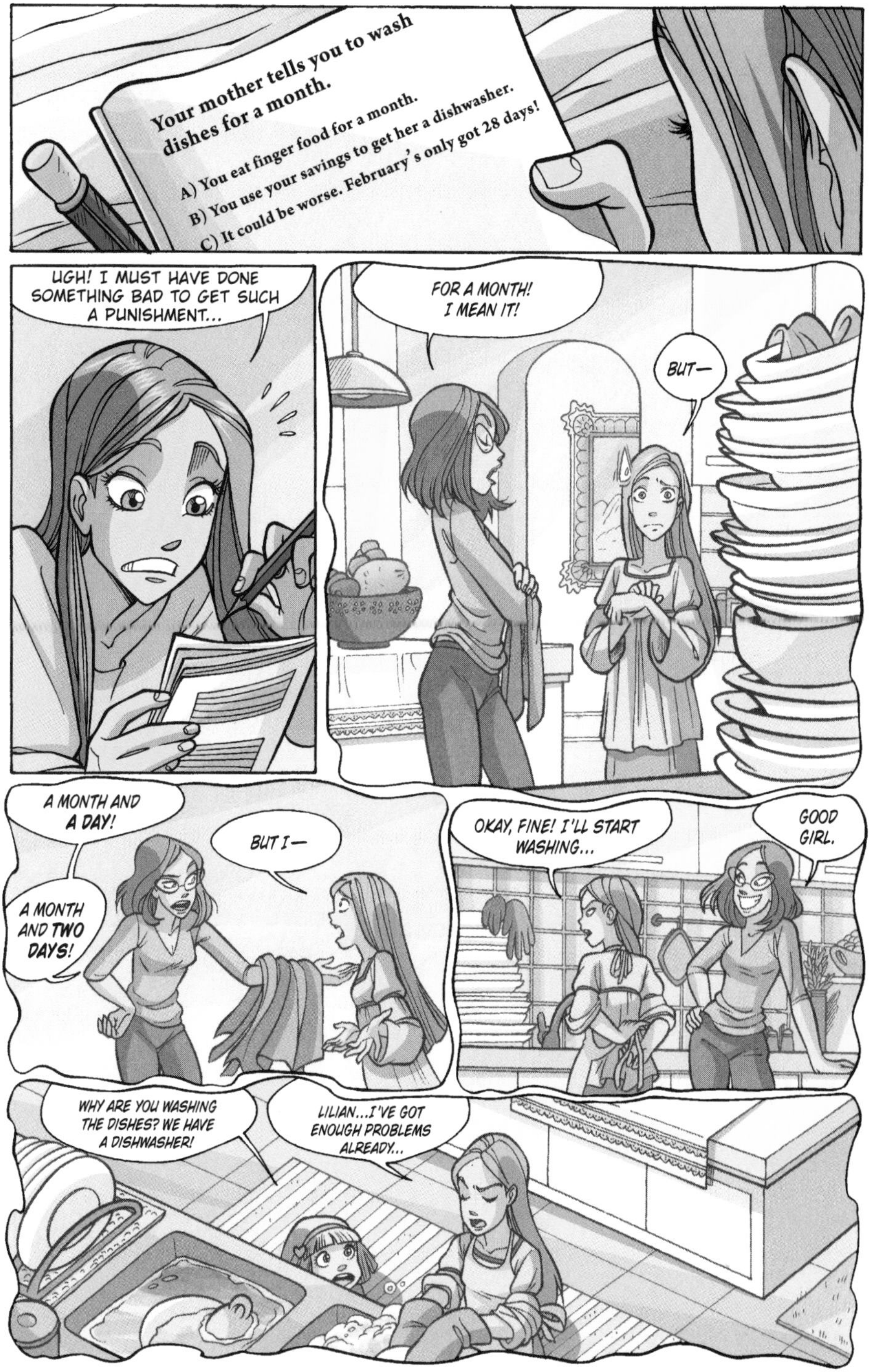

Your mother tells you to wash dishes for a month.
A) You eat finger food for a month.
B) You use your savings to get her a dishwasher.
C) It could be worse. February's only got 28 days!
UGH! I MUST HAVE DONE SOMETHING BAD TO GET SUCH A PUNISHMENT...
FOR A MONTH! I MEAN IT!
BUT—
A MONTH AND A DAY!
BUT I—
A MONTH AND TWO DAYS!
OKAY, FINE! I'LL START WASHING...
GOOD GIRL.
WHY ARE YOU WASHING THE DISHES? WE HAVE A DISHWASHER!
LILIAN...I'VE GOT ENOUGH PROBLEMS ALREADY...

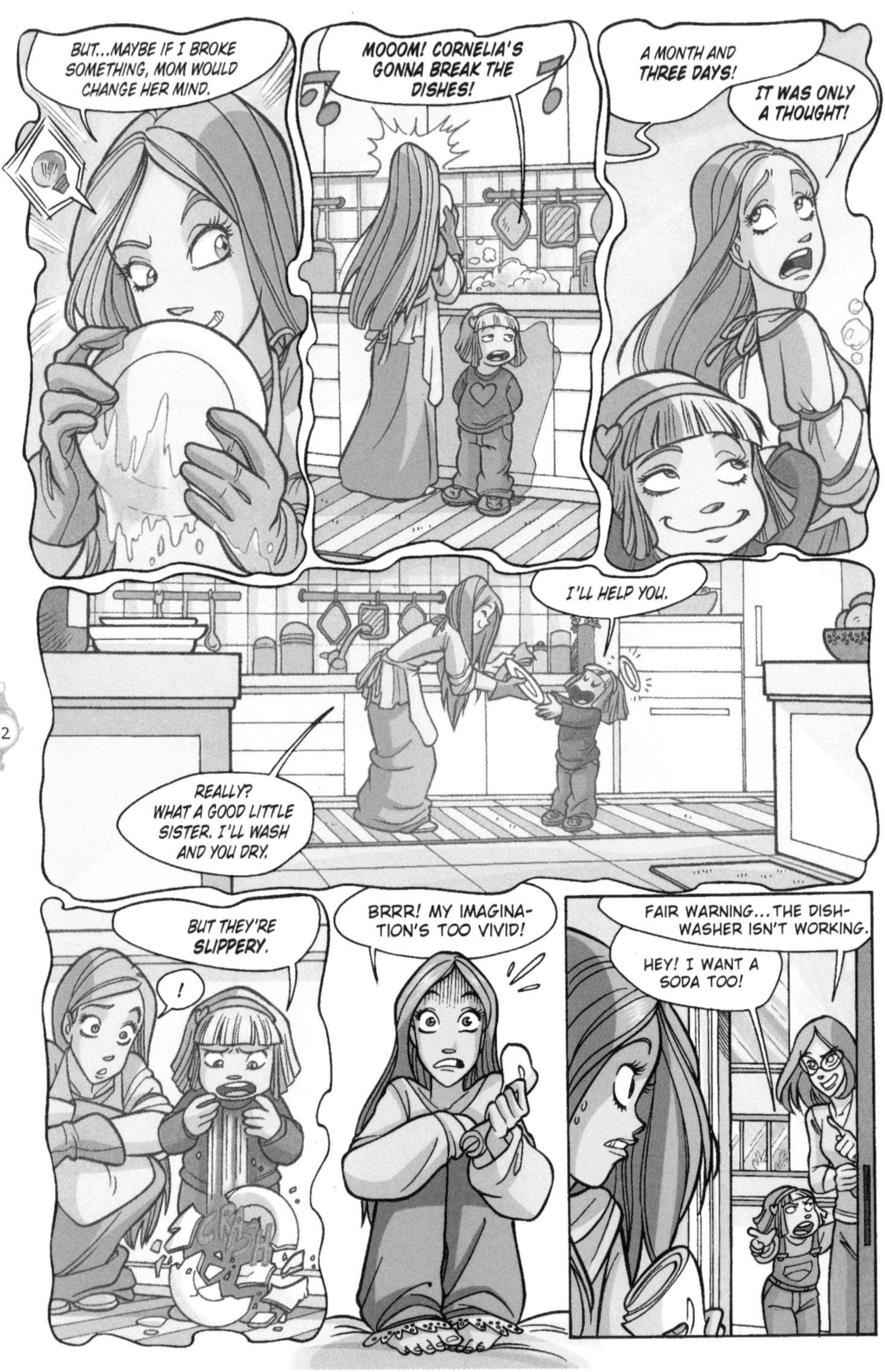
BUT...MAYBE IF I BROKE SOMETHING, MOM WOULD CHANGE HER MIND.
MOOOM! CORNELIA'S GONNA BREAK THE DISHES!
A MONTH AND THREE DAYS!
IT WAS ONLY A THOUGHT!
I'LL HELP YOU.
REALLY? WHAT A GOOD LITTLE SISTER. I'LL WASH AND YOU DRY.
BUT THEY'RE SLIPPERY.
!
CRASH
BRRR! MY IMAGINATION'S TOO VIVID!
FAIR WARNING...THE DISHWASHER ISN'T WORKING.
HEY! I WANT A SODA TOO!

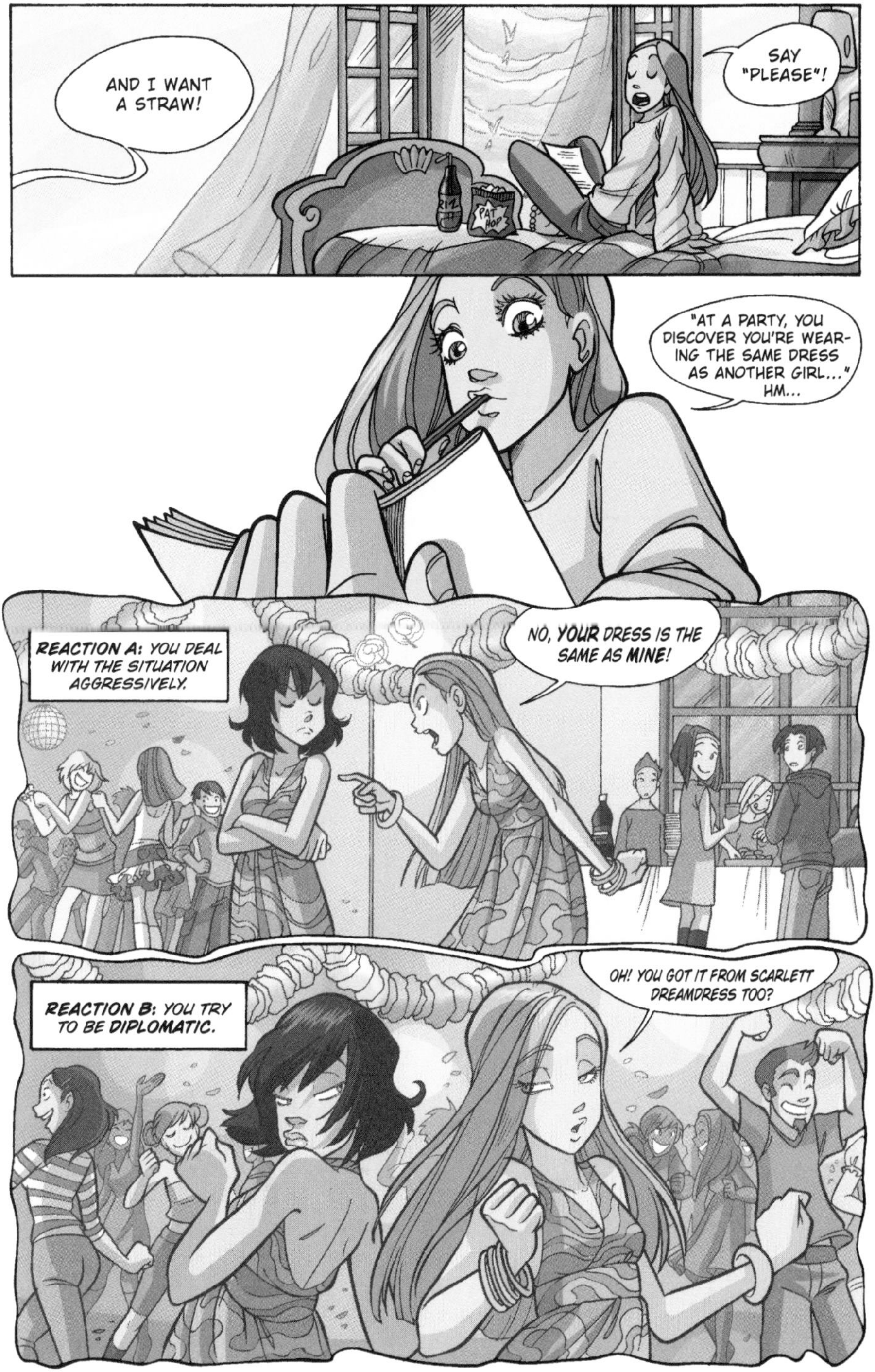
AND I WANT A STRAW!
SAY "PLEASE"!
"AT A PARTY, YOU DISCOVER YOU'RE WEAR-ING THE SAME DRESS AS ANOTHER GIRL..." HM...
REACTION A: YOU DEAL WITH THE SITUATION AGGRESSIVELY.
NO, YOUR DRESS IS THE SAME AS MINE!
REACTION B: YOU TRY TO BE DIPLOMATIC.
OH! YOU GOT IT FROM SCARLETT DREAMDRESS TOO?

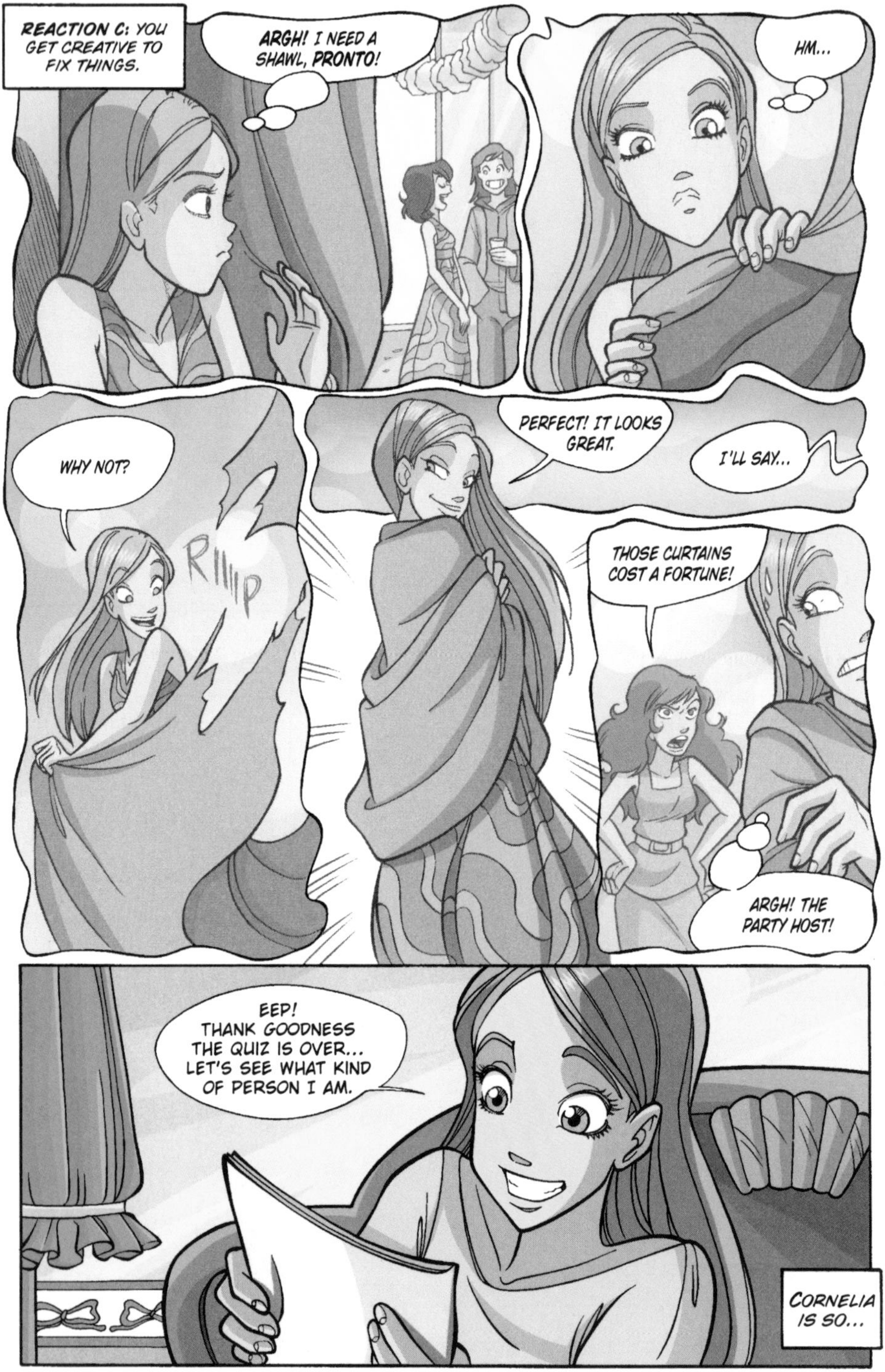
REACTION C: YOU GET CREATIVE TO FIX THINGS.
ARGH! I NEED A SHAWL, PRONTO!
HM...
WHY NOT?
RIIIIP
PERFECT! IT LOOKS GREAT.
I'LL SAY...
THOSE CURTAINS COST A FORTUNE!
ARGH! THE PARTY HOST!
EEP! THANK GOODNESS THE QUIZ IS OVER... LET'S SEE WHAT KIND OF PERSON I AM.
CORNELIA IS SO...

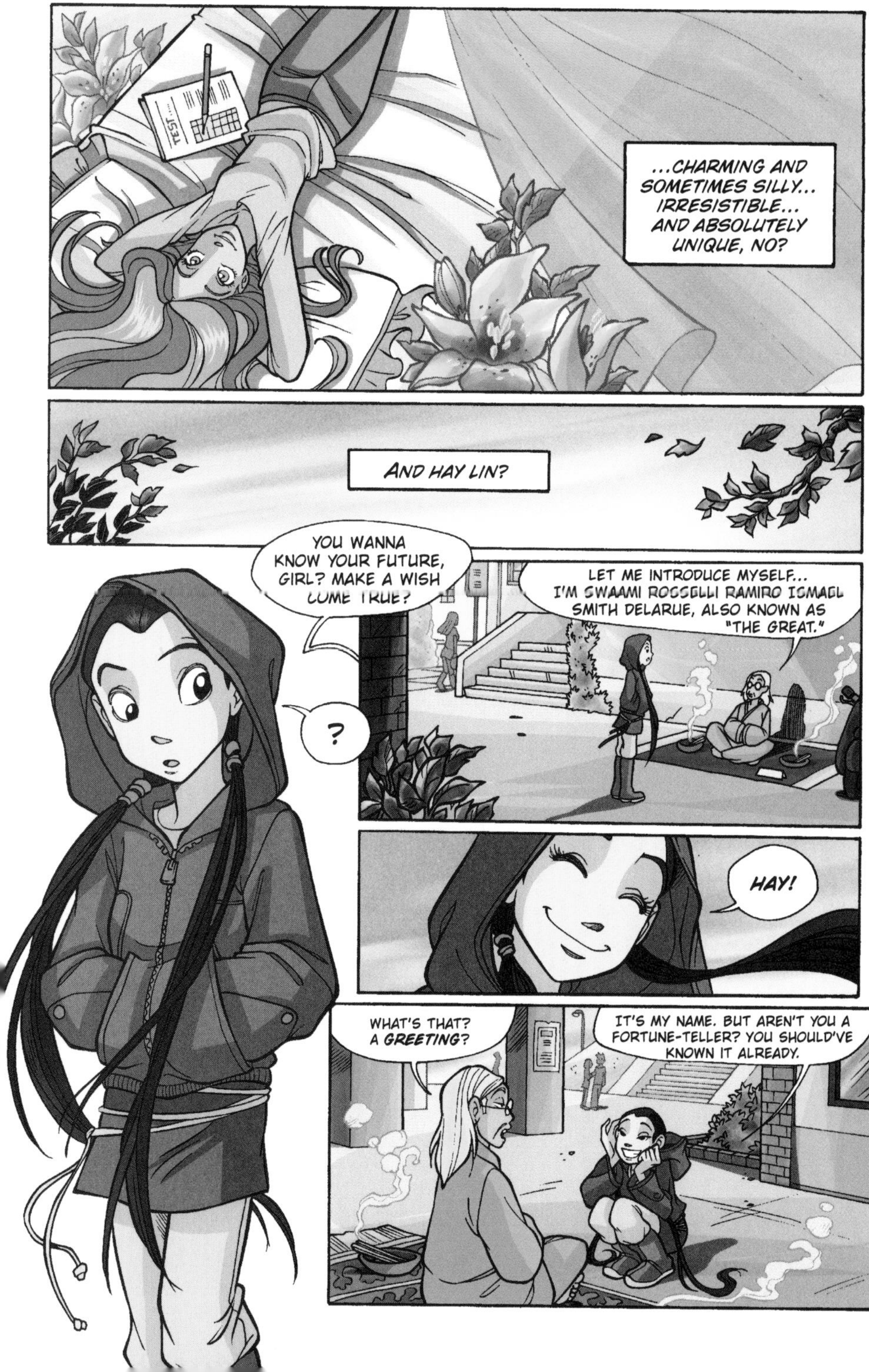
...CHARMING AND SOMETIMES SILLY... IRRESISTIBLE... AND ABSOLUTELY UNIQUE, NO?
AND HAY LIN?
YOU WANNA KNOW YOUR FUTURE, GIRL? MAKE A WISH COME TRUE?
LET ME INTRODUCE MYSELF... I'M SWAAMI ROSSELLI RAMIRO ISMAEL SMITH DELARUE, ALSO KNOWN AS "THE GREAT."
?
HAY!
WHAT'S THAT? A GREETING?
IT'S MY NAME. BUT AREN'T YOU A FORTUNE-TELLER? YOU SHOULD'VE KNOWN IT ALREADY.

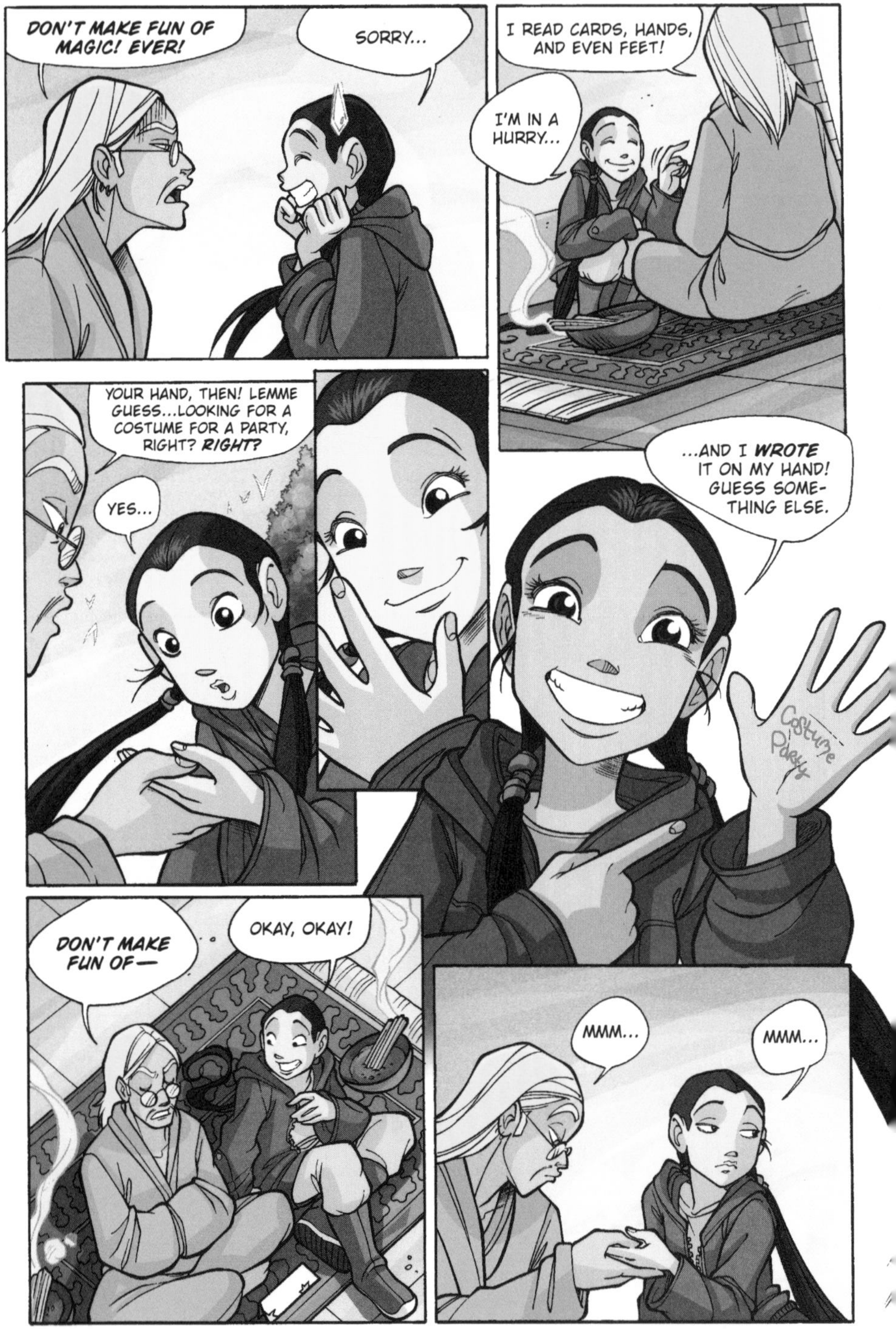
DON'T MAKE FUN OF MAGIC! EVER!
SORRY...
I READ CARDS, HANDS, AND EVEN FEET!
I'M IN A HURRY...
YOUR HAND, THEN! LEMME GUESS...LOOKING FOR A COSTUME FOR A PARTY, RIGHT? RIGHT?
YES...
...AND I WROTE IT ON MY HAND! GUESS SOMETHING ELSE.
Costume Party
DON'T MAKE FUN OF—
OKAY, OKAY!
MMM...
MMM...

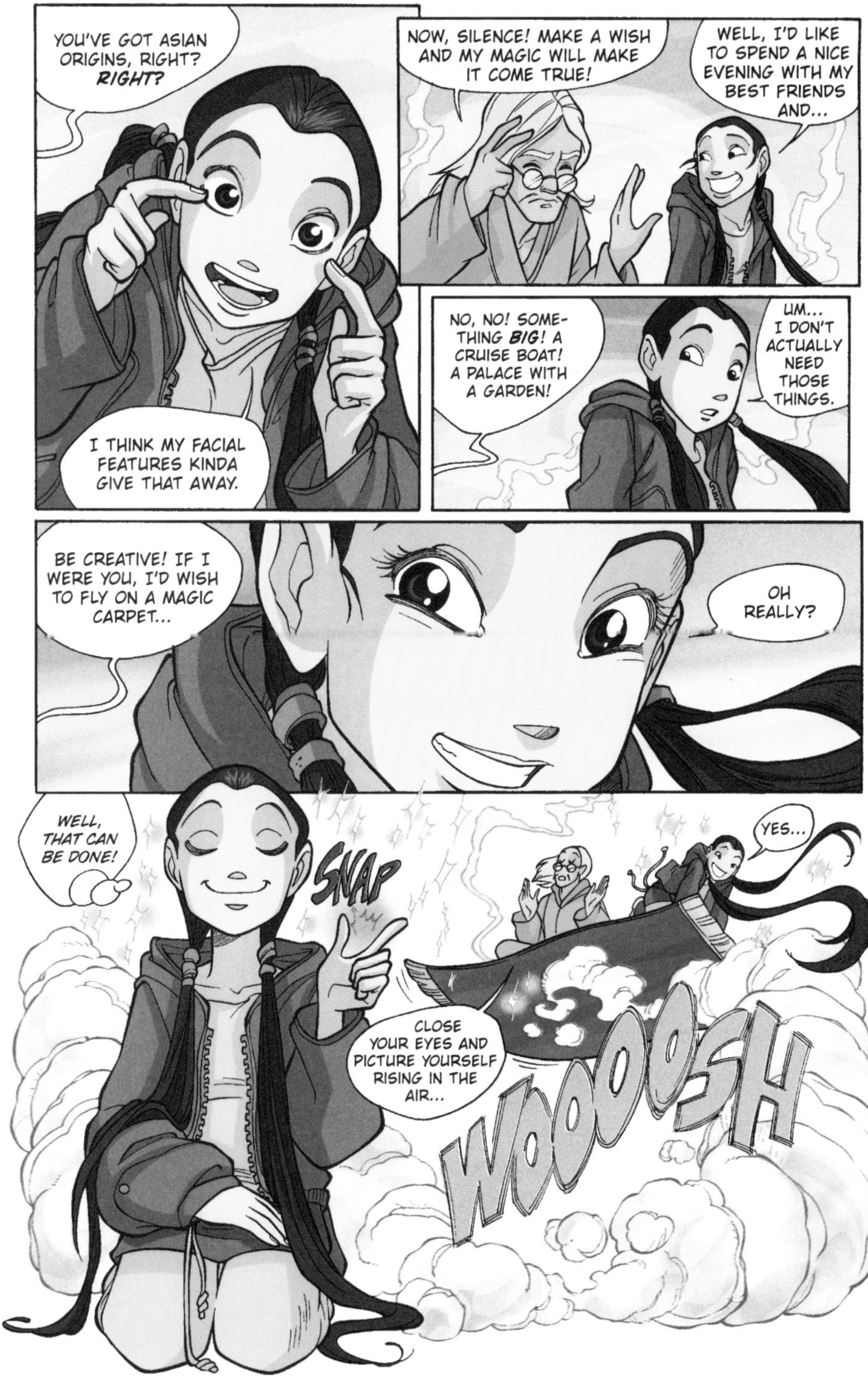
YOU'VE GOT ASIAN ORIGINS, RIGHT? ***RIGHT?***
I THINK MY FACIAL FEATURES KINDA GIVE THAT AWAY.
NOW, SILENCE! MAKE A WISH AND MY MAGIC WILL MAKE IT COME TRUE!
WELL, I'D LIKE TO SPEND A NICE EVENING WITH MY BEST FRIENDS AND...
NO, NO! SOMETHING ***BIG***! A CRUISE BOAT! A PALACE WITH A GARDEN!
UM... I DON'T ACTUALLY NEED THOSE THINGS.
BE CREATIVE! IF I WERE YOU, I'D WISH TO FLY ON A MAGIC CARPET...
OH REALLY?
WELL, THAT CAN BE DONE!
SNAP
YES...
CLOSE YOUR EYES AND PICTURE YOURSELF RISING IN THE AIR...
WOOOOSH

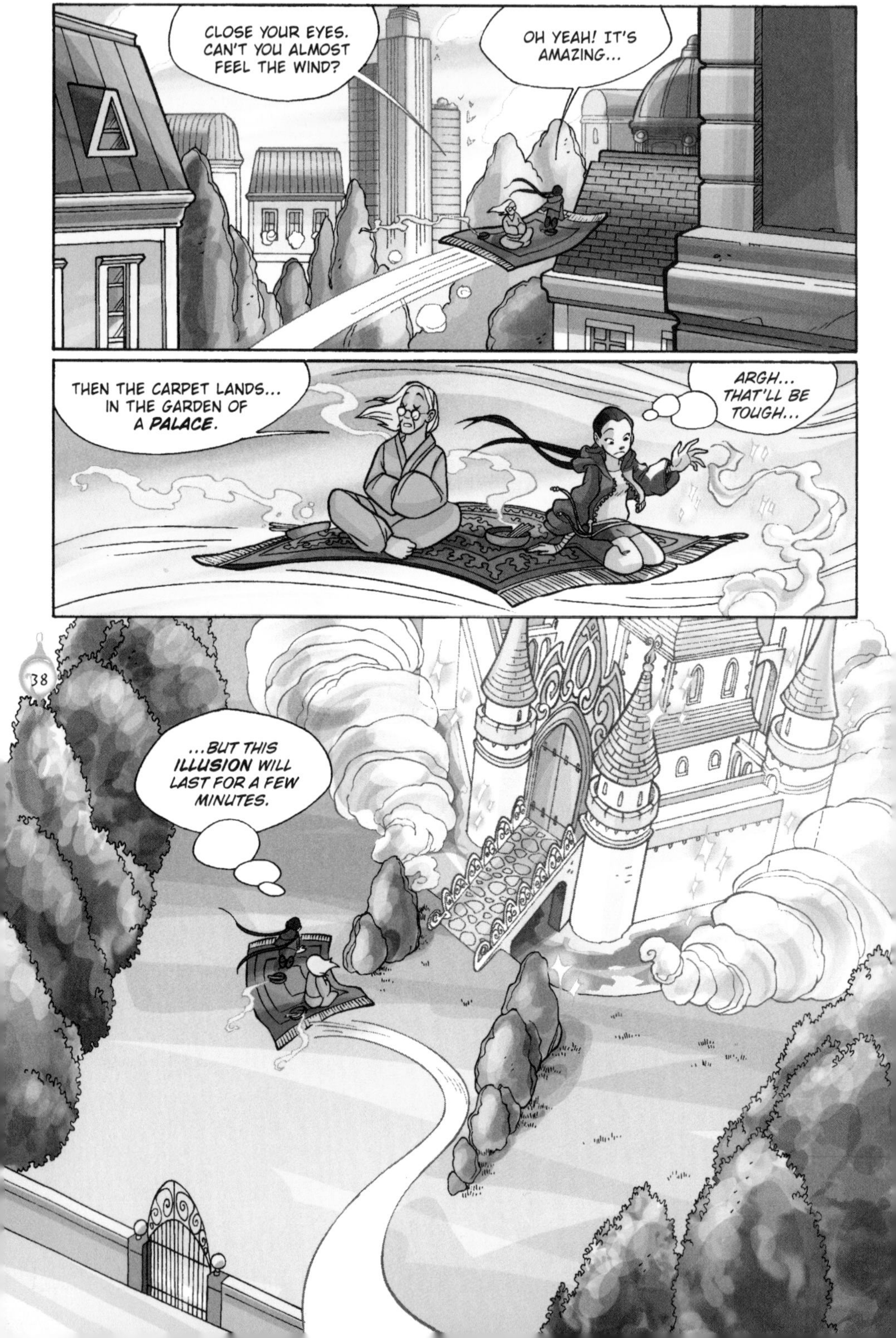

CLOSE YOUR EYES. CAN'T YOU ALMOST FEEL THE WIND?
OH YEAH! IT'S AMAZING...
THEN THE CARPET LANDS... IN THE GARDEN OF A **PALACE**.
ARGH... THAT'LL BE TOUGH...
...BUT THIS **ILLUSION** WILL LAST FOR A FEW MINUTES.

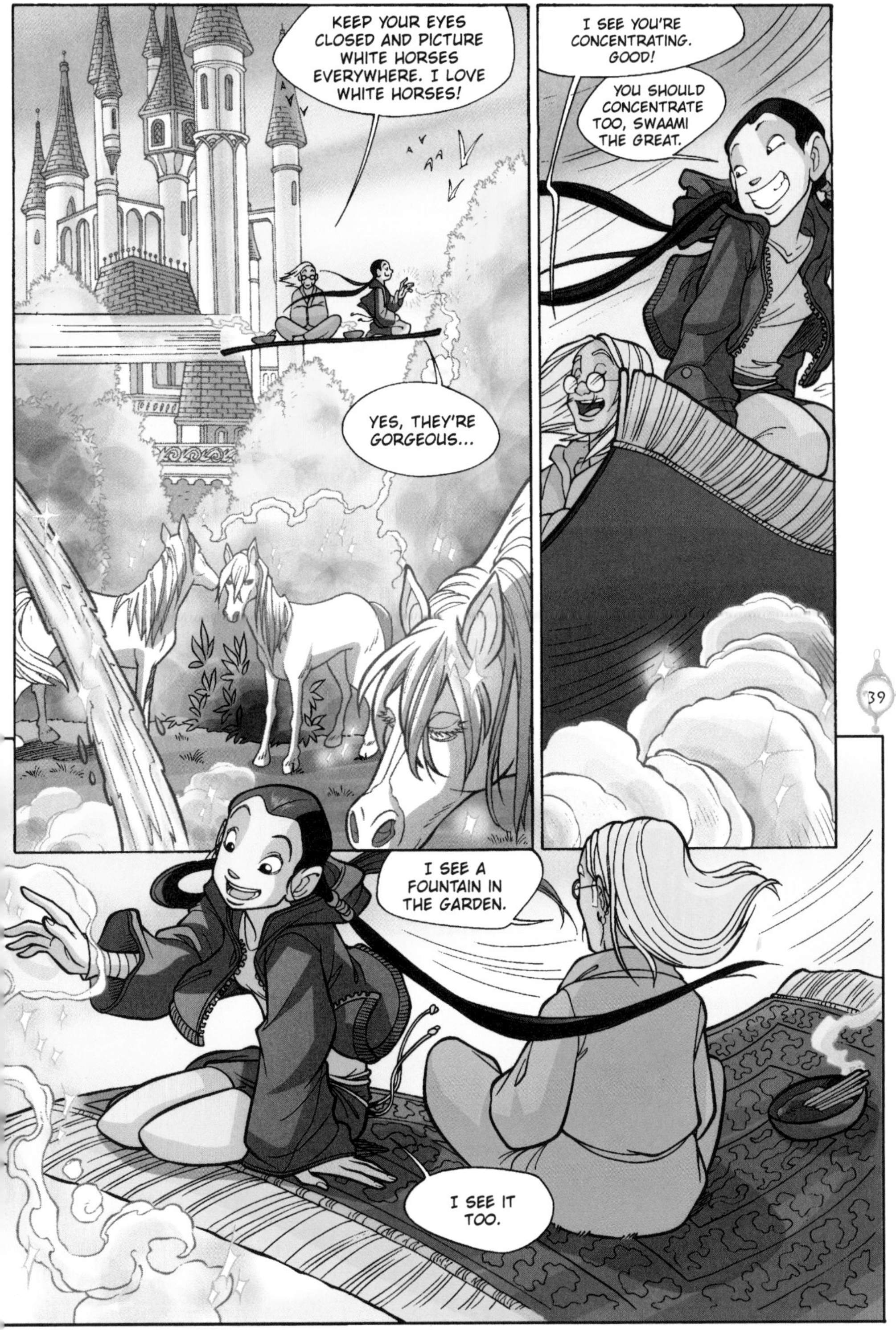
KEEP YOUR EYES CLOSED AND PICTURE WHITE HORSES EVERYWHERE. I LOVE WHITE HORSES!
YES, THEY'RE GORGEOUS...
I SEE YOU'RE CONCENTRATING. GOOD!
YOU SHOULD CONCENTRATE TOO, SWAAMI THE GREAT.
I SEE A FOUNTAIN IN THE GARDEN.
I SEE IT TOO.

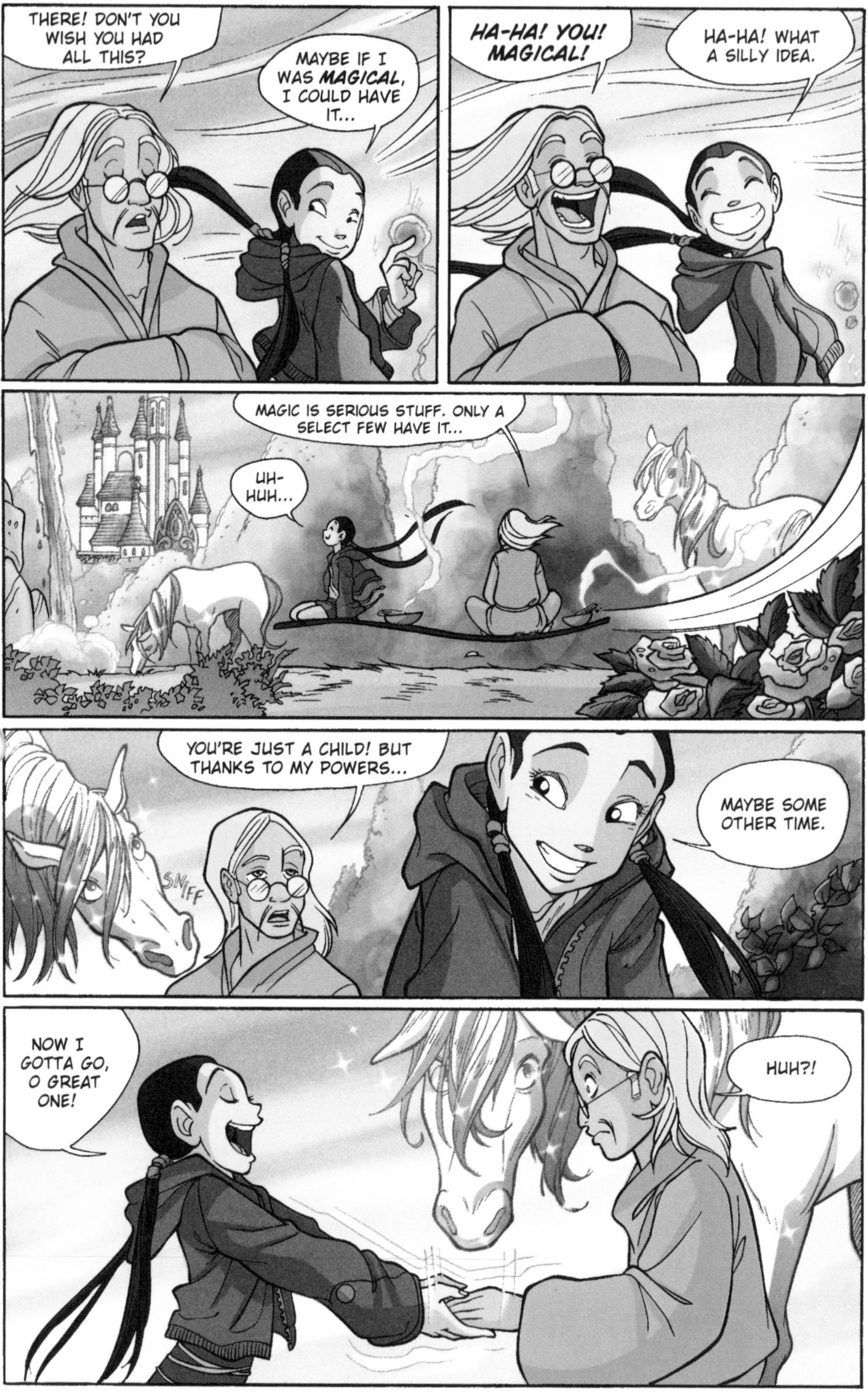
THERE! DON'T YOU WISH YOU HAD ALL THIS?
MAYBE IF I WAS MAGICAL, I COULD HAVE IT...
HA-HA! YOU! MAGICAL!
HA-HA! WHAT A SILLY IDEA.
MAGIC IS SERIOUS STUFF. ONLY A SELECT FEW HAVE IT...
UH-HUH...
YOU'RE JUST A CHILD! BUT THANKS TO MY POWERS...
SNIFF
MAYBE SOME OTHER TIME.
NOW I GOTTA GO, O GREAT ONE!
HUH?!

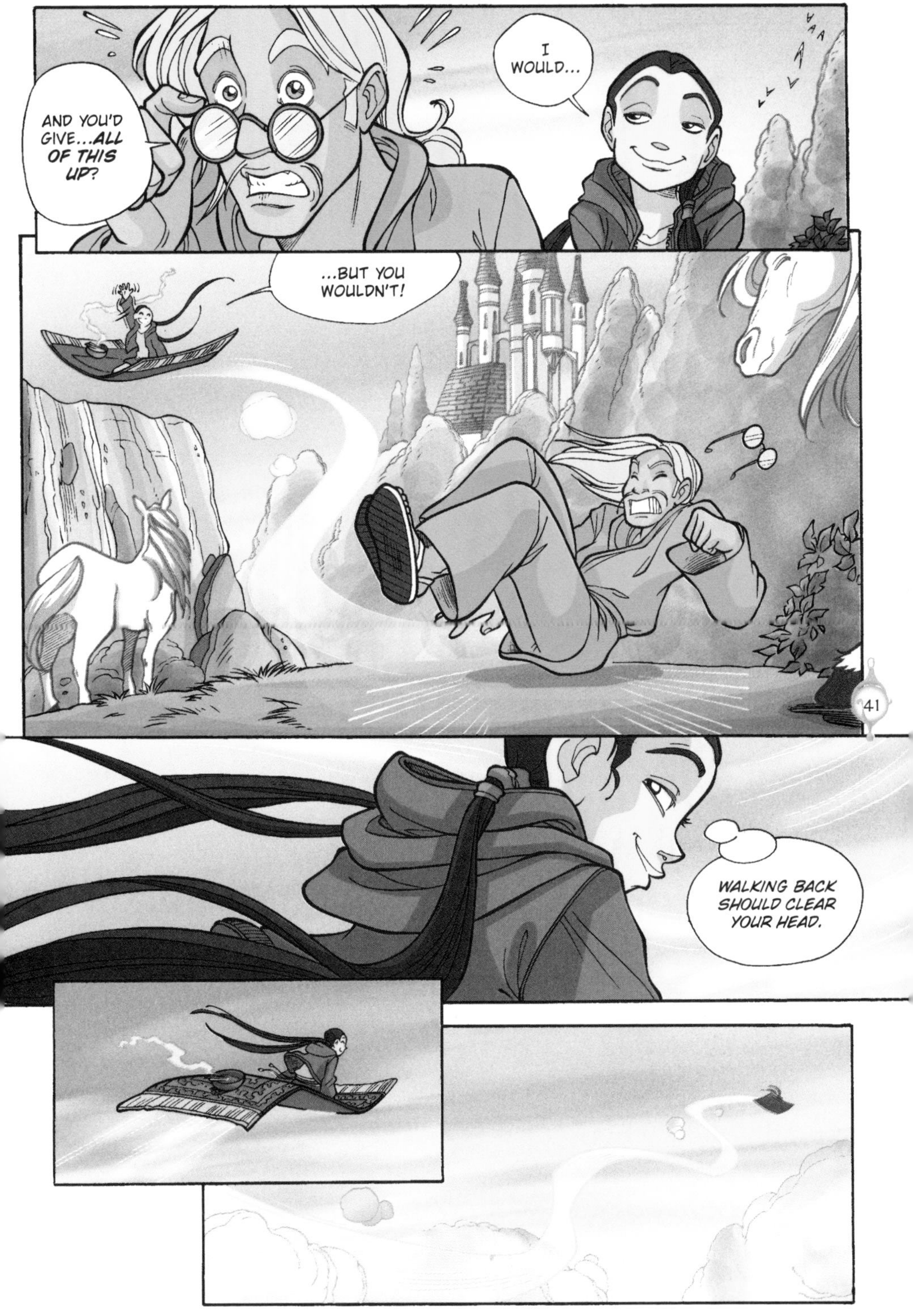
AND YOU'D GIVE...ALL OF THIS UP?
I WOULD...
...BUT YOU WOULDN'T!
WALKING BACK SHOULD CLEAR YOUR HEAD.

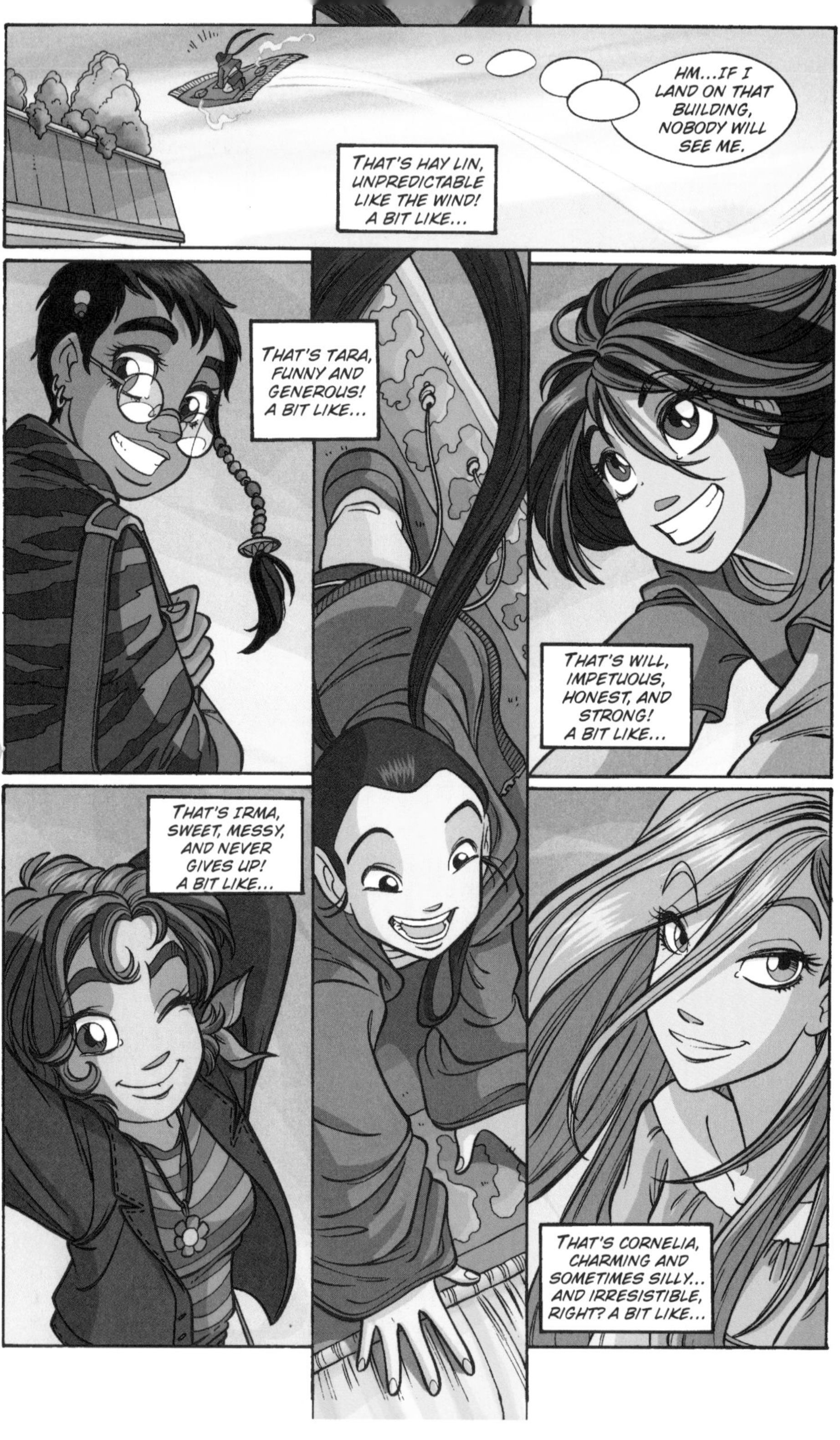

HM...IF I LAND ON THAT BUILDING, NOBODY WILL SEE ME.
THAT'S HAY LIN, UNPREDICTABLE LIKE THE WIND! A BIT LIKE...
THAT'S TARA, FUNNY AND GENEROUS! A BIT LIKE...
THAT'S WILL, IMPETUOUS, HONEST, AND STRONG! A BIT LIKE...
THAT'S IRMA, SWEET, MESSY, AND NEVER GIVES UP! A BIT LIKE...
THAT'S CORNELIA, CHARMING AND SOMETIMES SILLY... AND IRRESISTIBLE, RIGHT? A BIT LIKE...

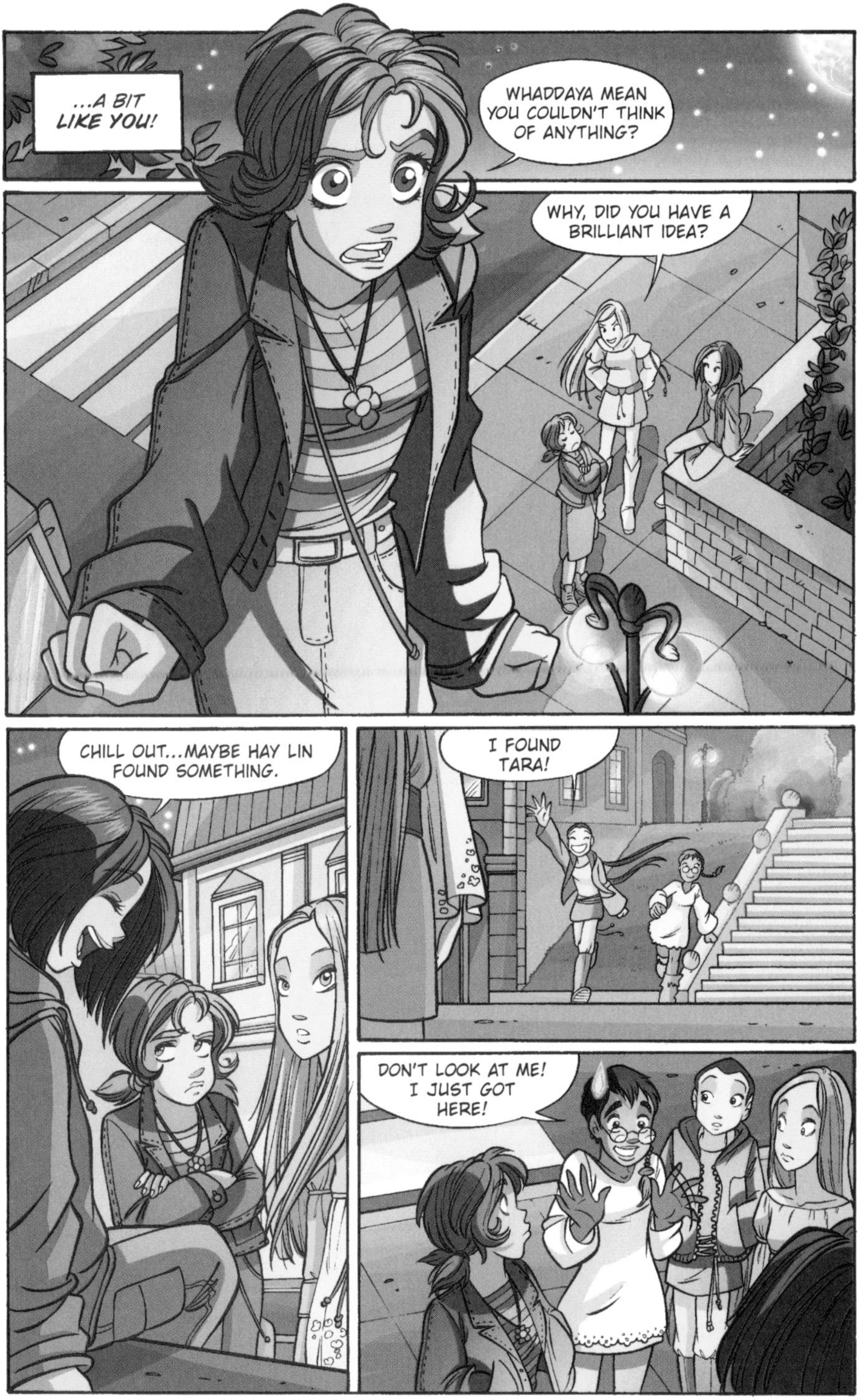
...A BIT LIKE YOU!
WHADDAYA MEAN YOU COULDN'T THINK OF ANYTHING?
WHY, DID YOU HAVE A BRILLIANT IDEA?
CHILL OUT...MAYBE HAY LIN FOUND SOMETHING.
I FOUND TARA!
DON'T LOOK AT ME! I JUST GOT HERE!

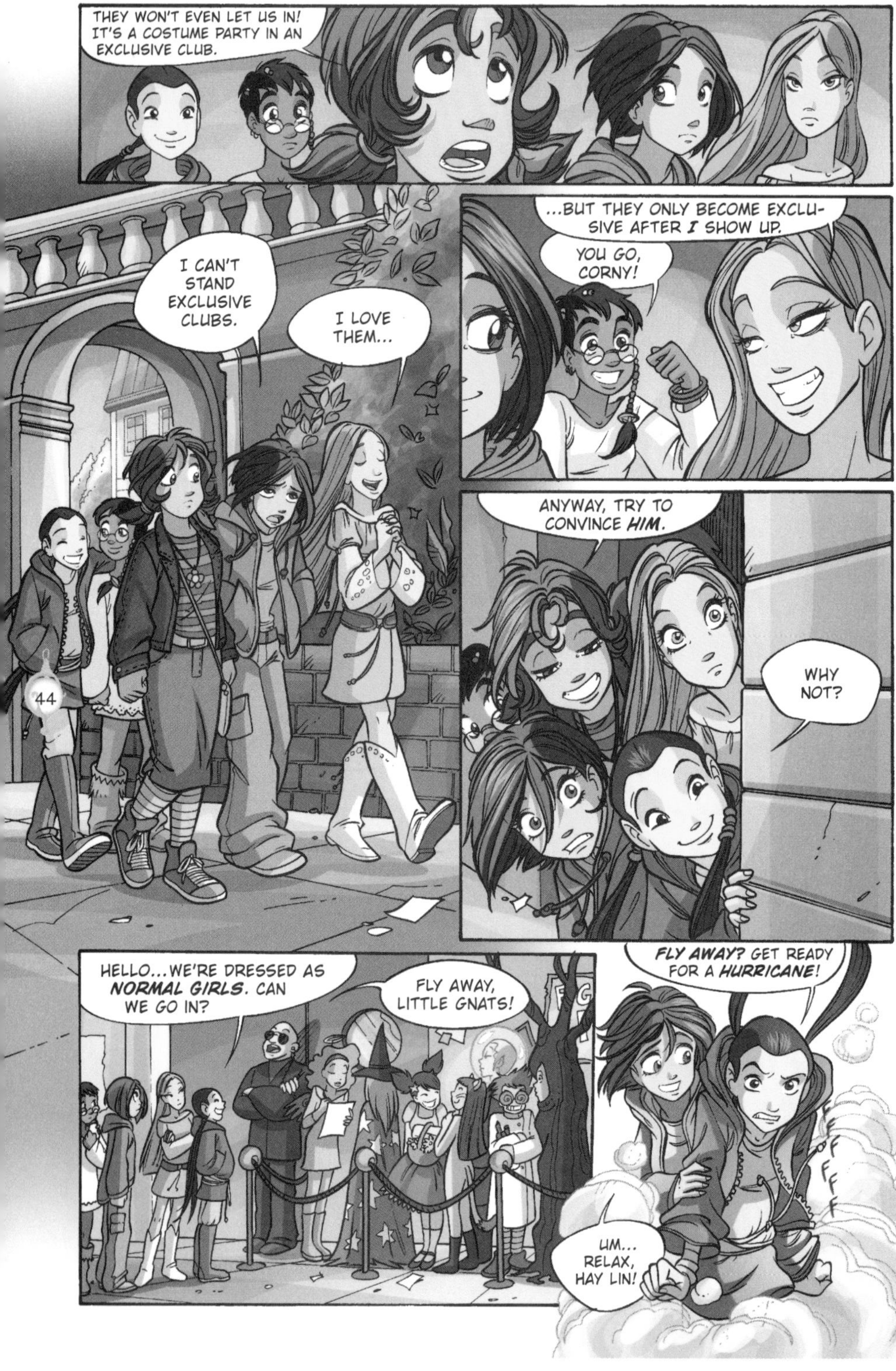
THEY WON'T EVEN LET US IN! IT'S A COSTUME PARTY IN AN EXCLUSIVE CLUB.
I CAN'T STAND EXCLUSIVE CLUBS.
I LOVE THEM...
...BUT THEY ONLY BECOME EXCLUSIVE AFTER I SHOW UP.
YOU GO, CORNY!
ANYWAY, TRY TO CONVINCE HIM.
WHY NOT?
HELLO... WE'RE DRESSED AS NORMAL GIRLS. CAN WE GO IN?
FLY AWAY, LITTLE GNATS!
FLY AWAY? GET READY FOR A HURRICANE!
UM... RELAX, HAY LIN!
FFFF

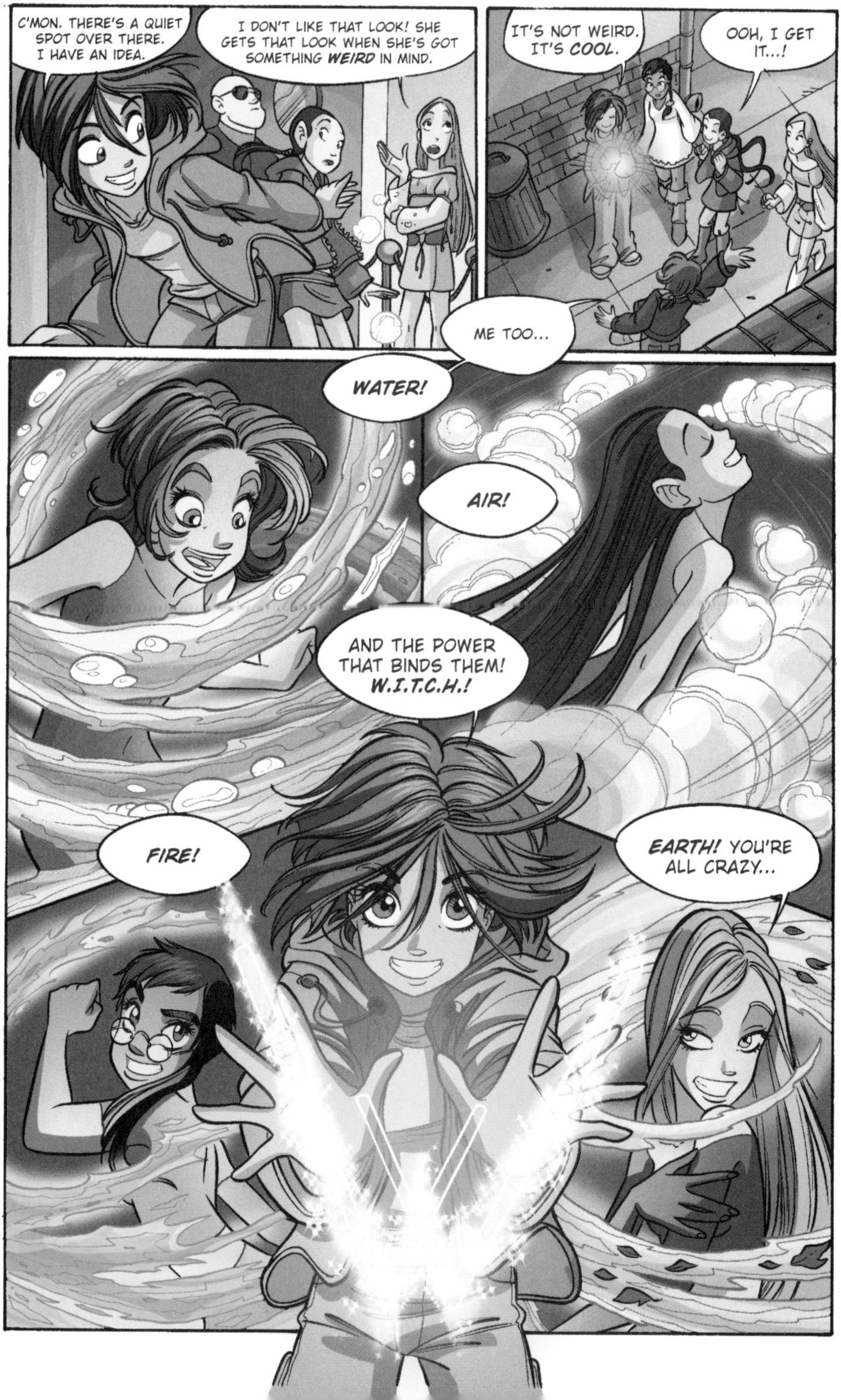
C'MON. THERE'S A QUIET SPOT OVER THERE. I HAVE AN IDEA.
I DON'T LIKE THAT LOOK! SHE GETS THAT LOOK WHEN SHE'S GOT SOMETHING WEIRD IN MIND.
IT'S NOT WEIRD. IT'S COOL.
OOH, I GET IT...!
ME TOO...
WATER!
AIR!
AND THE POWER THAT BINDS THEM! W.I.T.C.H.!
FIRE!
EARTH! YOU'RE ALL CRAZY...

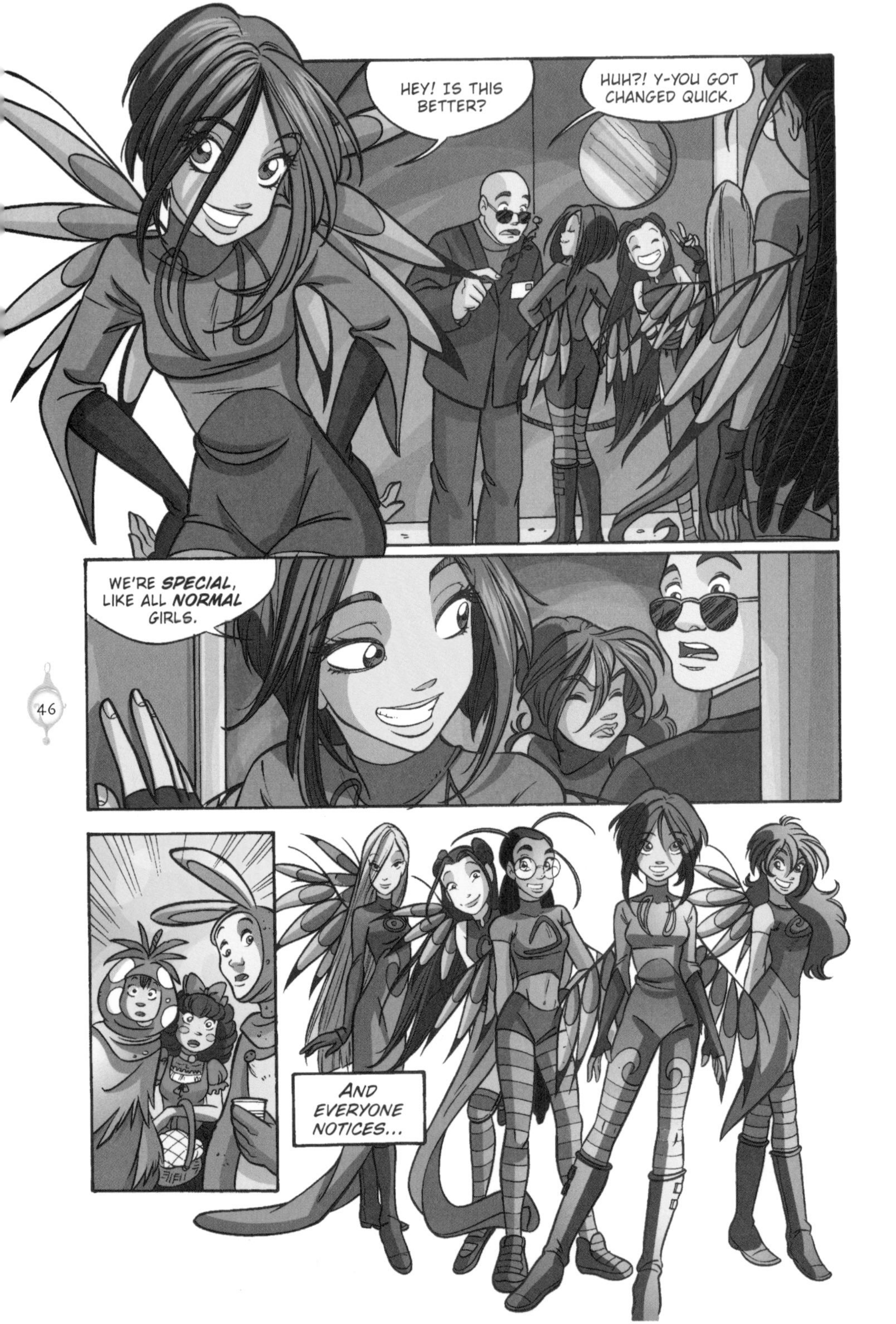
HEY! IS THIS BETTER?
HUH?! Y-YOU GOT CHANGED QUICK.
WE'RE **SPECIAL**, LIKE ALL **NORMAL** GIRLS.
AND EVERYONE NOTICES...

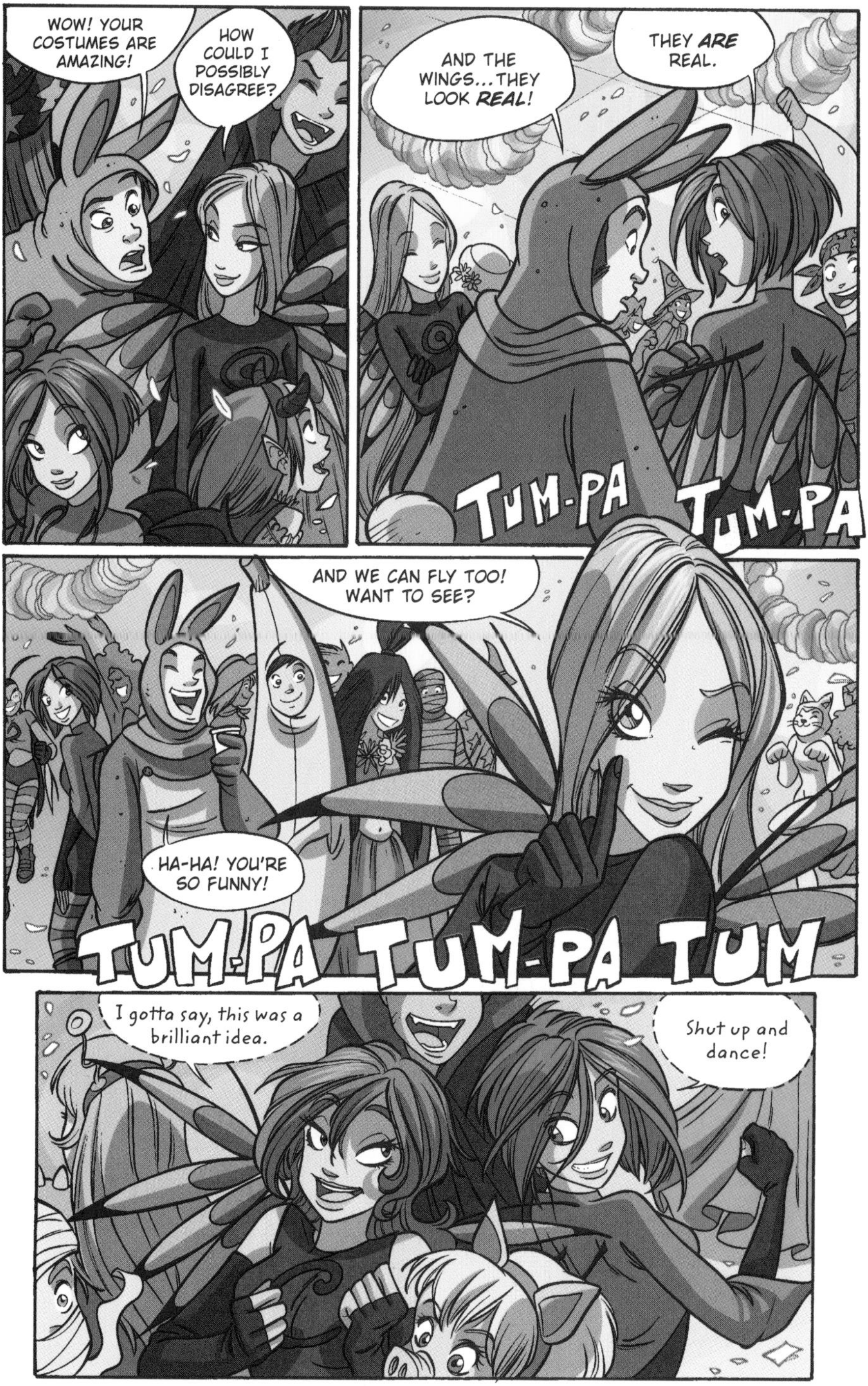
WOW! YOUR COSTUMES ARE AMAZING!
HOW COULD I POSSIBLY DISAGREE?
AND THE WINGS... THEY LOOK REAL!
THEY ARE REAL.
TUM-PA TUM-PA
AND WE CAN FLY TOO! WANT TO SEE?
HA-HA! YOU'RE SO FUNNY!
TUM-PA TUM-PA TUM
I gotta say, this was a brilliant idea.
Shut up and dance!

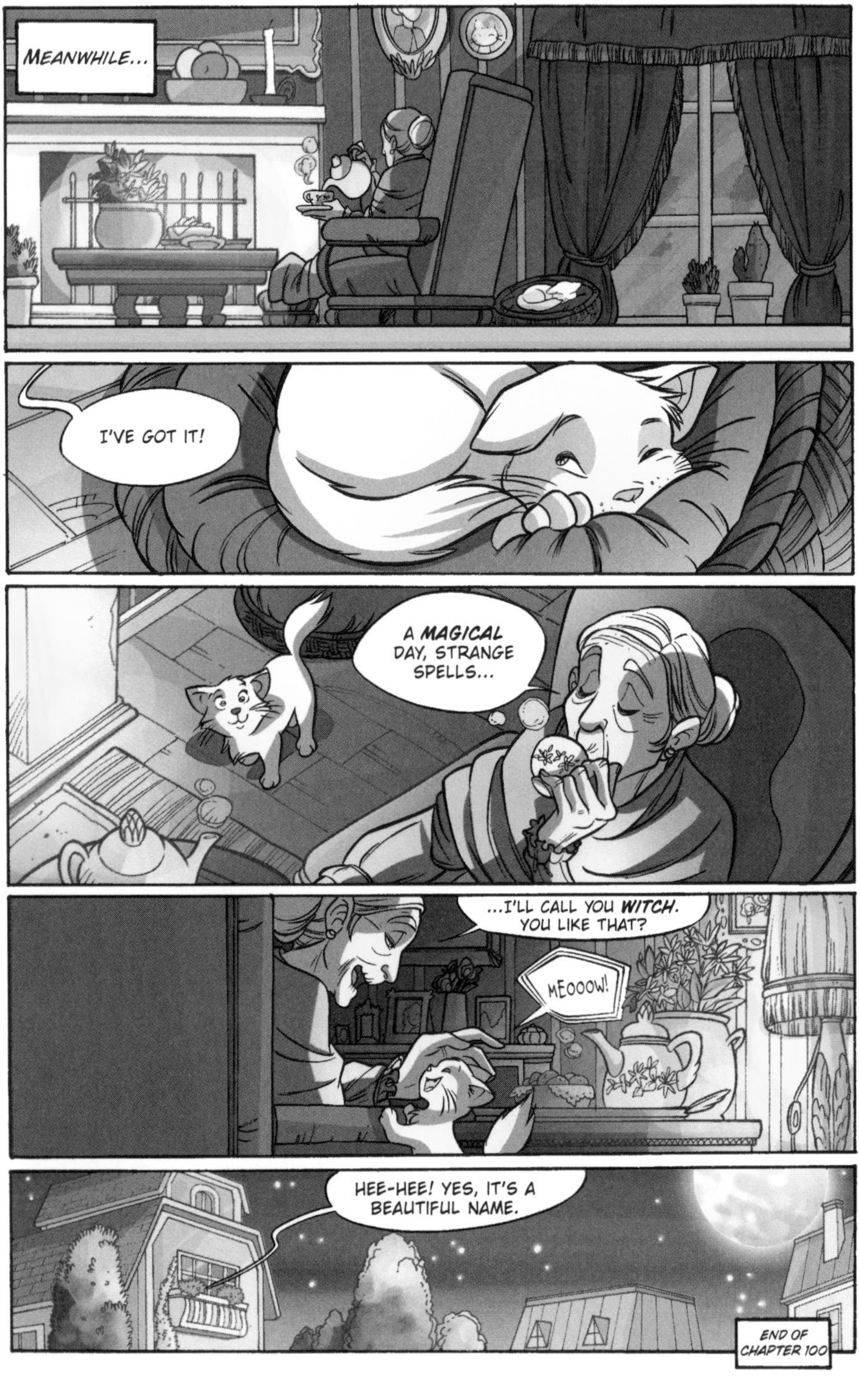
MEANWHILE...
I'VE GOT IT!
A MAGICAL DAY, STRANGE SPELLS...
...I'LL CALL YOU WITCH. YOU LIKE THAT?
MEOOOW!
HEE-HEE! YES, IT'S A BEAUTIFUL NAME.
END OF CHAPTER 100

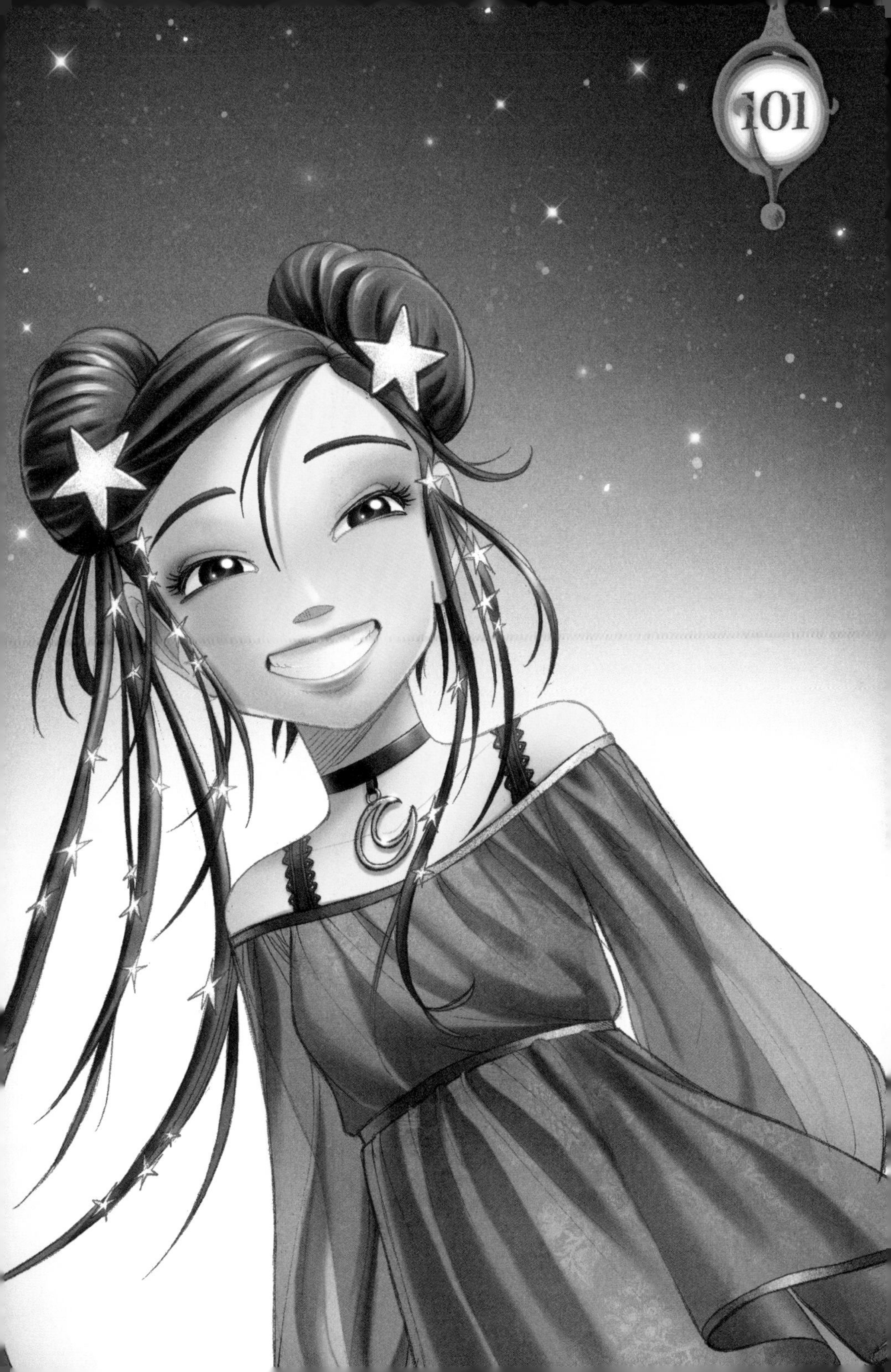
101

W.i.t.c.h.

Will Irma Taranee Cornelia Hay Lin

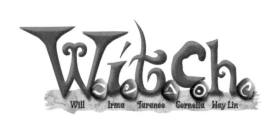

The Nascent Star

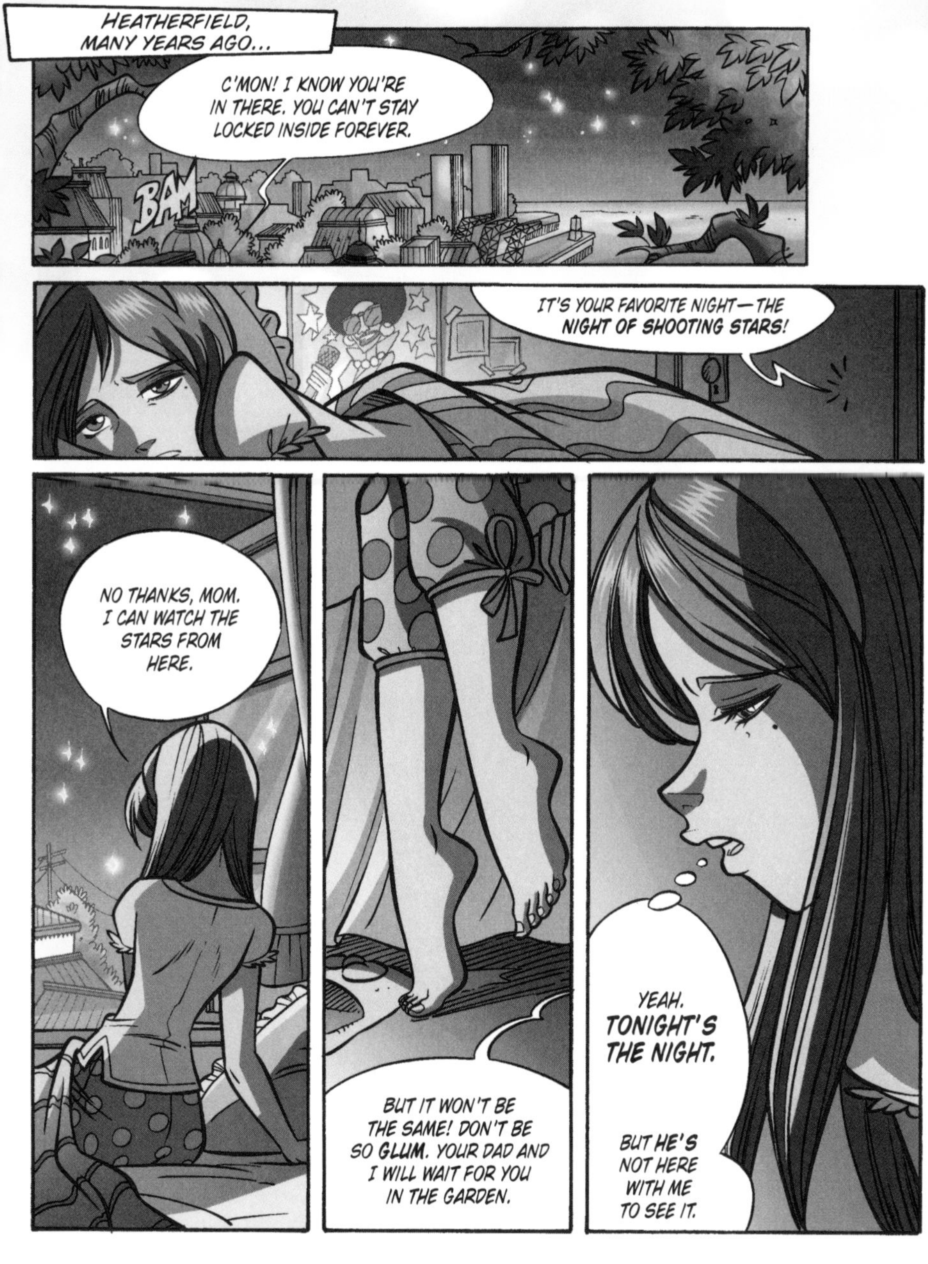

HEATHERFIELD, MANY YEARS AGO...
C'MON! I KNOW YOU'RE IN THERE. YOU CAN'T STAY LOCKED INSIDE FOREVER.
BAM
IT'S YOUR FAVORITE NIGHT—THE NIGHT OF SHOOTING STARS!
NO THANKS, MOM. I CAN WATCH THE STARS FROM HERE.
BUT IT WON'T BE THE SAME! DON'T BE SO GLUM. YOUR DAD AND I WILL WAIT FOR YOU IN THE GARDEN.
YEAH. TONIGHT'S THE NIGHT.
BUT HE'S NOT HERE WITH ME TO SEE IT.

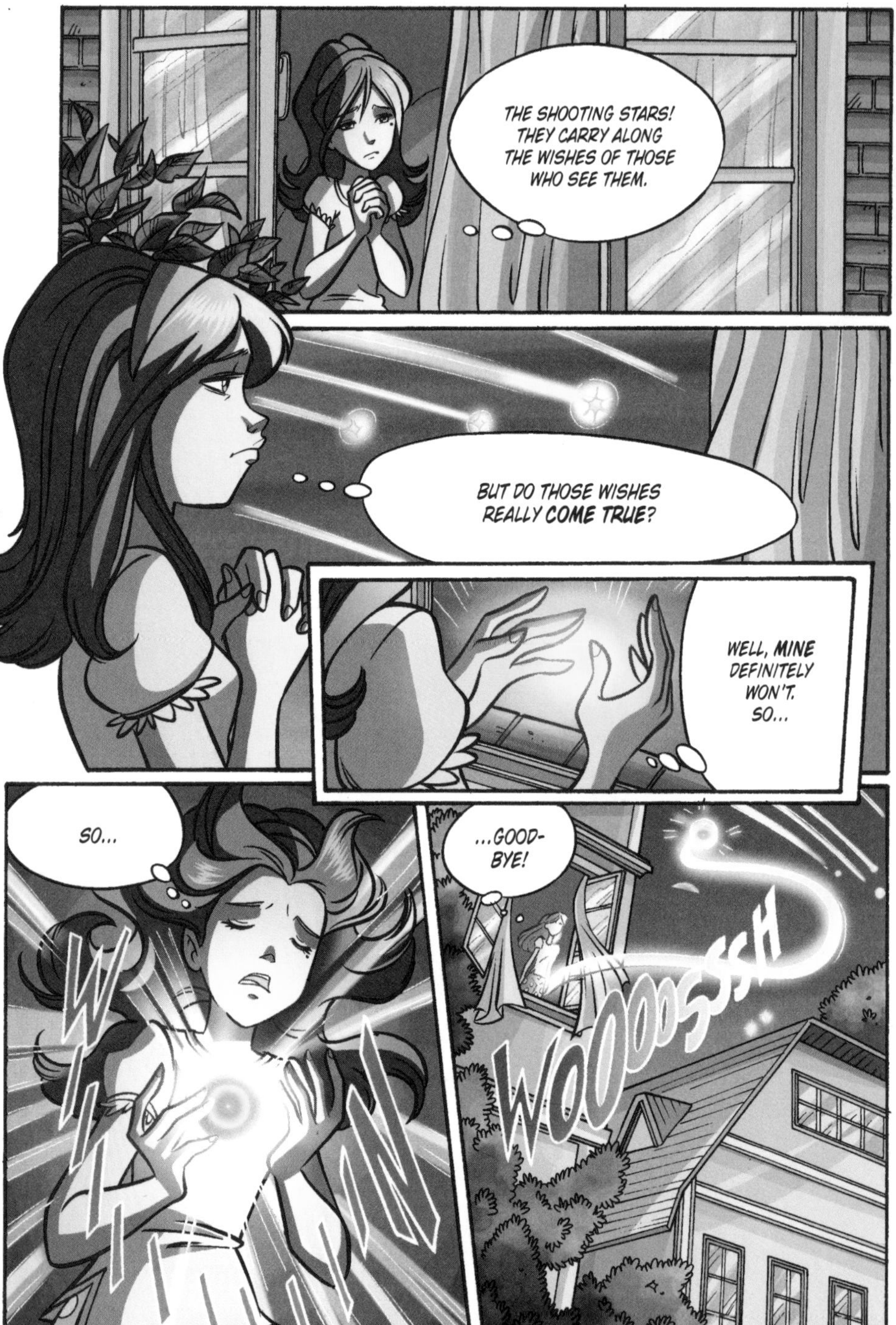
THE SHOOTING STARS! THEY CARRY ALONG THE WISHES OF THOSE WHO SEE THEM.
BUT DO THOSE WISHES REALLY **COME TRUE**?
WELL, **MINE** DEFINITELY WON'T. SO...
SO...
...GOOD-BYE!
WOOOOSSSH

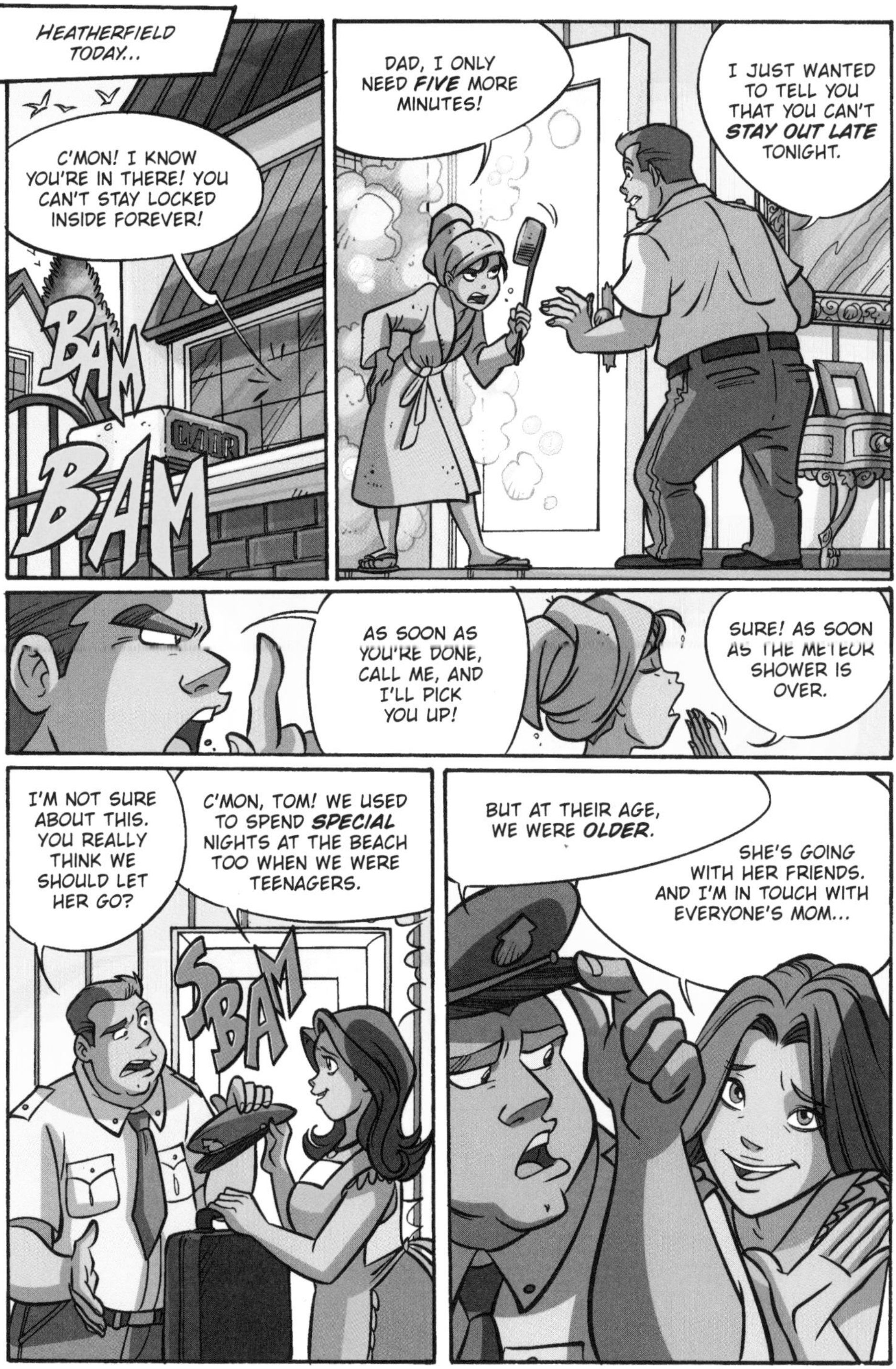
HEATHERFIELD TODAY...
C'MON! I KNOW YOU'RE IN THERE! YOU CAN'T STAY LOCKED INSIDE FOREVER!
BAM
BAM BAM
DAD, I ONLY NEED FIVE MORE MINUTES!
I JUST WANTED TO TELL YOU THAT YOU CAN'T STAY OUT LATE TONIGHT.
AS SOON AS YOU'RE DONE, CALL ME, AND I'LL PICK YOU UP!
SURE! AS SOON AS THE METEOR SHOWER IS OVER.
I'M NOT SURE ABOUT THIS. YOU REALLY THINK WE SHOULD LET HER GO?
C'MON, TOM! WE USED TO SPEND SPECIAL NIGHTS AT THE BEACH TOO WHEN WE WERE TEENAGERS.
SBAM
BUT AT THEIR AGE, WE WERE OLDER.
SHE'S GOING WITH HER FRIENDS. AND I'M IN TOUCH WITH EVERYONE'S MOM...

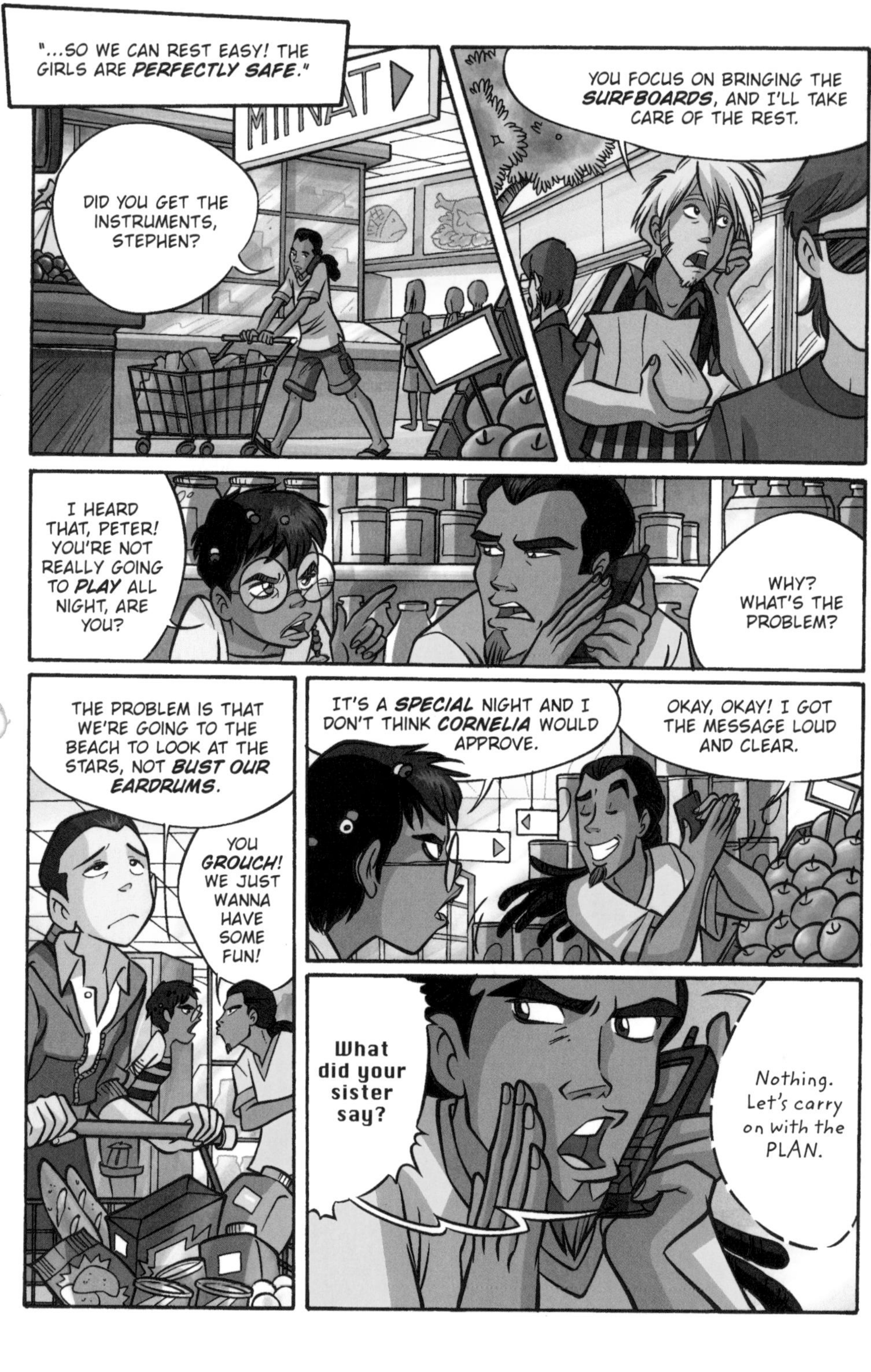
"...SO WE CAN REST EASY! THE GIRLS ARE ***PERFECTLY SAFE***."
MIINAT
DID YOU GET THE INSTRUMENTS, STEPHEN?
YOU FOCUS ON BRINGING THE ***SURFBOARDS***, AND I'LL TAKE CARE OF THE REST.
I HEARD THAT, PETER! YOU'RE NOT REALLY GOING TO ***PLAY*** ALL NIGHT, ARE YOU?
WHY? WHAT'S THE PROBLEM?
THE PROBLEM IS THAT WE'RE GOING TO THE BEACH TO LOOK AT THE STARS, NOT ***BUST OUR EARDRUMS***.
YOU ***GROUCH***! WE JUST WANNA HAVE SOME FUN!
IT'S A ***SPECIAL*** NIGHT AND I DON'T THINK ***CORNELIA*** WOULD APPROVE.
OKAY, OKAY! I GOT THE MESSAGE LOUD AND CLEAR.
What did your sister say?
Nothing. Let's carry on with the PLAN.

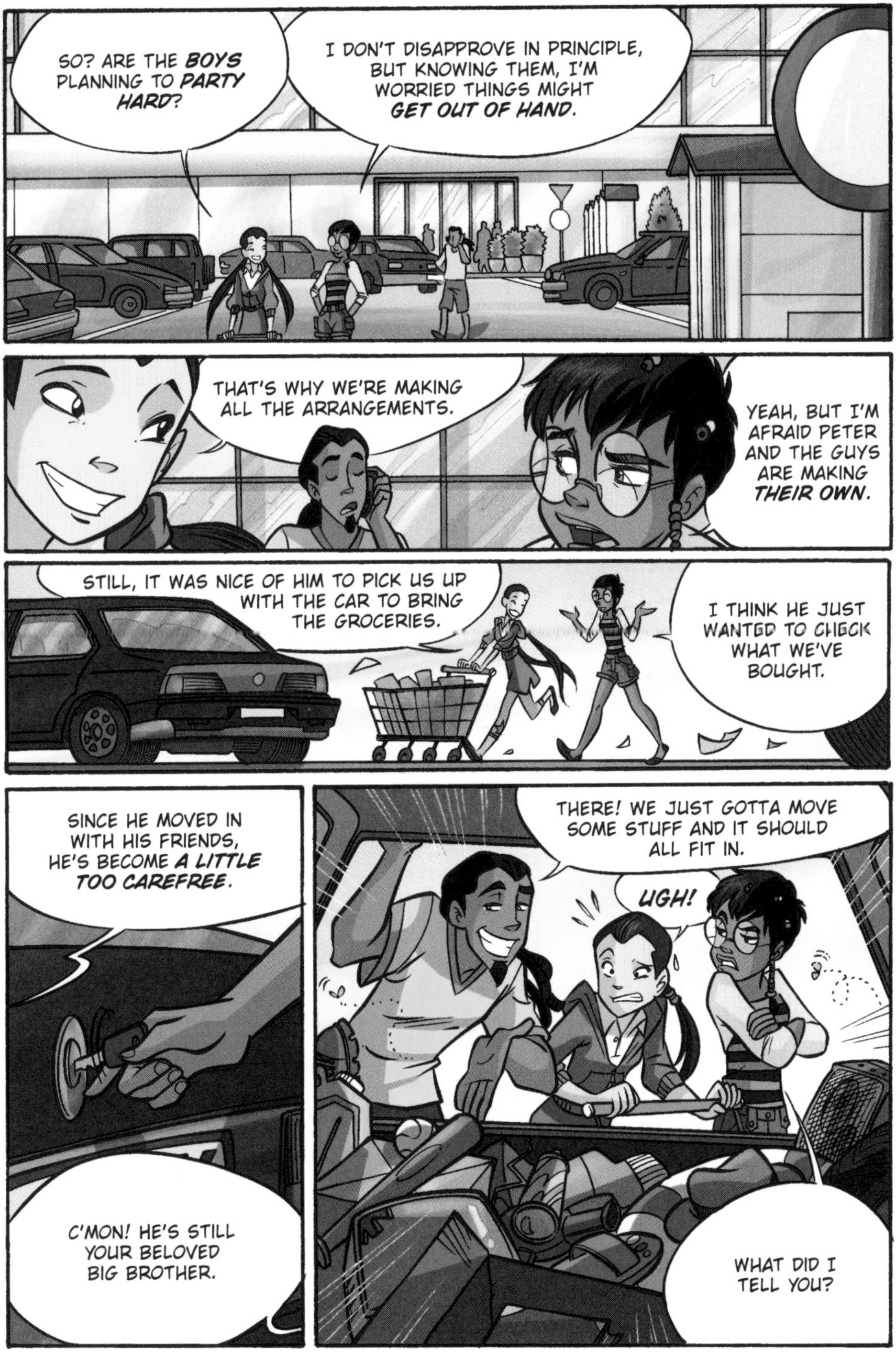
SO? ARE THE BOYS PLANNING TO PARTY HARD?
I DON'T DISAPPROVE IN PRINCIPLE, BUT KNOWING THEM, I'M WORRIED THINGS MIGHT GET OUT OF HAND.
THAT'S WHY WE'RE MAKING ALL THE ARRANGEMENTS.
YEAH, BUT I'M AFRAID PETER AND THE GUYS ARE MAKING THEIR OWN.
STILL, IT WAS NICE OF HIM TO PICK US UP WITH THE CAR TO BRING THE GROCERIES.
I THINK HE JUST WANTED TO CHECK WHAT WE'VE BOUGHT.
SINCE HE MOVED IN WITH HIS FRIENDS, HE'S BECOME A LITTLE TOO CAREFREE.
C'MON! HE'S STILL YOUR BELOVED BIG BROTHER.
THERE! WE JUST GOTTA MOVE SOME STUFF AND IT SHOULD ALL FIT IN.
UGH!
WHAT DID I TELL YOU?

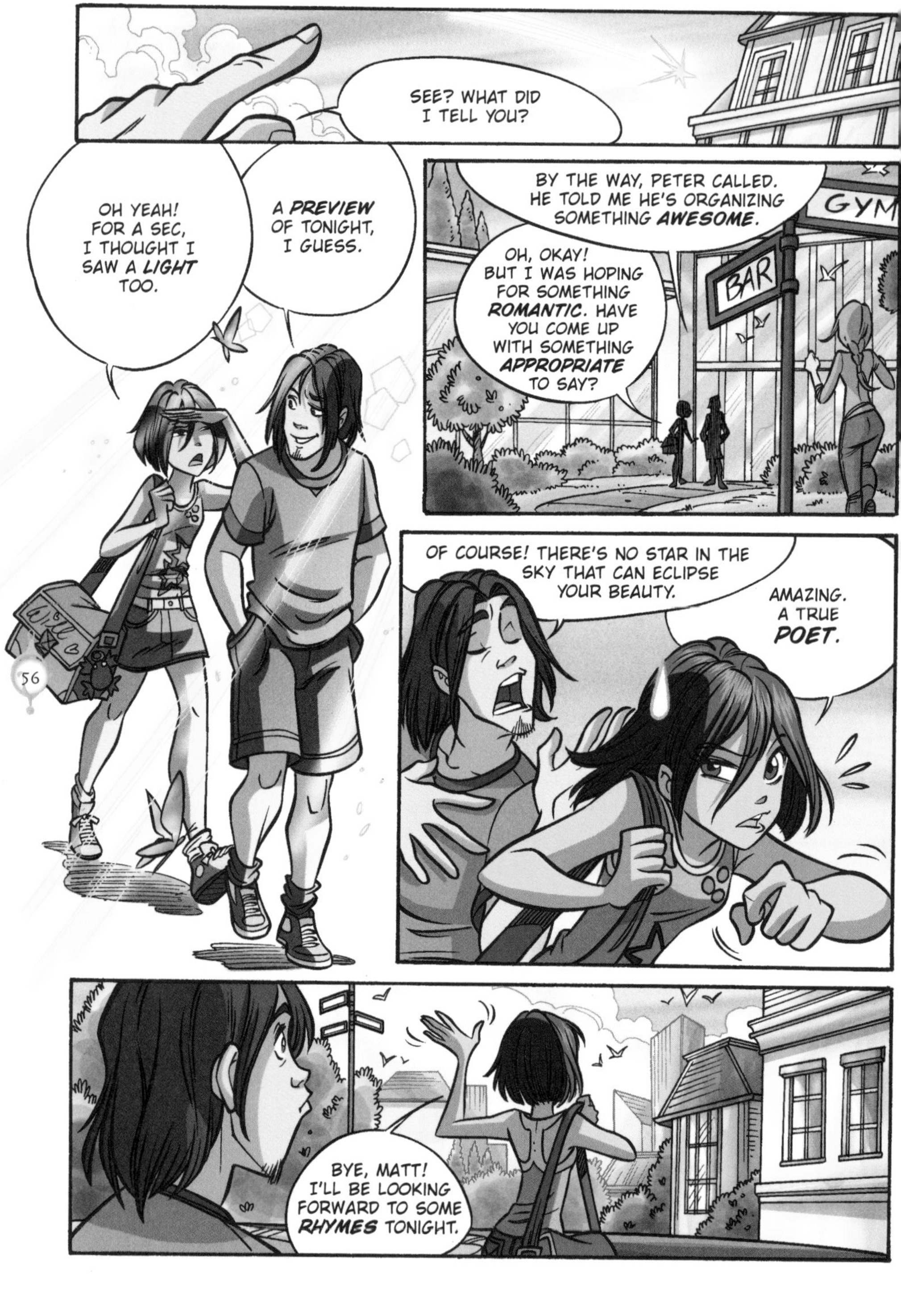

SEE? WHAT DID I TELL YOU?
OH YEAH! FOR A SEC, I THOUGHT I SAW A LIGHT TOO.
A PREVIEW OF TONIGHT, I GUESS.
BY THE WAY, PETER CALLED. HE TOLD ME HE'S ORGANIZING SOMETHING AWESOME.
OH, OKAY! BUT I WAS HOPING FOR SOMETHING ROMANTIC. HAVE YOU COME UP WITH SOMETHING APPROPRIATE TO SAY?
GYM
BAR
OF COURSE! THERE'S NO STAR IN THE SKY THAT CAN ECLIPSE YOUR BEAUTY.
AMAZING. A TRUE POET.
BYE, MATT! I'LL BE LOOKING FORWARD TO SOME RHYMES TONIGHT.

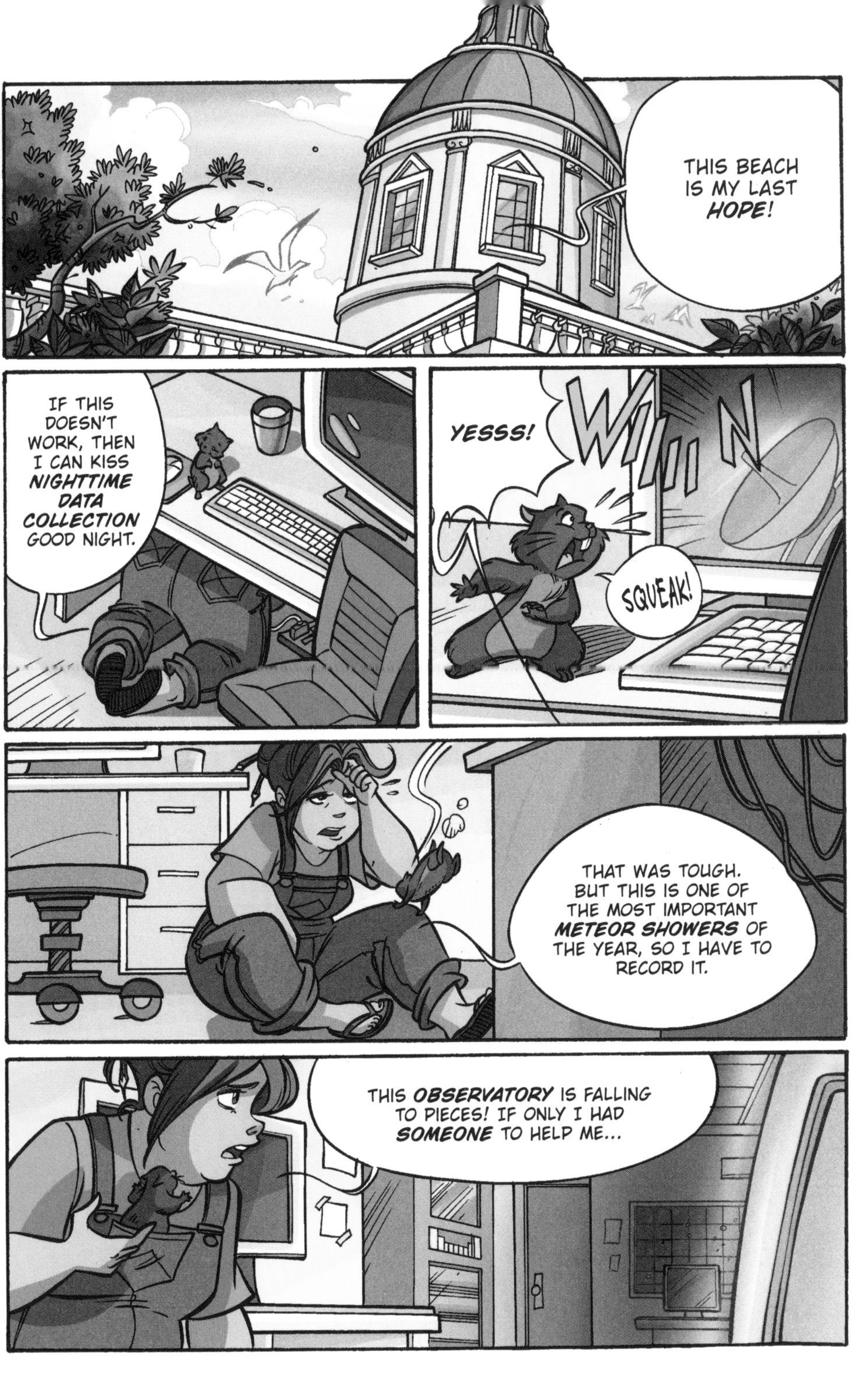
THIS BEACH IS MY LAST HOPE!
IF THIS DOESN'T WORK, THEN I CAN KISS NIGHTTIME DATA COLLECTION GOOD NIGHT.
YESSS!
WHIIIN
SQUEAK!
THAT WAS TOUGH. BUT THIS IS ONE OF THE MOST IMPORTANT METEOR SHOWERS OF THE YEAR, SO I HAVE TO RECORD IT.
THIS OBSERVATORY IS FALLING TO PIECES! IF ONLY I HAD SOMEONE TO HELP ME...

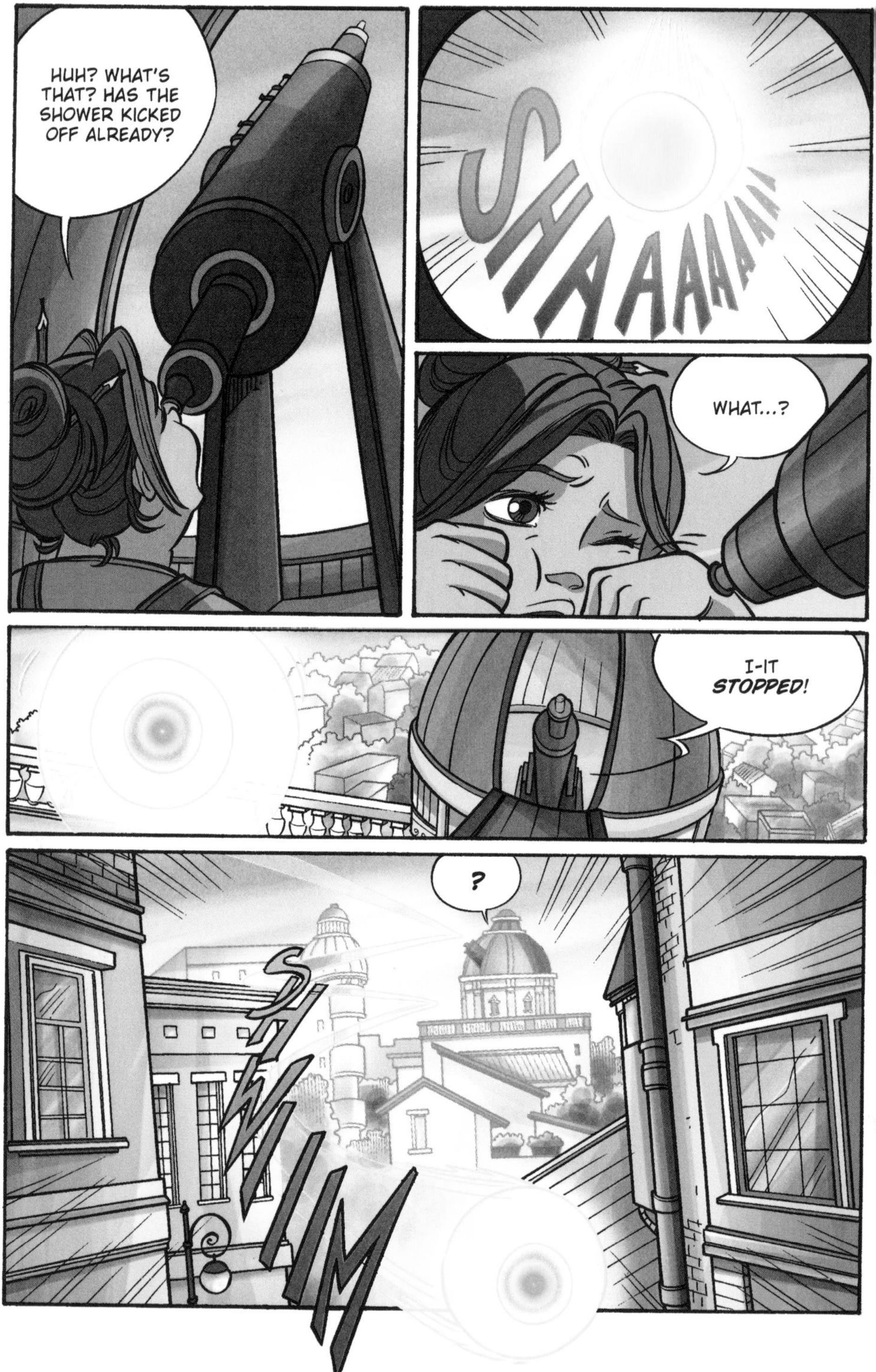
HUH? WHAT'S THAT? HAS THE SHOWER KICKED OFF ALREADY?
SHAAAAAA
WHAT...?
I-IT STOPPED!
?
SHWIIM

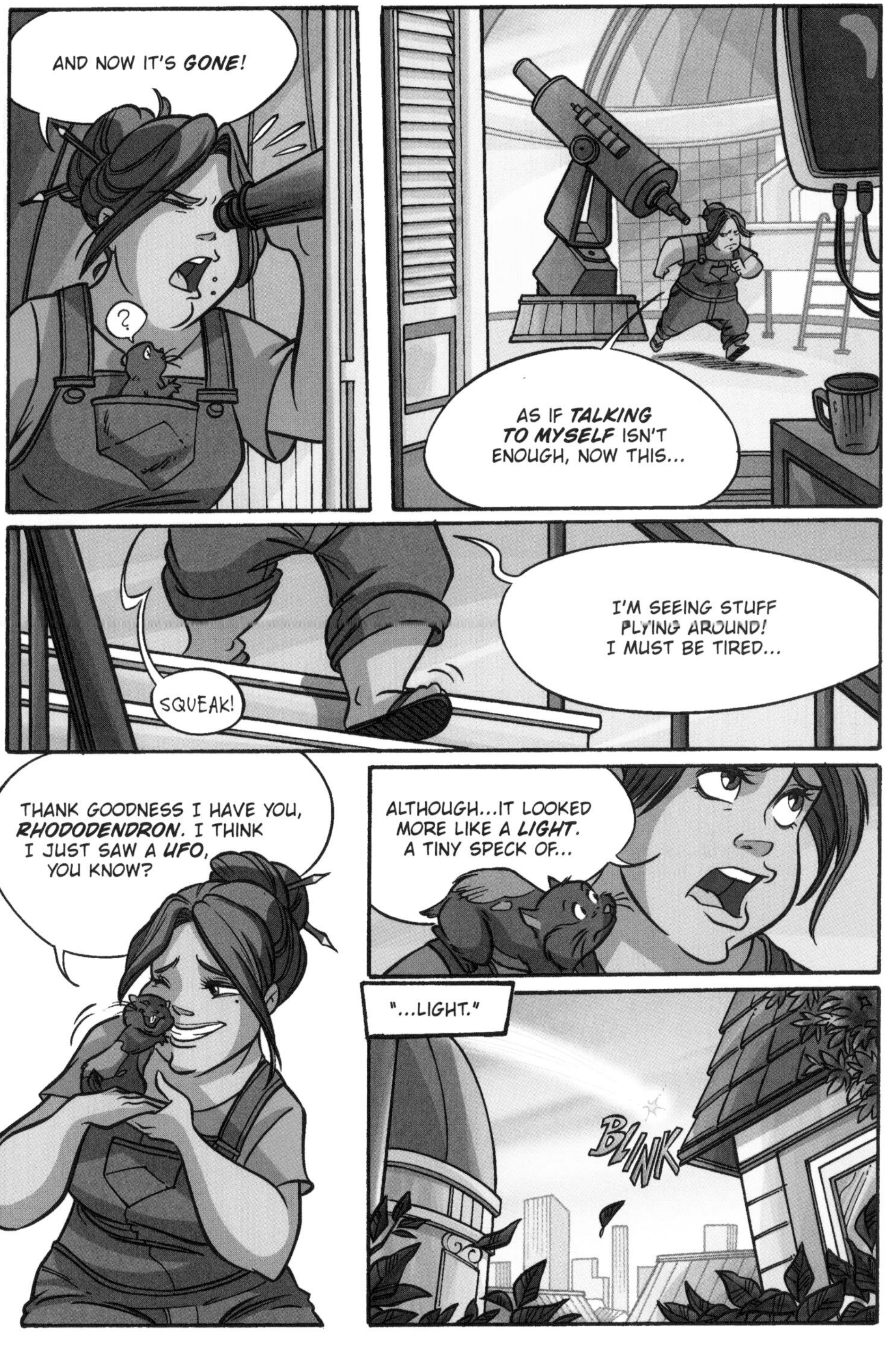
AND NOW IT'S GONE!
?
AS IF TALKING TO MYSELF ISN'T ENOUGH, NOW THIS...
SQUEAK!
I'M SEEING STUFF FLYING AROUND! I MUST BE TIRED...
THANK GOODNESS I HAVE YOU, RHODODENDRON. I THINK I JUST SAW A UFO, YOU KNOW?
ALTHOUGH...IT LOOKED MORE LIKE A LIGHT. A TINY SPECK OF...
"...LIGHT."
BLINK

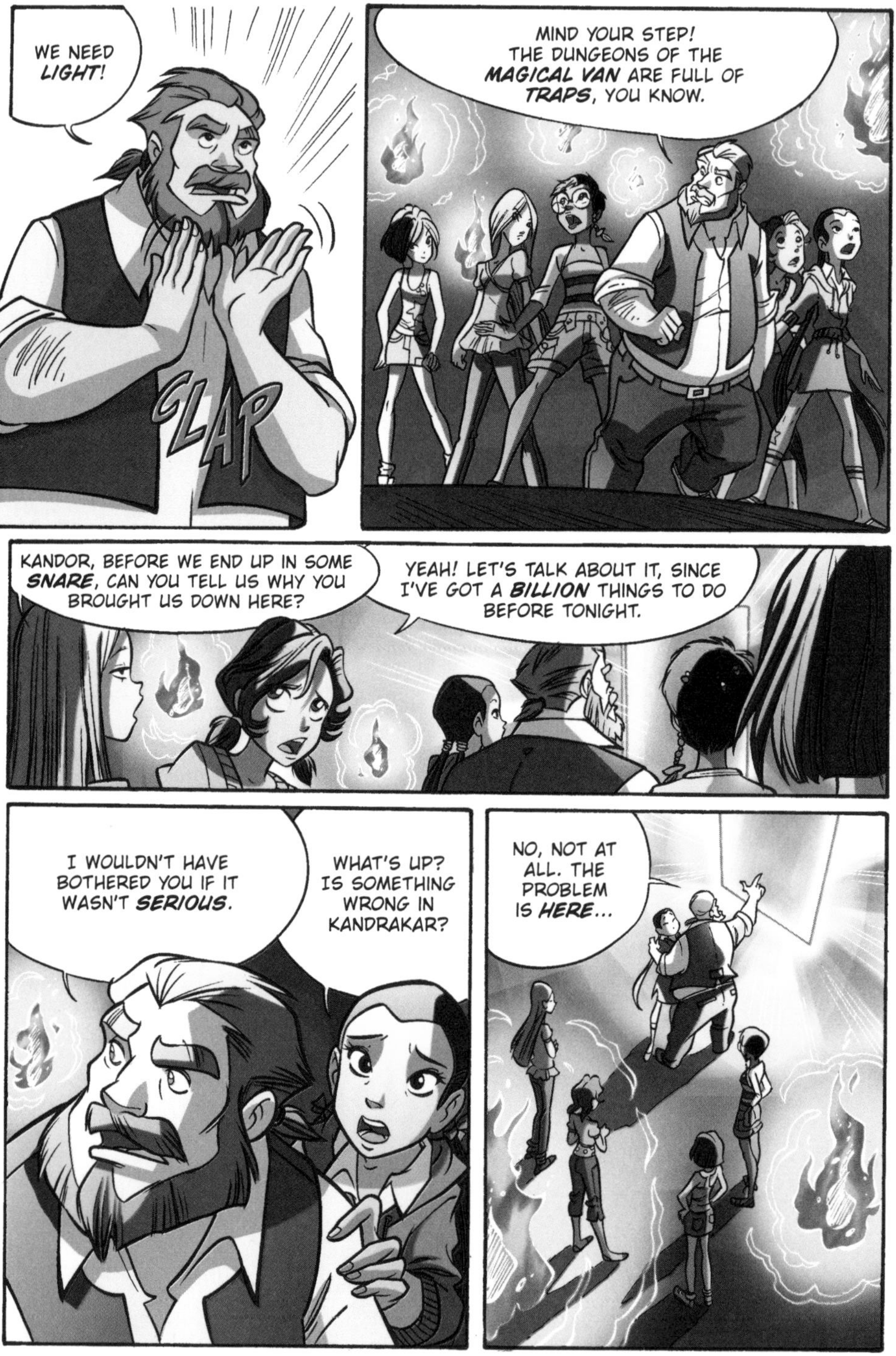

WE NEED LIGHT!
CLAP
MIND YOUR STEP! THE DUNGEONS OF THE MAGICAL VAN ARE FULL OF TRAPS, YOU KNOW.
KANDOR, BEFORE WE END UP IN SOME SNARE, CAN YOU TELL US WHY YOU BROUGHT US DOWN HERE?
YEAH! LET'S TALK ABOUT IT, SINCE I'VE GOT A BILLION THINGS TO DO BEFORE TONIGHT.
I WOULDN'T HAVE BOTHERED YOU IF IT WASN'T SERIOUS.
WHAT'S UP? IS SOMETHING WRONG IN KANDRAKAR?
NO, NOT AT ALL. THE PROBLEM IS HERE...

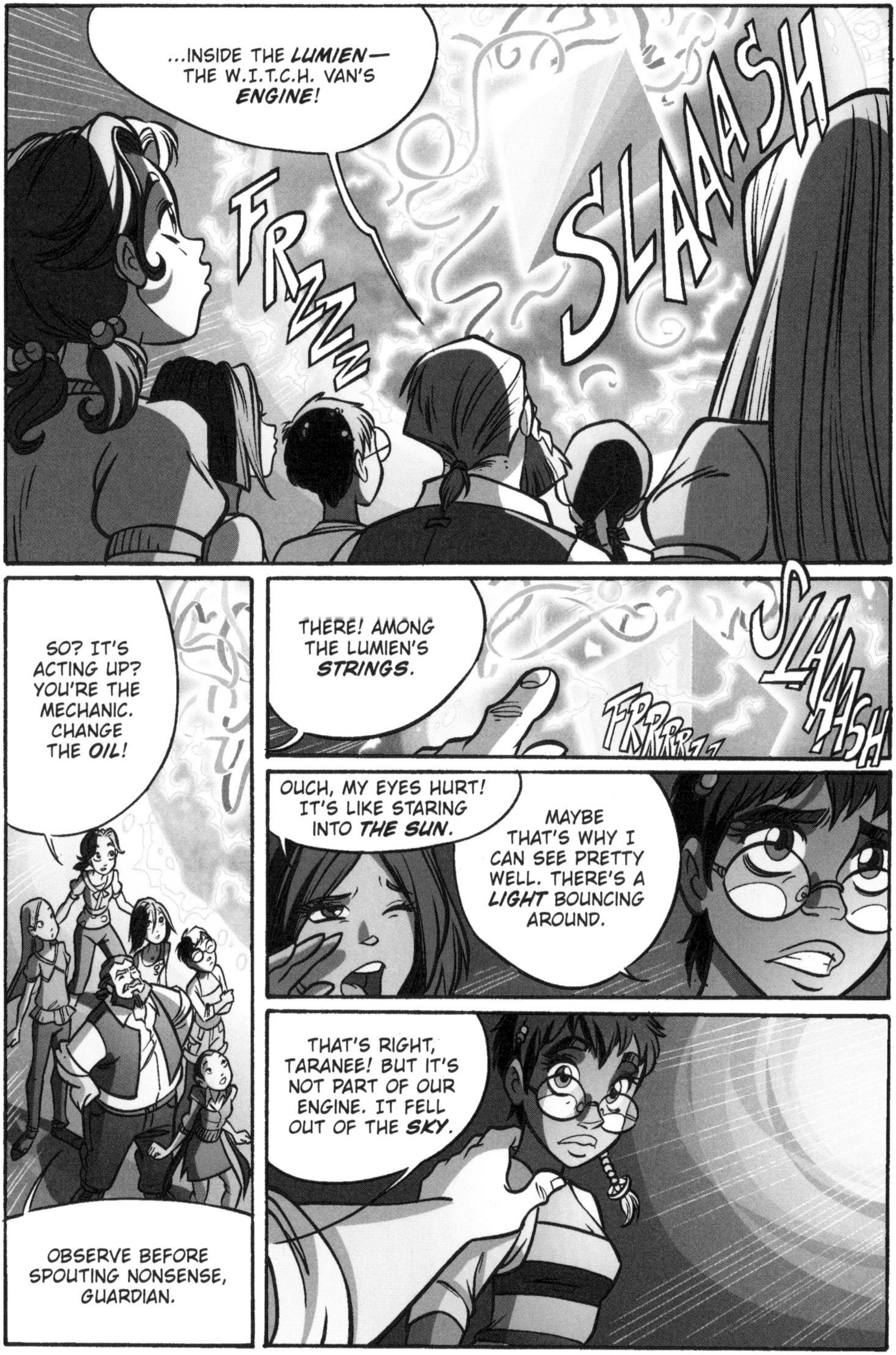
...INSIDE THE *LUMIEN*— THE W.I.T.C.H. VAN'S *ENGINE*!
FRZZZZ
SLAAASH
SO? IT'S ACTING UP? YOU'RE THE MECHANIC. CHANGE THE *OIL*!
OBSERVE BEFORE SPOUTING NONSENSE, GUARDIAN.
THERE! AMONG THE LUMIEN'S *STRINGS*.
SLAAASH
OUCH, MY EYES HURT! IT'S LIKE STARING INTO *THE SUN*.
MAYBE THAT'S WHY I CAN SEE PRETTY WELL. THERE'S A *LIGHT* BOUNCING AROUND.
THAT'S RIGHT, TARANEE! BUT IT'S NOT PART OF OUR ENGINE. IT FELL OUT OF THE *SKY*.

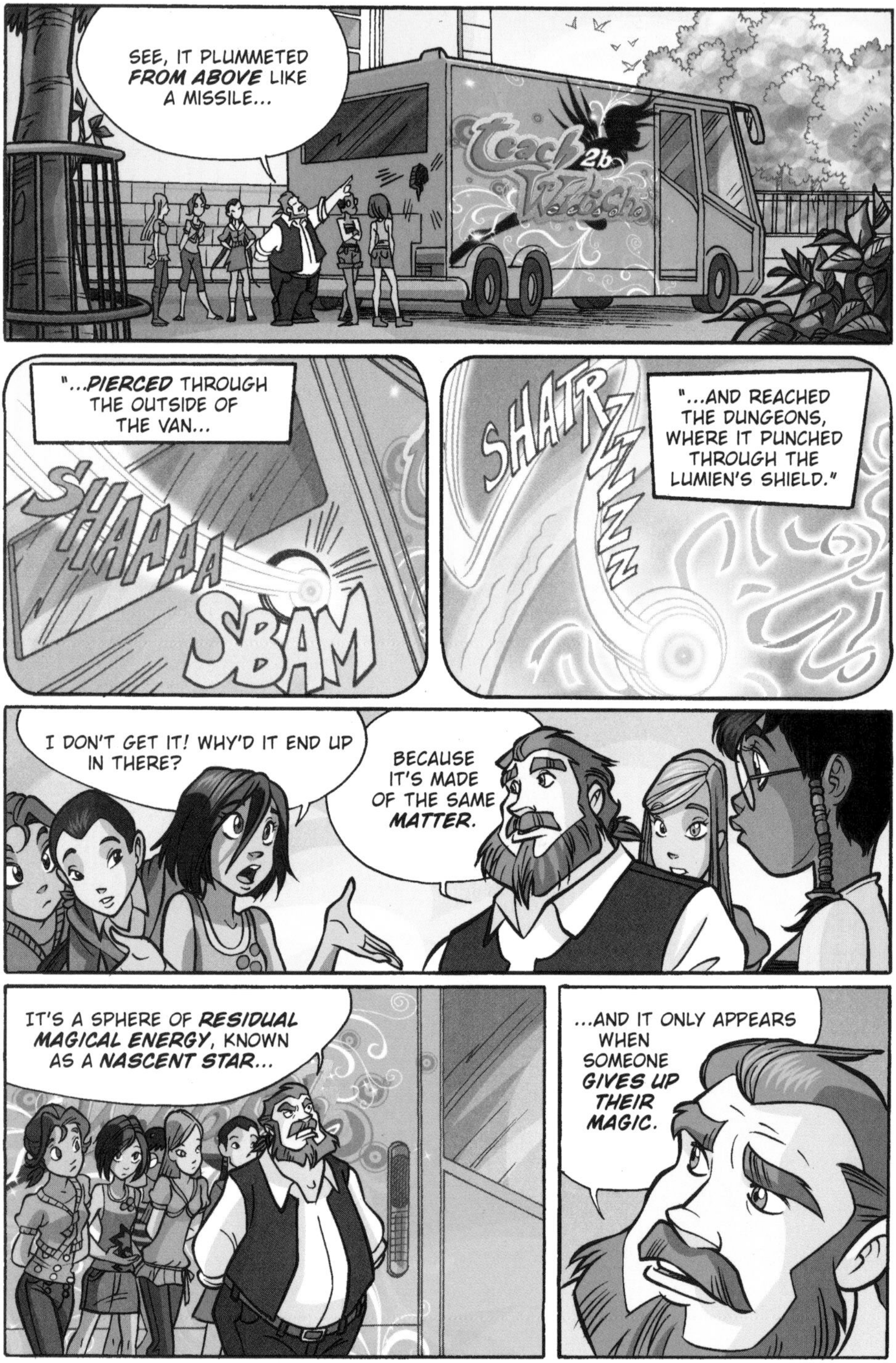
SEE, IT PLUMMETED FROM ABOVE LIKE A MISSILE...
Teach 2b Witch
"...PIERCED THROUGH THE OUTSIDE OF THE VAN...
SHAAAAA
SBAM
SHATRZZZNN
"...AND REACHED THE DUNGEONS, WHERE IT PUNCHED THROUGH THE LUMIEN'S SHIELD."
I DON'T GET IT! WHY'D IT END UP IN THERE?
BECAUSE IT'S MADE OF THE SAME MATTER.
IT'S A SPHERE OF RESIDUAL MAGICAL ENERGY, KNOWN AS A NASCENT STAR...
...AND IT ONLY APPEARS WHEN SOMEONE GIVES UP THEIR MAGIC.

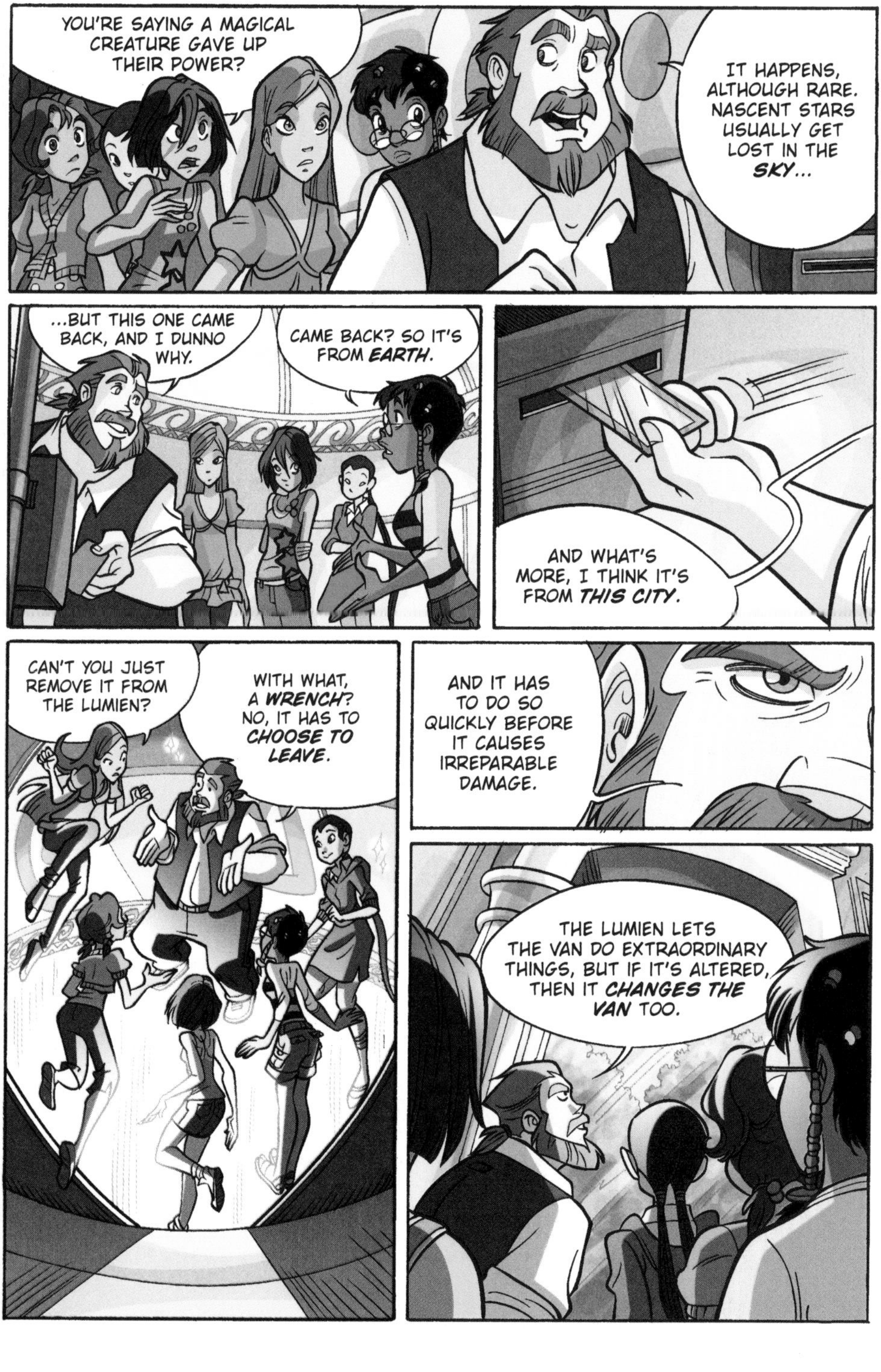
YOU'RE SAYING A MAGICAL CREATURE GAVE UP THEIR POWER?
IT HAPPENS, ALTHOUGH RARE. NASCENT STARS USUALLY GET LOST IN THE SKY...
...BUT THIS ONE CAME BACK, AND I DUNNO WHY.
CAME BACK? SO IT'S FROM EARTH.
AND WHAT'S MORE, I THINK IT'S FROM THIS CITY.
CAN'T YOU JUST REMOVE IT FROM THE LUMIEN?
WITH WHAT, A WRENCH? NO, IT HAS TO CHOOSE TO LEAVE.
AND IT HAS TO DO SO QUICKLY BEFORE IT CAUSES IRREPARABLE DAMAGE.
THE LUMIEN LETS THE VAN DO EXTRAORDINARY THINGS, BUT IF IT'S ALTERED, THEN IT CHANGES THE VAN TOO.

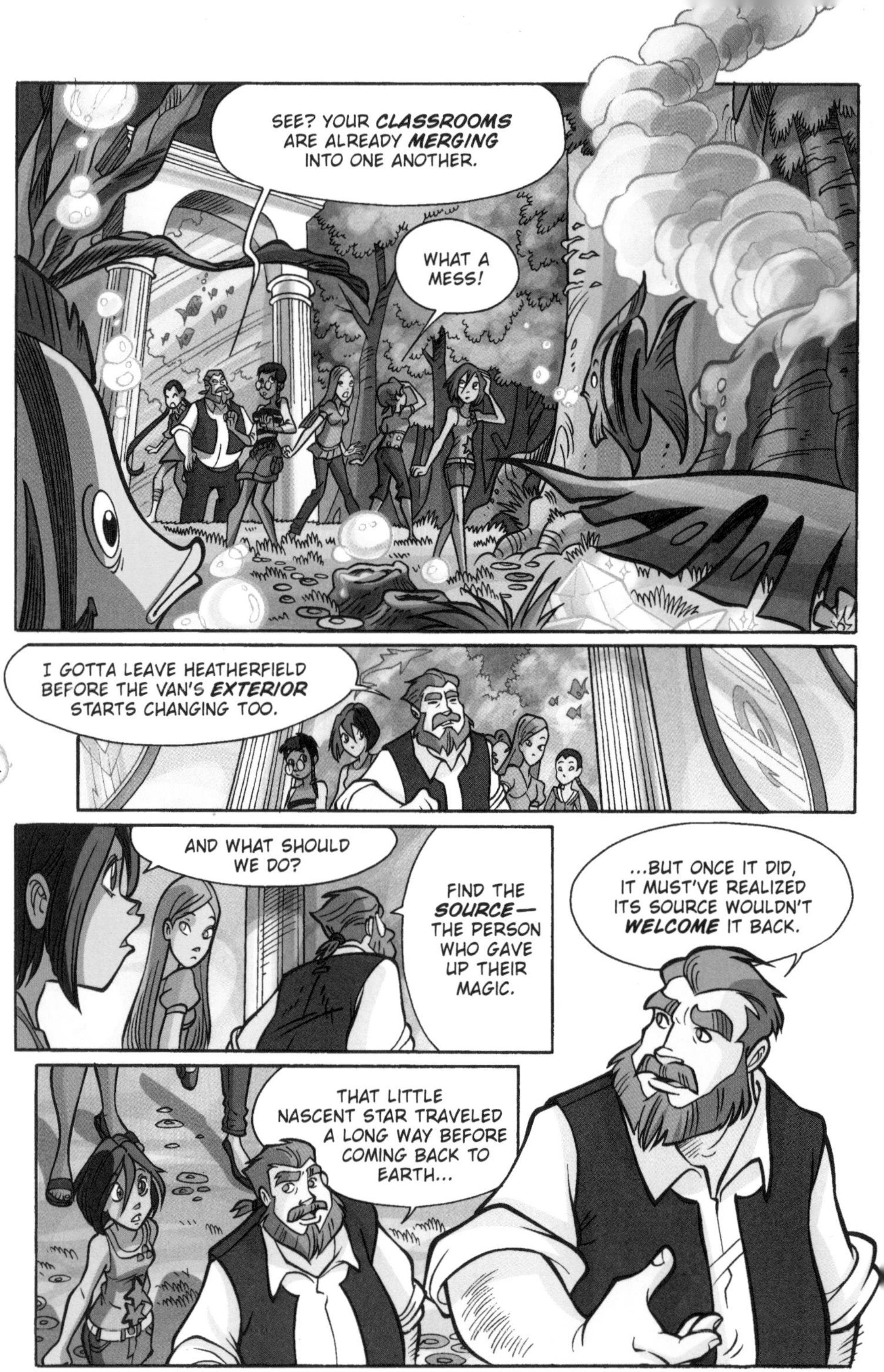
SEE? YOUR CLASSROOMS ARE ALREADY MERGING INTO ONE ANOTHER.
WHAT A MESS!
I GOTTA LEAVE HEATHERFIELD BEFORE THE VAN'S EXTERIOR STARTS CHANGING TOO.
AND WHAT SHOULD WE DO?
FIND THE SOURCE— THE PERSON WHO GAVE UP THEIR MAGIC.
THAT LITTLE NASCENT STAR TRAVELED A LONG WAY BEFORE COMING BACK TO EARTH...
...BUT ONCE IT DID, IT MUST'VE REALIZED ITS SOURCE WOULDN'T WELCOME IT BACK.

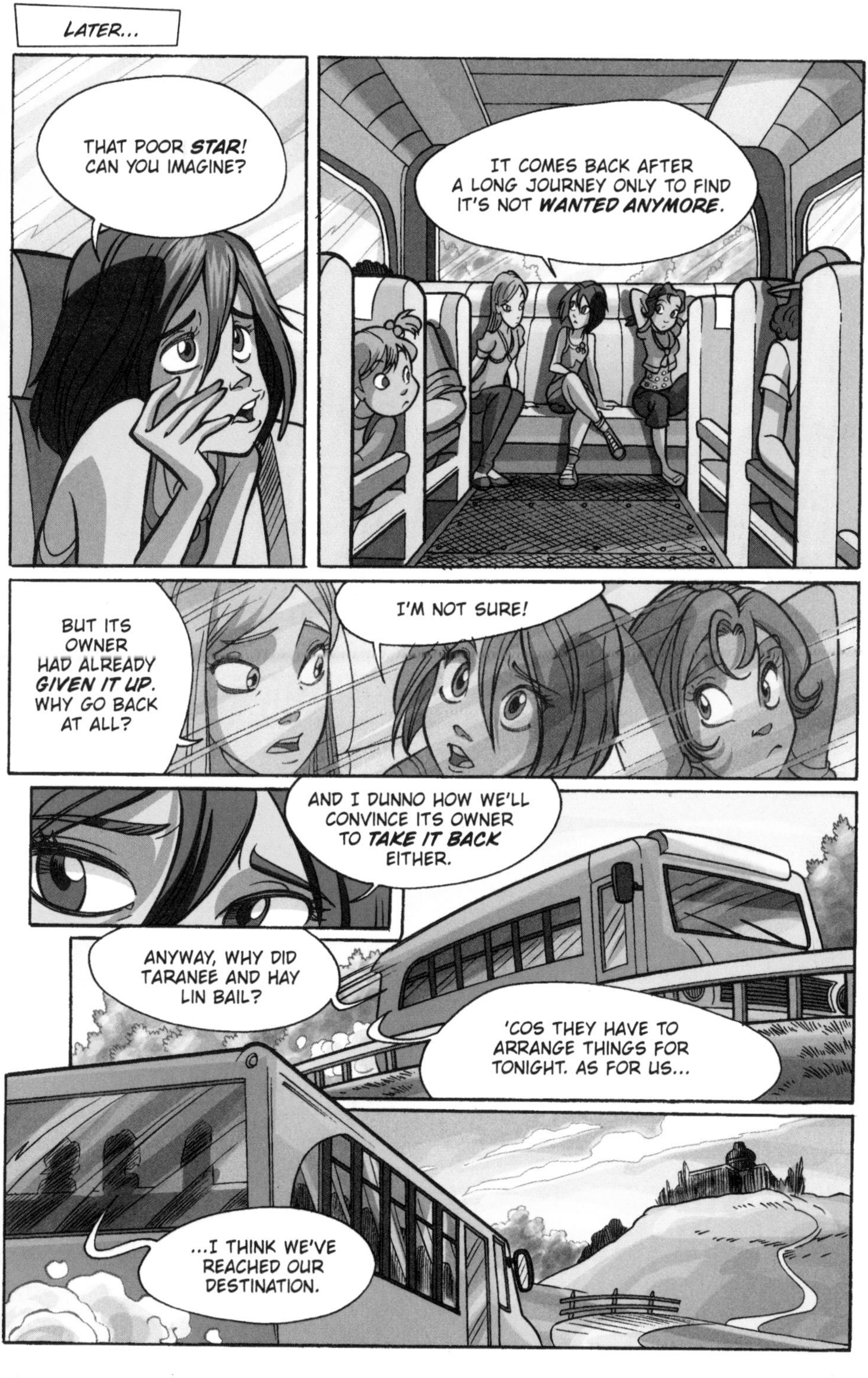
LATER...
THAT POOR STAR! CAN YOU IMAGINE?
IT COMES BACK AFTER A LONG JOURNEY ONLY TO FIND IT'S NOT WANTED ANYMORE.
BUT ITS OWNER HAD ALREADY GIVEN IT UP. WHY GO BACK AT ALL?
I'M NOT SURE!
AND I DUNNO HOW WE'LL CONVINCE ITS OWNER TO TAKE IT BACK EITHER.
ANYWAY, WHY DID TARANEE AND HAY LIN BAIL?
'COS THEY HAVE TO ARRANGE THINGS FOR TONIGHT. AS FOR US...
...I THINK WE'VE REACHED OUR DESTINATION.

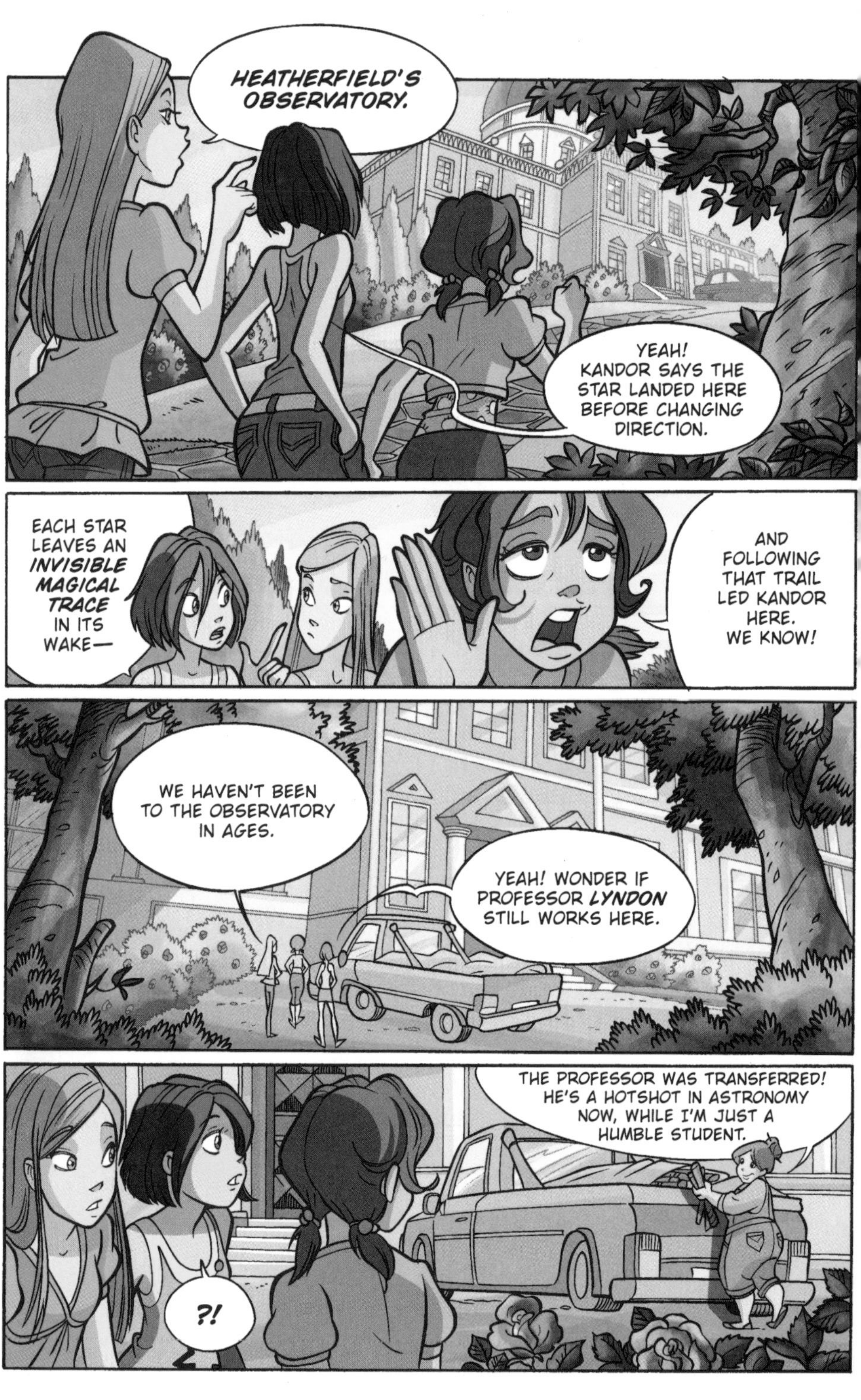
HEATHERFIELD'S OBSERVATORY.
YEAH! KANDOR SAYS THE STAR LANDED HERE BEFORE CHANGING DIRECTION.
EACH STAR LEAVES AN INVISIBLE MAGICAL TRACE IN ITS WAKE—
AND FOLLOWING THAT TRAIL LED KANDOR HERE. WE KNOW!
WE HAVEN'T BEEN TO THE OBSERVATORY IN AGES.
YEAH! WONDER IF PROFESSOR LYNDON STILL WORKS HERE.
THE PROFESSOR WAS TRANSFERRED! HE'S A HOTSHOT IN ASTRONOMY NOW, WHILE I'M JUST A HUMBLE STUDENT.
?!

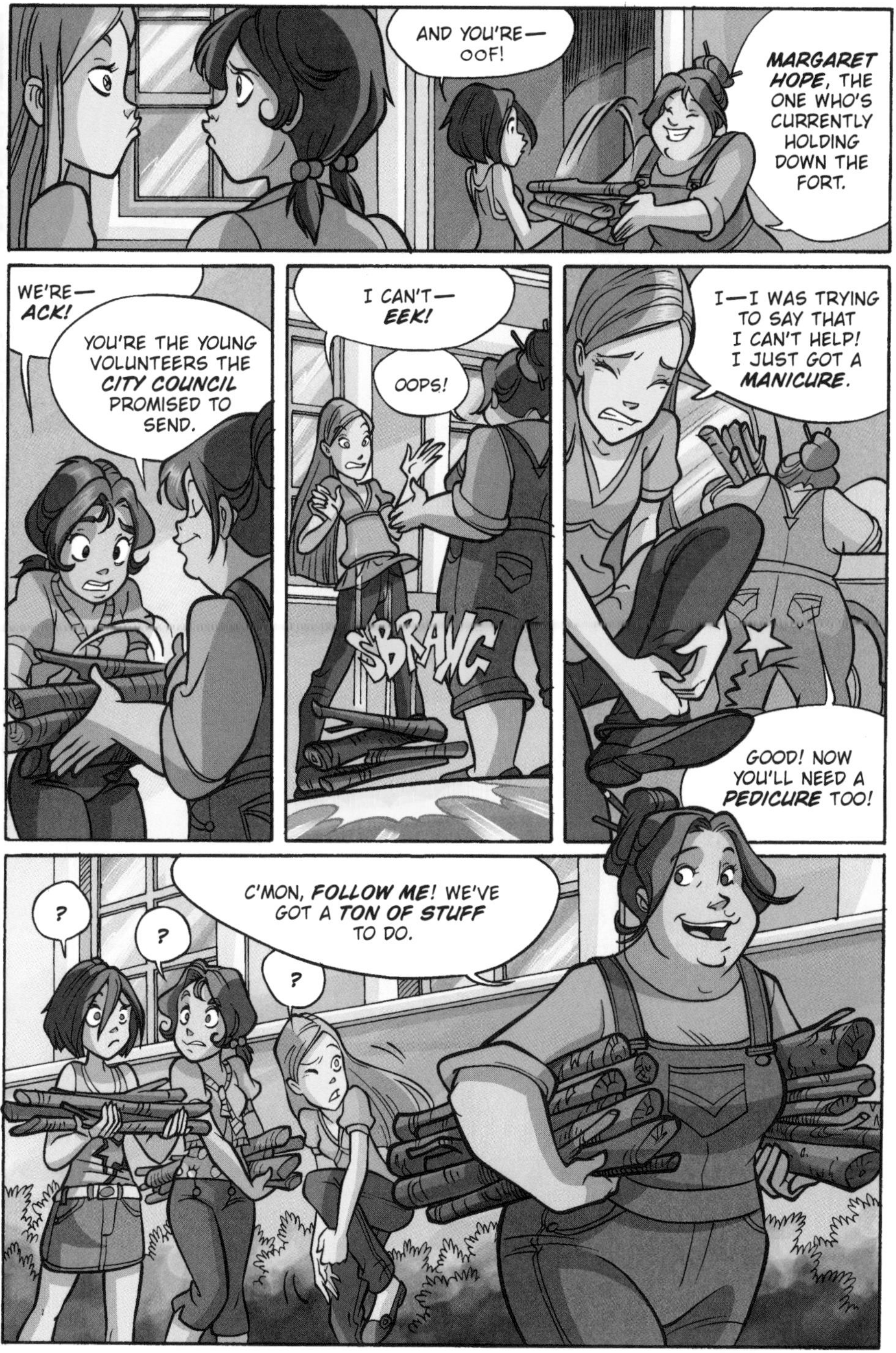

AND YOU'RE—
OOF!
MARGARET HOPE, THE ONE WHO'S CURRENTLY HOLDING DOWN THE FORT.
WE'RE—
ACK!
YOU'RE THE YOUNG VOLUNTEERS THE CITY COUNCIL PROMISED TO SEND.
I CAN'T—
EEK!
OOPS!
SBRANG
I—I WAS TRYING TO SAY THAT I CAN'T HELP! I JUST GOT A MANICURE.
GOOD! NOW YOU'LL NEED A PEDICURE TOO!
?
?
?
C'MON, FOLLOW ME! WE'VE GOT A TON OF STUFF TO DO.

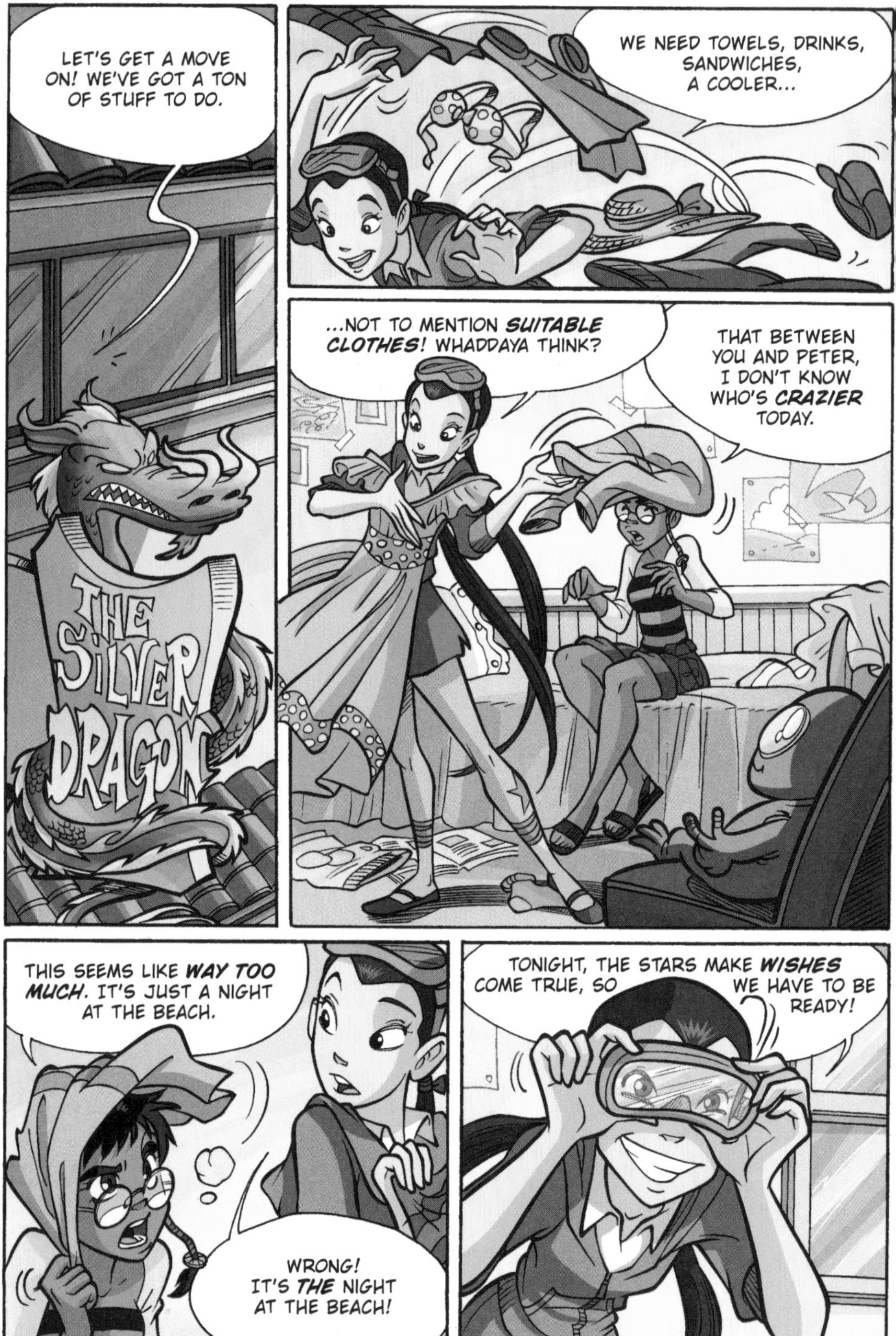
LET'S GET A MOVE ON! WE'VE GOT A TON OF STUFF TO DO.
WE NEED TOWELS, DRINKS, SANDWICHES, A COOLER...
THE SILVER DRAGON
...NOT TO MENTION SUITABLE CLOTHES! WHADDAYA THINK?
THAT BETWEEN YOU AND PETER, I DON'T KNOW WHO'S CRAZIER TODAY.
THIS SEEMS LIKE WAY TOO MUCH. IT'S JUST A NIGHT AT THE BEACH.
WRONG! IT'S THE NIGHT AT THE BEACH!
TONIGHT, THE STARS MAKE WISHES COME TRUE, SO
WE HAVE TO BE READY!

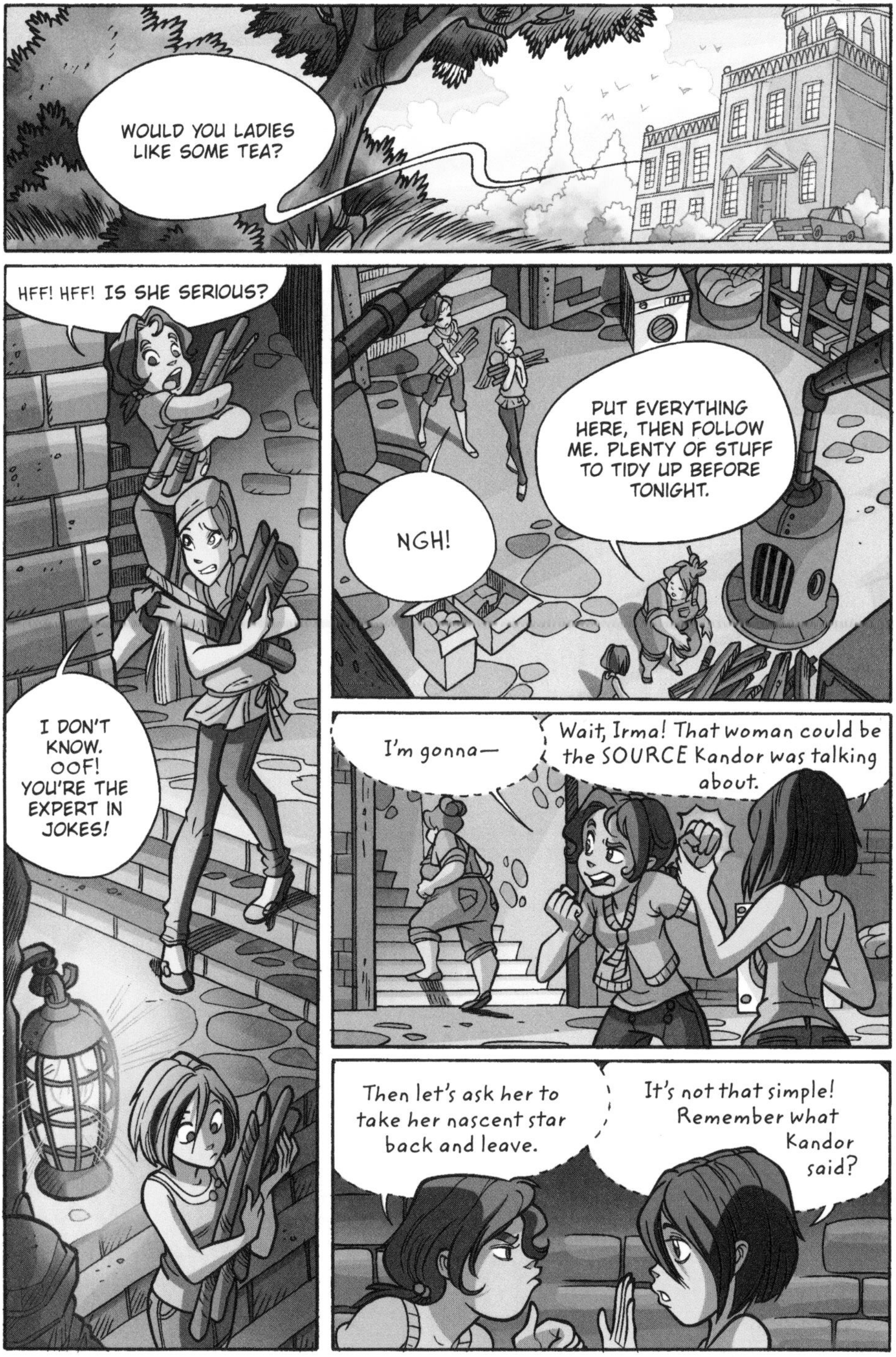
WOULD YOU LADIES LIKE SOME TEA?
HFF! HFF! IS SHE SERIOUS?
I DON'T KNOW. OOF! YOU'RE THE EXPERT IN JOKES!
PUT EVERYTHING HERE, THEN FOLLOW ME. PLENTY OF STUFF TO TIDY UP BEFORE TONIGHT.
NGH!
I'm gonna—
Wait, Irma! That woman could be the SOURCE Kandor was talking about.
Then let's ask her to take her nascent star back and leave.
It's not that simple! Remember what Kandor said?

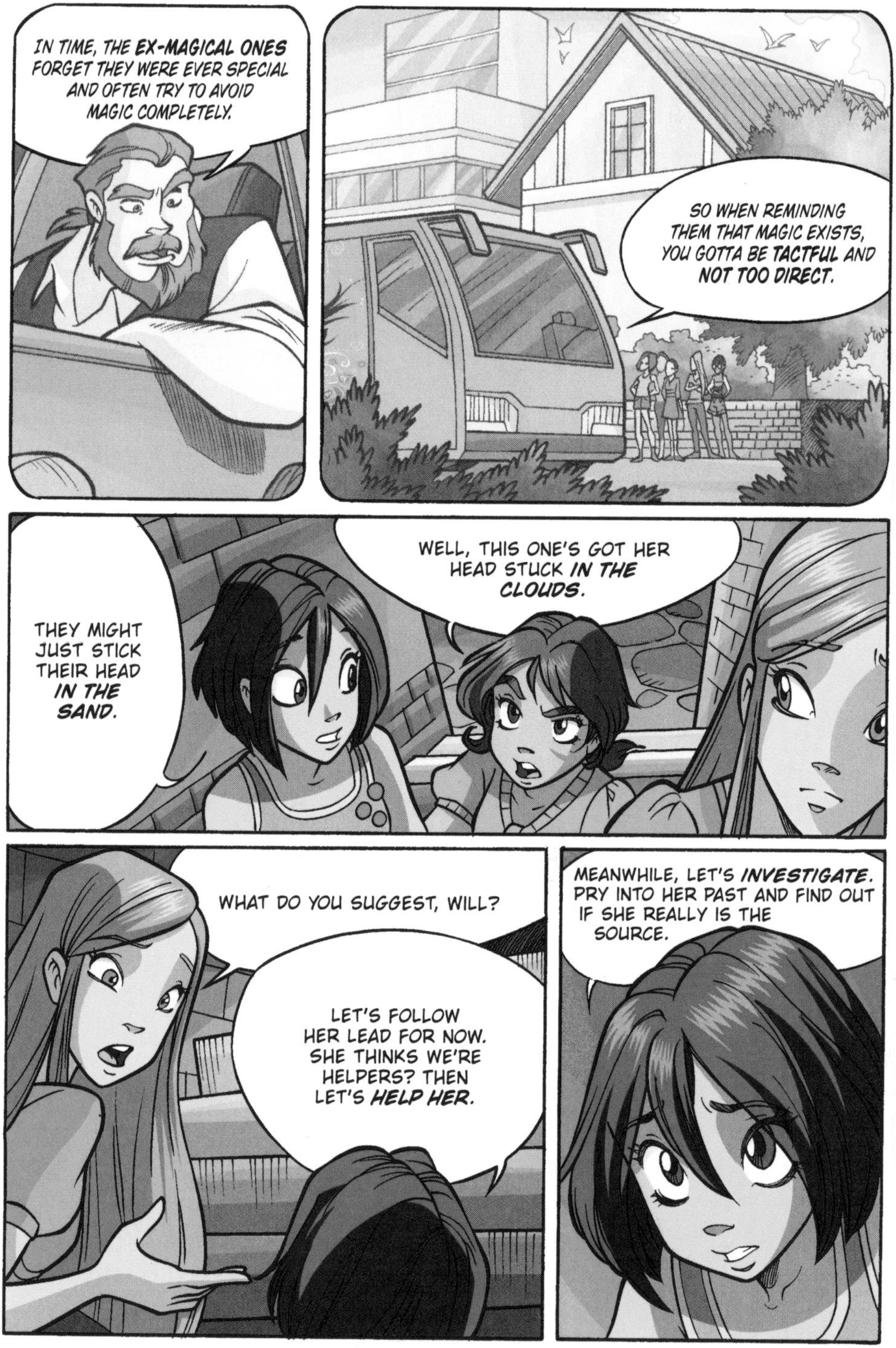
IN TIME, THE EX-MAGICAL ONES FORGET THEY WERE EVER SPECIAL AND OFTEN TRY TO AVOID MAGIC COMPLETELY.
SO WHEN REMINDING THEM THAT MAGIC EXISTS, YOU GOTTA BE TACTFUL AND NOT TOO DIRECT.
THEY MIGHT JUST STICK THEIR HEAD IN THE SAND.
WELL, THIS ONE'S GOT HER HEAD STUCK IN THE CLOUDS.
WHAT DO YOU SUGGEST, WILL?
LET'S FOLLOW HER LEAD FOR NOW. SHE THINKS WE'RE HELPERS? THEN LET'S HELP HER.
MEANWHILE, LET'S INVESTIGATE. PRY INTO HER PAST AND FIND OUT IF SHE REALLY IS THE SOURCE.

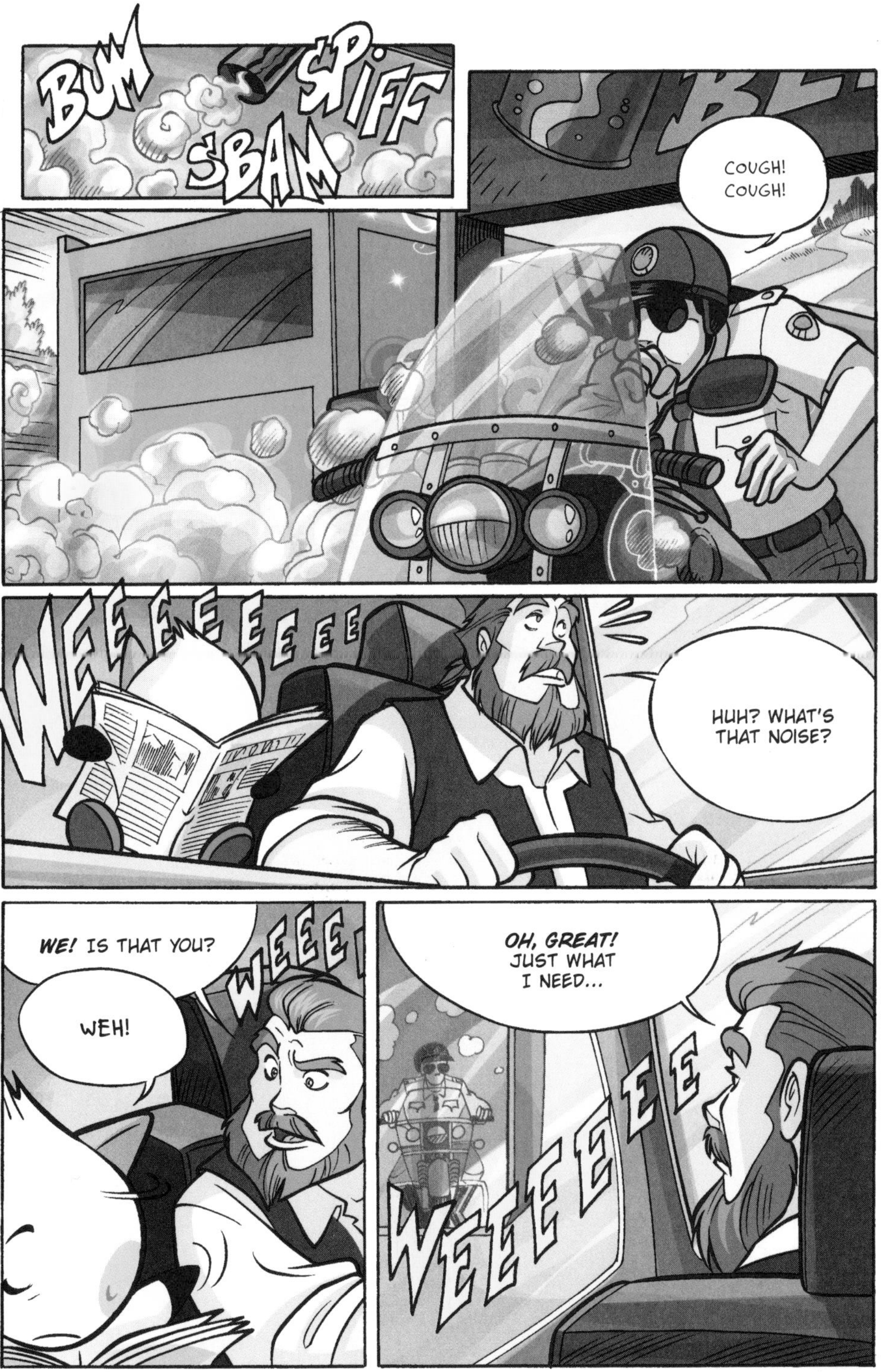
BUM
SPIFF
SBAM
COUGH!
COUGH!
WEEEEEEEE
HUH? WHAT'S THAT NOISE?
WE! IS THAT YOU?
WEH!
WEEE
OH, GREAT! JUST WHAT I NEED...
WEEEEEEE

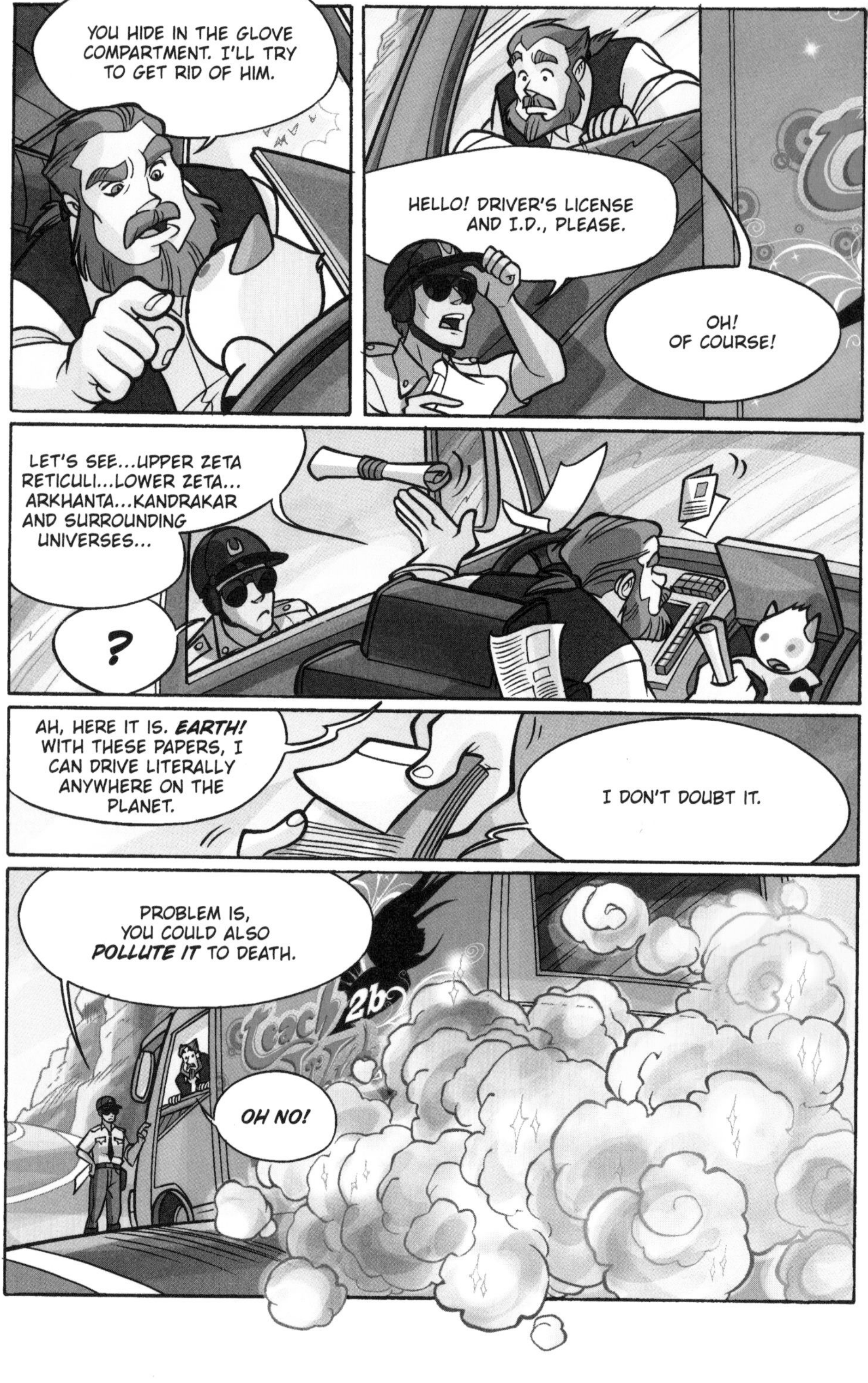
YOU HIDE IN THE GLOVE COMPARTMENT. I'LL TRY TO GET RID OF HIM.
HELLO! DRIVER'S LICENSE AND I.D., PLEASE.
OH! OF COURSE!
LET'S SEE...UPPER ZETA RETICULI...LOWER ZETA... ARKHANTA...KANDRAKAR AND SURROUNDING UNIVERSES...
?
AH, HERE IT IS. *EARTH!* WITH THESE PAPERS, I CAN DRIVE LITERALLY ANYWHERE ON THE PLANET.
I DON'T DOUBT IT.
PROBLEM IS, YOU COULD ALSO ***POLLUTE IT*** TO DEATH.
teach 2b
OH NO!

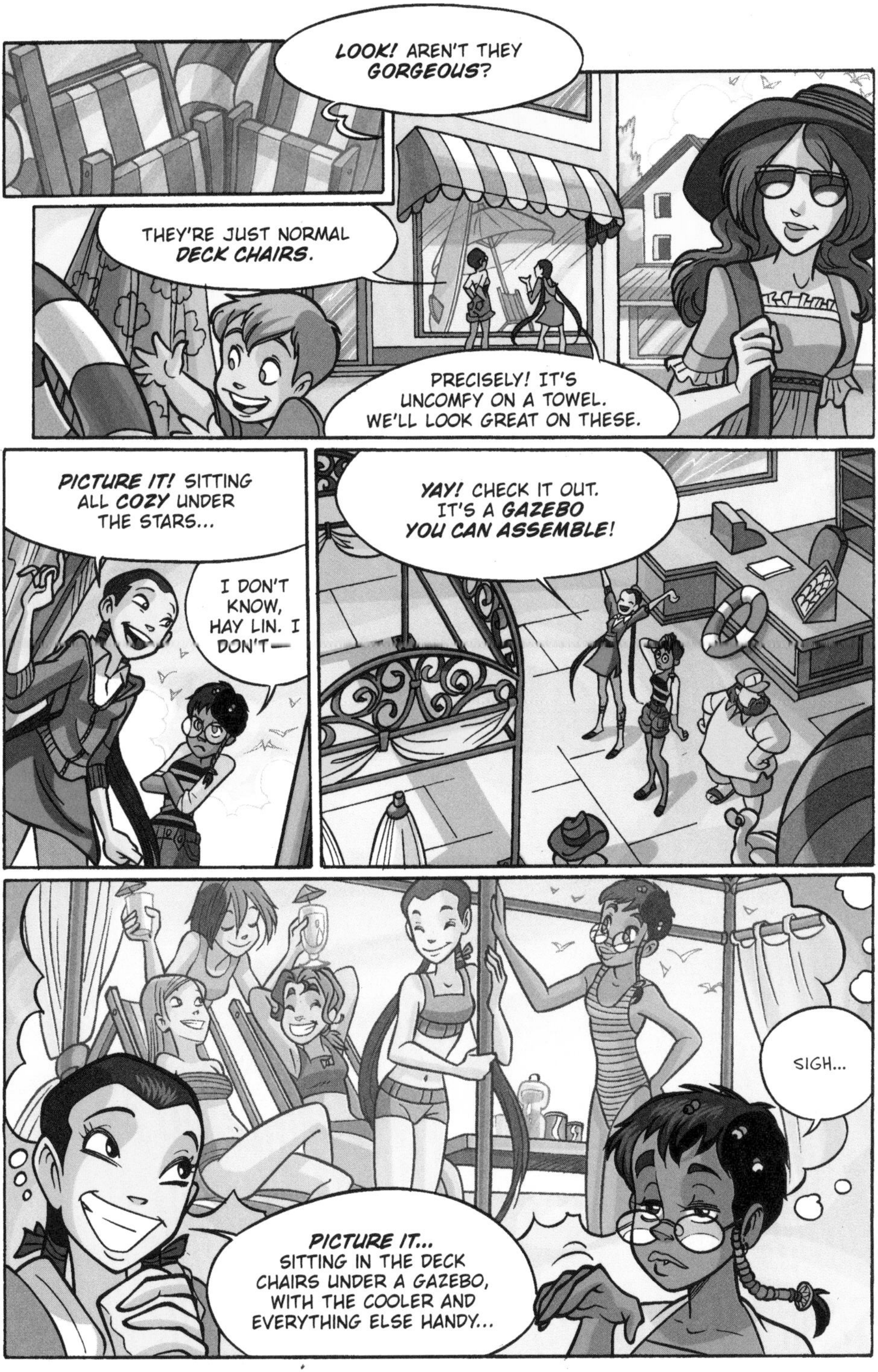
LOOK! AREN'T THEY GORGEOUS?
THEY'RE JUST NORMAL DECK CHAIRS.
PRECISELY! IT'S UNCOMFY ON A TOWEL. WE'LL LOOK GREAT ON THESE.
PICTURE IT! SITTING ALL COZY UNDER THE STARS...
I DON'T KNOW, HAY LIN. I DON'T—
YAY! CHECK IT OUT. IT'S A GAZEBO YOU CAN ASSEMBLE!
SIGH...
PICTURE IT... SITTING IN THE DECK CHAIRS UNDER A GAZEBO, WITH THE COOLER AND EVERYTHING ELSE HANDY...

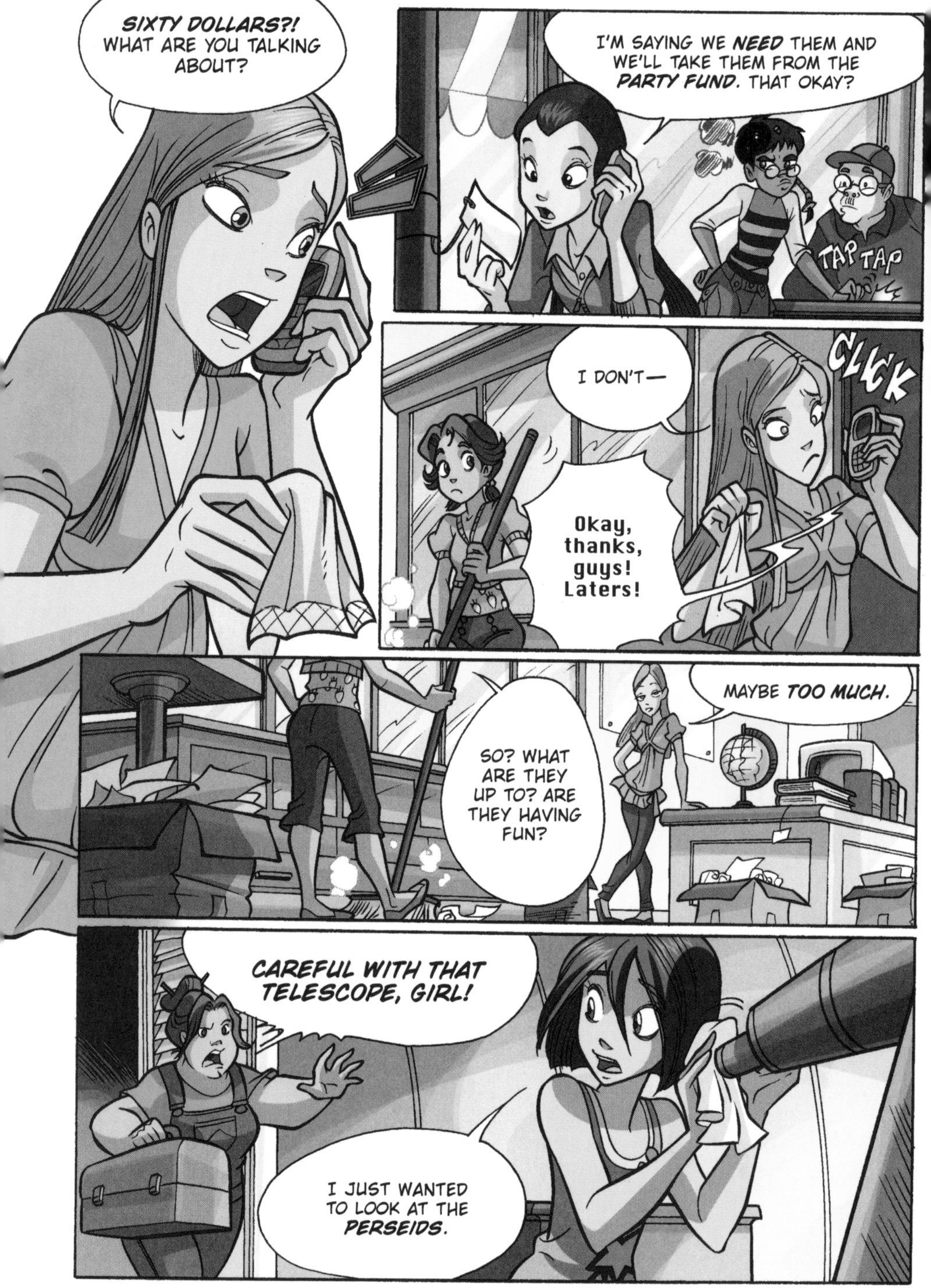
SIXTY DOLLARS?! WHAT ARE YOU TALKING ABOUT?
I'M SAYING WE NEED THEM AND WE'LL TAKE THEM FROM THE PARTY FUND. THAT OKAY?
TAP TAP
I DON'T—
CLICK
Okay, thanks, guys! Laters!
SO? WHAT ARE THEY UP TO? ARE THEY HAVING FUN?
MAYBE TOO MUCH.
CAREFUL WITH THAT TELESCOPE, GIRL!
I JUST WANTED TO LOOK AT THE PERSEIDS.

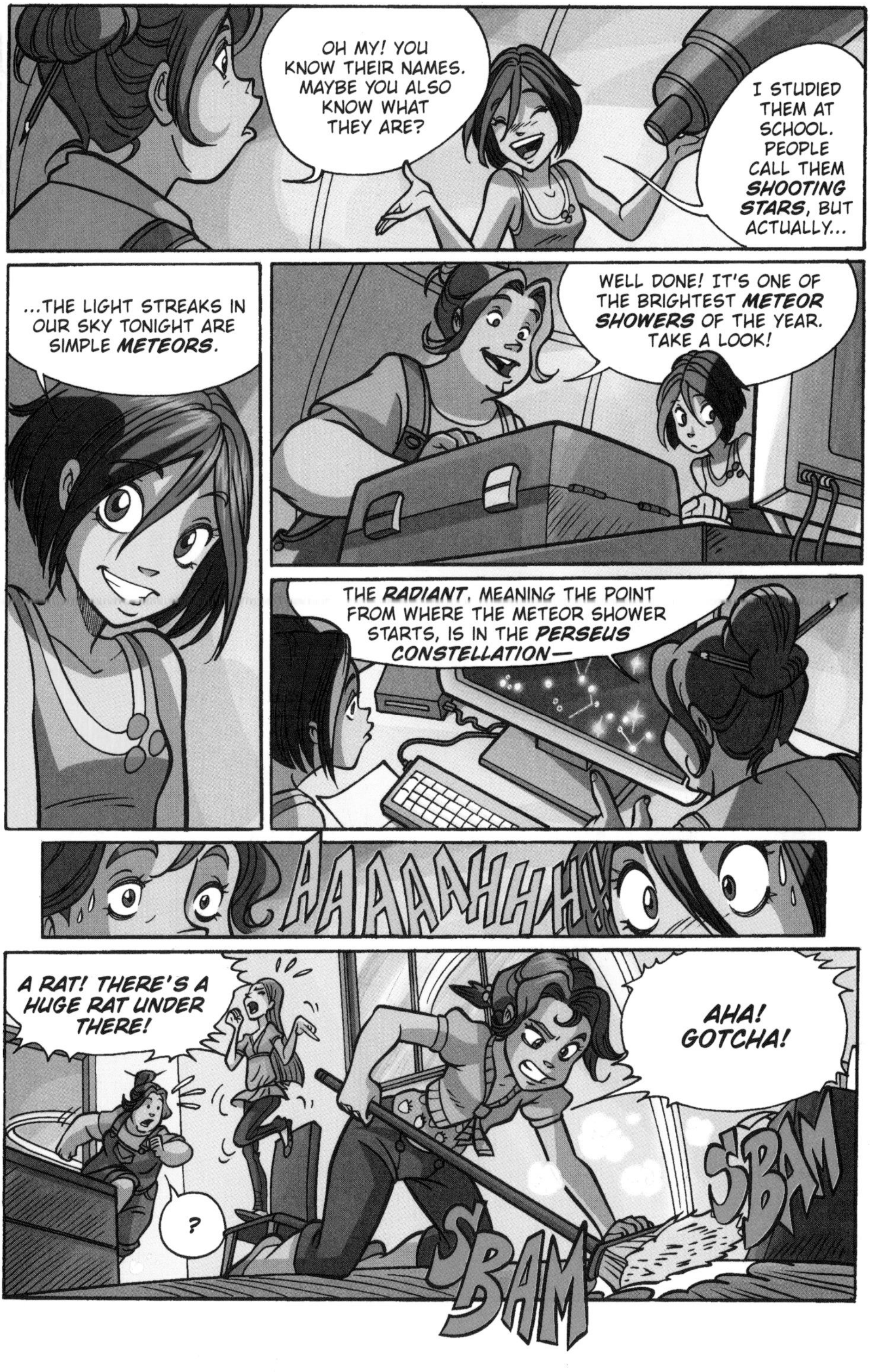
OH MY! YOU KNOW THEIR NAMES. MAYBE YOU ALSO KNOW WHAT THEY ARE?
I STUDIED THEM AT SCHOOL. PEOPLE CALL THEM **SHOOTING STARS**, BUT ACTUALLY...
...THE LIGHT STREAKS IN OUR SKY TONIGHT ARE SIMPLE **METEORS**.
WELL DONE! IT'S ONE OF THE BRIGHTEST **METEOR SHOWERS** OF THE YEAR. TAKE A LOOK!
THE **RADIANT**, MEANING THE POINT FROM WHERE THE METEOR SHOWER STARTS, IS IN THE **PERSEUS CONSTELLATION**—
AAAAAHHHH!
A RAT! THERE'S A HUGE RAT UNDER THERE!
AHA! GOTCHA!
?
SBAM
SBAM

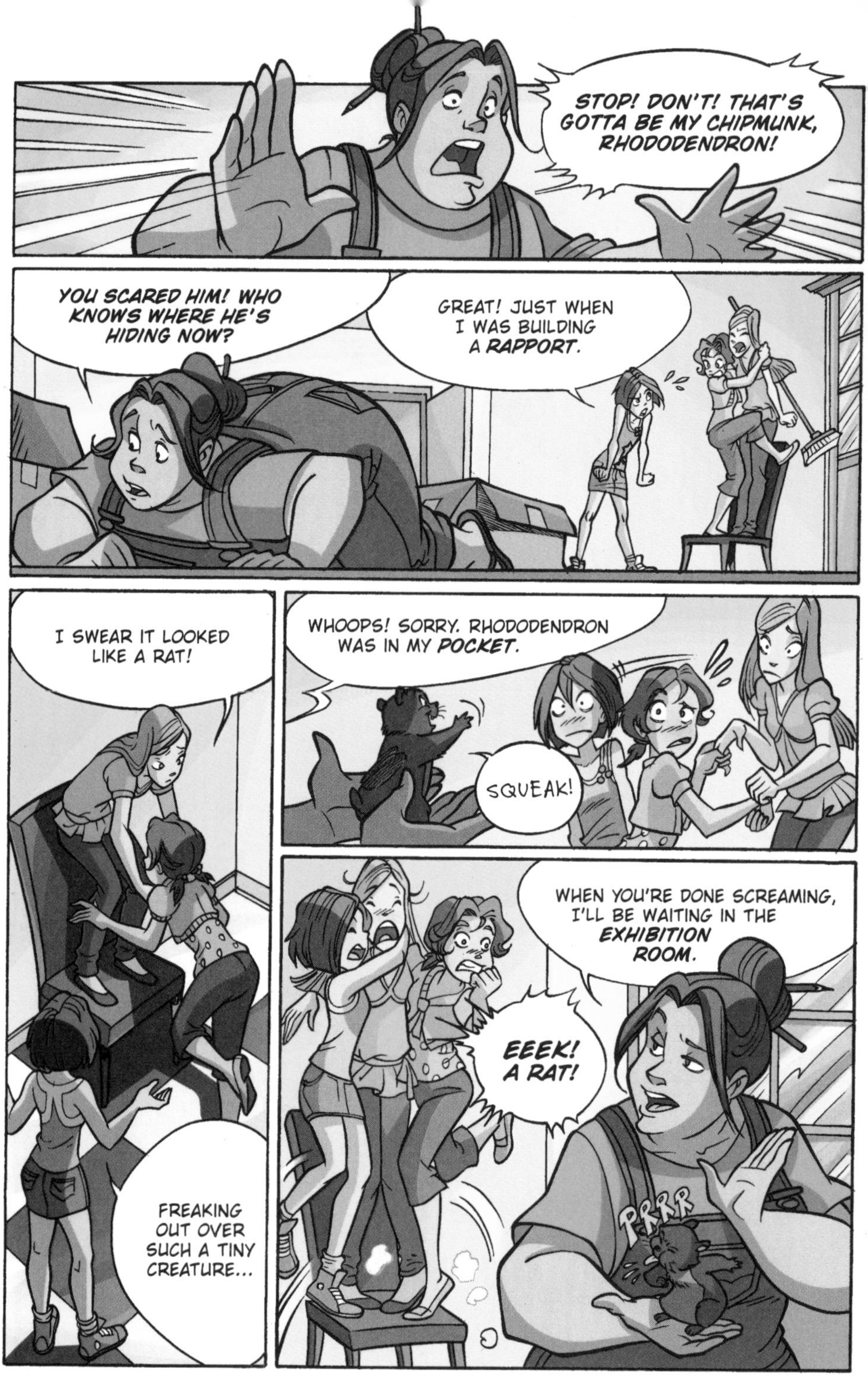
STOP! DON'T! THAT'S GOTTA BE MY CHIPMUNK, RHODODENDRON!
YOU SCARED HIM! WHO KNOWS WHERE HE'S HIDING NOW?
GREAT! JUST WHEN I WAS BUILDING A RAPPORT.
I SWEAR IT LOOKED LIKE A RAT!
FREAKING OUT OVER SUCH A TINY CREATURE...
WHOOPS! SORRY. RHODODENDRON WAS IN MY POCKET.
SQUEAK!
WHEN YOU'RE DONE SCREAMING, I'LL BE WAITING IN THE EXHIBITION ROOM.
EEEK! A RAT!
PRRR

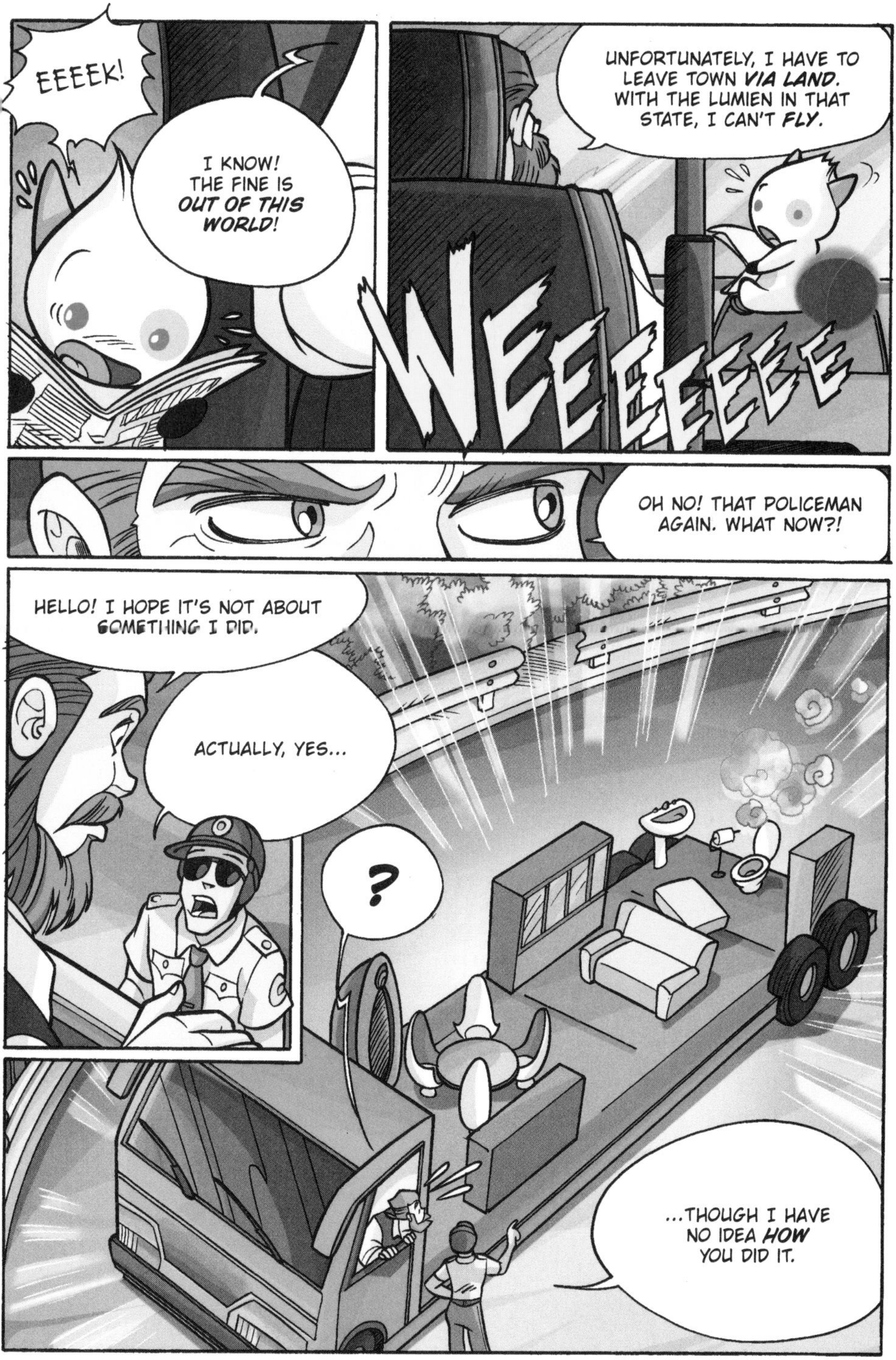
EEEEK!
I KNOW! THE FINE IS OUT OF THIS WORLD!
UNFORTUNATELY, I HAVE TO LEAVE TOWN VIA LAND. WITH THE LUMIEN IN THAT STATE, I CAN'T FLY.
WEEEEEEE
OH NO! THAT POLICEMAN AGAIN. WHAT NOW?!
HELLO! I HOPE IT'S NOT ABOUT SOMETHING I DID.
ACTUALLY, YES...
?
...THOUGH I HAVE NO IDEA HOW YOU DID IT.

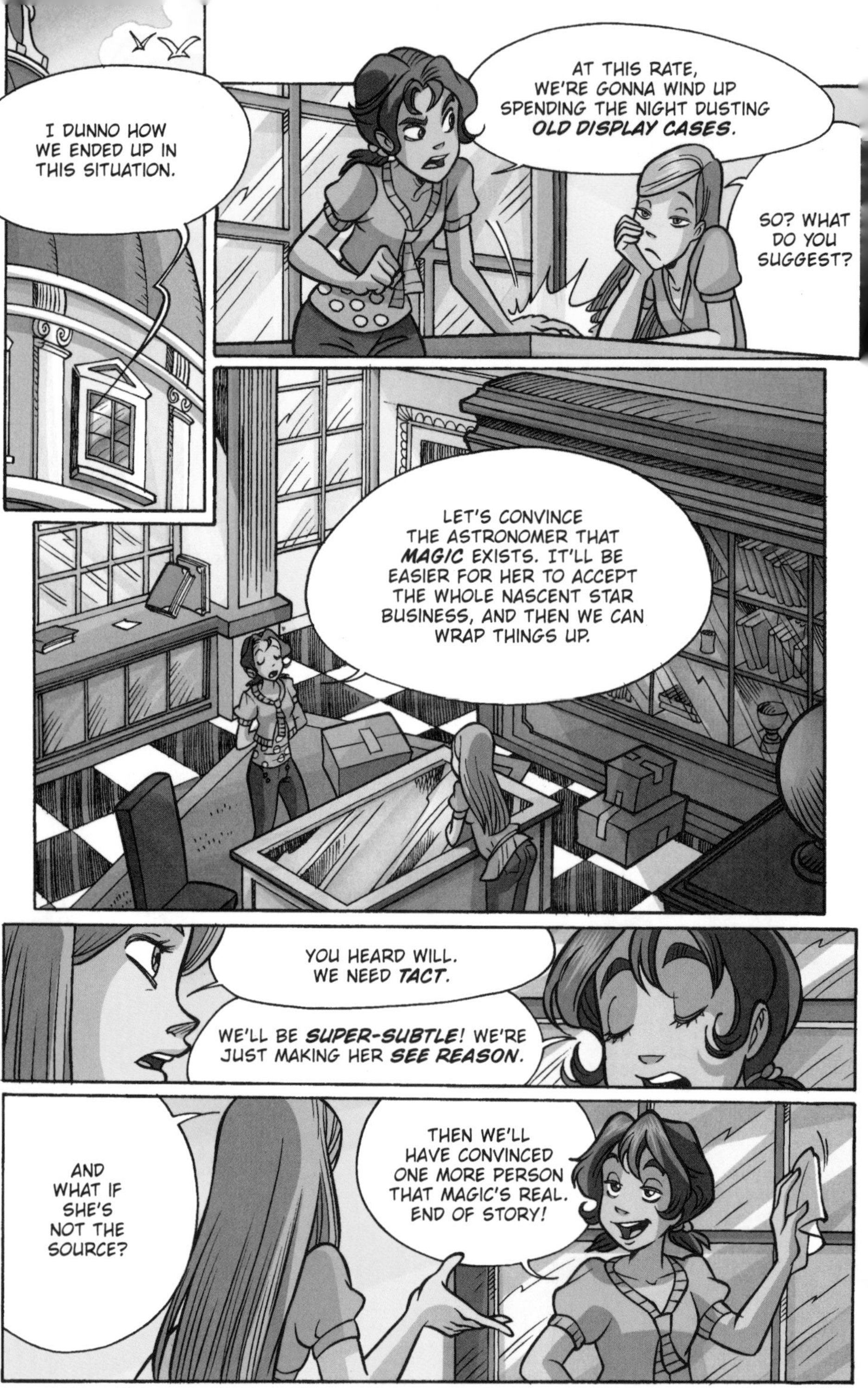
I DUNNO HOW WE ENDED UP IN THIS SITUATION.
AT THIS RATE, WE'RE GONNA WIND UP SPENDING THE NIGHT DUSTING OLD DISPLAY CASES.
SO? WHAT DO YOU SUGGEST?
LET'S CONVINCE THE ASTRONOMER THAT MAGIC EXISTS. IT'LL BE EASIER FOR HER TO ACCEPT THE WHOLE NASCENT STAR BUSINESS, AND THEN WE CAN WRAP THINGS UP.
YOU HEARD WILL. WE NEED TACT.
WE'LL BE SUPER-SUBTLE! WE'RE JUST MAKING HER SEE REASON.
AND WHAT IF SHE'S NOT THE SOURCE?
THEN WE'LL HAVE CONVINCED ONE MORE PERSON THAT MAGIC'S REAL. END OF STORY!

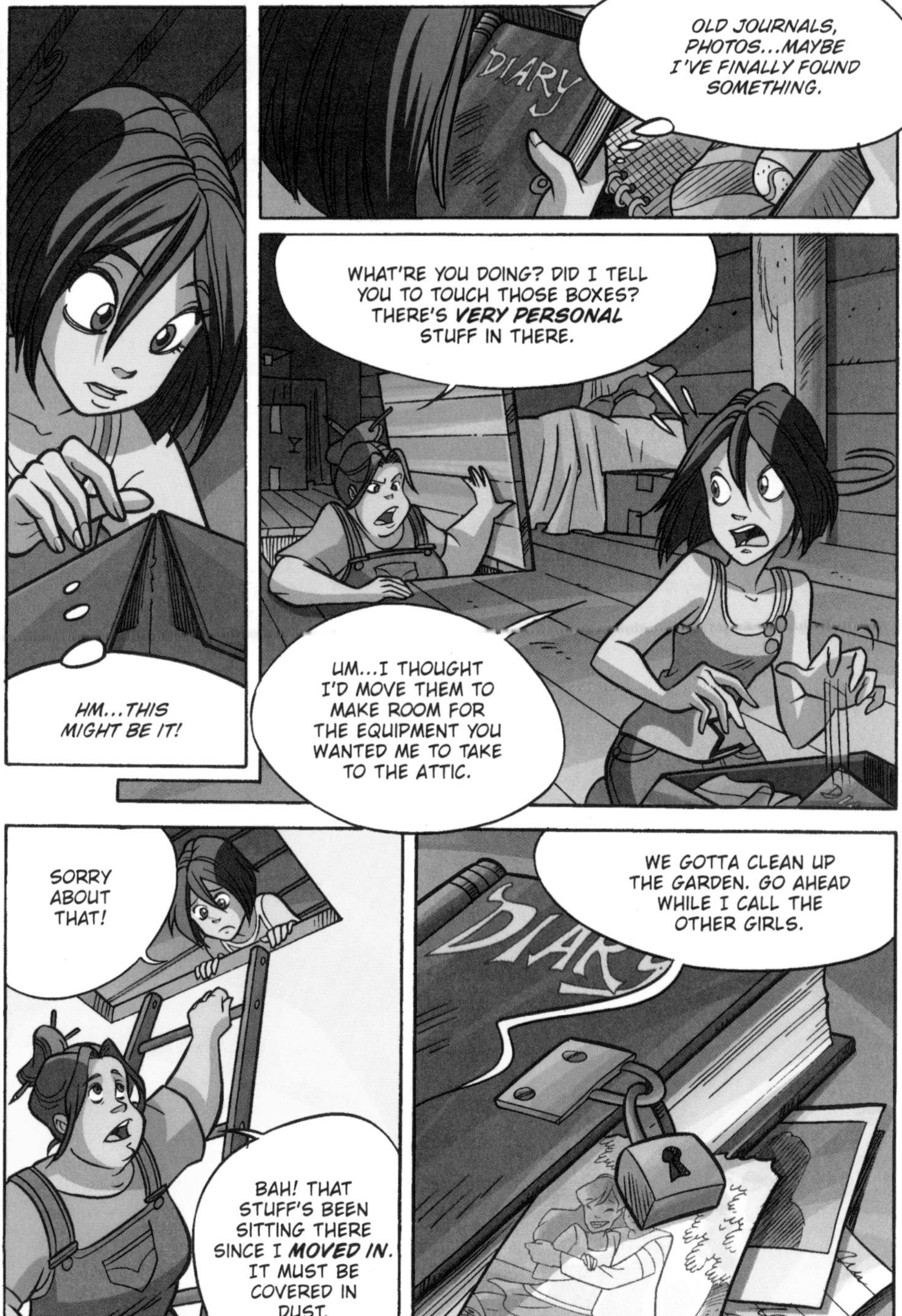
HM...THIS MIGHT BE IT!
OLD JOURNALS, PHOTOS...MAYBE I'VE FINALLY FOUND SOMETHING.
DIARY
WHAT'RE YOU DOING? DID I TELL YOU TO TOUCH THOSE BOXES? THERE'S **VERY PERSONAL** STUFF IN THERE.
UM...I THOUGHT I'D MOVE THEM TO MAKE ROOM FOR THE EQUIPMENT YOU WANTED ME TO TAKE TO THE ATTIC.
SORRY ABOUT THAT!
BAH! THAT STUFF'S BEEN SITTING THERE SINCE I **MOVED IN**. IT MUST BE COVERED IN DUST.
WE GOTTA CLEAN UP THE GARDEN. GO AHEAD WHILE I CALL THE OTHER GIRLS.
DIARY

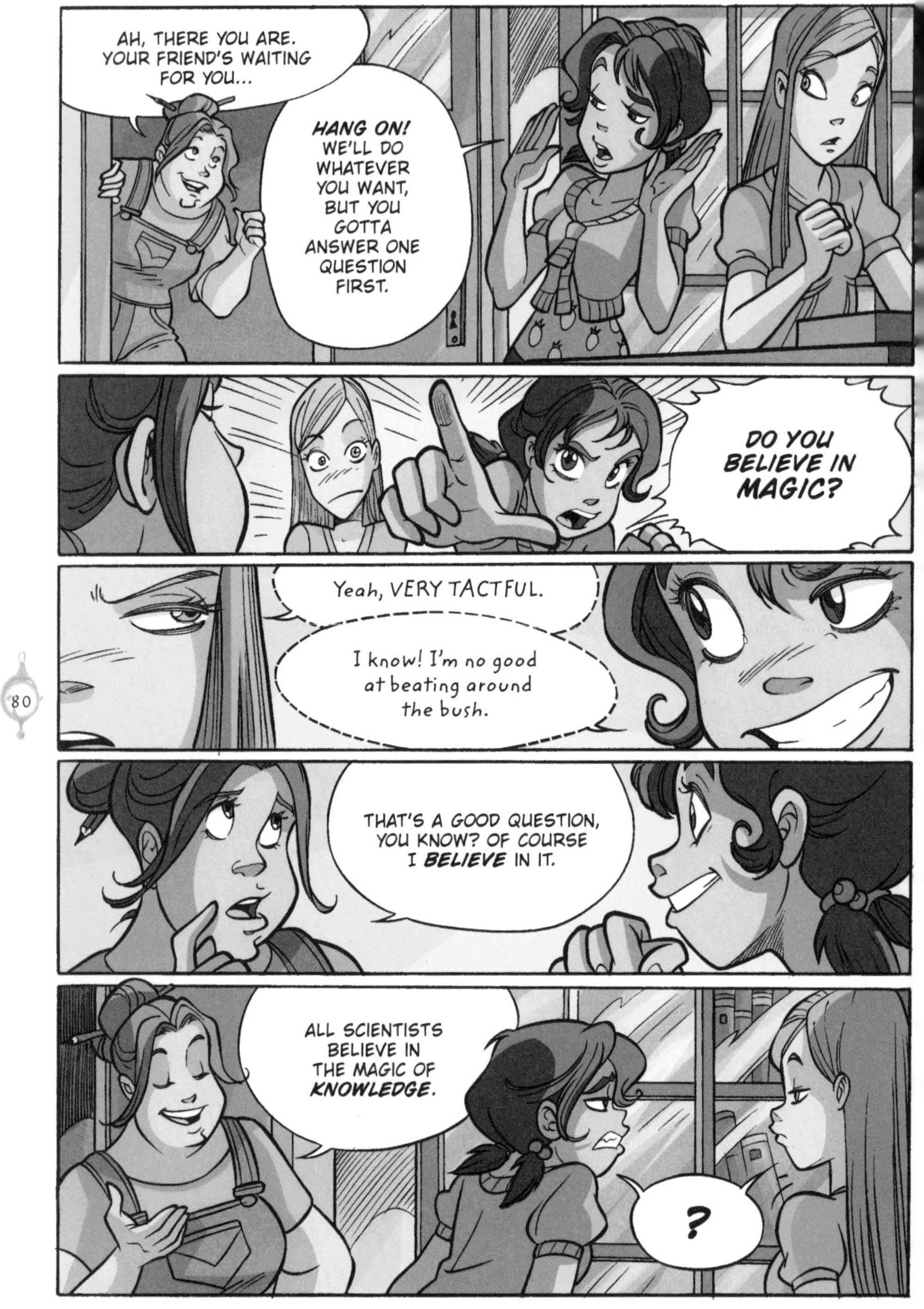
AH, THERE YOU ARE. YOUR FRIEND'S WAITING FOR YOU...
HANG ON! WE'LL DO WHATEVER YOU WANT, BUT YOU GOTTA ANSWER ONE QUESTION FIRST.
DO YOU BELIEVE IN MAGIC?
Yeah, VERY TACTFUL.
I know! I'm no good at beating around the bush.
THAT'S A GOOD QUESTION, YOU KNOW? OF COURSE I BELIEVE IN IT.
ALL SCIENTISTS BELIEVE IN THE MAGIC OF KNOWLEDGE.
?

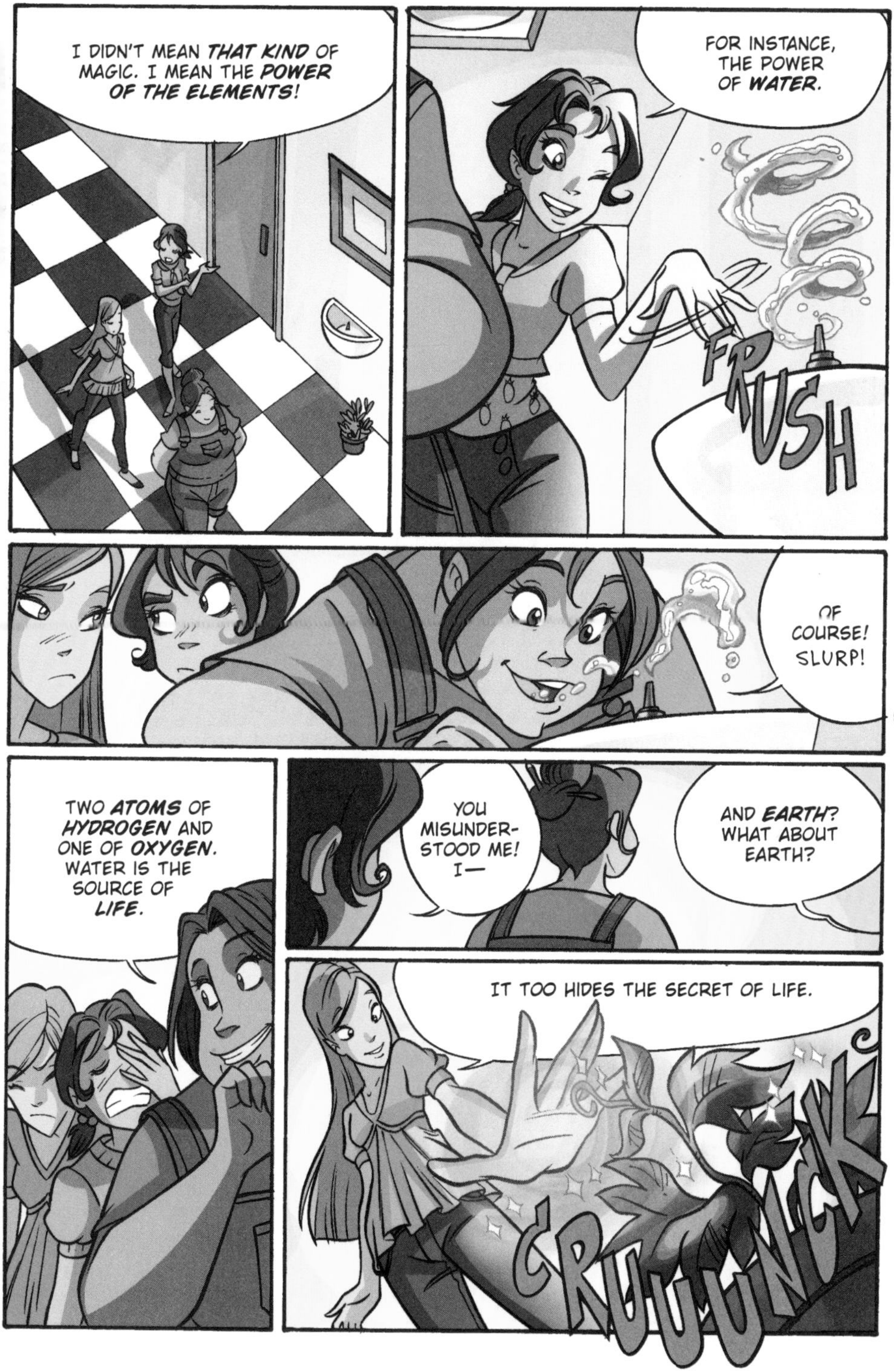

I DIDN'T MEAN THAT KIND OF MAGIC. I MEAN THE POWER OF THE ELEMENTS!
FOR INSTANCE, THE POWER OF WATER.
FRUSH
OF COURSE! SLURP!
TWO ATOMS OF HYDROGEN AND ONE OF OXYGEN. WATER IS THE SOURCE OF LIFE.
YOU MISUNDER-STOOD ME! I—
AND EARTH? WHAT ABOUT EARTH?
IT TOO HIDES THE SECRET OF LIFE.
CRUUUNCK

OH! I THOUGHT THAT PLANT HAD *DIED*.

ANYWAY, I LOVE EVERYTHING ABOUT THE EARTH. *GEOCHEMISTRY, MINERALOGY, STRATIGRAPHY,* AND SO ON!

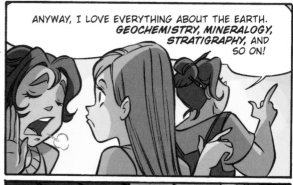

"TRUST ME, GIRLS. THERE'S NOTHING MORE MAGICAL THAN *SCIENCE.*

"IT HAS THE ANSWERS TO ALL YOUR QUESTIONS, AND MOST IMPORTANTLY...

"...IT WILL NEVER *LET YOU DOWN.*"

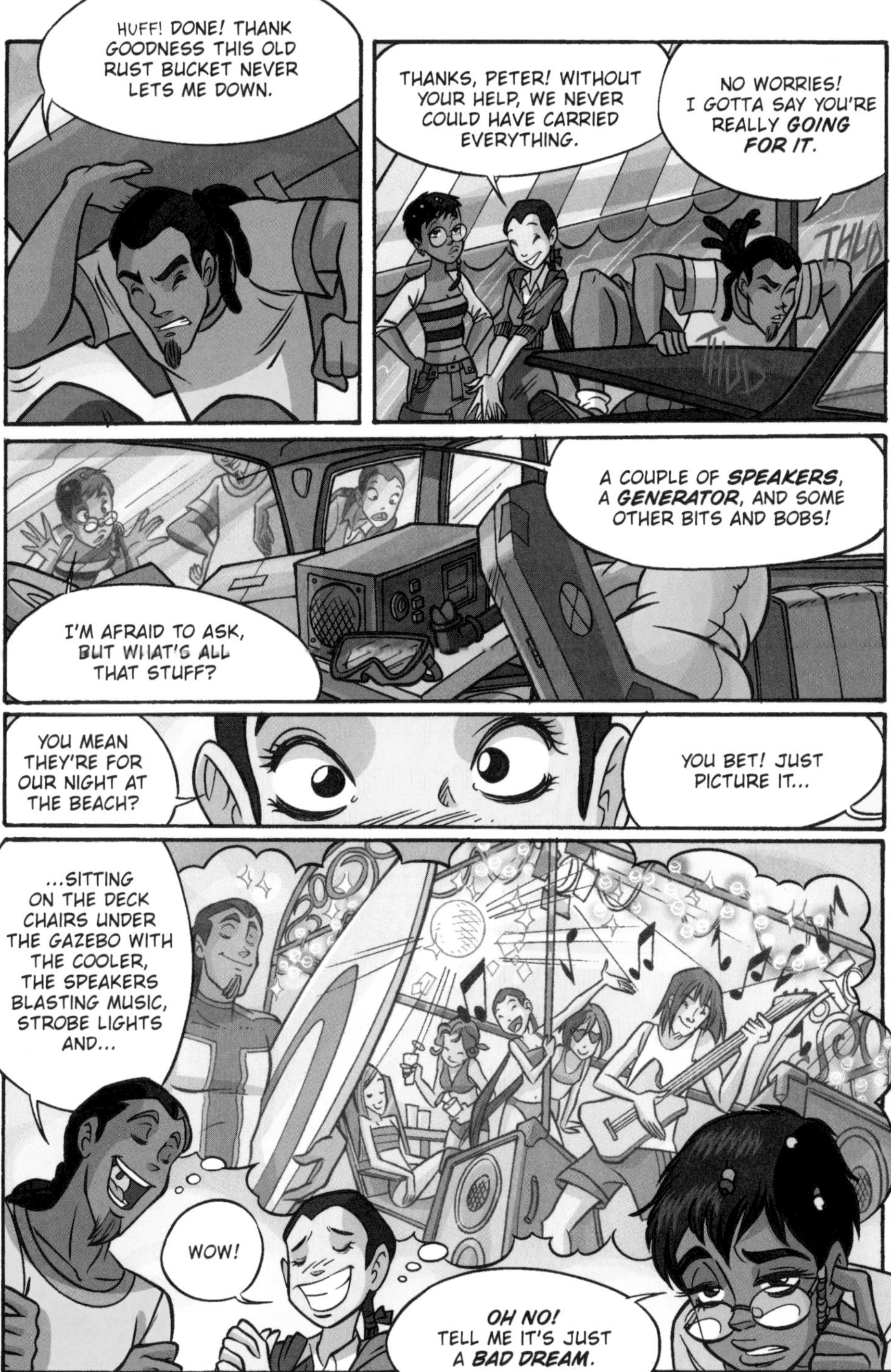
HUFF! DONE! THANK GOODNESS THIS OLD RUST BUCKET NEVER LETS ME DOWN.
THANKS, PETER! WITHOUT YOUR HELP, WE NEVER COULD HAVE CARRIED EVERYTHING.
NO WORRIES! I GOTTA SAY YOU'RE REALLY GOING FOR IT.
THUD
THUD
I'M AFRAID TO ASK, BUT WHAT'S ALL THAT STUFF?
A COUPLE OF SPEAKERS, A GENERATOR, AND SOME OTHER BITS AND BOBS!
YOU MEAN THEY'RE FOR OUR NIGHT AT THE BEACH?
YOU BET! JUST PICTURE IT...
...SITTING ON THE DECK CHAIRS UNDER THE GAZEBO WITH THE COOLER, THE SPEAKERS BLASTING MUSIC, STROBE LIGHTS AND...
WOW!
OH NO! TELL ME IT'S JUST A BAD DREAM.

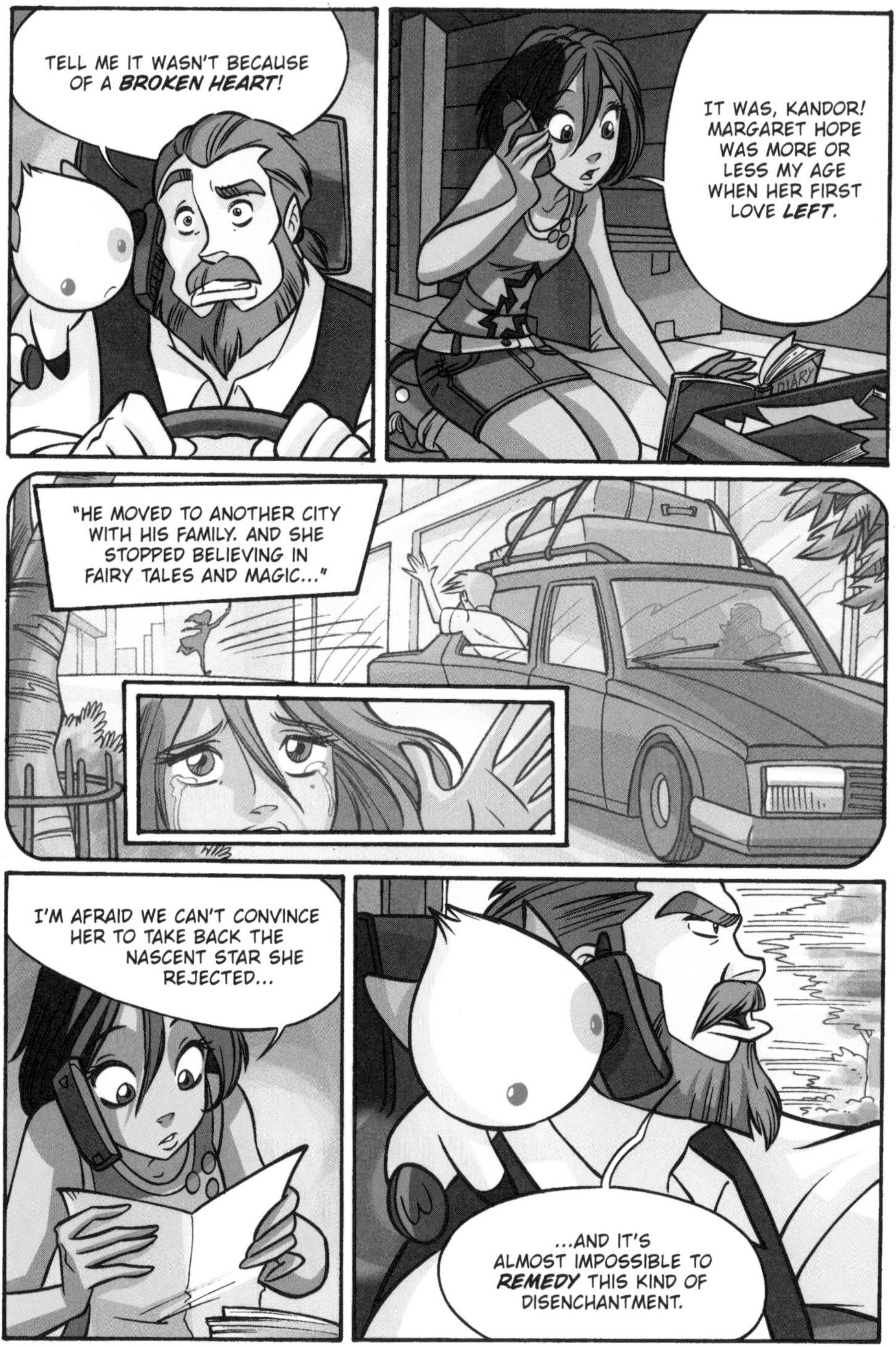

TELL ME IT WASN'T BECAUSE OF A BROKEN HEART!
IT WAS, KANDOR! MARGARET HOPE WAS MORE OR LESS MY AGE WHEN HER FIRST LOVE LEFT.
DIARY
"HE MOVED TO ANOTHER CITY WITH HIS FAMILY. AND SHE STOPPED BELIEVING IN FAIRY TALES AND MAGIC..."
I'M AFRAID WE CAN'T CONVINCE HER TO TAKE BACK THE NASCENT STAR SHE REJECTED...
...AND IT'S ALMOST IMPOSSIBLE TO REMEDY THIS KIND OF DISENCHANTMENT.

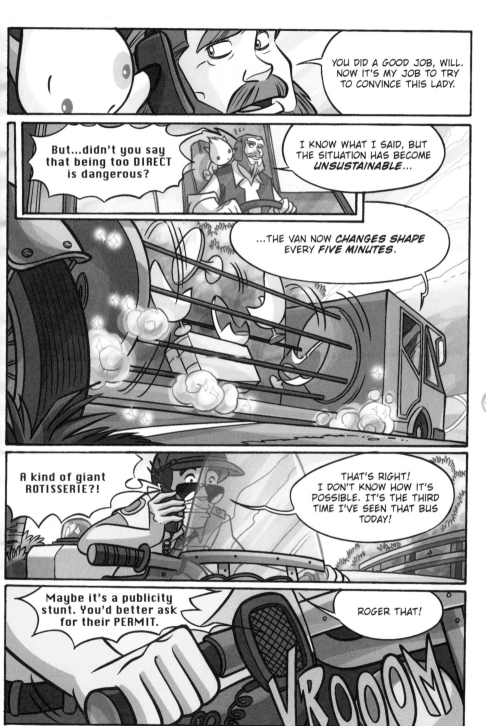

YOU DID A GOOD JOB, WILL. NOW IT'S MY JOB TO TRY TO CONVINCE THIS LADY.

But...didn't you say that being too DIRECT is dangerous?

I KNOW WHAT I SAID, BUT THE SITUATION HAS BECOME *UNSUSTAINABLE*...

...THE VAN NOW *CHANGES SHAPE* EVERY *FIVE MINUTES*.

A kind of giant ROTISSERIE?!

THAT'S RIGHT! I DON'T KNOW HOW IT'S POSSIBLE. IT'S THE THIRD TIME I'VE SEEN THAT BUS TODAY!

Maybe it's a publicity stunt. You'd better ask for their PERMIT.

ROGER THAT!

VROOOM

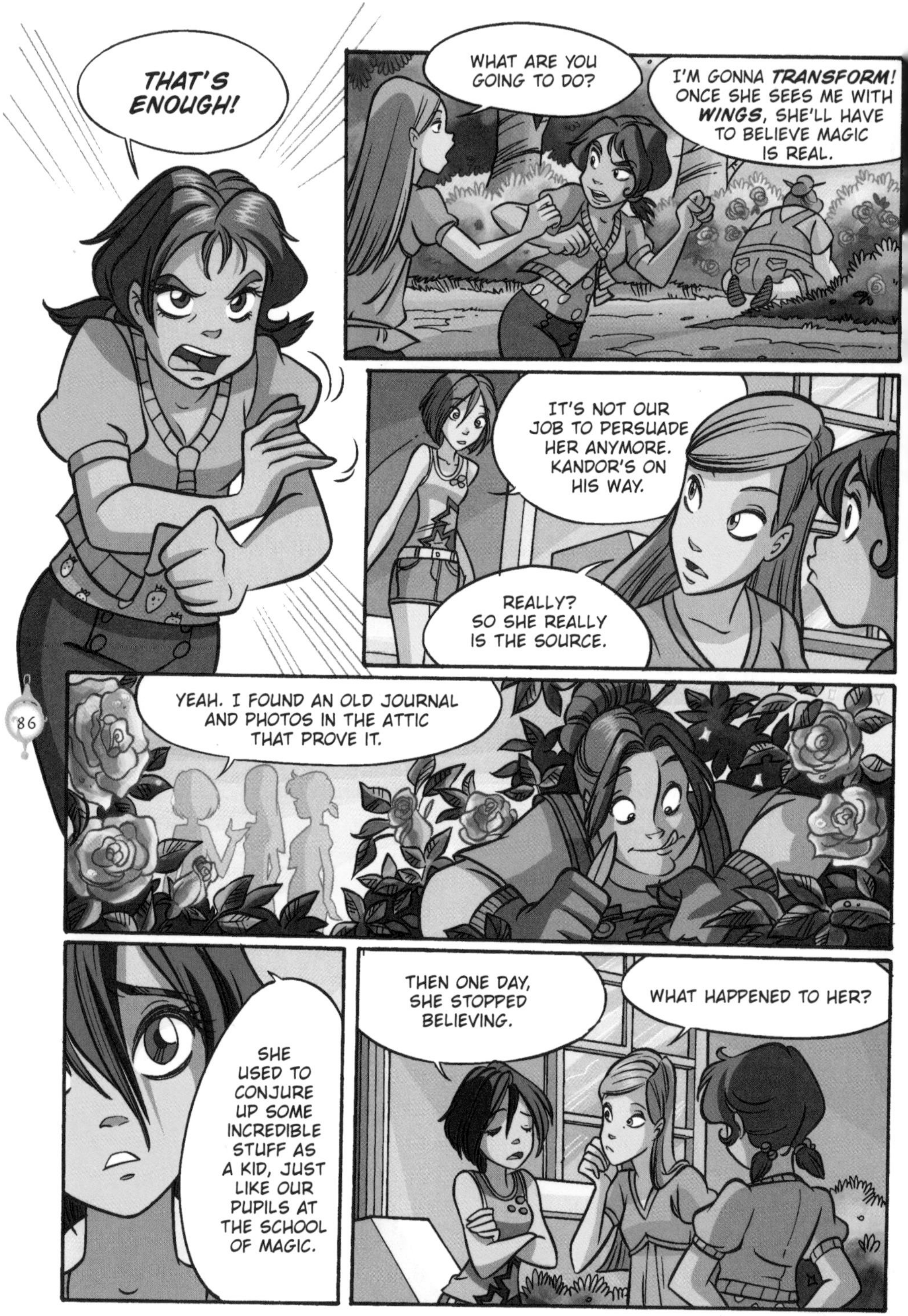
THAT'S ENOUGH!
WHAT ARE YOU GOING TO DO?
I'M GONNA TRANSFORM! ONCE SHE SEES ME WITH WINGS, SHE'LL HAVE TO BELIEVE MAGIC IS REAL.
IT'S NOT OUR JOB TO PERSUADE HER ANYMORE. KANDOR'S ON HIS WAY.
REALLY? SO SHE REALLY IS THE SOURCE.
YEAH. I FOUND AN OLD JOURNAL AND PHOTOS IN THE ATTIC THAT PROVE IT.
SHE USED TO CONJURE UP SOME INCREDIBLE STUFF AS A KID, JUST LIKE OUR PUPILS AT THE SCHOOL OF MAGIC.
THEN ONE DAY, SHE STOPPED BELIEVING.
WHAT HAPPENED TO HER?

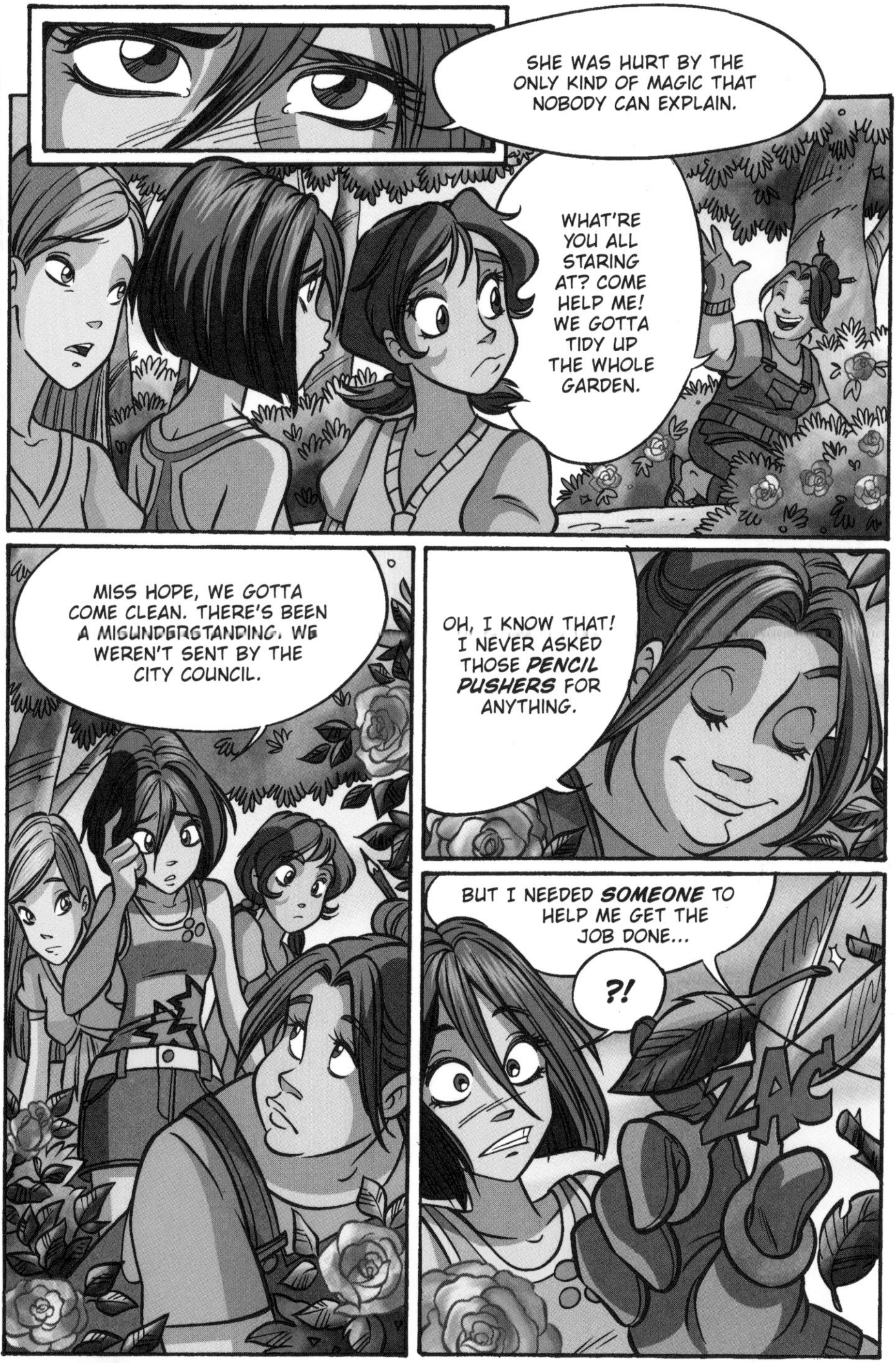
SHE WAS HURT BY THE ONLY KIND OF MAGIC THAT NOBODY CAN EXPLAIN.
WHAT'RE YOU ALL STARING AT? COME HELP ME! WE GOTTA TIDY UP THE WHOLE GARDEN.
MISS HOPE, WE GOTTA COME CLEAN. THERE'S BEEN A MISUNDERSTANDING. WE WEREN'T SENT BY THE CITY COUNCIL.
OH, I KNOW THAT! I NEVER ASKED THOSE PENCIL PUSHERS FOR ANYTHING.
BUT I NEEDED SOMEONE TO HELP ME GET THE JOB DONE...
?!
ZAC

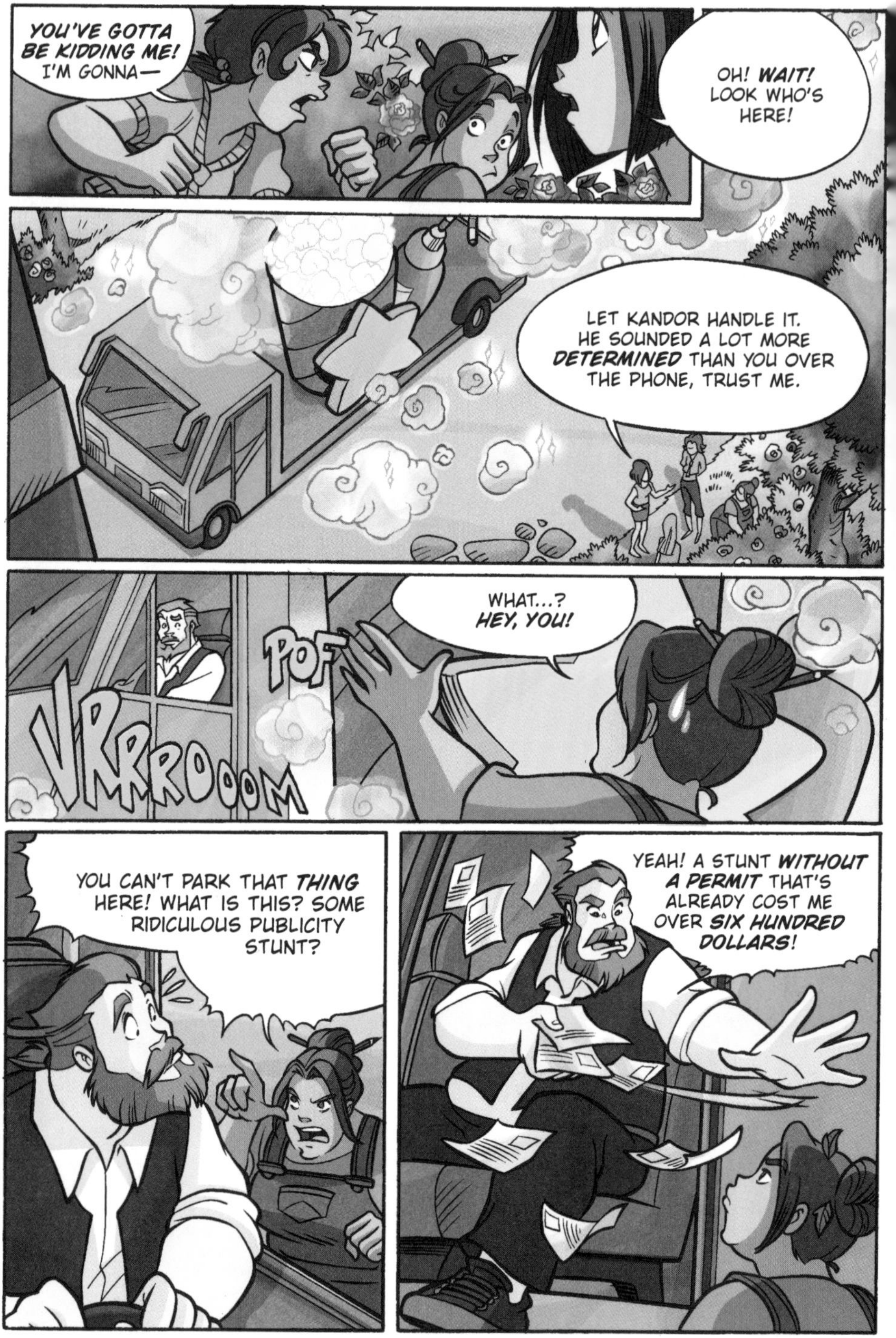
YOU'VE GOTTA BE KIDDING ME! I'M GONNA—
OH! WAIT! LOOK WHO'S HERE!
LET KANDOR HANDLE IT. HE SOUNDED A LOT MORE DETERMINED THAN YOU OVER THE PHONE, TRUST ME.
VRRROOOM
POF
WHAT...? HEY, YOU!
YOU CAN'T PARK THAT THING HERE! WHAT IS THIS? SOME RIDICULOUS PUBLICITY STUNT?
YEAH! A STUNT WITHOUT A PERMIT THAT'S ALREADY COST ME OVER SIX HUNDRED DOLLARS!

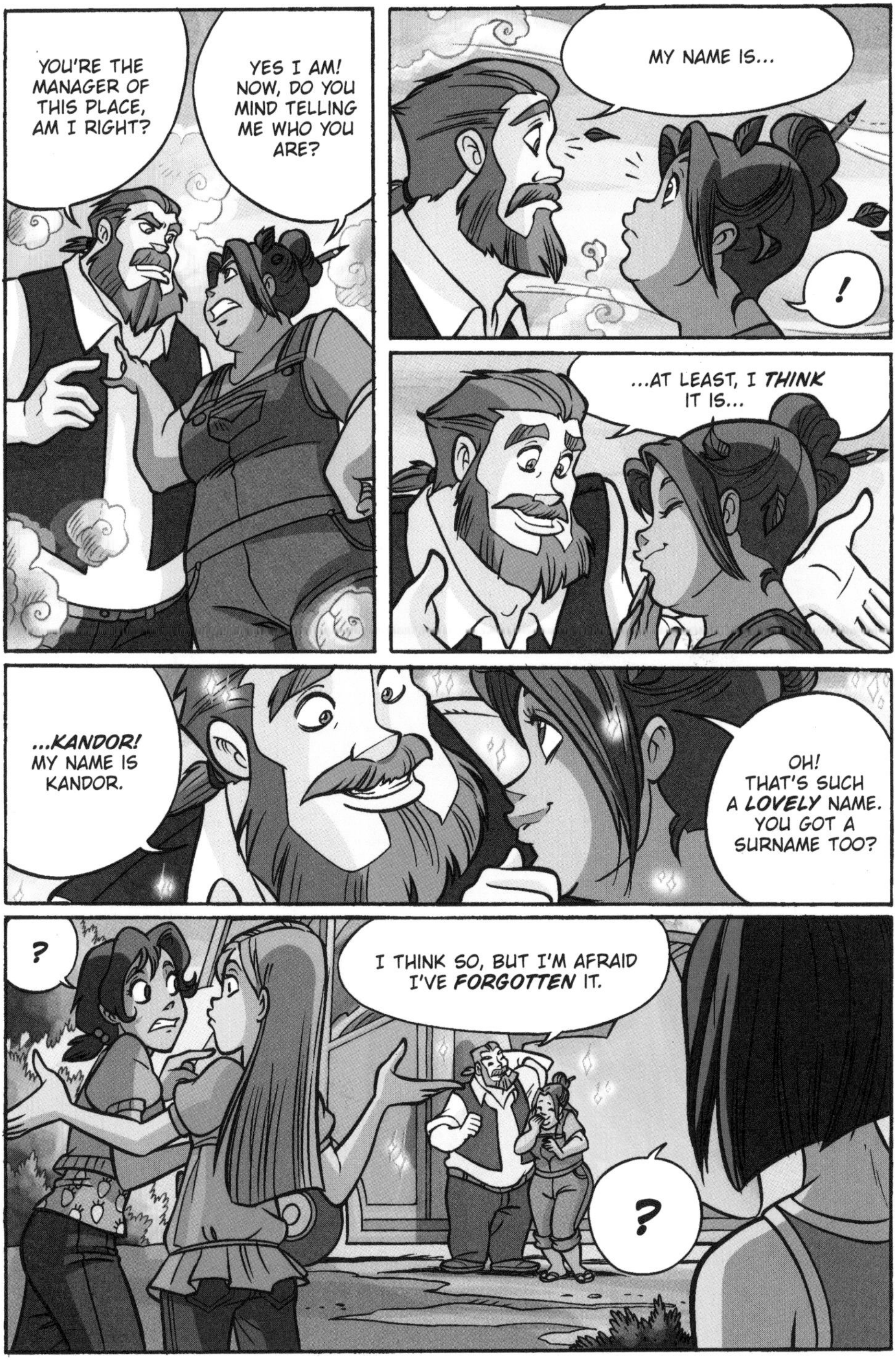
YOU'RE THE MANAGER OF THIS PLACE, AM I RIGHT?
YES I AM! NOW, DO YOU MIND TELLING ME WHO YOU ARE?
MY NAME IS...
!
...AT LEAST, I *THINK* IT IS...
...KANDOR! MY NAME IS KANDOR.
OH! THAT'S SUCH A *LOVELY* NAME. YOU GOT A SURNAME TOO?
?
I THINK SO, BUT I'M AFRAID I'VE *FORGOTTEN* IT.
?

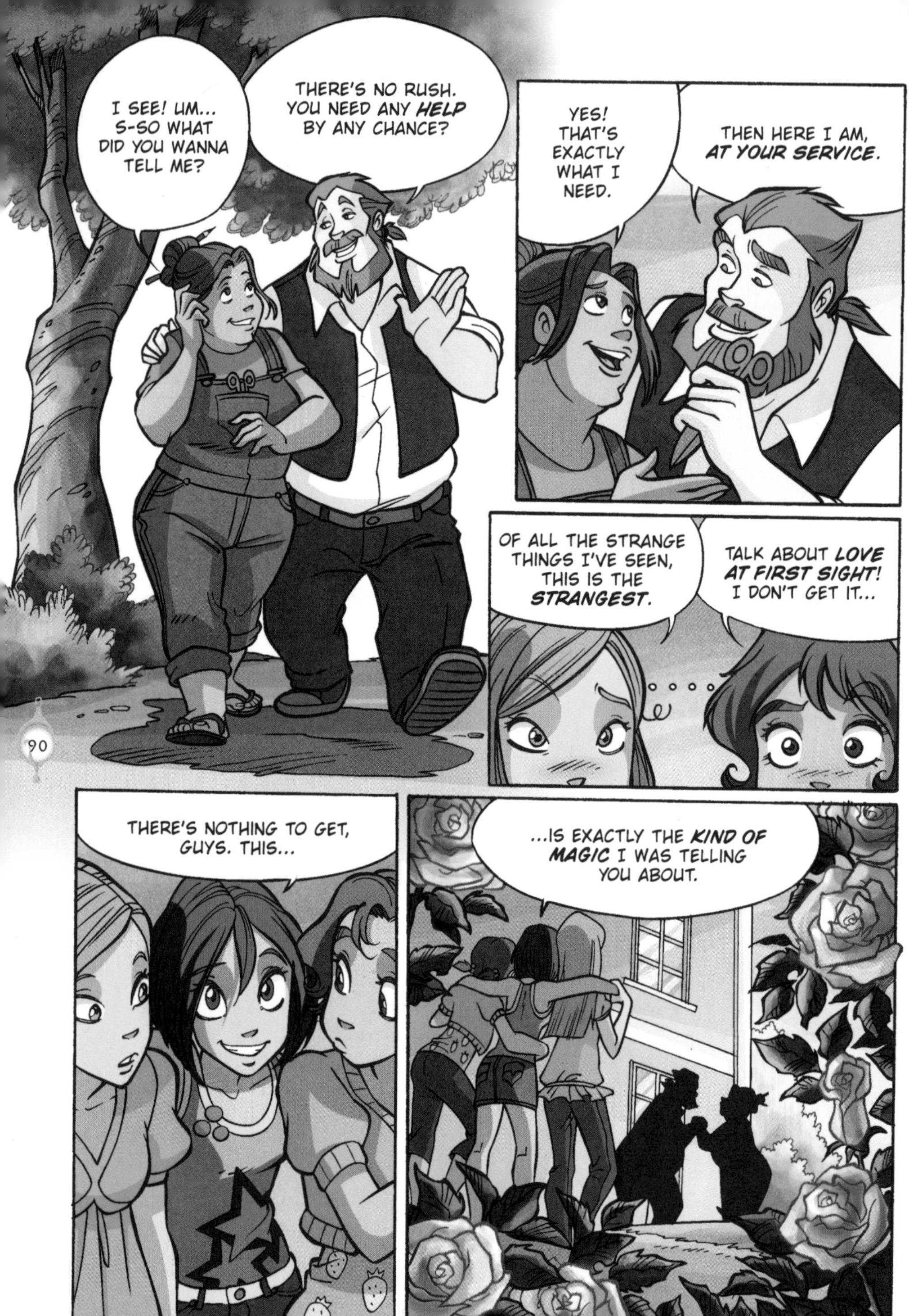
I SEE! UM... S-SO WHAT DID YOU WANNA TELL ME?
THERE'S NO RUSH. YOU NEED ANY HELP BY ANY CHANCE?
YES! THAT'S EXACTLY WHAT I NEED.
THEN HERE I AM, AT YOUR SERVICE.
OF ALL THE STRANGE THINGS I'VE SEEN, THIS IS THE STRANGEST.
TALK ABOUT LOVE AT FIRST SIGHT! I DON'T GET IT...
THERE'S NOTHING TO GET, GUYS. THIS...
...IS EXACTLY THE KIND OF MAGIC I WAS TELLING YOU ABOUT.

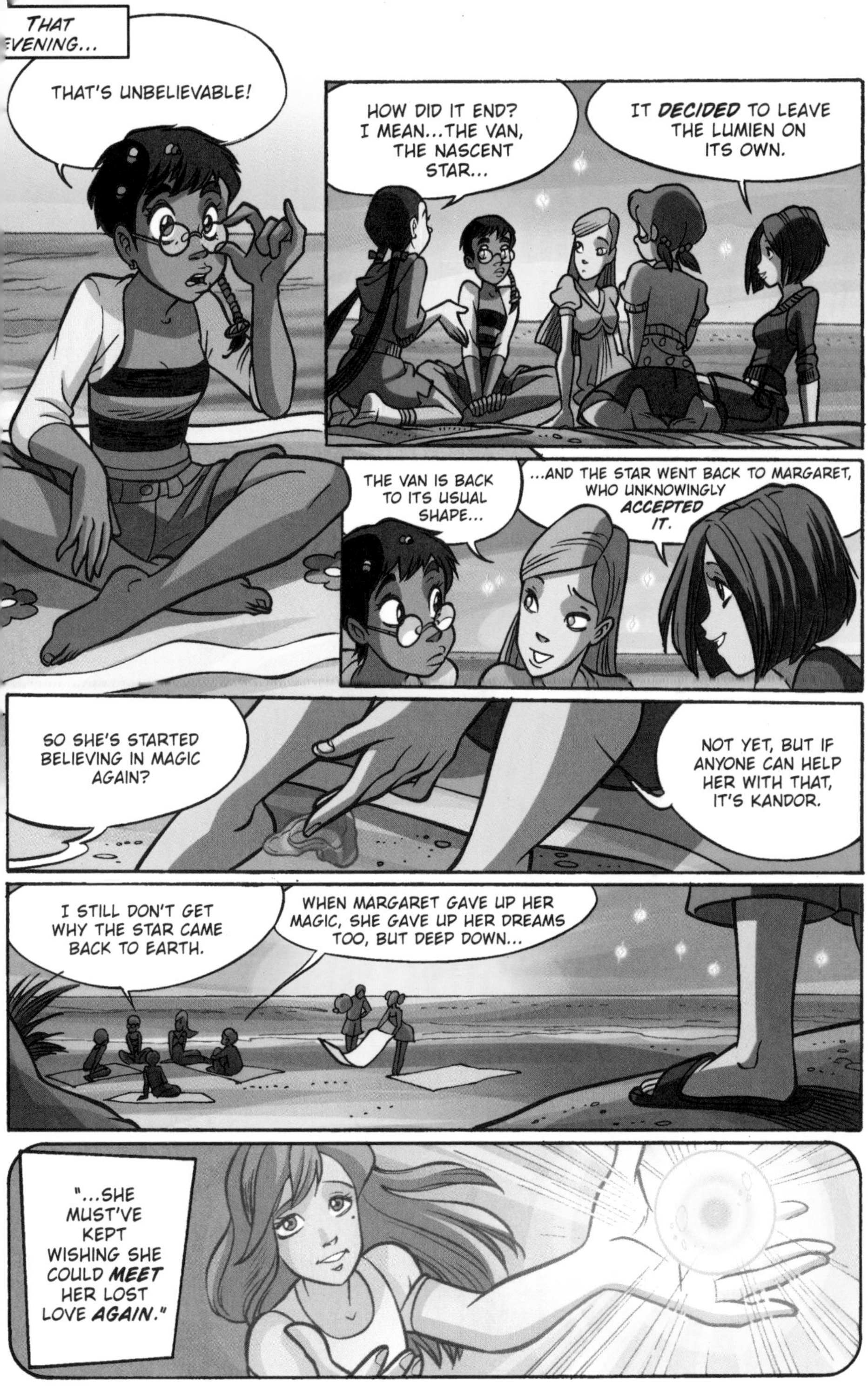
THAT EVENING...
THAT'S UNBELIEVABLE!
HOW DID IT END? I MEAN...THE VAN, THE NASCENT STAR...
IT DECIDED TO LEAVE THE LUMIEN ON ITS OWN.
THE VAN IS BACK TO ITS USUAL SHAPE...
...AND THE STAR WENT BACK TO MARGARET, WHO UNKNOWINGLY ACCEPTED IT.
SO SHE'S STARTED BELIEVING IN MAGIC AGAIN?
NOT YET, BUT IF ANYONE CAN HELP HER WITH THAT, IT'S KANDOR.
I STILL DON'T GET WHY THE STAR CAME BACK TO EARTH.
WHEN MARGARET GAVE UP HER MAGIC, SHE GAVE UP HER DREAMS TOO, BUT DEEP DOWN...
"...SHE MUST'VE KEPT WISHING SHE COULD MEET HER LOST LOVE AGAIN."

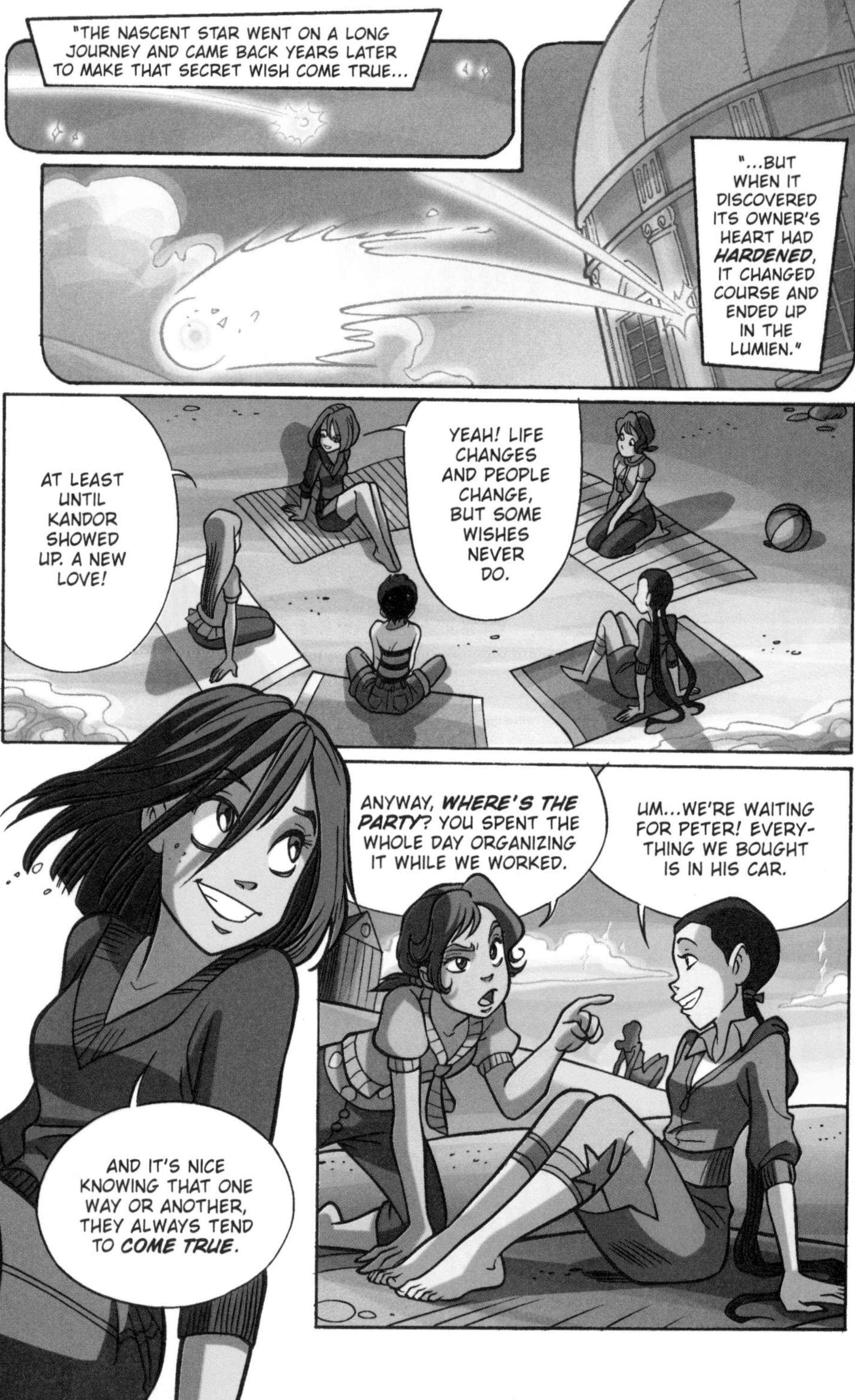
"THE NASCENT STAR WENT ON A LONG JOURNEY AND CAME BACK YEARS LATER TO MAKE THAT SECRET WISH COME TRUE...
"...BUT WHEN IT DISCOVERED ITS OWNER'S HEART HAD **HARDENED**, IT CHANGED COURSE AND ENDED UP IN THE LUMIEN."
AT LEAST UNTIL KANDOR SHOWED UP. A NEW LOVE!
YEAH! LIFE CHANGES AND PEOPLE CHANGE, BUT SOME WISHES NEVER DO.
AND IT'S NICE KNOWING THAT ONE WAY OR ANOTHER, THEY ALWAYS TEND TO **COME TRUE**.
ANYWAY, ***WHERE'S THE PARTY***? YOU SPENT THE WHOLE DAY ORGANIZING IT WHILE WE WORKED.
UM...WE'RE WAITING FOR PETER! EVERY-THING WE BOUGHT IS IN HIS CAR.

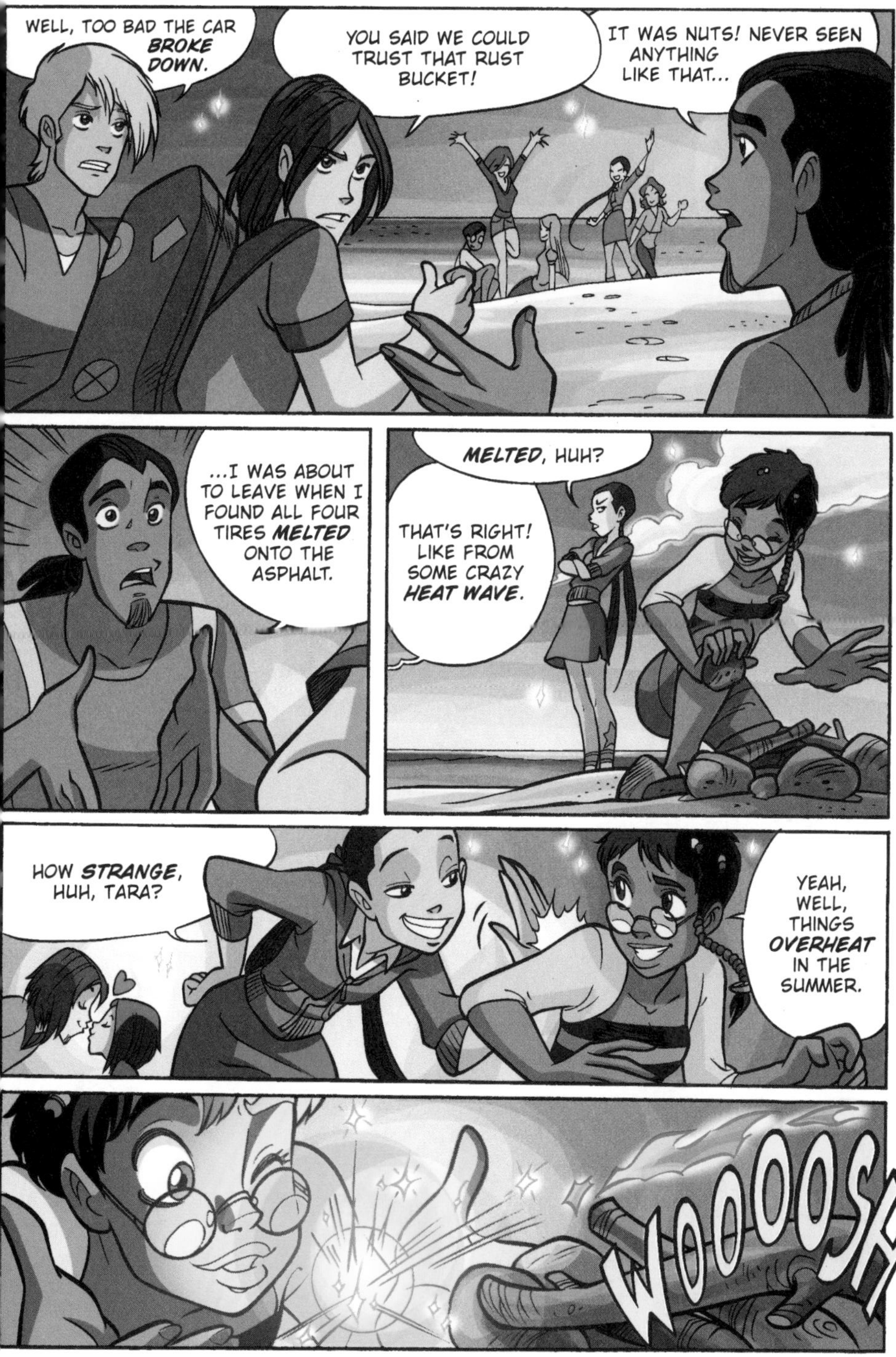
WELL, TOO BAD THE CAR BROKE DOWN.
YOU SAID WE COULD TRUST THAT RUST BUCKET!
IT WAS NUTS! NEVER SEEN ANYTHING LIKE THAT...
...I WAS ABOUT TO LEAVE WHEN I FOUND ALL FOUR TIRES MELTED ONTO THE ASPHALT.
MELTED, HUH?
THAT'S RIGHT! LIKE FROM SOME CRAZY HEAT WAVE.
HOW STRANGE, HUH, TARA?
YEAH, WELL, THINGS OVERHEAT IN THE SUMMER.
WOOOOSH

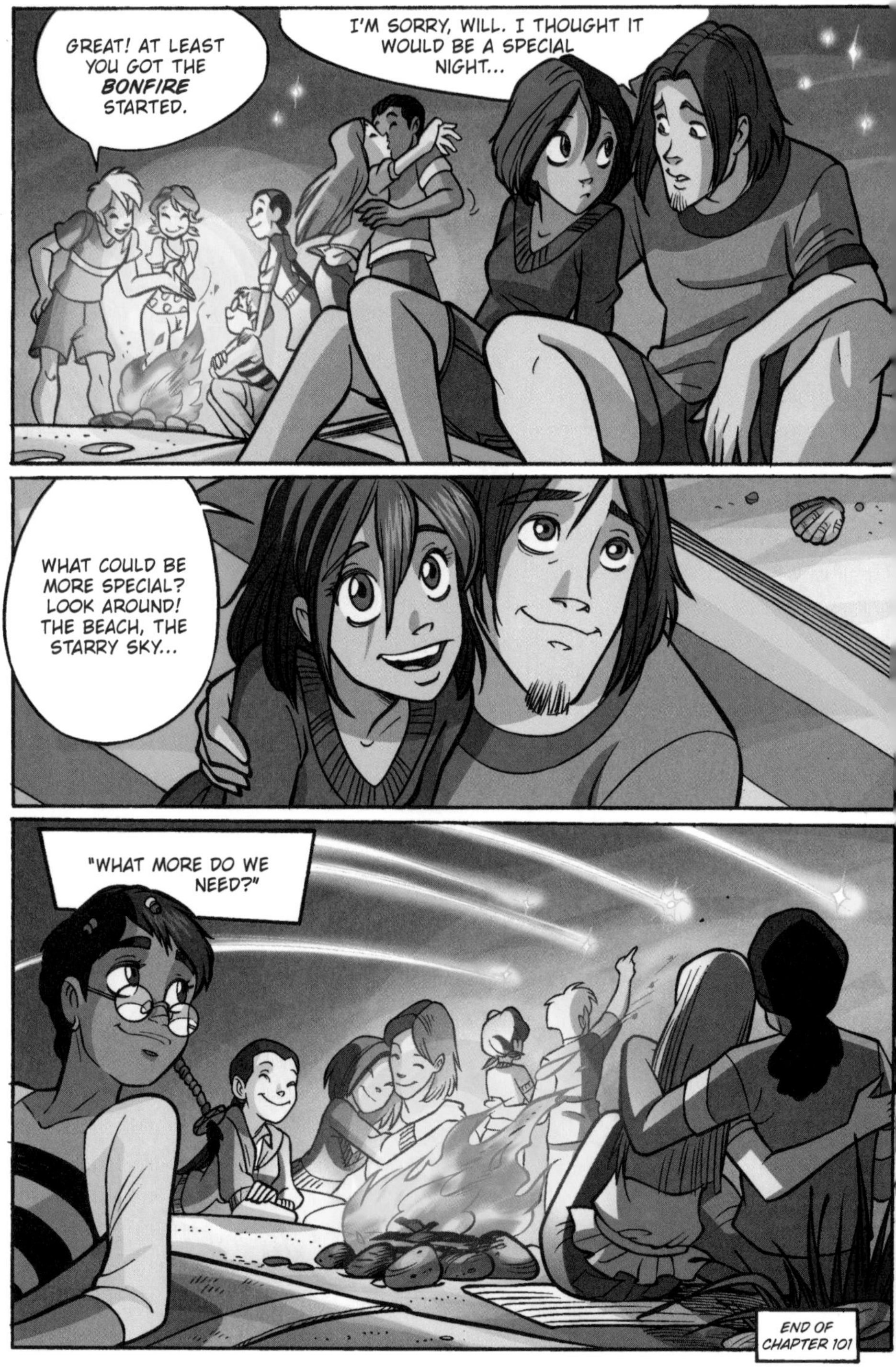
GREAT! AT LEAST YOU GOT THE **BONFIRE** STARTED.
I'M SORRY, WILL. I THOUGHT IT WOULD BE A SPECIAL NIGHT...
WHAT COULD BE MORE SPECIAL? LOOK AROUND! THE BEACH, THE STARRY SKY...
"WHAT MORE DO WE NEED?"
END OF CHAPTER 101

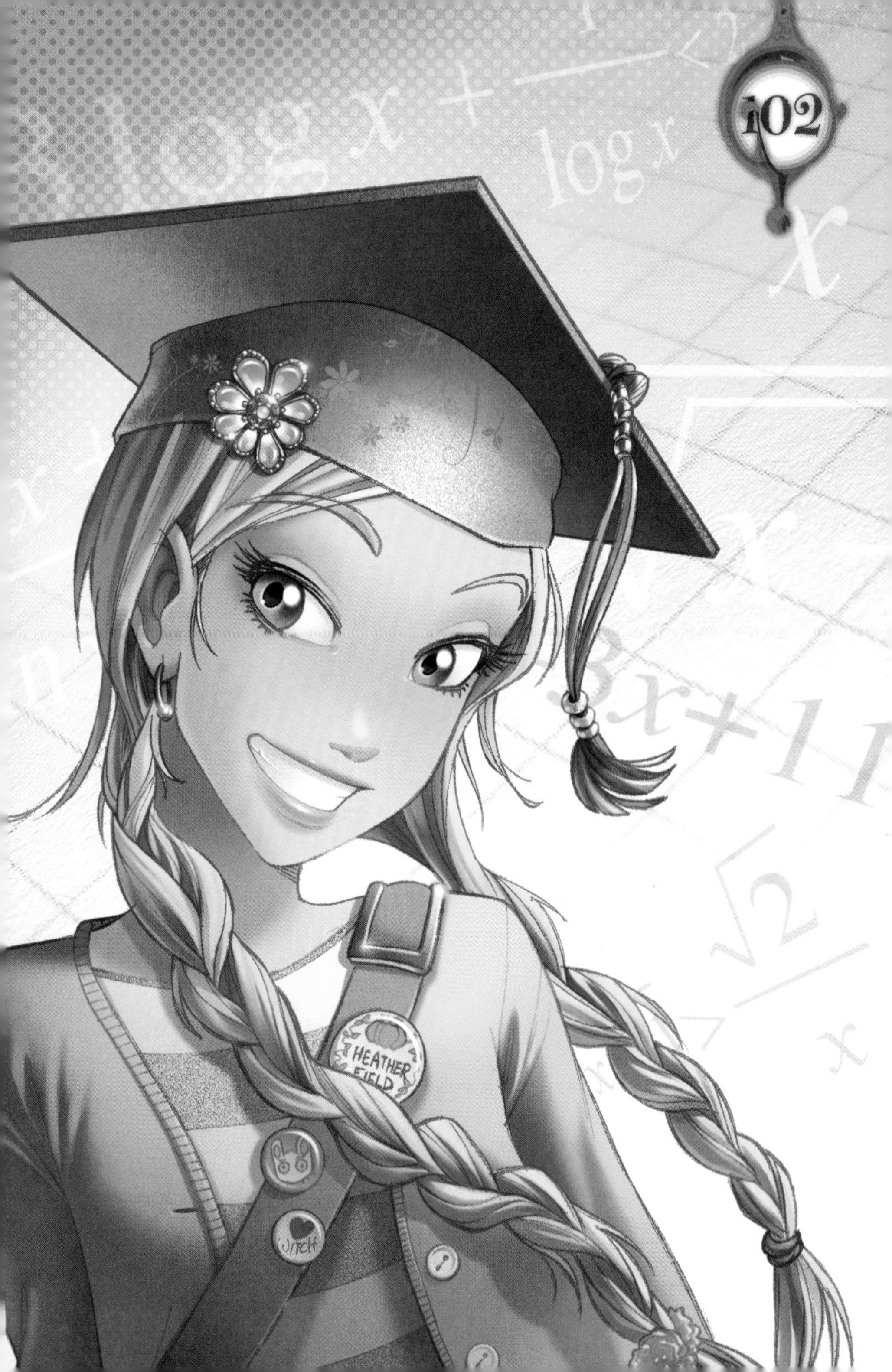
102
log x
HEATHER FIELD
WITCH

Will   Irma   Taranee   Cornelia   Hay Lin

The First Day

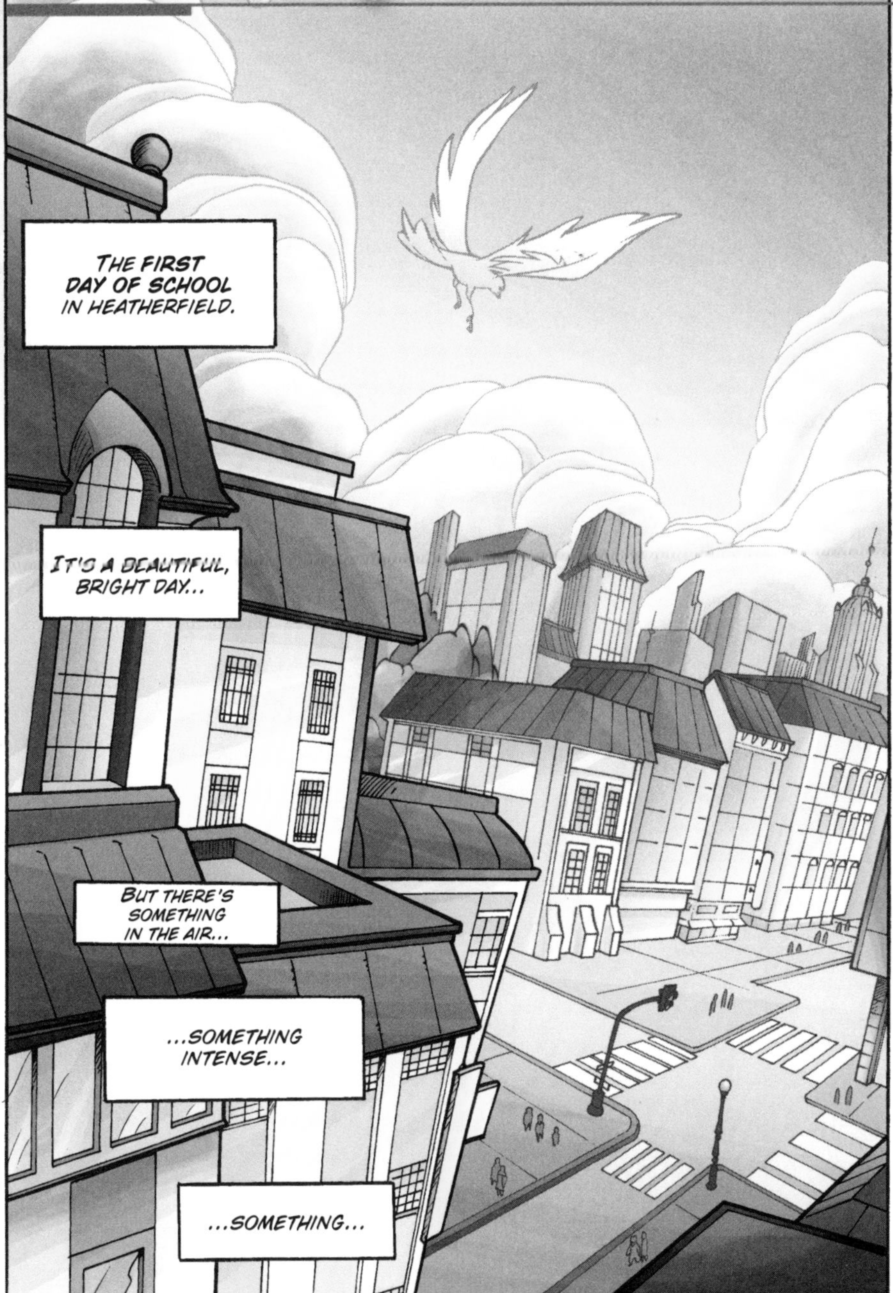

THE FIRST DAY OF SCHOOL IN HEATHERFIELD.
IT'S A BEAUTIFUL, BRIGHT DAY...
BUT THERE'S SOMETHING IN THE AIR...
...SOMETHING INTENSE...
...SOMETHING...

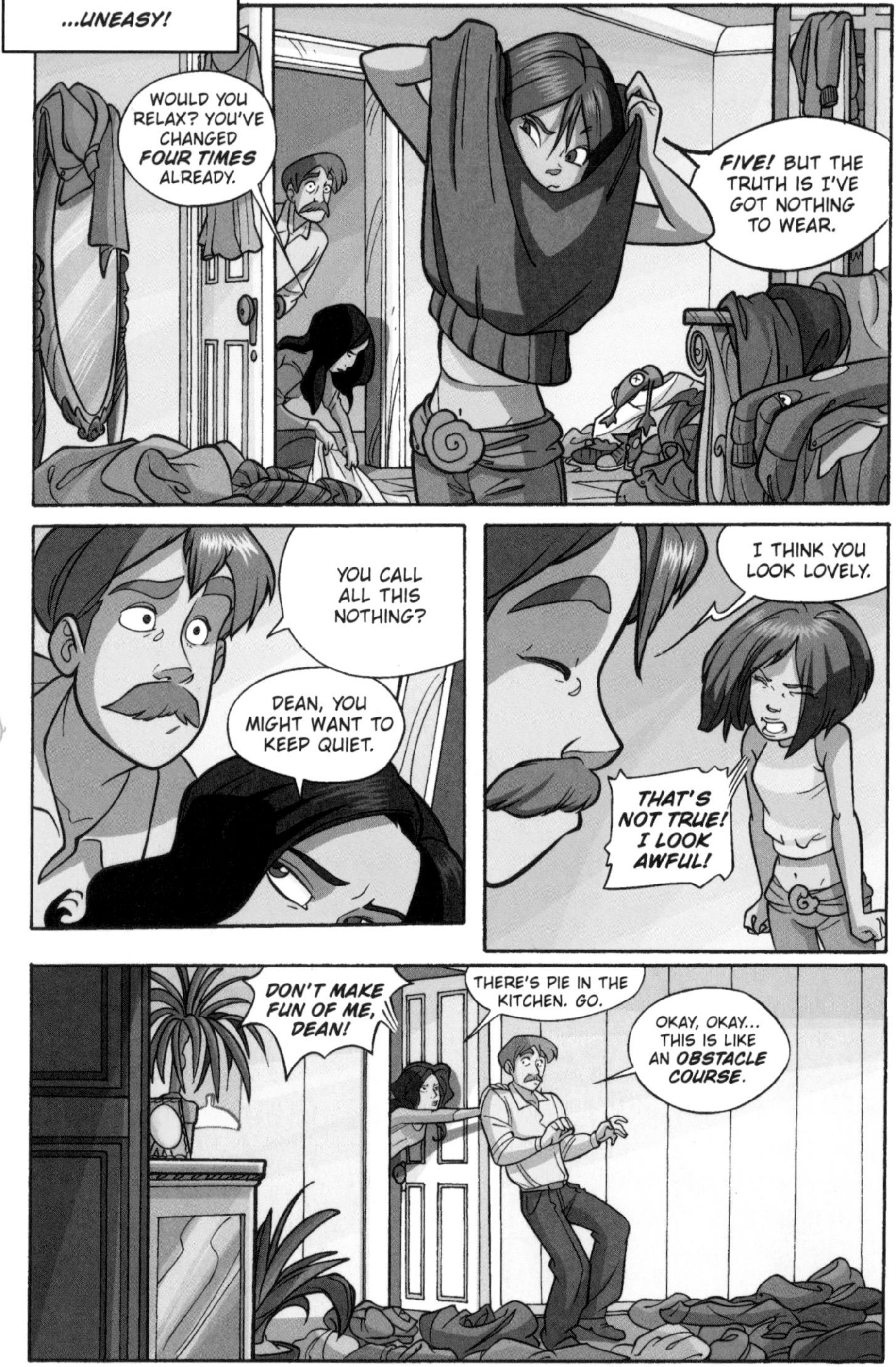
...UNEASY!
WOULD YOU RELAX? YOU'VE CHANGED FOUR TIMES ALREADY.
FIVE! BUT THE TRUTH IS I'VE GOT NOTHING TO WEAR.
YOU CALL ALL THIS NOTHING?
DEAN, YOU MIGHT WANT TO KEEP QUIET.
I THINK YOU LOOK LOVELY.
THAT'S NOT TRUE! I LOOK AWFUL!
DON'T MAKE FUN OF ME, DEAN!
THERE'S PIE IN THE KITCHEN. GO.
OKAY, OKAY... THIS IS LIKE AN OBSTACLE COURSE.

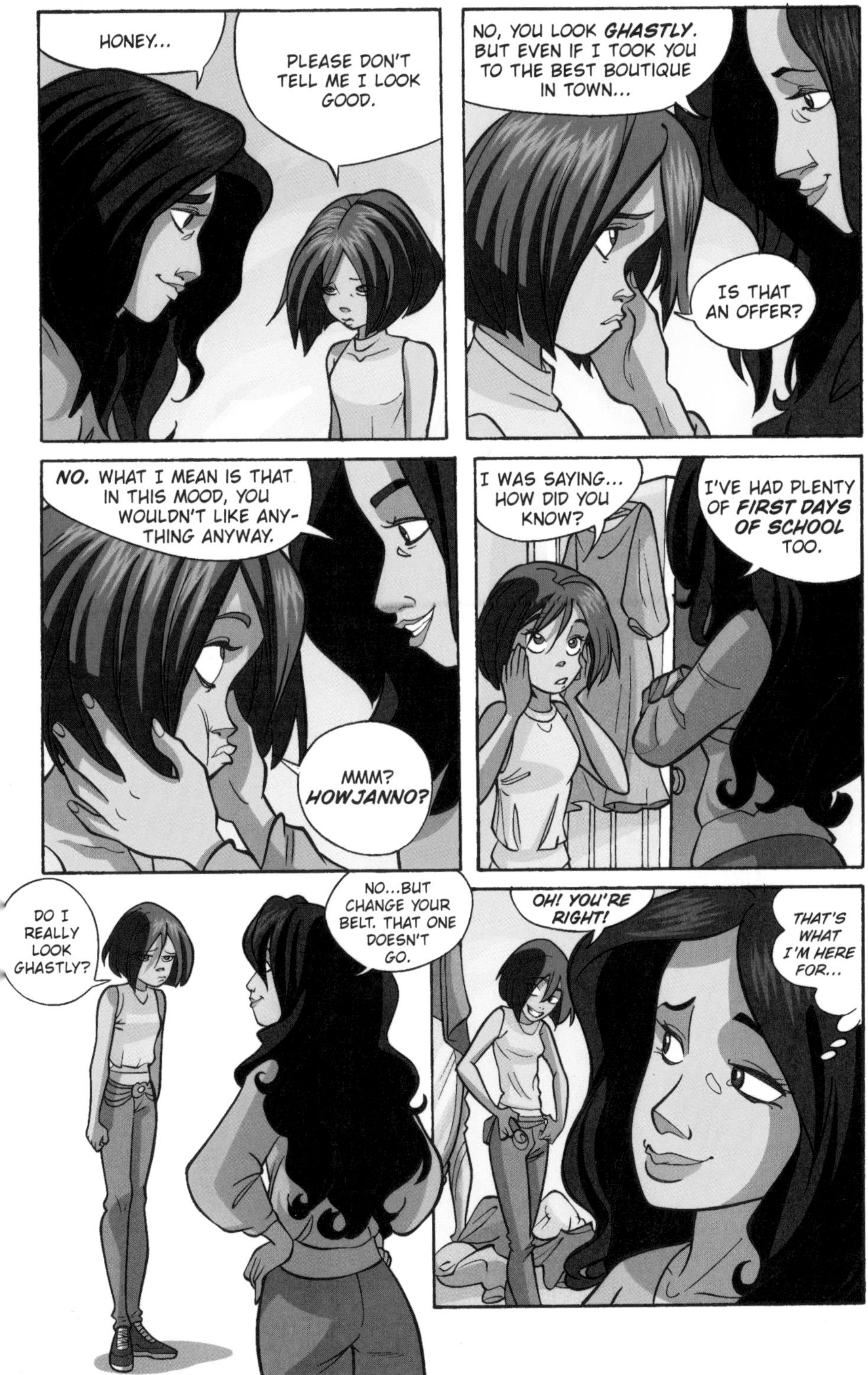
HONEY...
PLEASE DON'T TELL ME I LOOK GOOD.
NO, YOU LOOK *GHASTLY*. BUT EVEN IF I TOOK YOU TO THE BEST BOUTIQUE IN TOWN...
IS THAT AN OFFER?
NO. WHAT I MEAN IS THAT IN THIS MOOD, YOU WOULDN'T LIKE ANY-THING ANYWAY.
MMM? *HOWJANNO?*
I WAS SAYING... HOW DID YOU KNOW?
I'VE HAD PLENTY OF *FIRST DAYS OF SCHOOL* TOO.
DO I REALLY LOOK GHASTLY?
NO...BUT CHANGE YOUR BELT. THAT ONE DOESN'T GO.
OH! YOU'RE RIGHT!
THAT'S WHAT I'M HERE FOR...

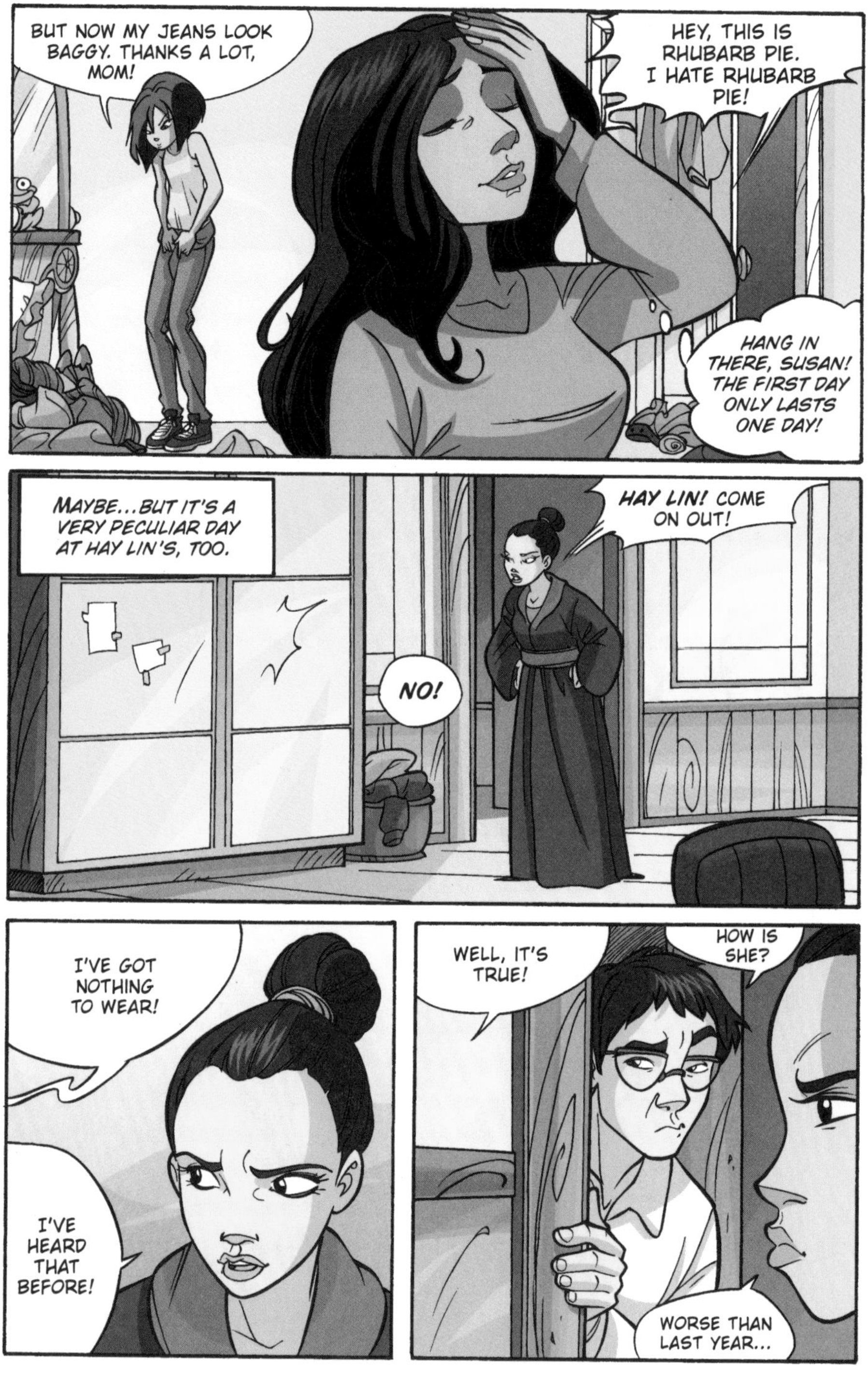
BUT NOW MY JEANS LOOK BAGGY. THANKS A LOT, MOM!
HEY, THIS IS RHUBARB PIE. I HATE RHUBARB PIE!
HANG IN THERE, SUSAN! THE FIRST DAY ONLY LASTS ONE DAY!
MAYBE... BUT IT'S A VERY PECULIAR DAY AT HAY LIN'S, TOO.
HAY LIN! COME ON OUT!
NO!
I'VE GOT NOTHING TO WEAR!
I'VE HEARD THAT BEFORE!
WELL, IT'S TRUE!
HOW IS SHE?
WORSE THAN LAST YEAR...

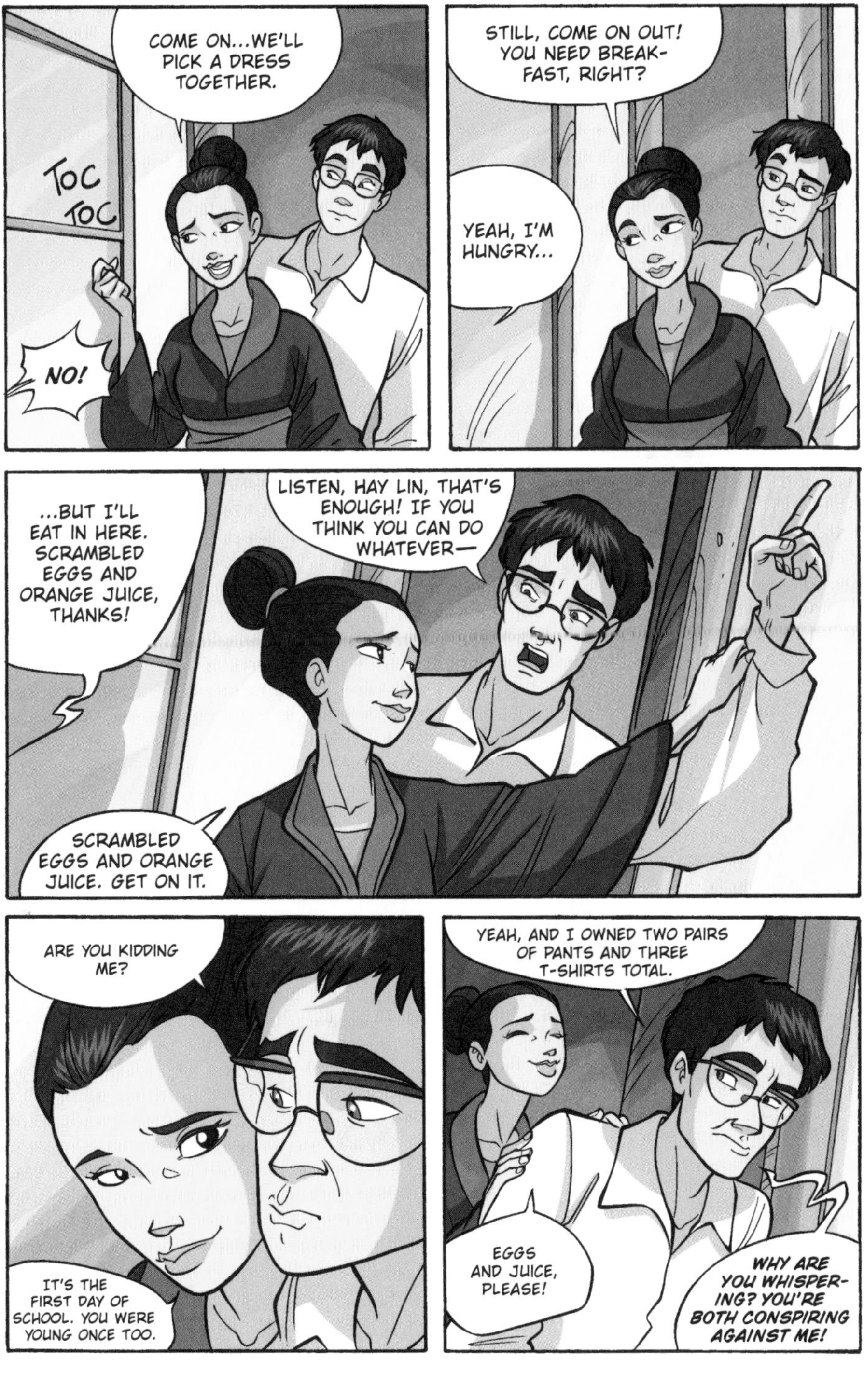

COME ON...WE'LL PICK A DRESS TOGETHER.
TOC TOC
NO!
STILL, COME ON OUT! YOU NEED BREAK-FAST, RIGHT?
YEAH, I'M HUNGRY...
...BUT I'LL EAT IN HERE. SCRAMBLED EGGS AND ORANGE JUICE, THANKS!
LISTEN, HAY LIN, THAT'S ENOUGH! IF YOU THINK YOU CAN DO WHATEVER—
SCRAMBLED EGGS AND ORANGE JUICE. GET ON IT.
ARE YOU KIDDING ME?
IT'S THE FIRST DAY OF SCHOOL. YOU WERE YOUNG ONCE TOO.
YEAH, AND I OWNED TWO PAIRS OF PANTS AND THREE T-SHIRTS TOTAL.
EGGS AND JUICE, PLEASE!
WHY ARE YOU WHISPER-ING? YOU'RE BOTH CONSPIRING AGAINST ME!

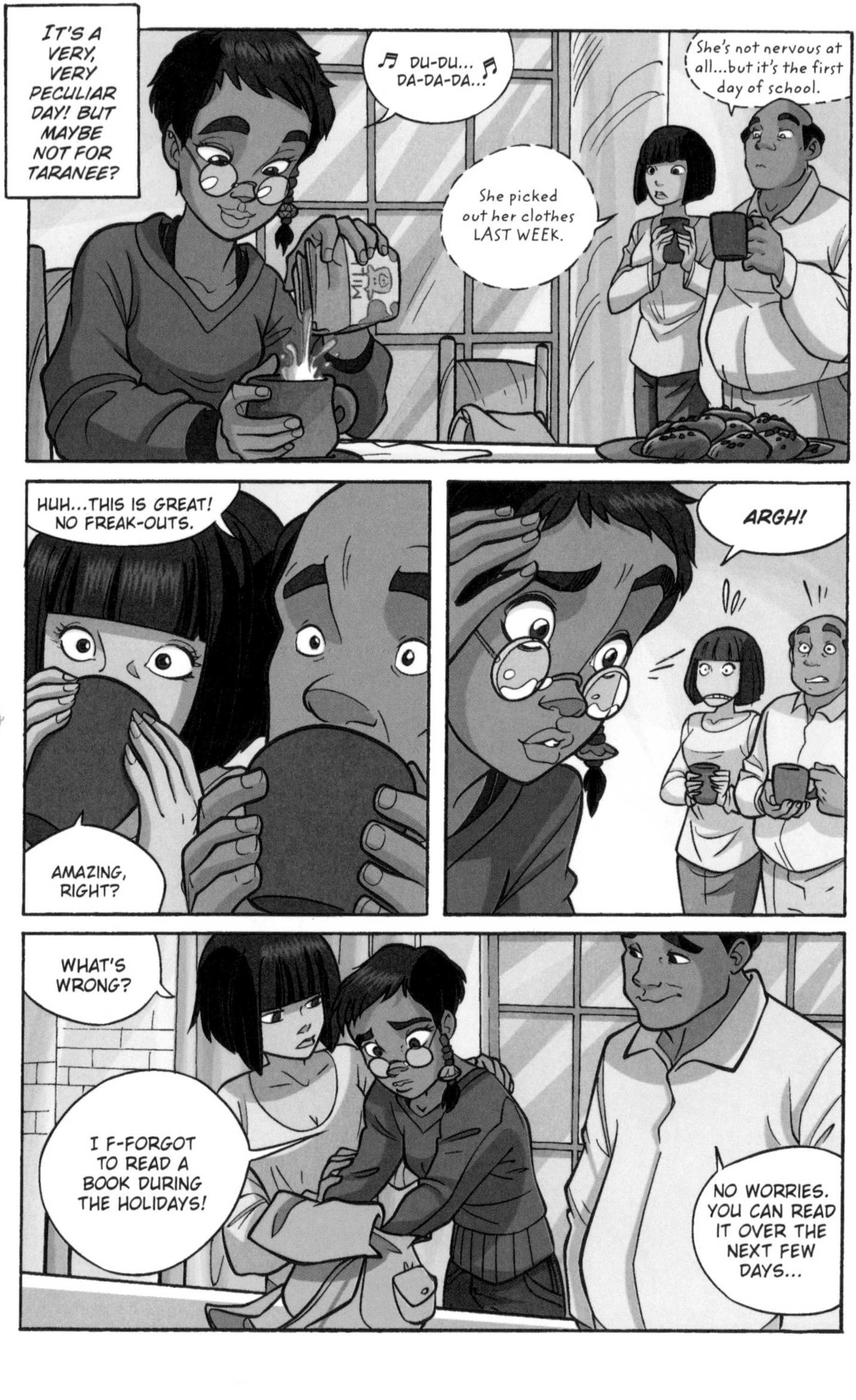
IT'S A VERY, VERY PECULIAR DAY! BUT MAYBE NOT FOR TARANEE?
♫ DU-DU... DA-DA-DA...♫
She's not nervous at all...but it's the first day of school.
She picked out her clothes LAST WEEK.
HUH...THIS IS GREAT! NO FREAK-OUTS.
AMAZING, RIGHT?
ARGH!
WHAT'S WRONG?
I F-FORGOT TO READ A BOOK DURING THE HOLIDAYS!
NO WORRIES. YOU CAN READ IT OVER THE NEXT FEW DAYS...

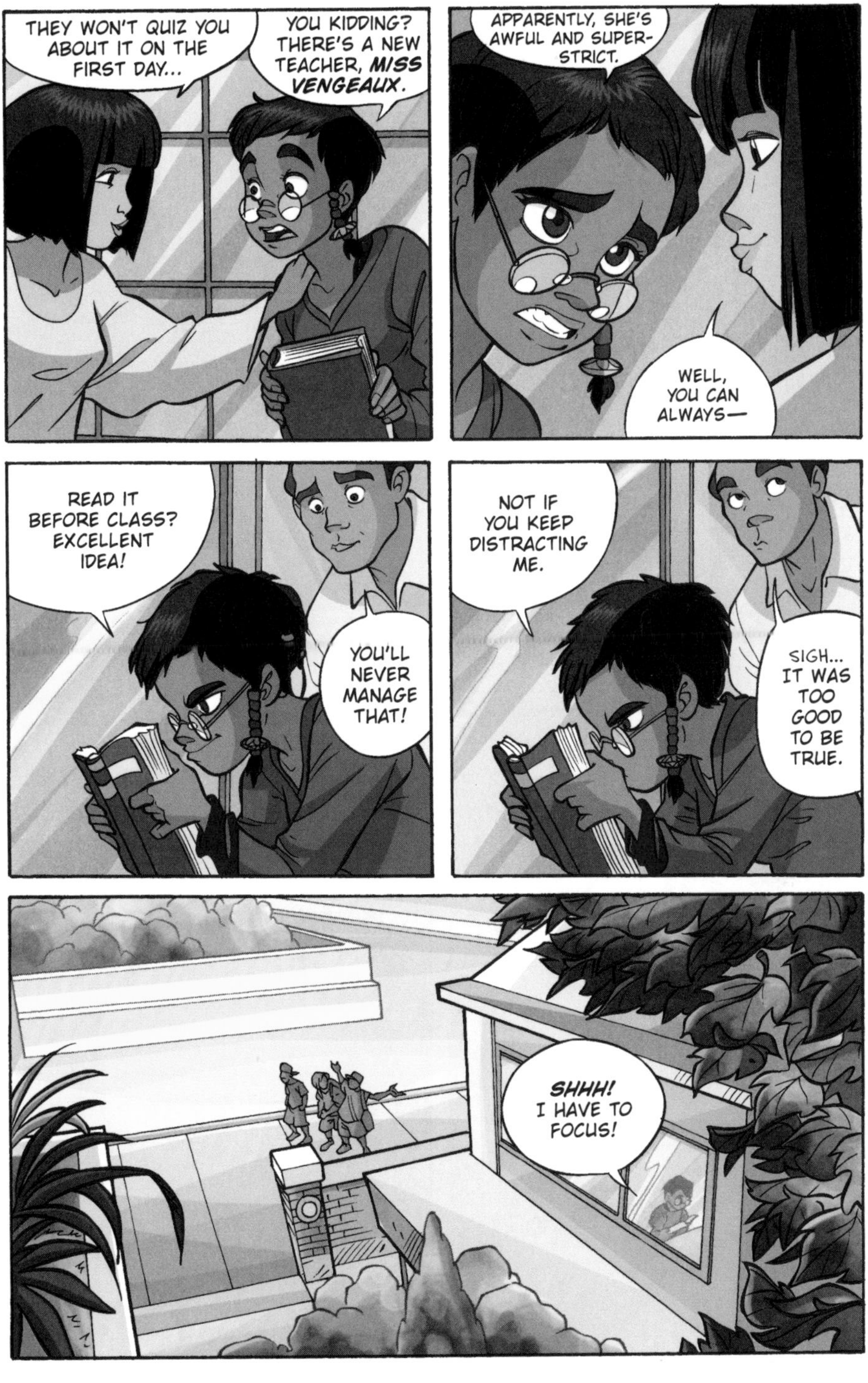
THEY WON'T QUIZ YOU ABOUT IT ON THE FIRST DAY...
YOU KIDDING? THERE'S A NEW TEACHER, MISS VENGEAUX.
APPARENTLY, SHE'S AWFUL AND SUPER-STRICT.
WELL, YOU CAN ALWAYS—
READ IT BEFORE CLASS? EXCELLENT IDEA!
YOU'LL NEVER MANAGE THAT!
NOT IF YOU KEEP DISTRACTING ME.
SIGH... IT WAS TOO GOOD TO BE TRUE.
SHHH! I HAVE TO FOCUS!

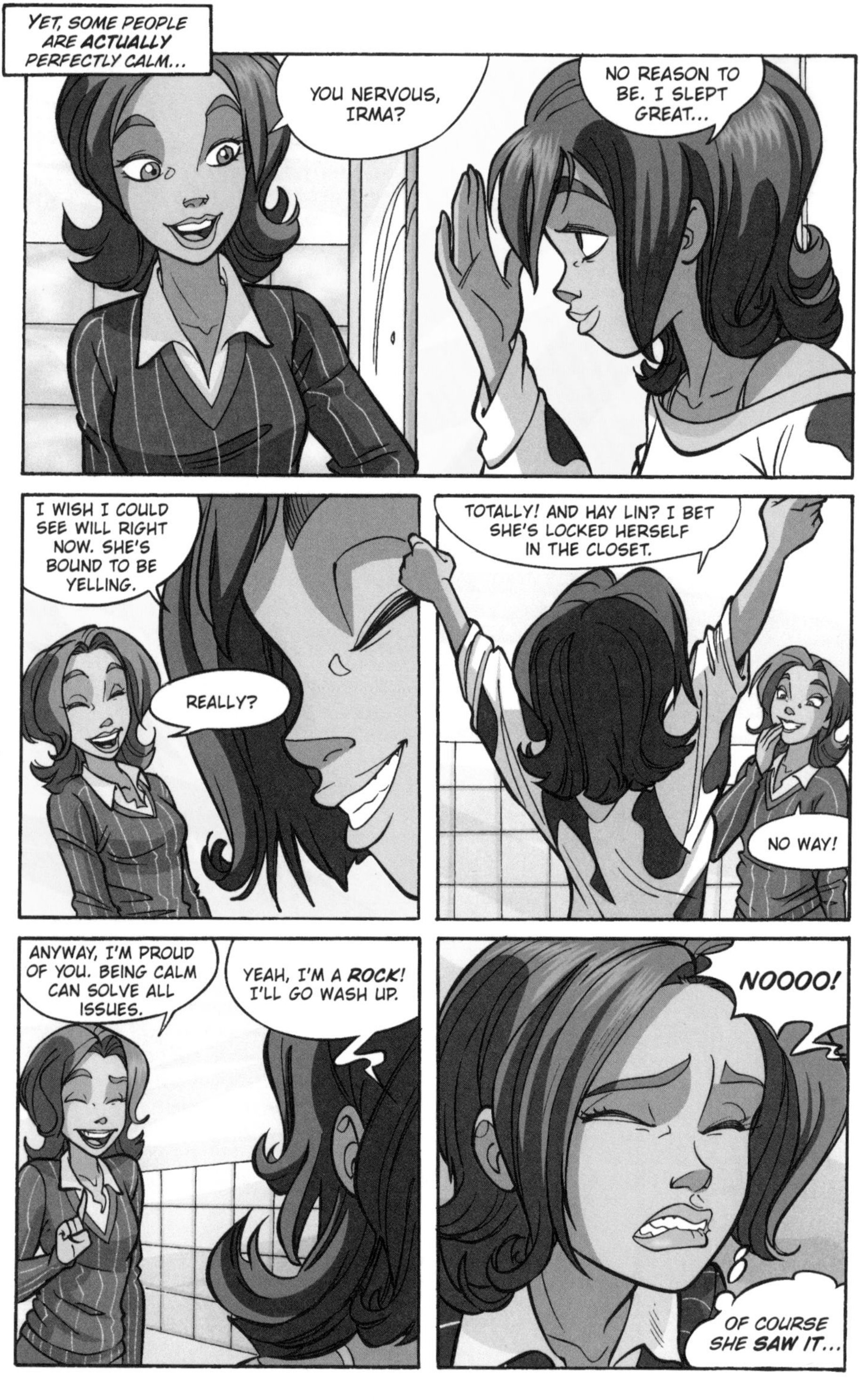
YET, SOME PEOPLE ARE **ACTUALLY** PERFECTLY CALM...
YOU NERVOUS, IRMA?
NO REASON TO BE. I SLEPT GREAT...
I WISH I COULD SEE WILL RIGHT NOW. SHE'S BOUND TO BE YELLING.
REALLY?
TOTALLY! AND HAY LIN? I BET SHE'S LOCKED HERSELF IN THE CLOSET.
NO WAY!
ANYWAY, I'M PROUD OF YOU. BEING CALM CAN SOLVE ALL ISSUES.
YEAH, I'M A **ROCK**! I'LL GO WASH UP.
NOOOO!
OF COURSE SHE **SAW IT**...

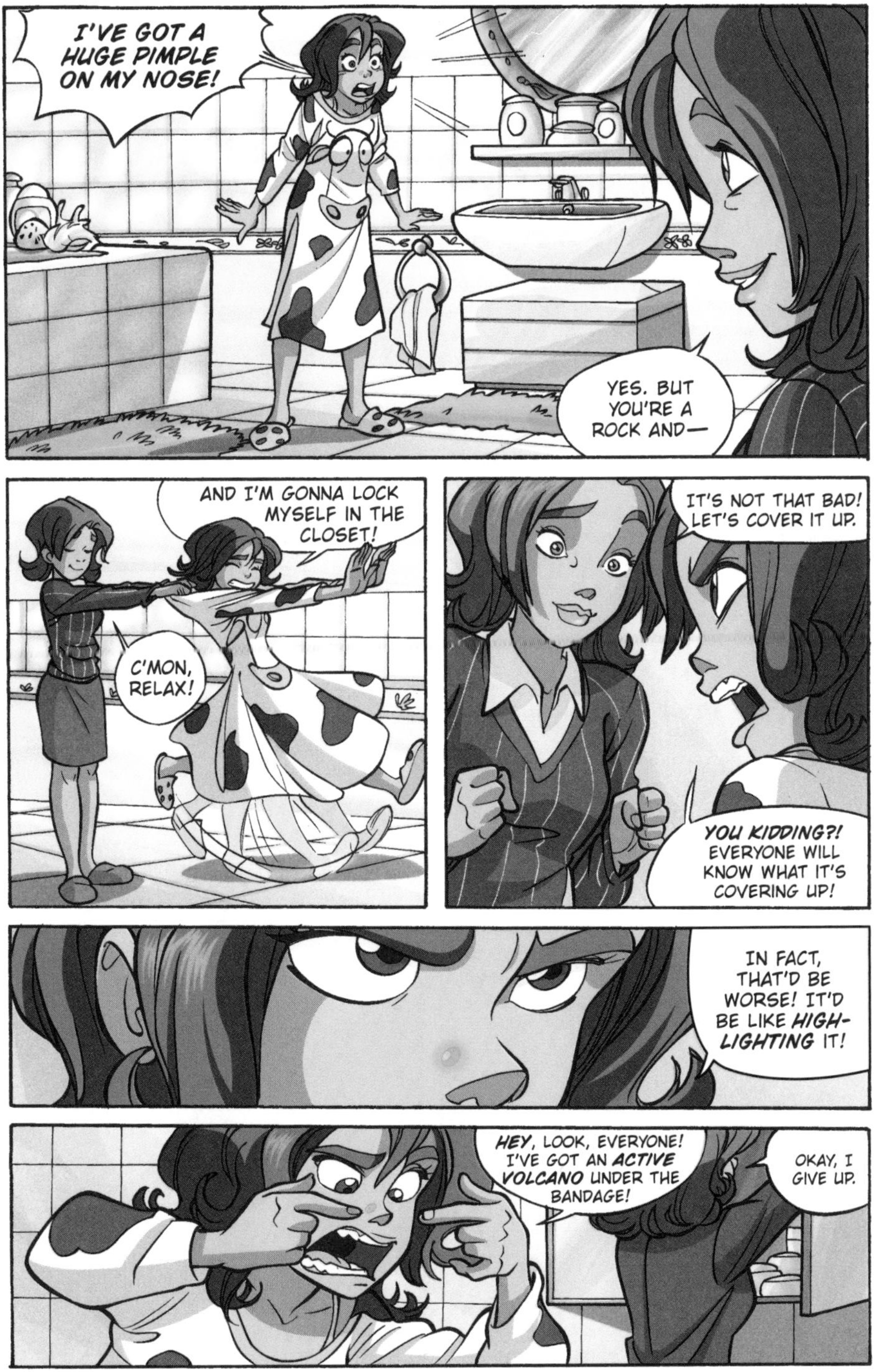
I'VE GOT A HUGE PIMPLE ON MY NOSE!
YES. BUT YOU'RE A ROCK AND—
AND I'M GONNA LOCK MYSELF IN THE CLOSET!
C'MON, RELAX!
IT'S NOT THAT BAD! LET'S COVER IT UP.
YOU KIDDING?! EVERYONE WILL KNOW WHAT IT'S COVERING UP!
IN FACT, THAT'D BE WORSE! IT'D BE LIKE HIGH-LIGHTING IT!
HEY, LOOK, EVERYONE! I'VE GOT AN ACTIVE VOLCANO UNDER THE BANDAGE!
OKAY, I GIVE UP.

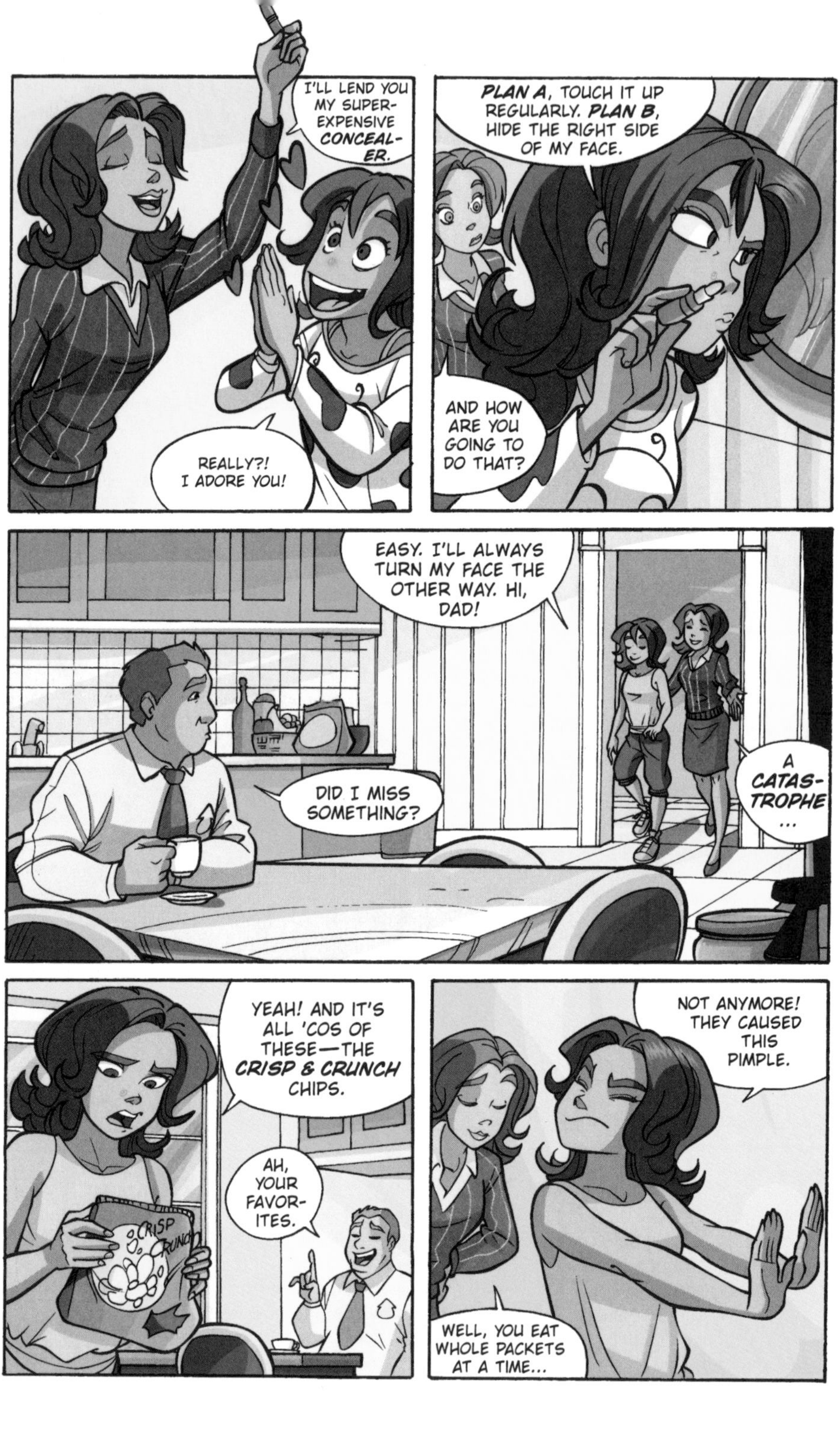
I'LL LEND YOU MY SUPER-EXPENSIVE CONCEAL-ER.
REALLY?! I ADORE YOU!
PLAN A, TOUCH IT UP REGULARLY. PLAN B, HIDE THE RIGHT SIDE OF MY FACE.
AND HOW ARE YOU GOING TO DO THAT?
EASY. I'LL ALWAYS TURN MY FACE THE OTHER WAY. HI, DAD!
A CATAS-TROPHE...
DID I MISS SOMETHING?
YEAH! AND IT'S ALL 'COS OF THESE—THE CRISP & CRUNCH CHIPS.
CRISP CRUNCH
AH, YOUR FAVOR-ITES.
NOT ANYMORE! THEY CAUSED THIS PIMPLE.
WELL, YOU EAT WHOLE PACKETS AT A TIME...

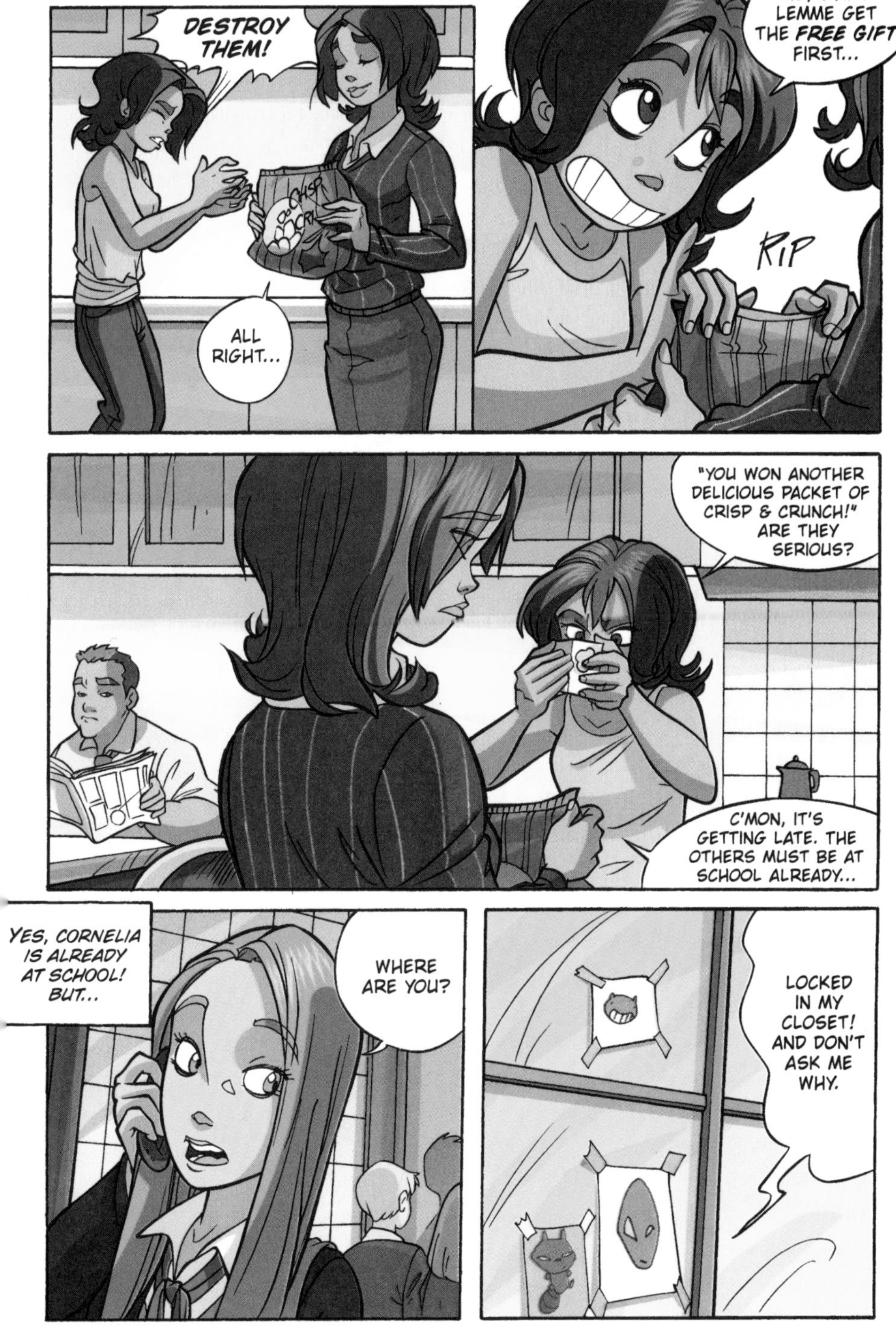

DESTROY THEM!
ALL RIGHT...
CRISP CRU
NO, WAIT! LEMME GET THE FREE GIFT FIRST...
RIP
"YOU WON ANOTHER DELICIOUS PACKET OF CRISP & CRUNCH!" ARE THEY SERIOUS?
C'MON, IT'S GETTING LATE. THE OTHERS MUST BE AT SCHOOL ALREADY...
YES, CORNELIA IS ALREADY AT SCHOOL! BUT...
WHERE ARE YOU?
LOCKED IN MY CLOSET! AND DON'T ASK ME WHY.

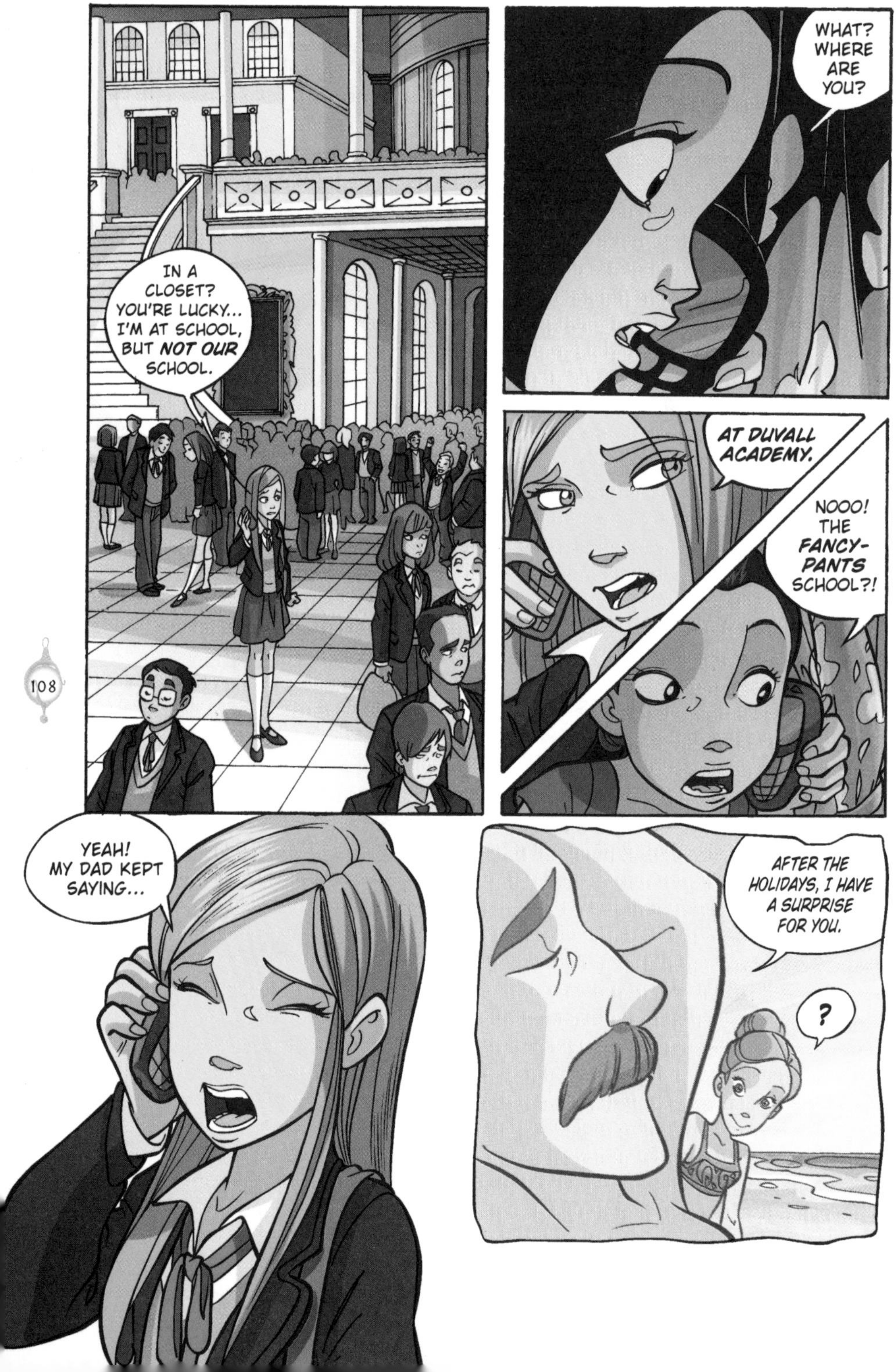

IN A CLOSET? YOU'RE LUCKY... I'M AT SCHOOL, BUT **NOT OUR** SCHOOL.
WHAT? WHERE ARE YOU?
AT DUVALL ACADEMY.
NOOO! THE ***FANCY-PANTS*** SCHOOL?!
YEAH! MY DAD KEPT SAYING...
AFTER THE HOLIDAYS, I HAVE A SURPRISE FOR YOU.
?

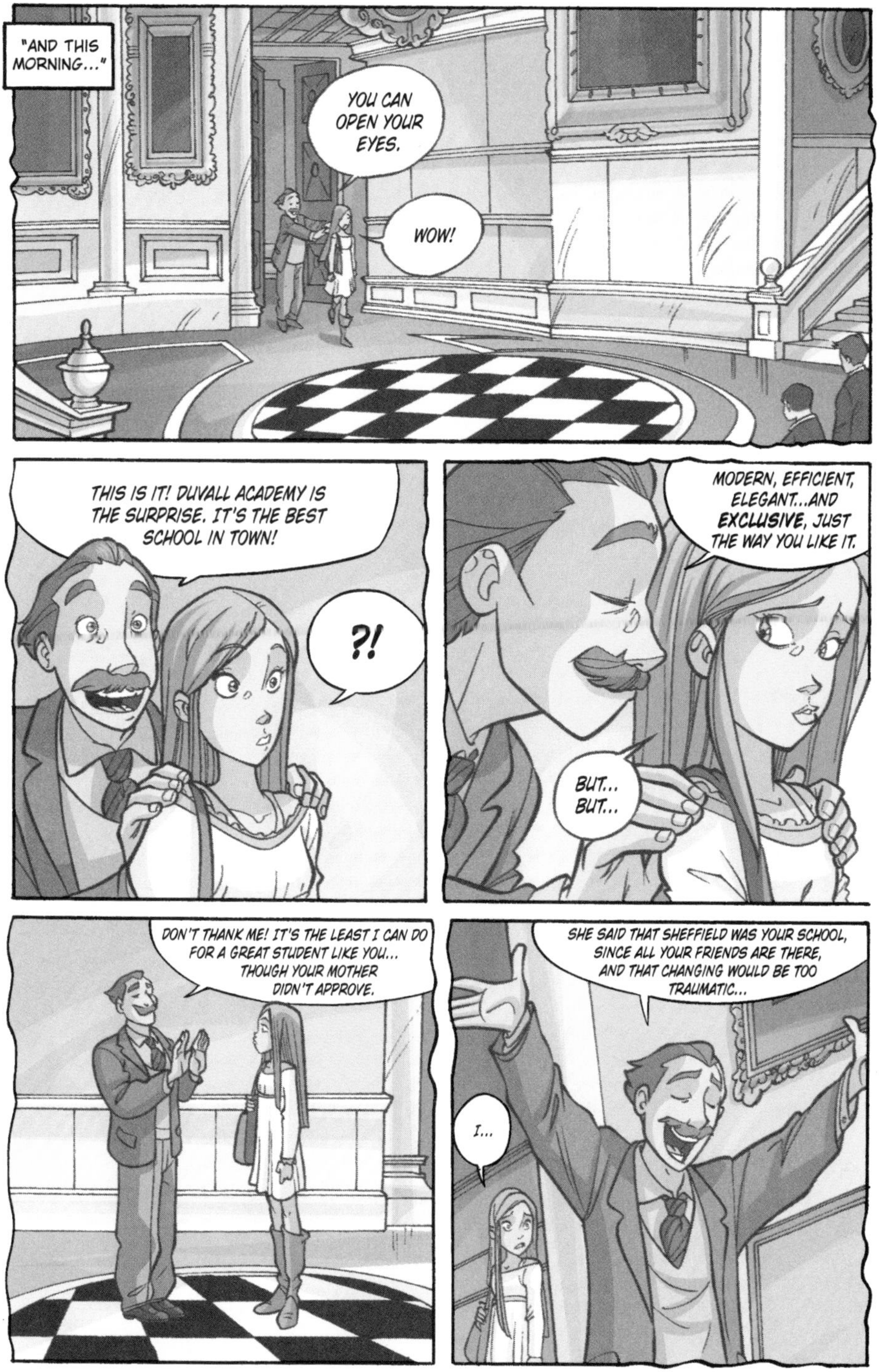
"AND THIS MORNING..."
YOU CAN OPEN YOUR EYES.
WOW!
THIS IS IT! DUVALL ACADEMY IS THE SURPRISE. IT'S THE BEST SCHOOL IN TOWN!
?!
MODERN, EFFICIENT, ELEGANT...AND EXCLUSIVE, JUST THE WAY YOU LIKE IT.
BUT... BUT...
DON'T THANK ME! IT'S THE LEAST I CAN DO FOR A GREAT STUDENT LIKE YOU... THOUGH YOUR MOTHER DIDN'T APPROVE.
SHE SAID THAT SHEFFIELD WAS YOUR SCHOOL, SINCE ALL YOUR FRIENDS ARE THERE, AND THAT CHANGING WOULD BE TOO TRAUMATIC...
I...

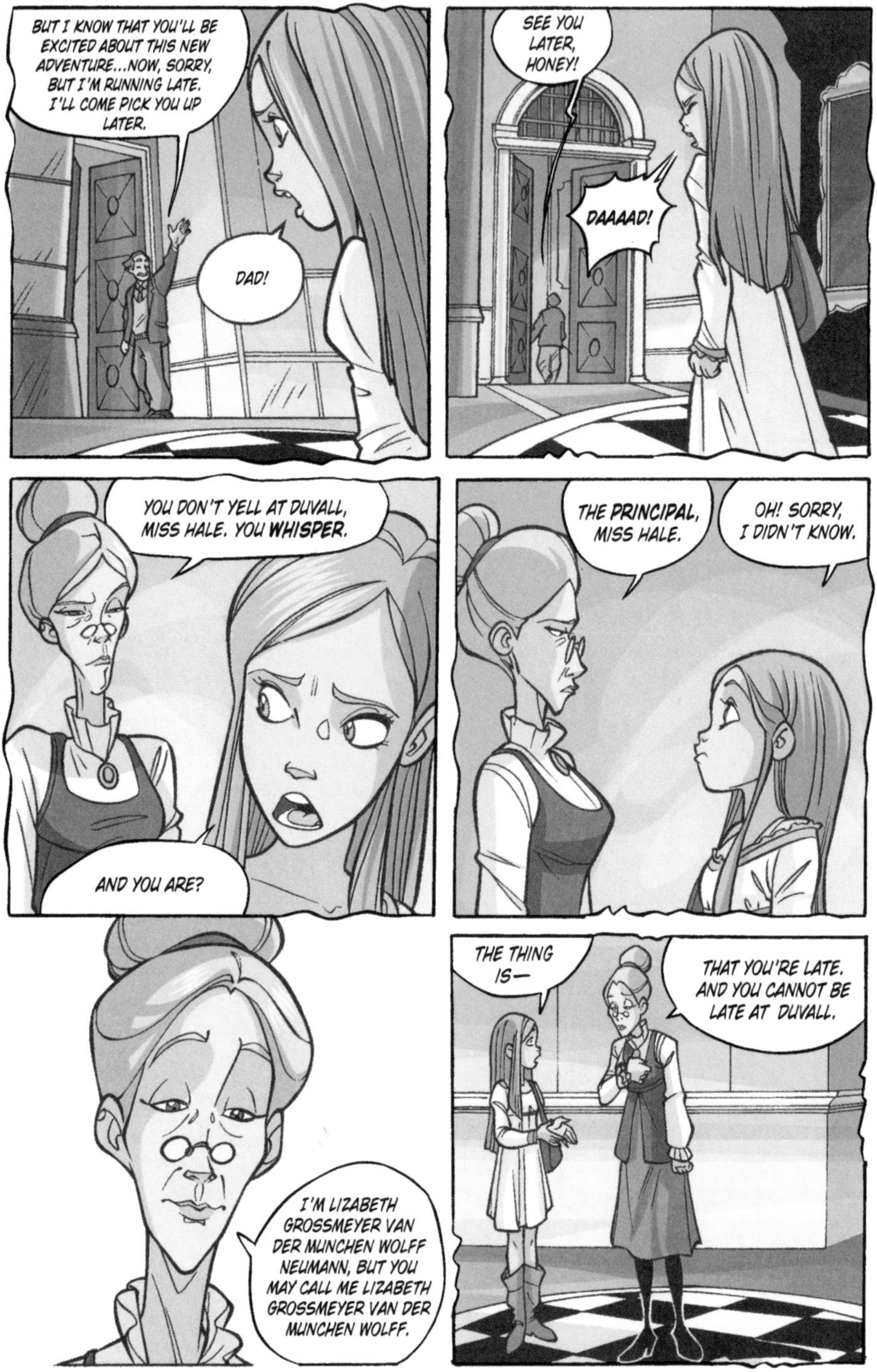
BUT I KNOW THAT YOU'LL BE EXCITED ABOUT THIS NEW ADVENTURE...NOW, SORRY, BUT I'M RUNNING LATE. I'LL COME PICK YOU UP LATER.
DAD!
SEE YOU LATER, HONEY!
DAAAAD!
YOU DON'T YELL AT DUVALL, MISS HALE. YOU WHISPER.
AND YOU ARE?
THE PRINCIPAL, MISS HALE.
OH! SORRY, I DIDN'T KNOW.
I'M LIZABETH GROSSMEYER VAN DER MUNCHEN WOLFF NEUMANN, BUT YOU MAY CALL ME LIZABETH GROSSMEYER VAN DER MUNCHEN WOLFF.
THE THING IS—
THAT YOU'RE LATE. AND YOU CANNOT BE LATE AT DUVALL.

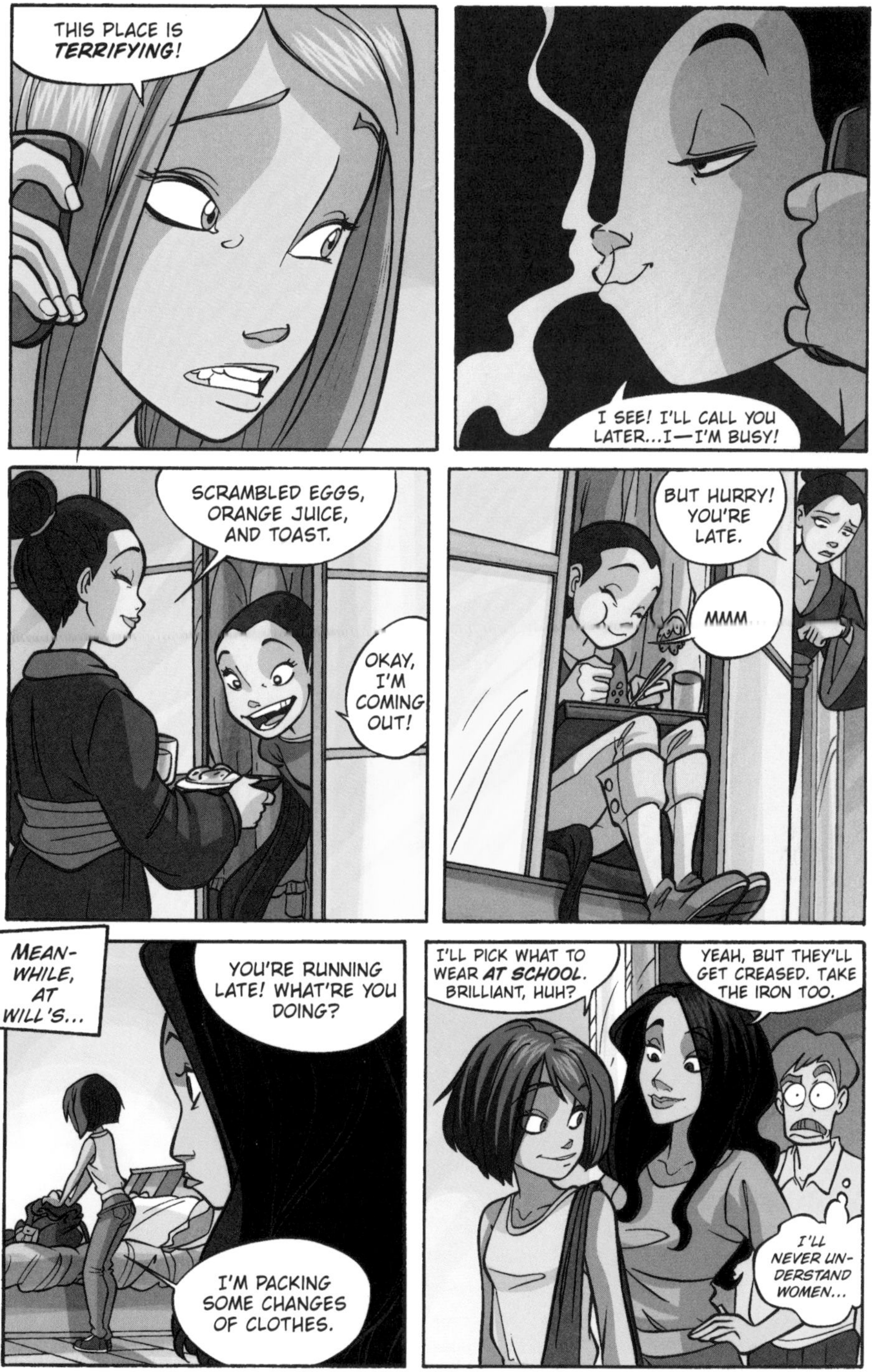
THIS PLACE IS TERRIFYING!
I SEE! I'LL CALL YOU LATER...I—I'M BUSY!
SCRAMBLED EGGS, ORANGE JUICE, AND TOAST.
OKAY, I'M COMING OUT!
BUT HURRY! YOU'RE LATE.
MMM...
MEAN-WHILE, AT WILL'S...
YOU'RE RUNNING LATE! WHAT'RE YOU DOING?
I'M PACKING SOME CHANGES OF CLOTHES.
I'LL PICK WHAT TO WEAR AT SCHOOL. BRILLIANT, HUH?
YEAH, BUT THEY'LL GET CREASED. TAKE THE IRON TOO.
I'LL NEVER UN-DERSTAND WOMEN...

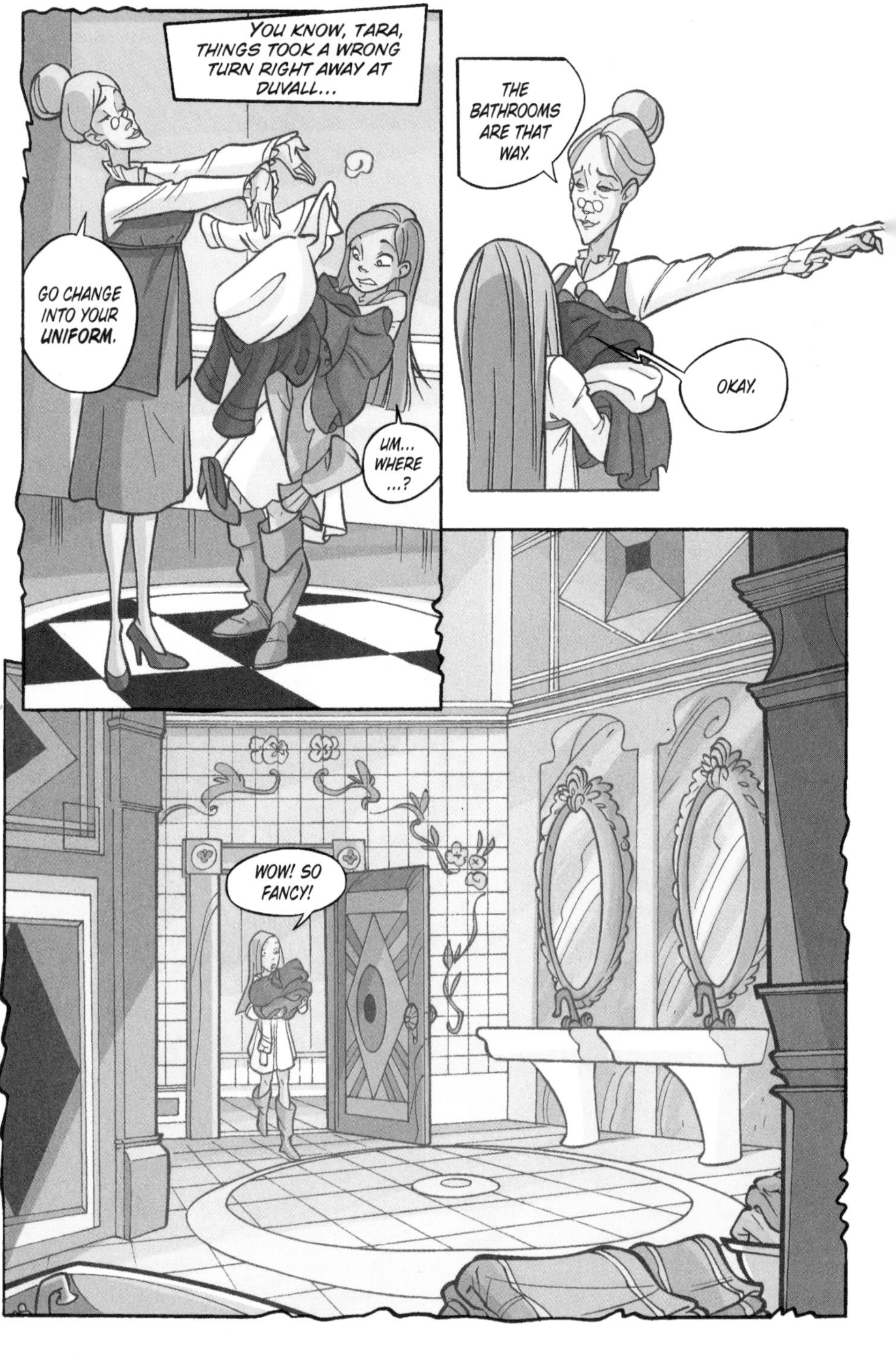
YOU KNOW, TARA, THINGS TOOK A WRONG TURN RIGHT AWAY AT DUVALL...
GO CHANGE INTO YOUR **UNIFORM**.
UM... WHERE ...?
THE BATHROOMS ARE THAT WAY.
OKAY.
WOW! SO FANCY!

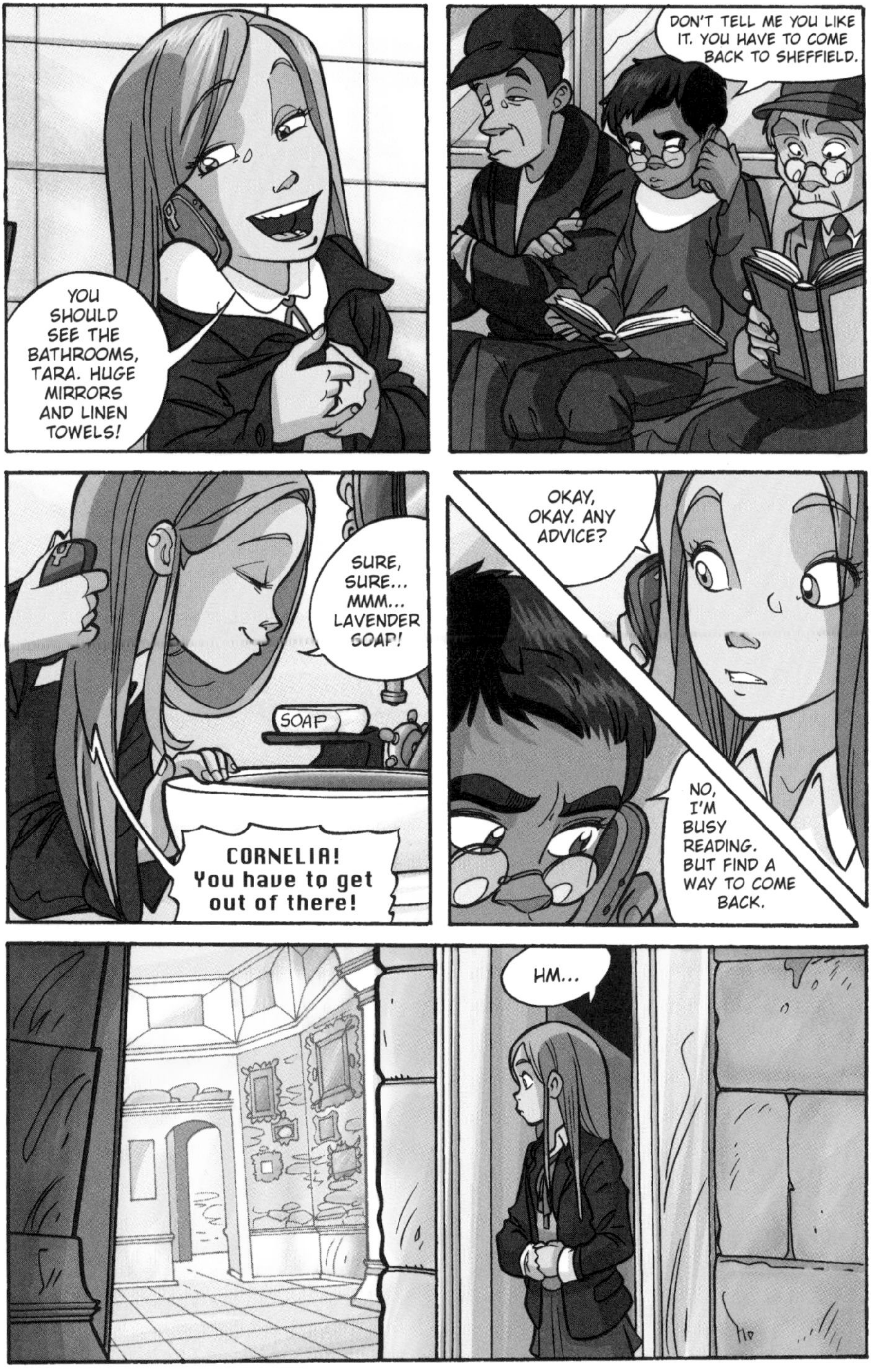
YOU SHOULD SEE THE BATHROOMS, TARA. HUGE MIRRORS AND LINEN TOWELS!
DON'T TELL ME YOU LIKE IT. YOU HAVE TO COME BACK TO SHEFFIELD.
SURE, SURE... MMM... LAVENDER SOAP!
SOAP
CORNELIA! You have to get out of there!
OKAY, OKAY. ANY ADVICE?
NO, I'M BUSY READING. BUT FIND A WAY TO COME BACK.
HM...

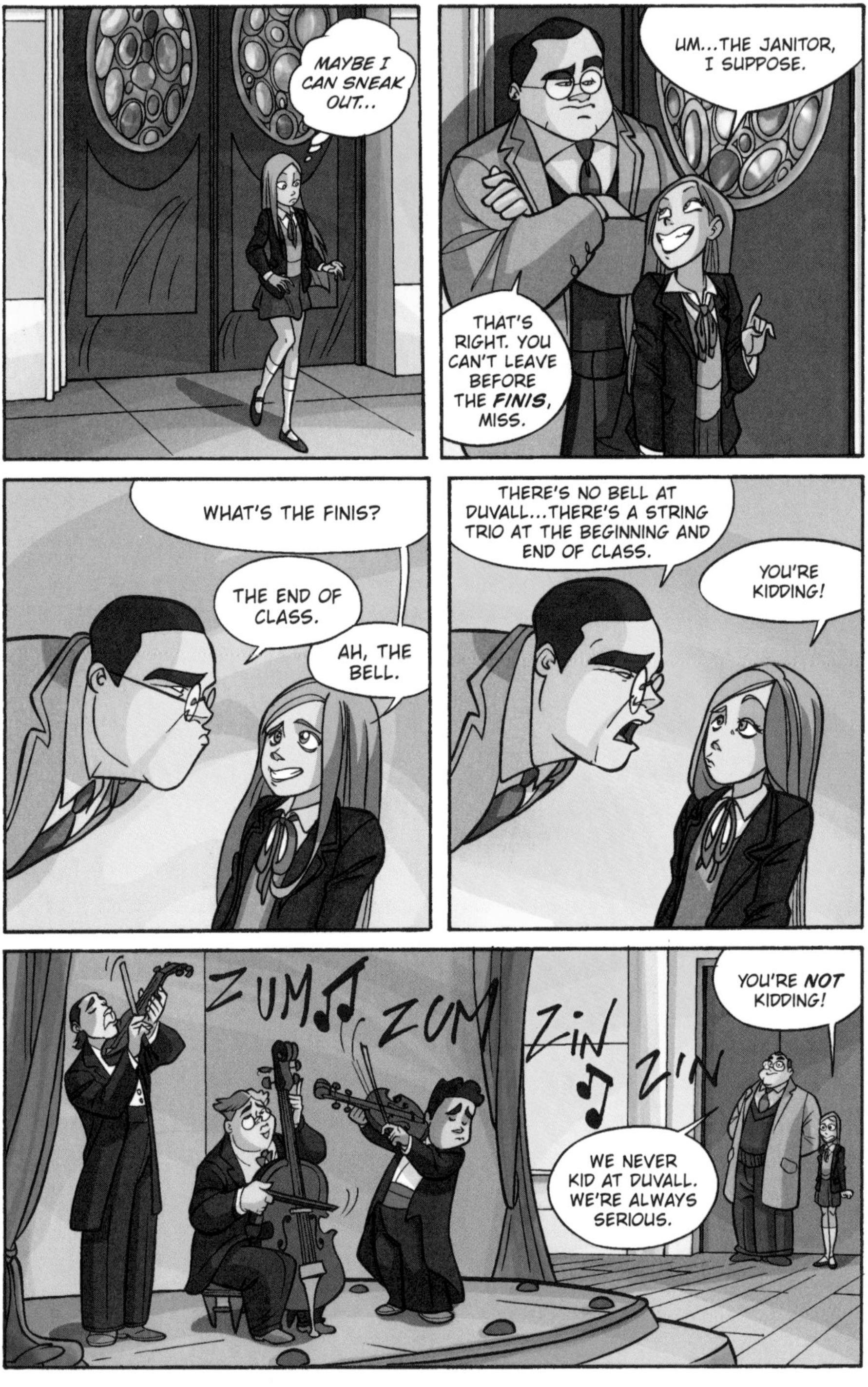
MAYBE I CAN SNEAK OUT...
UM...THE JANITOR, I SUPPOSE.
THAT'S RIGHT. YOU CAN'T LEAVE BEFORE THE *FINIS*, MISS.
WHAT'S THE FINIS?
THE END OF CLASS.
AH, THE BELL.
THERE'S NO BELL AT DUVALL...THERE'S A STRING TRIO AT THE BEGINNING AND END OF CLASS.
YOU'RE KIDDING!
ZUM ZUM
ZIN ZIN
YOU'RE *NOT* KIDDING!
WE NEVER KID AT DUVALL. WE'RE ALWAYS SERIOUS.

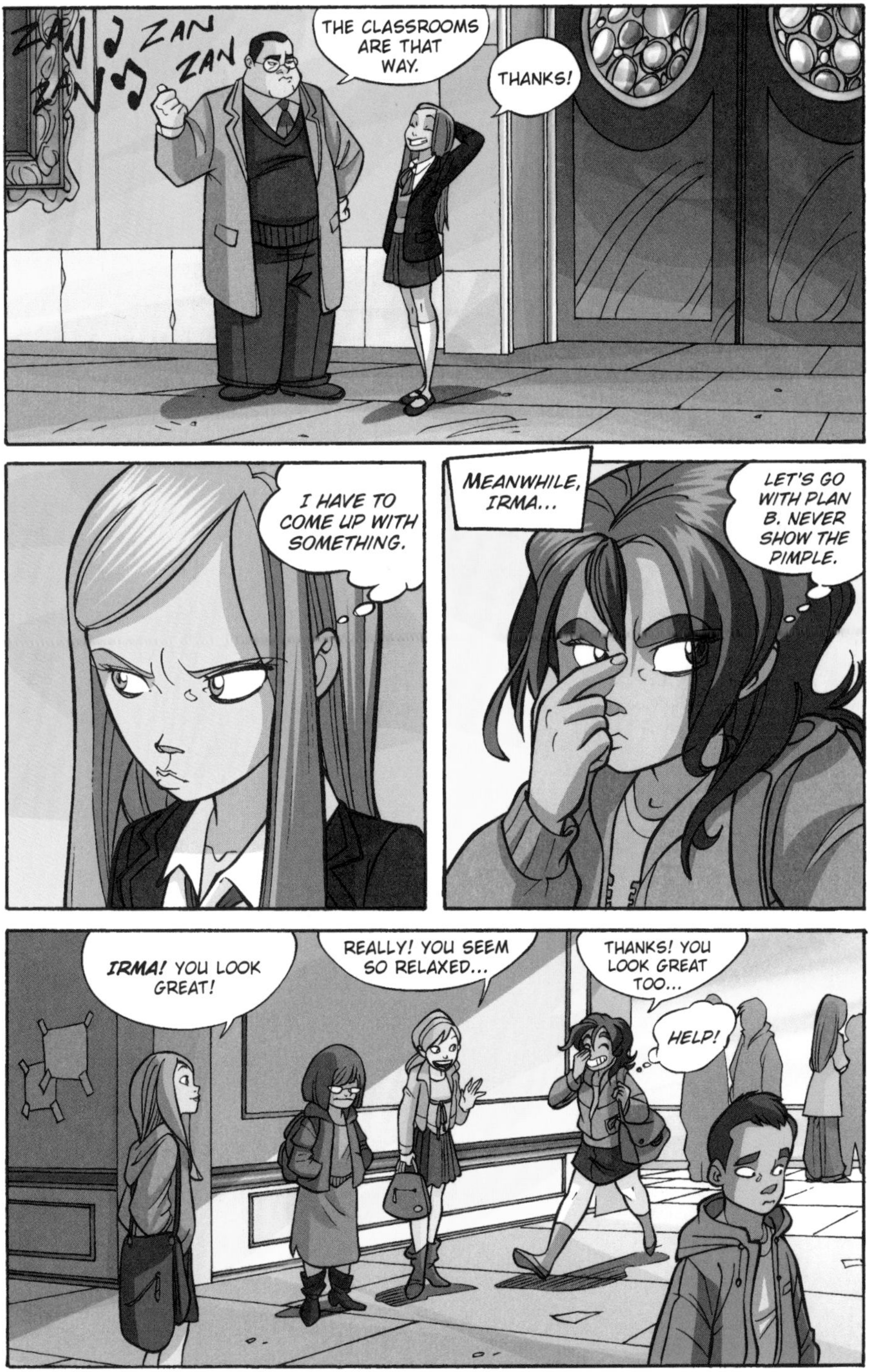
ZAN ZAN ZAN ZAN ZAN
THE CLASSROOMS ARE THAT WAY.
THANKS!
I HAVE TO COME UP WITH SOMETHING.
MEANWHILE, IRMA...
LET'S GO WITH PLAN B. NEVER SHOW THE PIMPLE.
IRMA! YOU LOOK GREAT!
REALLY! YOU SEEM SO RELAXED...
THANKS! YOU LOOK GREAT TOO...
HELP!

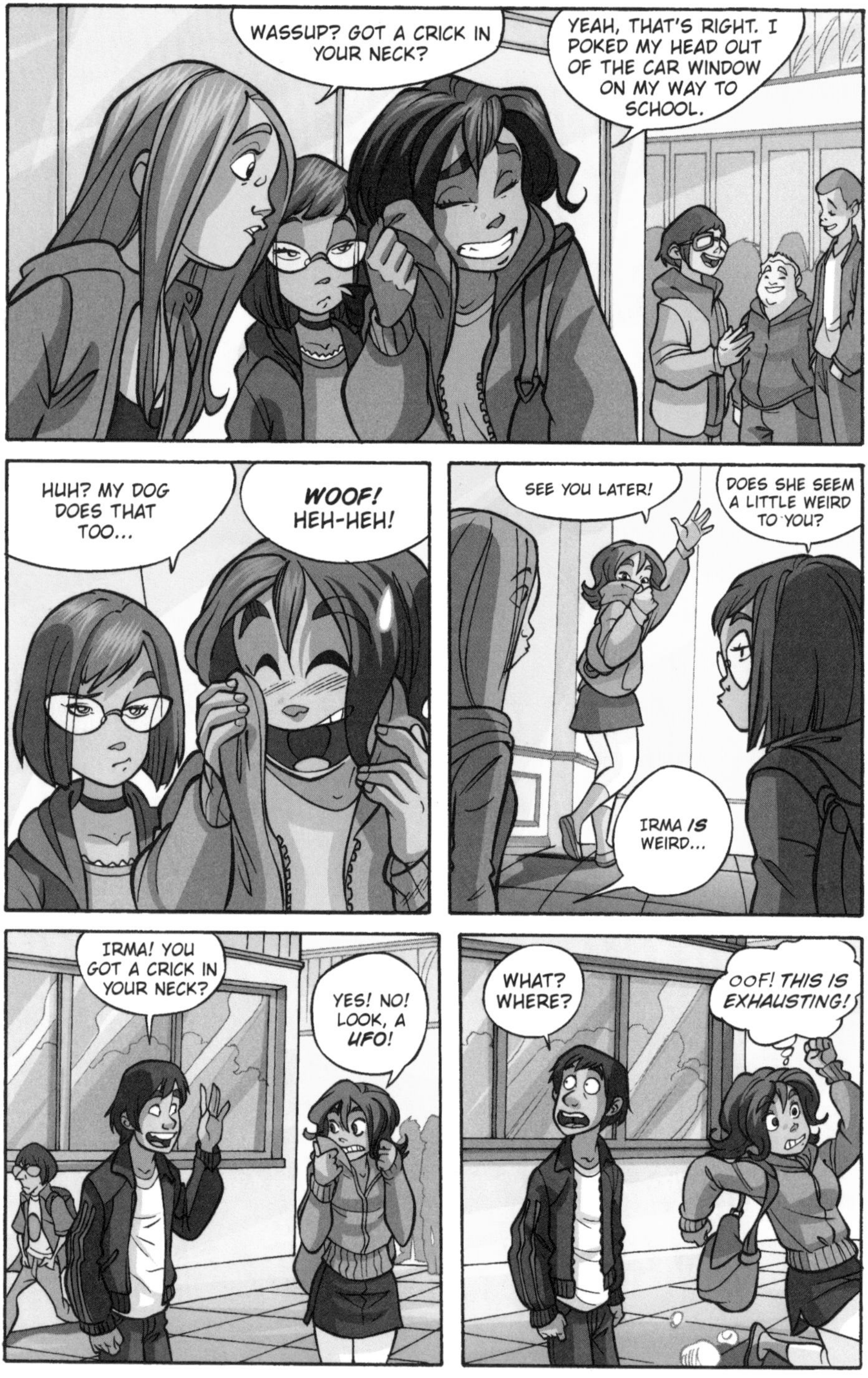
WASSUP? GOT A CRICK IN YOUR NECK?
YEAH, THAT'S RIGHT. I POKED MY HEAD OUT OF THE CAR WINDOW ON MY WAY TO SCHOOL.
HUH? MY DOG DOES THAT TOO...
WOOF! HEH-HEH!
SEE YOU LATER!
DOES SHE SEEM A LITTLE WEIRD TO YOU?
IRMA IS WEIRD...
IRMA! YOU GOT A CRICK IN YOUR NECK?
YES! NO! LOOK, A UFO!
WHAT? WHERE?
OOF! THIS IS EXHAUSTING!

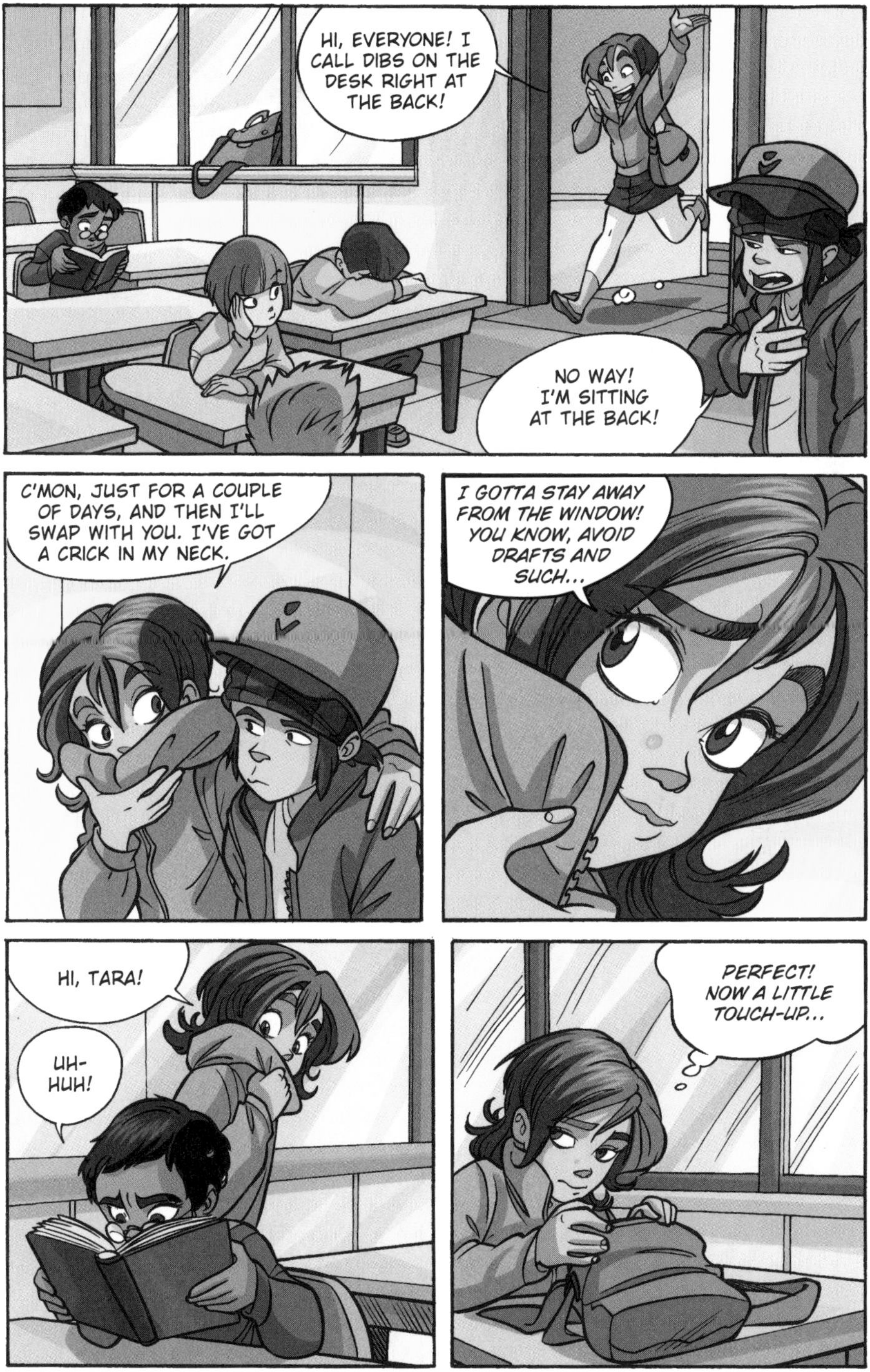
HI, EVERYONE! I CALL DIBS ON THE DESK RIGHT AT THE BACK!
NO WAY! I'M SITTING AT THE BACK!
C'MON, JUST FOR A COUPLE OF DAYS, AND THEN I'LL SWAP WITH YOU. I'VE GOT A CRICK IN MY NECK.
I GOTTA STAY AWAY FROM THE WINDOW! YOU KNOW, AVOID DRAFTS AND SUCH...
HI, TARA!
UH-HUH!
PERFECT! NOW A LITTLE TOUCH-UP...

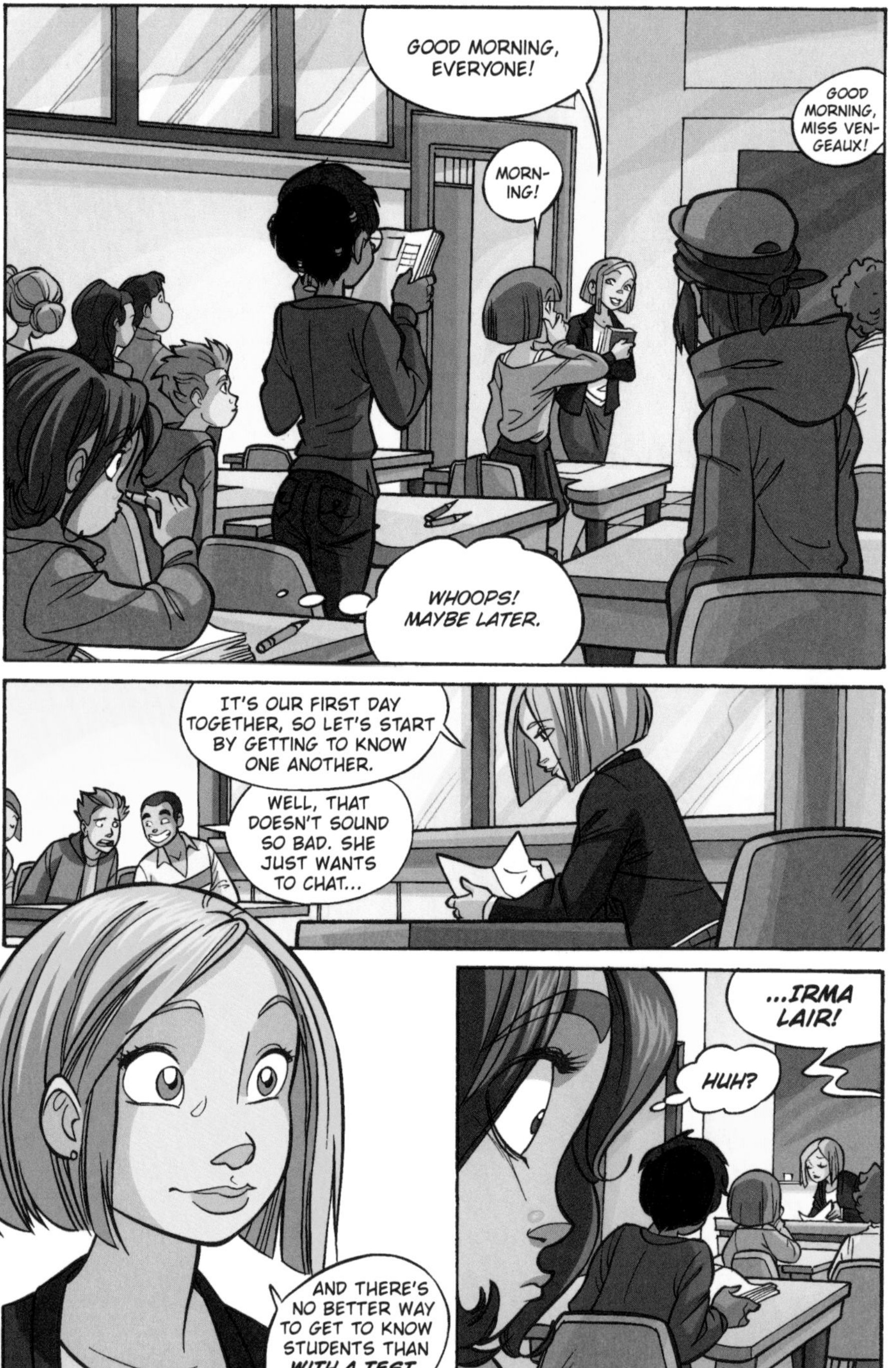
GOOD MORNING, EVERYONE!
MORN- ING!
GOOD MORNING, MISS VEN- GEAUX!
WHOOPS! MAYBE LATER.
IT'S OUR FIRST DAY TOGETHER, SO LET'S START BY GETTING TO KNOW ONE ANOTHER.
WELL, THAT DOESN'T SOUND SO BAD. SHE JUST WANTS TO CHAT...
AND THERE'S NO BETTER WAY TO GET TO KNOW STUDENTS THAN *WITH A TEST*. LET'S SEE...
...IRMA LAIR!
HUH?

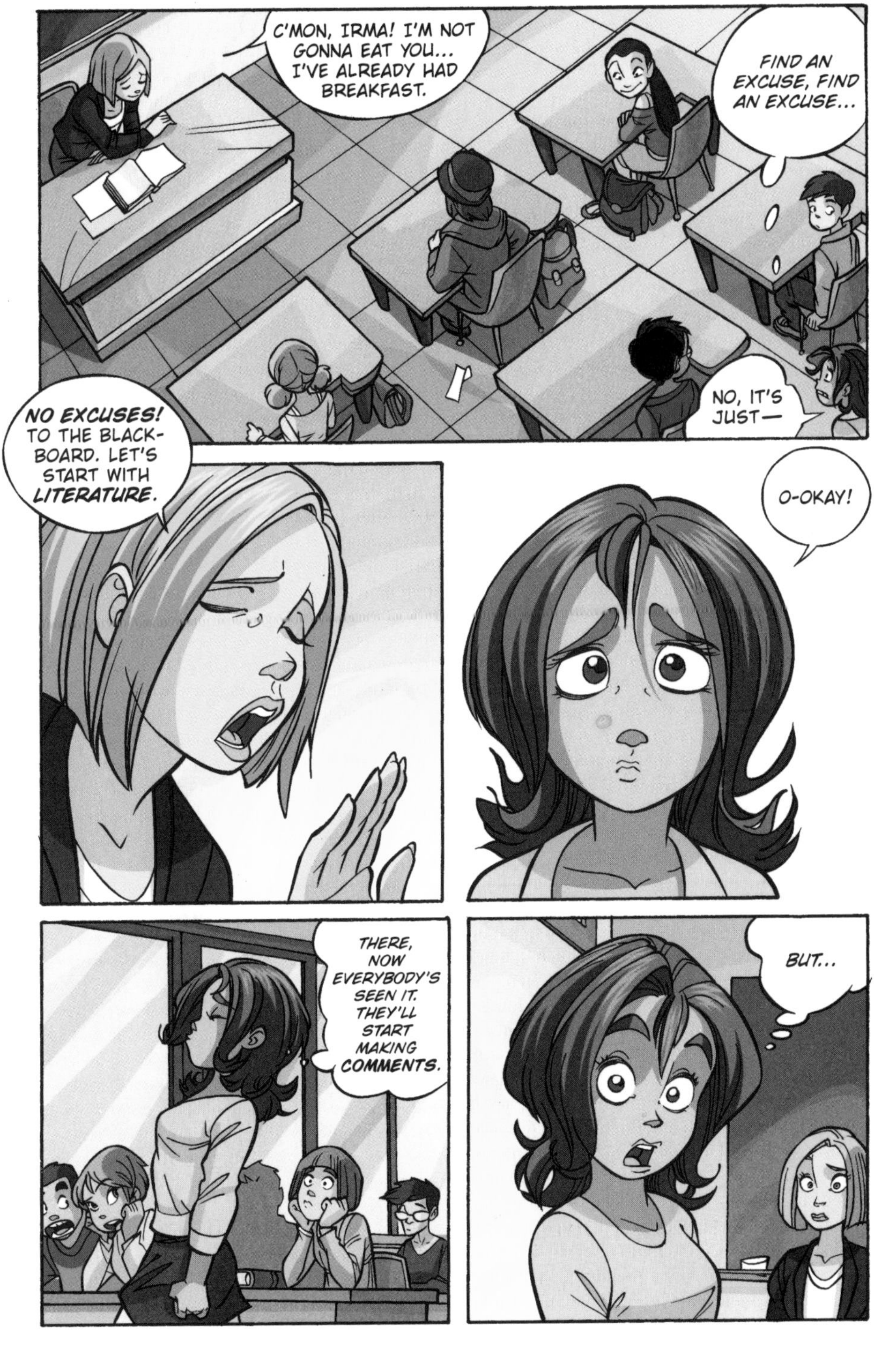
C'MON, IRMA! I'M NOT GONNA EAT YOU... I'VE ALREADY HAD BREAKFAST.
FIND AN EXCUSE, FIND AN EXCUSE...
NO, IT'S JUST—
NO EXCUSES! TO THE BLACKBOARD. LET'S START WITH LITERATURE.
O-OKAY!
THERE, NOW EVERYBODY'S SEEN IT. THEY'LL START MAKING COMMENTS.
BUT...

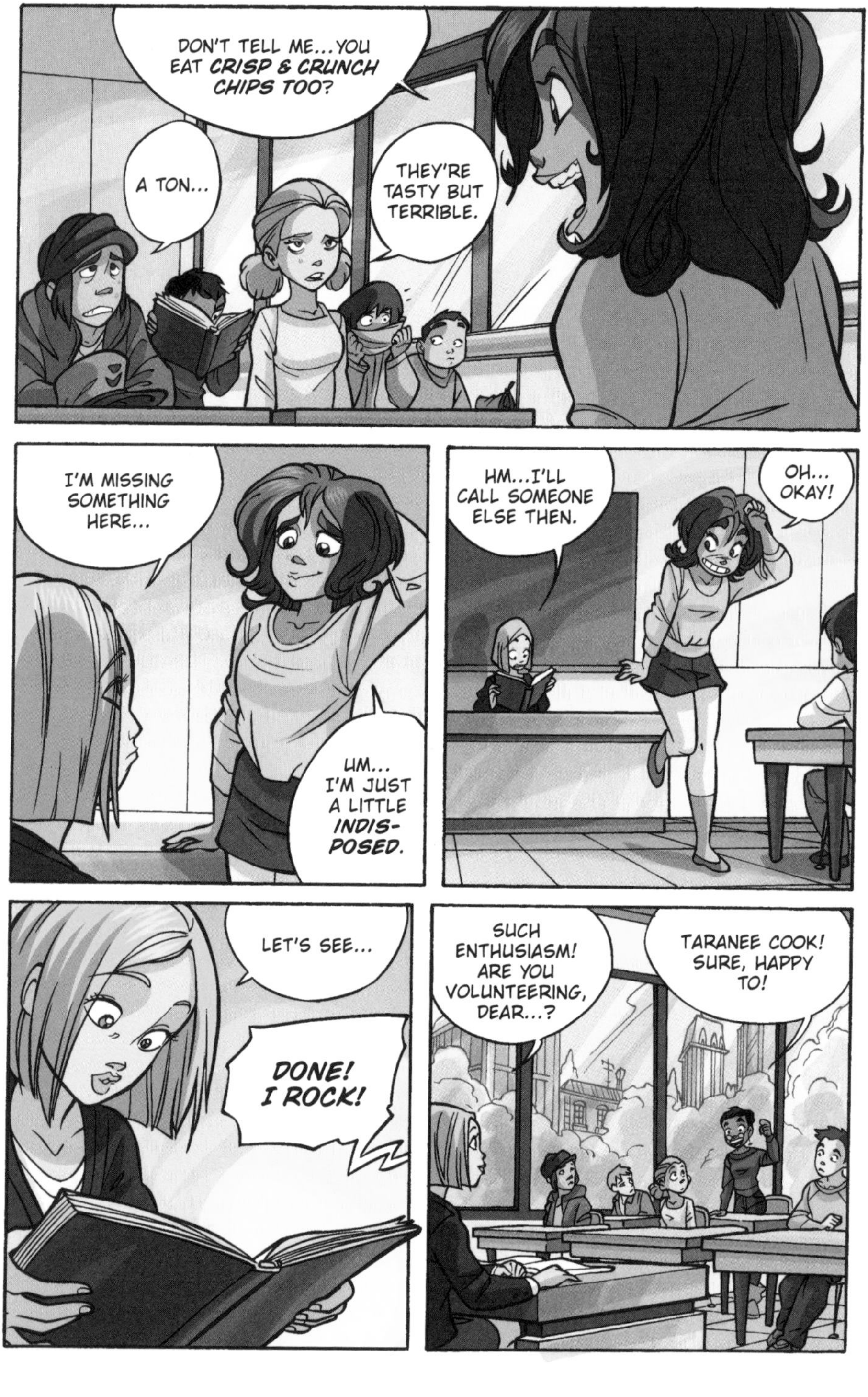
DON'T TELL ME...YOU EAT CRISP & CRUNCH CHIPS TOO?
A TON...
THEY'RE TASTY BUT TERRIBLE.
I'M MISSING SOMETHING HERE...
UM... I'M JUST A LITTLE INDIS-POSED.
HM...I'LL CALL SOMEONE ELSE THEN.
OH... OKAY!
LET'S SEE...
DONE! I ROCK!
SUCH ENTHUSIASM! ARE YOU VOLUNTEERING, DEAR...?
TARANEE COOK! SURE, HAPPY TO!

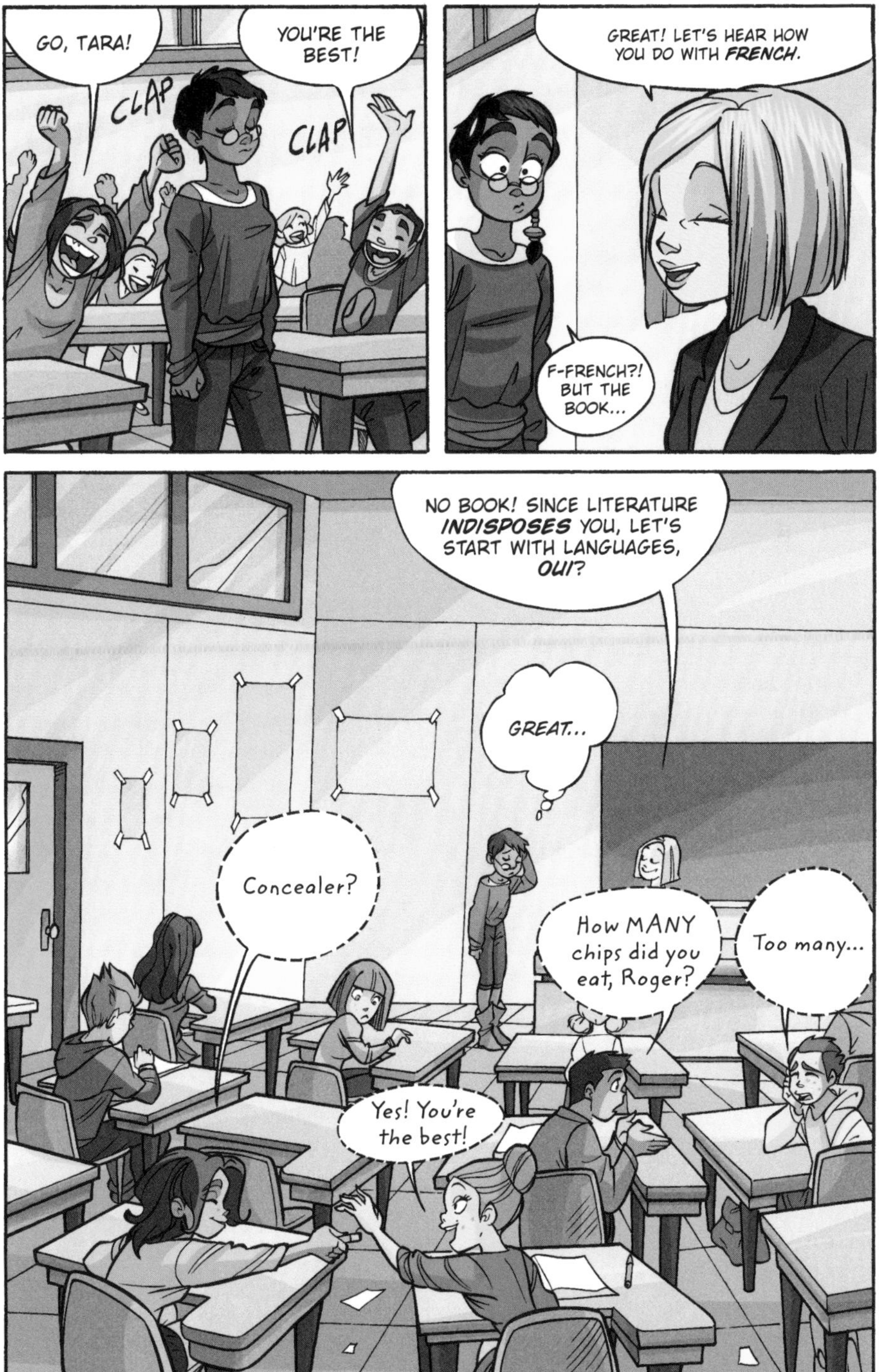
GO, TARA!
YOU'RE THE BEST!
CLAP
CLAP
GREAT! LET'S HEAR HOW YOU DO WITH FRENCH.
F-FRENCH?! BUT THE BOOK...
NO BOOK! SINCE LITERATURE INDISPOSES YOU, LET'S START WITH LANGUAGES, OUI?
GREAT...
Concealer?
How MANY chips did you eat, Roger?
Too many...
Yes! You're the best!

121

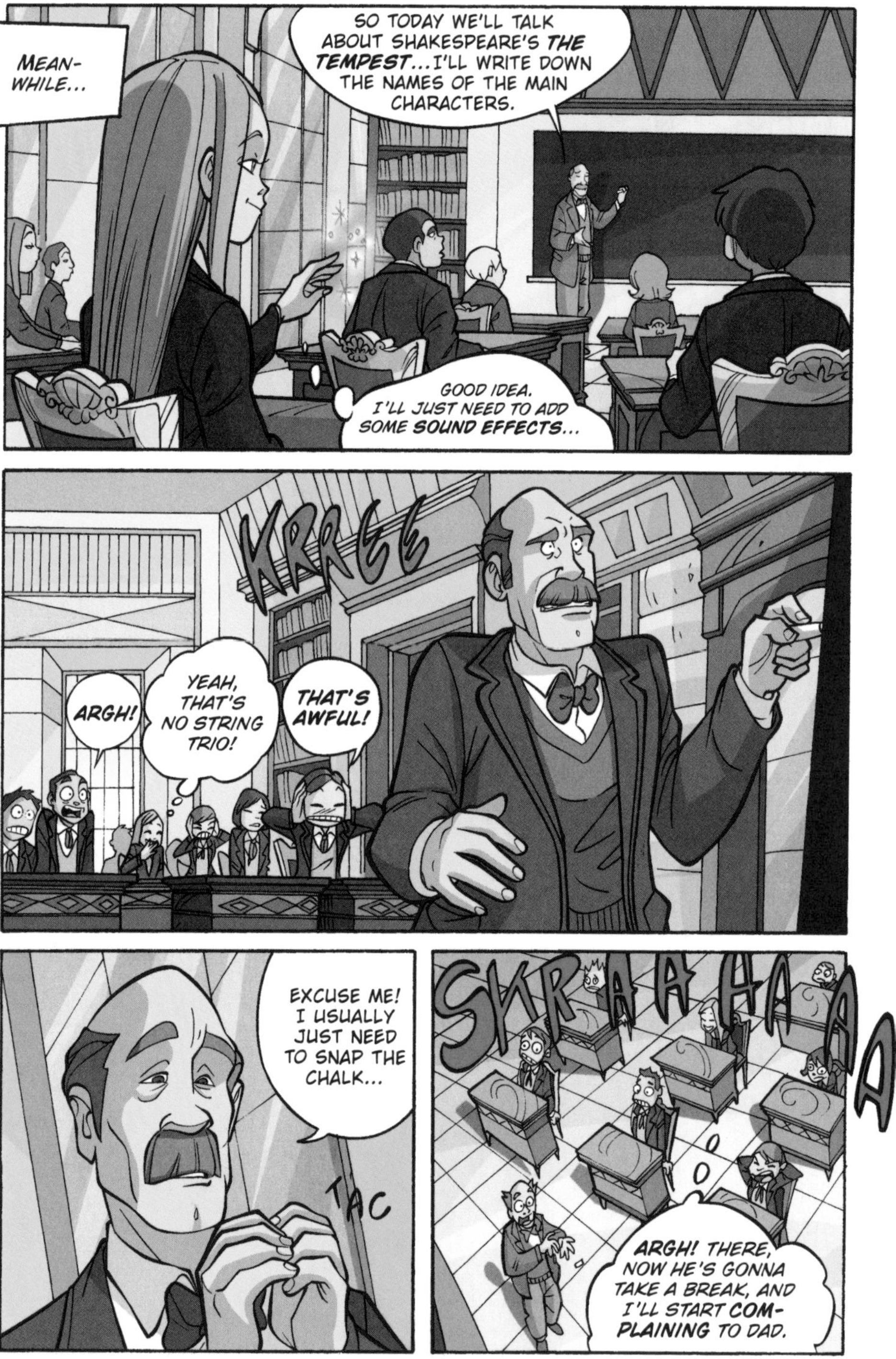
MEAN-WHILE...
SO TODAY WE'LL TALK ABOUT SHAKESPEARE'S *THE TEMPEST*... I'LL WRITE DOWN THE NAMES OF THE MAIN CHARACTERS.
GOOD IDEA. I'LL JUST NEED TO ADD SOME **SOUND EFFECTS**...
KRREE
ARGH!
YEAH, THAT'S NO STRING TRIO!
THAT'S AWFUL!
EXCUSE ME! I USUALLY JUST NEED TO SNAP THE CHALK...
TAC
SKRAAAAAA
ARGH! THERE, NOW HE'S GONNA TAKE A BREAK, AND I'LL START **COM-PLAINING** TO DAD.

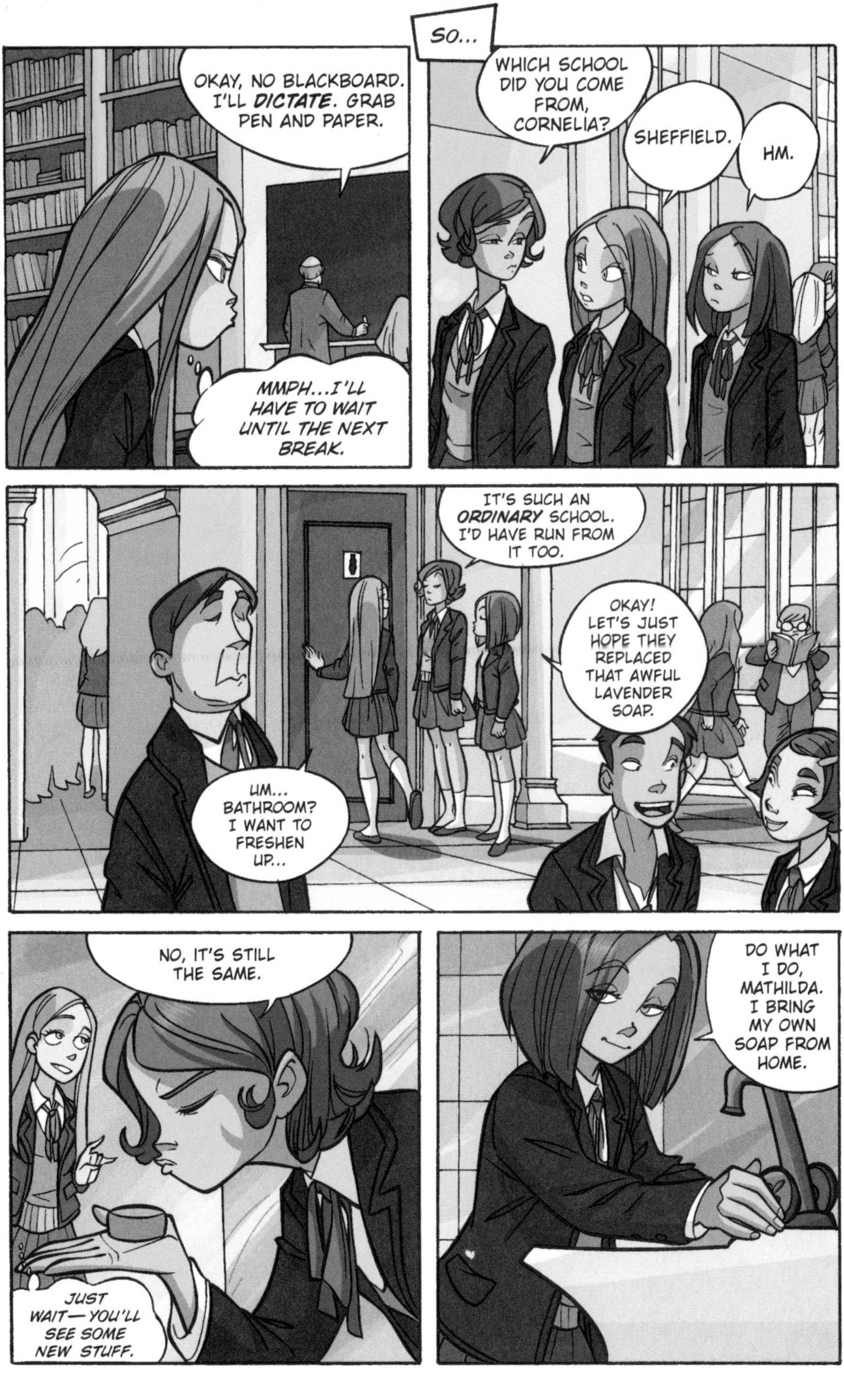
SO...
OKAY, NO BLACKBOARD. I'LL *DICTATE*. GRAB PEN AND PAPER.
MMPH...I'LL HAVE TO WAIT UNTIL THE NEXT BREAK.
WHICH SCHOOL DID YOU COME FROM, CORNELIA?
SHEFFIELD.
HM.
IT'S SUCH AN *ORDINARY* SCHOOL. I'D HAVE RUN FROM IT TOO.
OKAY! LET'S JUST HOPE THEY REPLACED THAT AWFUL LAVENDER SOAP.
UM... BATHROOM? I WANT TO FRESHEN UP...
NO, IT'S STILL THE SAME.
JUST WAIT—YOU'LL SEE SOME NEW STUFF.
DO WHAT I DO, MATHILDA. I BRING MY OWN SOAP FROM HOME.

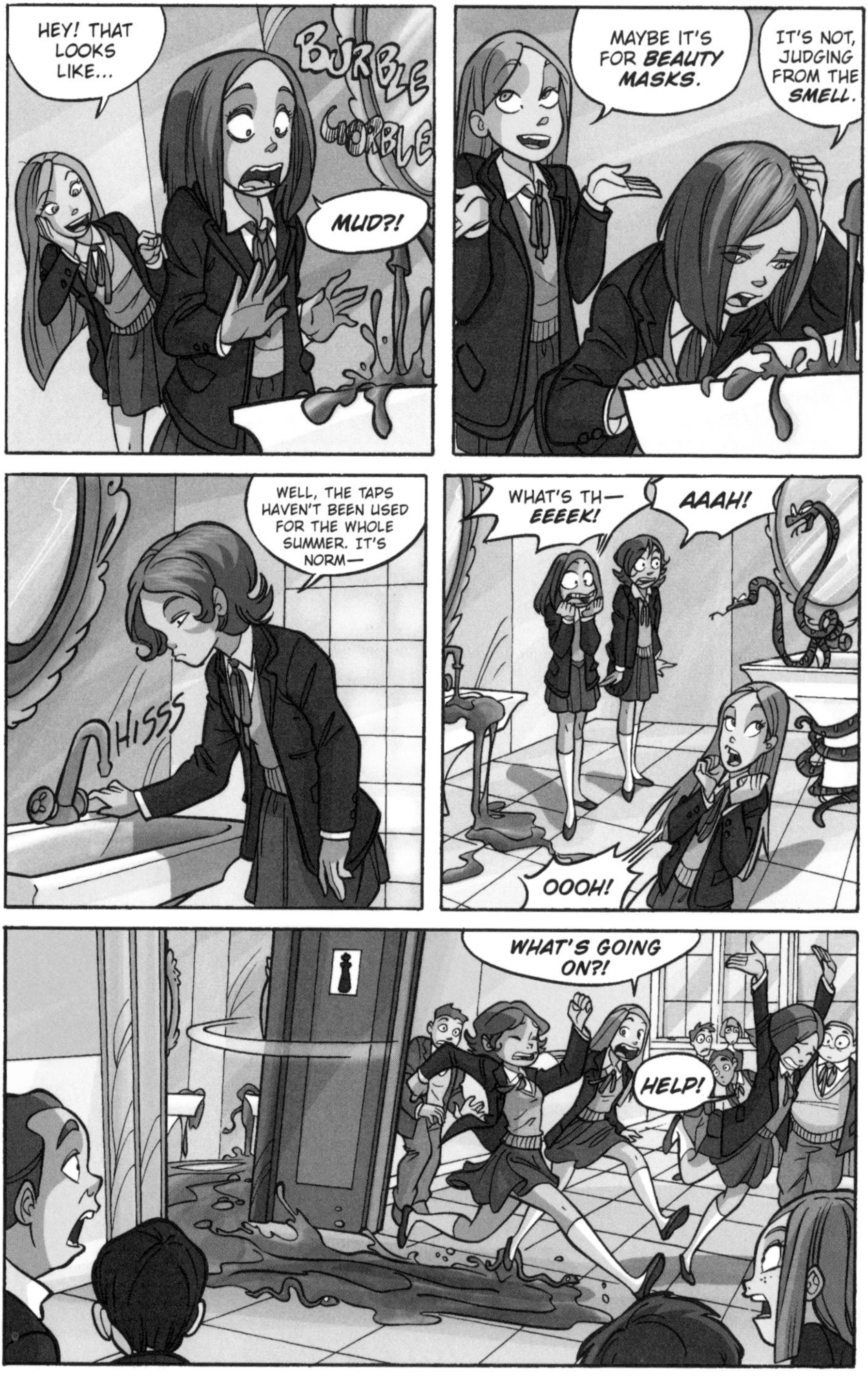
HEY! THAT LOOKS LIKE...
BURBLE
GORBLE
MUD?!
MAYBE IT'S FOR BEAUTY MASKS.
IT'S NOT, JUDGING FROM THE SMELL.
WELL, THE TAPS HAVEN'T BEEN USED FOR THE WHOLE SUMMER. IT'S NORM—
HISSS
WHAT'S TH— EEEEK!
AAAH!
OOOH!
WHAT'S GOING ON?!
HELP!

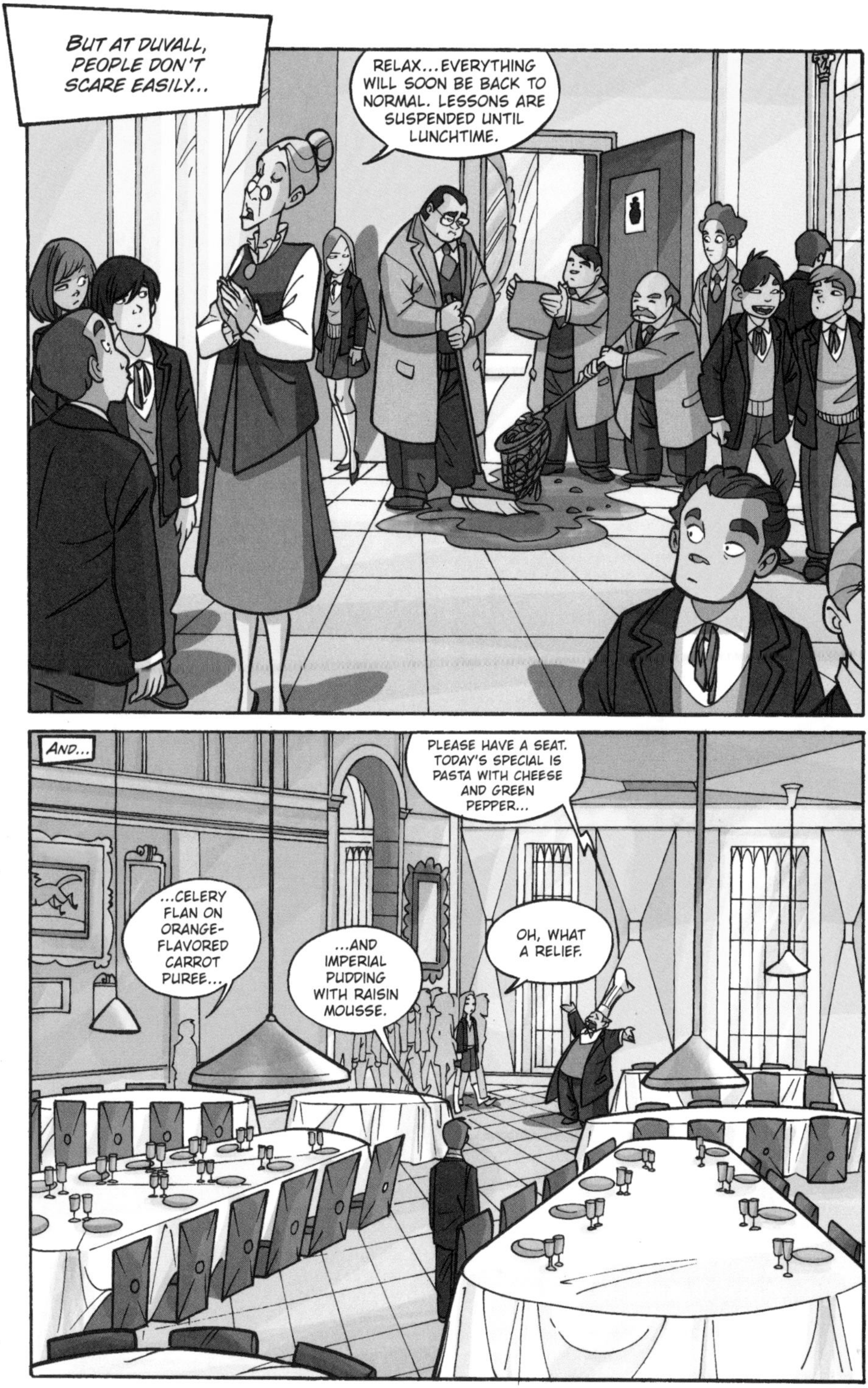
BUT AT DUVALL, PEOPLE DON'T SCARE EASILY...
RELAX... EVERYTHING WILL SOON BE BACK TO NORMAL. LESSONS ARE SUSPENDED UNTIL LUNCHTIME.
AND...
PLEASE HAVE A SEAT. TODAY'S SPECIAL IS PASTA WITH CHEESE AND GREEN PEPPER...
...CELERY FLAN ON ORANGE-FLAVORED CARROT PUREE...
...AND IMPERIAL PUDDING WITH RAISIN MOUSSE.
OH, WHAT A RELIEF.

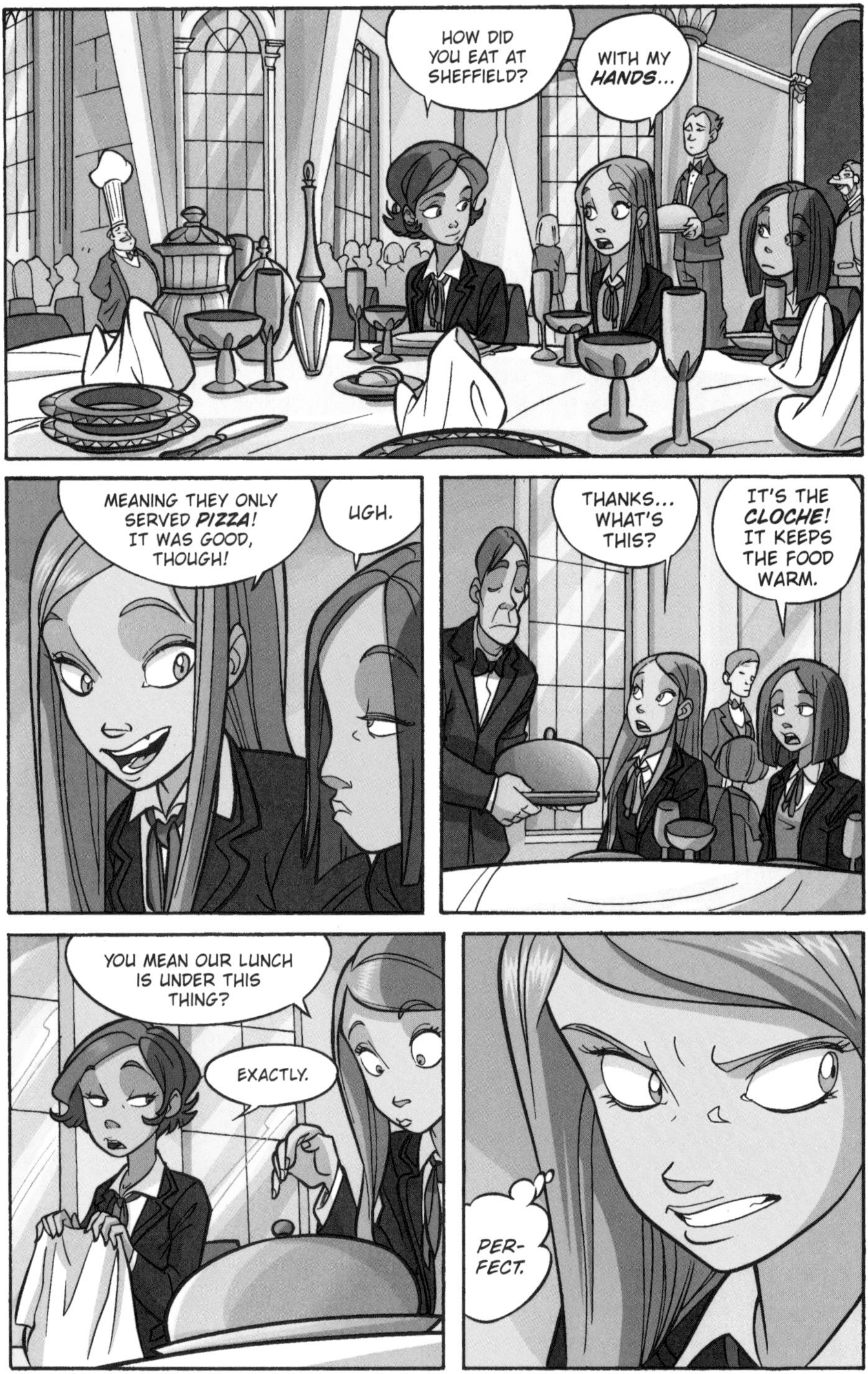
HOW DID YOU EAT AT SHEFFIELD?
WITH MY *HANDS*...
MEANING THEY ONLY SERVED *PIZZA*! IT WAS GOOD, THOUGH!
UGH.
THANKS... WHAT'S THIS?
IT'S THE *CLOCHE*! IT KEEPS THE FOOD WARM.
YOU MEAN OUR LUNCH IS UNDER THIS THING?
EXACTLY.
PER-FECT.

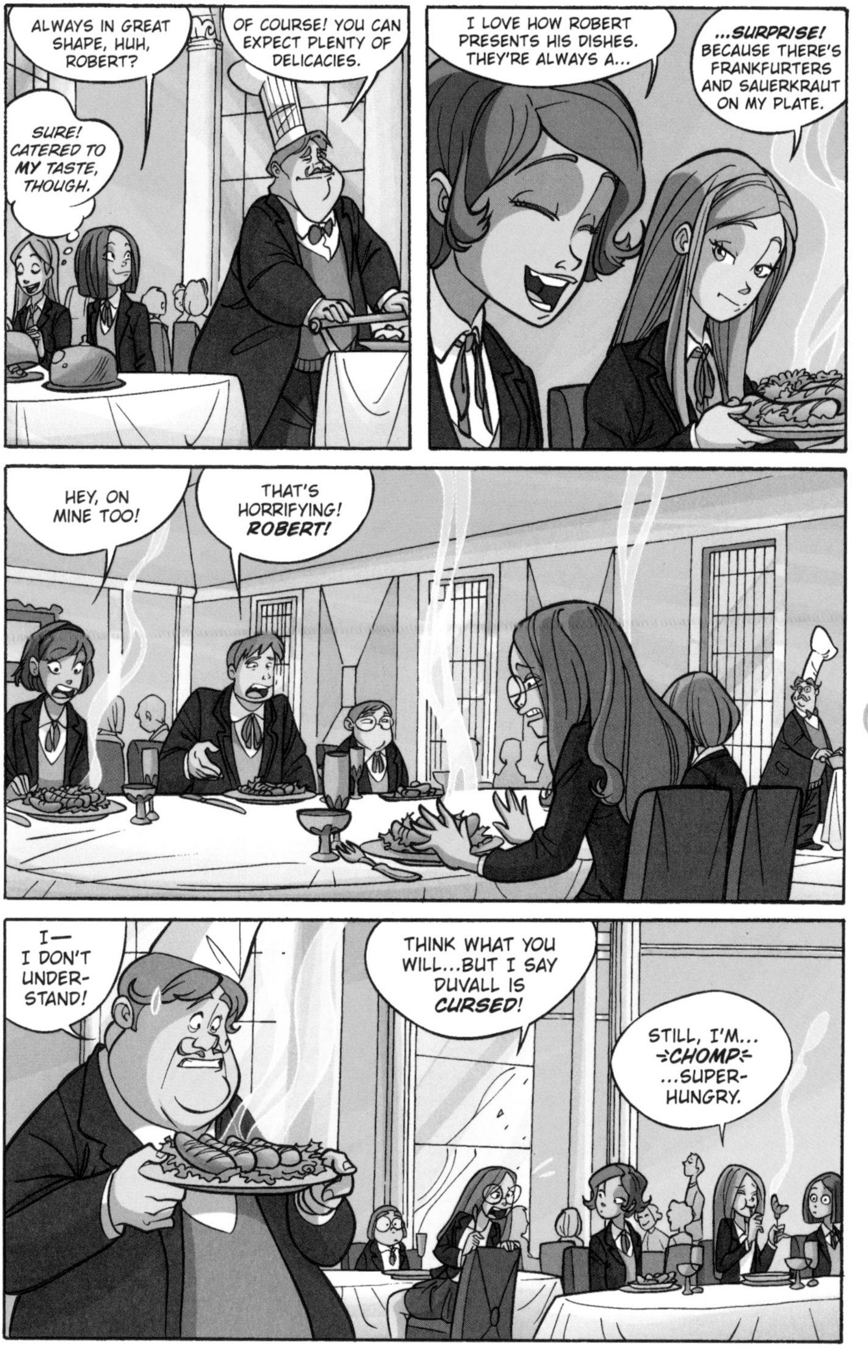
ALWAYS IN GREAT SHAPE, HUH, ROBERT?
SURE! CATERED TO MY TASTE, THOUGH.
OF COURSE! YOU CAN EXPECT PLENTY OF DELICACIES.
I LOVE HOW ROBERT PRESENTS HIS DISHES. THEY'RE ALWAYS A...
...SURPRISE! BECAUSE THERE'S FRANKFURTERS AND SAUERKRAUT ON MY PLATE.
HEY, ON MINE TOO!
THAT'S HORRIFYING! ROBERT!
I— I DON'T UNDER-STAND!
THINK WHAT YOU WILL...BUT I SAY DUVALL IS CURSED!
STILL, I'M... CHOMP ...SUPER-HUNGRY.

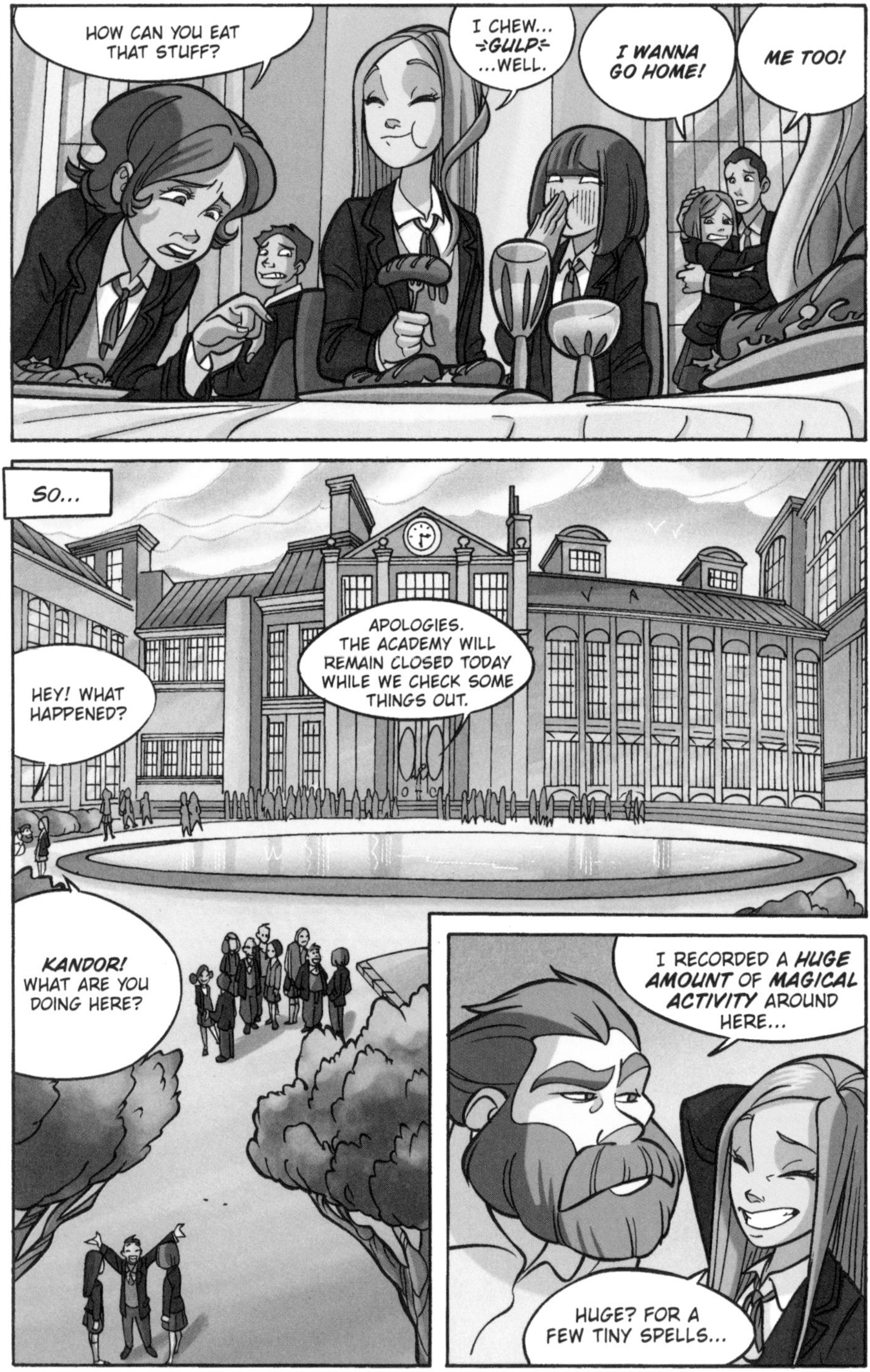
HOW CAN YOU EAT THAT STUFF?
I CHEW... GULP ...WELL.
I WANNA GO HOME!
ME TOO!
SO...
HEY! WHAT HAPPENED?
APOLOGIES. THE ACADEMY WILL REMAIN CLOSED TODAY WHILE WE CHECK SOME THINGS OUT.
KANDOR! WHAT ARE YOU DOING HERE?
I RECORDED A HUGE AMOUNT OF MAGICAL ACTIVITY AROUND HERE...
HUGE? FOR A FEW TINY SPELLS...

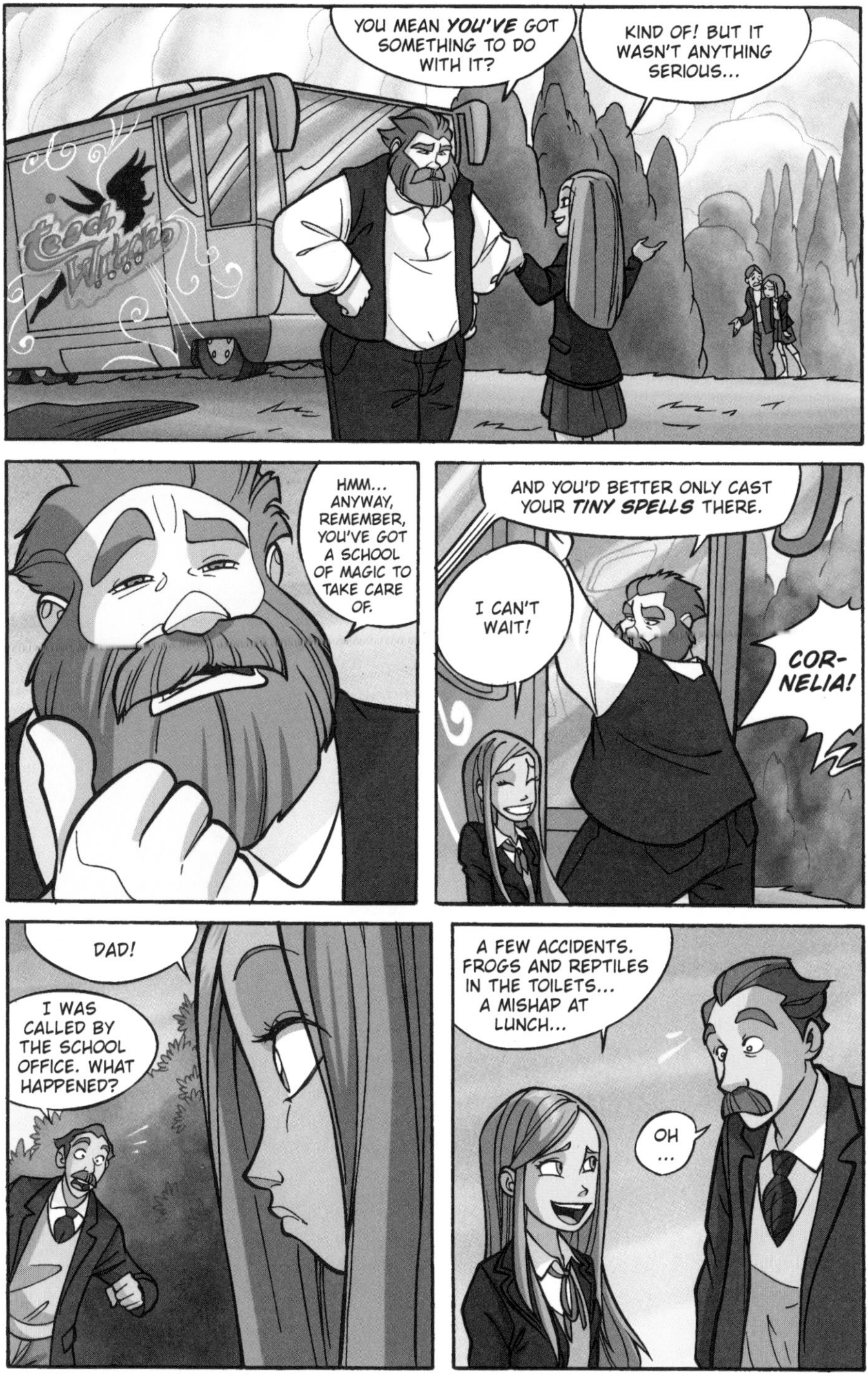
YOU MEAN *YOU'VE* GOT SOMETHING TO DO WITH IT?
KIND OF! BUT IT WASN'T ANYTHING SERIOUS...
HMM... ANYWAY, REMEMBER, YOU'VE GOT A SCHOOL OF MAGIC TO TAKE CARE OF.
AND YOU'D BETTER ONLY CAST YOUR *TINY SPELLS* THERE.
I CAN'T WAIT!
COR-NELIA!
DAD!
I WAS CALLED BY THE SCHOOL OFFICE. WHAT HAPPENED?
A FEW ACCIDENTS. FROGS AND REPTILES IN THE TOILETS... A MISHAP AT LUNCH...
OH ...

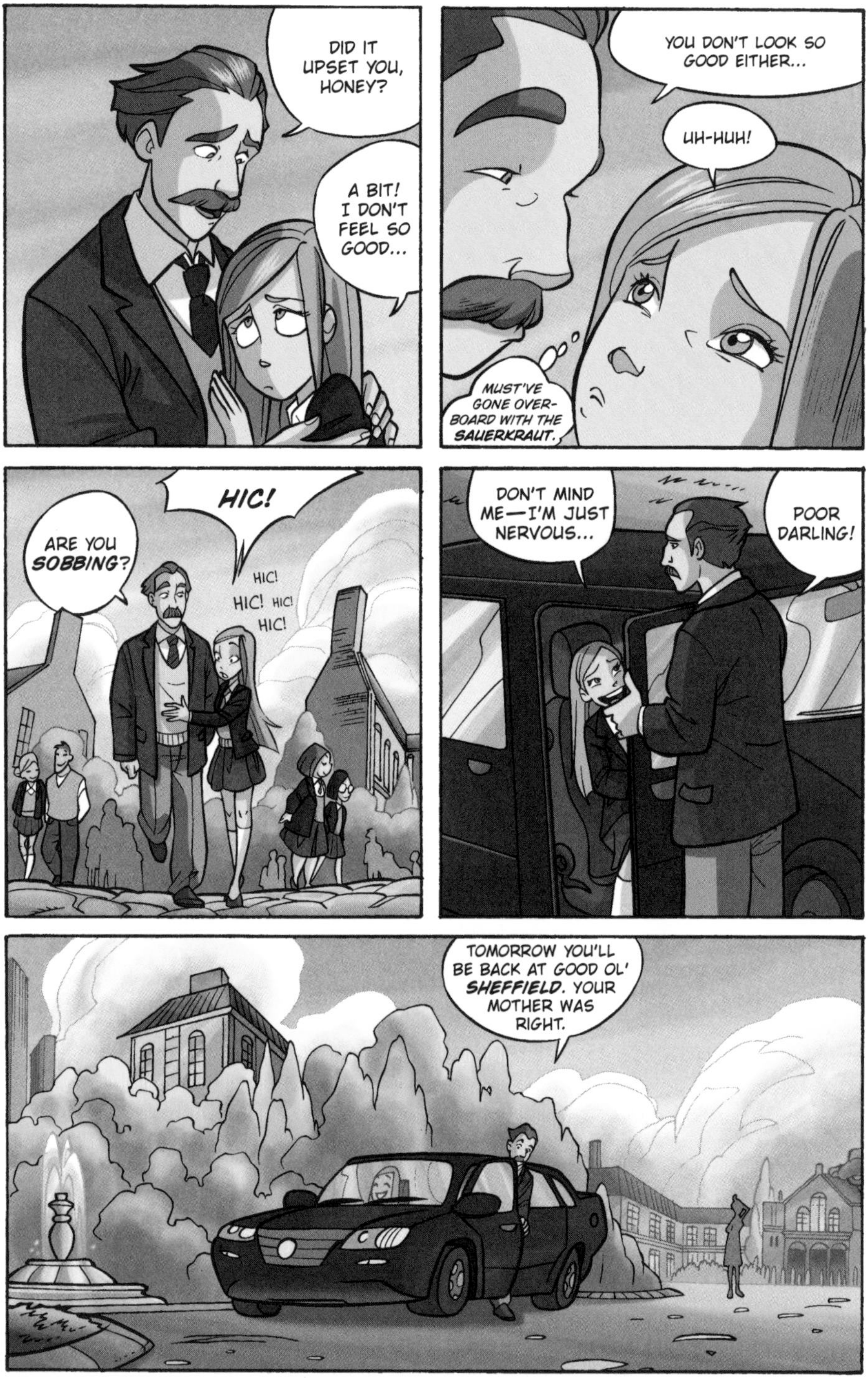
DID IT UPSET YOU, HONEY?
A BIT! I DON'T FEEL SO GOOD...
YOU DON'T LOOK SO GOOD EITHER...
UH-HUH!
MUST'VE GONE OVER-BOARD WITH THE SAUERKRAUT.
ARE YOU SOBBING?
HIC!
HIC! HIC! HIC! HIC!
DON'T MIND ME—I'M JUST NERVOUS...
POOR DARLING!
TOMORROW YOU'LL BE BACK AT GOOD OL' SHEFFIELD. YOUR MOTHER WAS RIGHT.

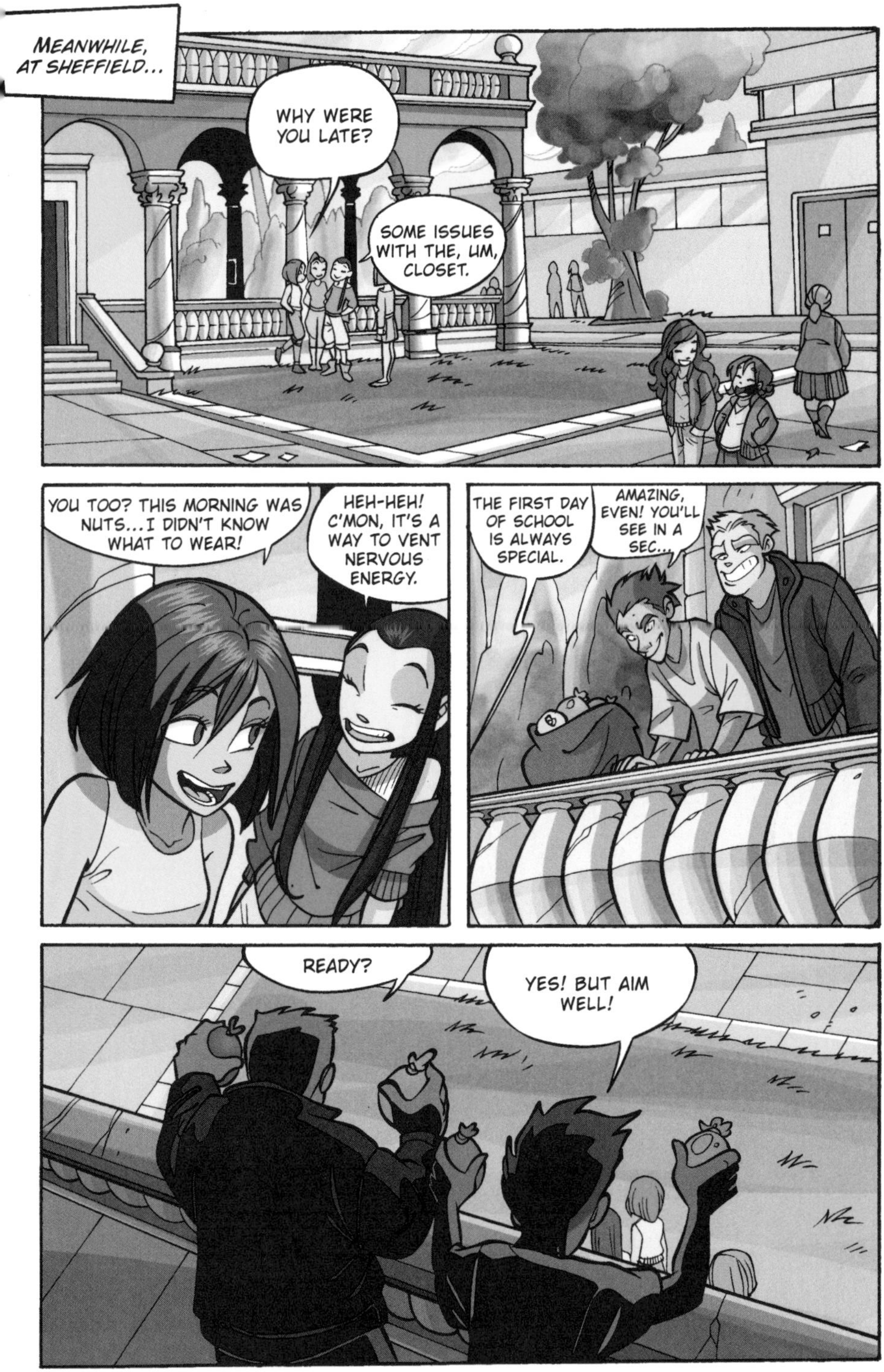
MEANWHILE, AT SHEFFIELD...
WHY WERE YOU LATE?
SOME ISSUES WITH THE, UM, CLOSET.
YOU TOO? THIS MORNING WAS NUTS...I DIDN'T KNOW WHAT TO WEAR!
HEH-HEH! C'MON, IT'S A WAY TO VENT NERVOUS ENERGY.
THE FIRST DAY OF SCHOOL IS ALWAYS SPECIAL.
AMAZING, EVEN! YOU'LL SEE IN A SEC...
READY?
YES! BUT AIM WELL!

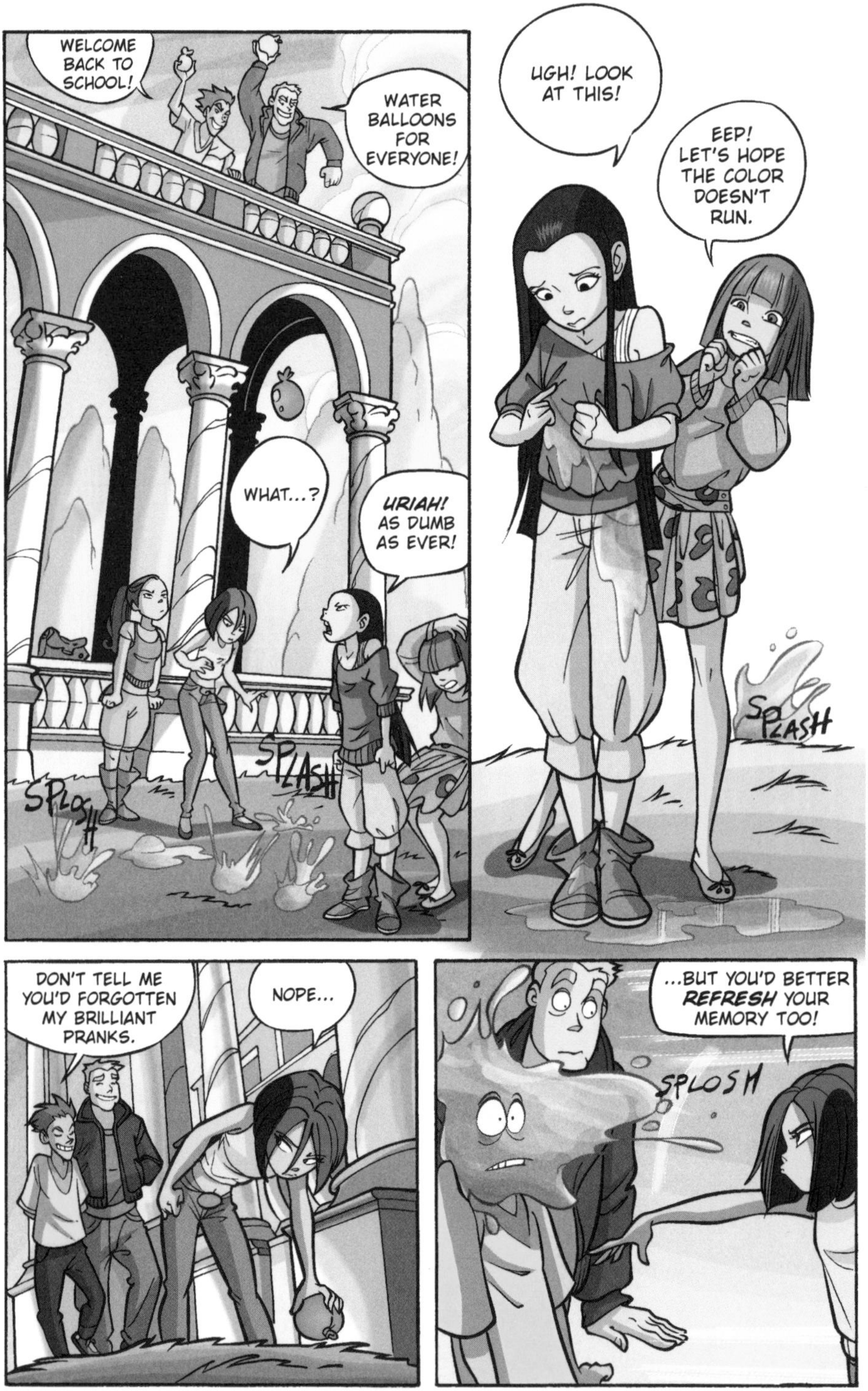
WELCOME BACK TO SCHOOL!
WATER BALLOONS FOR EVERYONE!
WHAT...?
URIAH! AS DUMB AS EVER!
SPLOSH
SPLASH
UGH! LOOK AT THIS!
EEP! LET'S HOPE THE COLOR DOESN'T RUN.
SPLASH
DON'T TELL ME YOU'D FORGOTTEN MY BRILLIANT PRANKS.
NOPE...
...BUT YOU'D BETTER REFRESH YOUR MEMORY TOO!
SPLOSH

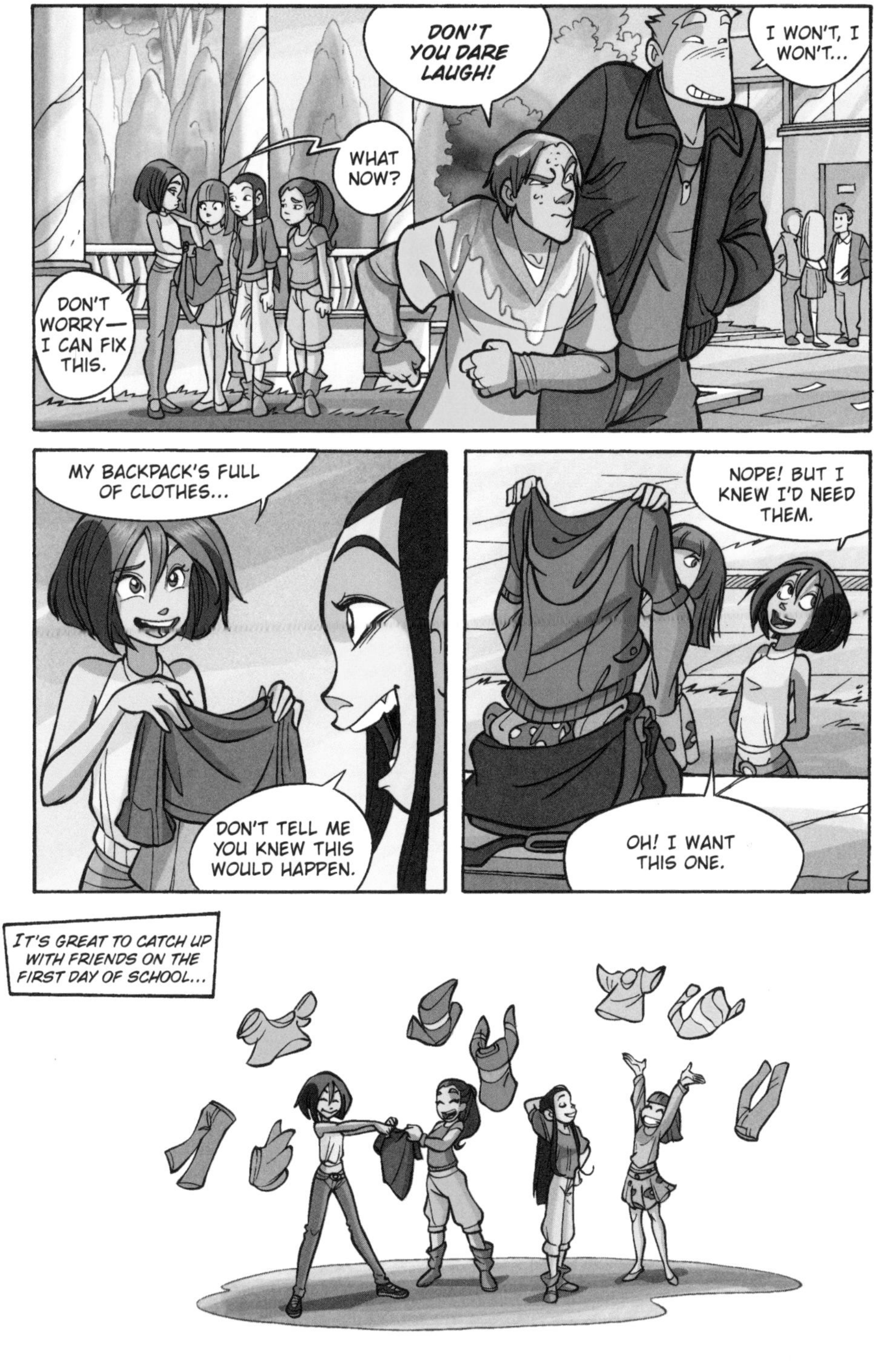
DON'T YOU DARE LAUGH!
I WON'T, I WON'T...
WHAT NOW?
DON'T WORRY—I CAN FIX THIS.
MY BACKPACK'S FULL OF CLOTHES...
DON'T TELL ME YOU KNEW THIS WOULD HAPPEN.
NOPE! BUT I KNEW I'D NEED THEM.
OH! I WANT THIS ONE.
IT'S GREAT TO CATCH UP WITH FRIENDS ON THE FIRST DAY OF SCHOOL...

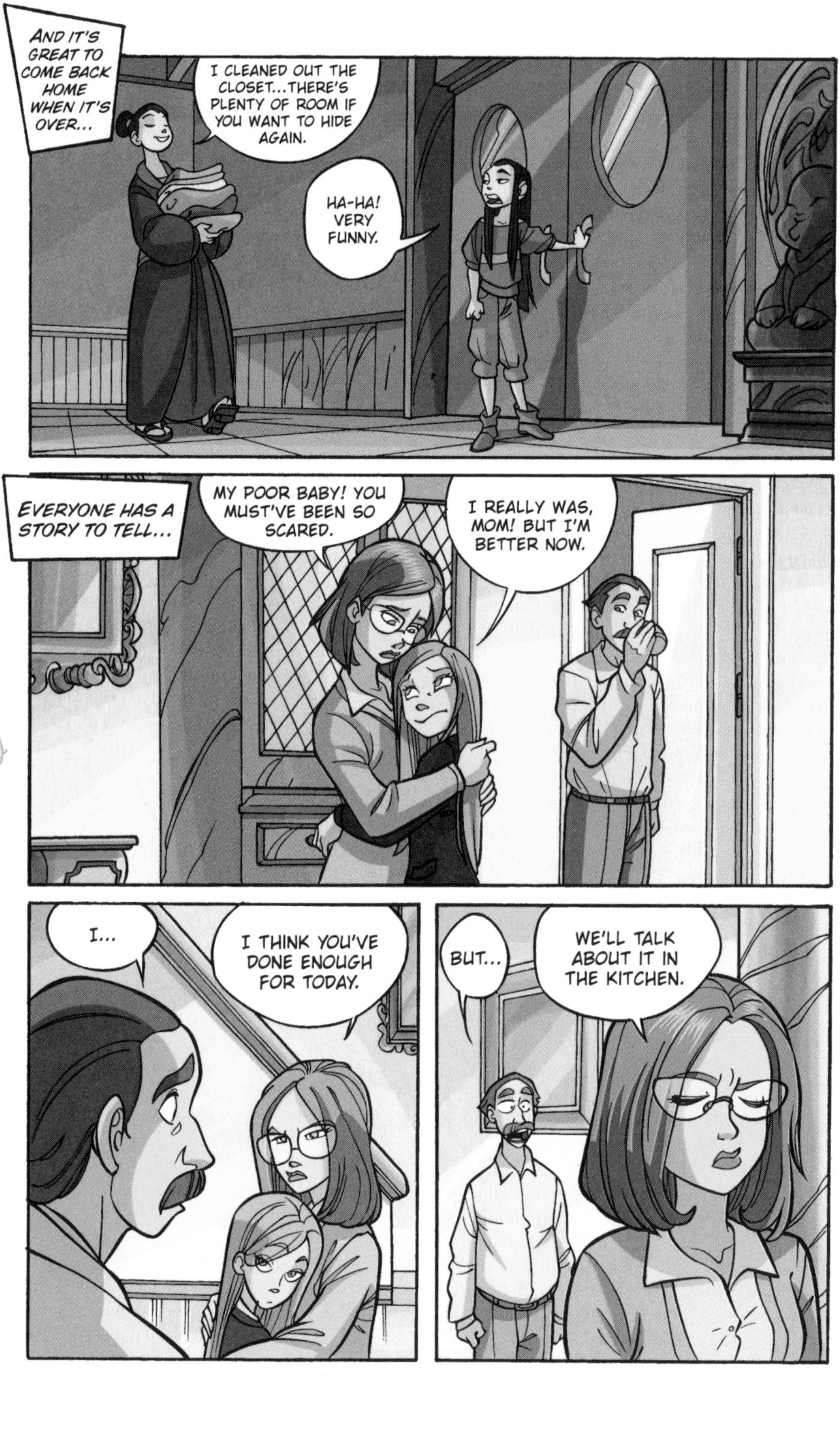
AND IT'S GREAT TO COME BACK HOME WHEN IT'S OVER...
I CLEANED OUT THE CLOSET...THERE'S PLENTY OF ROOM IF YOU WANT TO HIDE AGAIN.
HA-HA! VERY FUNNY.
EVERYONE HAS A STORY TO TELL...
MY POOR BABY! YOU MUST'VE BEEN SO SCARED.
I REALLY WAS, MOM! BUT I'M BETTER NOW.
I...
I THINK YOU'VE DONE ENOUGH FOR TODAY.
BUT...
WE'LL TALK ABOUT IT IN THE KITCHEN.

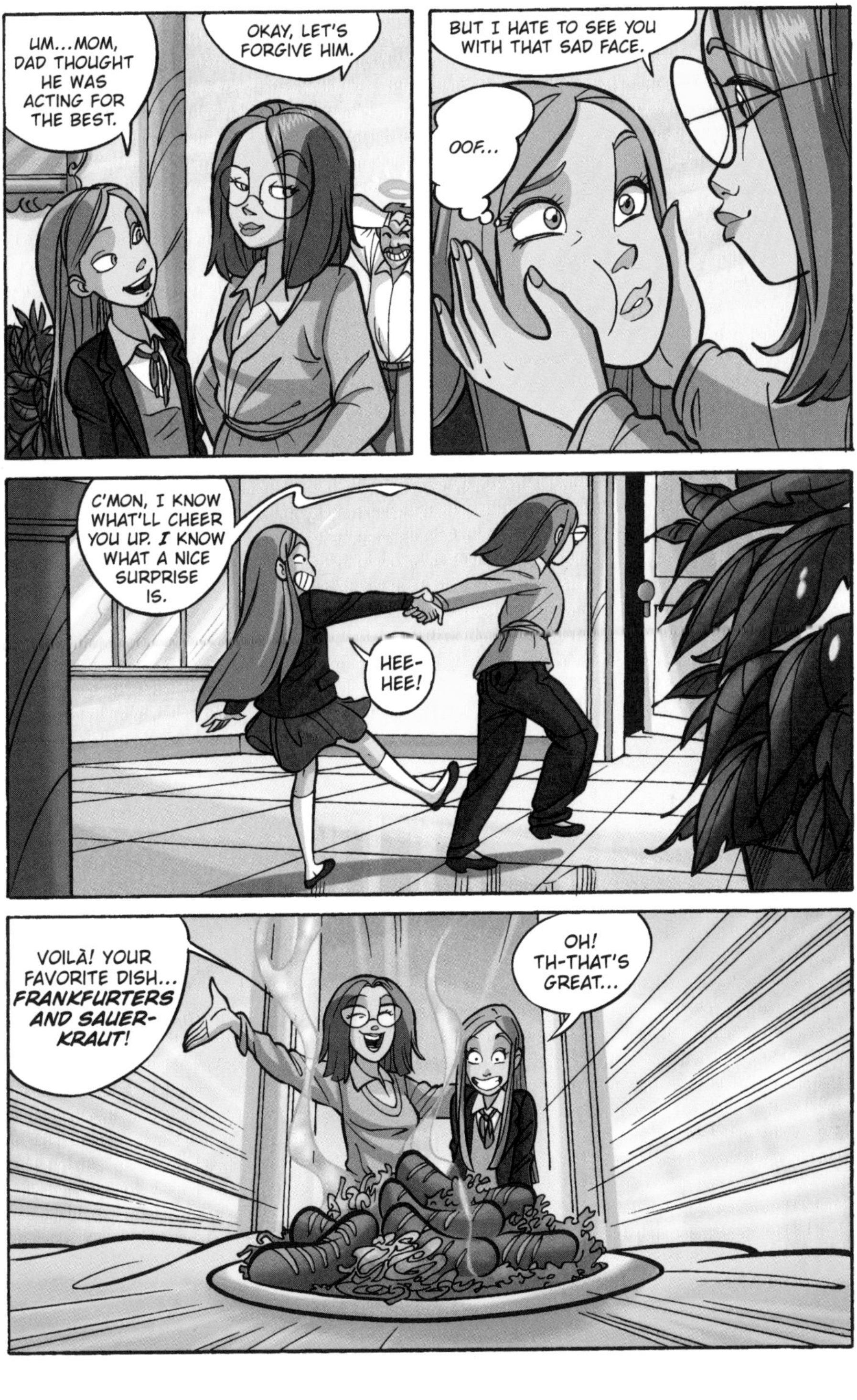
UM...MOM, DAD THOUGHT HE WAS ACTING FOR THE BEST.
OKAY, LET'S FORGIVE HIM.
BUT I HATE TO SEE YOU WITH THAT SAD FACE.
OOF...
C'MON, I KNOW WHAT'LL CHEER YOU UP. *I* KNOW WHAT A NICE SURPRISE IS.
HEE-HEE!
VOILÀ! YOUR FAVORITE DISH... ***FRANKFURTERS AND SAUER-KRAUT!***
OH! TH-THAT'S GREAT...

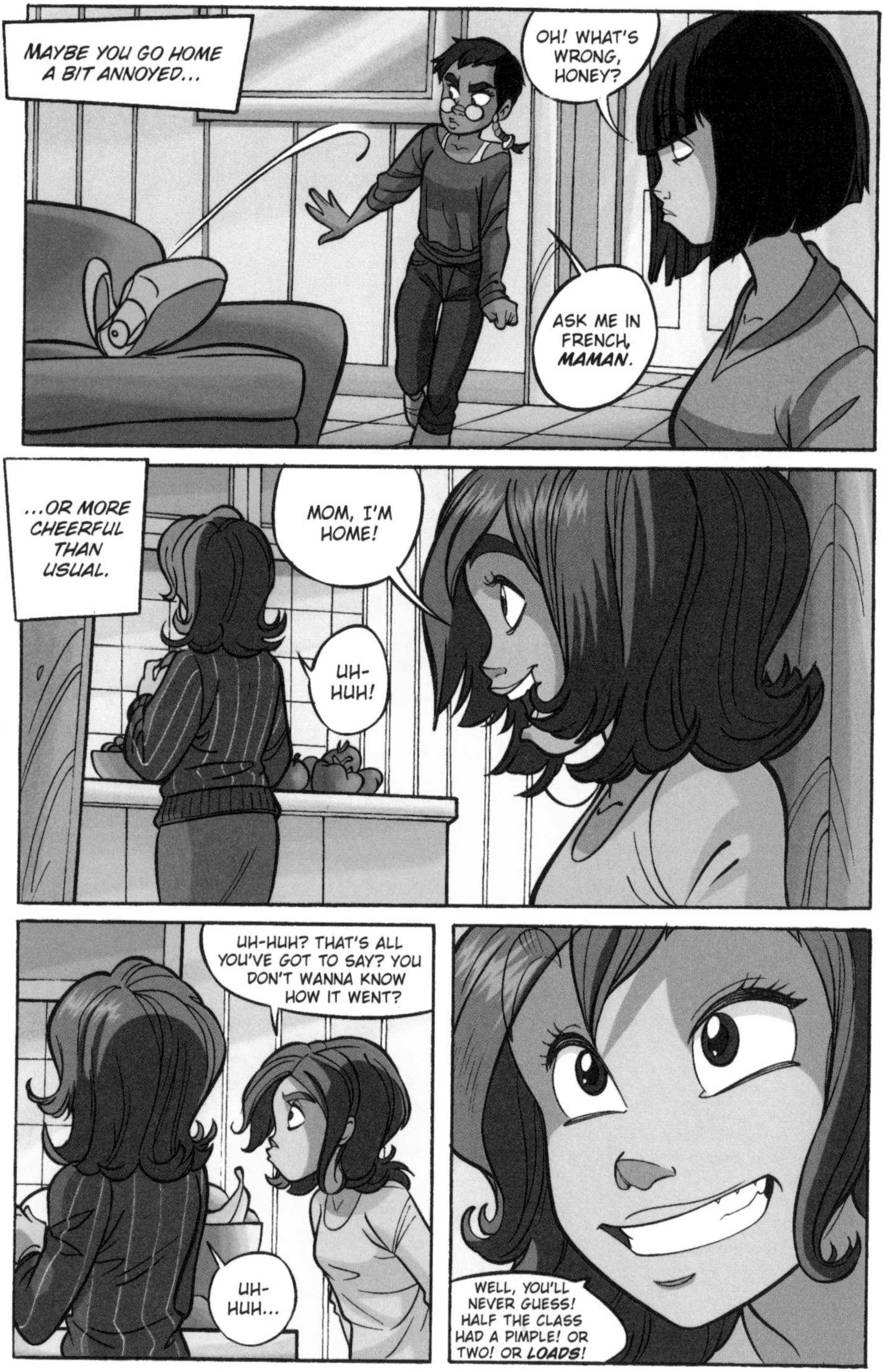
MAYBE YOU GO HOME A BIT ANNOYED...
OH! WHAT'S WRONG, HONEY?
ASK ME IN FRENCH, *MAMAN*.
...OR MORE CHEERFUL THAN USUAL.
MOM, I'M HOME!
UH-HUH!
UH-HUH? THAT'S ALL YOU'VE GOT TO SAY? YOU DON'T WANNA KNOW HOW IT WENT?
UH-HUH...
WELL, YOU'LL NEVER GUESS! HALF THE CLASS HAD A PIMPLE! OR TWO! OR ***LOADS***!

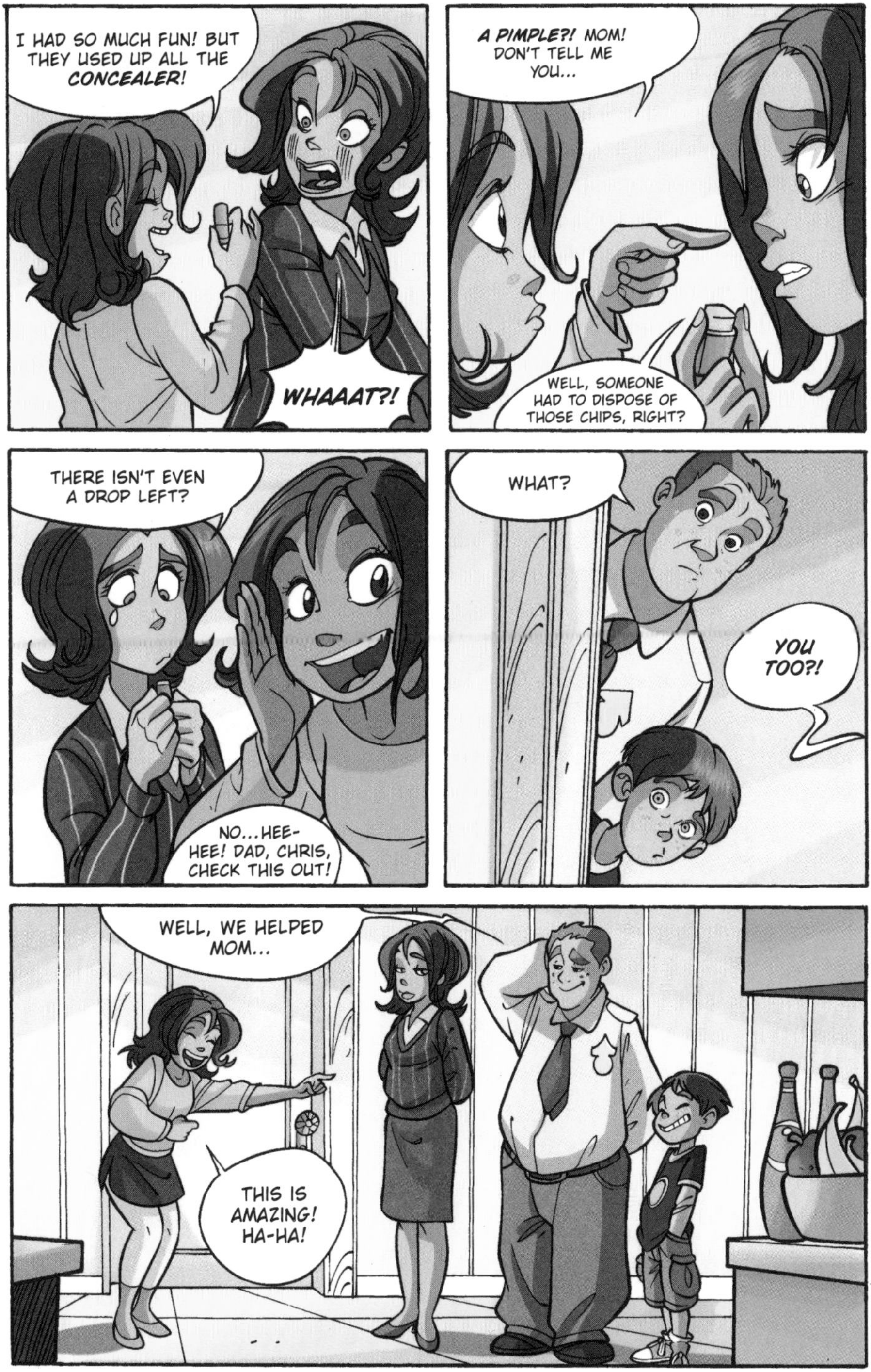

I HAD SO MUCH FUN! BUT THEY USED UP ALL THE **CONCEALER**!
WHAAAT?!
A PIMPLE?! MOM! DON'T TELL ME YOU...
WELL, SOMEONE HAD TO DISPOSE OF THOSE CHIPS, RIGHT?
THERE ISN'T EVEN A DROP LEFT?
NO...HEE-HEE! DAD, CHRIS, CHECK THIS OUT!
WHAT?
YOU TOO?!
WELL, WE HELPED MOM...
THIS IS AMAZING! HA-HA!

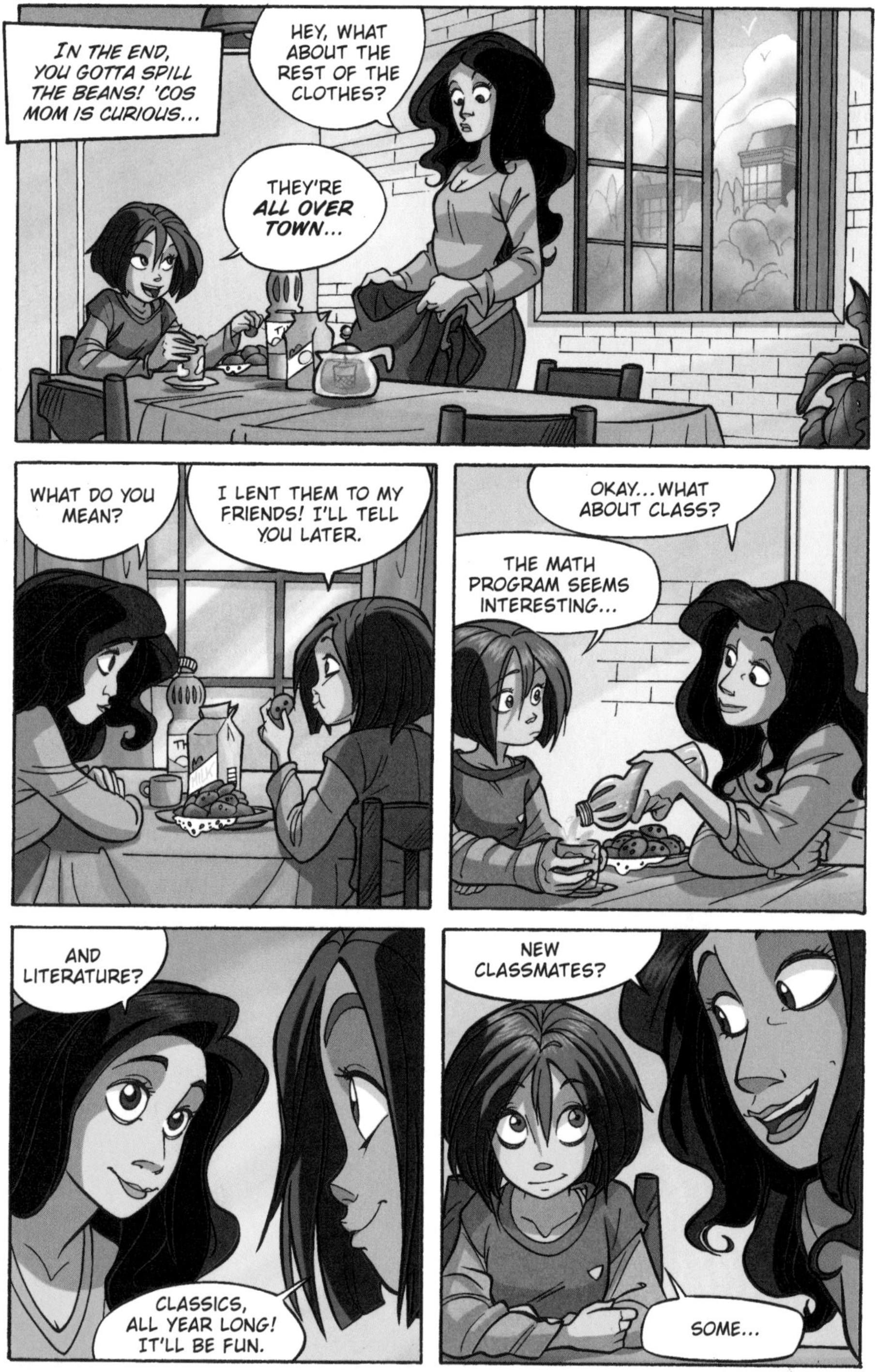

IN THE END, YOU GOTTA SPILL THE BEANS! 'COS MOM IS CURIOUS...
HEY, WHAT ABOUT THE REST OF THE CLOTHES?
THEY'RE ALL OVER TOWN...
WHAT DO YOU MEAN?
I LENT THEM TO MY FRIENDS! I'LL TELL YOU LATER.
OKAY...WHAT ABOUT CLASS?
THE MATH PROGRAM SEEMS INTERESTING...
AND LITERATURE?
CLASSICS, ALL YEAR LONG! IT'LL BE FUN.
NEW CLASSMATES?
SOME...

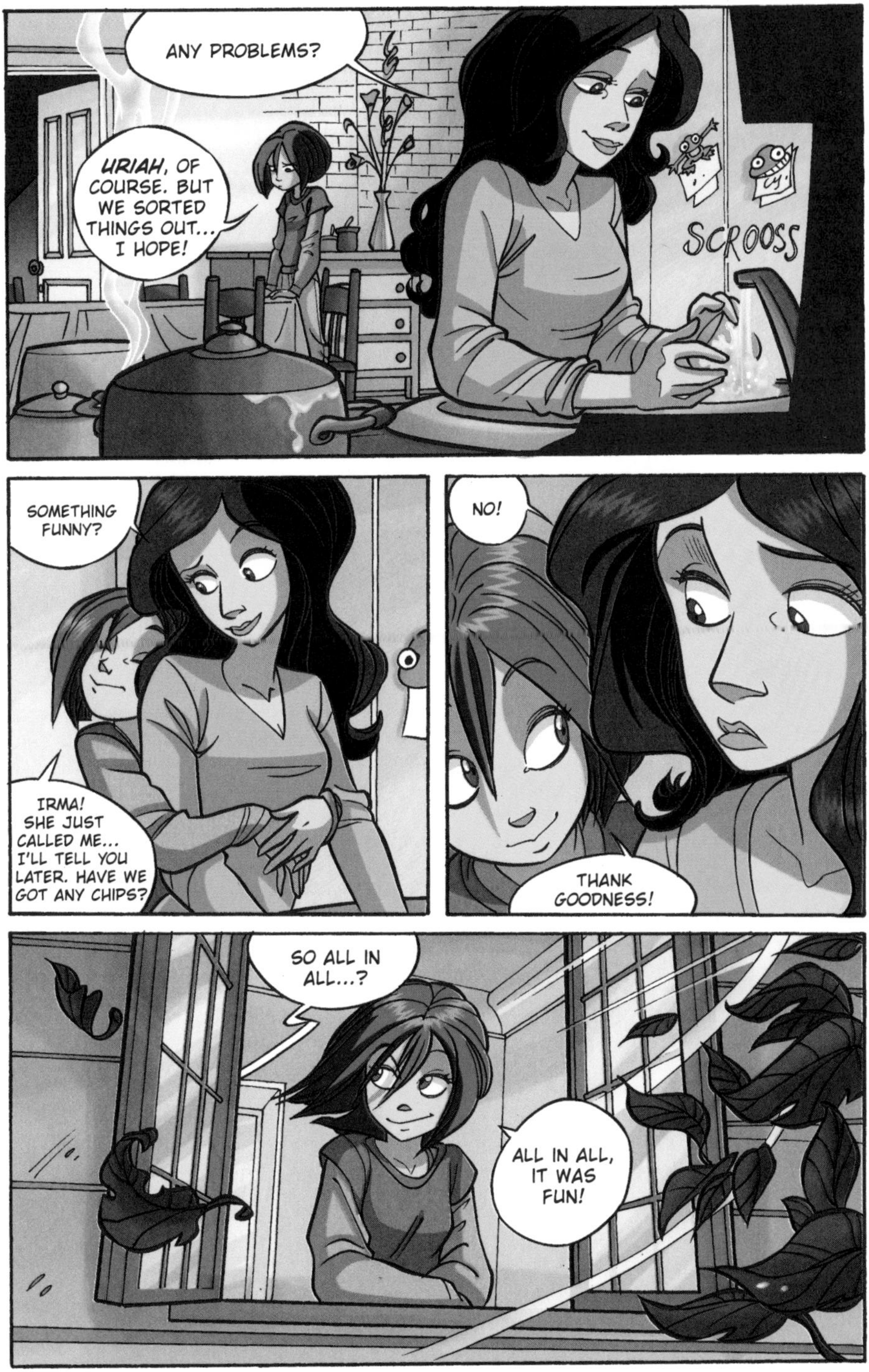
ANY PROBLEMS?
URIAH, OF COURSE. BUT WE SORTED THINGS OUT... I HOPE!
SCROOSS
SOMETHING FUNNY?
IRMA! SHE JUST CALLED ME... I'LL TELL YOU LATER. HAVE WE GOT ANY CHIPS?
NO!
THANK GOODNESS!
SO ALL IN ALL...?
ALL IN ALL, IT WAS FUN!

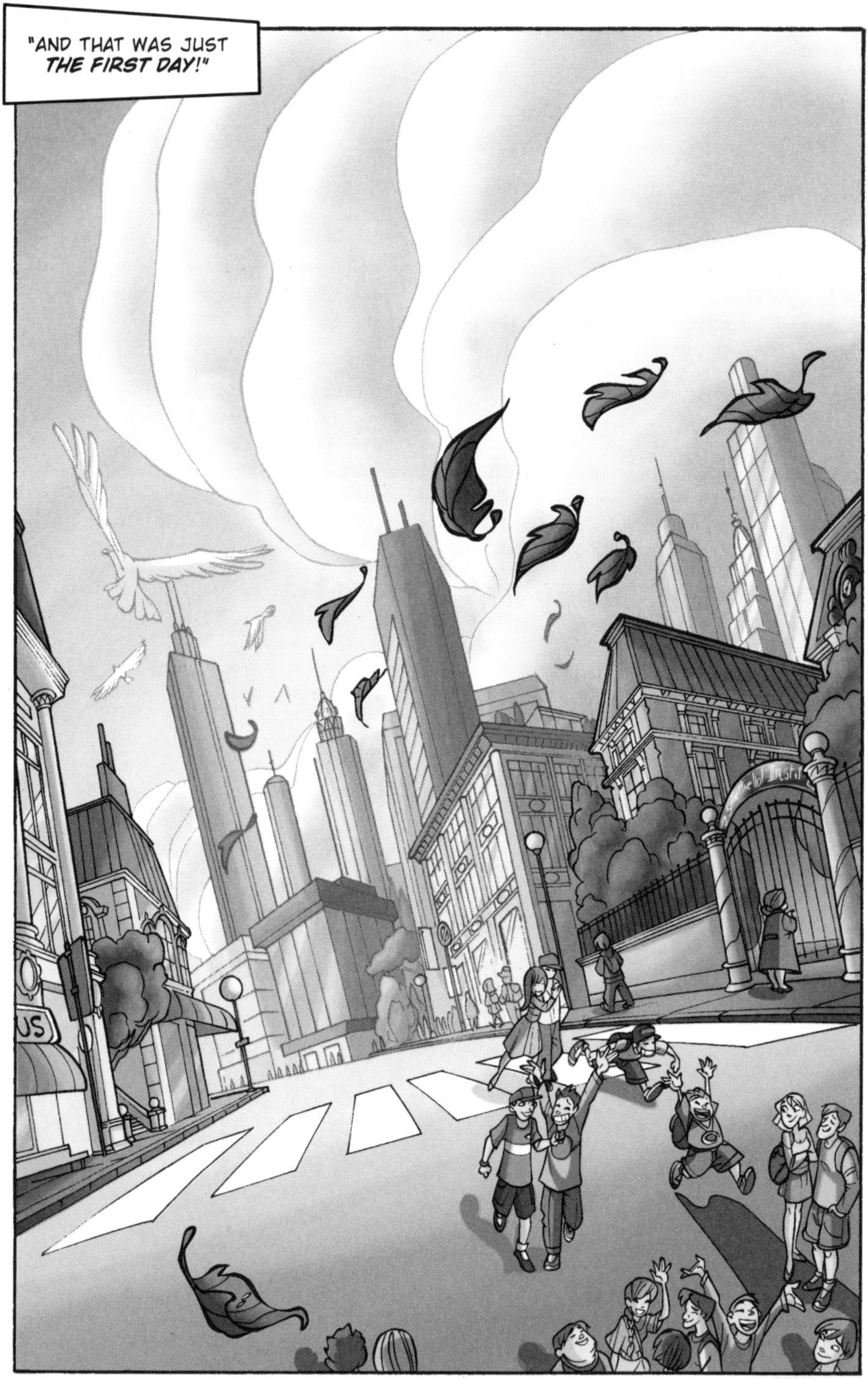
"AND THAT WAS JUST *THE FIRST DAY!*"

END OF CHAPTER 102

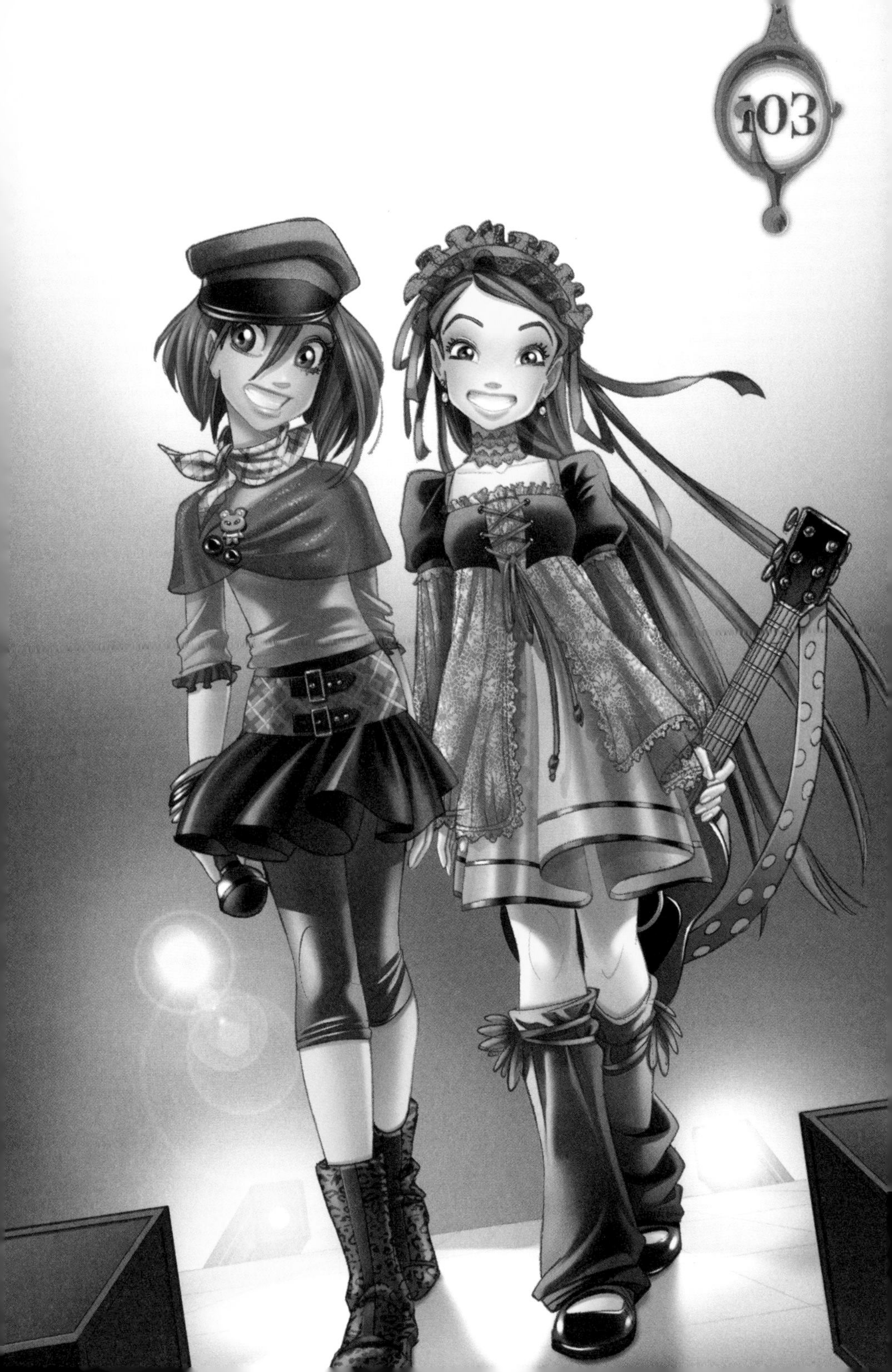
103

W.i.t.c.h.

Will Irma Taranee Cornelia Hay Lin

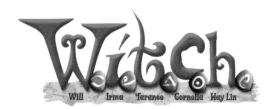

The One You're Not

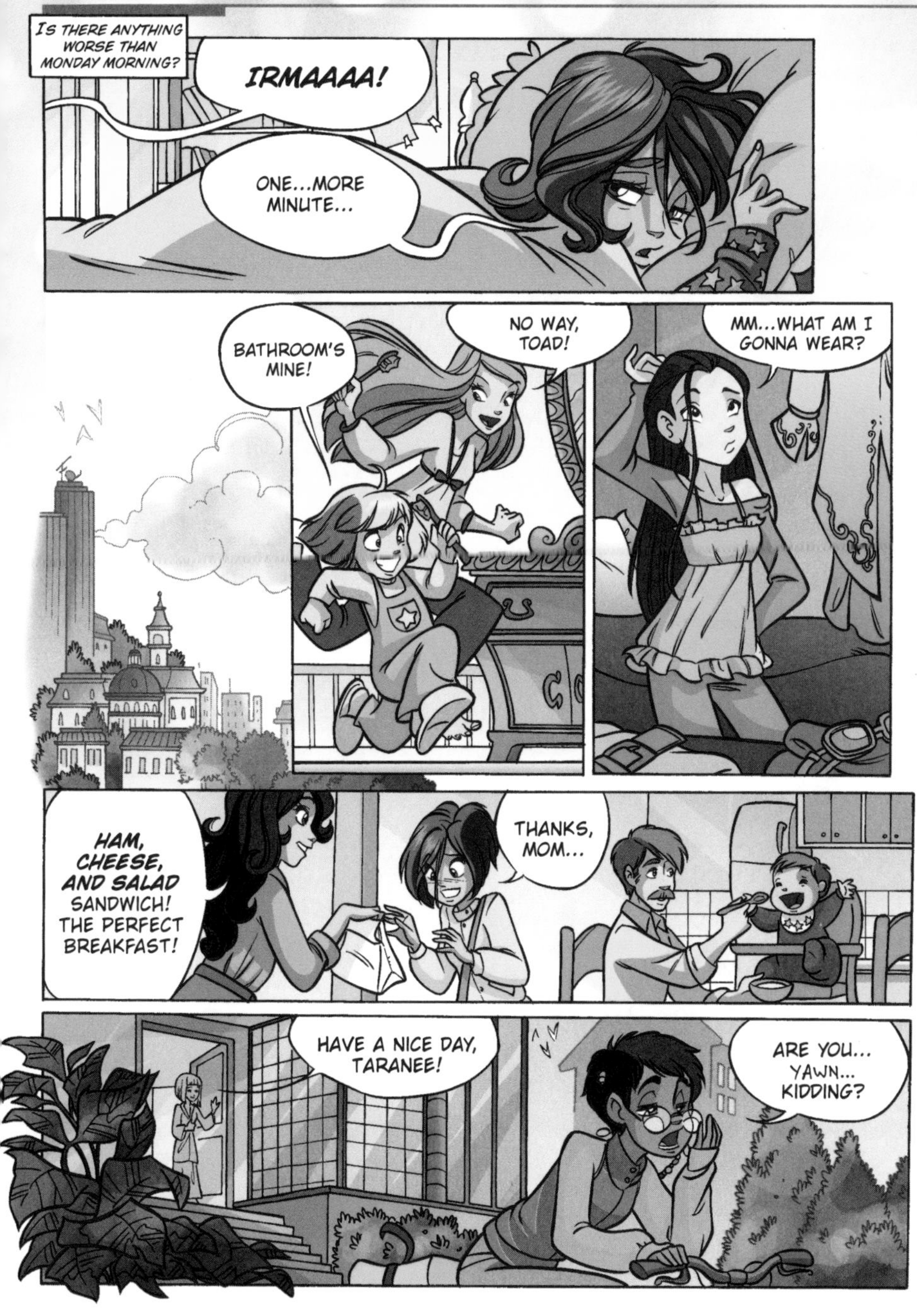

IS THERE ANYTHING WORSE THAN MONDAY MORNING?
IRMAAAA!
ONE...MORE MINUTE...
BATHROOM'S MINE!
NO WAY, TOAD!
MM...WHAT AM I GONNA WEAR?
HAM, CHEESE, AND SALAD SANDWICH! THE PERFECT BREAKFAST!
THANKS, MOM...
HAVE A NICE DAY, TARANEE!
ARE YOU... YAWN... KIDDING?

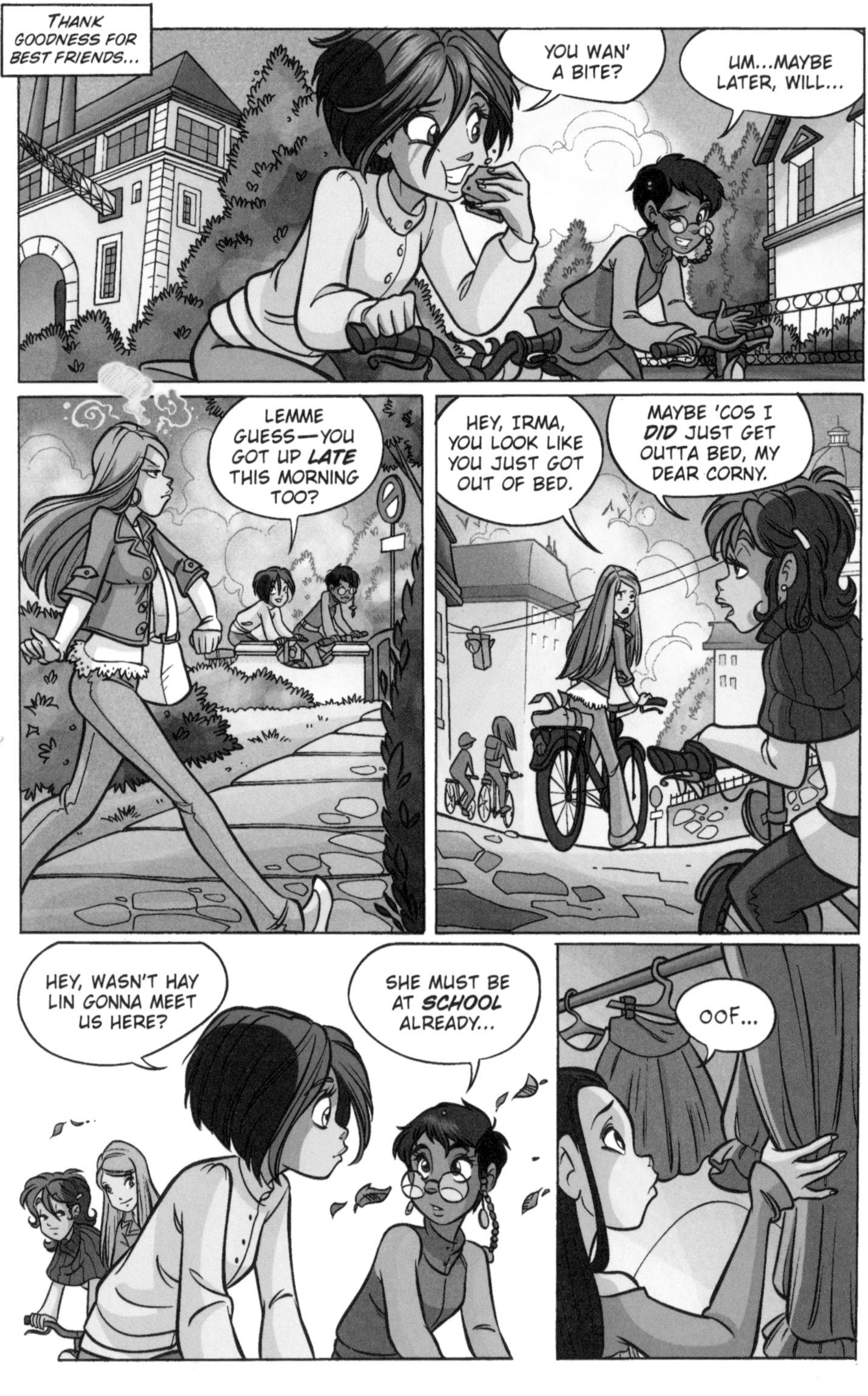
THANK GOODNESS FOR BEST FRIENDS...
YOU WAN' A BITE?
UM...MAYBE LATER, WILL...
LEMME GUESS—YOU GOT UP LATE THIS MORNING TOO?
HEY, IRMA, YOU LOOK LIKE YOU JUST GOT OUT OF BED.
MAYBE 'COS I DID JUST GET OUTTA BED, MY DEAR CORNY.
HEY, WASN'T HAY LIN GONNA MEET US HERE?
SHE MUST BE AT SCHOOL ALREADY...
OOF...

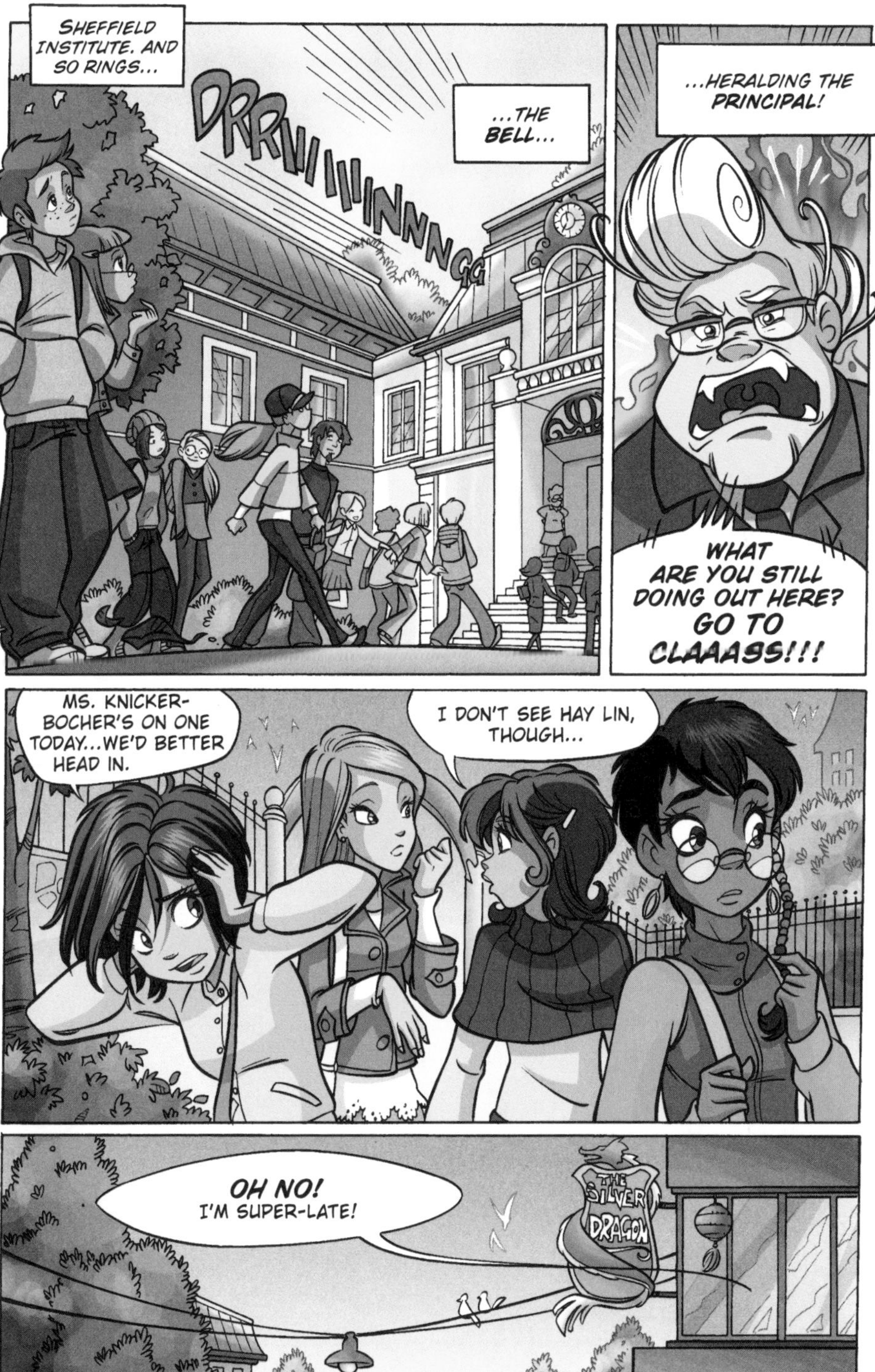
SHEFFIELD INSTITUTE. AND SO RINGS...
DRRWIIIIINNNNGG
...THE BELL...
...HERALDING THE PRINCIPAL!
WHAT ARE YOU STILL DOING OUT HERE? GO TO CLAAASS!!!
MS. KNICKER-BOCHER'S ON ONE TODAY...WE'D BETTER HEAD IN.
I DON'T SEE HAY LIN, THOUGH...
OH NO! I'M SUPER-LATE!
THE SILVER DRAGON

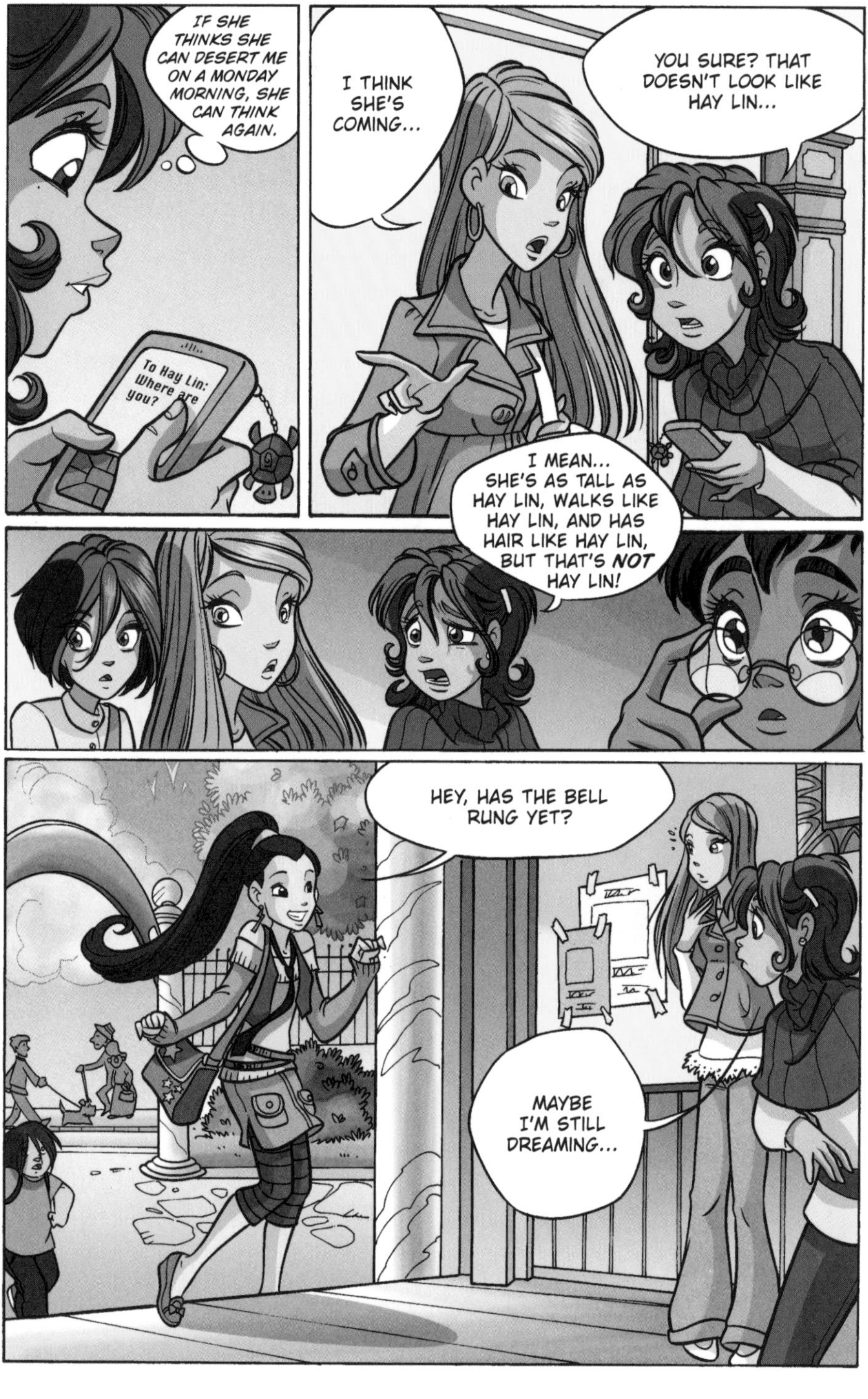
IF SHE THINKS SHE CAN DESERT ME ON A MONDAY MORNING, SHE CAN THINK AGAIN.
To Hay Lin: Where are you?
I THINK SHE'S COMING...
YOU SURE? THAT DOESN'T LOOK LIKE HAY LIN...
I MEAN... SHE'S AS TALL AS HAY LIN, WALKS LIKE HAY LIN, AND HAS HAIR LIKE HAY LIN, BUT THAT'S **NOT** HAY LIN!
HEY, HAS THE BELL RUNG YET?
MAYBE I'M STILL DREAMING...

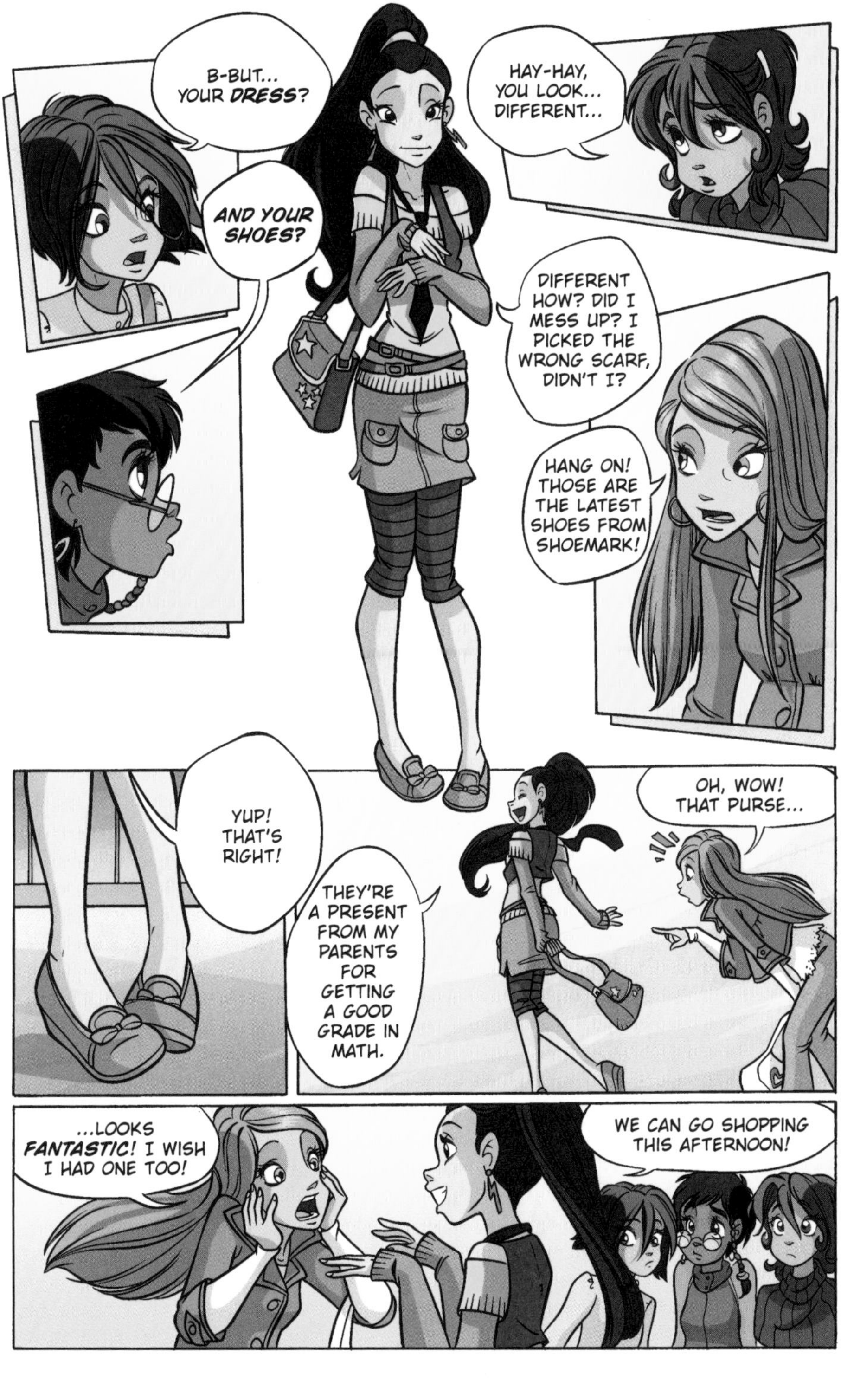
B-BUT... YOUR DRESS?
HAY-HAY, YOU LOOK... DIFFERENT...
AND YOUR SHOES?
DIFFERENT HOW? DID I MESS UP? I PICKED THE WRONG SCARF, DIDN'T I?
HANG ON! THOSE ARE THE LATEST SHOES FROM SHOEMARK!
YUP! THAT'S RIGHT!
THEY'RE A PRESENT FROM MY PARENTS FOR GETTING A GOOD GRADE IN MATH.
OH, WOW! THAT PURSE...
...LOOKS FANTASTIC! I WISH I HAD ONE TOO!
WE CAN GO SHOPPING THIS AFTERNOON!

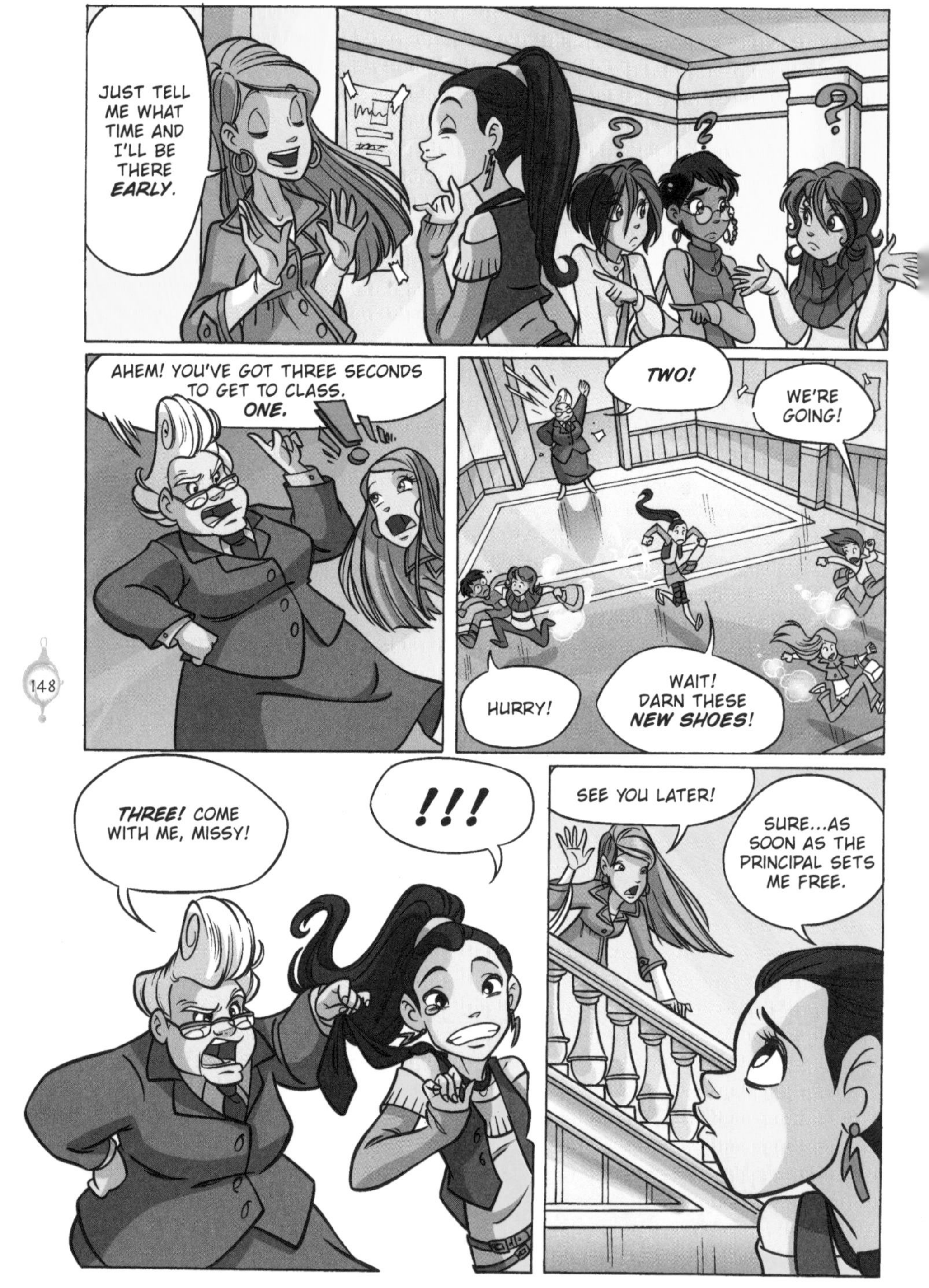

JUST TELL ME WHAT TIME AND I'LL BE THERE *EARLY*.
AHEM! YOU'VE GOT THREE SECONDS TO GET TO CLASS. *ONE.*
TWO!
WE'RE GOING!
HURRY!
WAIT! DARN THESE *NEW SHOES*!
THREE! COME WITH ME, MISSY!
!!!
SEE YOU LATER!
SURE...AS SOON AS THE PRINCIPAL SETS ME FREE.

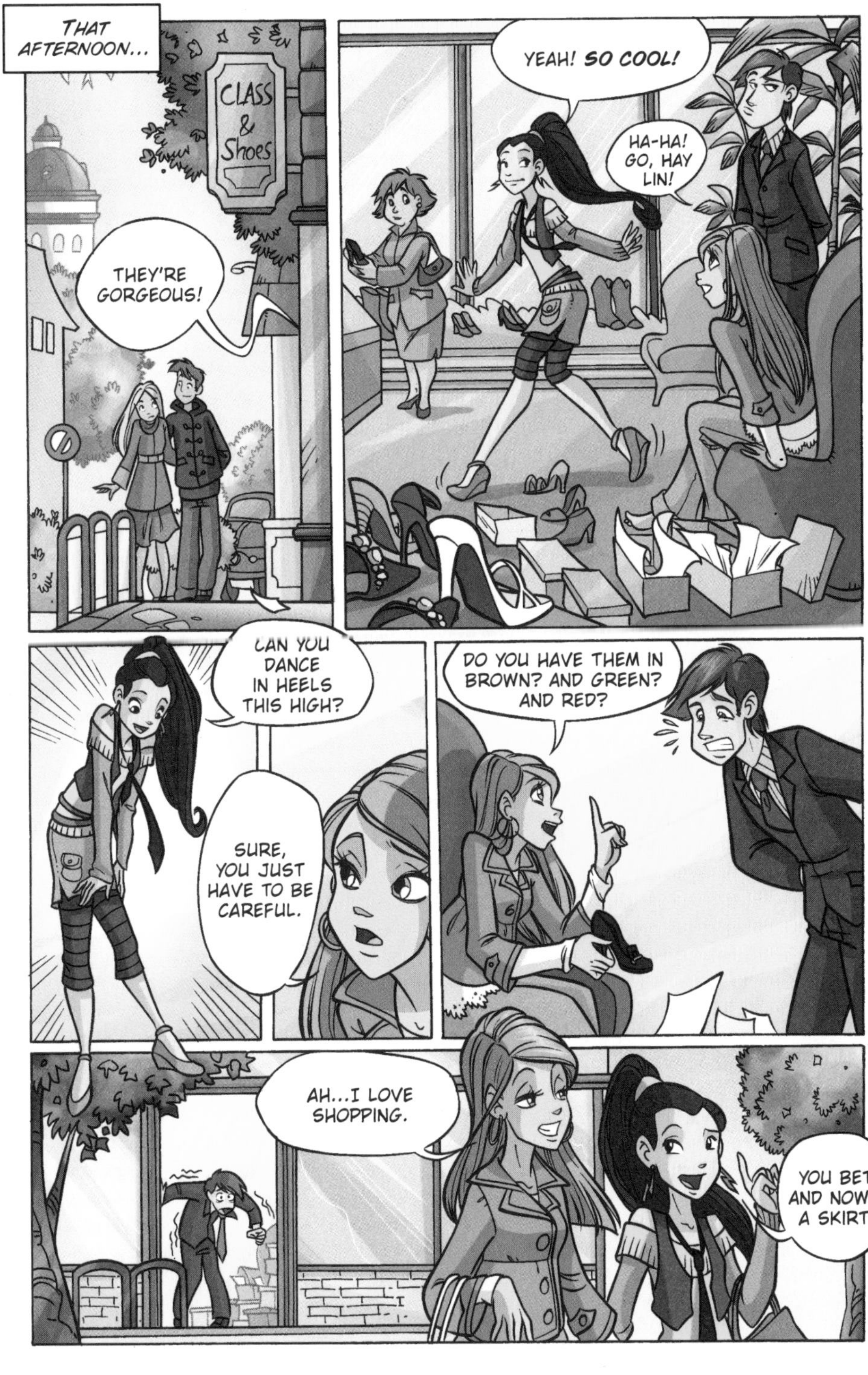
THAT AFTERNOON...
CLASS & Shoes
THEY'RE GORGEOUS!
YEAH! SO COOL!
HA-HA! GO, HAY LIN!
CAN YOU DANCE IN HEELS THIS HIGH?
SURE, YOU JUST HAVE TO BE CAREFUL.
DO YOU HAVE THEM IN BROWN? AND GREEN? AND RED?
AH...I LOVE SHOPPING.
YOU BET. AND NOW... A SKIRT!

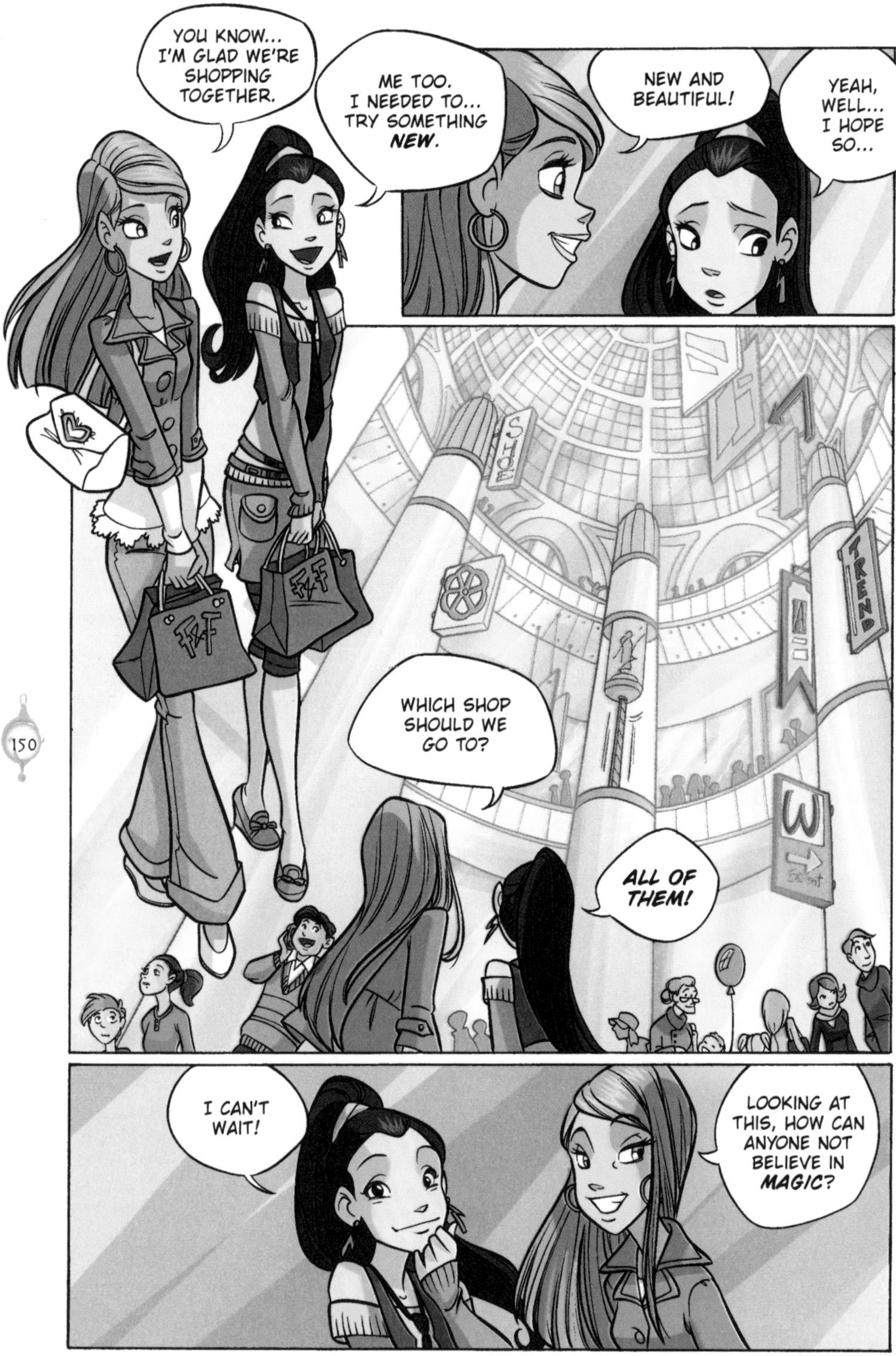
YOU KNOW... I'M GLAD WE'RE SHOPPING TOGETHER.
ME TOO. I NEEDED TO... TRY SOMETHING **NEW**.
NEW AND BEAUTIFUL!
YEAH, WELL... I HOPE SO...
SHOE
TREND
WHICH SHOP SHOULD WE GO TO?
W
ALL OF THEM!
I CAN'T WAIT!
LOOKING AT THIS, HOW CAN ANYONE NOT BELIEVE IN ***MAGIC***?

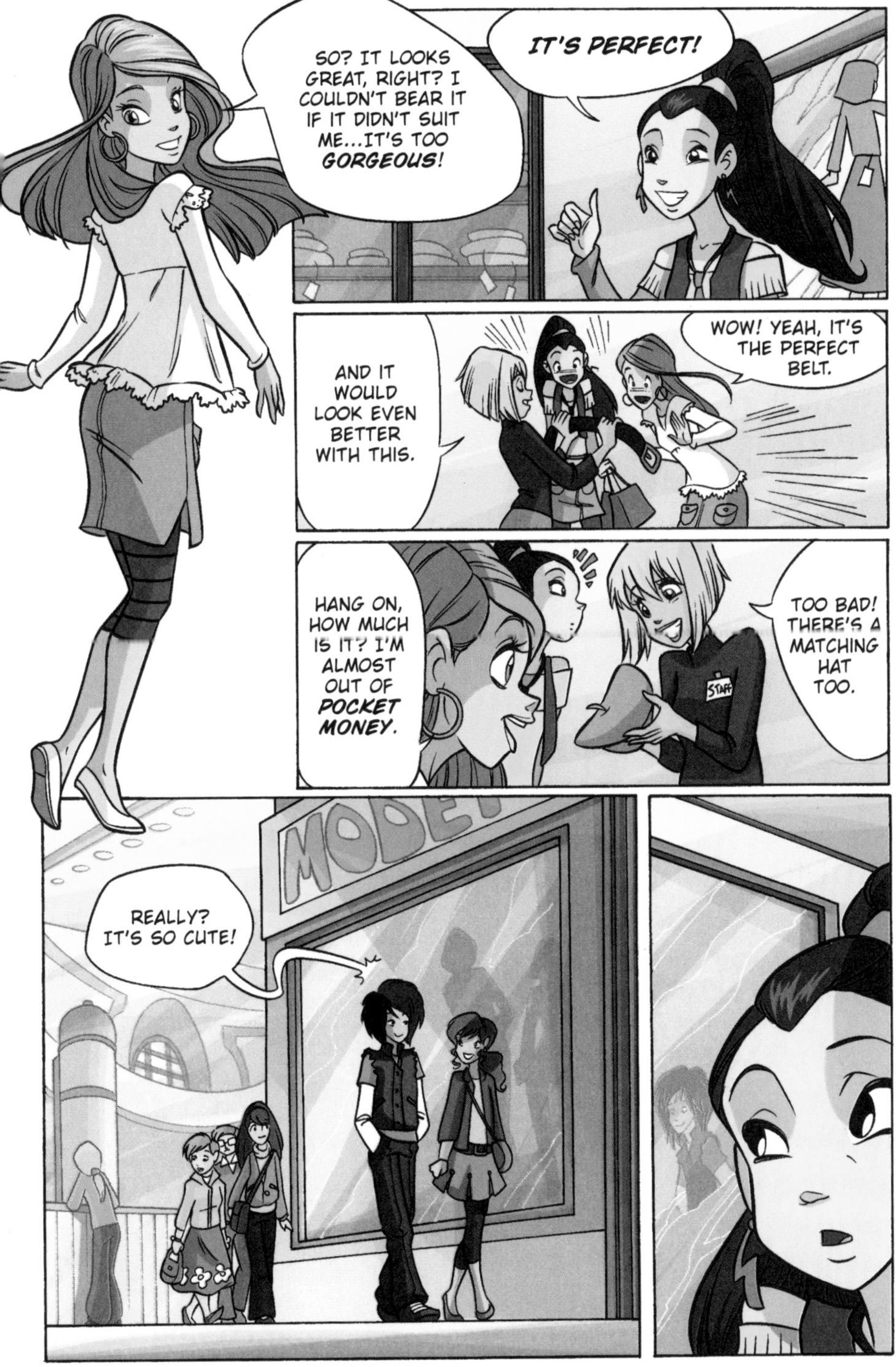
SO? IT LOOKS GREAT, RIGHT? I COULDN'T BEAR IT IF IT DIDN'T SUIT ME...IT'S TOO GORGEOUS!
IT'S PERFECT!
AND IT WOULD LOOK EVEN BETTER WITH THIS.
WOW! YEAH, IT'S THE PERFECT BELT.
HANG ON, HOW MUCH IS IT? I'M ALMOST OUT OF POCKET MONEY.
TOO BAD! THERE'S A MATCHING HAT TOO.
STAFF
MODE
REALLY? IT'S SO CUTE!

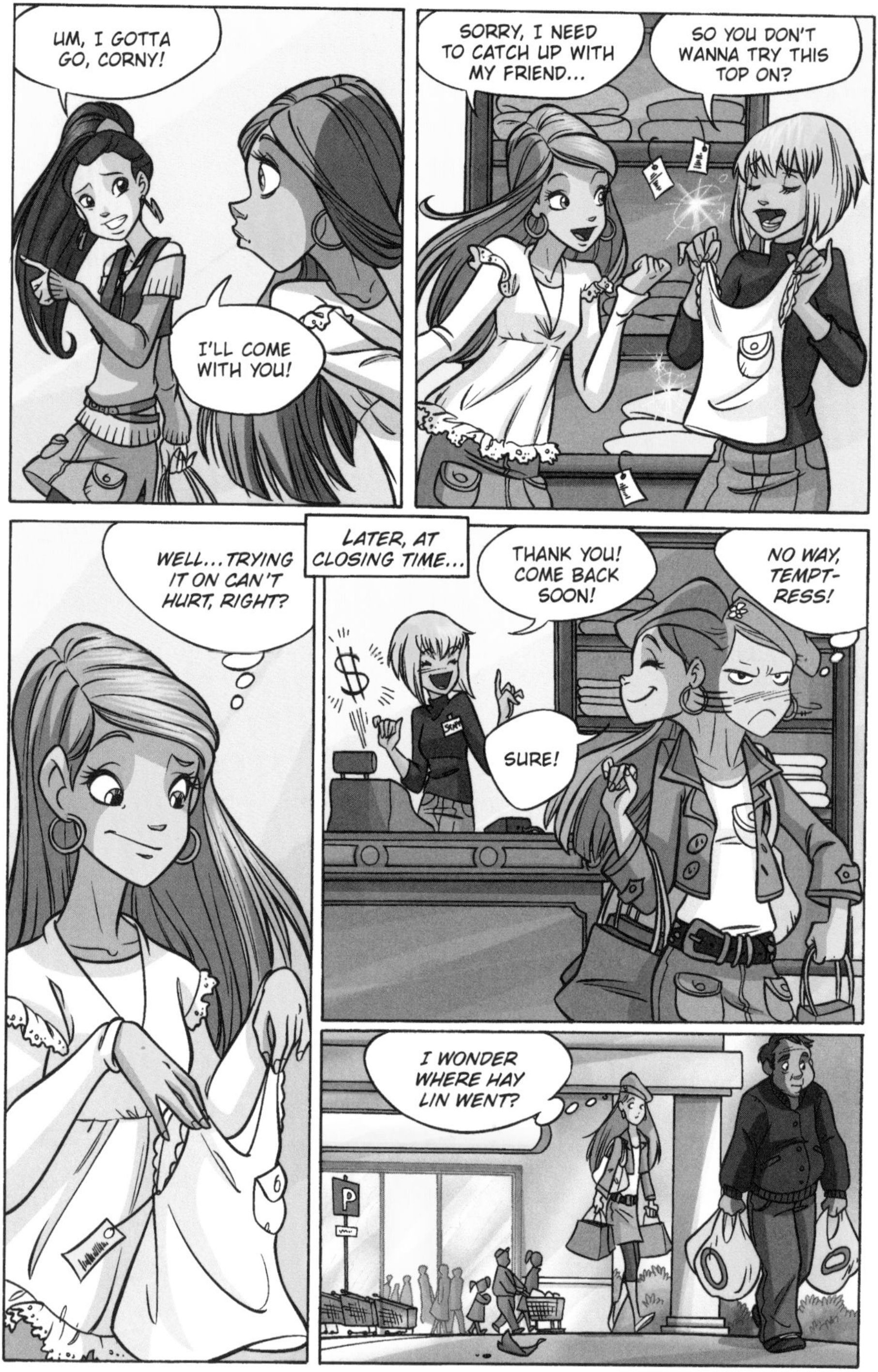
UM, I GOTTA GO, CORNY!
I'LL COME WITH YOU!
SORRY, I NEED TO CATCH UP WITH MY FRIEND...
SO YOU DON'T WANNA TRY THIS TOP ON?
WELL...TRYING IT ON CAN'T HURT, RIGHT?
LATER, AT CLOSING TIME...
THANK YOU! COME BACK SOON!
NO WAY, TEMPT-RESS!
SURE!
I WONDER WHERE HAY LIN WENT?

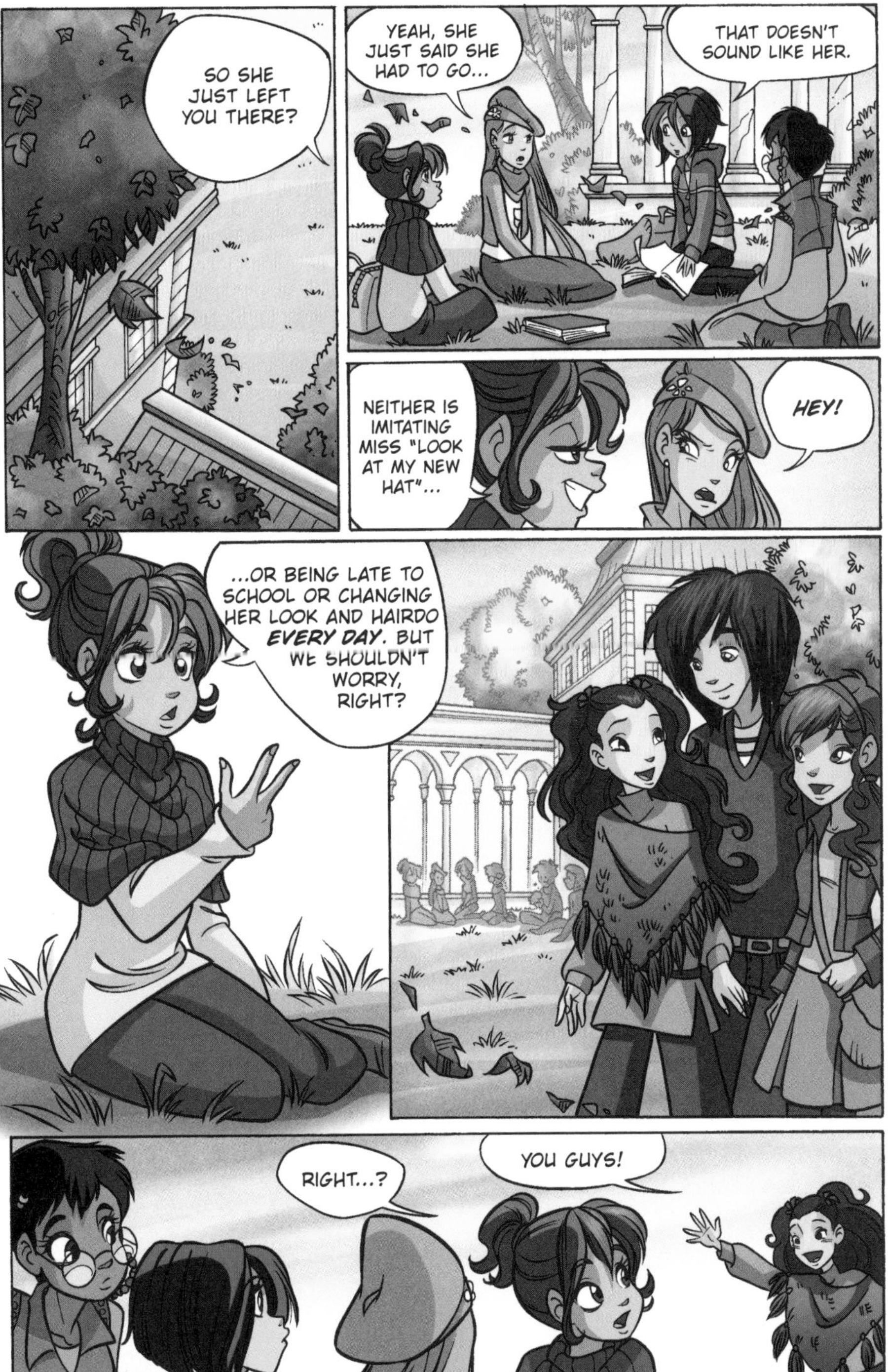
SO SHE JUST LEFT YOU THERE?
YEAH, SHE JUST SAID SHE HAD TO GO...
THAT DOESN'T SOUND LIKE HER.
NEITHER IS IMITATING MISS "LOOK AT MY NEW HAT"...
HEY!
...OR BEING LATE TO SCHOOL OR CHANGING HER LOOK AND HAIRDO EVERY DAY. BUT WE SHOULDN'T WORRY, RIGHT?
RIGHT...?
YOU GUYS!

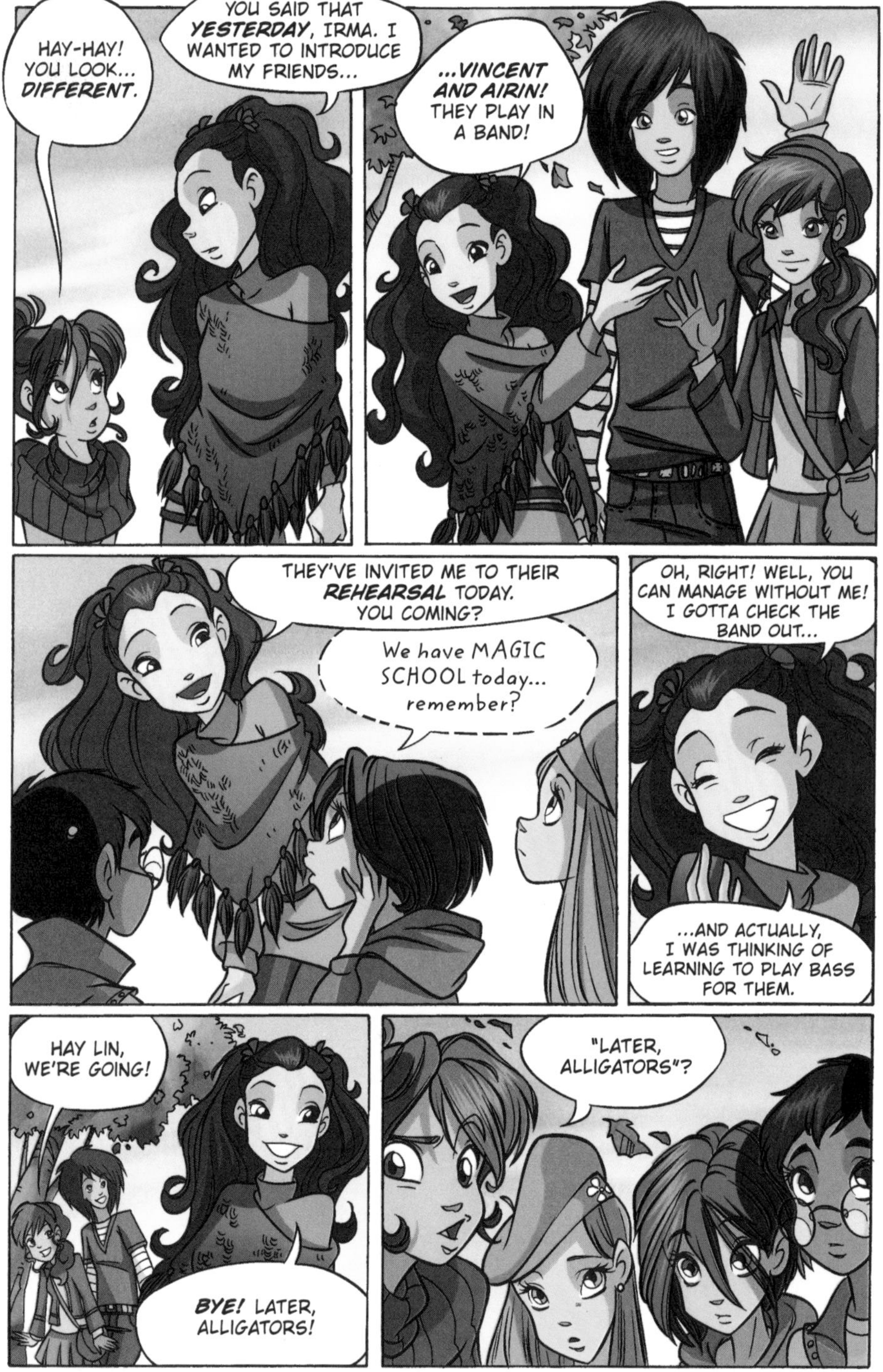
HAY-HAY! YOU LOOK... DIFFERENT.
YOU SAID THAT YESTERDAY, IRMA. I WANTED TO INTRODUCE MY FRIENDS...
...VINCENT AND AIRIN! THEY PLAY IN A BAND!
THEY'VE INVITED ME TO THEIR REHEARSAL TODAY. YOU COMING?
We have MAGIC SCHOOL today... remember?
OH, RIGHT! WELL, YOU CAN MANAGE WITHOUT ME! I GOTTA CHECK THE BAND OUT...
...AND ACTUALLY, I WAS THINKING OF LEARNING TO PLAY BASS FOR THEM.
HAY LIN, WE'RE GOING!
BYE! LATER, ALLIGATORS!
"LATER, ALLIGATORS"?

DON'T YOU **SEE**?

IT LOOKS **TERRIBLE**!

BUT IT'S YOUR FAVORITE DRESS!

IT **WAS**, MOM. I HATE IT NOW, AND ALL THE OTHERS TOO.

I HAVE A REHEARSAL TO GO TO...

...AND I'VE GOT **NOTHING** TO WEAR!

MAYBE WE SHOULD'VE OPENED A BOUTIQUE, NOT A RESTAURANT...

LEAVE IT TO ME... HUH?

Sheffield Inst.
Astronomy, the
science of stars

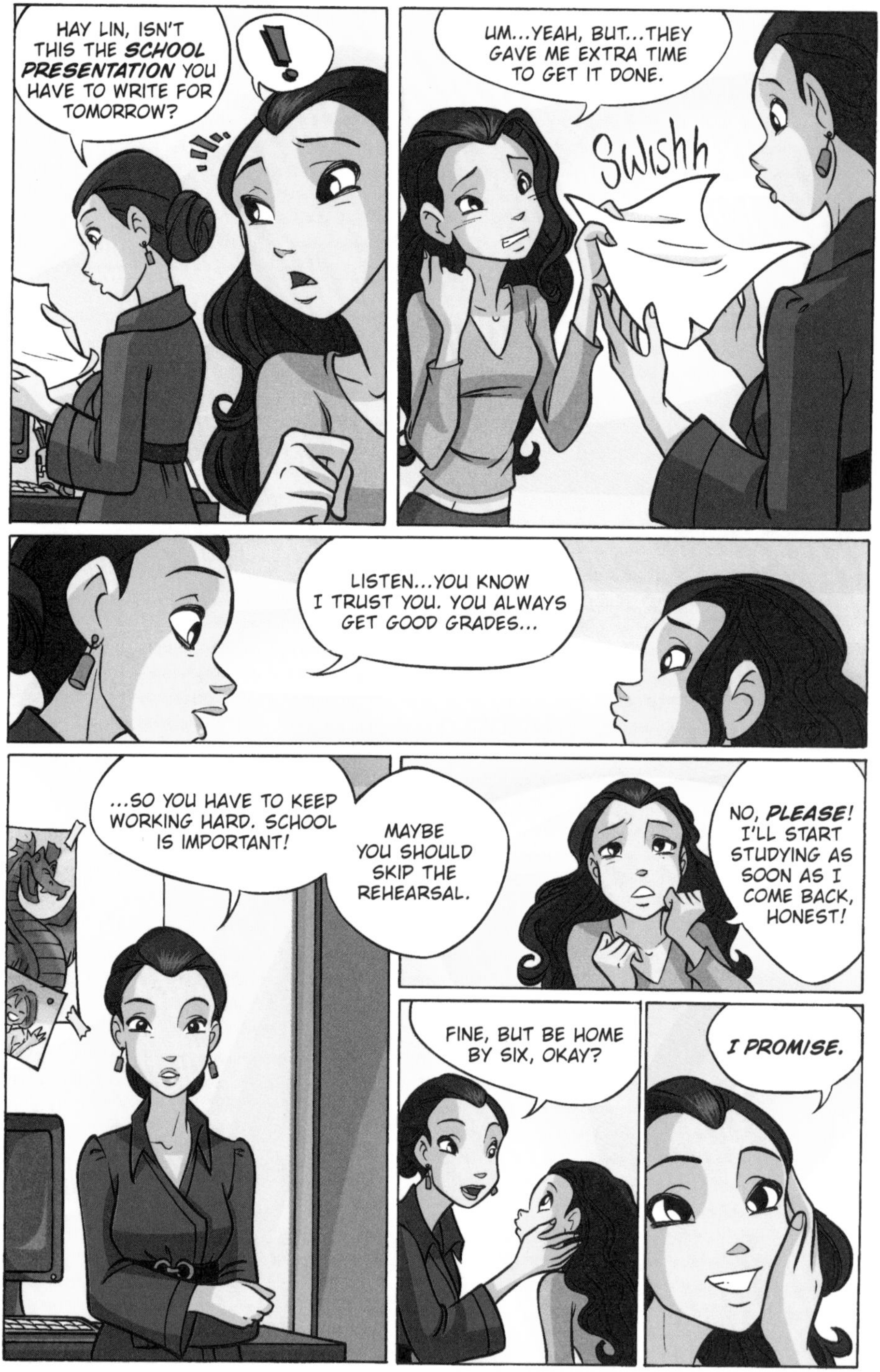
HAY LIN, ISN'T THIS THE SCHOOL PRESENTATION YOU HAVE TO WRITE FOR TOMORROW?
!
UM...YEAH, BUT...THEY GAVE ME EXTRA TIME TO GET IT DONE.
SWISHH
LISTEN...YOU KNOW I TRUST YOU. YOU ALWAYS GET GOOD GRADES...
...SO YOU HAVE TO KEEP WORKING HARD. SCHOOL IS IMPORTANT!
MAYBE YOU SHOULD SKIP THE REHEARSAL.
NO, PLEASE! I'LL START STUDYING AS SOON AS I COME BACK, HONEST!
FINE, BUT BE HOME BY SIX, OKAY?
I PROMISE.

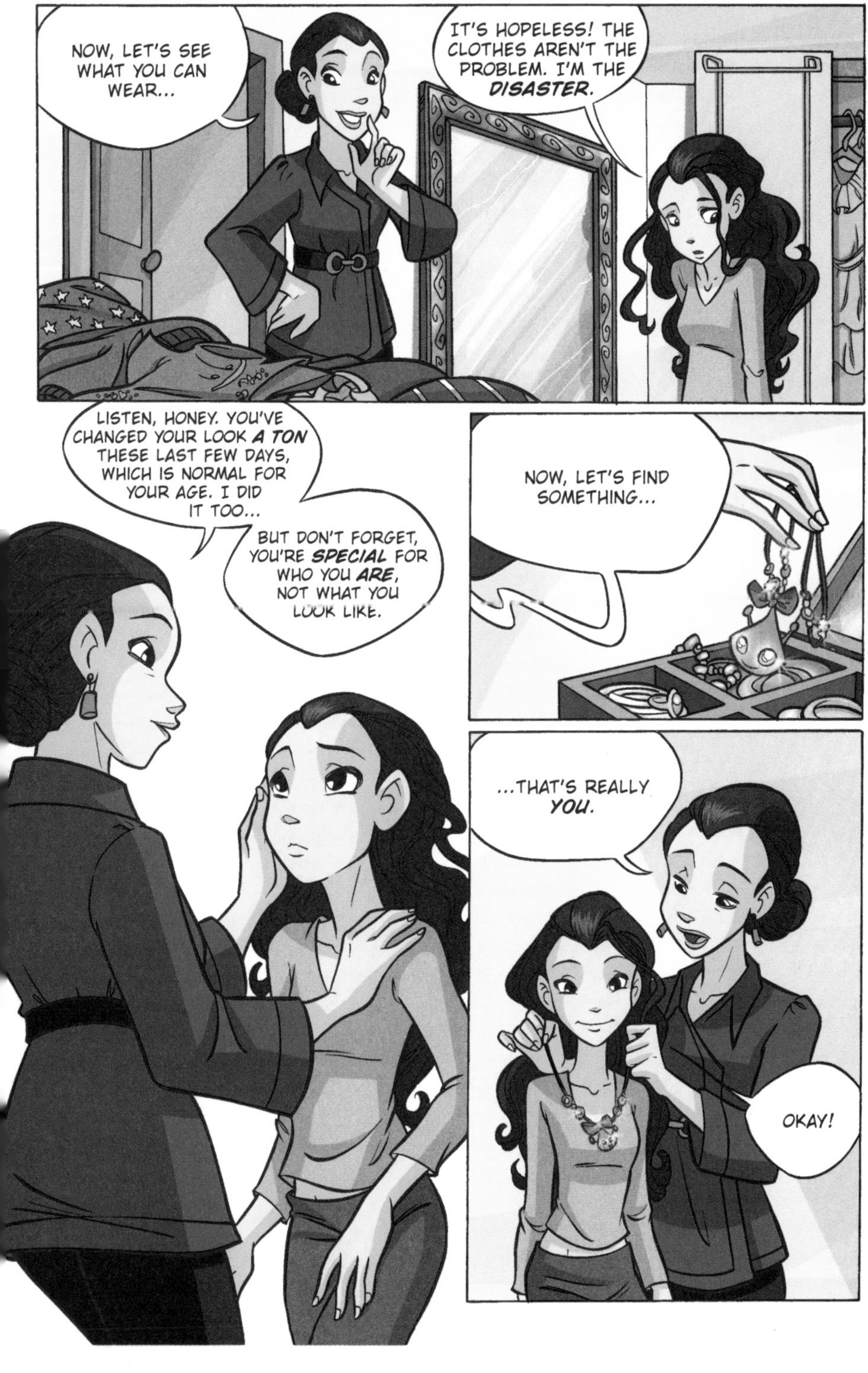
NOW, LET'S SEE WHAT YOU CAN WEAR...
IT'S HOPELESS! THE CLOTHES AREN'T THE PROBLEM. I'M THE DISASTER.
LISTEN, HONEY. YOU'VE CHANGED YOUR LOOK A TON THESE LAST FEW DAYS, WHICH IS NORMAL FOR YOUR AGE. I DID IT TOO...
BUT DON'T FORGET, YOU'RE SPECIAL FOR WHO YOU ARE, NOT WHAT YOU LOOK LIKE.
NOW, LET'S FIND SOMETHING...
...THAT'S REALLY YOU.
OKAY!

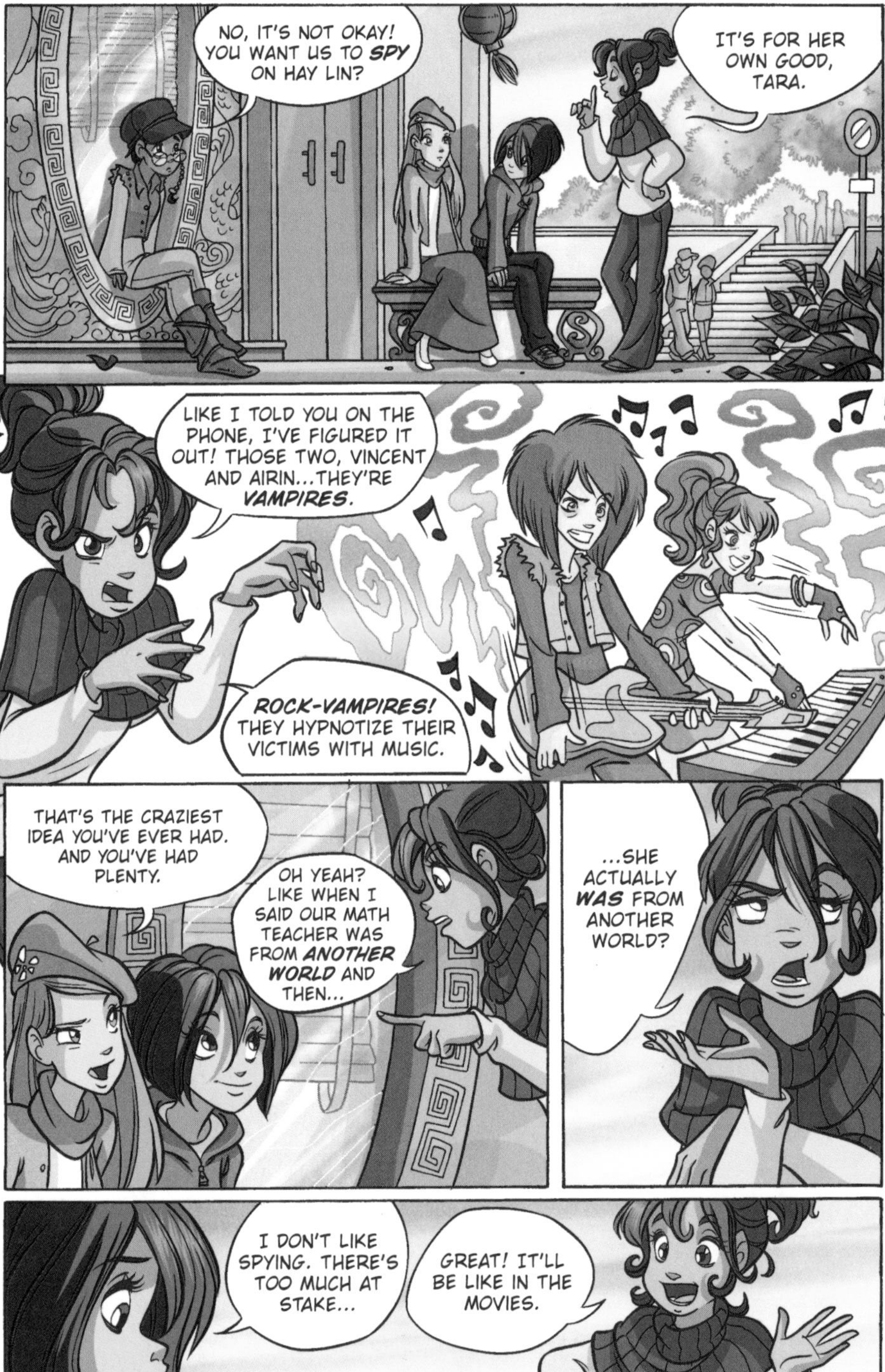
NO, IT'S NOT OKAY! YOU WANT US TO SPY ON HAY LIN?
IT'S FOR HER OWN GOOD, TARA.
LIKE I TOLD YOU ON THE PHONE, I'VE FIGURED IT OUT! THOSE TWO, VINCENT AND AIRIN...THEY'RE VAMPIRES.
ROCK-VAMPIRES! THEY HYPNOTIZE THEIR VICTIMS WITH MUSIC.
THAT'S THE CRAZIEST IDEA YOU'VE EVER HAD. AND YOU'VE HAD PLENTY.
OH YEAH? LIKE WHEN I SAID OUR MATH TEACHER WAS FROM ANOTHER WORLD AND THEN...
...SHE ACTUALLY WAS FROM ANOTHER WORLD?
I DON'T LIKE SPYING. THERE'S TOO MUCH AT STAKE...
GREAT! IT'LL BE LIKE IN THE MOVIES.

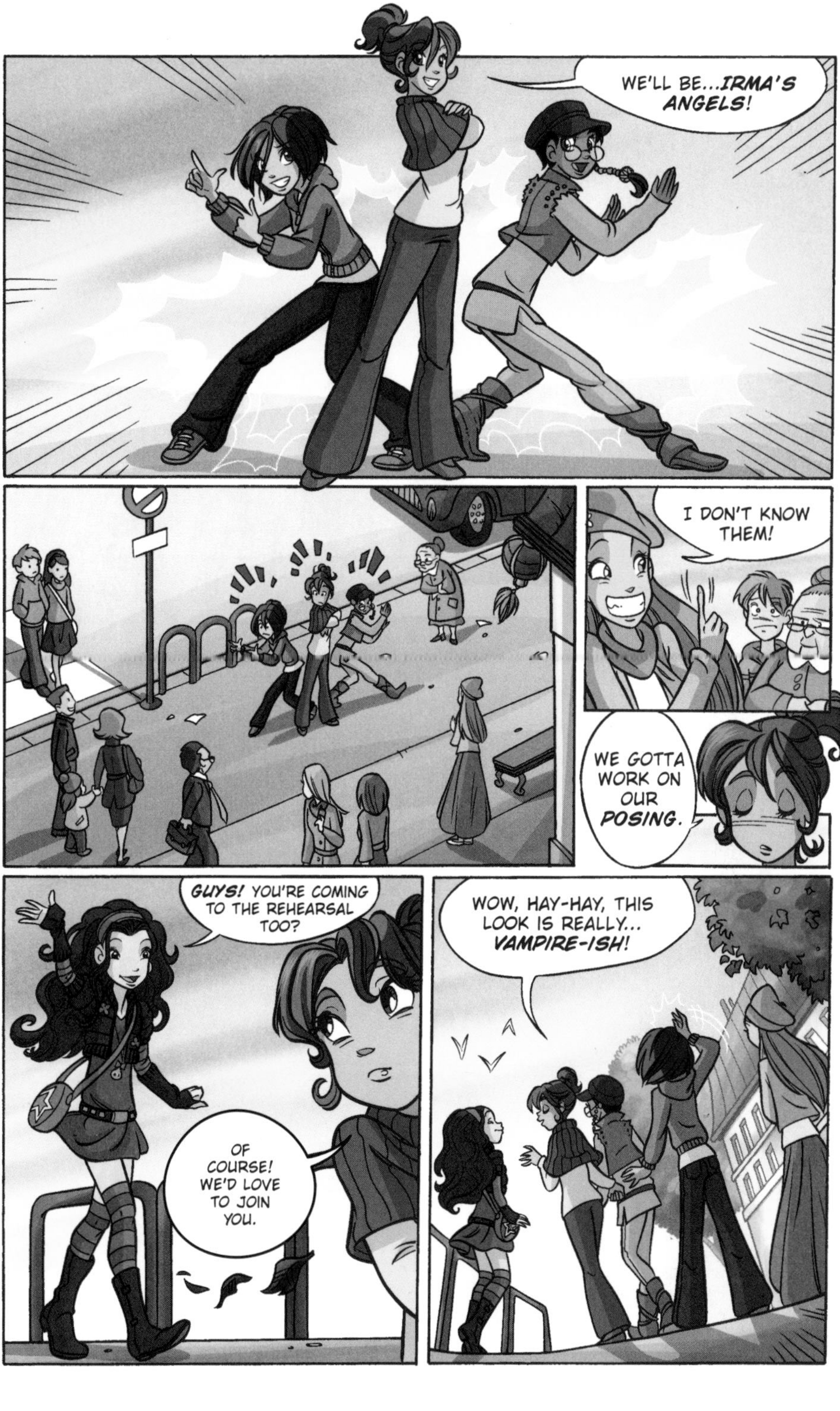
WE'LL BE...IRMA'S ANGELS!
I DON'T KNOW THEM!
WE GOTTA WORK ON OUR POSING.
GUYS! YOU'RE COMING TO THE REHEARSAL TOO?
OF COURSE! WE'D LOVE TO JOIN YOU.
WOW, HAY-HAY, THIS LOOK IS REALLY... VAMPIRE-ISH!

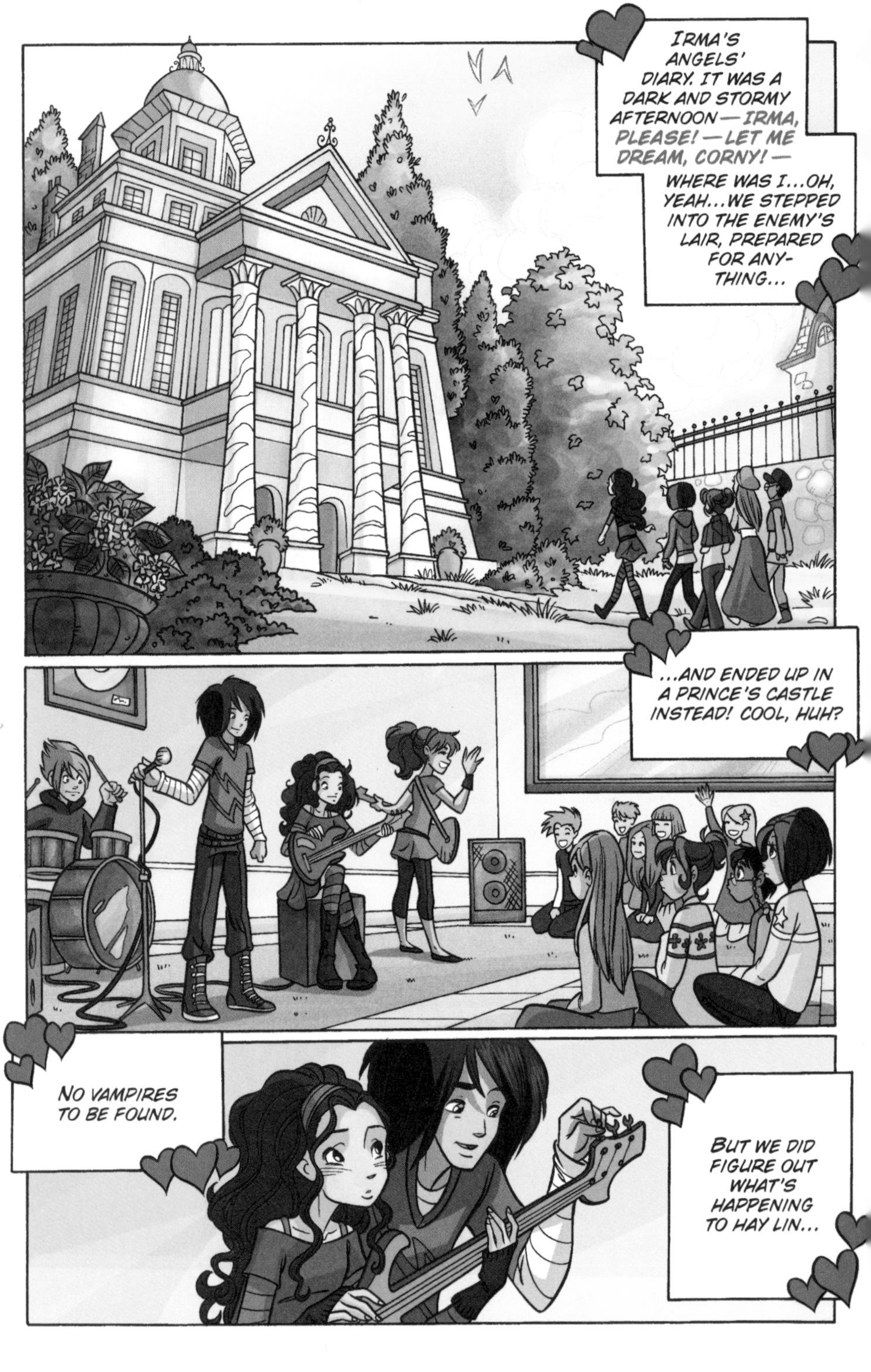
IRMA'S ANGELS' DIARY. IT WAS A DARK AND STORMY AFTERNOON—IRMA, PLEASE!—LET ME DREAM, CORNY!—
WHERE WAS I...OH, YEAH...WE STEPPED INTO THE ENEMY'S LAIR, PREPARED FOR ANYTHING...
...AND ENDED UP IN A PRINCE'S CASTLE INSTEAD! COOL, HUH?
NO VAMPIRES TO BE FOUND.
BUT WE DID FIGURE OUT WHAT'S HAPPENING TO HAY LIN...

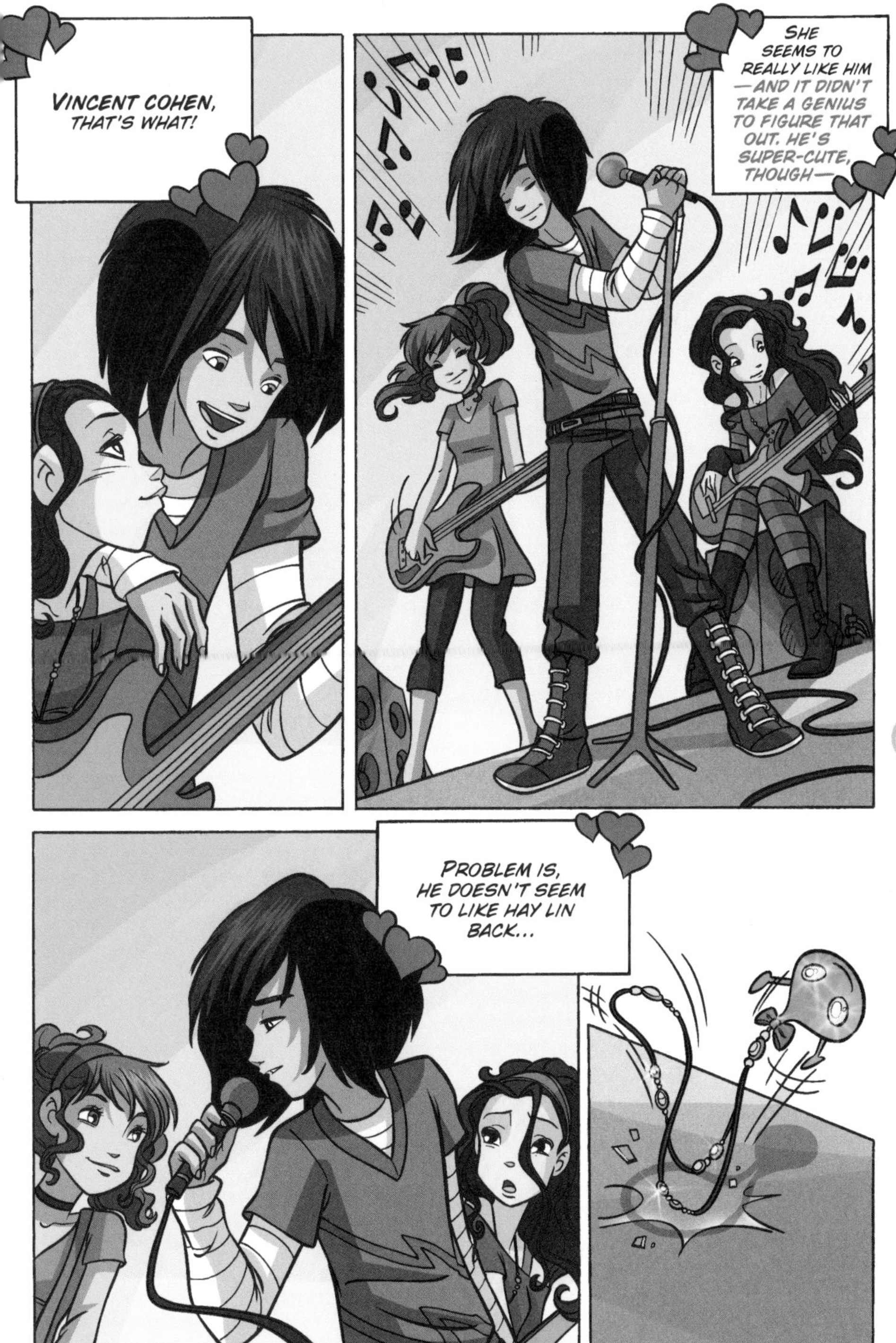
VINCENT COHEN, THAT'S WHAT!
SHE SEEMS TO REALLY LIKE HIM —AND IT DIDN'T TAKE A GENIUS TO FIGURE THAT OUT. HE'S SUPER-CUTE, THOUGH—
PROBLEM IS, HE DOESN'T SEEM TO LIKE HAY LIN BACK...

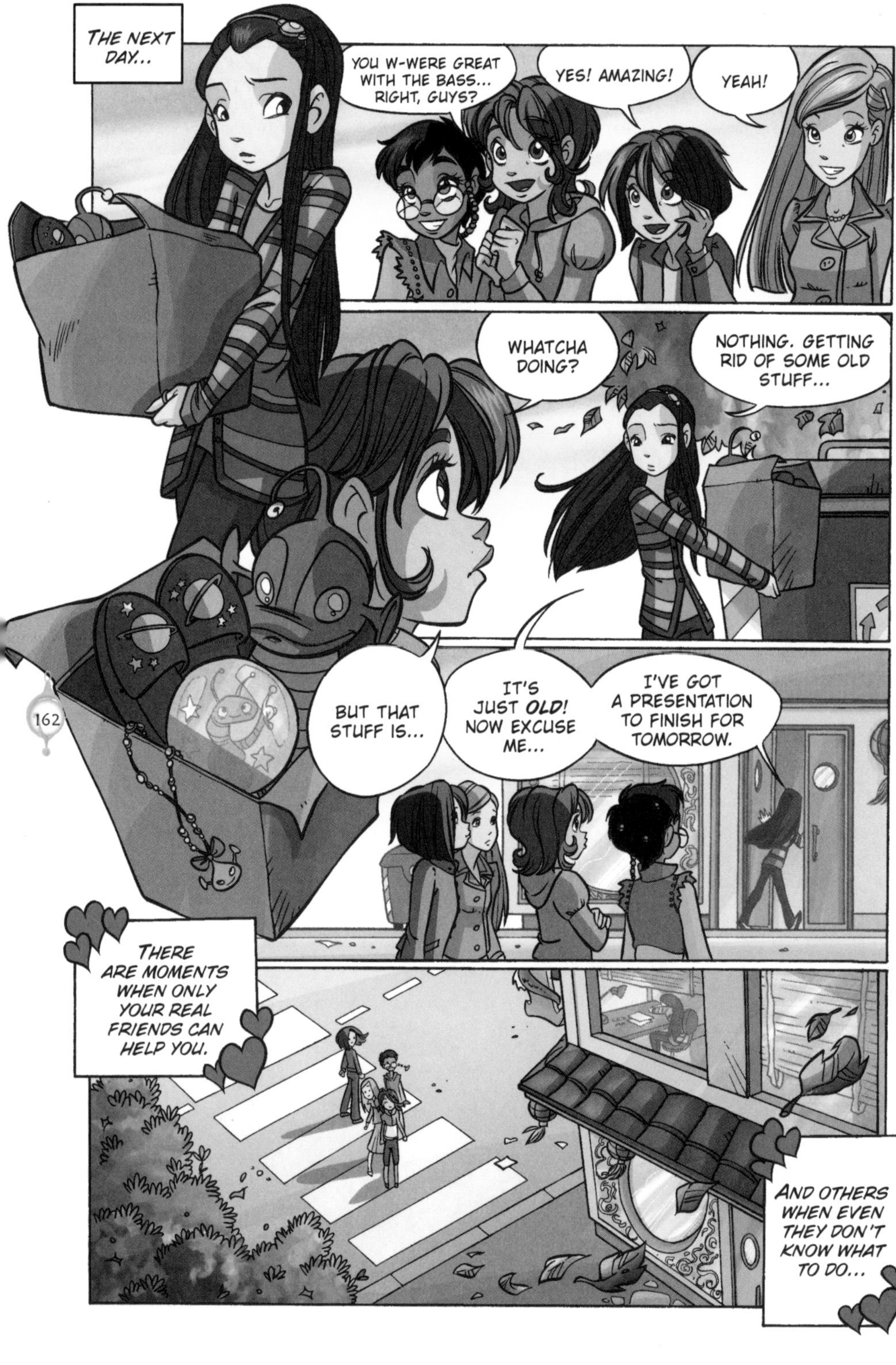
THE NEXT DAY...
YOU W-WERE GREAT WITH THE BASS... RIGHT, GUYS?
YES! AMAZING!
YEAH!
WHATCHA DOING?
NOTHING. GETTING RID OF SOME OLD STUFF...
BUT THAT STUFF IS...
IT'S JUST OLD! NOW EXCUSE ME...
I'VE GOT A PRESENTATION TO FINISH FOR TOMORROW.
THERE ARE MOMENTS WHEN ONLY YOUR REAL FRIENDS CAN HELP YOU.
AND OTHERS WHEN EVEN THEY DON'T KNOW WHAT TO DO...

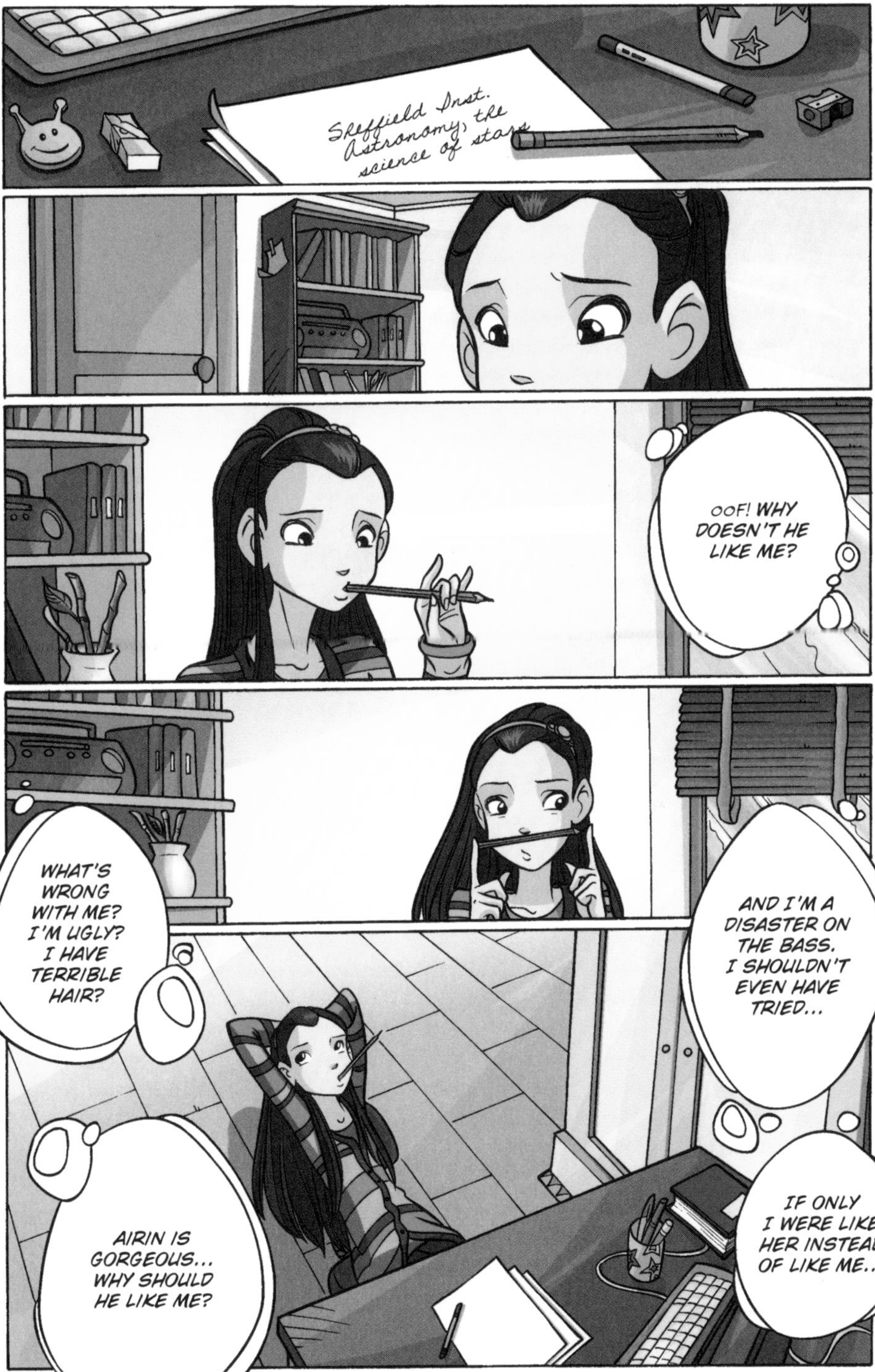
Sheffield Inst.
Astronomy, the science of stars
OOF! WHY DOESN'T HE LIKE ME?
WHAT'S WRONG WITH ME? I'M UGLY? I HAVE TERRIBLE HAIR?
AND I'M A DISASTER ON THE BASS. I SHOULDN'T EVEN HAVE TRIED...
AIRIN IS GORGEOUS... WHY SHOULD HE LIKE ME?
IF ONLY I WERE LIKE HER INSTEAD OF LIKE ME...

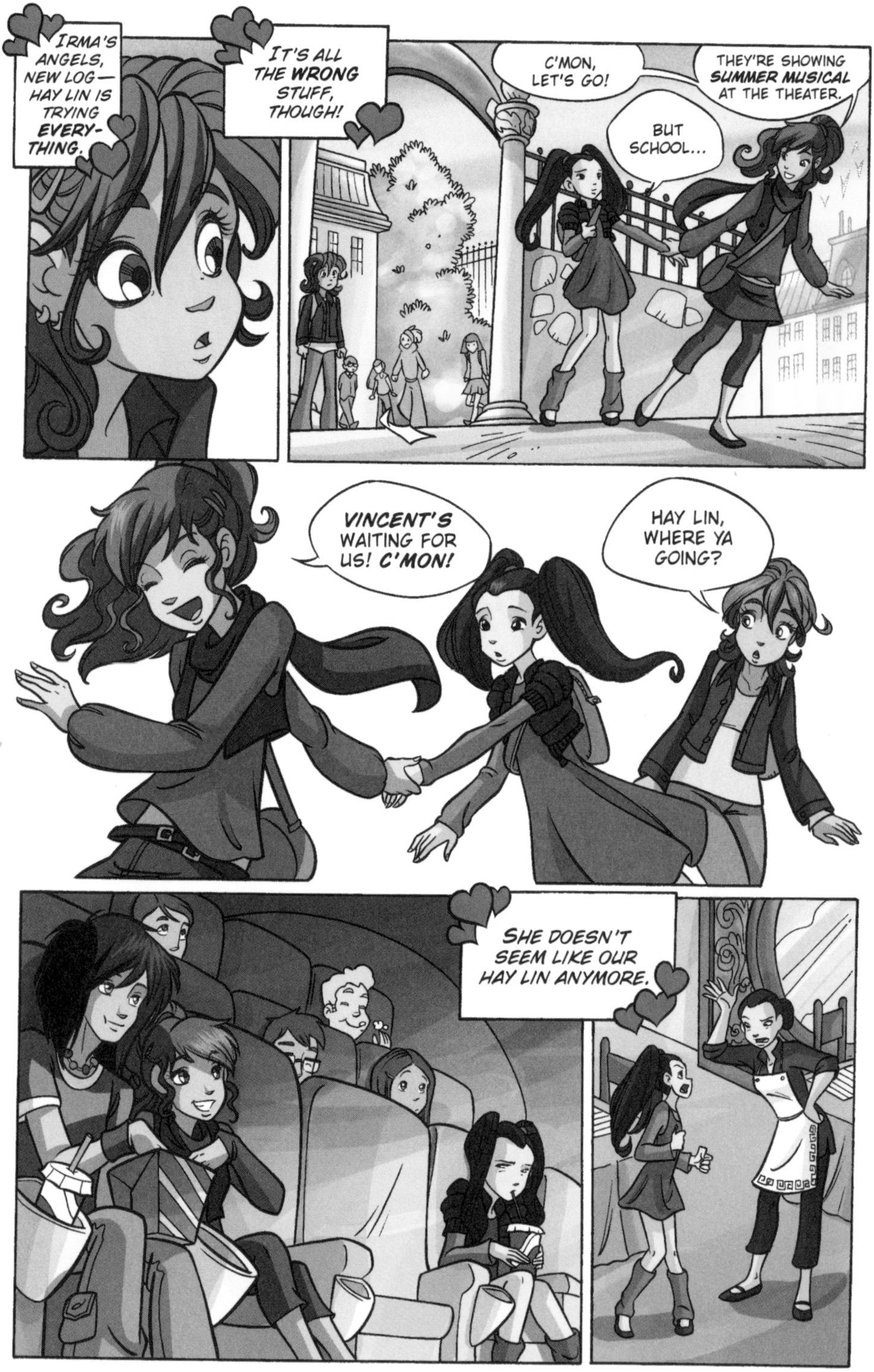
IRMA'S ANGELS, NEW LOG—HAY LIN IS TRYING EVERYTHING.
IT'S ALL THE WRONG STUFF, THOUGH!
C'MON, LET'S GO!
THEY'RE SHOWING SUMMER MUSICAL AT THE THEATER.
BUT SCHOOL...
VINCENT'S WAITING FOR US! C'MON!
HAY LIN, WHERE YA GOING?
SHE DOESN'T SEEM LIKE OUR HAY LIN ANYMORE.

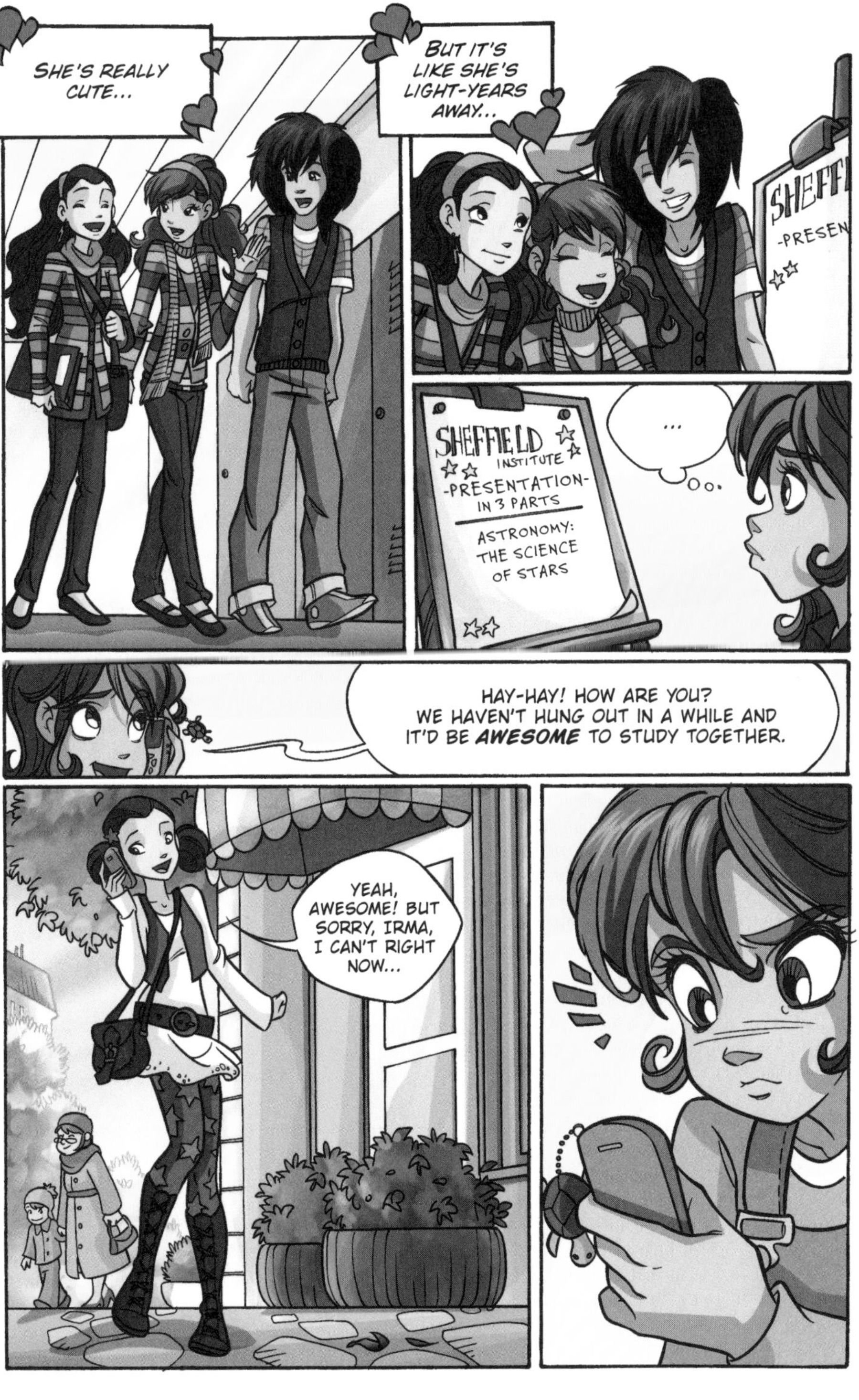
SHE'S REALLY CUTE...
BUT IT'S LIKE SHE'S LIGHT-YEARS AWAY...
SHEFFI
-PRESEN
SHEFFIELD INSTITUTE
-PRESENTATION-
IN 3 PARTS
ASTRONOMY: THE SCIENCE OF STARS
...
HAY-HAY! HOW ARE YOU? WE HAVEN'T HUNG OUT IN A WHILE AND IT'D BE ***AWESOME*** TO STUDY TOGETHER.
YEAH, AWESOME! BUT SORRY, IRMA, I CAN'T RIGHT NOW...

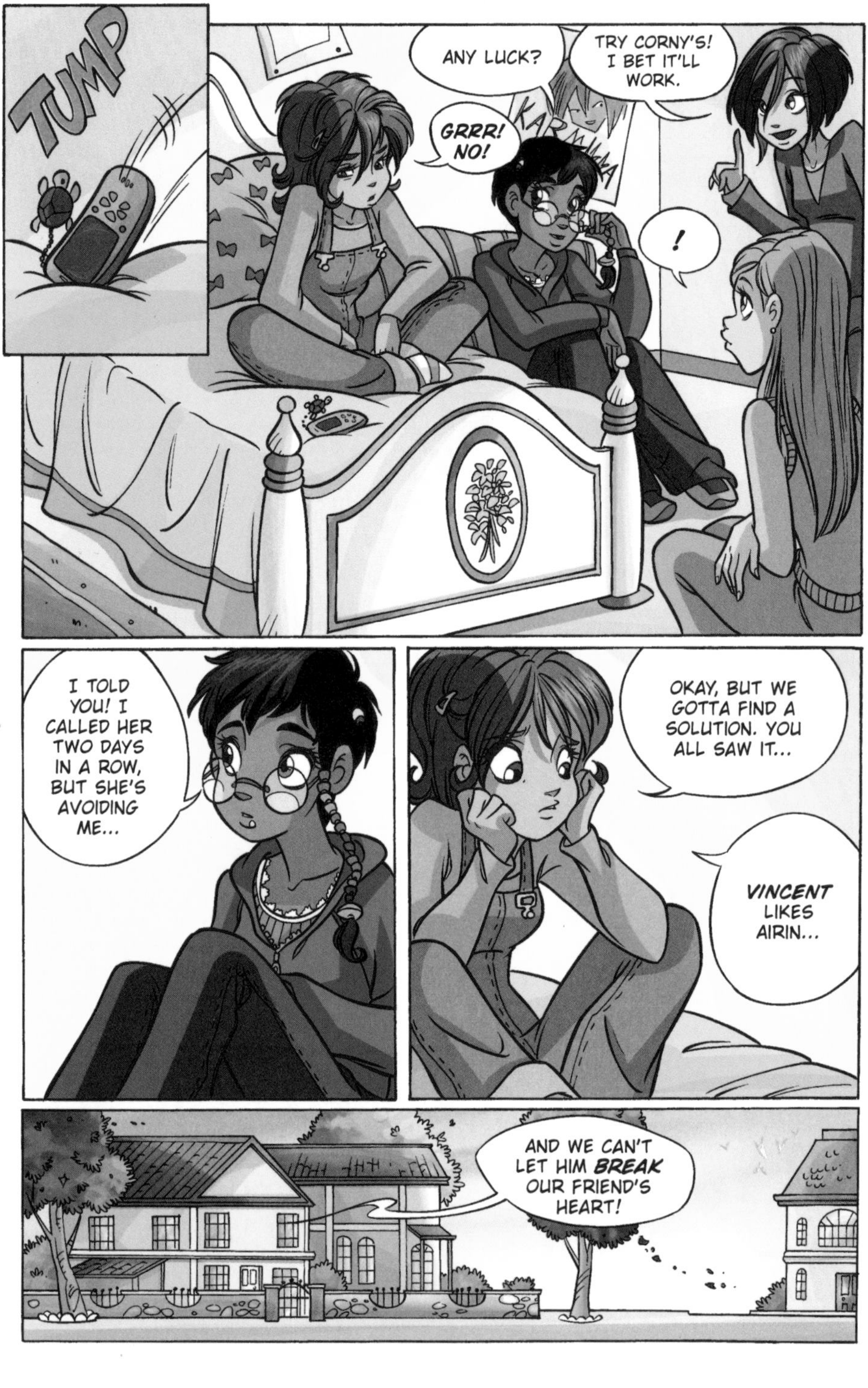
TUMP
ANY LUCK?
GRRR! NO!
TRY CORNY'S! I BET IT'LL WORK.
!
I TOLD YOU! I CALLED HER TWO DAYS IN A ROW, BUT SHE'S AVOIDING ME...
OKAY, BUT WE GOTTA FIND A SOLUTION. YOU ALL SAW IT...
VINCENT LIKES AIRIN...
AND WE CAN'T LET HIM BREAK OUR FRIEND'S HEART!

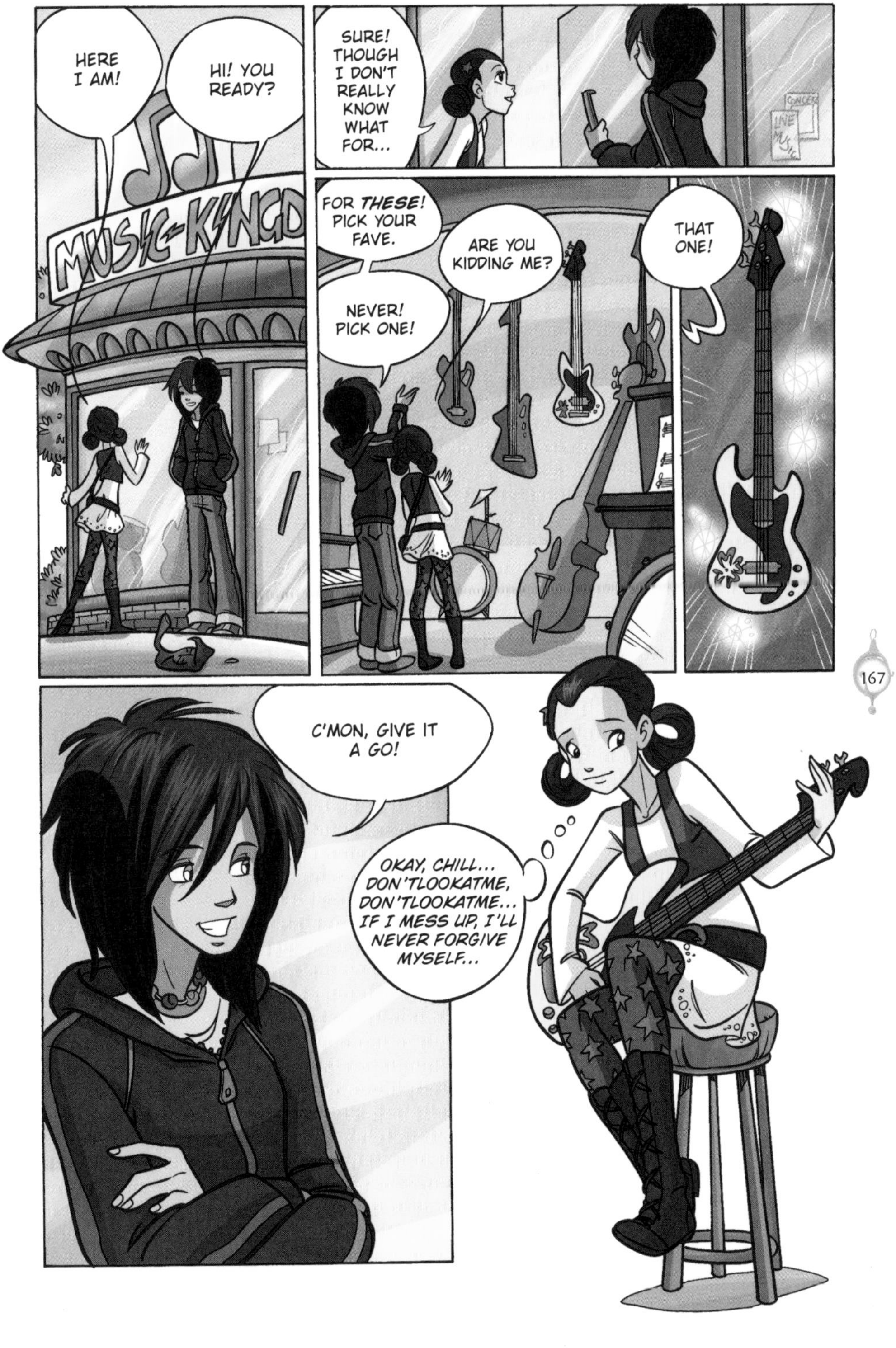
HERE I AM!
HI! YOU READY?
MUSIC KINGD
SURE! THOUGH I DON'T REALLY KNOW WHAT FOR...
CONCERT
LIVE MUSIC
FOR *THESE*! PICK YOUR FAVE.
ARE YOU KIDDING ME?
NEVER! PICK ONE!
THAT ONE!
C'MON, GIVE IT A GO!
OKAY, CHILL... DON'TLOOKATME, DON'TLOOKATME... IF I MESS UP, I'LL NEVER FORGIVE MYSELF...

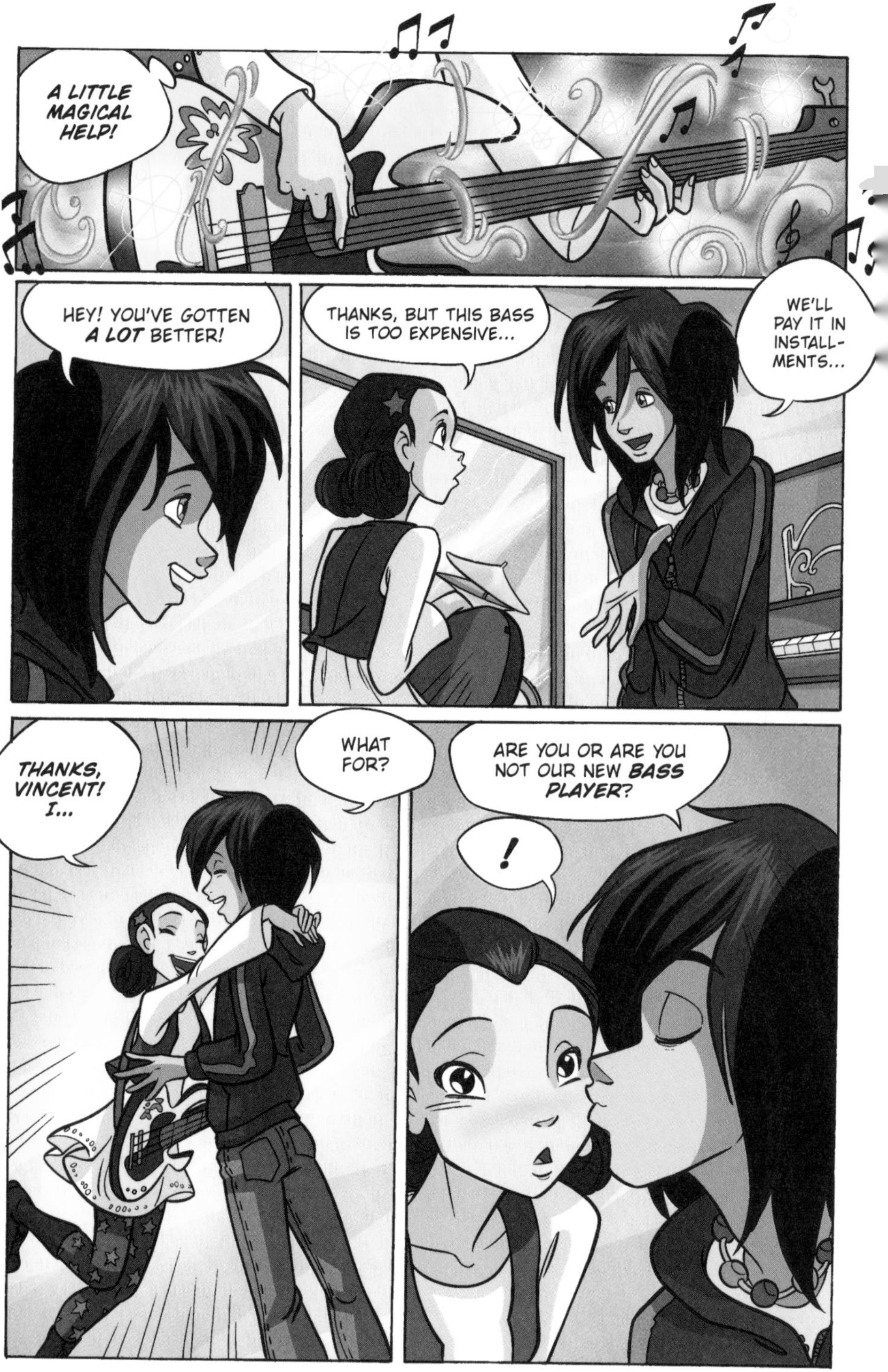
A LITTLE MAGICAL HELP!
HEY! YOU'VE GOTTEN A LOT BETTER!
THANKS, BUT THIS BASS IS TOO EXPENSIVE...
WE'LL PAY IT IN INSTALL-MENTS...
THANKS, VINCENT! I...
WHAT FOR?
ARE YOU OR ARE YOU NOT OUR NEW BASS PLAYER?
!

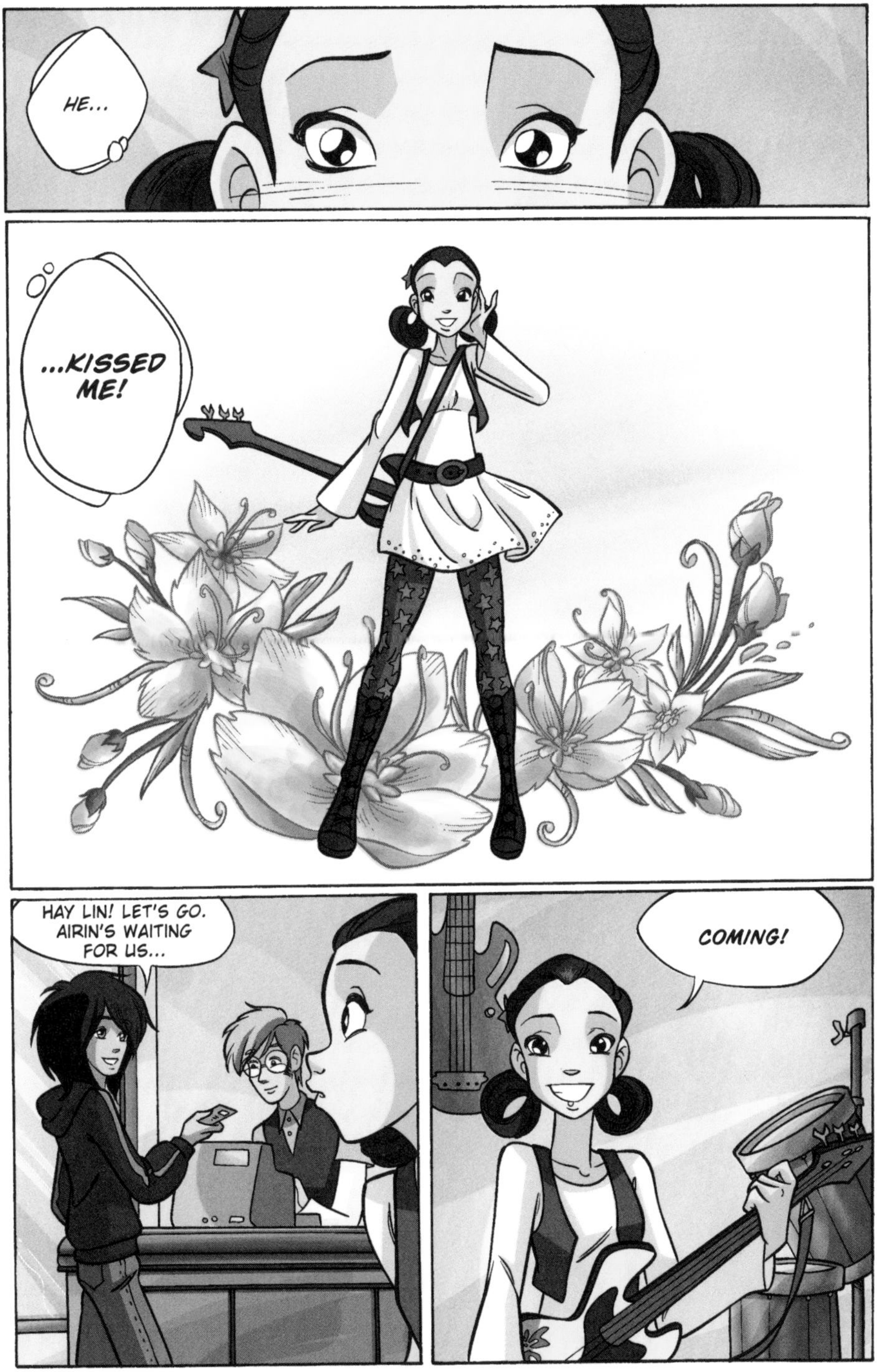
HE...
...KISSED ME!
HAY LIN! LET'S GO. AIRIN'S WAITING FOR US...
COMING!

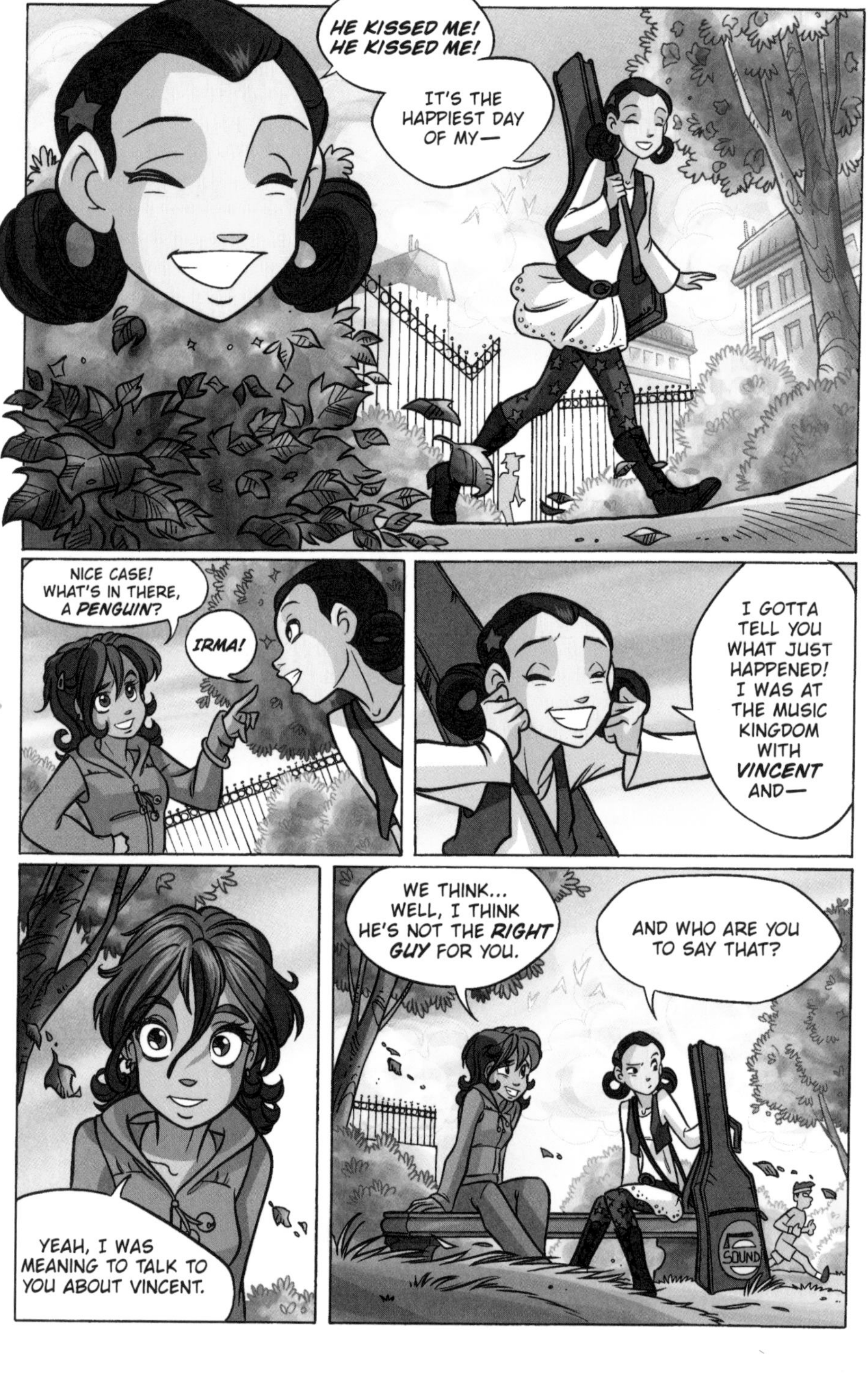

HE KISSED ME! HE KISSED ME!
IT'S THE HAPPIEST DAY OF MY—
NICE CASE! WHAT'S IN THERE, A PENGUIN?
IRMA!
I GOTTA TELL YOU WHAT JUST HAPPENED! I WAS AT THE MUSIC KINGDOM WITH VINCENT AND—
YEAH, I WAS MEANING TO TALK TO YOU ABOUT VINCENT.
WE THINK... WELL, I THINK HE'S NOT THE RIGHT GUY FOR YOU.
AND WHO ARE YOU TO SAY THAT?
SOUND

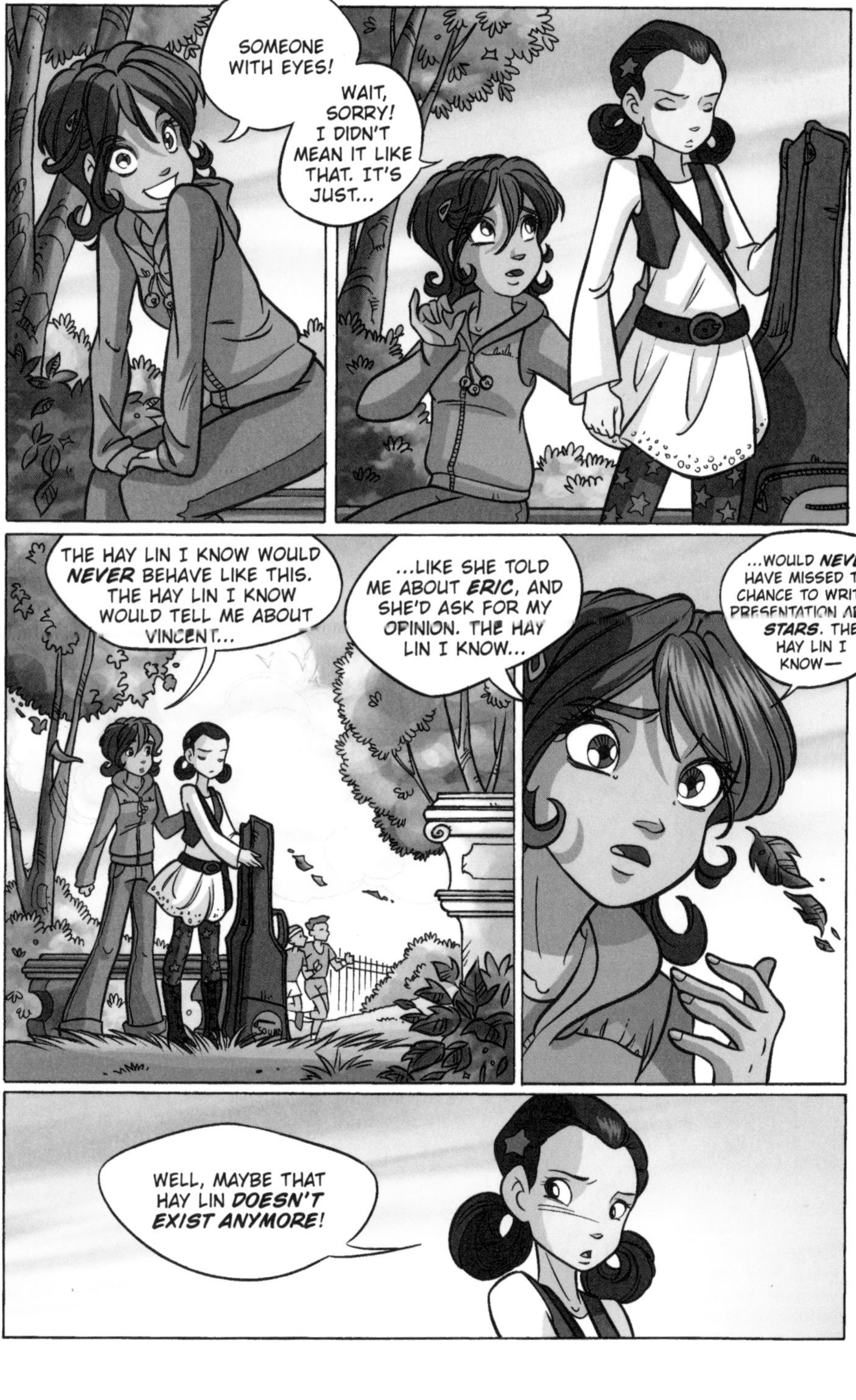
SOMEONE WITH EYES!
WAIT, SORRY! I DIDN'T MEAN IT LIKE THAT. IT'S JUST...
THE HAY LIN I KNOW WOULD **NEVER** BEHAVE LIKE THIS. THE HAY LIN I KNOW WOULD TELL ME ABOUT VINCENT...
...LIKE SHE TOLD ME ABOUT **ERIC**, AND SHE'D ASK FOR MY OPINION. THE HAY LIN I KNOW...
...WOULD **NEVER** HAVE MISSED THE CHANCE TO WRITE A PRESENTATION ABOUT **STARS**. THE HAY LIN I KNOW—
WELL, MAYBE THAT HAY LIN ***DOESN'T EXIST ANYMORE***!

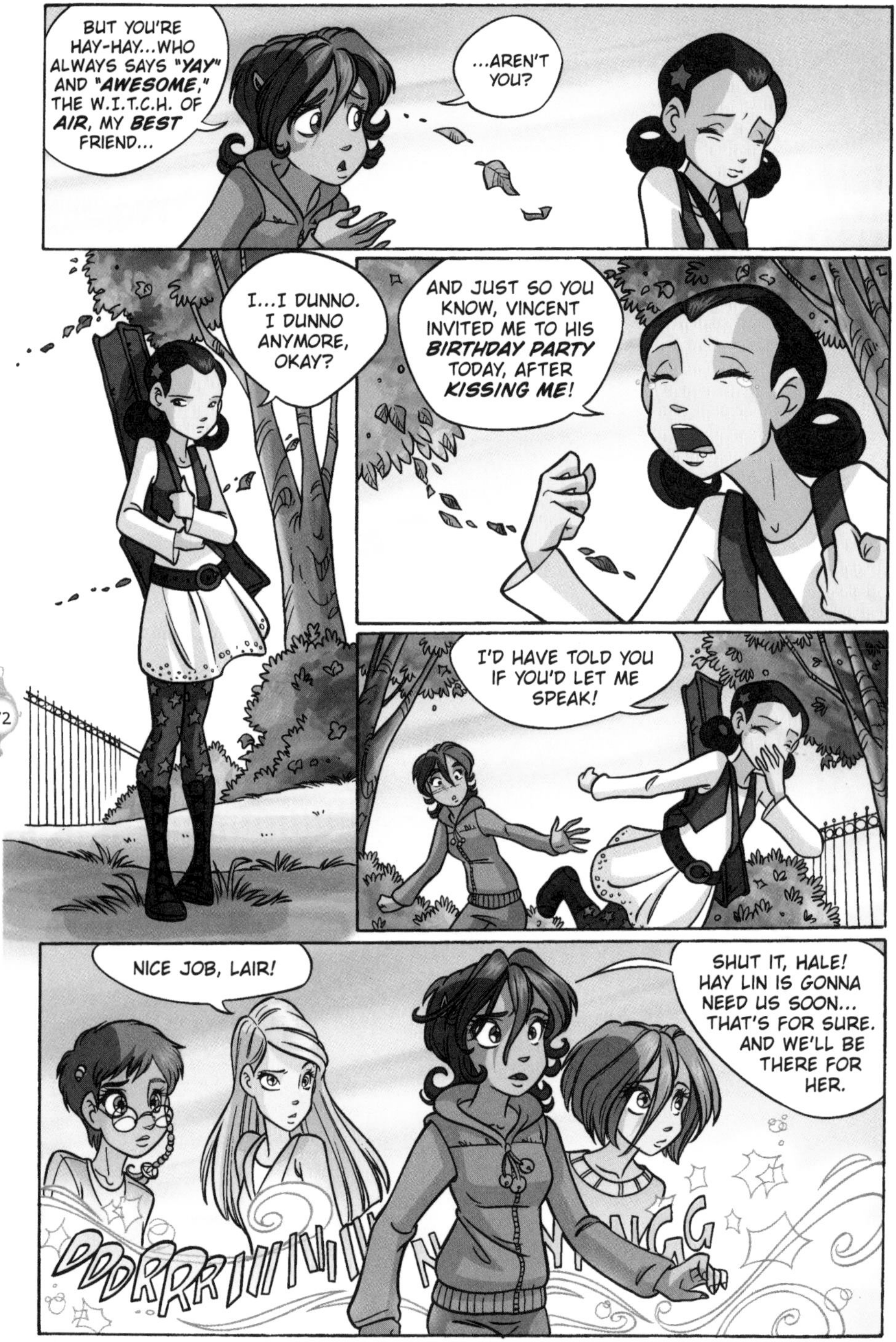
BUT YOU'RE HAY-HAY...WHO ALWAYS SAYS "YAY" AND "AWESOME," THE W.I.T.C.H. OF AIR, MY BEST FRIEND...
...AREN'T YOU?
I...I DUNNO. I DUNNO ANYMORE, OKAY?
AND JUST SO YOU KNOW, VINCENT INVITED ME TO HIS BIRTHDAY PARTY TODAY, AFTER KISSING ME!
I'D HAVE TOLD YOU IF YOU'D LET ME SPEAK!
NICE JOB, LAIR!
SHUT IT, HALE! HAY LIN IS GONNA NEED US SOON... THAT'S FOR SURE. AND WE'LL BE THERE FOR HER.
DDDRRRRIIIINNNNNNGG

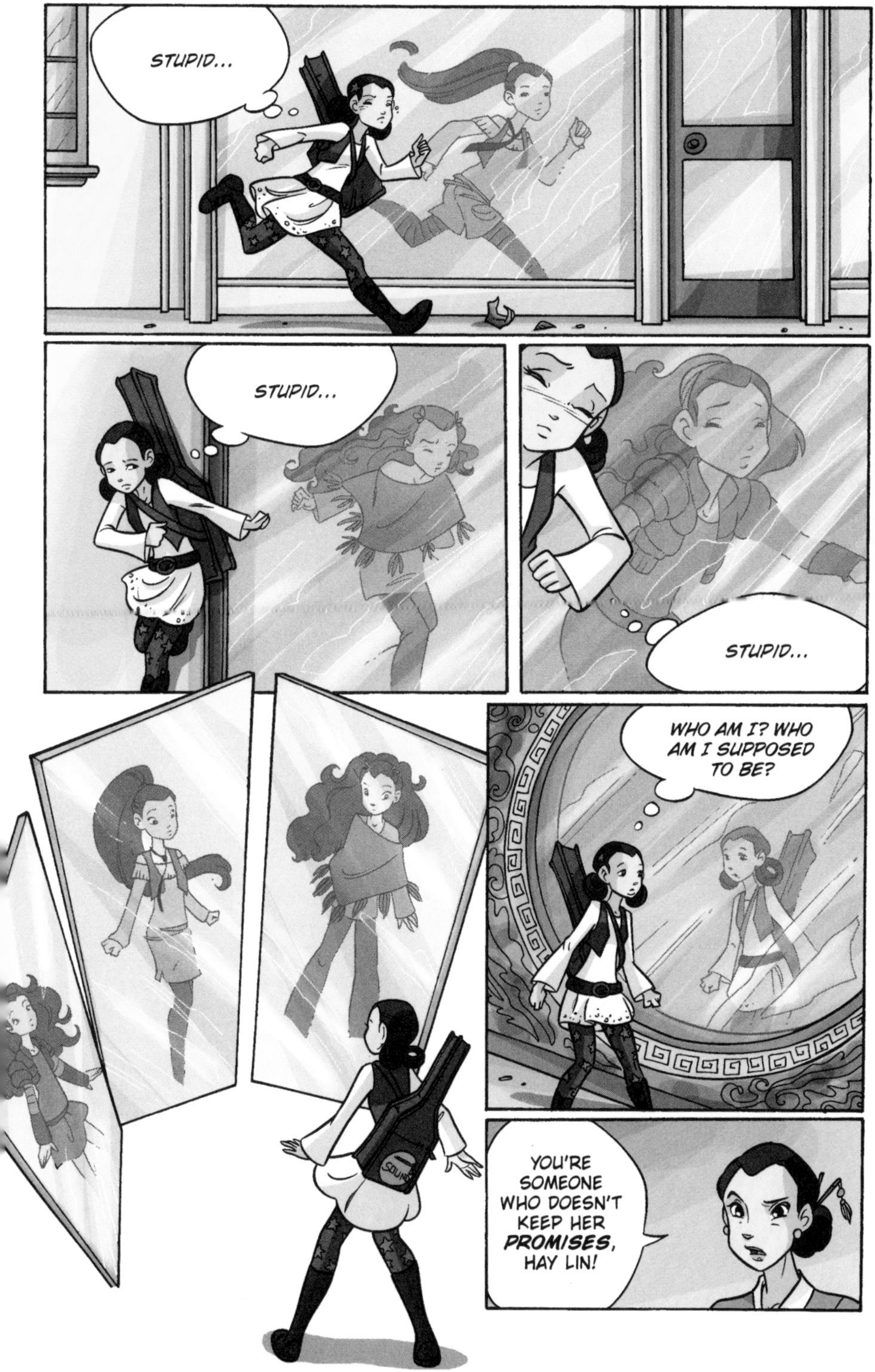
STUPID...
STUPID...
STUPID...
WHO AM I? WHO AM I SUPPOSED TO BE?
YOU'RE SOMEONE WHO DOESN'T KEEP HER **PROMISES**, HAY LIN!

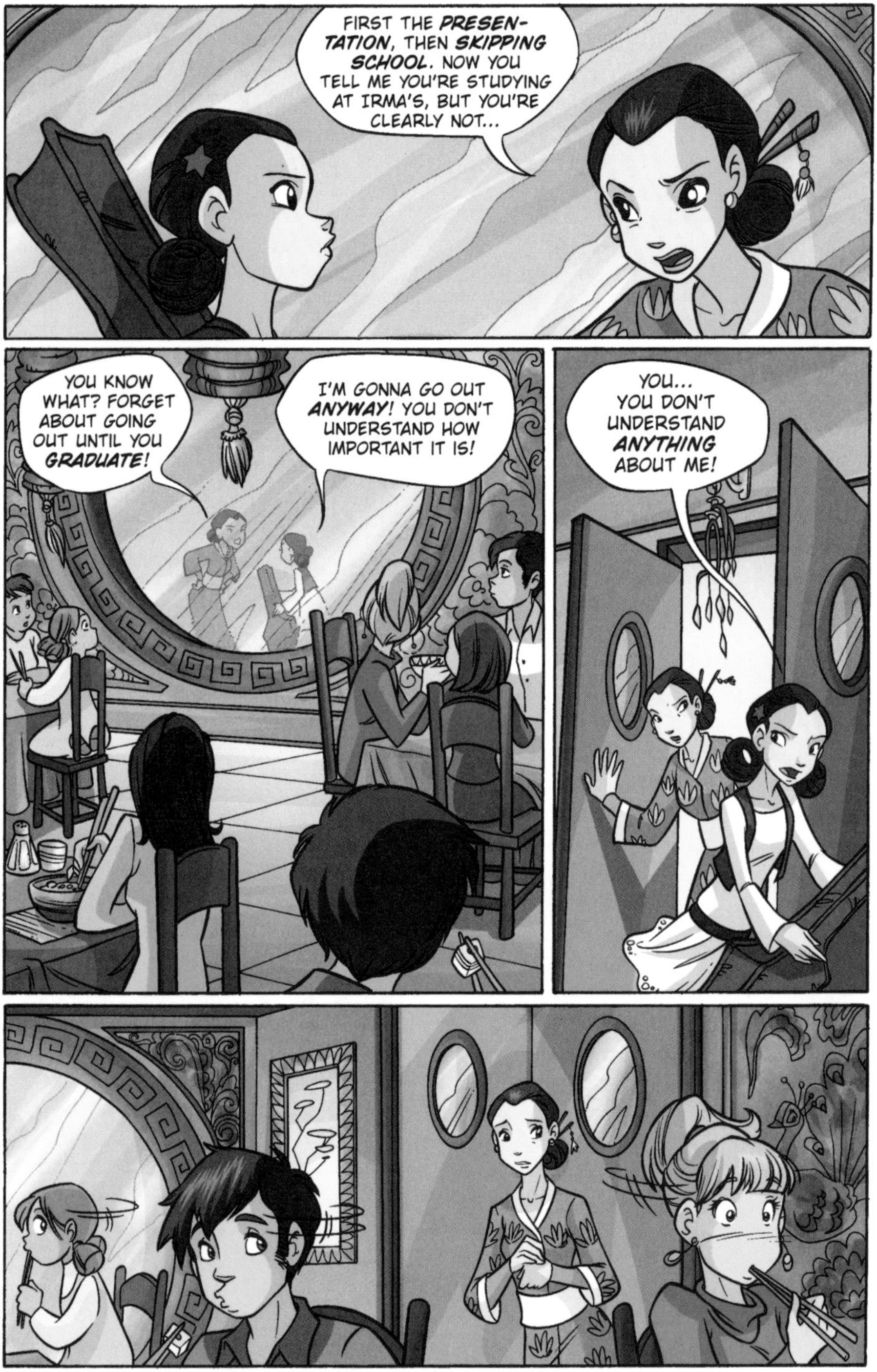
FIRST THE PRESENTATION, THEN SKIPPING SCHOOL. NOW YOU TELL ME YOU'RE STUDYING AT IRMA'S, BUT YOU'RE CLEARLY NOT...
YOU KNOW WHAT? FORGET ABOUT GOING OUT UNTIL YOU GRADUATE!
I'M GONNA GO OUT ANYWAY! YOU DON'T UNDERSTAND HOW IMPORTANT IT IS!
YOU... YOU DON'T UNDERSTAND ANYTHING ABOUT ME!

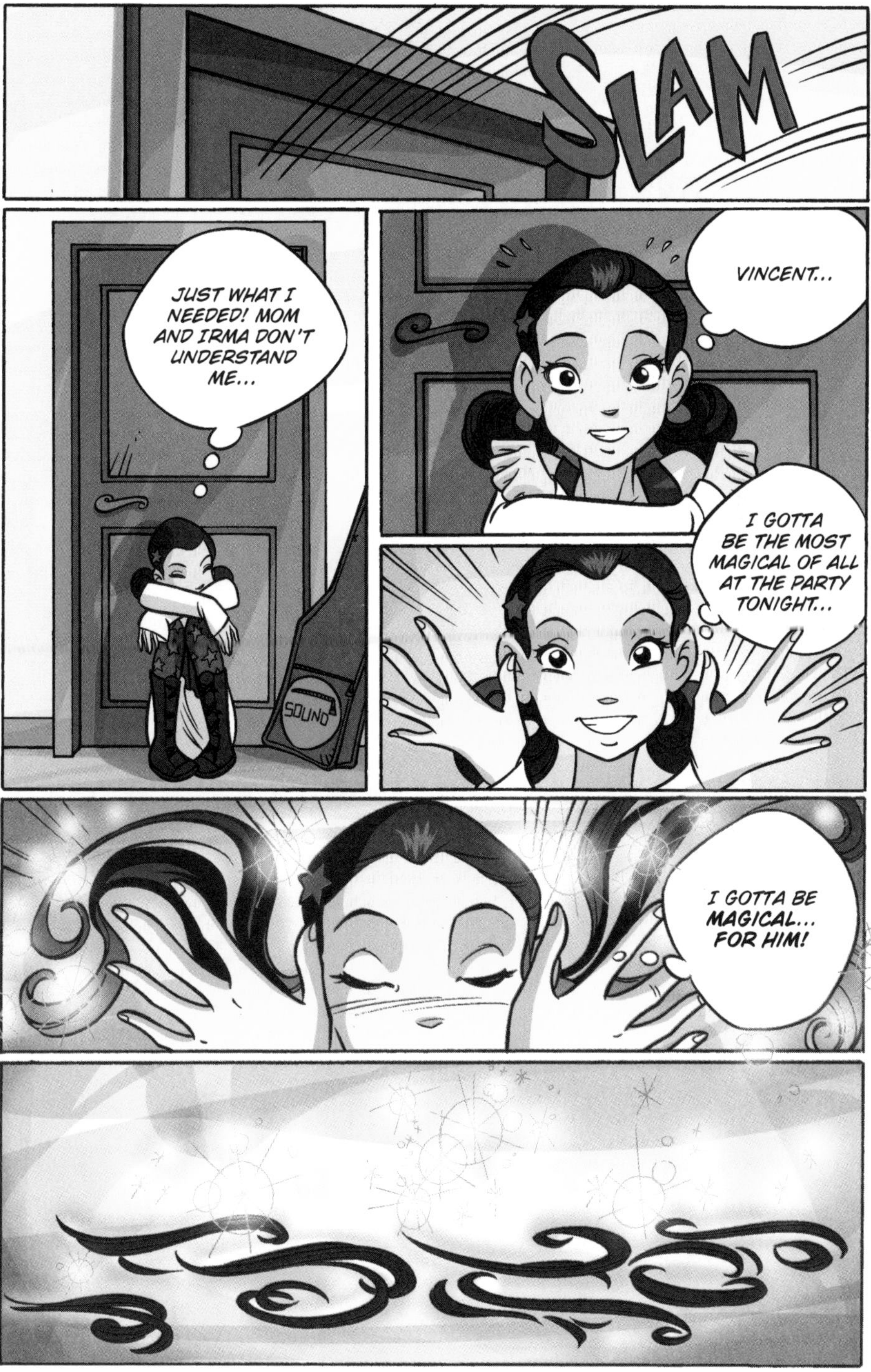
SLAM
JUST WHAT I NEEDED! MOM AND IRMA DON'T UNDERSTAND ME...
SOUND
VINCENT...
I GOTTA BE THE MOST MAGICAL OF ALL AT THE PARTY TONIGHT...
I GOTTA BE **MAGICAL... FOR HIM!**

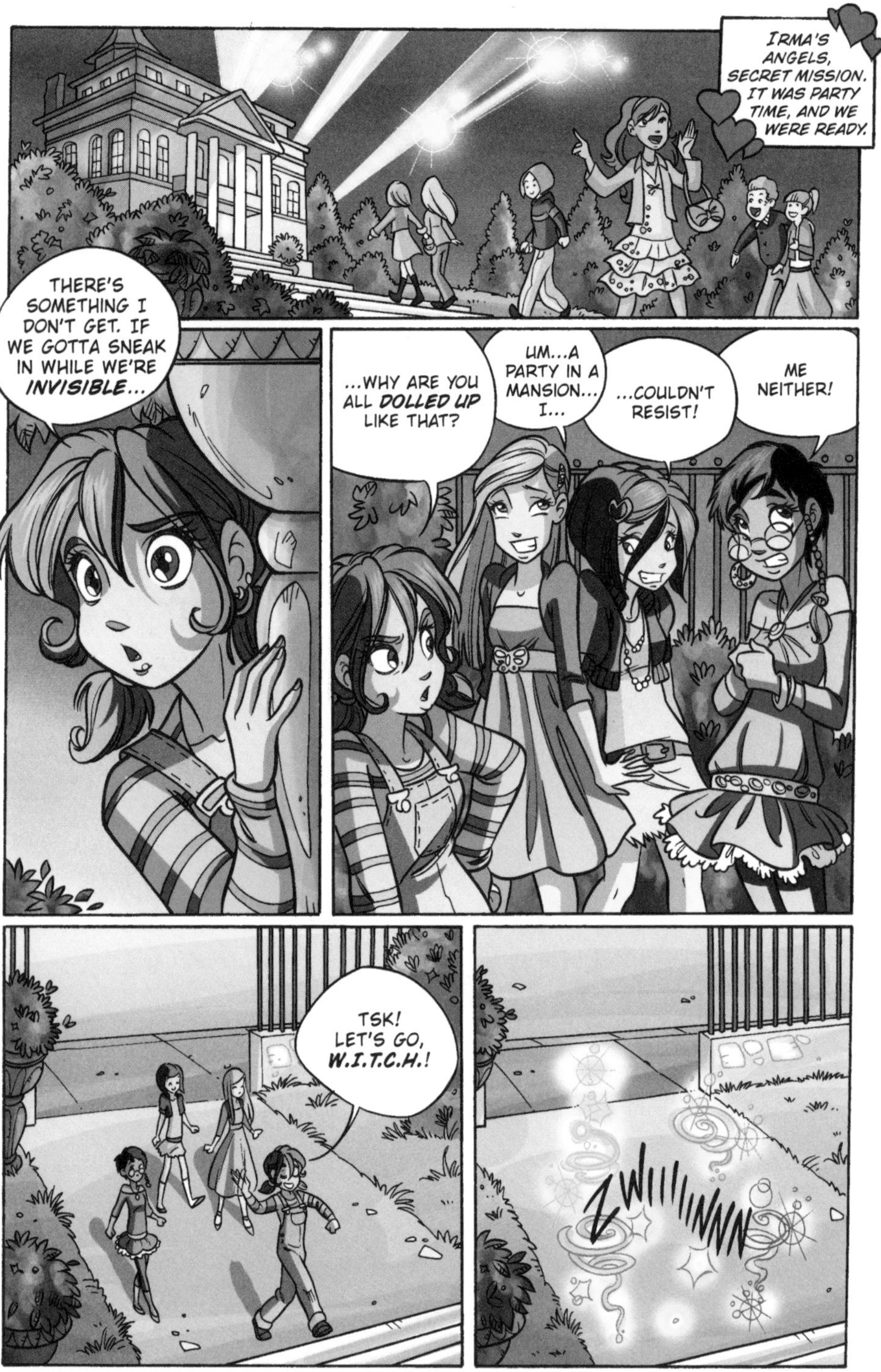
IRMA'S ANGELS, SECRET MISSION. IT WAS PARTY TIME, AND WE WERE READY.
THERE'S SOMETHING I DON'T GET. IF WE GOTTA SNEAK IN WHILE WE'RE INVISIBLE...
...WHY ARE YOU ALL DOLLED UP LIKE THAT?
UM...A PARTY IN A MANSION... I...
...COULDN'T RESIST!
ME NEITHER!
TSK! LET'S GO, W.I.T.C.H.!
ZWIIIINNN

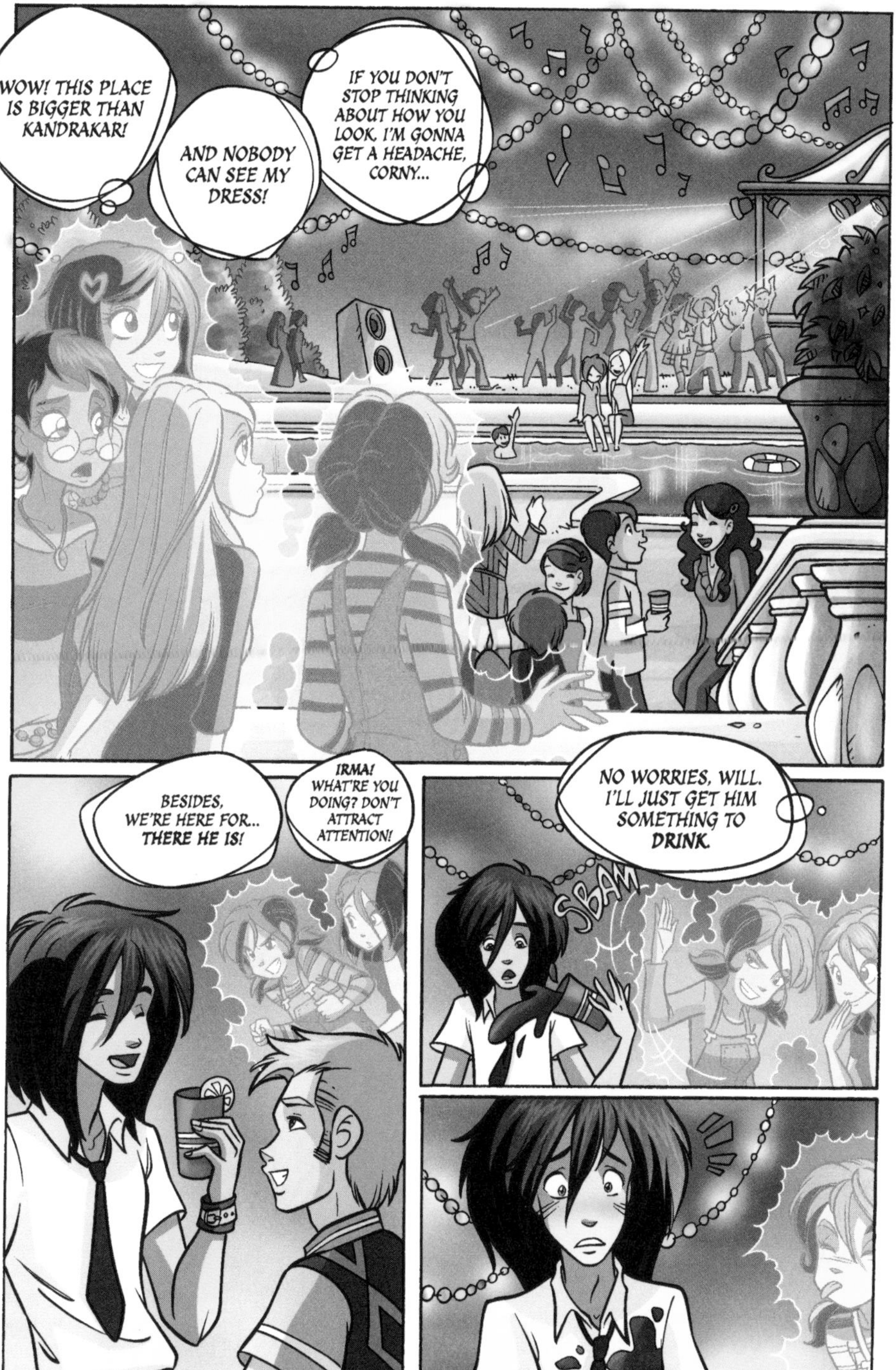
WOW! THIS PLACE IS BIGGER THAN KANDRAKAR!
AND NOBODY CAN SEE MY DRESS!
IF YOU DON'T STOP THINKING ABOUT HOW YOU LOOK, I'M GONNA GET A HEADACHE, CORNY...
BESIDES, WE'RE HERE FOR... THERE HE IS!
IRMA! WHAT'RE YOU DOING? DON'T ATTRACT ATTENTION!
NO WORRIES, WILL. I'LL JUST GET HIM SOMETHING TO DRINK.
SBAM

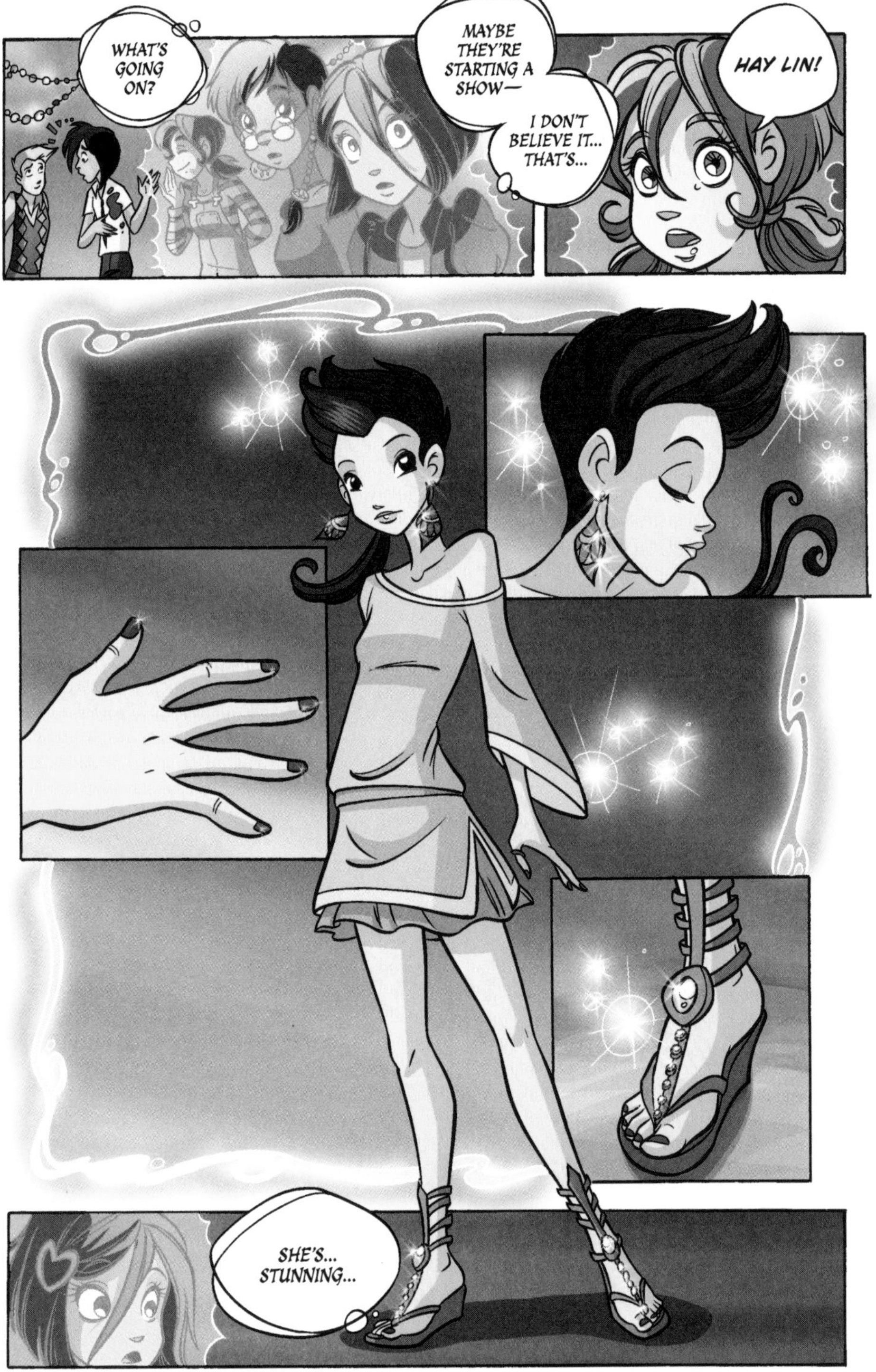
WHAT'S GOING ON?
MAYBE THEY'RE STARTING A SHOW—
I DON'T BELIEVE IT... THAT'S...
HAY LIN!
SHE'S... STUNNING...

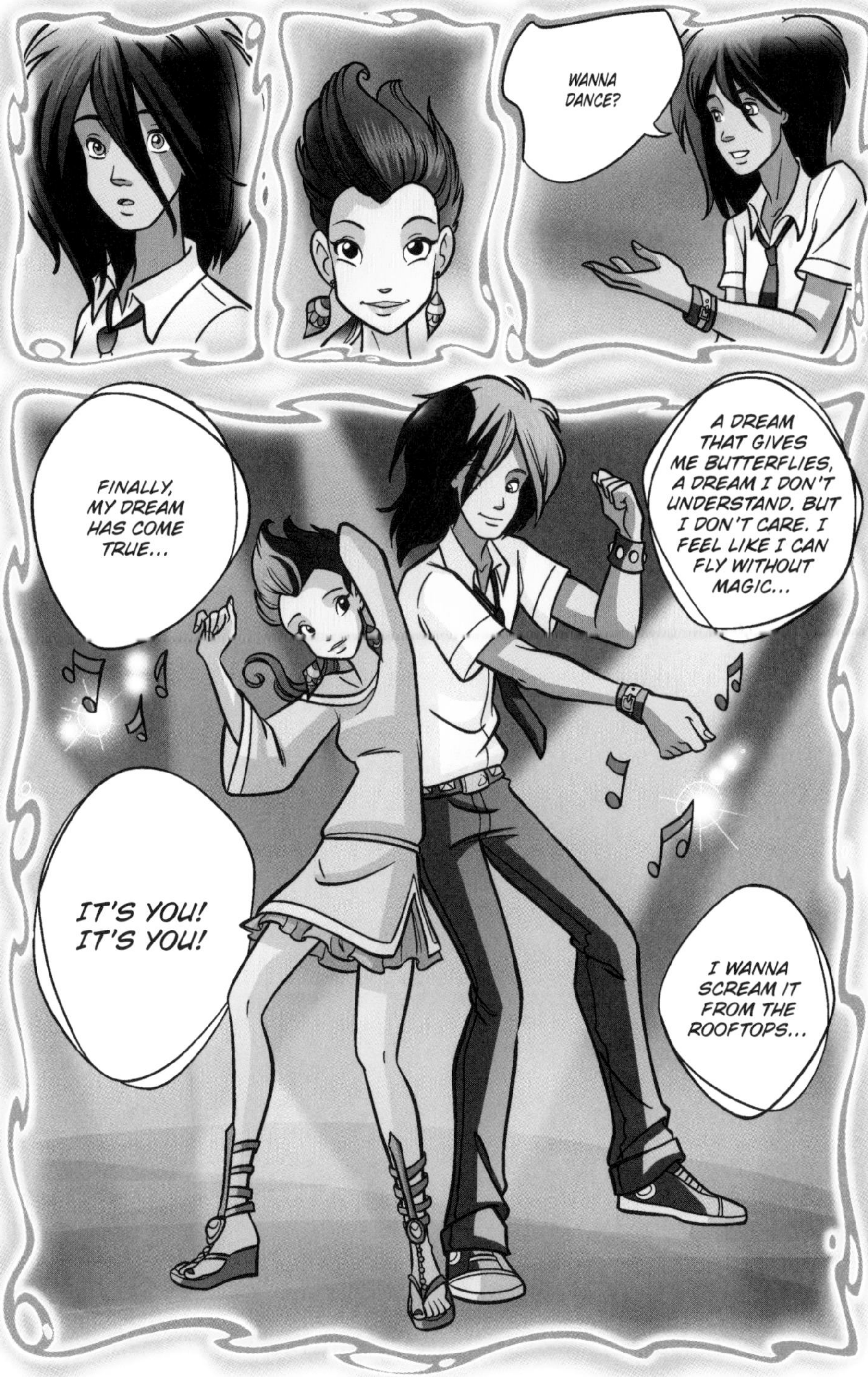
WANNA DANCE?
FINALLY, MY DREAM HAS COME TRUE...
A DREAM THAT GIVES ME BUTTERFLIES, A DREAM I DON'T UNDERSTAND. BUT I DON'T CARE. I FEEL LIKE I CAN FLY WITHOUT MAGIC...
IT'S YOU! IT'S YOU!
I WANNA SCREAM IT FROM THE ROOFTOPS...

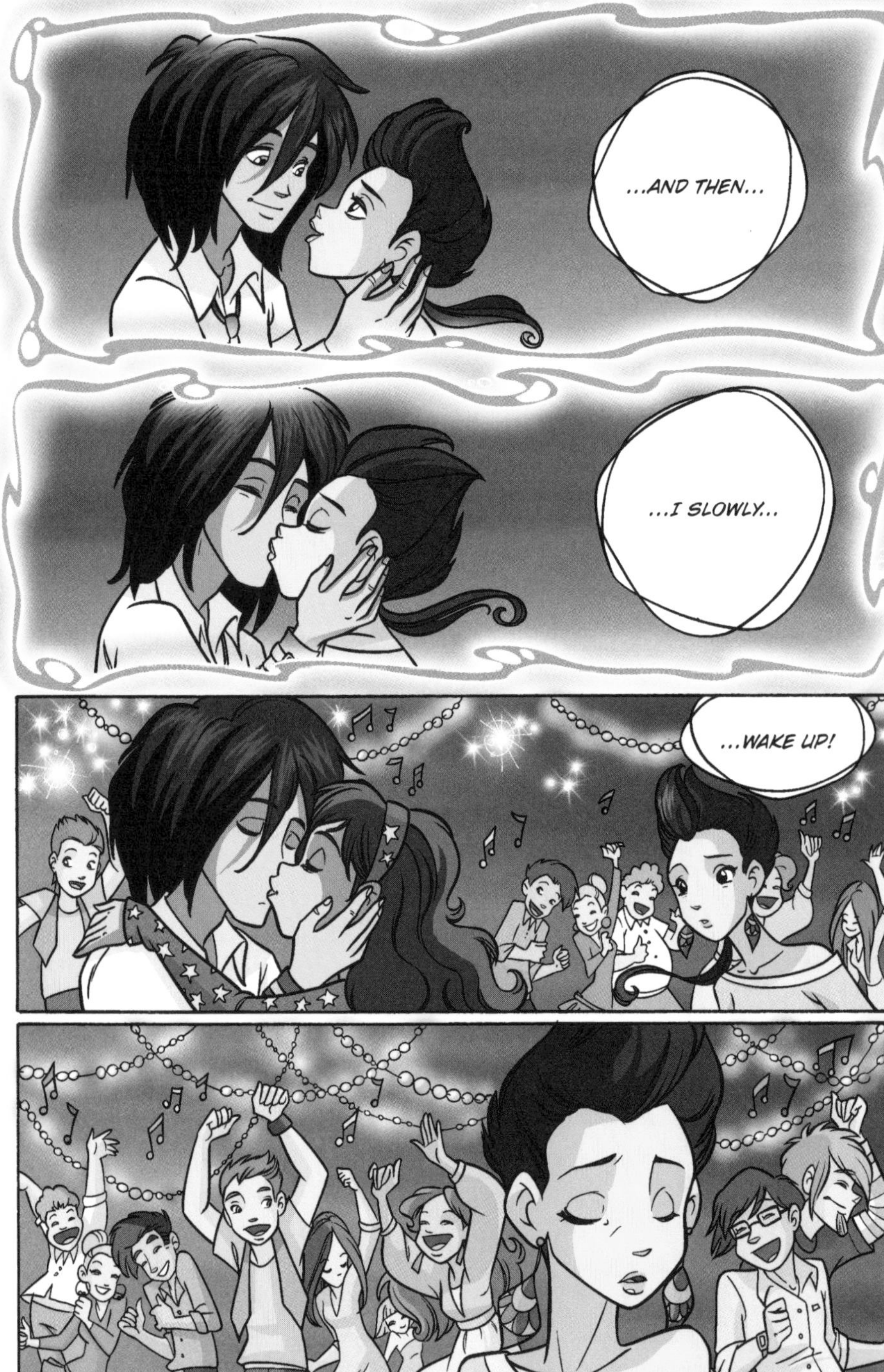
...AND THEN...
...I SLOWLY...
...WAKE UP!

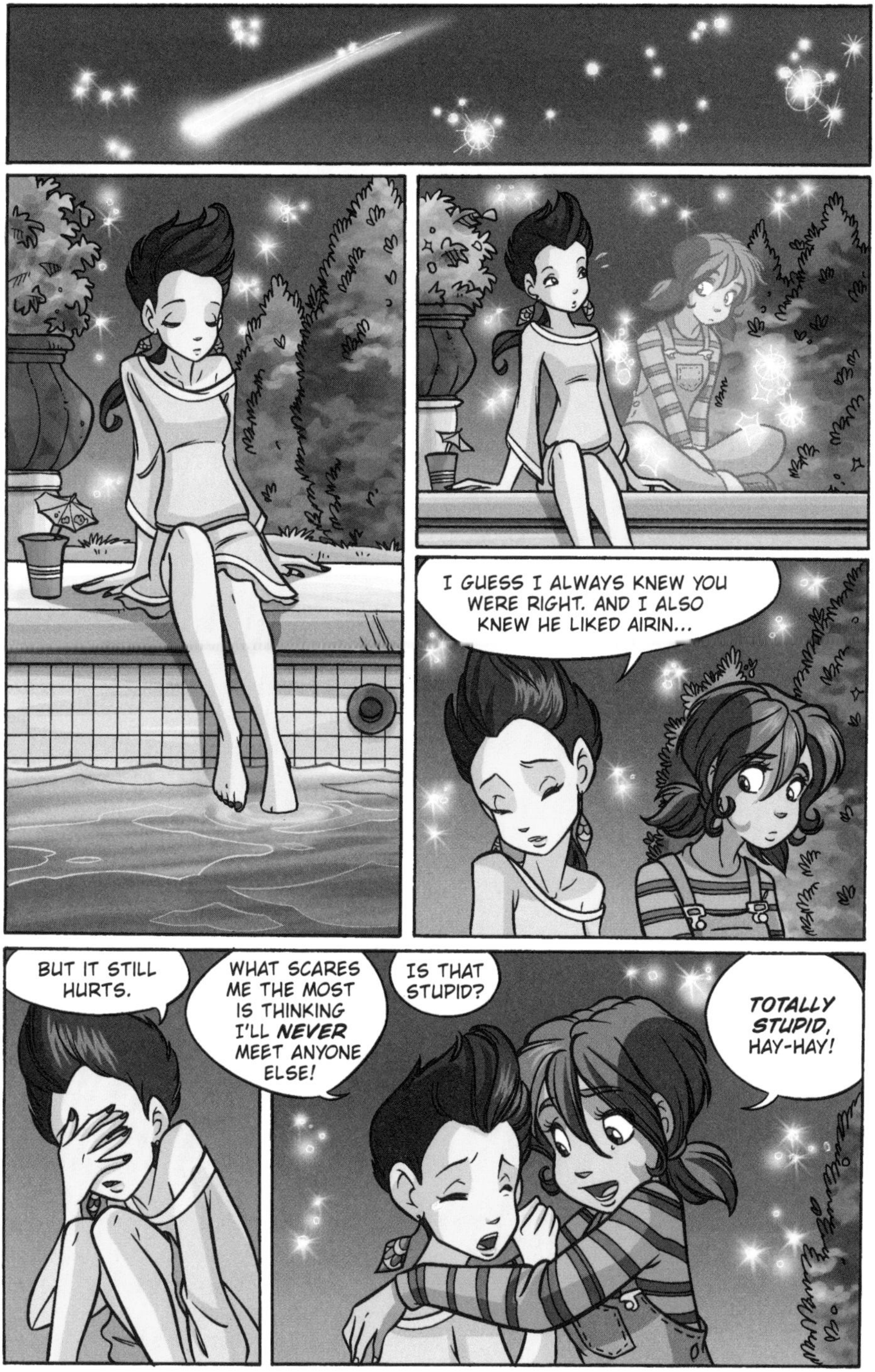

I GUESS I ALWAYS KNEW YOU WERE RIGHT. AND I ALSO KNEW HE LIKED AIRIN...
BUT IT STILL HURTS.
WHAT SCARES ME THE MOST IS THINKING I'LL ***NEVER*** MEET ANYONE ELSE!
IS THAT STUPID?
TOTALLY STUPID, HAY-HAY!

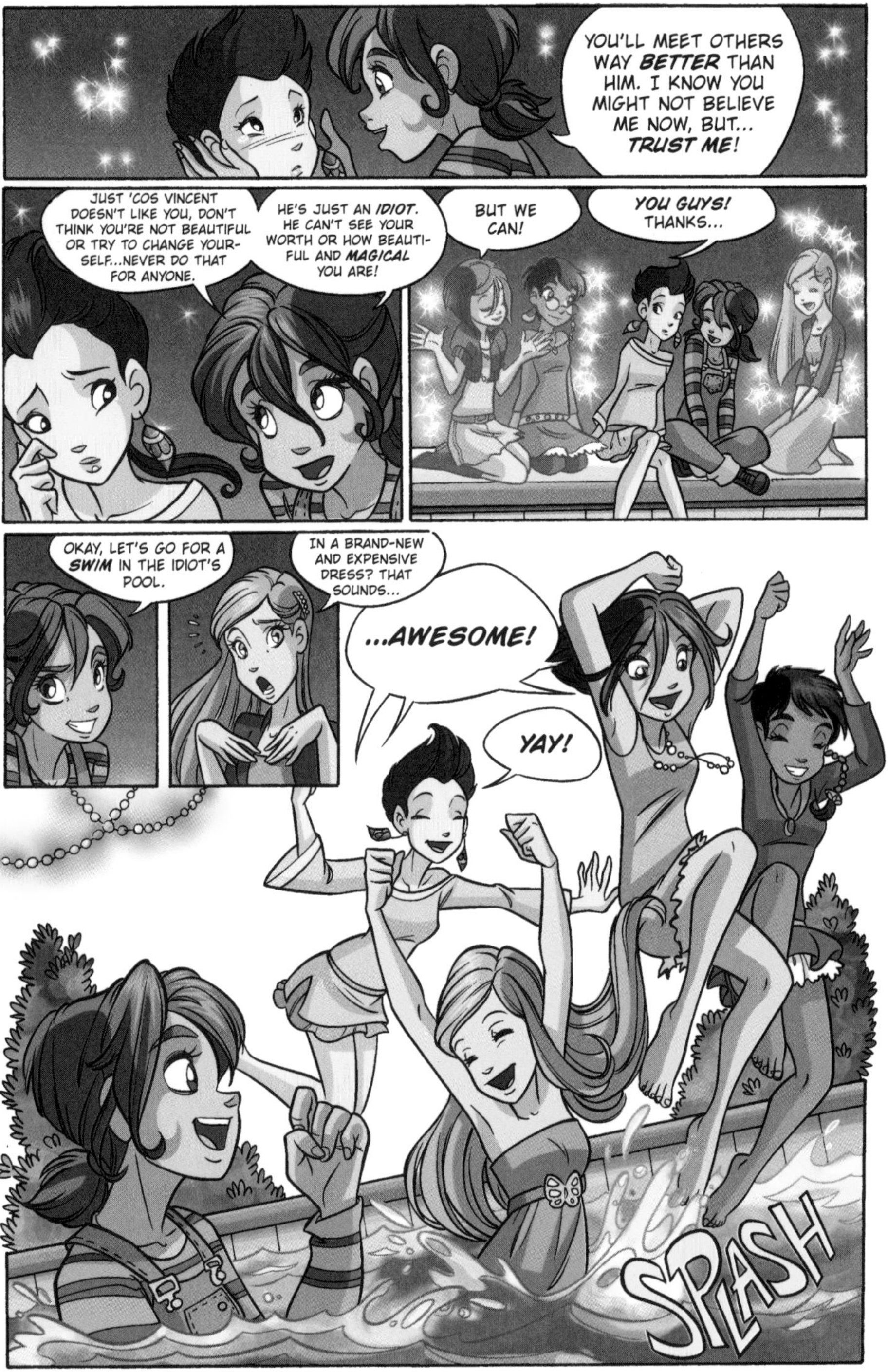
YOU'LL MEET OTHERS WAY BETTER THAN HIM. I KNOW YOU MIGHT NOT BELIEVE ME NOW, BUT... TRUST ME!
JUST 'COS VINCENT DOESN'T LIKE YOU, DON'T THINK YOU'RE NOT BEAUTIFUL OR TRY TO CHANGE YOURSELF...NEVER DO THAT FOR ANYONE.
HE'S JUST AN IDIOT. HE CAN'T SEE YOUR WORTH OR HOW BEAUTIFUL AND MAGICAL YOU ARE!
BUT WE CAN!
YOU GUYS! THANKS...
OKAY, LET'S GO FOR A SWIM IN THE IDIOT'S POOL.
IN A BRAND-NEW AND EXPENSIVE DRESS? THAT SOUNDS...
...AWESOME!
YAY!
SPLASH

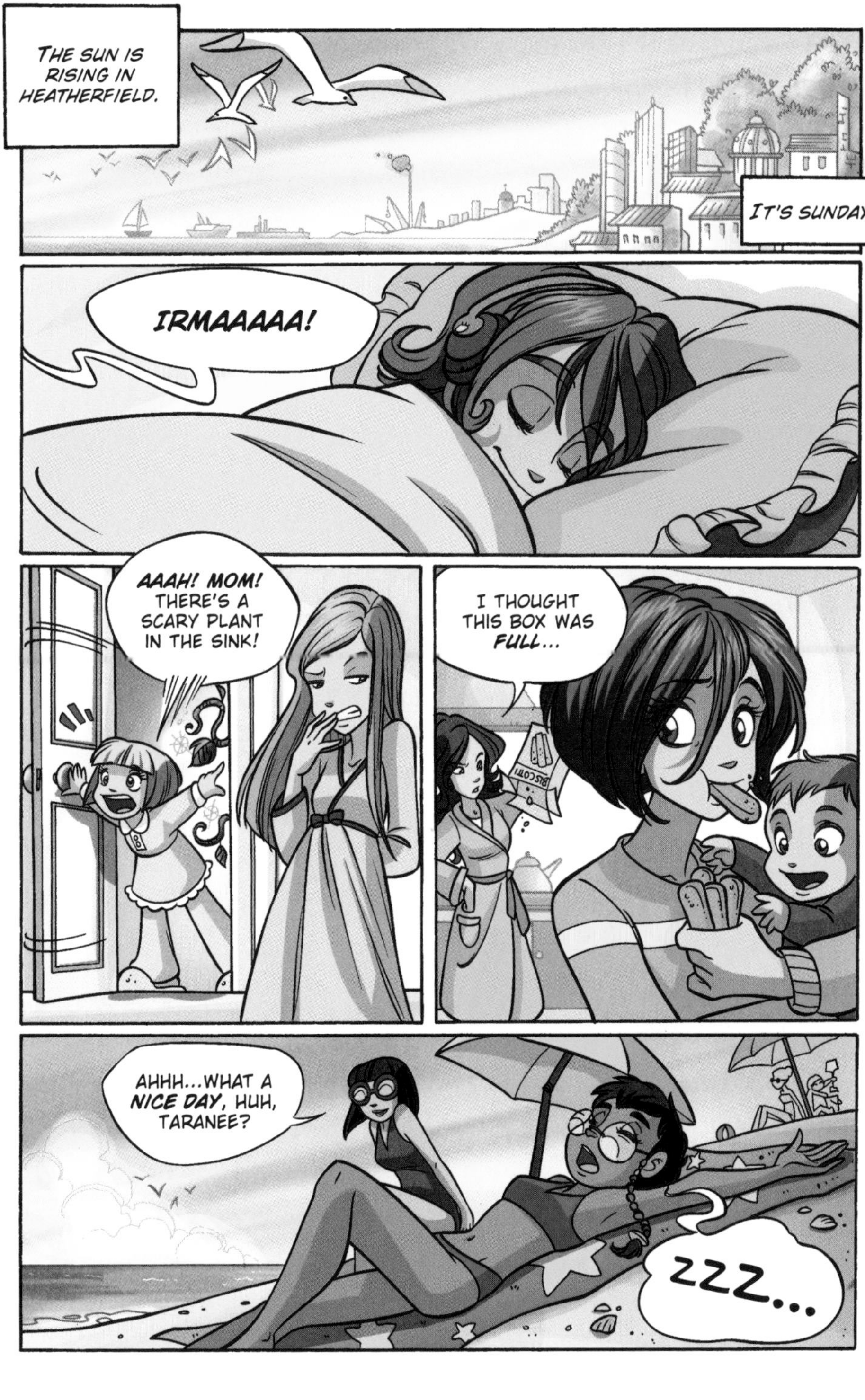
THE SUN IS RISING IN HEATHERFIELD.
IT'S SUNDAY.
IRMAAAAAA!
AAAH! MOM! THERE'S A SCARY PLANT IN THE SINK!
I THOUGHT THIS BOX WAS FULL...
BISCOTTI
AHHH...WHAT A NICE DAY, HUH, TARANEE?
ZZZ...

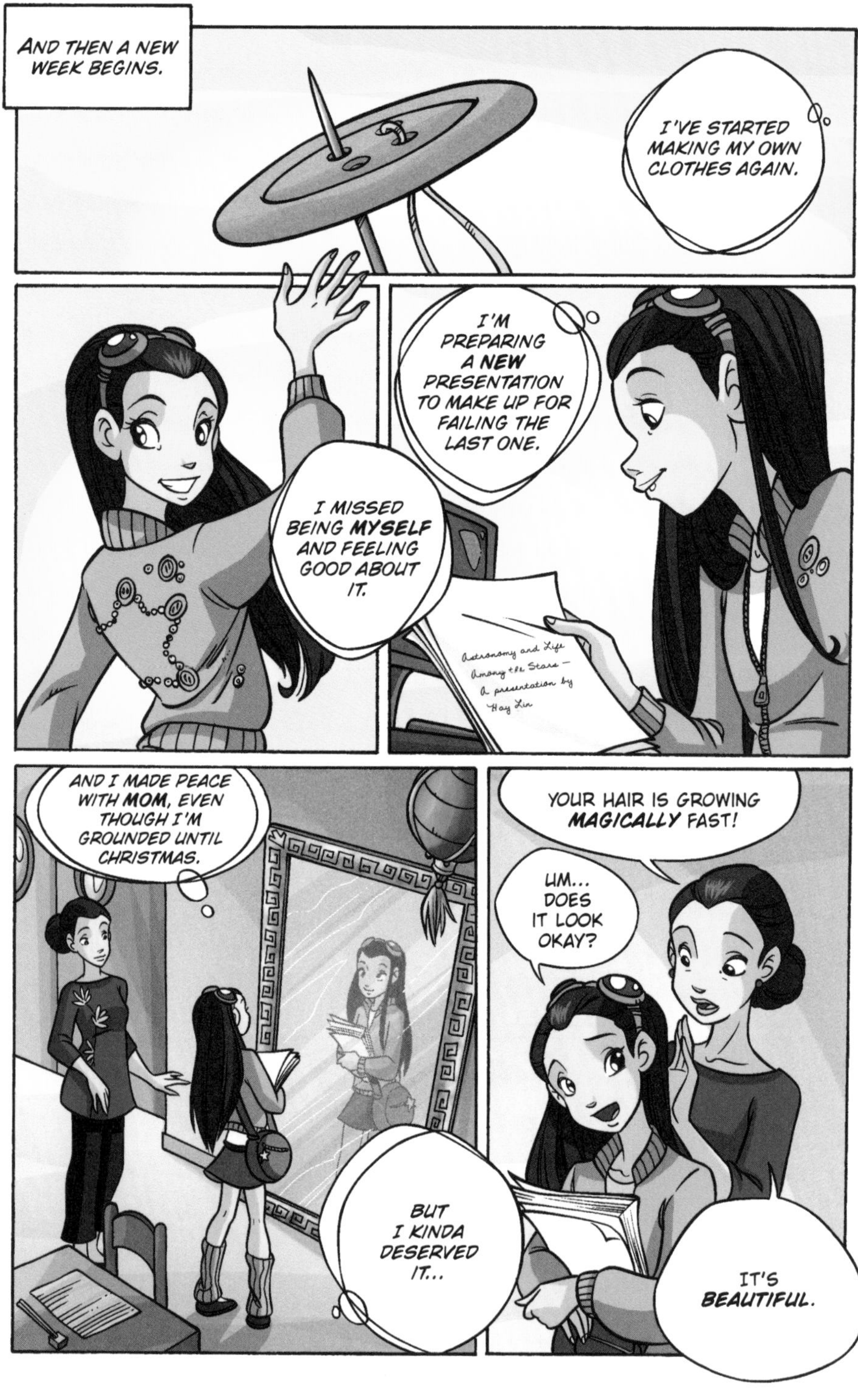
AND THEN A NEW WEEK BEGINS.
I'VE STARTED MAKING MY OWN CLOTHES AGAIN.
I MISSED BEING MYSELF AND FEELING GOOD ABOUT IT.
I'M PREPARING A NEW PRESENTATION TO MAKE UP FOR FAILING THE LAST ONE.
Astronomy and Life Among the Stars — A presentation by Hay Lin
AND I MADE PEACE WITH MOM, EVEN THOUGH I'M GROUNDED UNTIL CHRISTMAS.
BUT I KINDA DESERVED IT...
YOUR HAIR IS GROWING MAGICALLY FAST!
UM... DOES IT LOOK OKAY?
IT'S BEAUTIFUL.

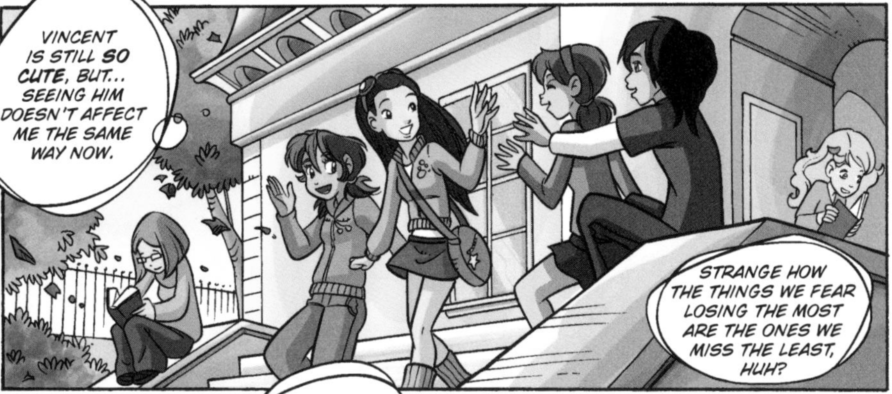
VINCENT IS STILL **SO CUTE**, BUT... SEEING HIM DOESN'T AFFECT ME THE SAME WAY NOW.
STRANGE HOW THE THINGS WE FEAR LOSING THE MOST ARE THE ONES WE MISS THE LEAST, HUH?

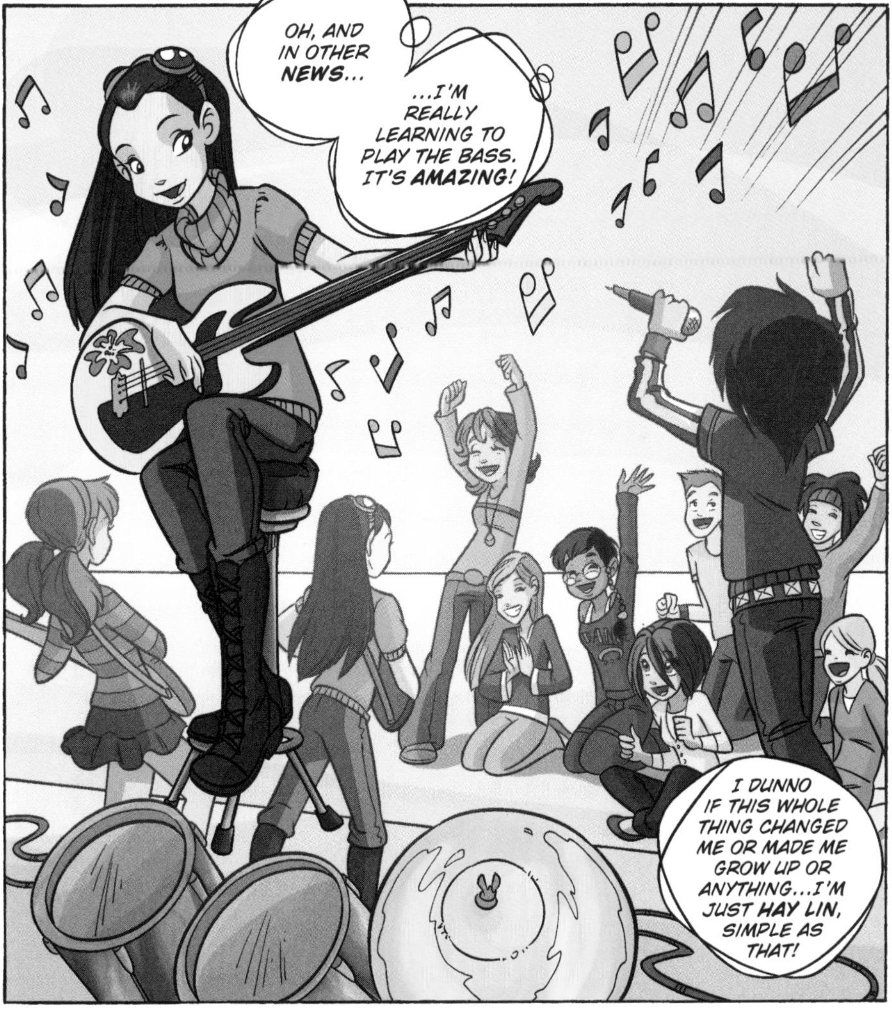
OH, AND IN OTHER **NEWS**...
...I'M REALLY LEARNING TO PLAY THE BASS. IT'S **AMAZING**!
I DUNNO IF THIS WHOLE THING CHANGED ME OR MADE ME GROW UP OR ANYTHING...I'M JUST **HAY LIN**, SIMPLE AS THAT!

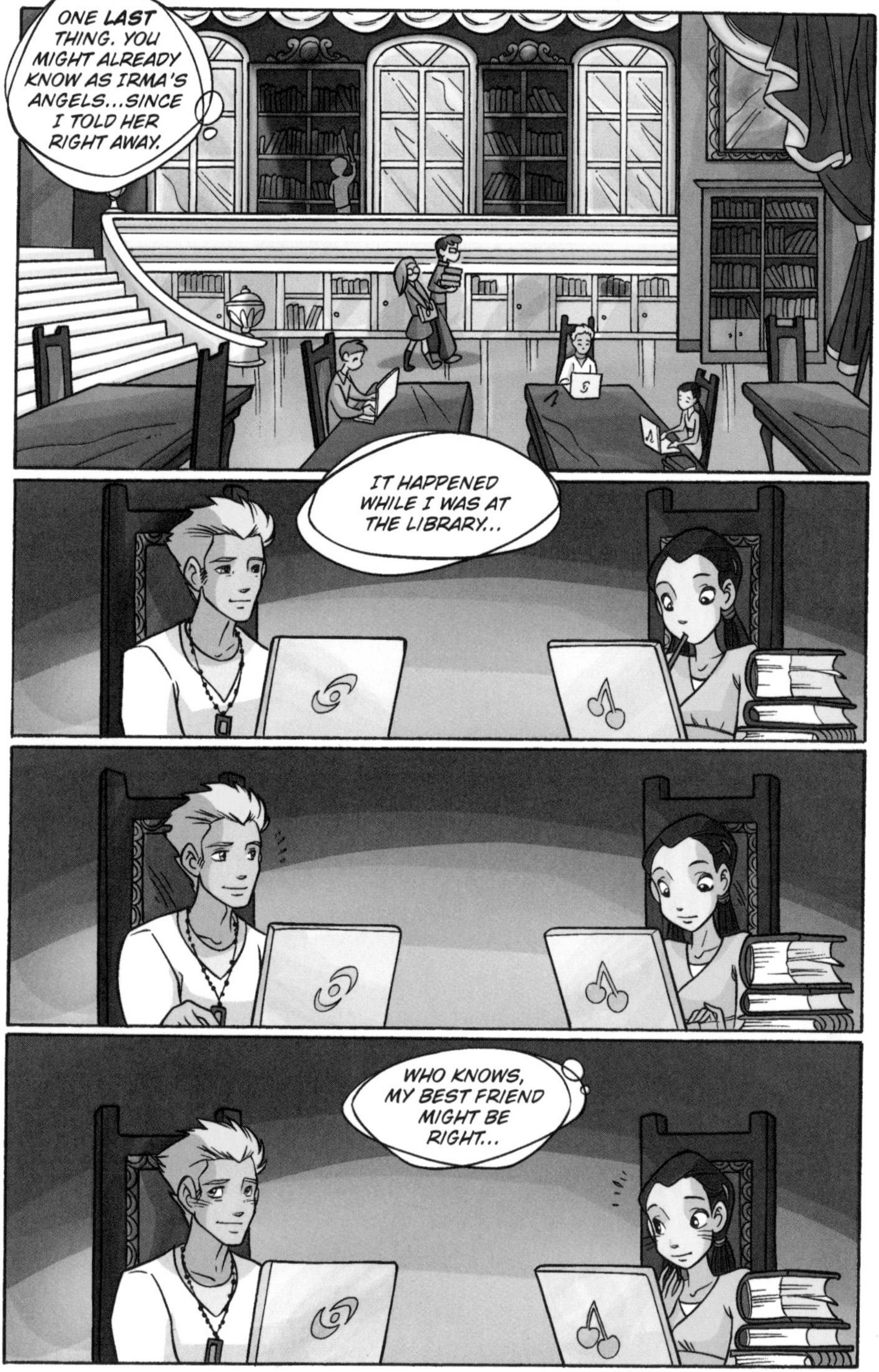
ONE LAST THING. YOU MIGHT ALREADY KNOW AS IRMA'S ANGELS...SINCE I TOLD HER RIGHT AWAY.
IT HAPPENED WHILE I WAS AT THE LIBRARY...
WHO KNOWS, MY BEST FRIEND MIGHT BE RIGHT...

END OF CHAPTER 103

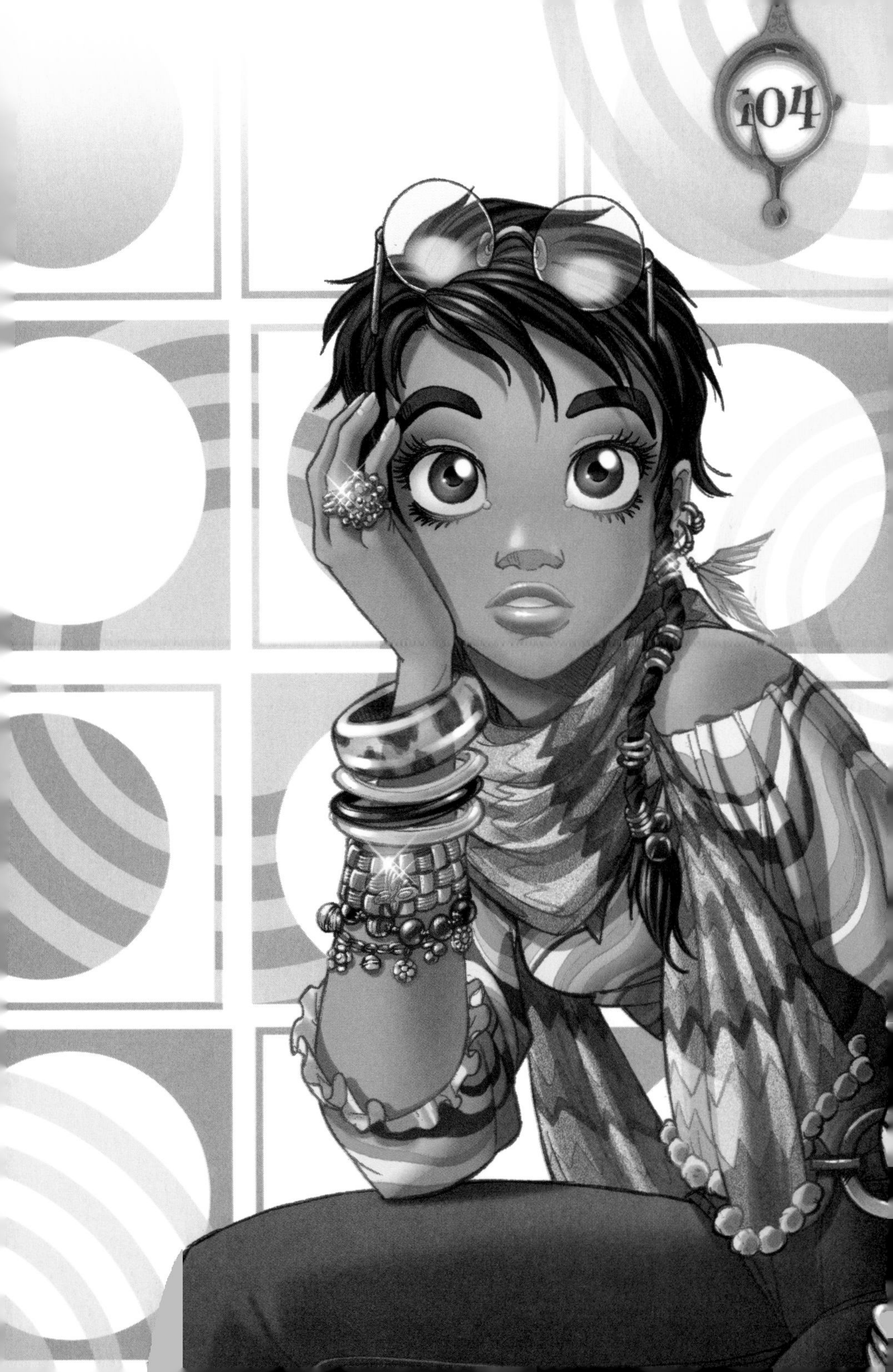
104

W.i.t.c.h.

Will Irma Taranee Cornelia Hay Lin

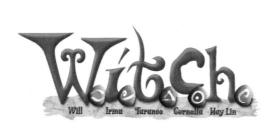

Another World

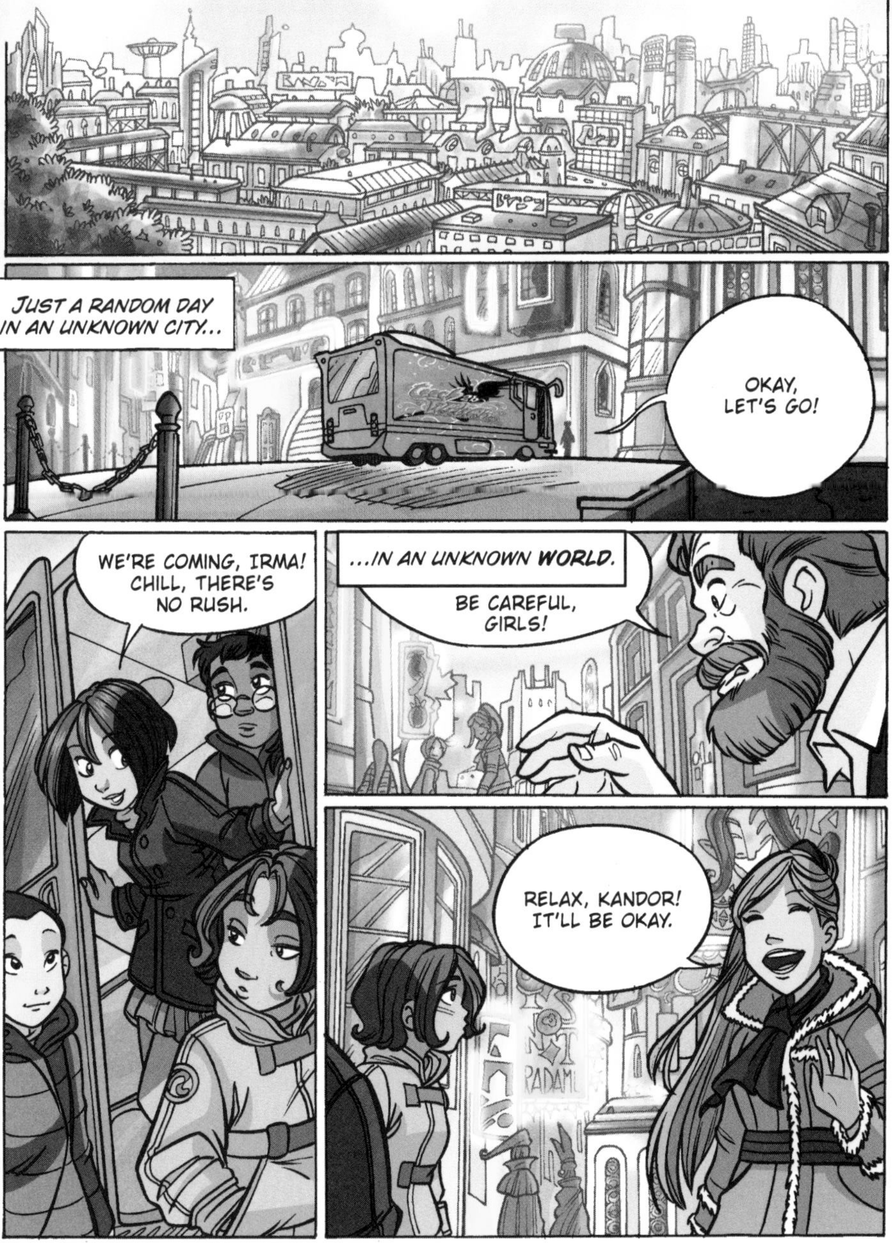

JUST A RANDOM DAY IN AN UNKNOWN CITY...
OKAY, LET'S GO!
WE'RE COMING, IRMA! CHILL, THERE'S NO RUSH.
...IN AN UNKNOWN WORLD.
BE CAREFUL, GIRLS!
RELAX, KANDOR! IT'LL BE OKAY.

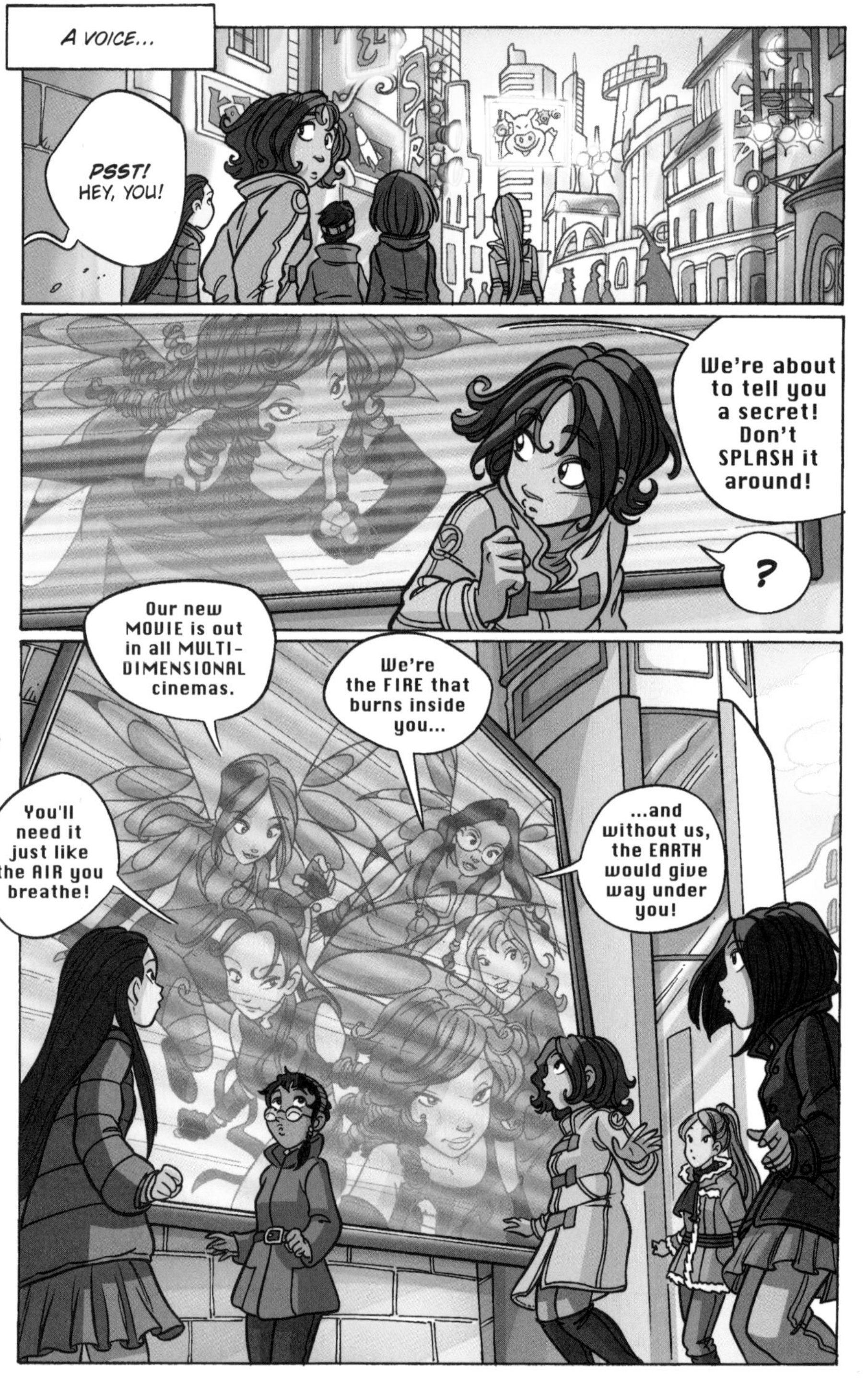
A VOICE...
PSST! HEY, YOU!
We're about to tell you a secret! Don't SPLASH it around!
?
Our new MOVIE is out in all MULTI-DIMENSIONAL cinemas.
We're the FIRE that burns inside you...
You'll need it just like the AIR you breathe!
...and without us, the EARTH would give way under you!

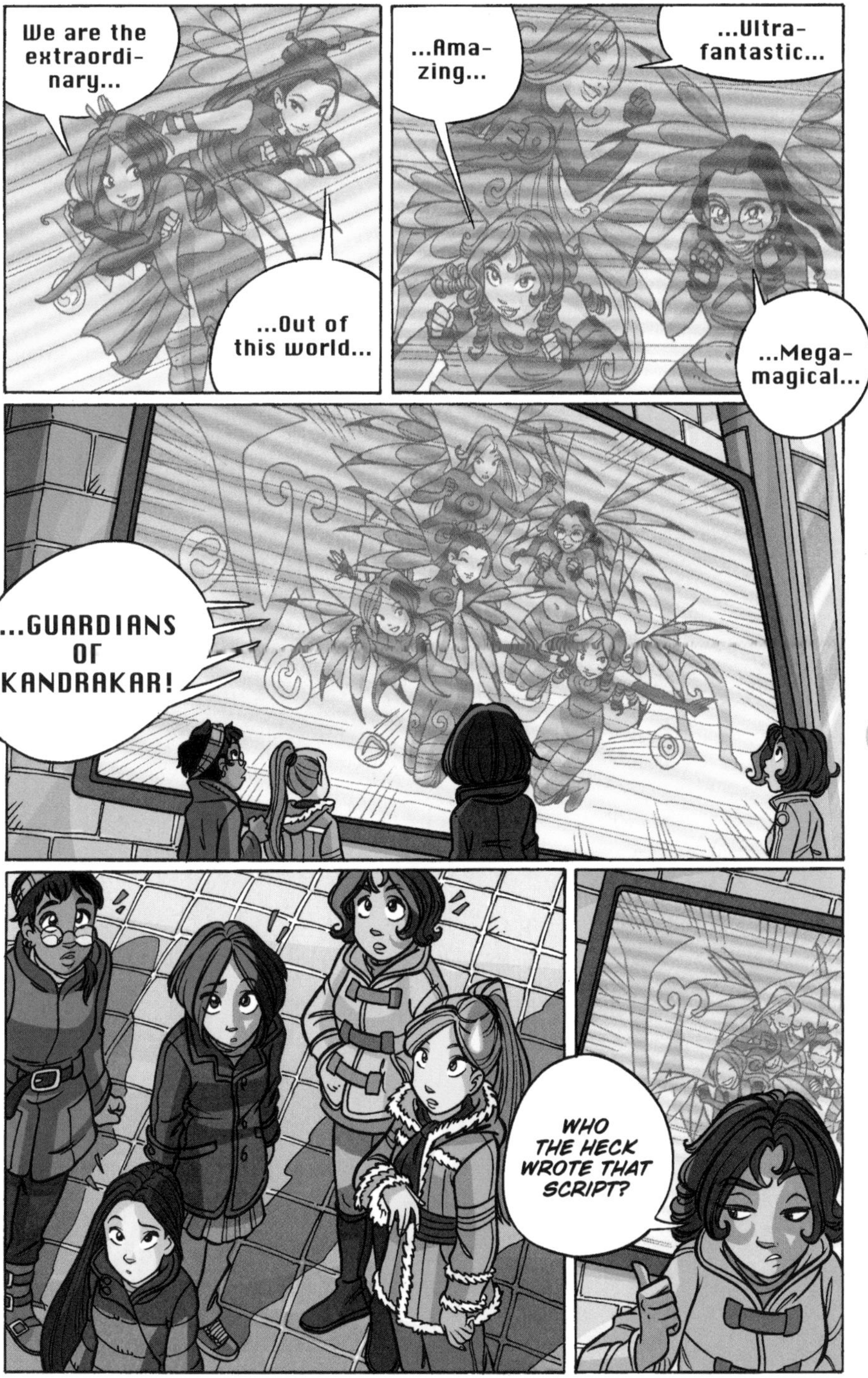
We are the extraordinary...
...Out of this world...
...Amazing...
...Ultra-fantastic...
...Mega-magical...
...GUARDIANS OF KANDRAKAR!
WHO THE HECK WROTE THAT SCRIPT?

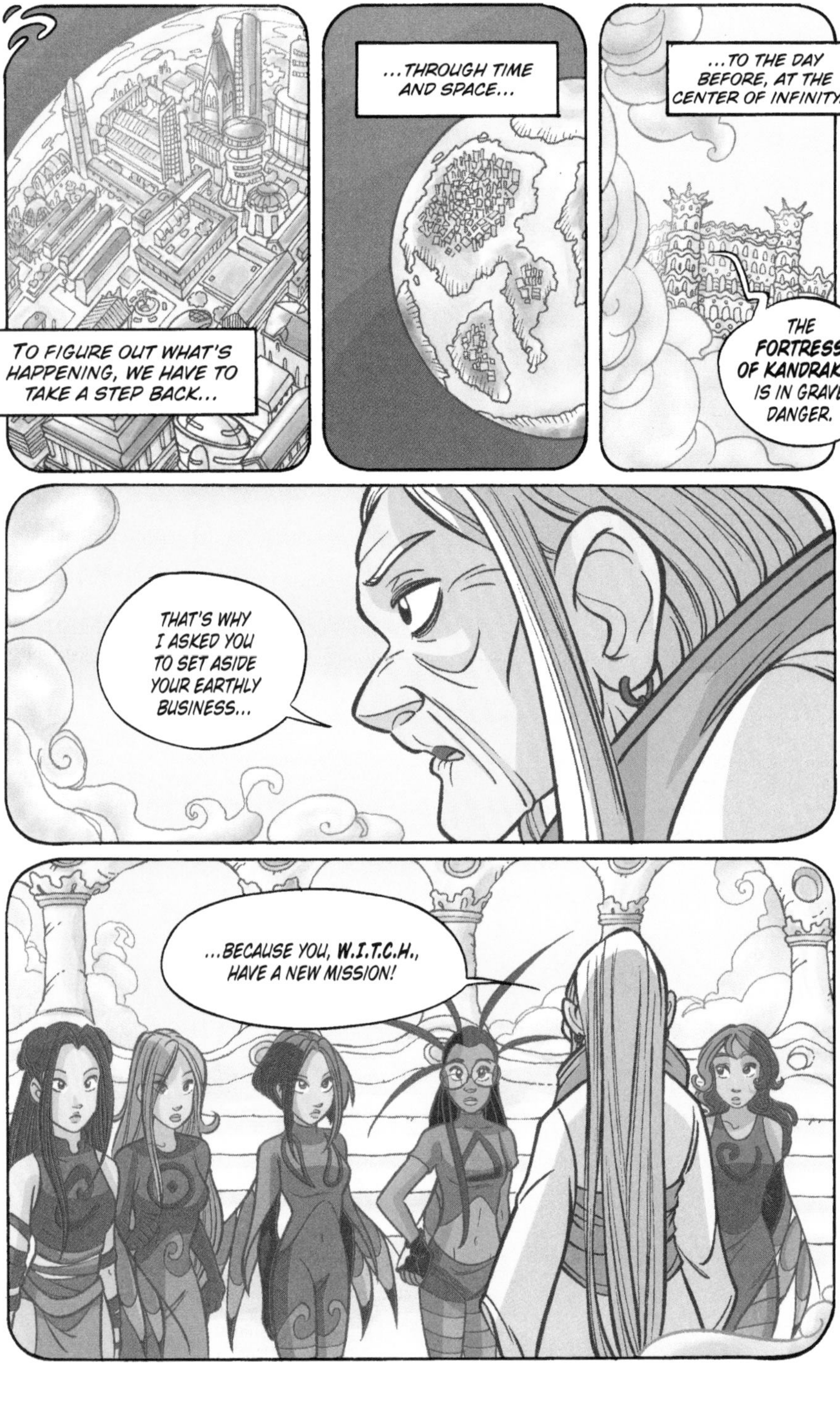
TO FIGURE OUT WHAT'S HAPPENING, WE HAVE TO TAKE A STEP BACK...
...THROUGH TIME AND SPACE...
...TO THE DAY BEFORE, AT THE CENTER OF INFINITY...
THE FORTRESS OF KANDRAKAR IS IN GRAVE DANGER.
THAT'S WHY I ASKED YOU TO SET ASIDE YOUR EARTHLY BUSINESS...
...BECAUSE YOU, W.I.T.C.H., HAVE A NEW MISSION!

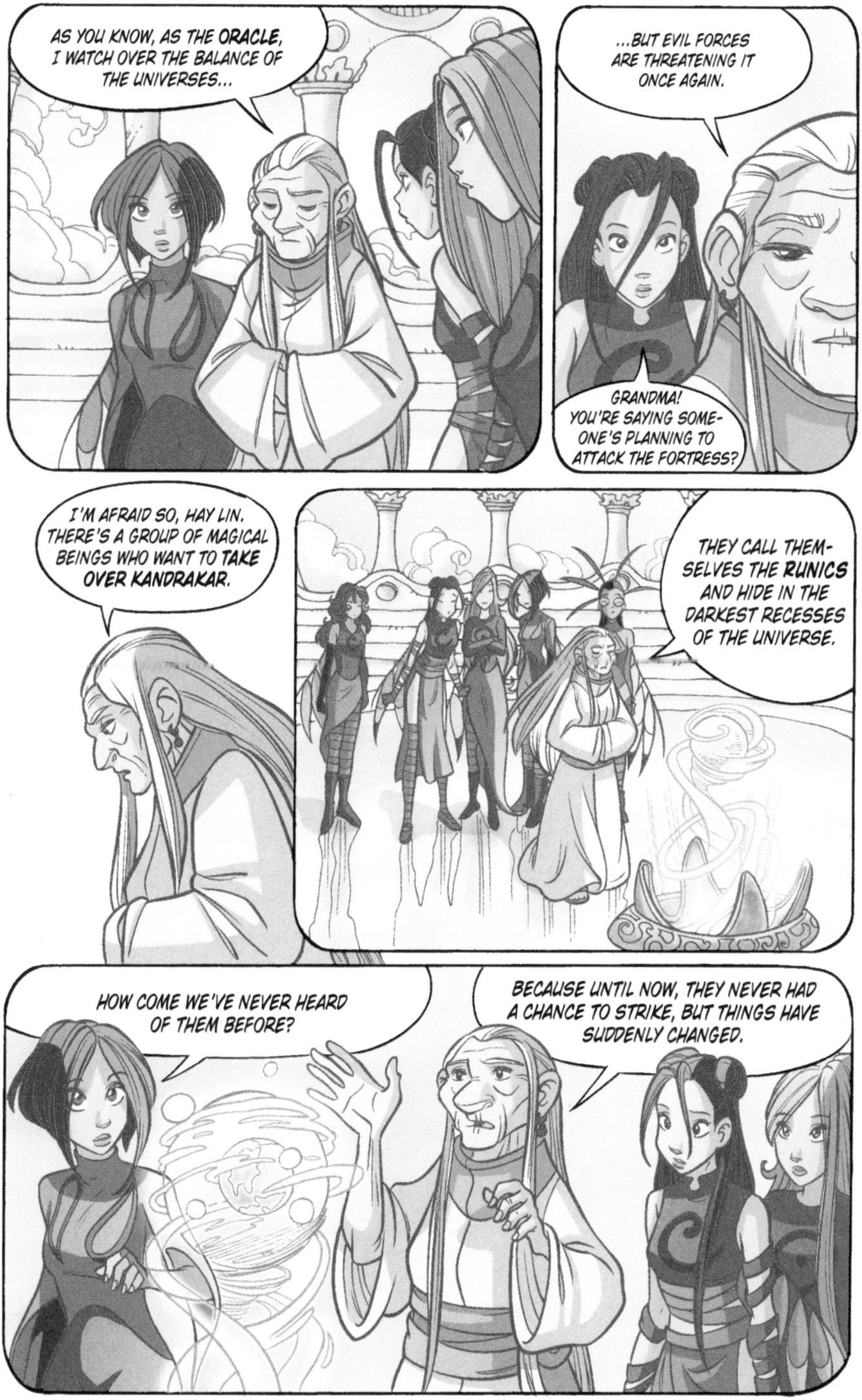
AS YOU KNOW, AS THE ORACLE, I WATCH OVER THE BALANCE OF THE UNIVERSES...
...BUT EVIL FORCES ARE THREATENING IT ONCE AGAIN.
GRANDMA! YOU'RE SAYING SOME-ONE'S PLANNING TO ATTACK THE FORTRESS?
I'M AFRAID SO, HAY LIN. THERE'S A GROUP OF MAGICAL BEINGS WHO WANT TO TAKE OVER KANDRAKAR.
THEY CALL THEM-SELVES THE RUNICS AND HIDE IN THE DARKEST RECESSES OF THE UNIVERSE.
HOW COME WE'VE NEVER HEARD OF THEM BEFORE?
BECAUSE UNTIL NOW, THEY NEVER HAD A CHANCE TO STRIKE, BUT THINGS HAVE SUDDENLY CHANGED.

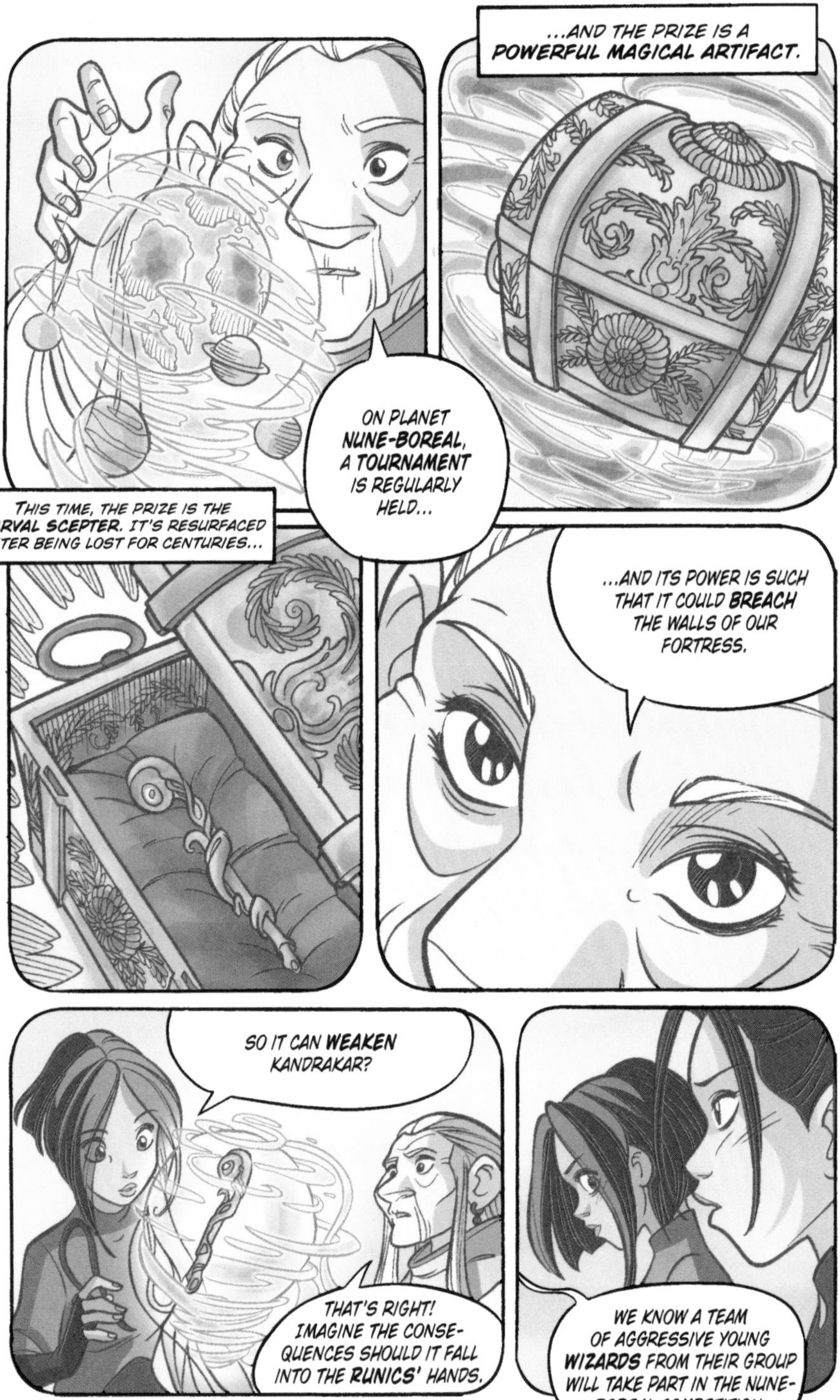

ON PLANET NUNE-BOREAL, A TOURNAMENT IS REGULARLY HELD...
...AND THE PRIZE IS A POWERFUL MAGICAL ARTIFACT.
THIS TIME, THE PRIZE IS THE NARVAL SCEPTER. IT'S RESURFACED AFTER BEING LOST FOR CENTURIES...
...AND ITS POWER IS SUCH THAT IT COULD BREACH THE WALLS OF OUR FORTRESS.
SO IT CAN WEAKEN KANDRAKAR?
THAT'S RIGHT! IMAGINE THE CONSE-QUENCES SHOULD IT FALL INTO THE RUNICS' HANDS.
WE KNOW A TEAM OF AGGRESSIVE YOUNG WIZARDS FROM THEIR GROUP WILL TAKE PART IN THE NUNE-BOREAL COMPETITION.

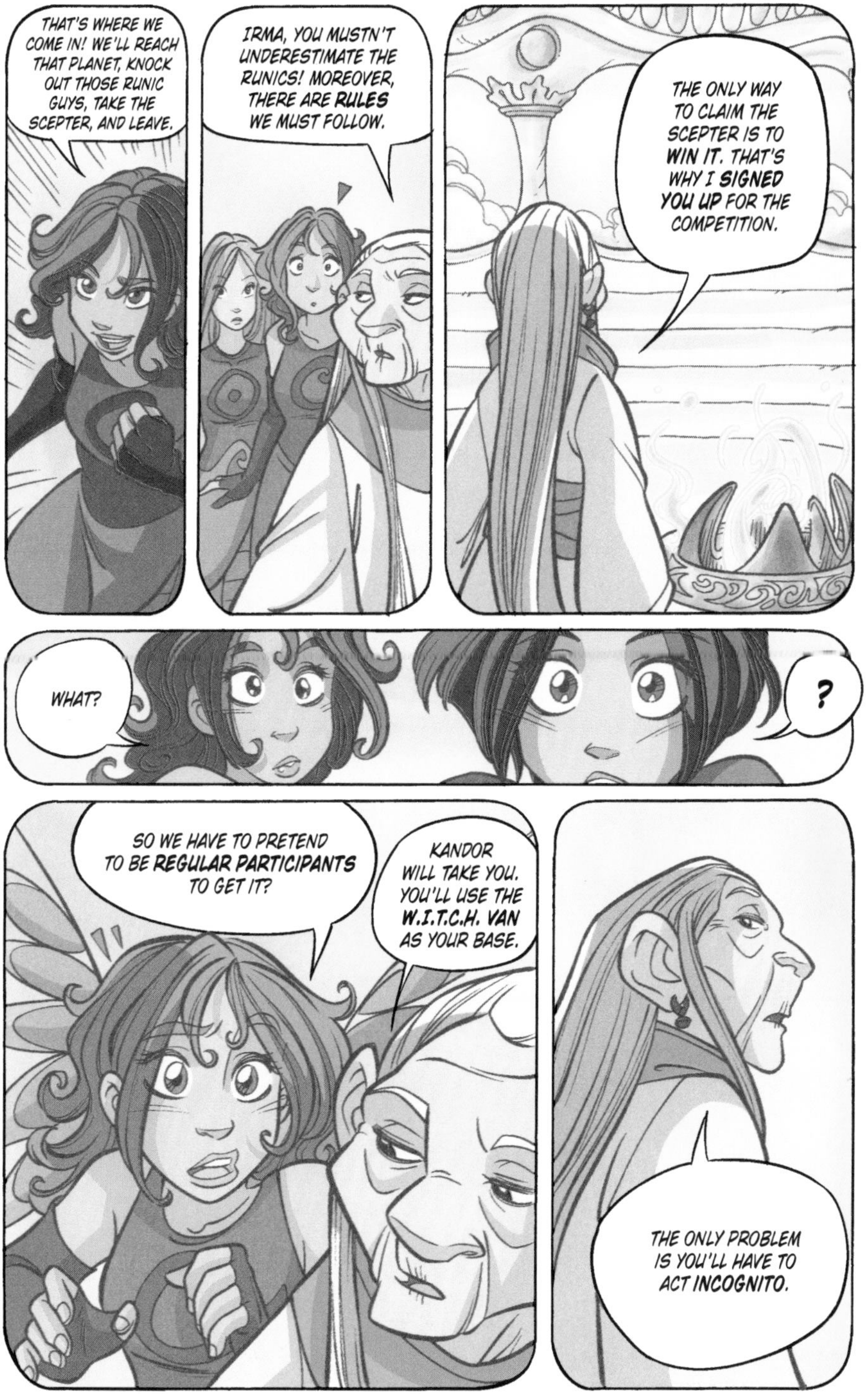
THAT'S WHERE WE COME IN! WE'LL REACH THAT PLANET, KNOCK OUT THOSE RUNIC GUYS, TAKE THE SCEPTER, AND LEAVE.
IRMA, YOU MUSTN'T UNDERESTIMATE THE RUNICS! MOREOVER, THERE ARE RULES WE MUST FOLLOW.
THE ONLY WAY TO CLAIM THE SCEPTER IS TO WIN IT. THAT'S WHY I SIGNED YOU UP FOR THE COMPETITION.
WHAT?
?
SO WE HAVE TO PRETEND TO BE REGULAR PARTICIPANTS TO GET IT?
KANDOR WILL TAKE YOU. YOU'LL USE THE W.I.T.C.H. VAN AS YOUR BASE.
THE ONLY PROBLEM IS YOU'LL HAVE TO ACT INCOGNITO.

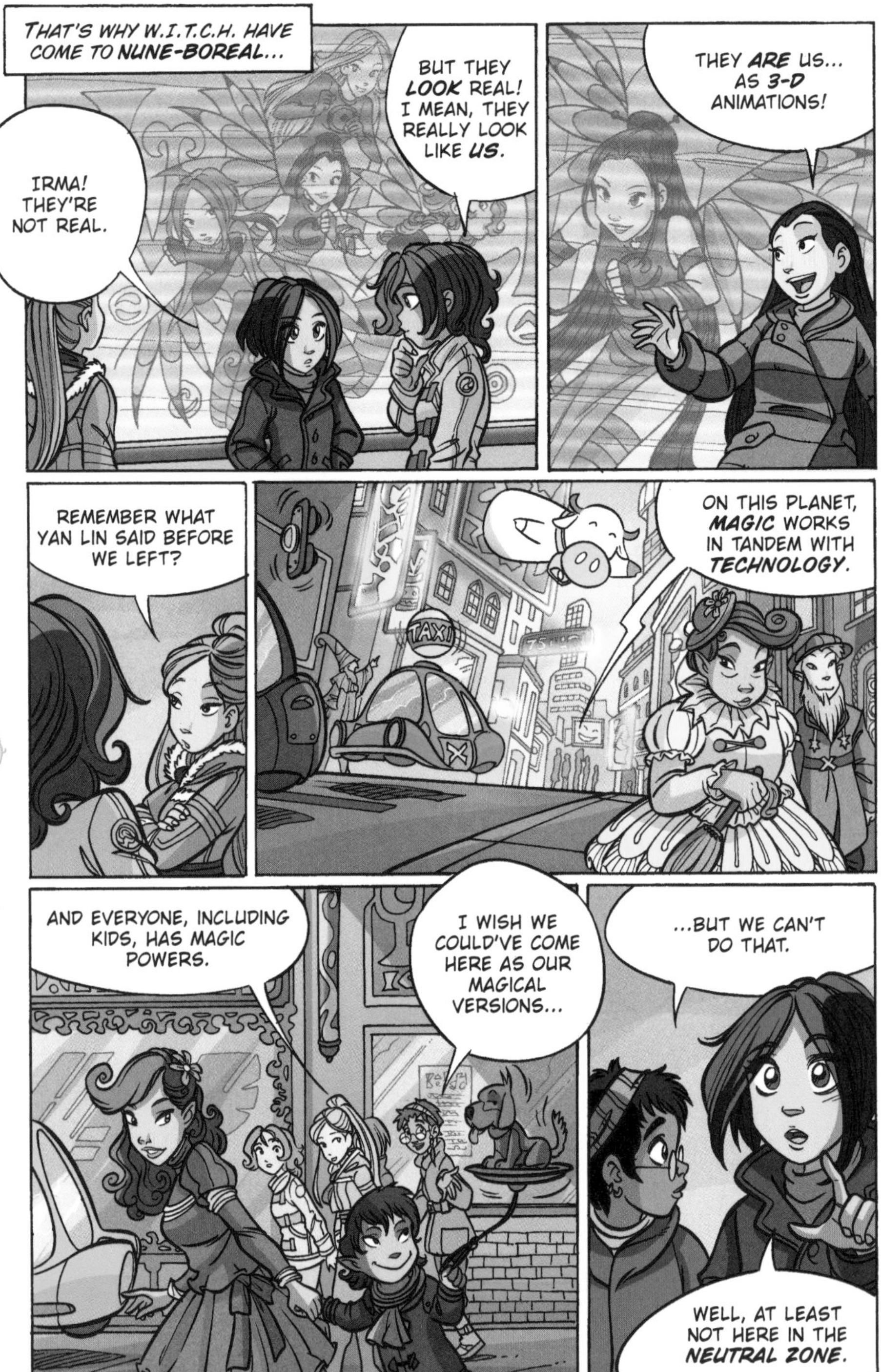
THAT'S WHY W.I.T.C.H. HAVE COME TO **NUNE-BOREAL**...
IRMA! THEY'RE NOT REAL.
BUT THEY **LOOK** REAL! I MEAN, THEY REALLY LOOK LIKE **US**.
THEY **ARE** US... AS **3-D** ANIMATIONS!
REMEMBER WHAT YAN LIN SAID BEFORE WE LEFT?
TAXI
ON THIS PLANET, **MAGIC** WORKS IN TANDEM WITH **TECHNOLOGY**.
AND EVERYONE, INCLUDING KIDS, HAS MAGIC POWERS.
I WISH WE COULD'VE COME HERE AS OUR MAGICAL VERSIONS...
...BUT WE CAN'T DO THAT.
WELL, AT LEAST NOT HERE IN THE **NEUTRAL ZONE**.

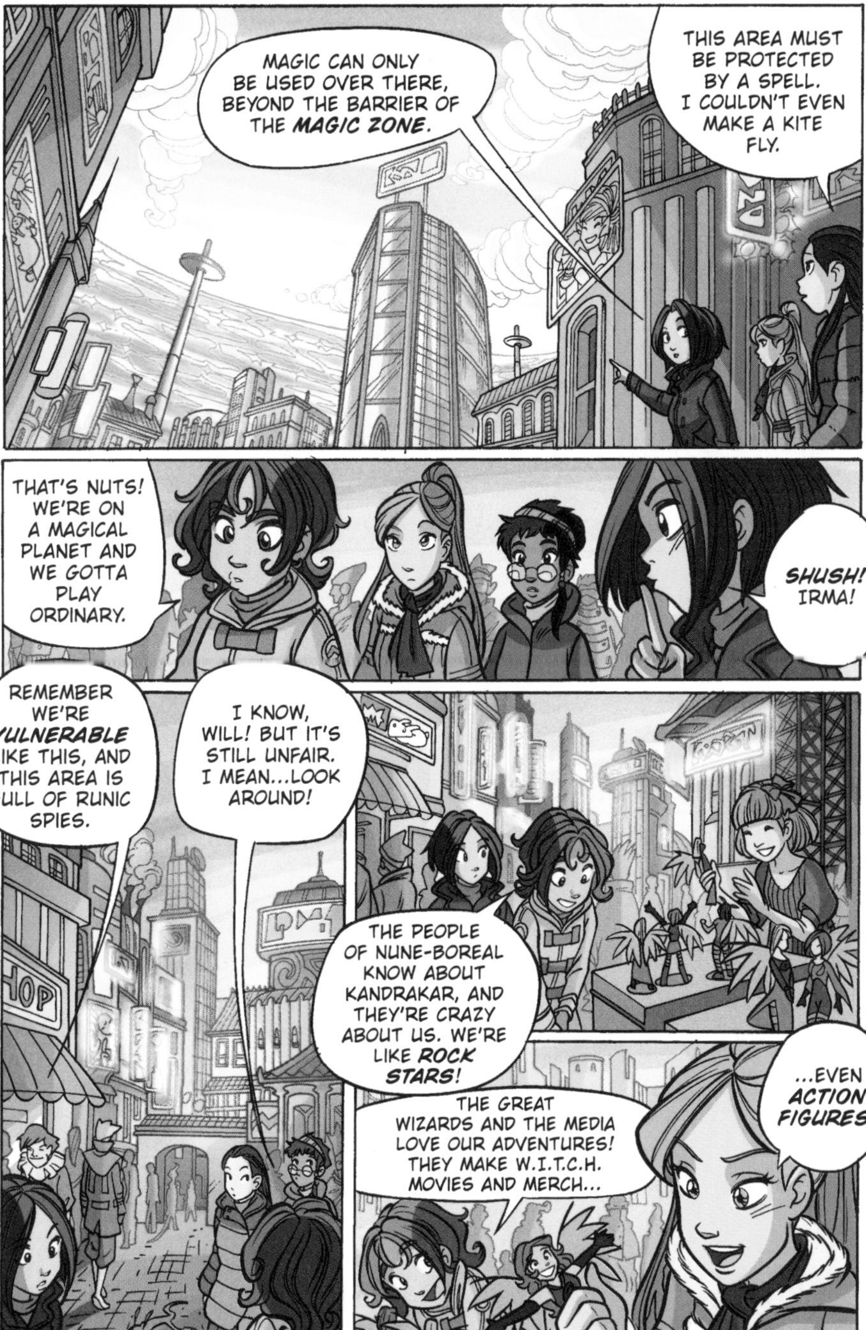
MAGIC CAN ONLY BE USED OVER THERE, BEYOND THE BARRIER OF THE ***MAGIC ZONE***.
THIS AREA MUST BE PROTECTED BY A SPELL. I COULDN'T EVEN MAKE A KITE FLY.
THAT'S NUTS! WE'RE ON A MAGICAL PLANET AND WE GOTTA PLAY ORDINARY.
SHUSH! IRMA!
REMEMBER WE'RE ***VULNERABLE*** LIKE THIS, AND THIS AREA IS FULL OF RUNIC SPIES.
I KNOW, WILL! BUT IT'S STILL UNFAIR. I MEAN...LOOK AROUND!
HOP
THE PEOPLE OF NUNE-BOREAL KNOW ABOUT KANDRAKAR, AND THEY'RE CRAZY ABOUT US. WE'RE LIKE ***ROCK STARS***!
THE GREAT WIZARDS AND THE MEDIA LOVE OUR ADVENTURES! THEY MAKE W.I.T.C.H. MOVIES AND MERCH...
...EVEN ***ACTION FIGURES***!

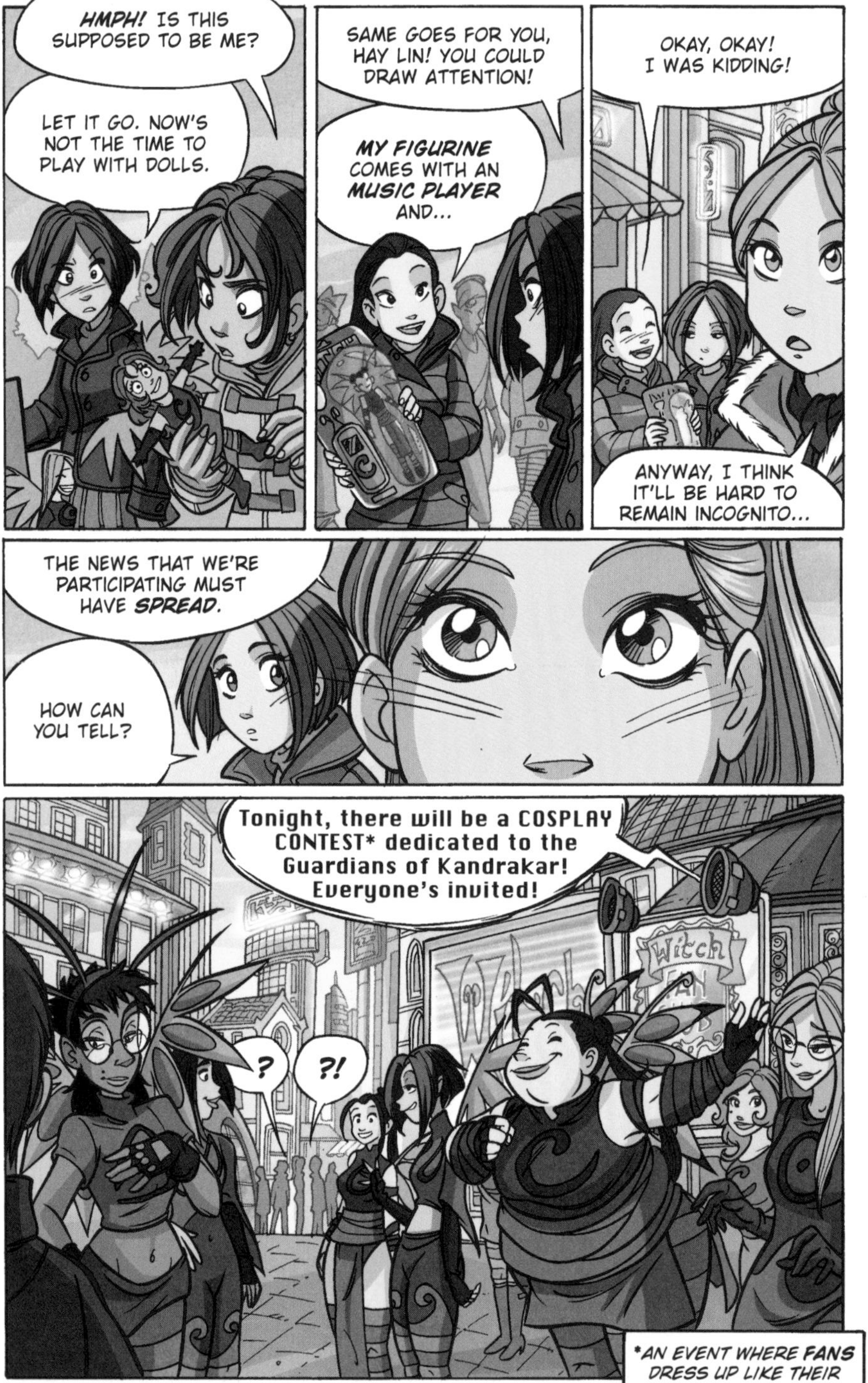
HMPH! IS THIS SUPPOSED TO BE ME?
LET IT GO. NOW'S NOT THE TIME TO PLAY WITH DOLLS.
SAME GOES FOR YOU, HAY LIN! YOU COULD DRAW ATTENTION!
MY FIGURINE COMES WITH AN MUSIC PLAYER AND...
OKAY, OKAY! I WAS KIDDING!
ANYWAY, I THINK IT'LL BE HARD TO REMAIN INCOGNITO...
THE NEWS THAT WE'RE PARTICIPATING MUST HAVE SPREAD.
HOW CAN YOU TELL?
Tonight, there will be a COSPLAY CONTEST* dedicated to the Guardians of Kandrakar! Everyone's invited!
?
?!
Witch
*AN EVENT WHERE FANS DRESS UP LIKE THEIR FAVORITE CHARACTERS.

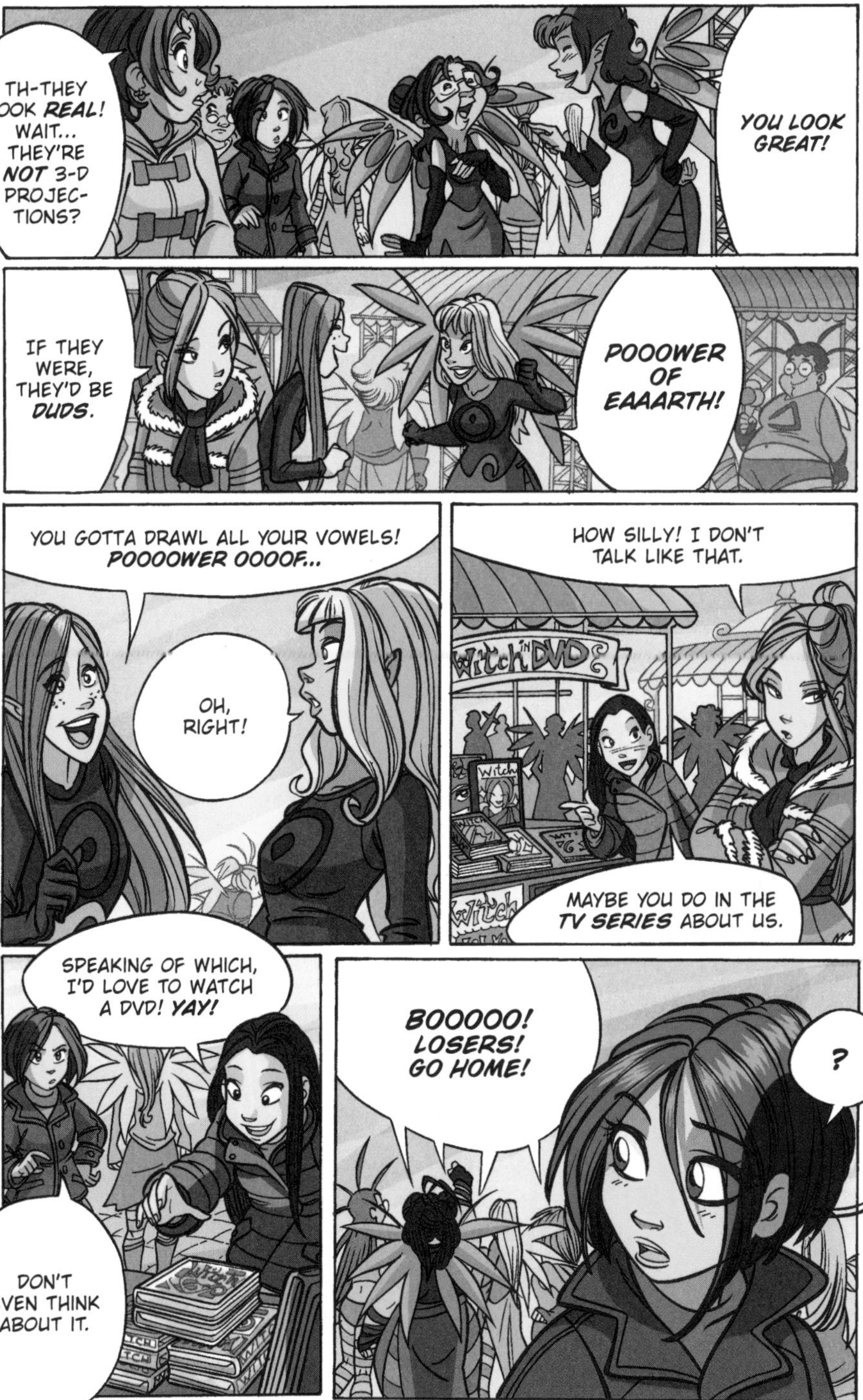
TH-THEY LOOK REAL! WAIT... THEY'RE NOT 3-D PROJECTIONS?
YOU LOOK GREAT!
IF THEY WERE, THEY'D BE DUDS.
POOOWER OF EAAARTH!
YOU GOTTA DRAWL ALL YOUR VOWELS! POOOOWER OOOOF...
OH, RIGHT!
HOW SILLY! I DON'T TALK LIKE THAT.
Witch in DVD
MAYBE YOU DO IN THE TV SERIES ABOUT US.
SPEAKING OF WHICH, I'D LOVE TO WATCH A DVD! YAY!
DON'T EVEN THINK ABOUT IT.
BOOOOO! LOSERS! GO HOME!
?

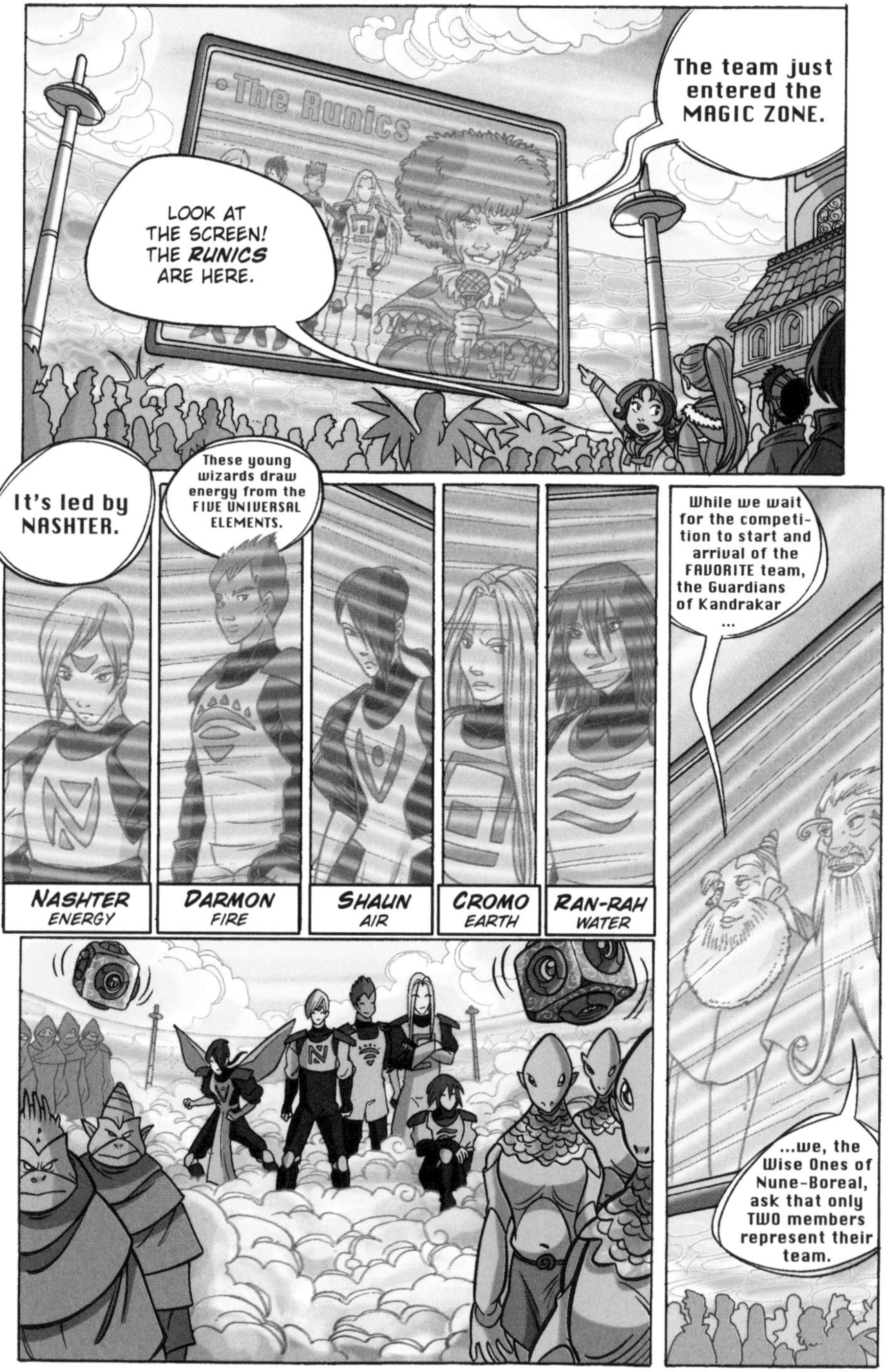
The Runics
The team just entered the MAGIC ZONE.
LOOK AT THE SCREEN! THE RUNICS ARE HERE.
It's led by NASHTER.
These young wizards draw energy from the FIVE UNIVERSAL ELEMENTS.
NASHTER ENERGY
DARMON FIRE
SHAUN AIR
CROMO EARTH
RAN-RAH WATER
While we wait for the competition to start and arrival of the FAVORITE team, the Guardians of Kandrakar ...
...we, the Wise Ones of Nune-Boreal, ask that only TWO members represent their team.

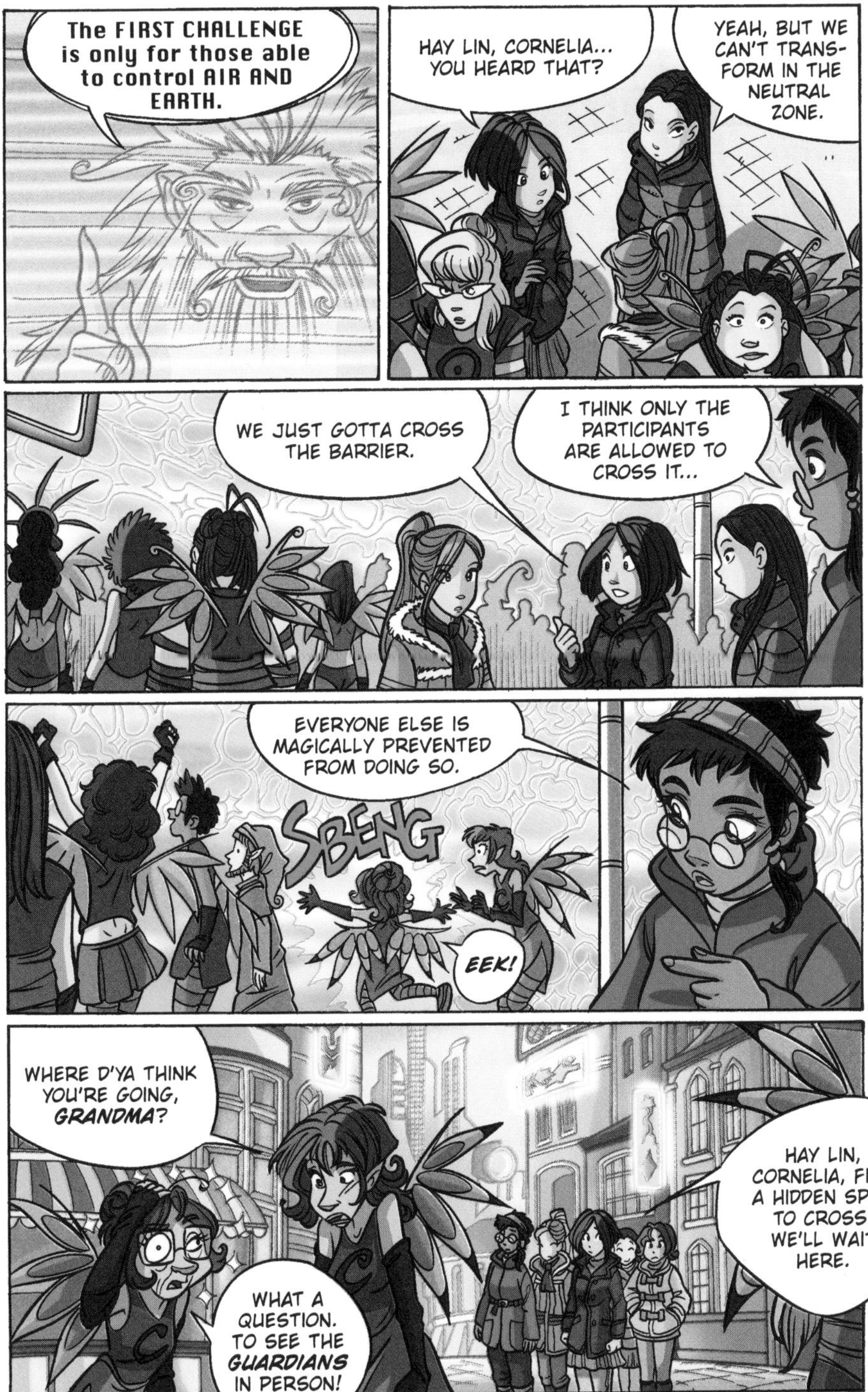
The FIRST CHALLENGE is only for those able to control AIR AND EARTH.
HAY LIN, CORNELIA... YOU HEARD THAT?
YEAH, BUT WE CAN'T TRANS-FORM IN THE NEUTRAL ZONE.
WE JUST GOTTA CROSS THE BARRIER.
I THINK ONLY THE PARTICIPANTS ARE ALLOWED TO CROSS IT...
EVERYONE ELSE IS MAGICALLY PREVENTED FROM DOING SO.
SBENG
EEK!
WHERE D'YA THINK YOU'RE GOING, GRANDMA?
WHAT A QUESTION. TO SEE THE GUARDIANS IN PERSON!
HAY LIN, CORNELIA, FIND A HIDDEN SPOT TO CROSS. WE'LL WAIT HERE.

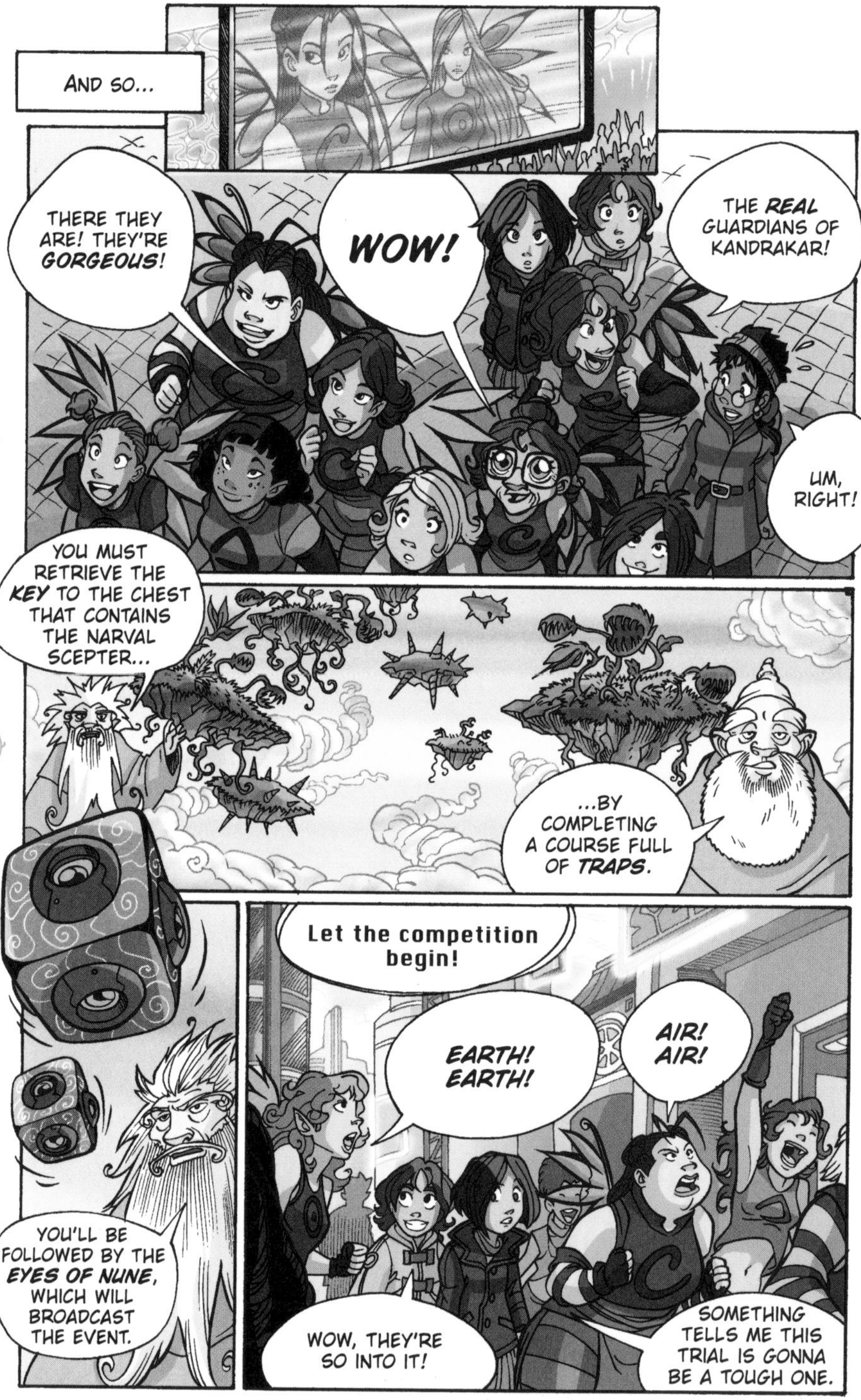
AND SO...
THERE THEY ARE! THEY'RE GORGEOUS!
WOW!
THE REAL GUARDIANS OF KANDRAKAR!
UM, RIGHT!
YOU MUST RETRIEVE THE KEY TO THE CHEST THAT CONTAINS THE NARVAL SCEPTER...
...BY COMPLETING A COURSE FULL OF TRAPS.
YOU'LL BE FOLLOWED BY THE EYES OF NUNE, WHICH WILL BROADCAST THE EVENT.
Let the competition begin!
EARTH! EARTH!
AIR! AIR!
WOW, THEY'RE SO INTO IT!
SOMETHING TELLS ME THIS TRIAL IS GONNA BE A TOUGH ONE.

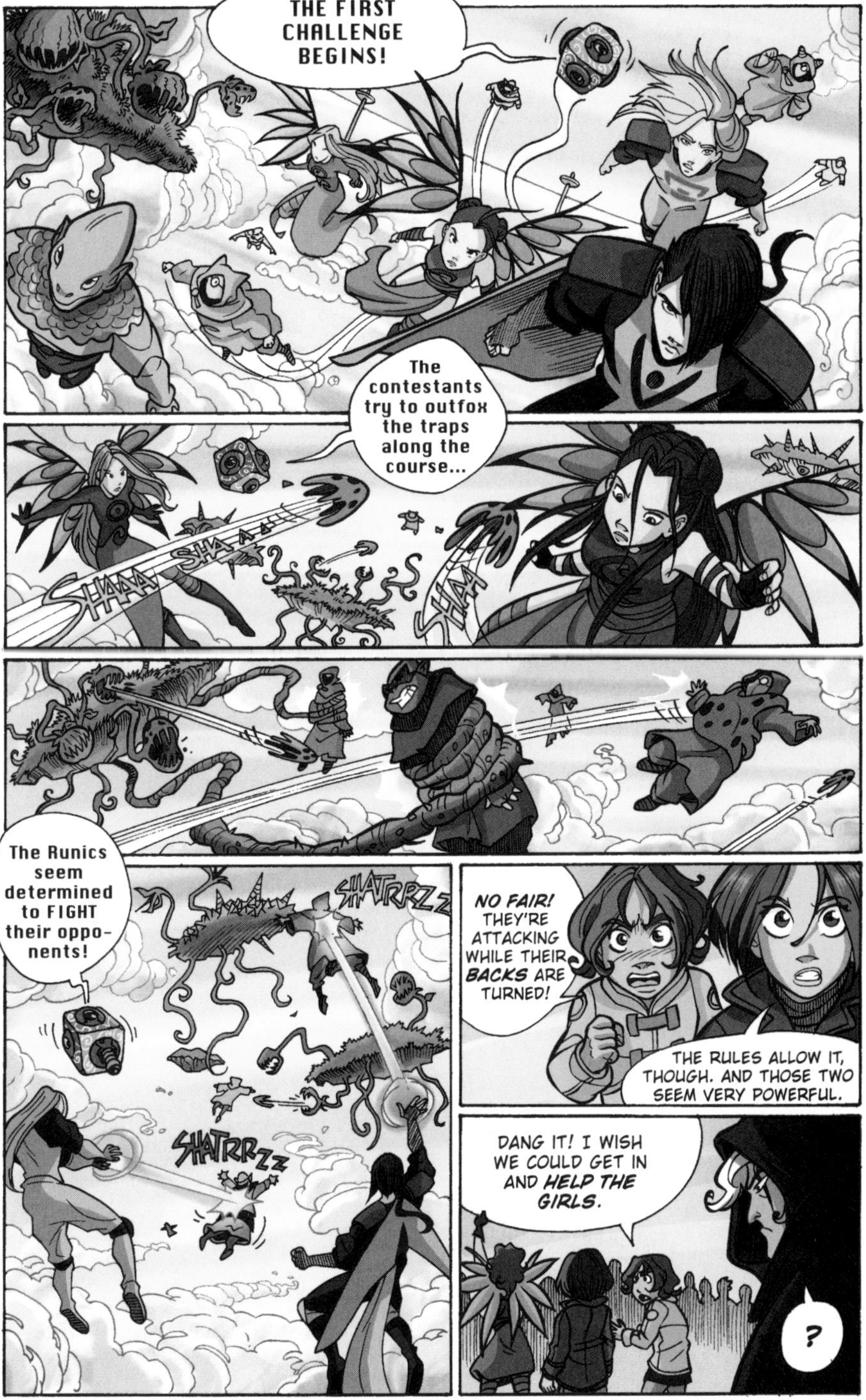

THE FIRST CHALLENGE BEGINS!
The contestants try to outfox the traps along the course...
SHAAA SHAAA
SHAA
The Runics seem determined to FIGHT their opponents!
SHATRRZZ
SHATRRZz
NO FAIR! THEY'RE ATTACKING WHILE THEIR BACKS ARE TURNED!
THE RULES ALLOW IT, THOUGH. AND THOSE TWO SEEM VERY POWERFUL.
DANG IT! I WISH WE COULD GET IN AND HELP THE GIRLS.
?

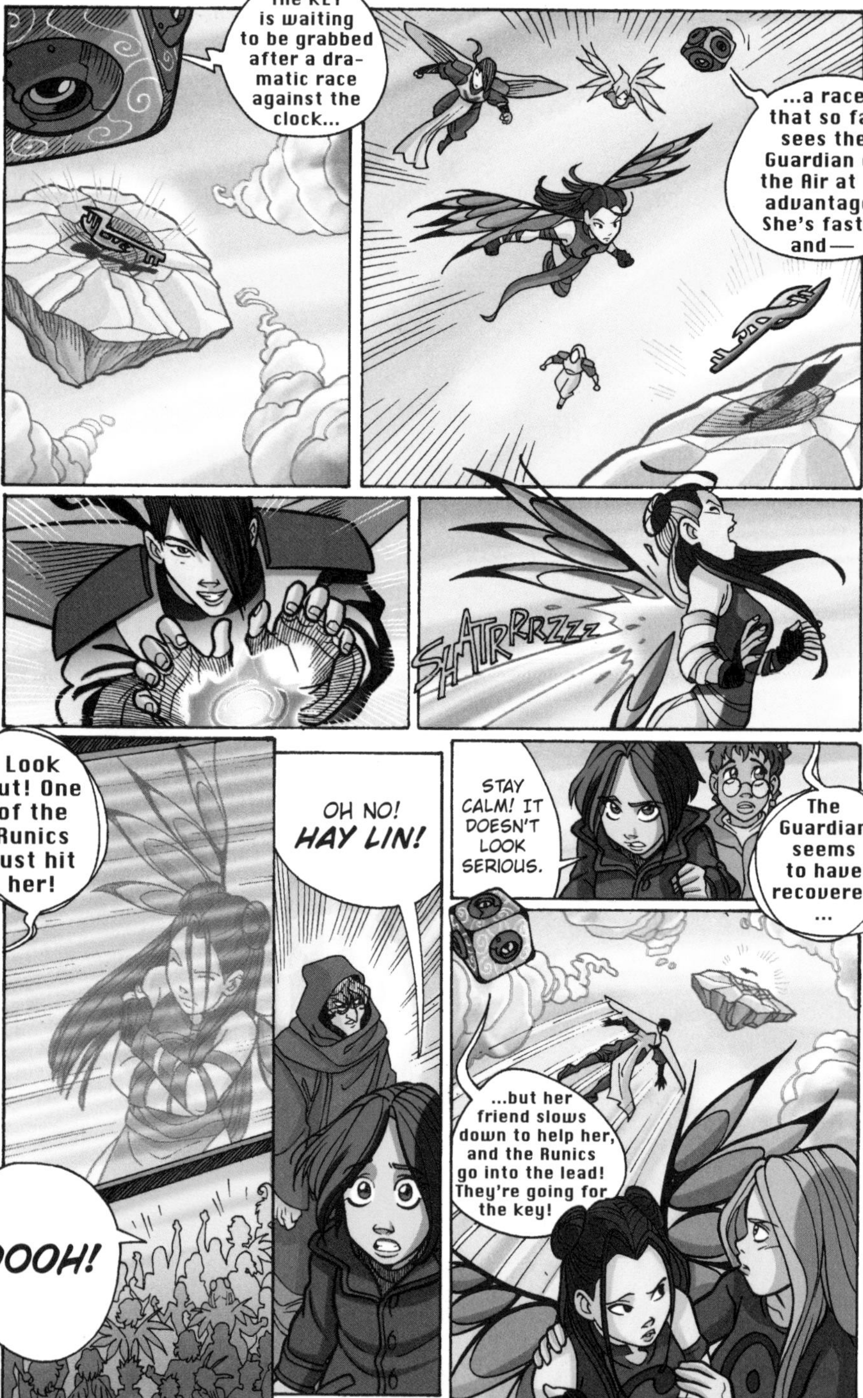
The KEY is waiting to be grabbed after a dramatic race against the clock...
...a race that so far sees the Guardian of the Air at an advantage! She's faster and—
SHATRRRZZZ
Look out! One of the Runics just hit her!
OOOH!
OH NO! HAY LIN!
STAY CALM! IT DOESN'T LOOK SERIOUS.
The Guardian seems to have recovered...
...but her friend slows down to help her, and the Runics go into the lead! They're going for the key!

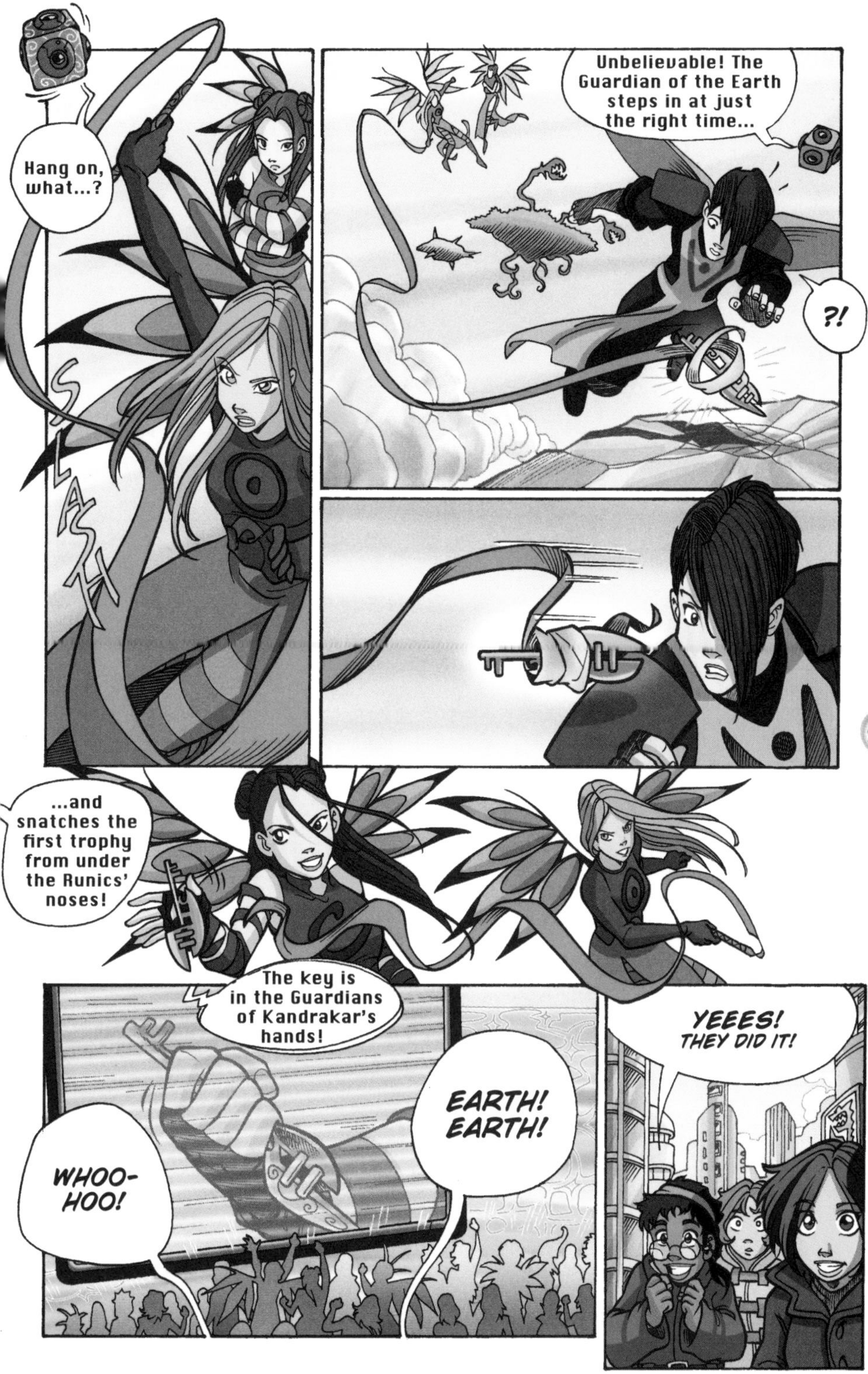
Hang on, what...?
SLASH
Unbelievable! The Guardian of the Earth steps in at just the right time...
?!
...and snatches the first trophy from under the Runics' noses!
The key is in the Guardians of Kandrakar's hands!
WHOO-HOO!
EARTH! EARTH!
YEEES! THEY DID IT!

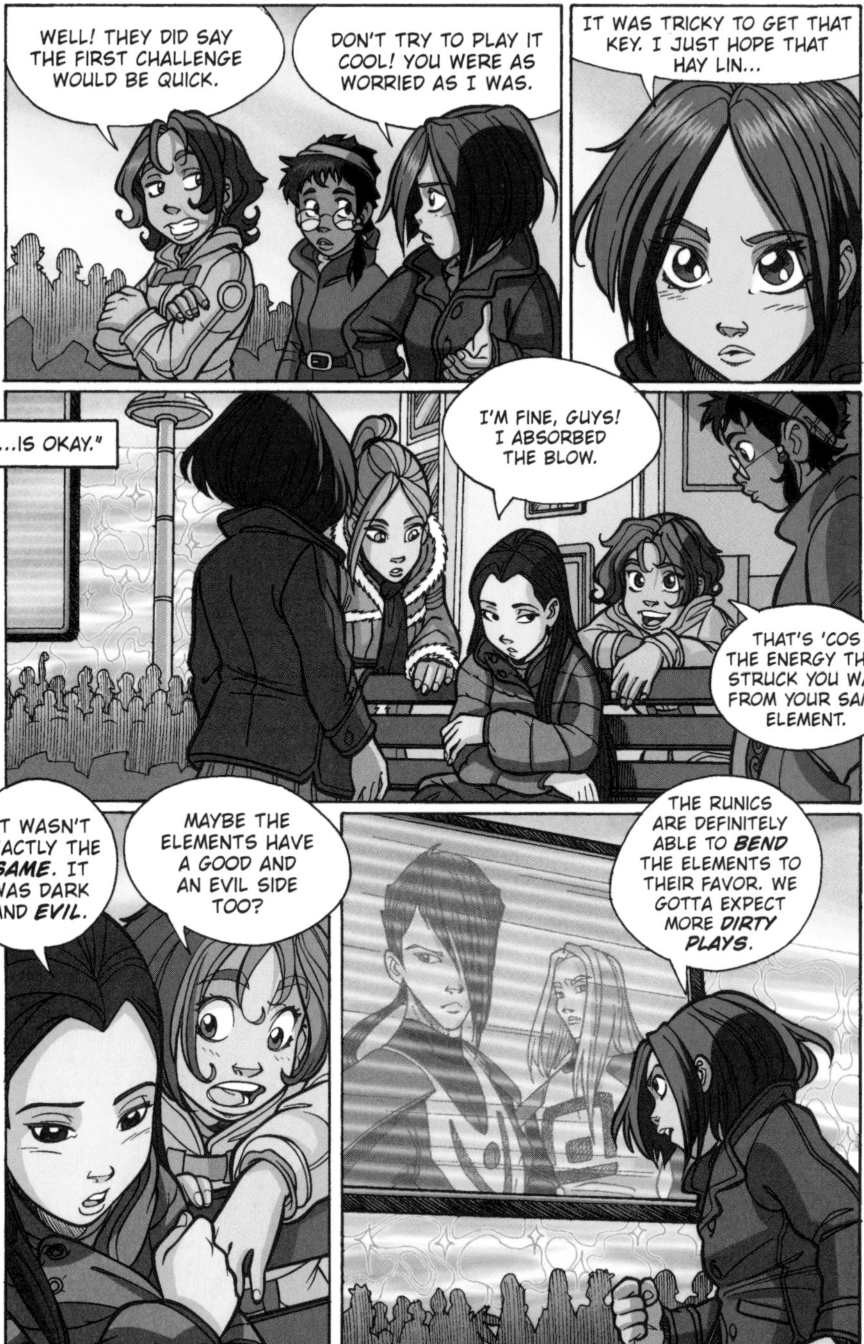
WELL! THEY DID SAY THE FIRST CHALLENGE WOULD BE QUICK.
DON'T TRY TO PLAY IT COOL! YOU WERE AS WORRIED AS I WAS.
IT WAS TRICKY TO GET THAT KEY. I JUST HOPE THAT HAY LIN...
"...IS OKAY."
I'M FINE, GUYS! I ABSORBED THE BLOW.
THAT'S 'COS THE ENERGY THAT STRUCK YOU WAS FROM YOUR SAME ELEMENT.
IT WASN'T EXACTLY THE SAME. IT WAS DARK AND EVIL.
MAYBE THE ELEMENTS HAVE A GOOD AND AN EVIL SIDE TOO?
THE RUNICS ARE DEFINITELY ABLE TO BEND THE ELEMENTS TO THEIR FAVOR. WE GOTTA EXPECT MORE DIRTY PLAYS.

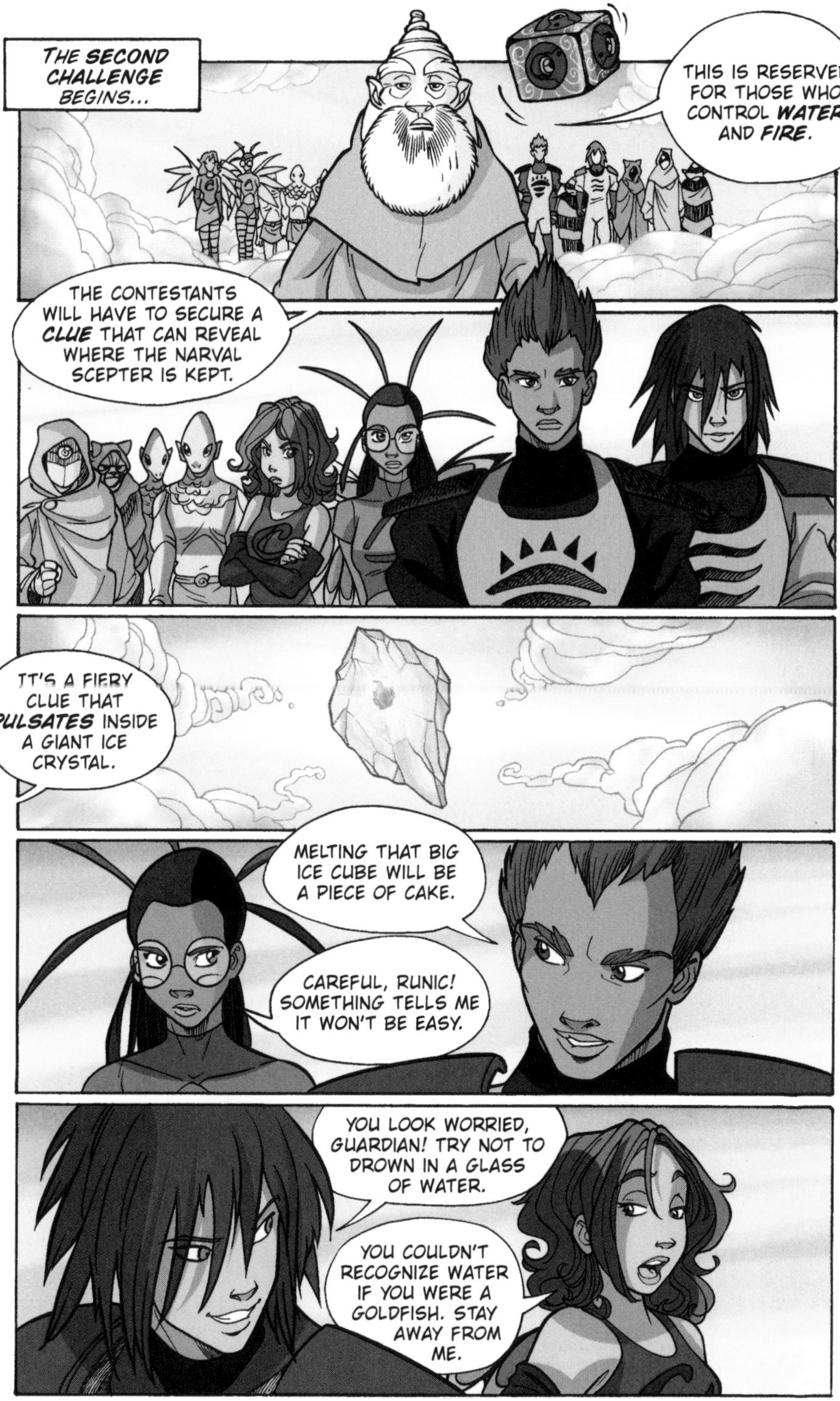
THE SECOND CHALLENGE BEGINS...
THIS IS RESERVED FOR THOSE WHO CONTROL WATER AND FIRE.
THE CONTESTANTS WILL HAVE TO SECURE A CLUE THAT CAN REVEAL WHERE THE NARVAL SCEPTER IS KEPT.
IT'S A FIERY CLUE THAT PULSATES INSIDE A GIANT ICE CRYSTAL.
MELTING THAT BIG ICE CUBE WILL BE A PIECE OF CAKE.
CAREFUL, RUNIC! SOMETHING TELLS ME IT WON'T BE EASY.
YOU LOOK WORRIED, GUARDIAN! TRY NOT TO DROWN IN A GLASS OF WATER.
YOU COULDN'T RECOGNIZE WATER IF YOU WERE A GOLDFISH. STAY AWAY FROM ME.

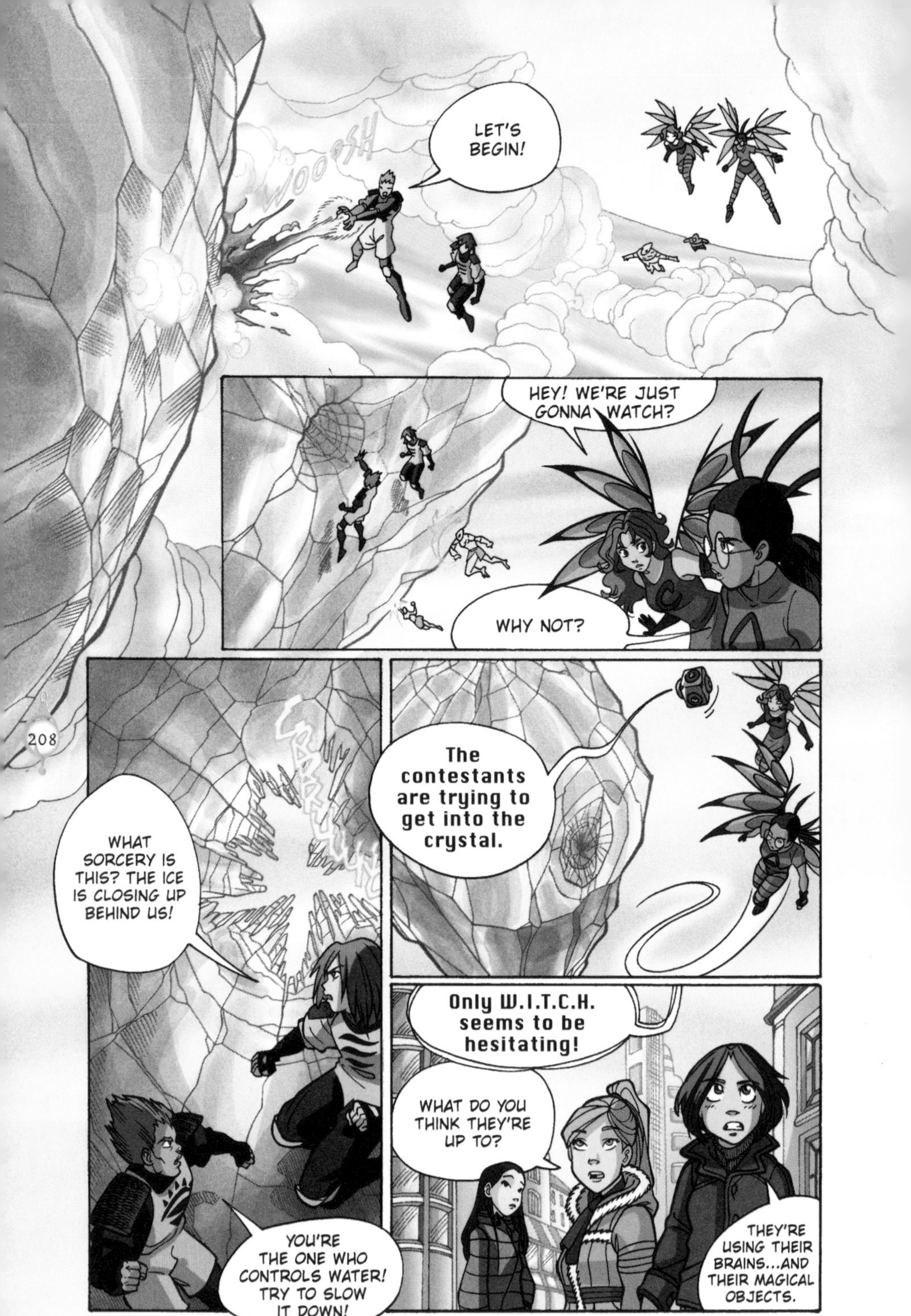
WOOOSH
LET'S BEGIN!
HEY! WE'RE JUST GONNA WATCH?
WHY NOT?
WHAT SORCERY IS THIS? THE ICE IS CLOSING UP BEHIND US!
YOU'RE THE ONE WHO CONTROLS WATER! TRY TO SLOW IT DOWN!
The contestants are trying to get into the crystal.
Only W.I.T.C.H. seems to be hesitating!
WHAT DO YOU THINK THEY'RE UP TO?
THEY'RE USING THEIR BRAINS...AND THEIR MAGICAL OBJECTS.

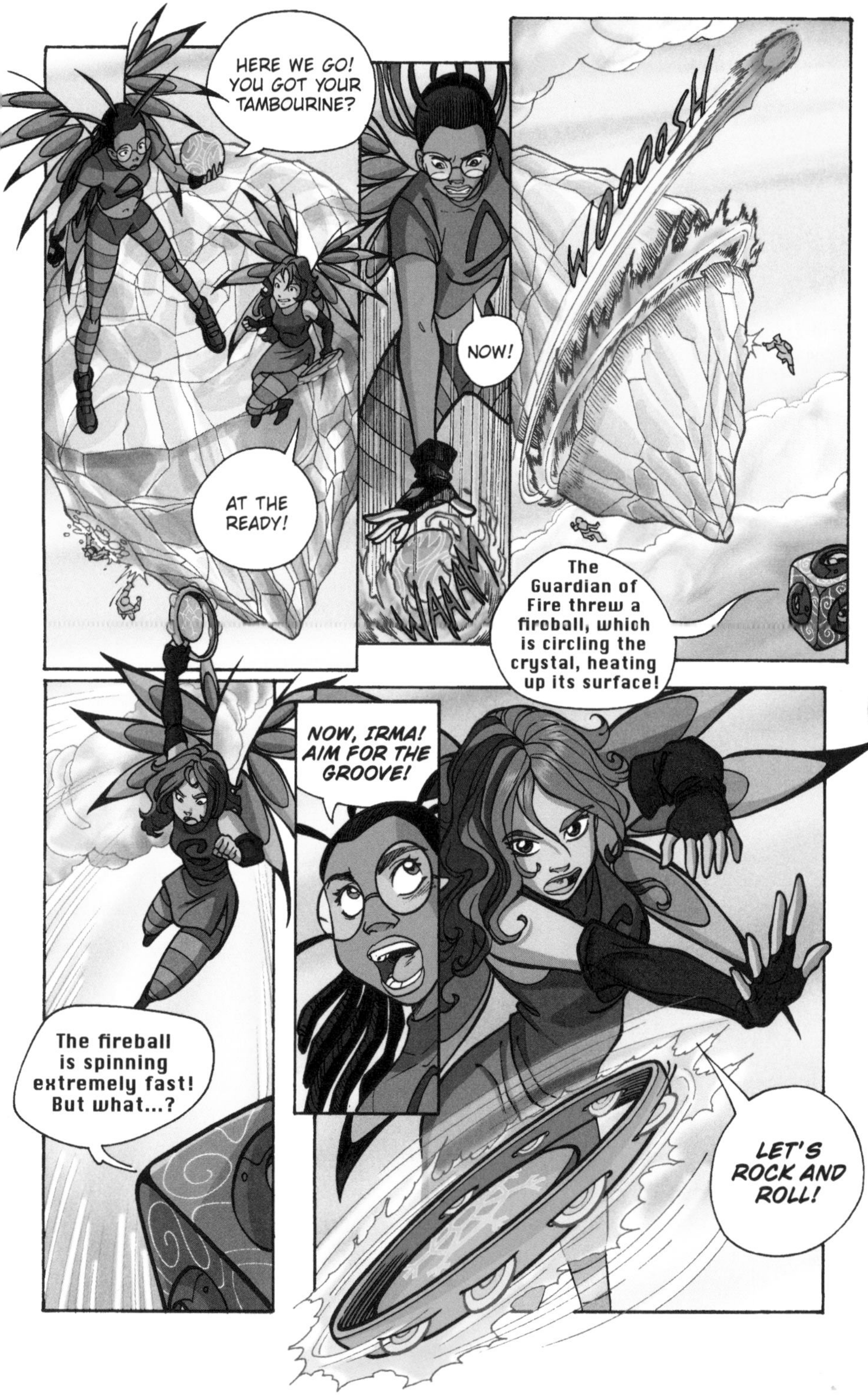
HERE WE GO! YOU GOT YOUR TAMBOURINE?
AT THE READY!
NOW!
WAAAM
WOOOOOSH
The Guardian of Fire threw a fireball, which is circling the crystal, heating up its surface!
NOW, IRMA! AIM FOR THE GROOVE!
The fireball is spinning extremely fast! But what...?
LET'S ROCK AND ROLL!

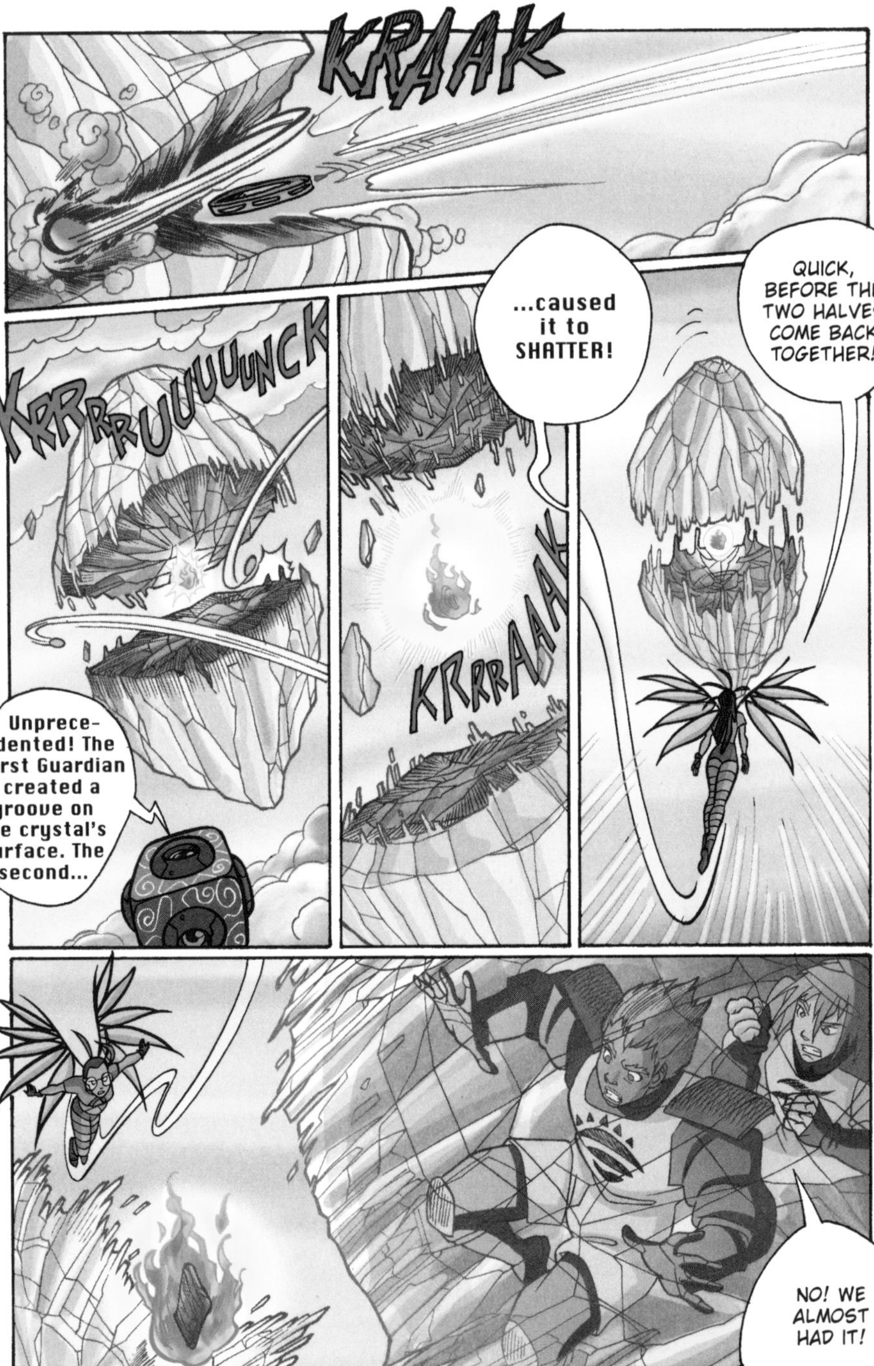
KRAAK
KRRRRUUUUUNCK
Unprece-dented! The first Guardian created a groove on the crystal's surface. The second...
KRRRAAAK
...caused it to SHATTER!
QUICK, BEFORE THE TWO HALVES COME BACK TOGETHER!
NO! WE ALMOST HAD IT!

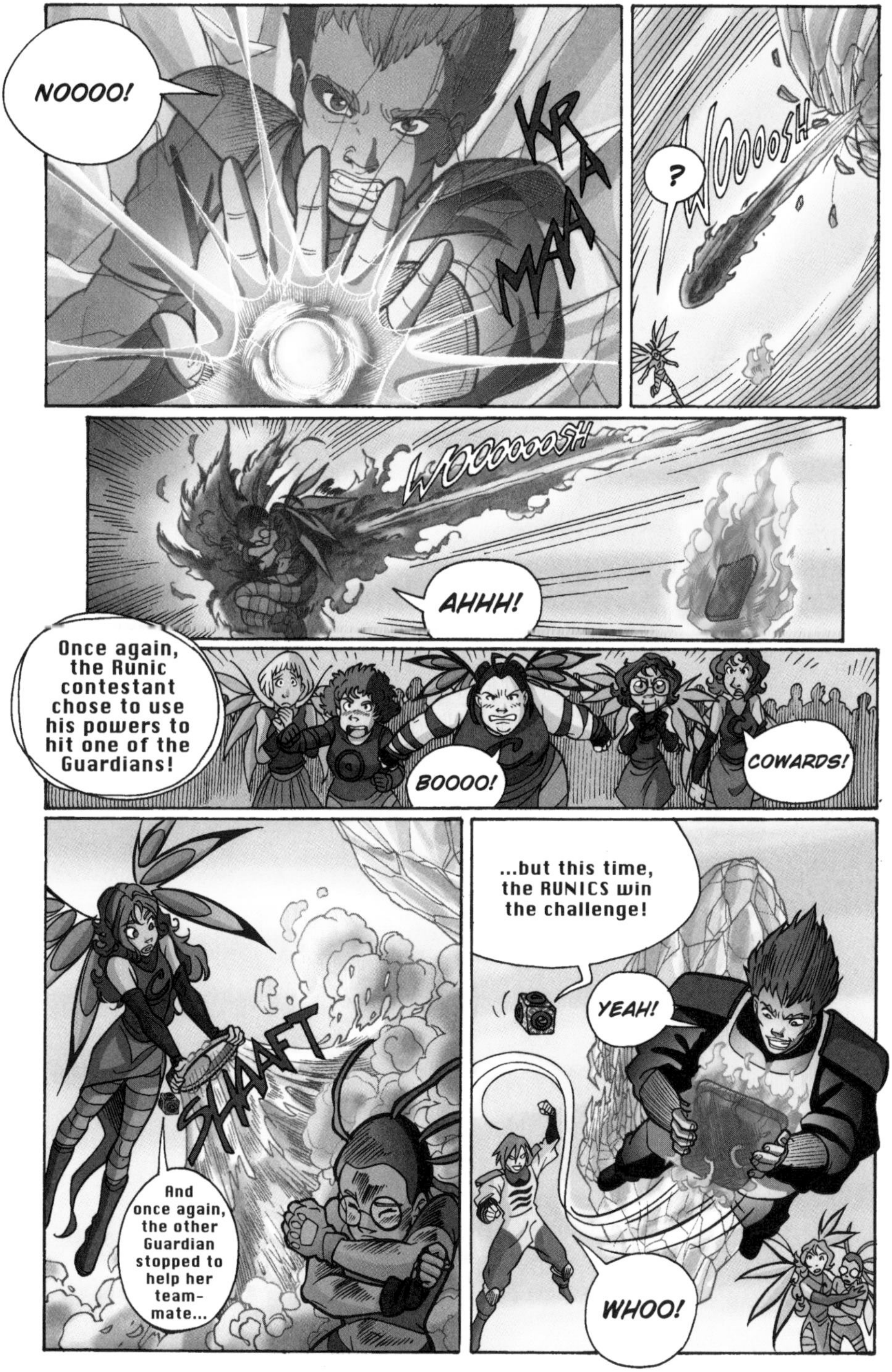
NOOOO!
KRAMAA
?
WOOOOSH
WOOOOOOSH
AHHH!
Once again, the Runic contestant chose to use his powers to hit one of the Guardians!
BOOOO!
COWARDS!
SHAAFT
And once again, the other Guardian stopped to help her team-mate...
...but this time, the RUNICS win the challenge!
YEAH!
WHOO!

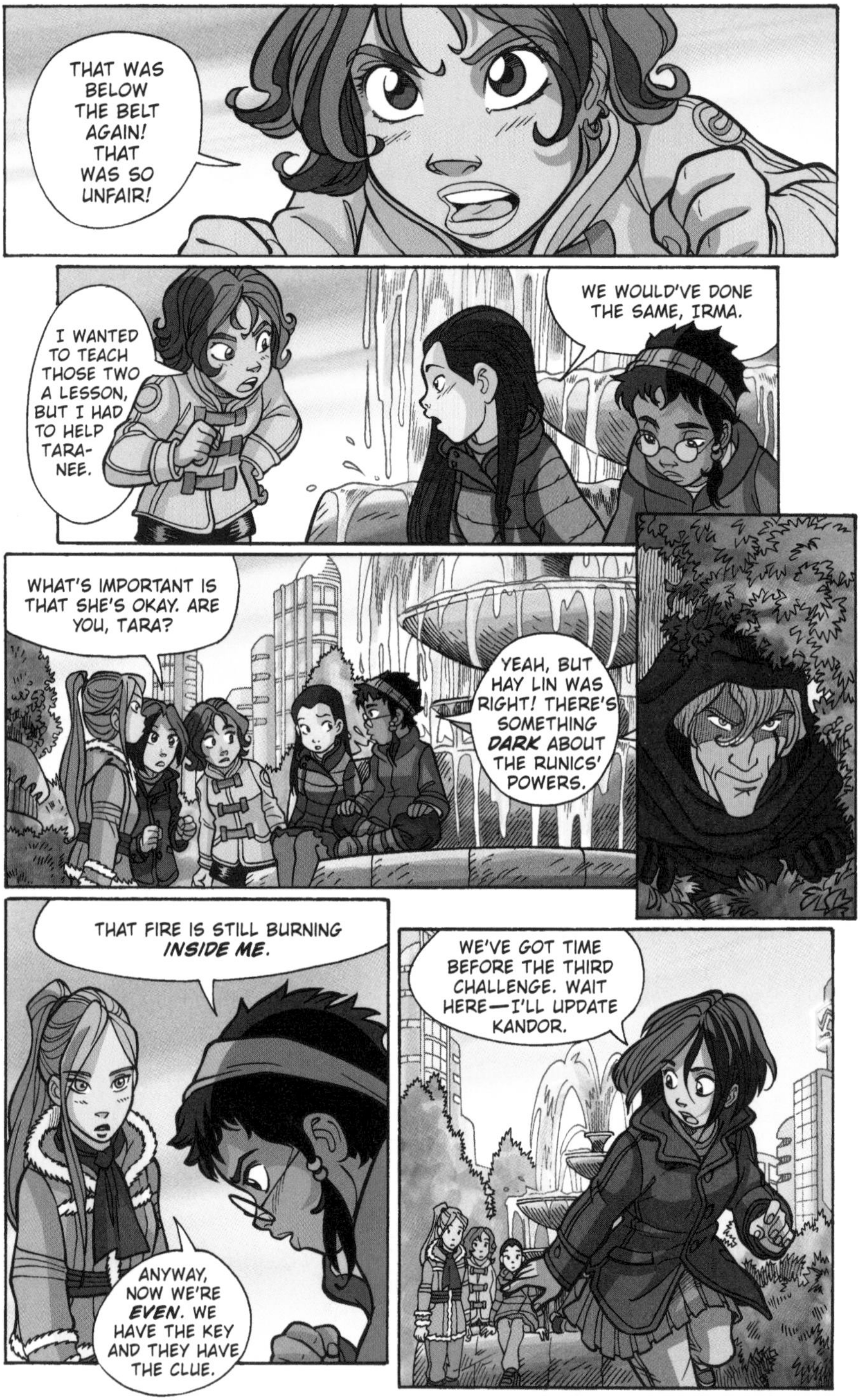

THAT WAS BELOW THE BELT AGAIN! THAT WAS SO UNFAIR!
I WANTED TO TEACH THOSE TWO A LESSON, BUT I HAD TO HELP TARA-NEE.
WE WOULD'VE DONE THE SAME, IRMA.
WHAT'S IMPORTANT IS THAT SHE'S OKAY. ARE YOU, TARA?
YEAH, BUT HAY LIN WAS RIGHT! THERE'S SOMETHING **DARK** ABOUT THE RUNICS' POWERS.
THAT FIRE IS STILL BURNING **INSIDE ME**.
ANYWAY, NOW WE'RE **EVEN**. WE HAVE THE KEY AND THEY HAVE THE CLUE.
WE'VE GOT TIME BEFORE THE THIRD CHALLENGE. WAIT HERE—I'LL UPDATE KANDOR.

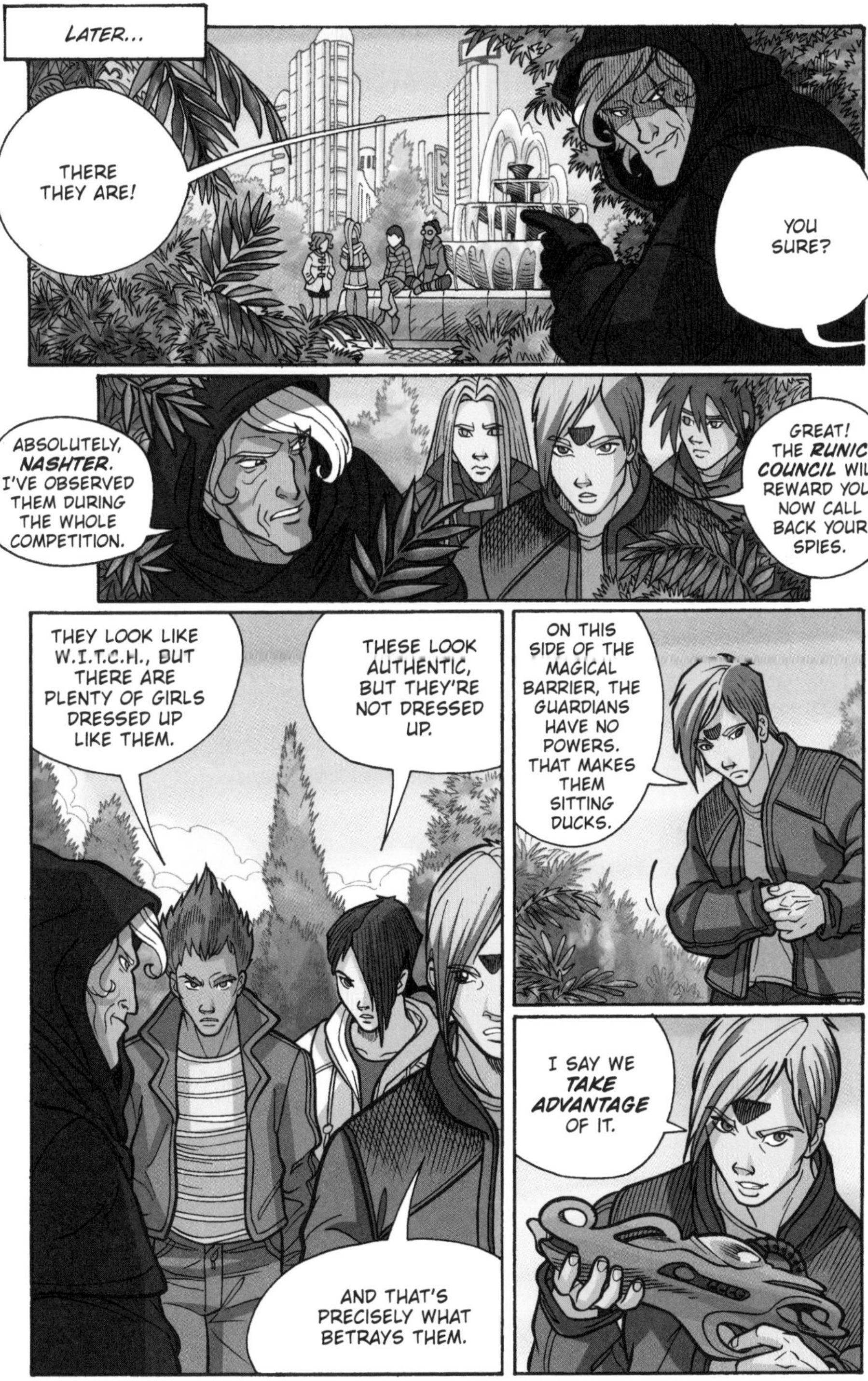

LATER...
THERE THEY ARE!
YOU SURE?
ABSOLUTELY, NASHTER. I'VE OBSERVED THEM DURING THE WHOLE COMPETITION.
GREAT! THE RUNIC COUNCIL WILL REWARD YOU. NOW CALL BACK YOUR SPIES.
THEY LOOK LIKE W.I.T.C.H., BUT THERE ARE PLENTY OF GIRLS DRESSED UP LIKE THEM.
THESE LOOK AUTHENTIC, BUT THEY'RE NOT DRESSED UP.
AND THAT'S PRECISELY WHAT BETRAYS THEM.
ON THIS SIDE OF THE MAGICAL BARRIER, THE GUARDIANS HAVE NO POWERS. THAT MAKES THEM SITTING DUCKS.
I SAY WE TAKE ADVANTAGE OF IT.

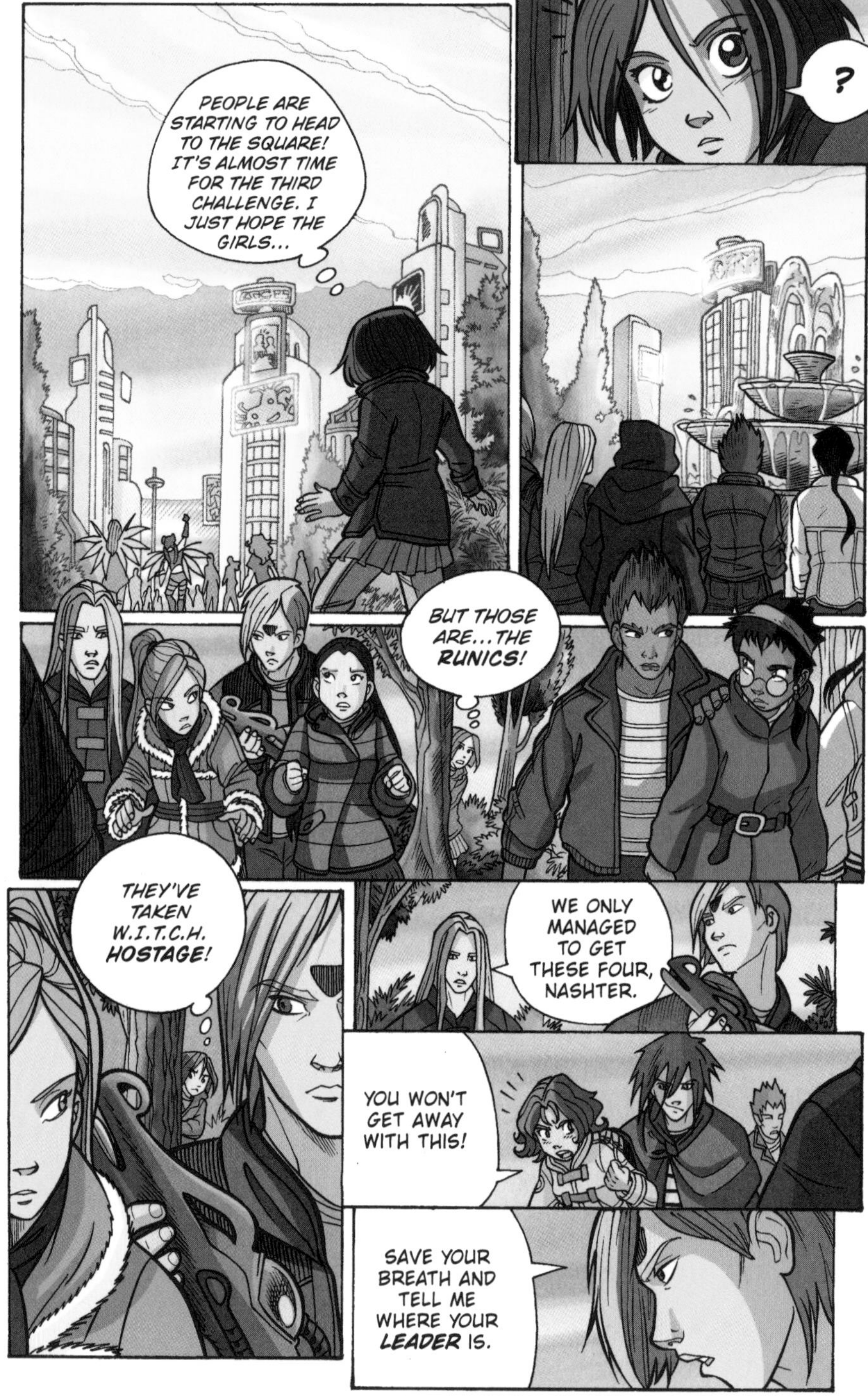
PEOPLE ARE STARTING TO HEAD TO THE SQUARE! IT'S ALMOST TIME FOR THE THIRD CHALLENGE. I JUST HOPE THE GIRLS...
?
BUT THOSE ARE...THE RUNICS!
THEY'VE TAKEN W.I.T.C.H. HOSTAGE!
WE ONLY MANAGED TO GET THESE FOUR, NASHTER.
YOU WON'T GET AWAY WITH THIS!
SAVE YOUR BREATH AND TELL ME WHERE YOUR LEADER IS.

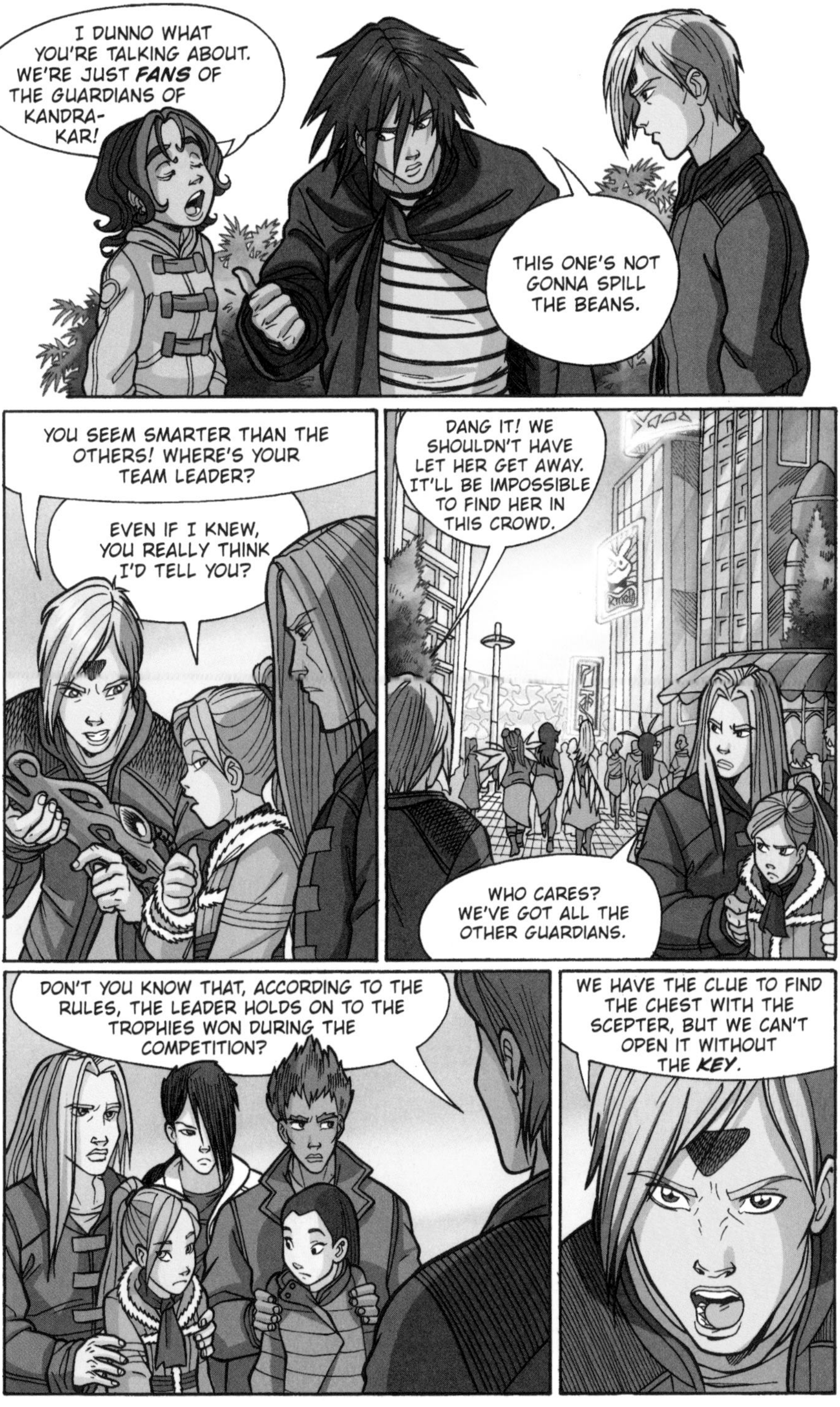

I DUNNO WHAT YOU'RE TALKING ABOUT. WE'RE JUST FANS OF THE GUARDIANS OF KANDRA-KAR!
THIS ONE'S NOT GONNA SPILL THE BEANS.
YOU SEEM SMARTER THAN THE OTHERS! WHERE'S YOUR TEAM LEADER?
EVEN IF I KNEW, YOU REALLY THINK I'D TELL YOU?
DANG IT! WE SHOULDN'T HAVE LET HER GET AWAY. IT'LL BE IMPOSSIBLE TO FIND HER IN THIS CROWD.
WHO CARES? WE'VE GOT ALL THE OTHER GUARDIANS.
DON'T YOU KNOW THAT, ACCORDING TO THE RULES, THE LEADER HOLDS ON TO THE TROPHIES WON DURING THE COMPETITION?
WE HAVE THE CLUE TO FIND THE CHEST WITH THE SCEPTER, BUT WE CAN'T OPEN IT WITHOUT THE KEY.

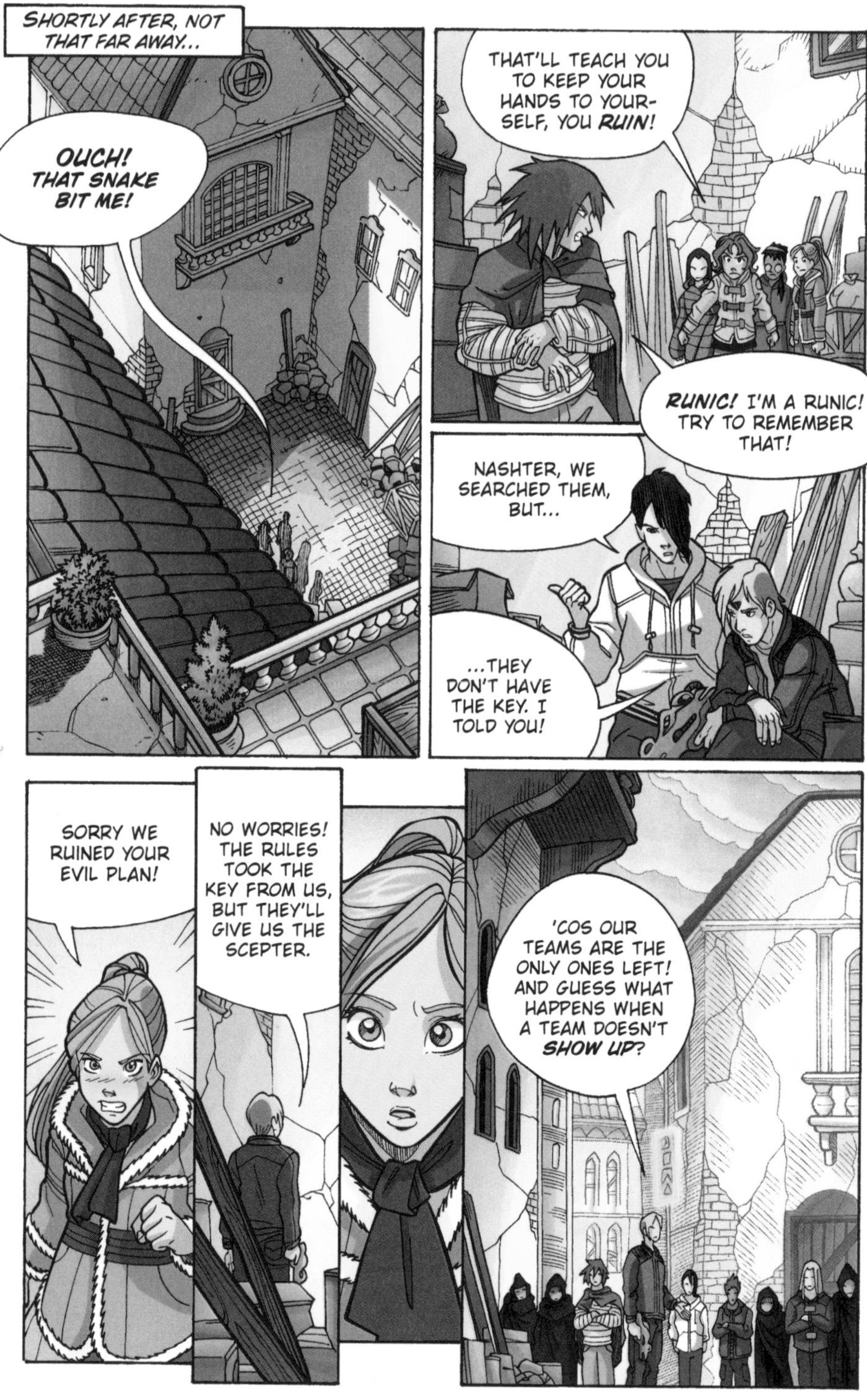
SHORTLY AFTER, NOT THAT FAR AWAY...
OUCH! THAT SNAKE BIT ME!
THAT'LL TEACH YOU TO KEEP YOUR HANDS TO YOURSELF, YOU RUIN!
RUNIC! I'M A RUNIC! TRY TO REMEMBER THAT!
NASHTER, WE SEARCHED THEM, BUT...
...THEY DON'T HAVE THE KEY. I TOLD YOU!
SORRY WE RUINED YOUR EVIL PLAN!
NO WORRIES! THE RULES TOOK THE KEY FROM US, BUT THEY'LL GIVE US THE SCEPTER.
'COS OUR TEAMS ARE THE ONLY ONES LEFT! AND GUESS WHAT HAPPENS WHEN A TEAM DOESN'T SHOW UP?

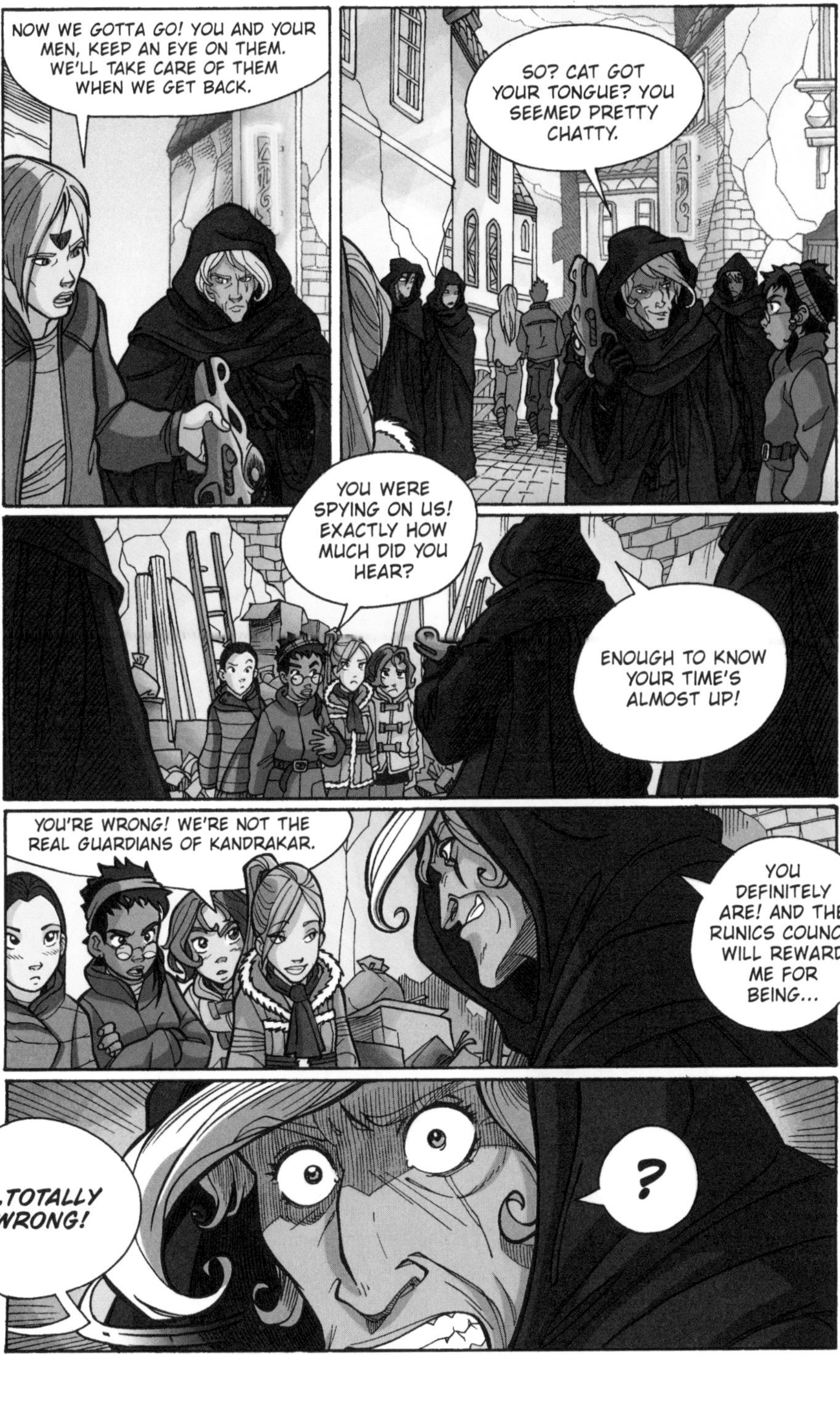
NOW WE GOTTA GO! YOU AND YOUR MEN, KEEP AN EYE ON THEM. WE'LL TAKE CARE OF THEM WHEN WE GET BACK.
SO? CAT GOT YOUR TONGUE? YOU SEEMED PRETTY CHATTY.
YOU WERE SPYING ON US! EXACTLY HOW MUCH DID YOU HEAR?
ENOUGH TO KNOW YOUR TIME'S ALMOST UP!
YOU'RE WRONG! WE'RE NOT THE REAL GUARDIANS OF KANDRAKAR.
YOU DEFINITELY ARE! AND THE RUNICS COUNCIL WILL REWARD ME FOR BEING...
...TOTALLY WRONG!
?

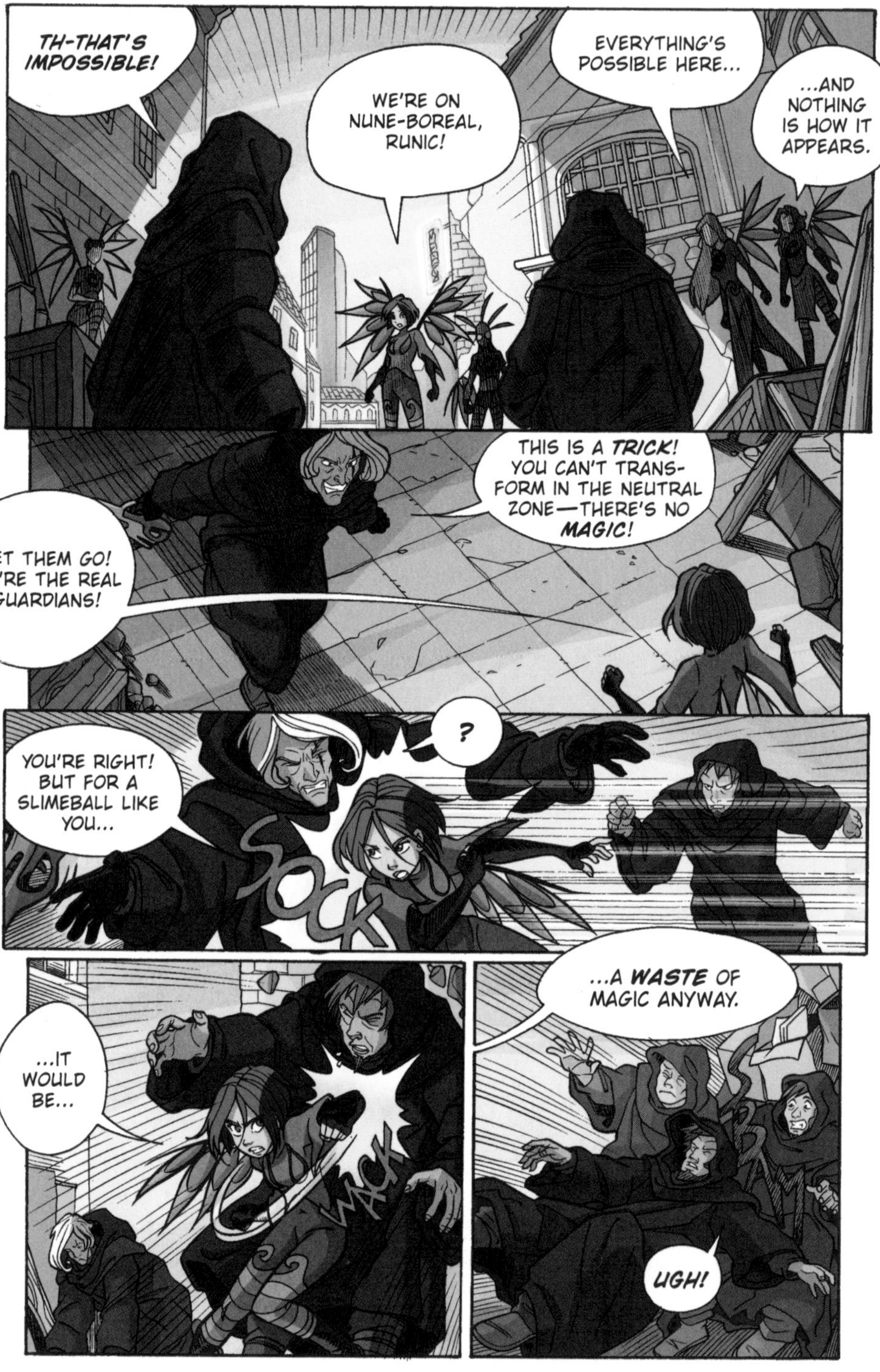
TH-THAT'S IMPOSSIBLE!
WE'RE ON NUNE-BOREAL, RUNIC!
EVERYTHING'S POSSIBLE HERE...
...AND NOTHING IS HOW IT APPEARS.
THIS IS A TRICK! YOU CAN'T TRANS-FORM IN THE NEUTRAL ZONE—THERE'S NO MAGIC!
LET THEM GO! WE'RE THE REAL GUARDIANS!
YOU'RE RIGHT! BUT FOR A SLIMEBALL LIKE YOU...
?
SOCK
...IT WOULD BE...
WHACK
...A WASTE OF MAGIC ANYWAY.
UGH!

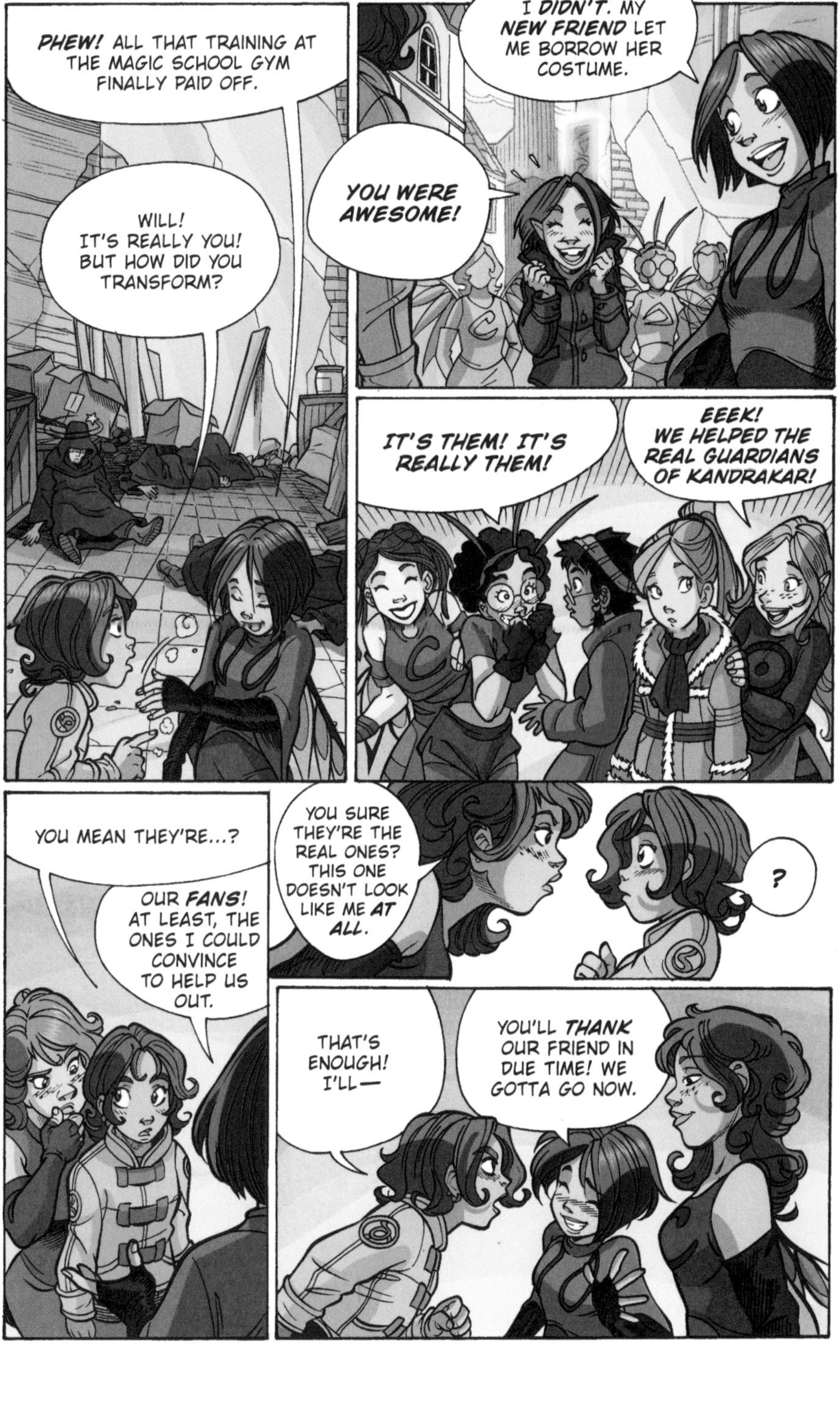
PHEW! ALL THAT TRAINING AT THE MAGIC SCHOOL GYM FINALLY PAID OFF.
WILL! IT'S REALLY YOU! BUT HOW DID YOU TRANSFORM?
I DIDN'T. MY NEW FRIEND LET ME BORROW HER COSTUME.
YOU WERE AWESOME!
IT'S THEM! IT'S REALLY THEM!
EEEK! WE HELPED THE REAL GUARDIANS OF KANDRAKAR!
YOU MEAN THEY'RE...?
OUR FANS! AT LEAST, THE ONES I COULD CONVINCE TO HELP US OUT.
YOU SURE THEY'RE THE REAL ONES? THIS ONE DOESN'T LOOK LIKE ME AT ALL.
?
THAT'S ENOUGH! I'LL—
YOU'LL THANK OUR FRIEND IN DUE TIME! WE GOTTA GO NOW.

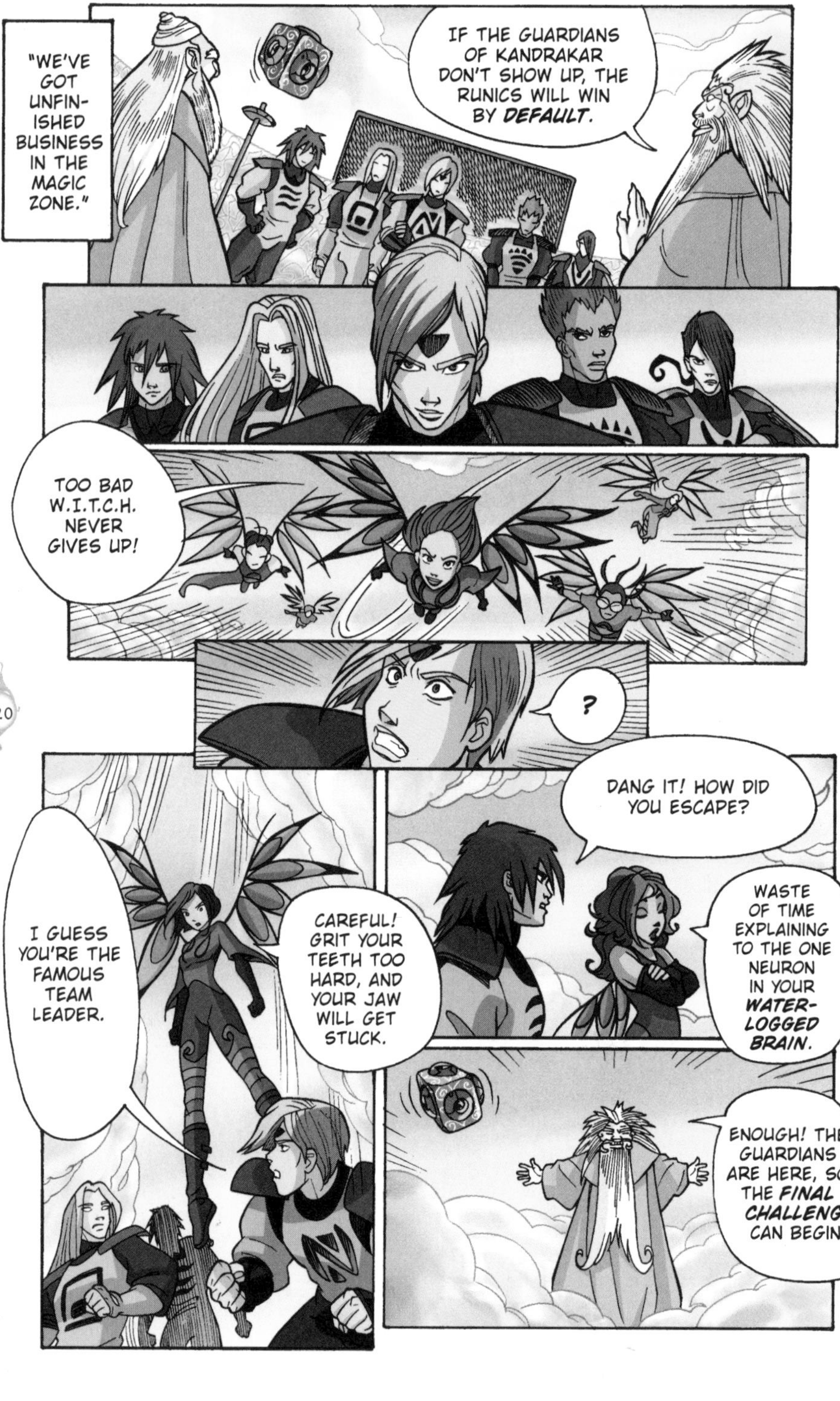
"WE'VE GOT UNFINISHED BUSINESS IN THE MAGIC ZONE."
IF THE GUARDIANS OF KANDRAKAR DON'T SHOW UP, THE RUNICS WILL WIN BY DEFAULT.
TOO BAD W.I.T.C.H. NEVER GIVES UP!
?
I GUESS YOU'RE THE FAMOUS TEAM LEADER.
CAREFUL! GRIT YOUR TEETH TOO HARD, AND YOUR JAW WILL GET STUCK.
DANG IT! HOW DID YOU ESCAPE?
WASTE OF TIME EXPLAINING TO THE ONE NEURON IN YOUR WATER-LOGGED BRAIN.
ENOUGH! THE GUARDIANS ARE HERE, SO THE FINAL CHALLENGE CAN BEGIN.
220

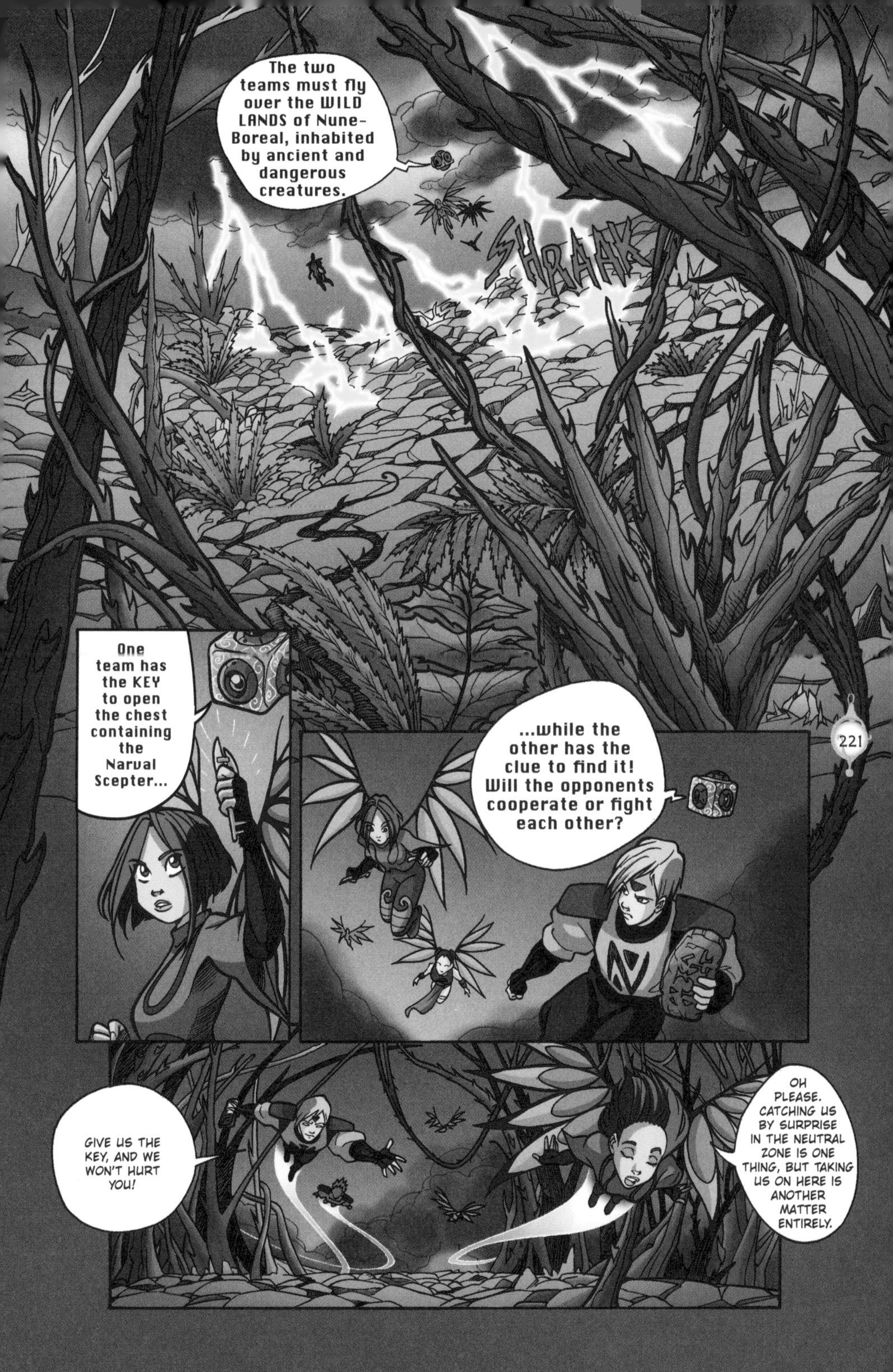
The two teams must fly over the WILD LANDS of Nune-Boreal, inhabited by ancient and dangerous creatures.
SHRAAK
One team has the KEY to open the chest containing the Narval Scepter...
...while the other has the clue to find it! Will the opponents cooperate or fight each other?
GIVE US THE KEY, AND WE WON'T HURT YOU!
OH PLEASE. CATCHING US BY SURPRISE IN THE NEUTRAL ZONE IS ONE THING, BUT TAKING US ON HERE IS ANOTHER MATTER ENTIRELY.

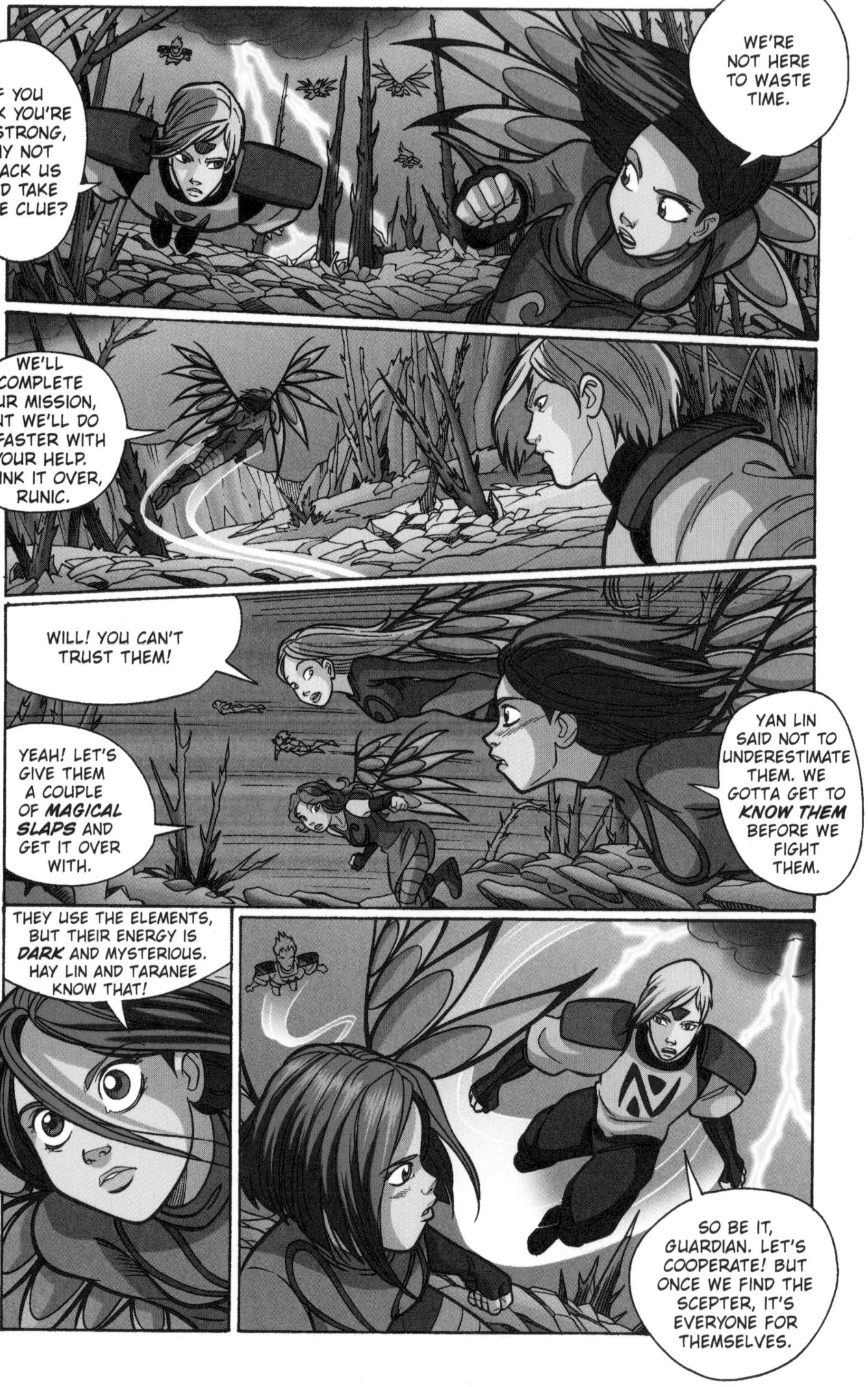
IF YOU THINK YOU'RE SO STRONG, WHY NOT ATTACK US AND TAKE THE CLUE?
WE'RE NOT HERE TO WASTE TIME.
WE'LL COMPLETE OUR MISSION, BUT WE'LL DO IT FASTER WITH YOUR HELP. THINK IT OVER, RUNIC.
WILL! YOU CAN'T TRUST THEM!
YEAH! LET'S GIVE THEM A COUPLE OF MAGICAL SLAPS AND GET IT OVER WITH.
YAN LIN SAID NOT TO UNDERESTIMATE THEM. WE GOTTA GET TO KNOW THEM BEFORE WE FIGHT THEM.
THEY USE THE ELEMENTS, BUT THEIR ENERGY IS DARK AND MYSTERIOUS. HAY LIN AND TARANEE KNOW THAT!
SO BE IT, GUARDIAN. LET'S COOPERATE! BUT ONCE WE FIND THE SCEPTER, IT'S EVERYONE FOR THEMSELVES.

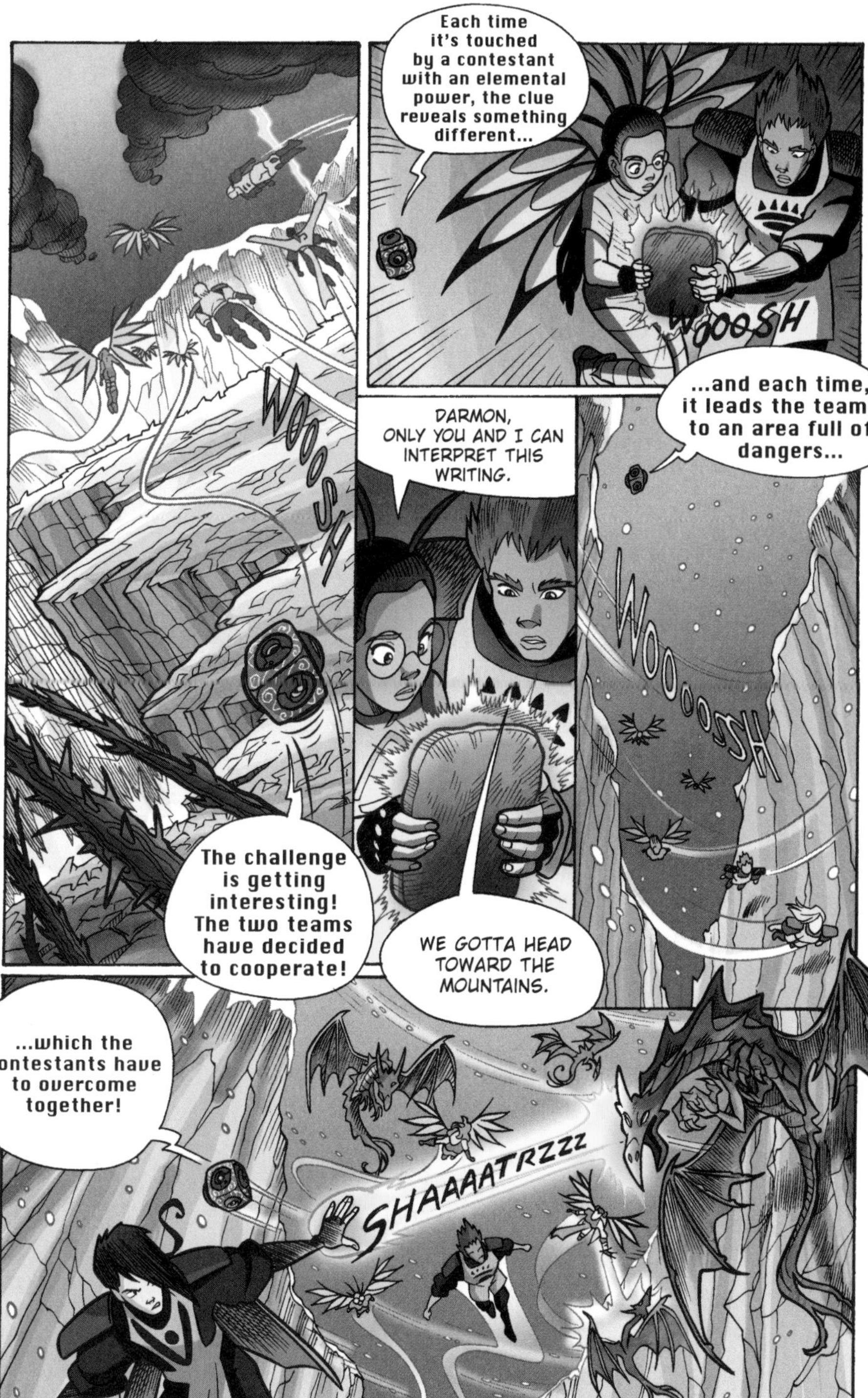
WOOOSH
Each time it's touched by a contestant with an elemental power, the clue reveals something different...
WOOOSH
DARMON, ONLY YOU AND I CAN INTERPRET THIS WRITING.
...and each time, it leads the teams to an area full of dangers...
WOOOOOSH
The challenge is getting interesting! The two teams have decided to cooperate!
WE GOTTA HEAD TOWARD THE MOUNTAINS.
...which the contestants have to overcome together!
SHAAAATRZZZ

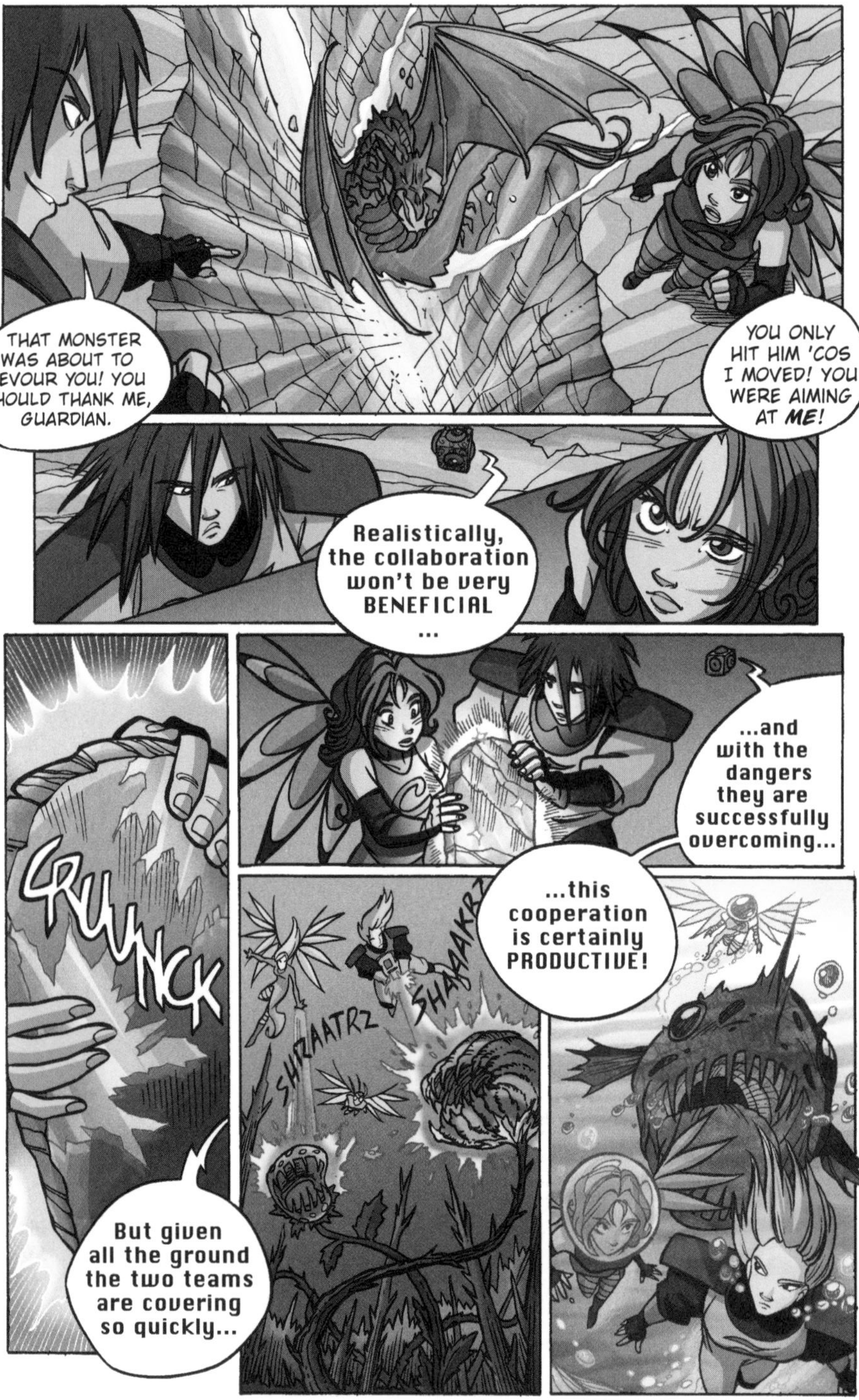
THAT MONSTER WAS ABOUT TO DEVOUR YOU! YOU SHOULD THANK ME, GUARDIAN.
YOU ONLY HIT HIM 'COS I MOVED! YOU WERE AIMING AT ME!
Realistically, the collaboration won't be very BENEFICIAL ...
...and with the dangers they are successfully overcoming...
CRUUNCK
...this cooperation is certainly PRODUCTIVE!
SHRAATRZ
SHAAAKRZ
But given all the ground the two teams are covering so quickly...

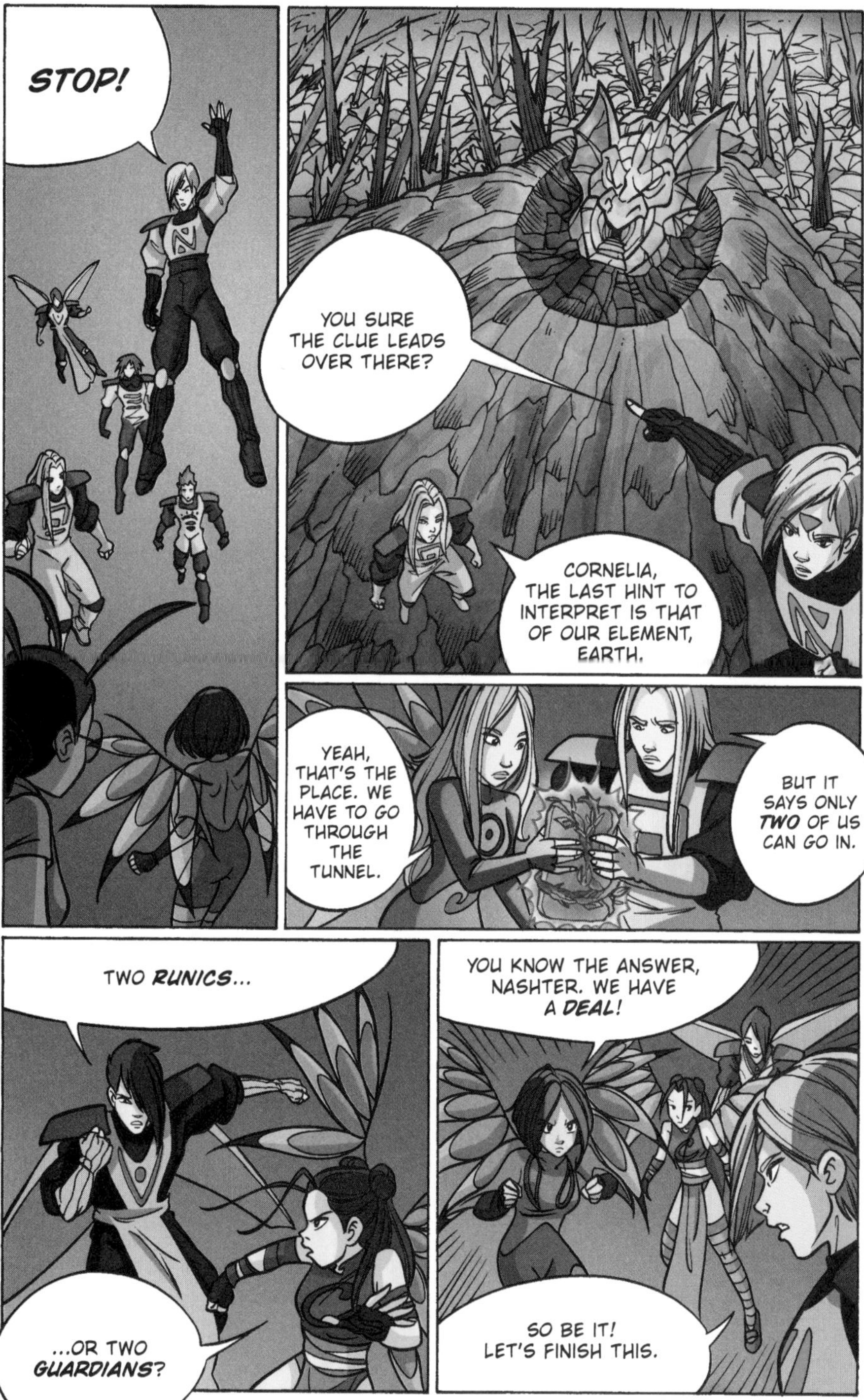
STOP!
YOU SURE THE CLUE LEADS OVER THERE?
CORNELIA, THE LAST HINT TO INTERPRET IS THAT OF OUR ELEMENT, EARTH.
YEAH, THAT'S THE PLACE. WE HAVE TO GO THROUGH THE TUNNEL.
BUT IT SAYS ONLY TWO OF US CAN GO IN.
TWO RUNICS...
...OR TWO GUARDIANS?
YOU KNOW THE ANSWER, NASHTER. WE HAVE A DEAL!
SO BE IT! LET'S FINISH THIS.

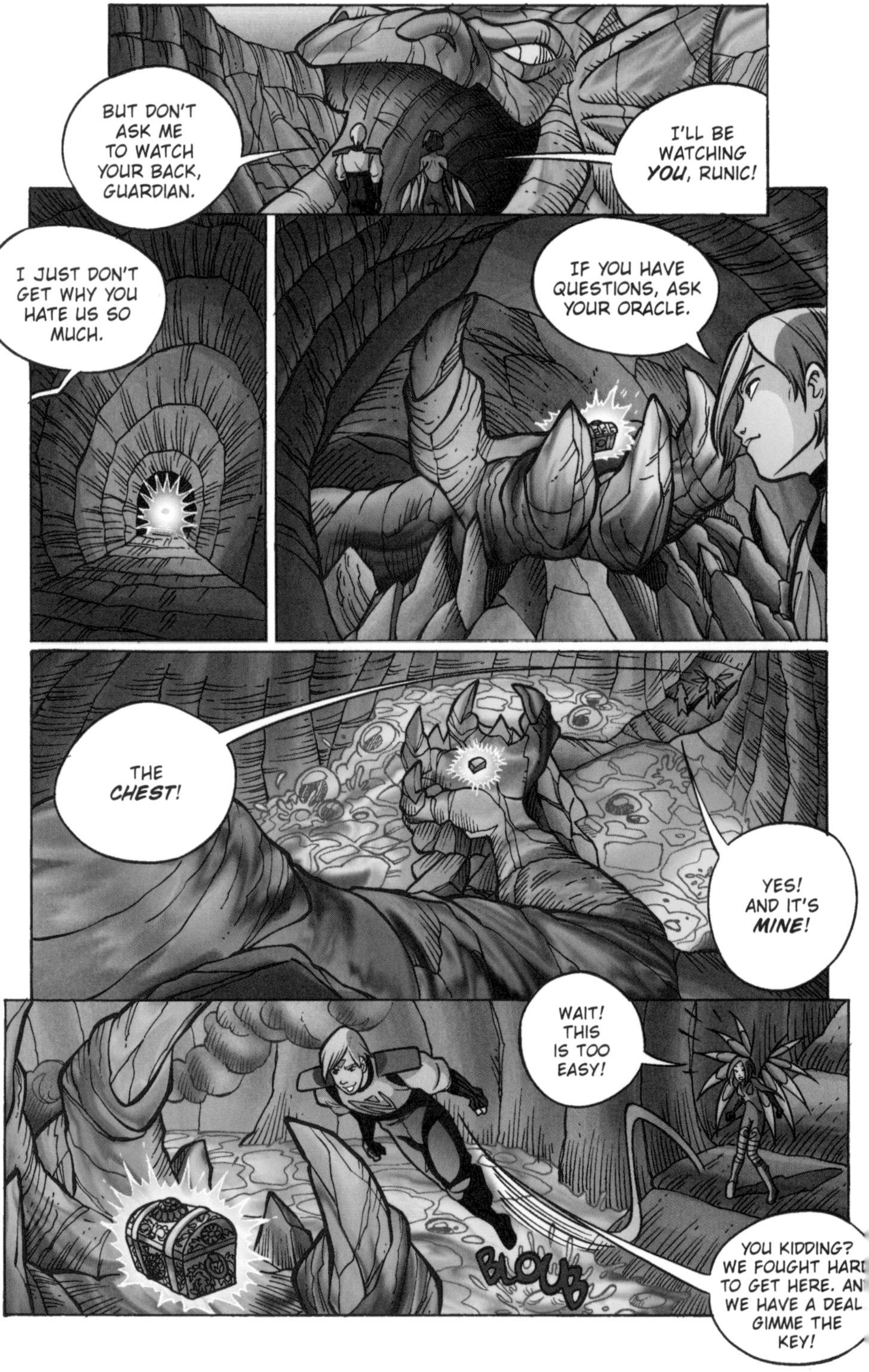

BUT DON'T ASK ME TO WATCH YOUR BACK, GUARDIAN.
I'LL BE WATCHING *YOU*, RUNIC!
I JUST DON'T GET WHY YOU HATE US SO MUCH.
IF YOU HAVE QUESTIONS, ASK YOUR ORACLE.
THE *CHEST*!
YES! AND IT'S *MINE*!
WAIT! THIS IS TOO EASY!
BLOUB
YOU KIDDING? WE FOUGHT HARD TO GET HERE. AND WE HAVE A DEAL. GIMME THE KEY!

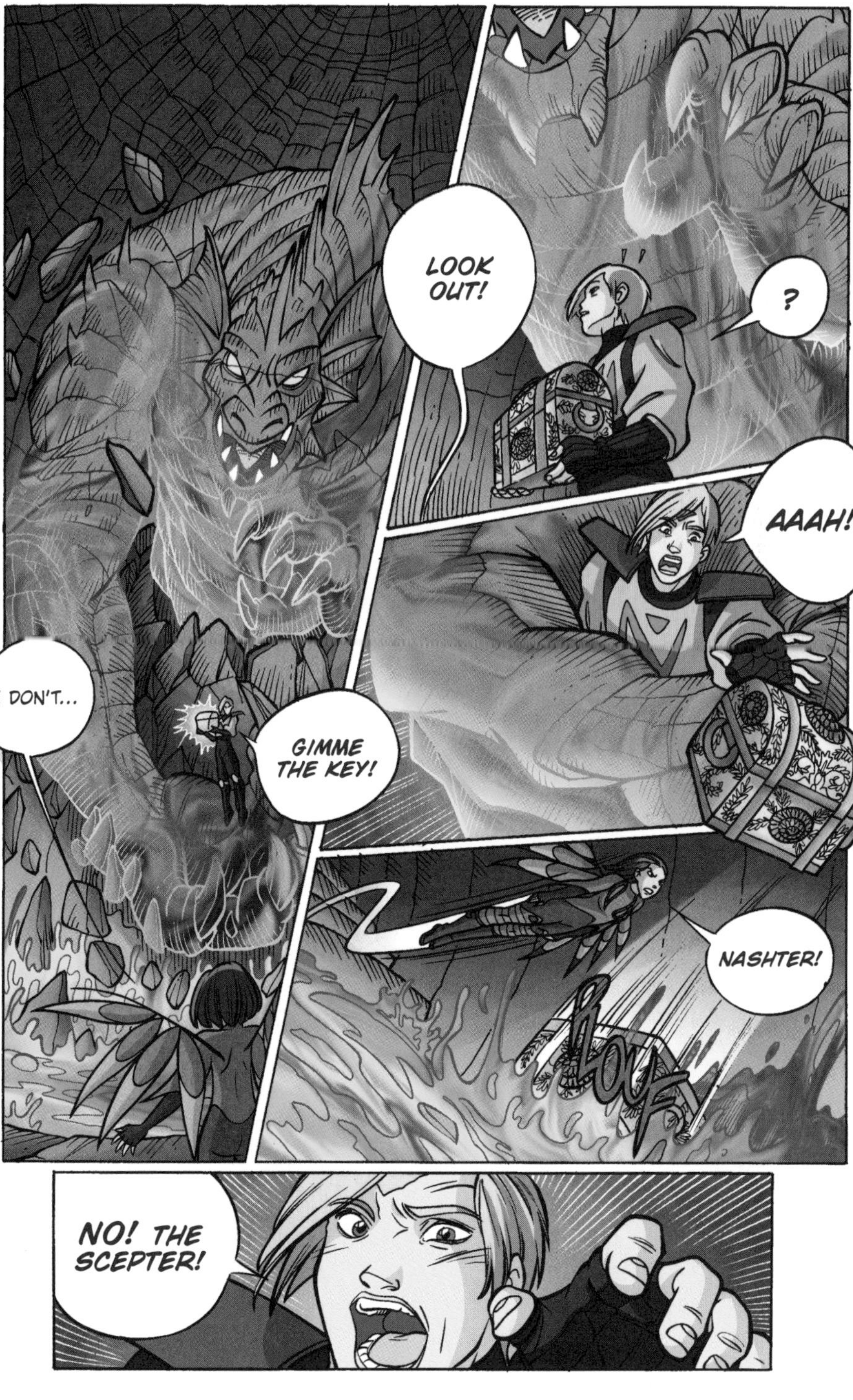
LOOK OUT!
?
AAAH!
I DON'T...
GIMME THE KEY!
NASHTER!
NO! THE SCEPTER!

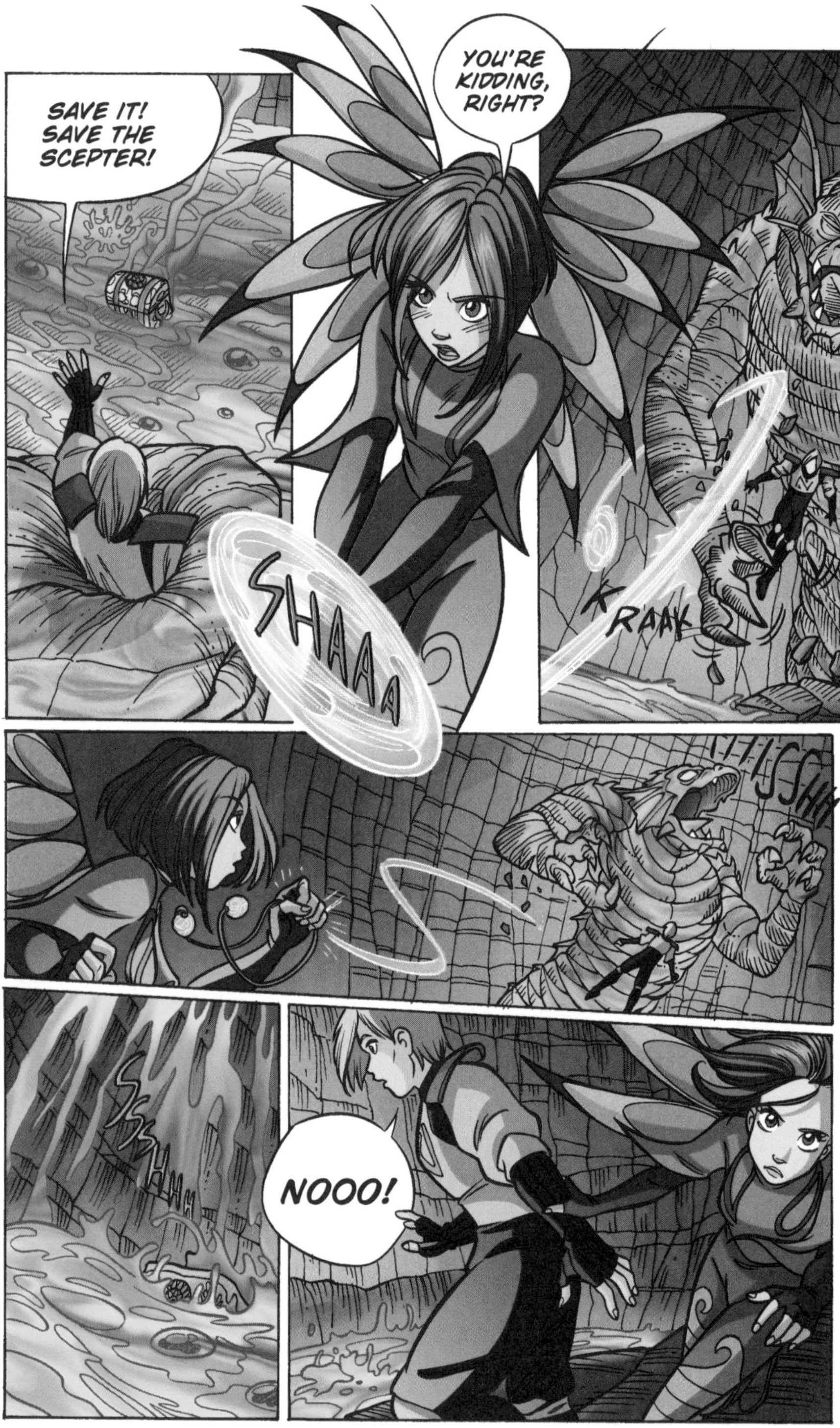
SAVE IT! SAVE THE SCEPTER!
YOU'RE KIDDING, RIGHT?
SHAAAA
KRAAK
HISSHH
SSSHHH
NOOO!

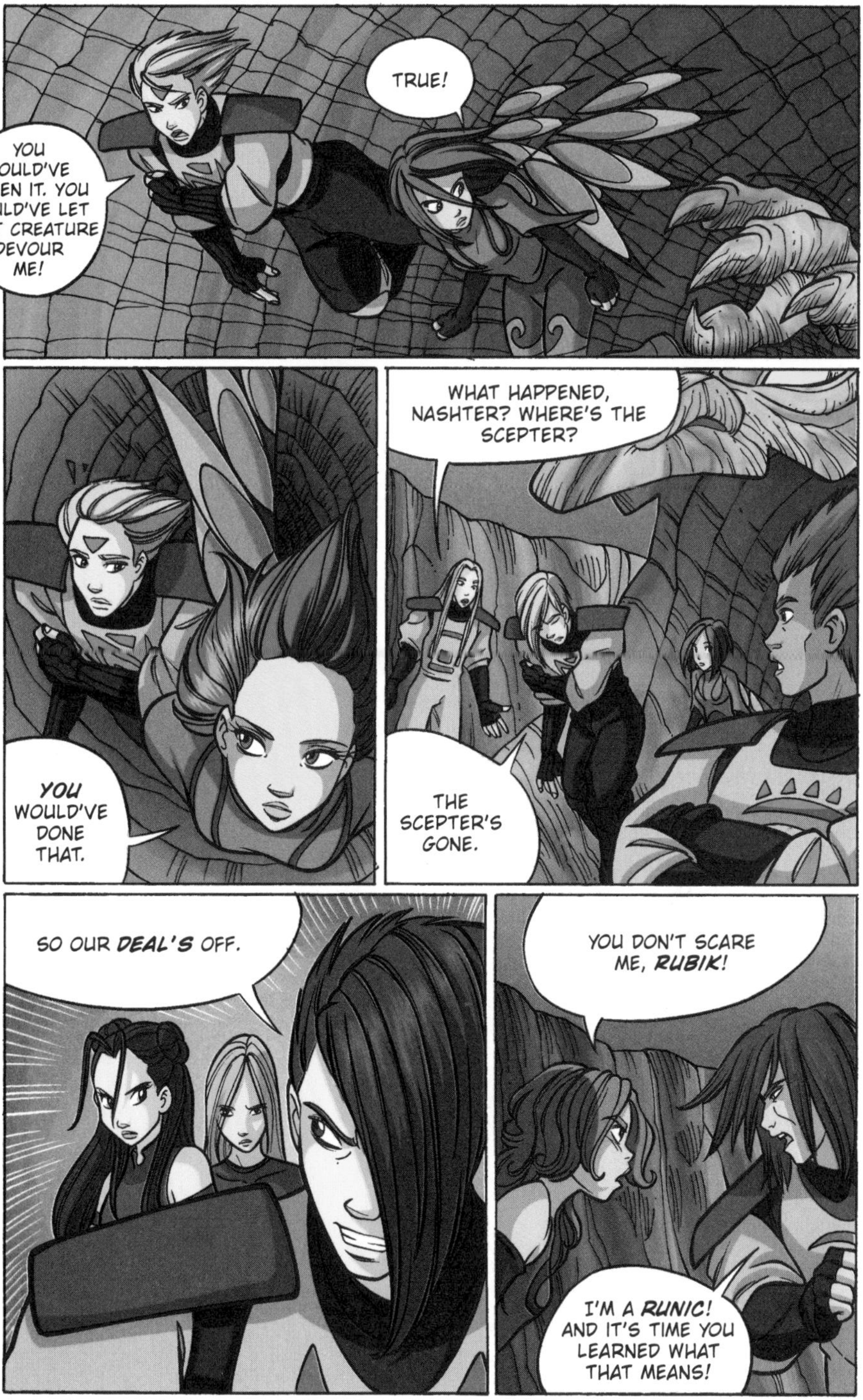
TRUE!
YOU COULD'VE TAKEN IT. YOU COULD'VE LET THAT CREATURE DEVOUR ME!
YOU WOULD'VE DONE THAT.
WHAT HAPPENED, NASHTER? WHERE'S THE SCEPTER?
THE SCEPTER'S GONE.
SO OUR ***DEAL'S*** OFF.
YOU DON'T SCARE ME, ***RUBIK***!
I'M A ***RUNIC***! AND IT'S TIME YOU LEARNED WHAT THAT MEANS!

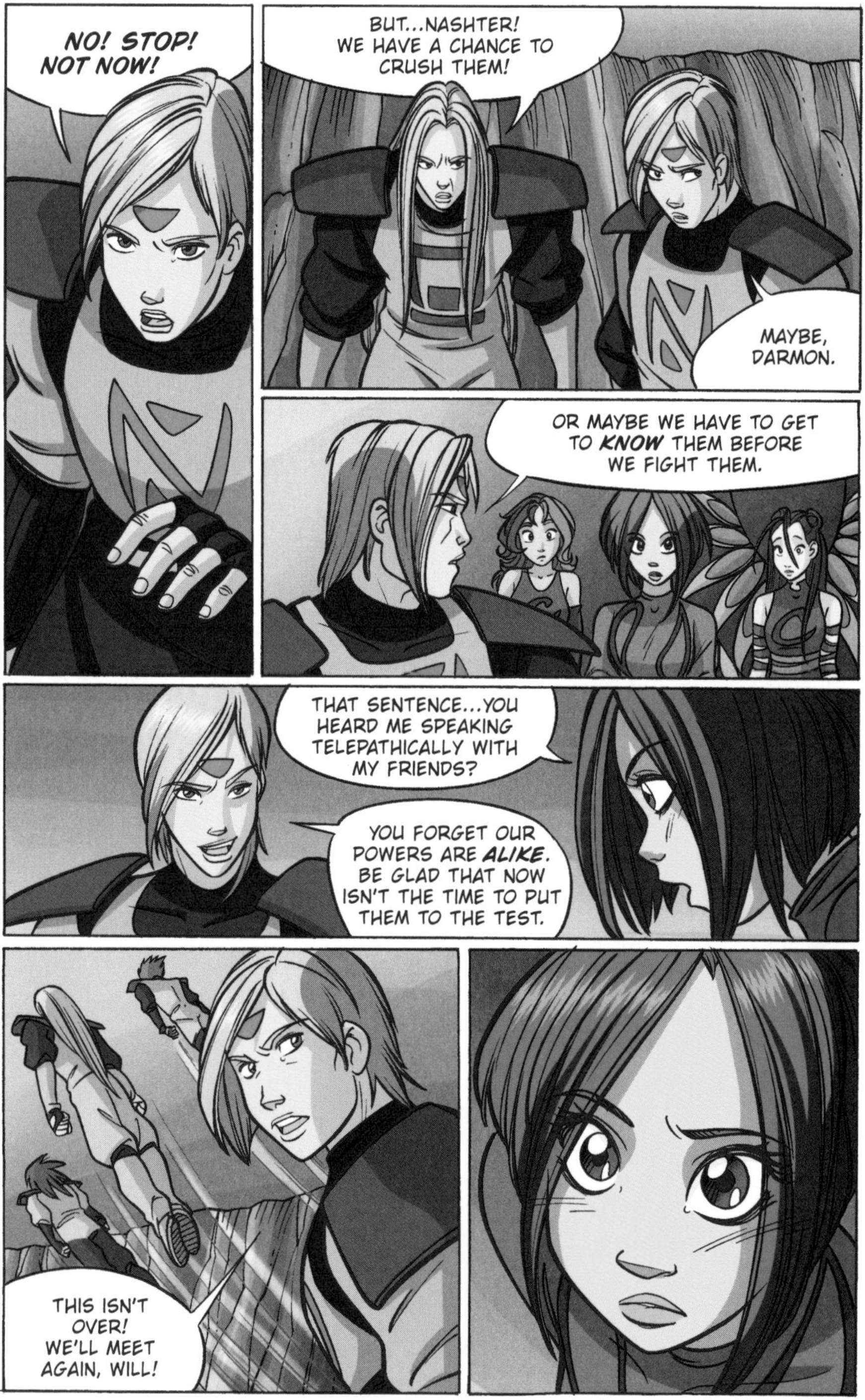
NO! STOP! NOT NOW!
BUT...NASHTER! WE HAVE A CHANCE TO CRUSH THEM!
MAYBE, DARMON.
OR MAYBE WE HAVE TO GET TO KNOW THEM BEFORE WE FIGHT THEM.
THAT SENTENCE...YOU HEARD ME SPEAKING TELEPATHICALLY WITH MY FRIENDS?
YOU FORGET OUR POWERS ARE ALIKE. BE GLAD THAT NOW ISN'T THE TIME TO PUT THEM TO THE TEST.
THIS ISN'T OVER! WE'LL MEET AGAIN, WILL!

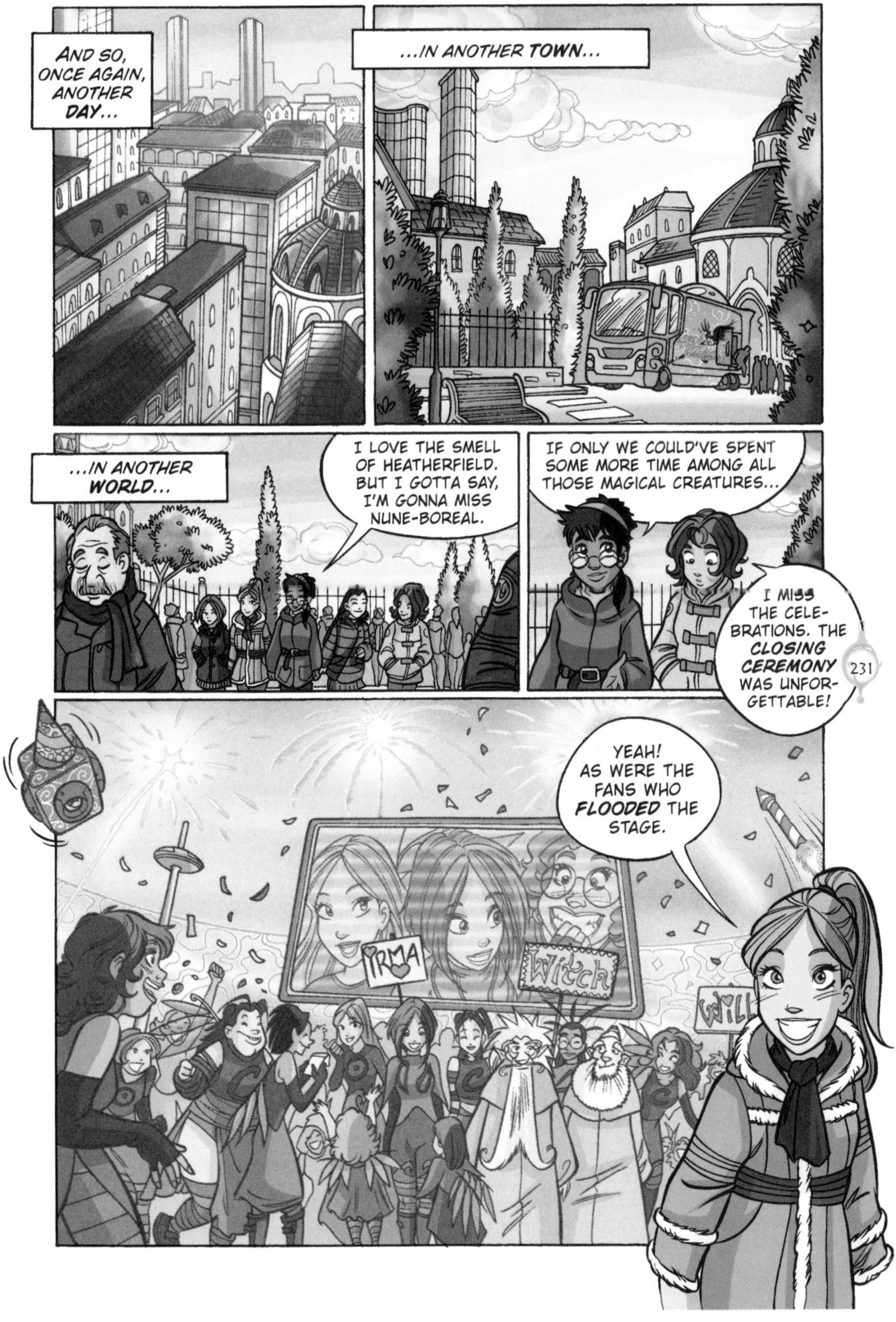
AND SO, ONCE AGAIN, ANOTHER DAY...
...IN ANOTHER TOWN...
...IN ANOTHER WORLD...
I LOVE THE SMELL OF HEATHERFIELD. BUT I GOTTA SAY, I'M GONNA MISS NUNE-BOREAL.
IF ONLY WE COULD'VE SPENT SOME MORE TIME AMONG ALL THOSE MAGICAL CREATURES...
I MISS THE CELE-BRATIONS. THE CLOSING CEREMONY WAS UNFOR-GETTABLE!
YEAH! AS WERE THE FANS WHO FLOODED THE STAGE.
IRMA
Witch
Will

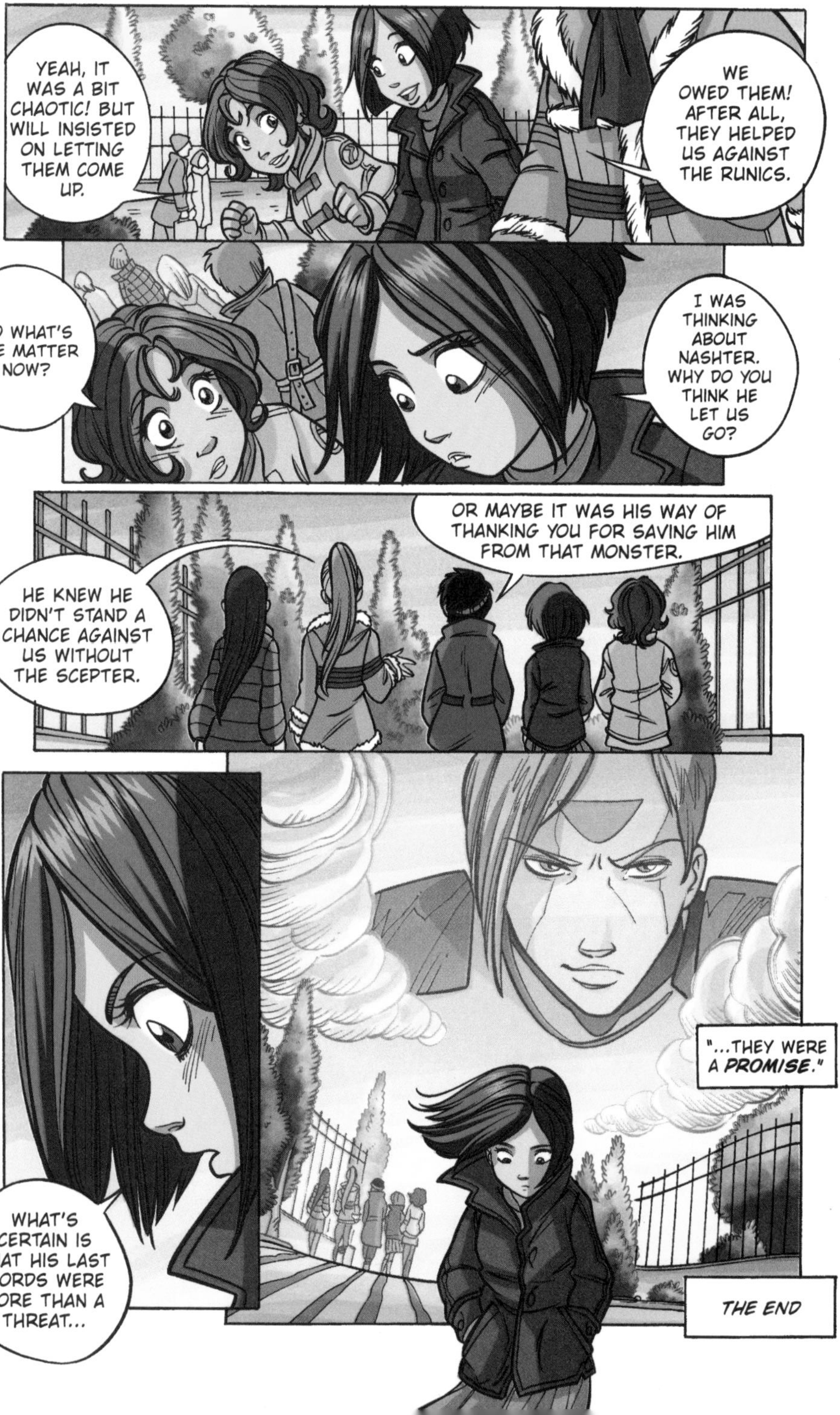
YEAH, IT WAS A BIT CHAOTIC! BUT WILL INSISTED ON LETTING THEM COME UP.
WE OWED THEM! AFTER ALL, THEY HELPED US AGAINST THE RUNICS.
SO WHAT'S THE MATTER NOW?
I WAS THINKING ABOUT NASHTER. WHY DO YOU THINK HE LET US GO?
HE KNEW HE DIDN'T STAND A CHANCE AGAINST US WITHOUT THE SCEPTER.
OR MAYBE IT WAS HIS WAY OF THANKING YOU FOR SAVING HIM FROM THAT MONSTER.
WHAT'S CERTAIN IS THAT HIS LAST WORDS WERE MORE THAN A THREAT...
"...THEY WERE A ***PROMISE***."
THE END

Read on in Volume 27!

100 snapshots, just for you

100 snapshots, one for each
chapter! 100 drawings that we
dedicate to the people who matter
the most to us—our readers!

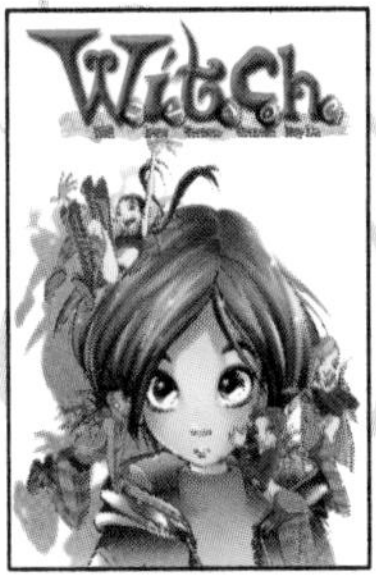
W.i.t.c.h.
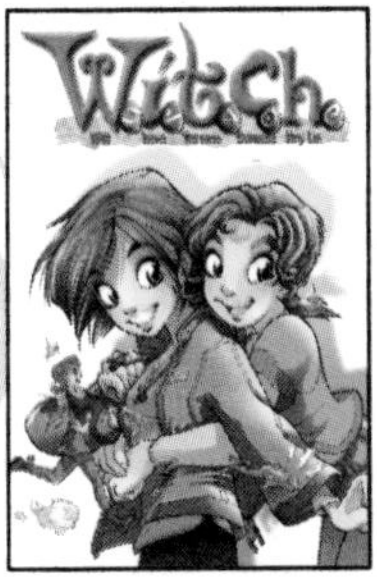
W.i.t.c.h.
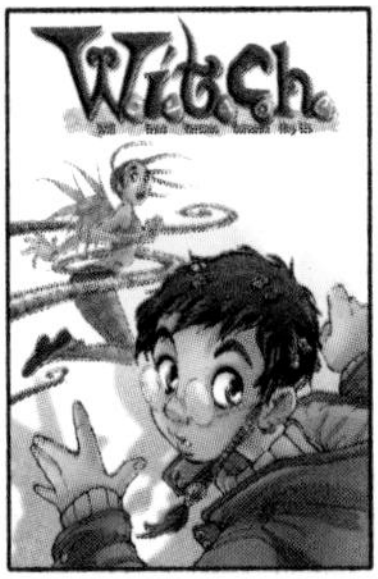
W.i.t.c.h.
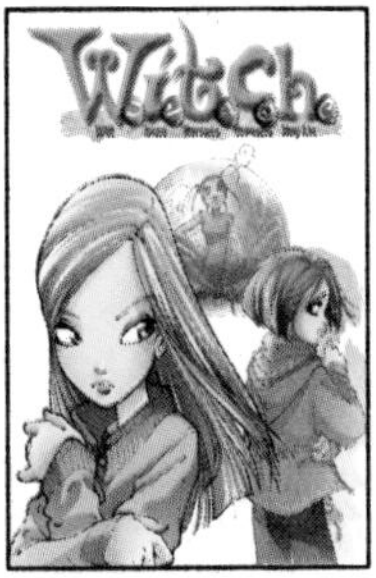
W.i.t.c.h.
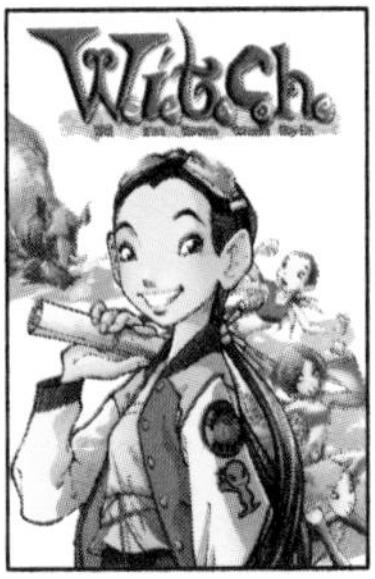
W.i.t.c.h.
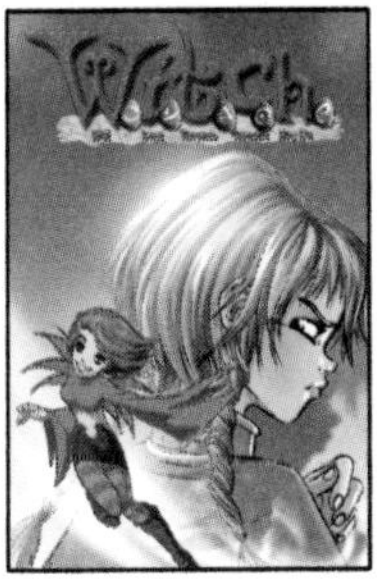
W.i.t.c.h.
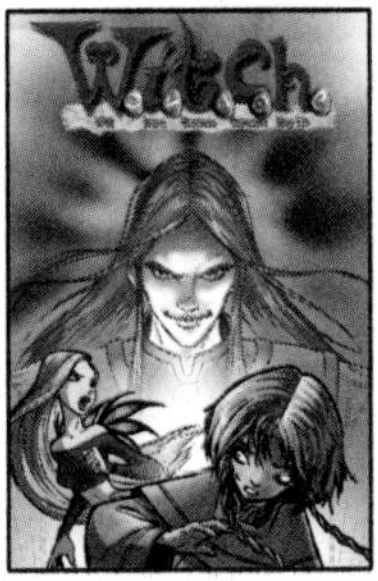
W.i.t.c.h.
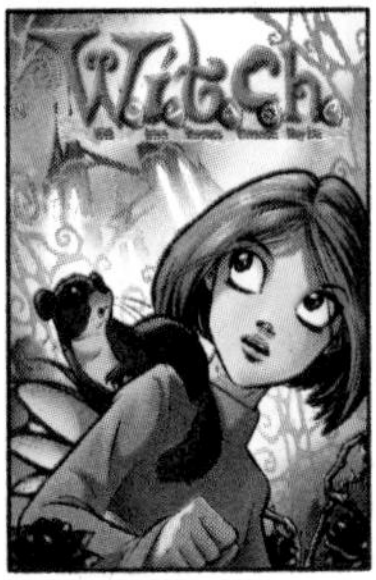
W.i.t.c.h.
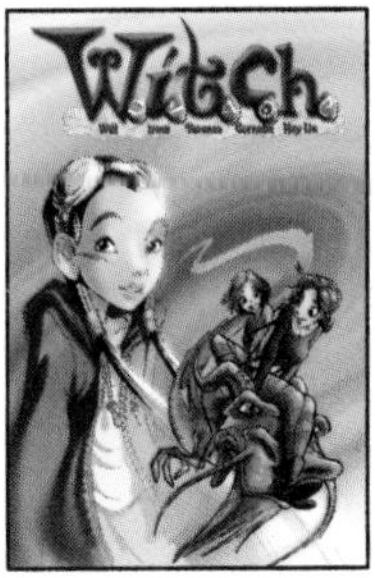
W.i.t.c.h.
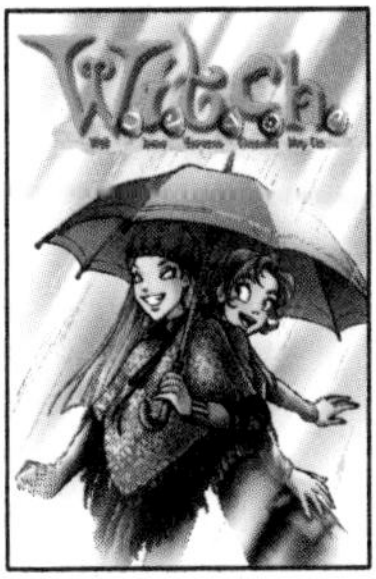
W.i.t.c.h.
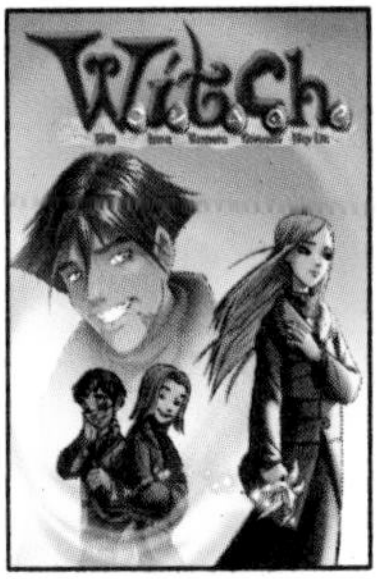
W.i.t.c.h.
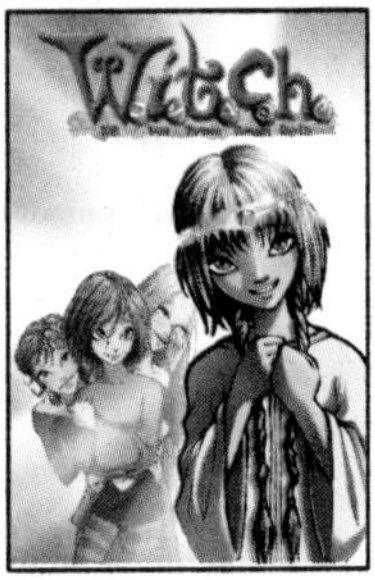
W.i.t.c.h.
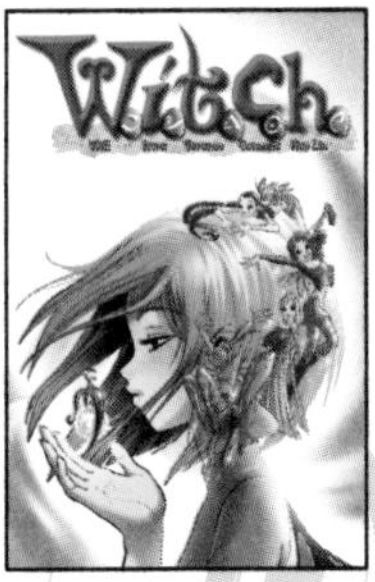
W.i.t.c.h.
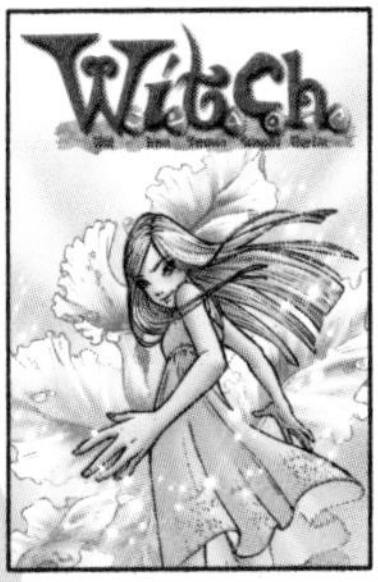
W.i.t.c.h.
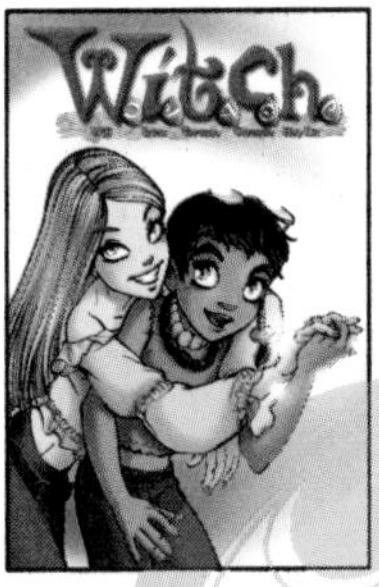
W.i.t.c.h.
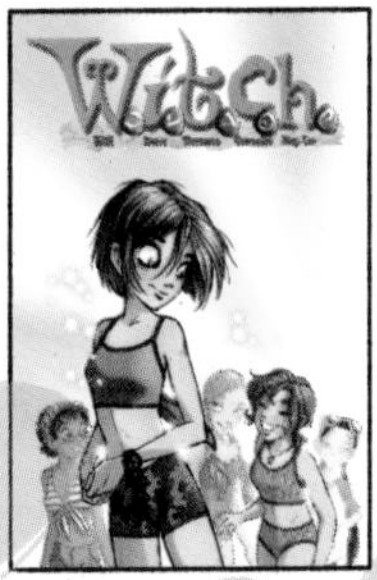
W.i.t.c.h.
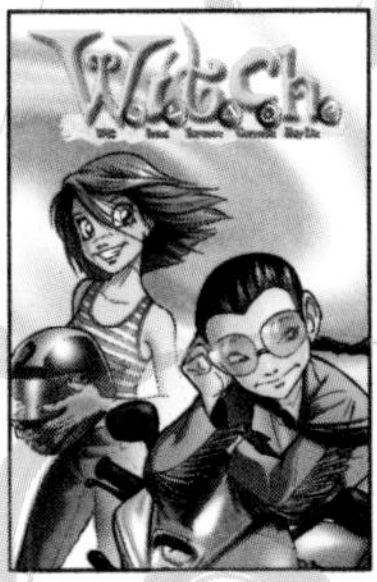
W.i.t.c.h.
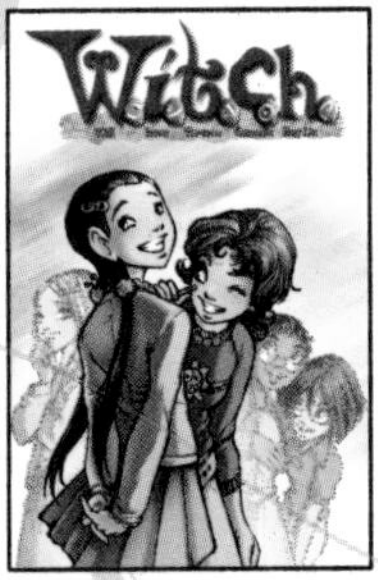
W.i.t.c.h.
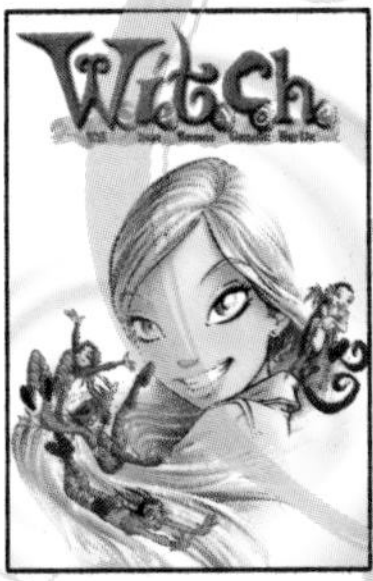
W.i.t.c.h.
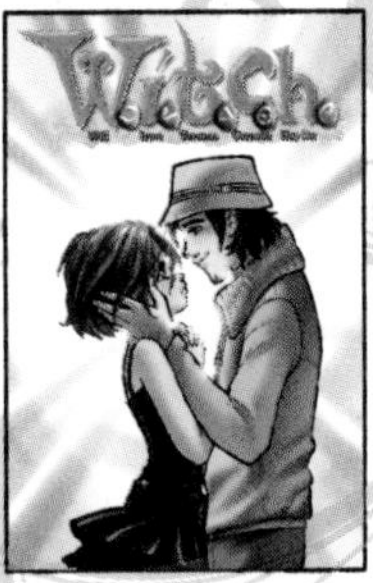
W.i.t.c.h.

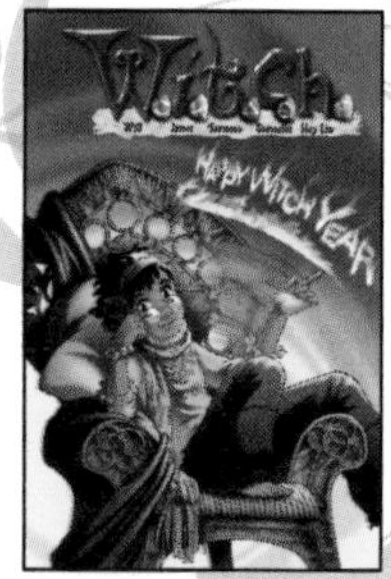
W.i.t.c.h.
HAPPY WITCH YEAR
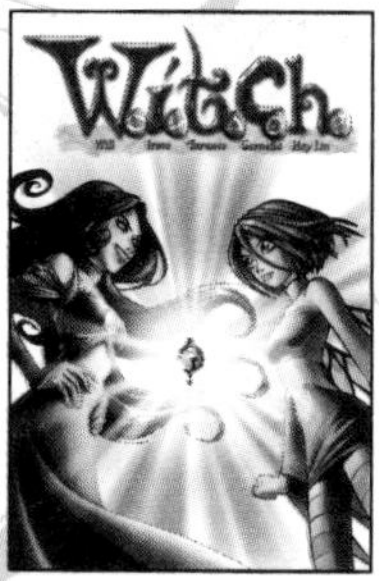
W.i.t.c.h.
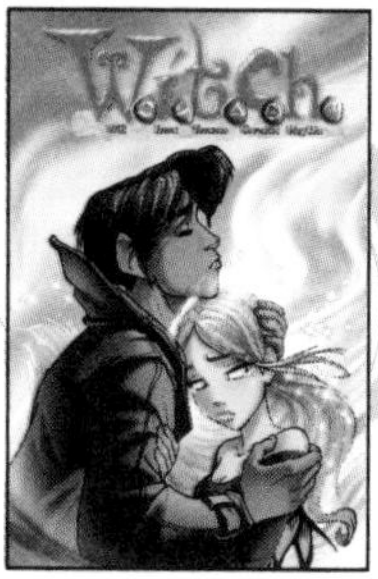
W.i.t.c.h.
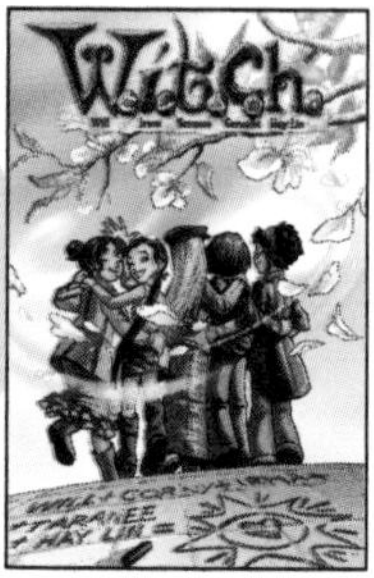
W.i.t.c.h.
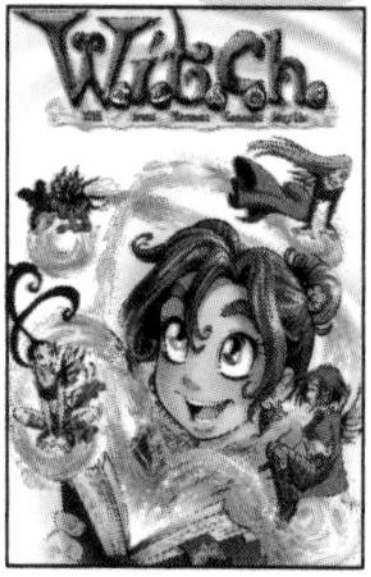
W.i.t.c.h.
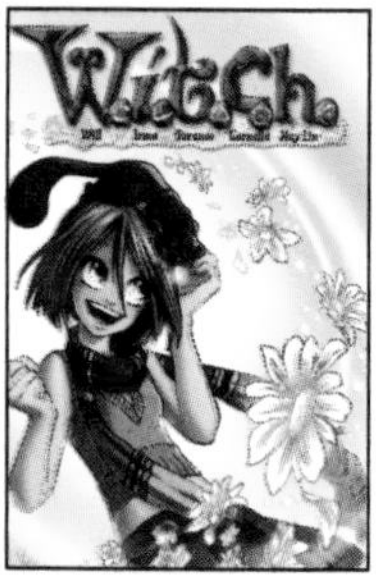
W.i.t.c.h.
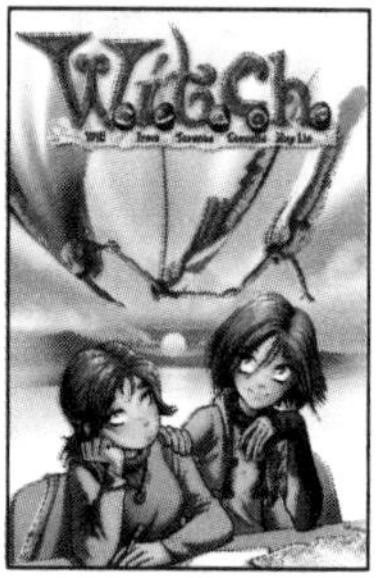
W.i.t.c.h.
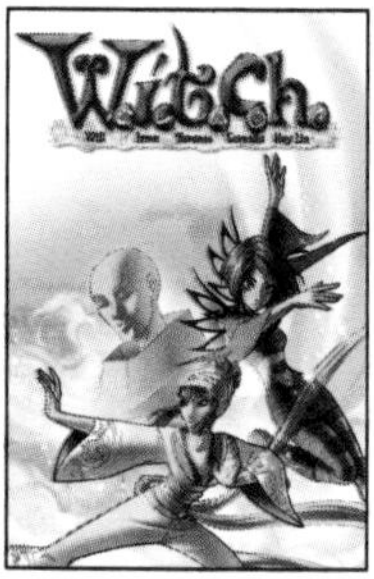
W.i.t.c.h.
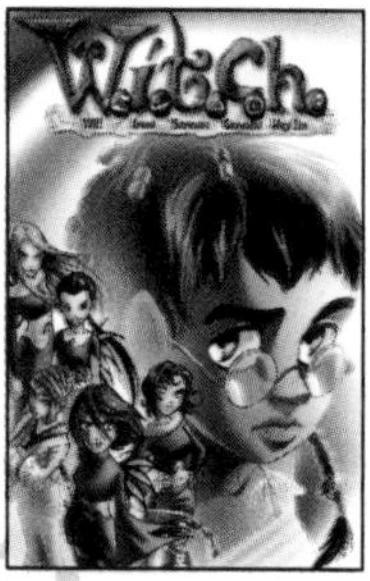
W.i.t.c.h.
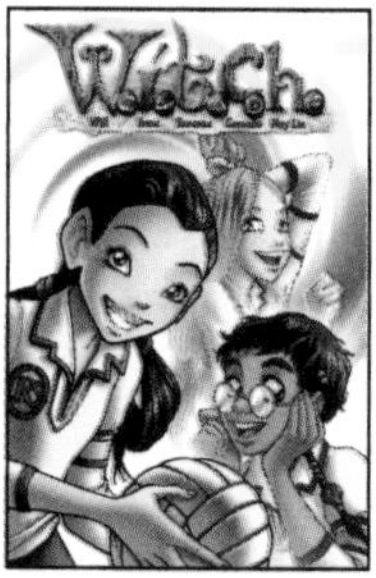
W.i.t.c.h.
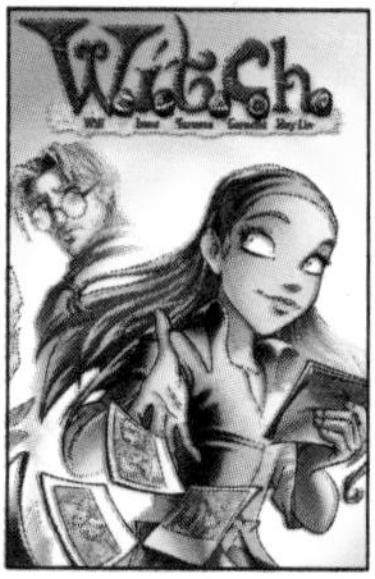
W.i.t.c.h.
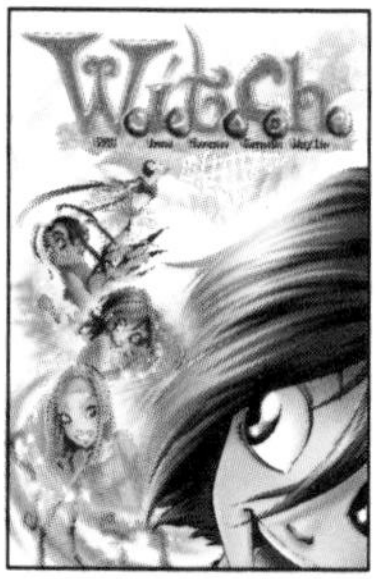
W.i.t.c.h.
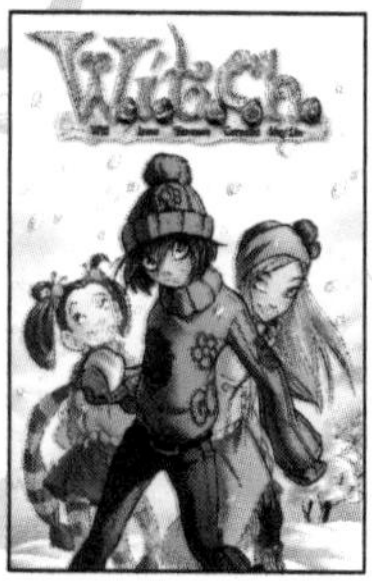
W.i.t.c.h.
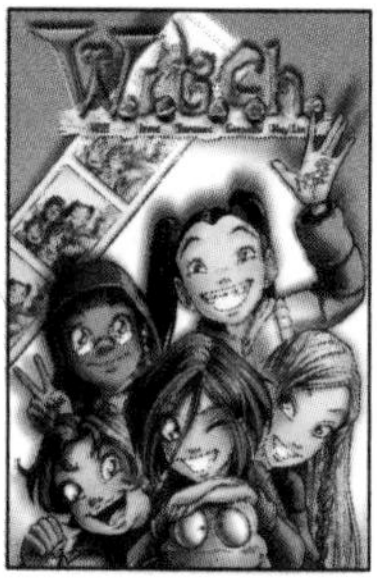
W.i.t.c.h.
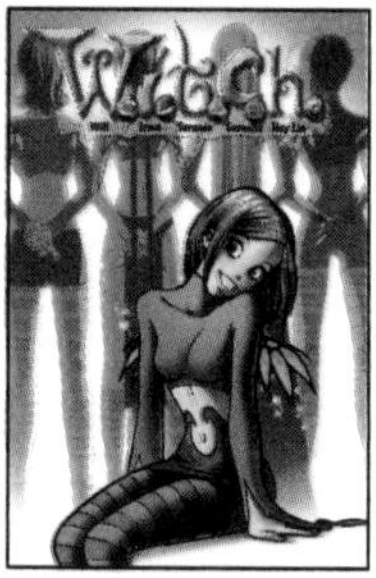
W.i.t.c.h.
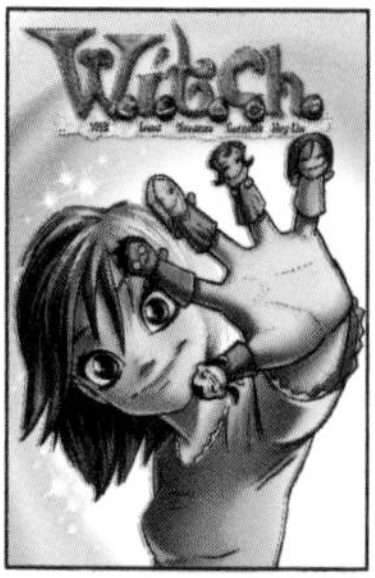
W.i.t.c.h.
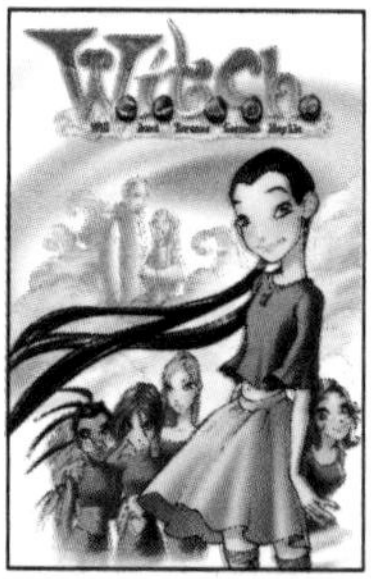
W.i.t.c.h.
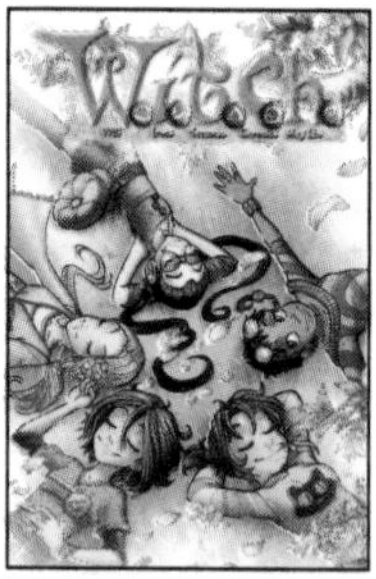
W.i.t.c.h.
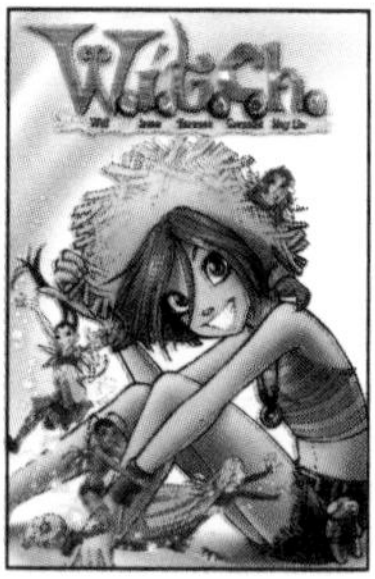
W.i.t.c.h.
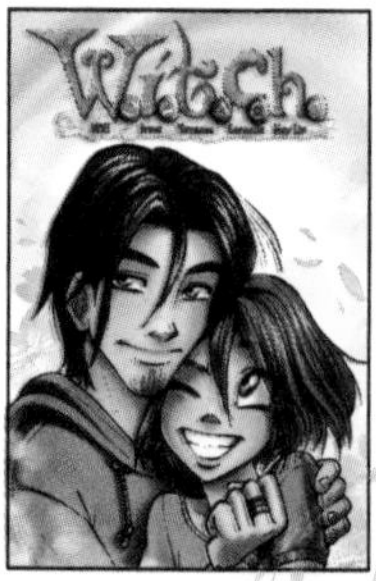
W.i.t.c.h.

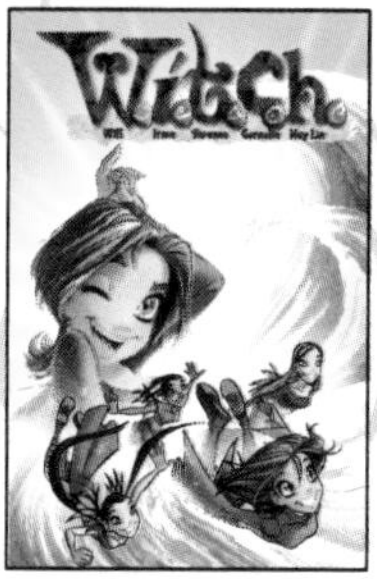
W.i.t.c.h.
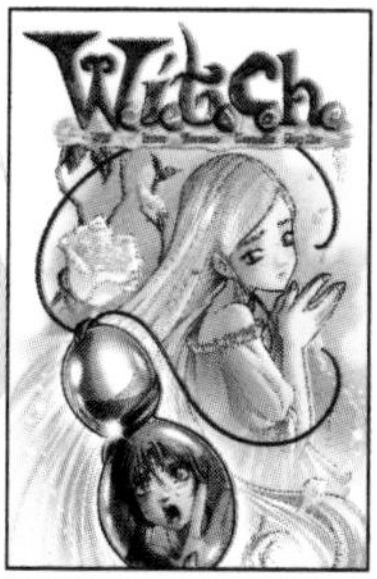
W.i.t.c.h.
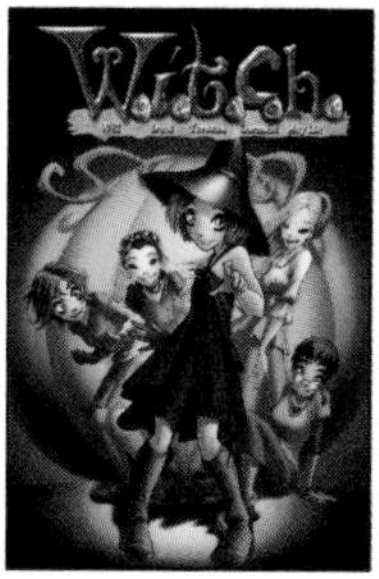
W.i.t.c.h.
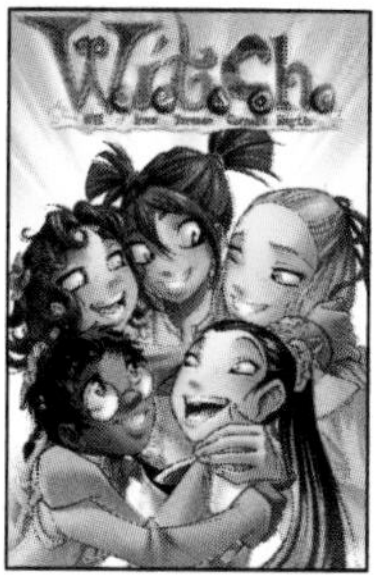
W.i.t.c.h.
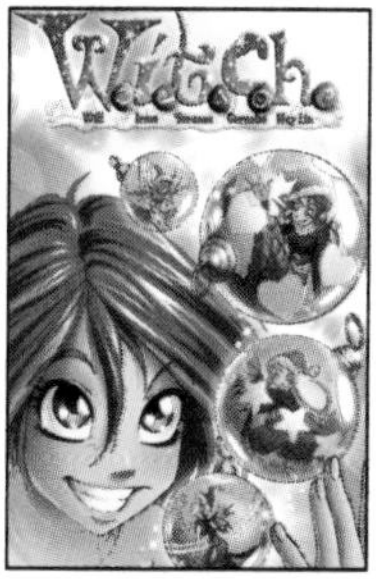
W.i.t.c.h.
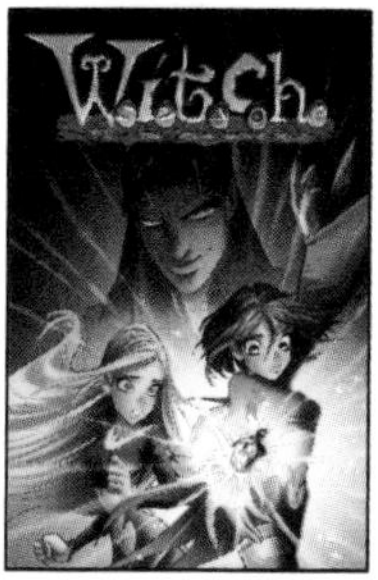
W.i.t.c.h.
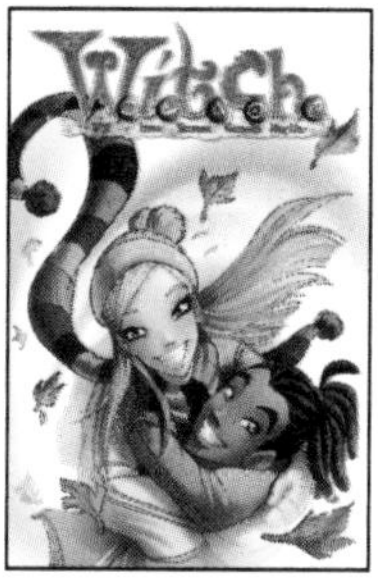
W.i.t.c.h.
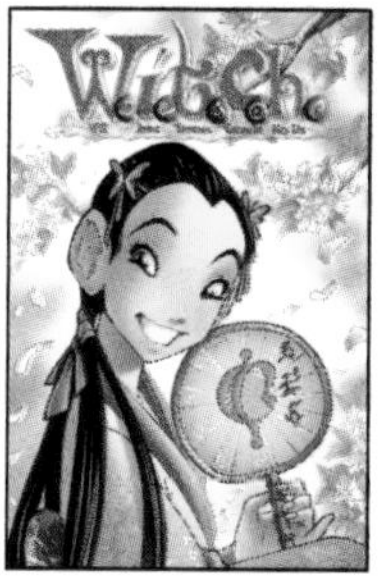
W.i.t.c.h.
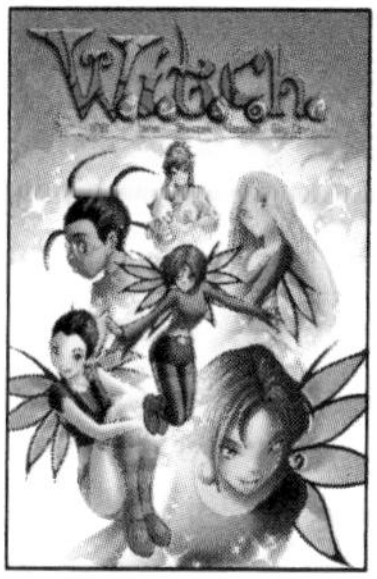
W.i.t.c.h.
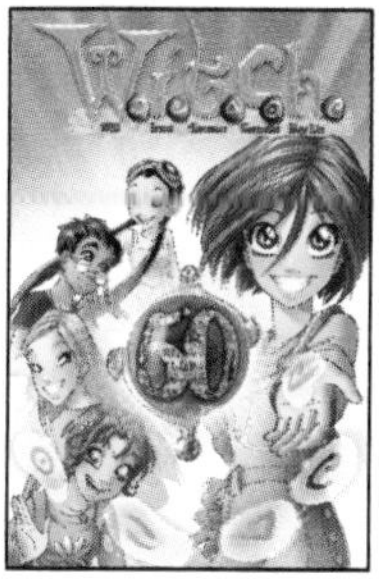
W.i.t.c.h.
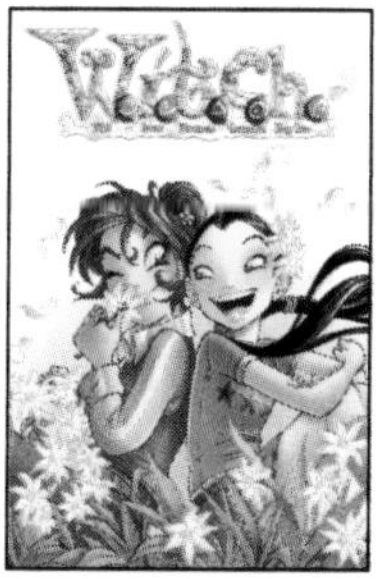
W.i.t.c.h.
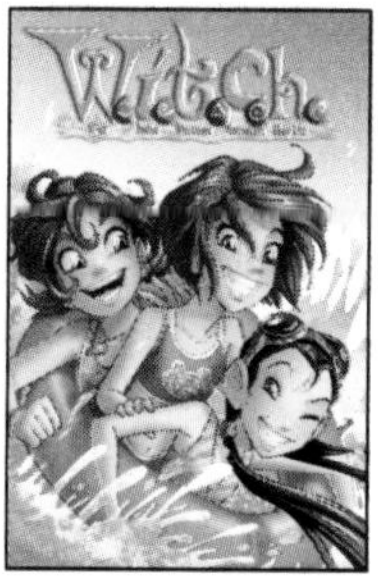
W.i.t.c.h.
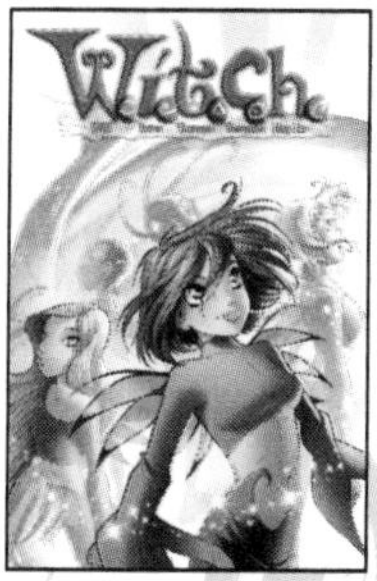
W.i.t.c.h.
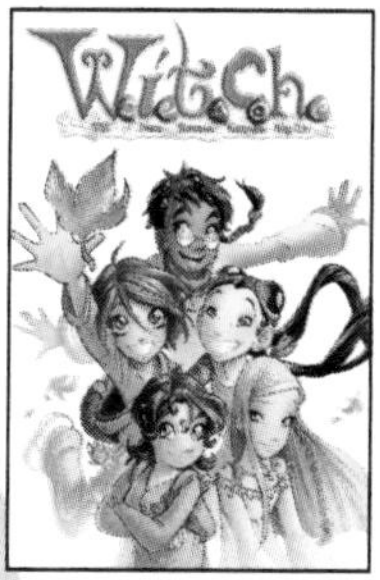
W.i.t.c.h.
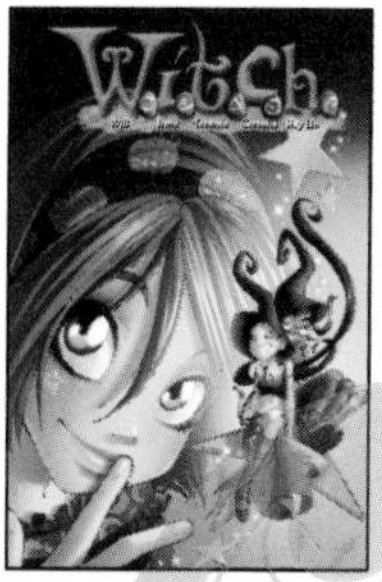
W.i.t.c.h.
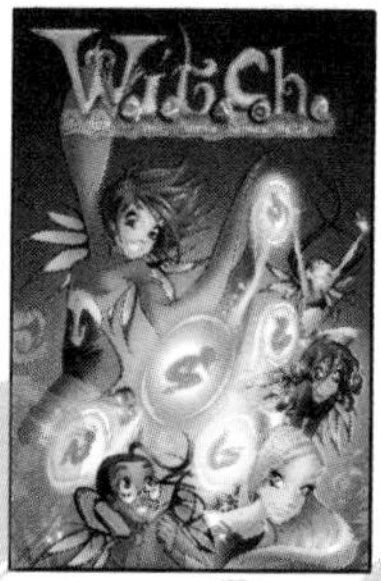
W.i.t.c.h.
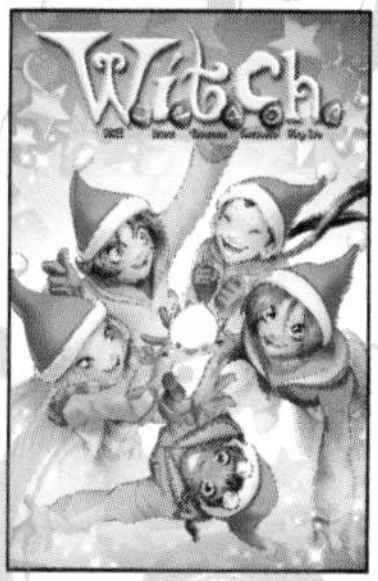
W.i.t.c.h.
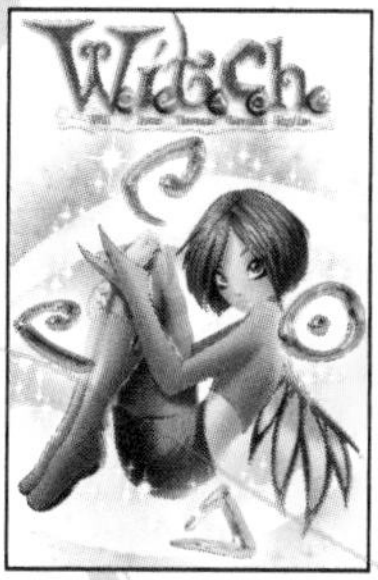
W.i.t.c.h.
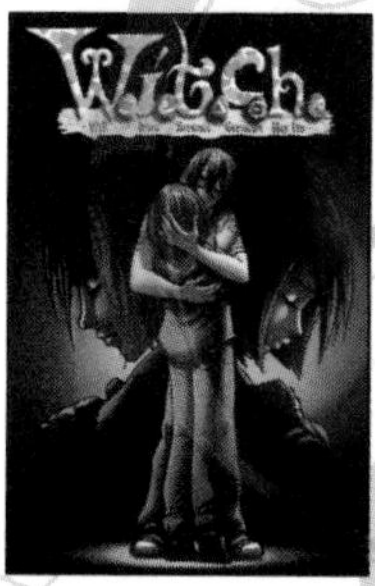
W.i.t.c.h.
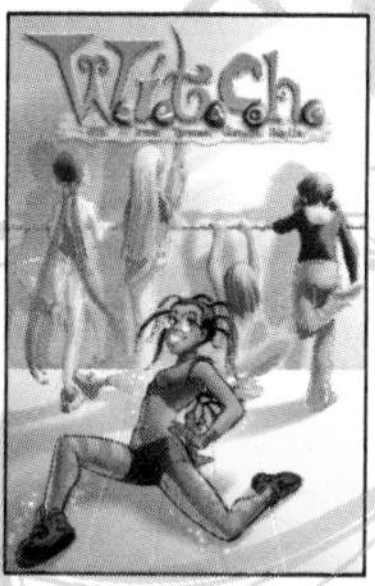
W.i.t.c.h.

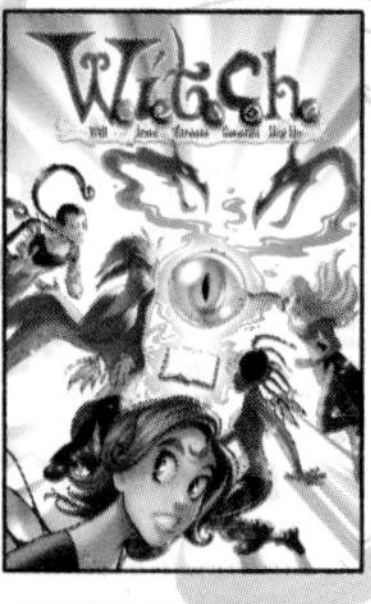
W.i.t.c.h.
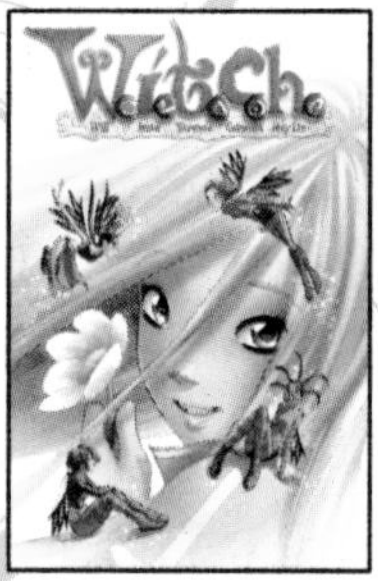
W.i.t.c.h.
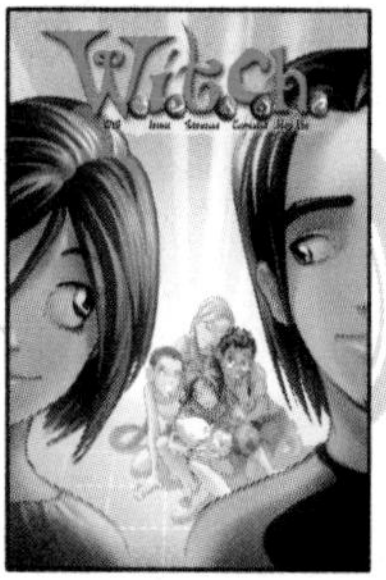
W.i.t.c.h.
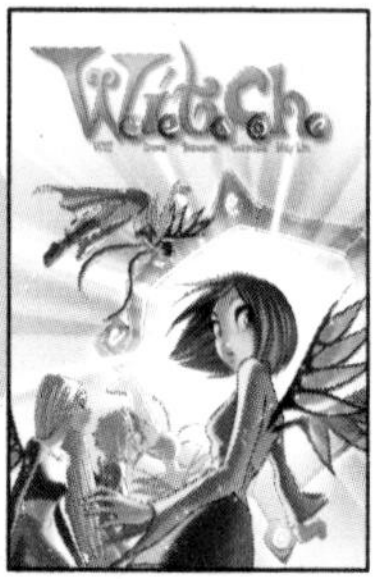
W.i.t.c.h.
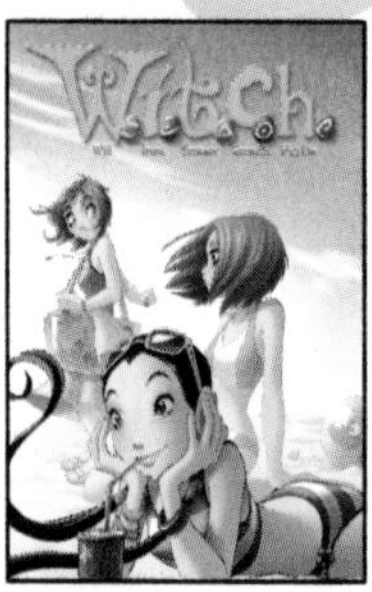
W.i.t.c.h.
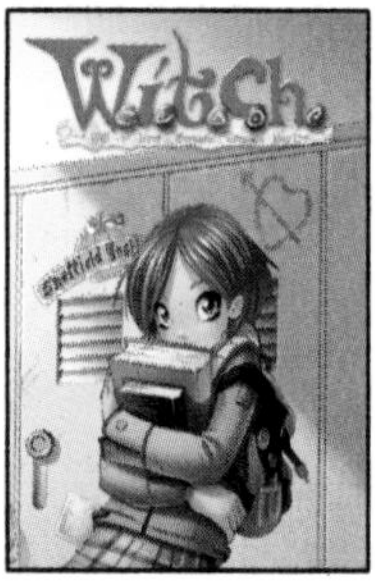
W.i.t.c.h.
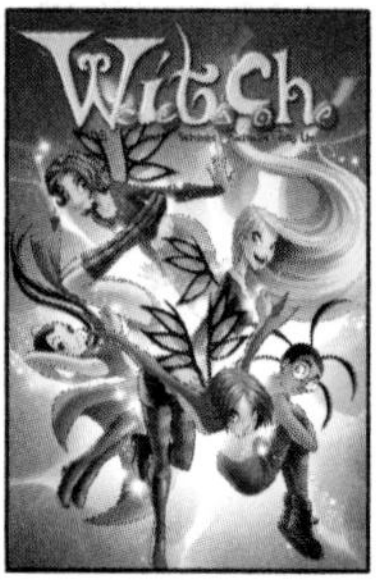
W.i.t.c.h.
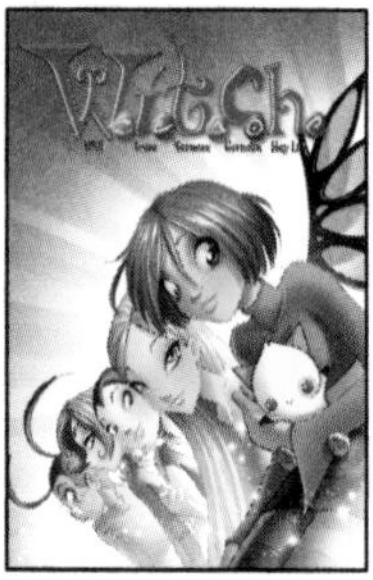
W.i.t.c.h.
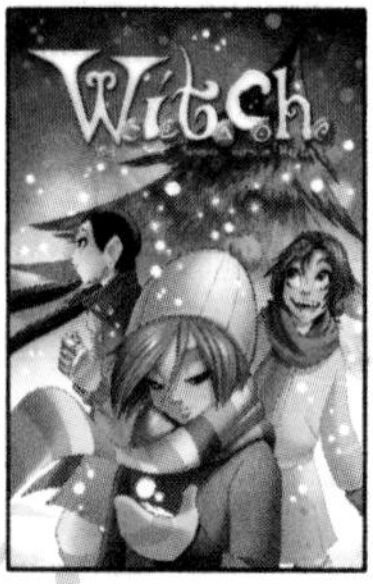
W.i.t.c.h.
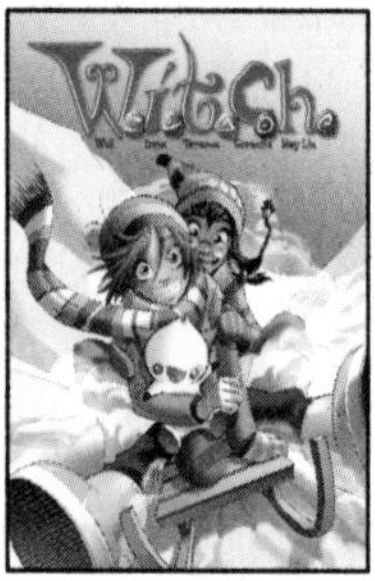
W.i.t.c.h.
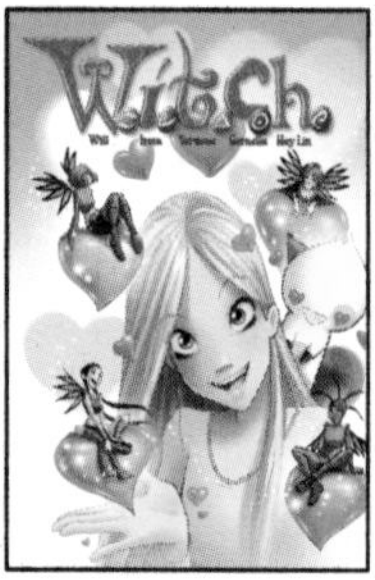
W.i.t.c.h.
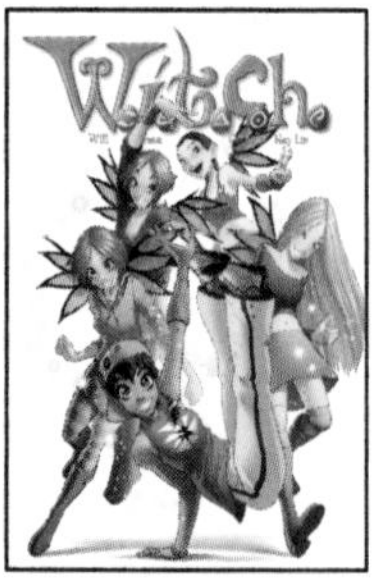
W.i.t.c.h.
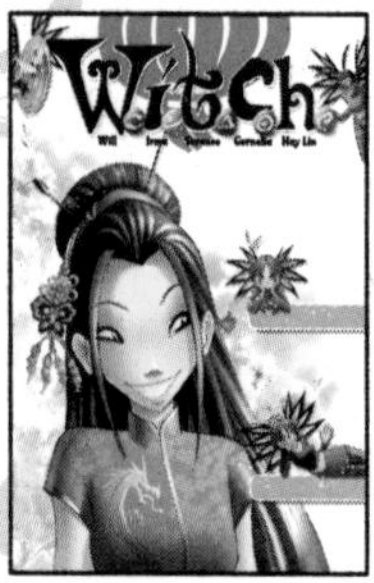
W.i.t.c.h.
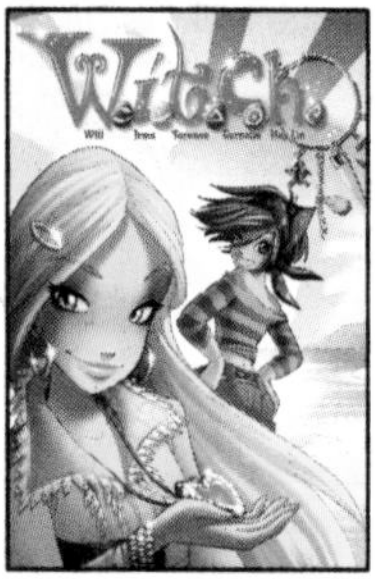
W.i.t.c.h.
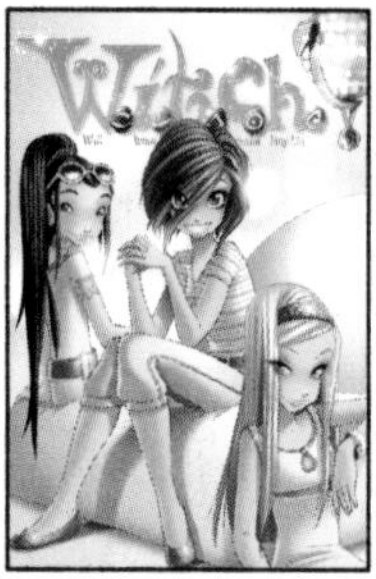
W.i.t.c.h.
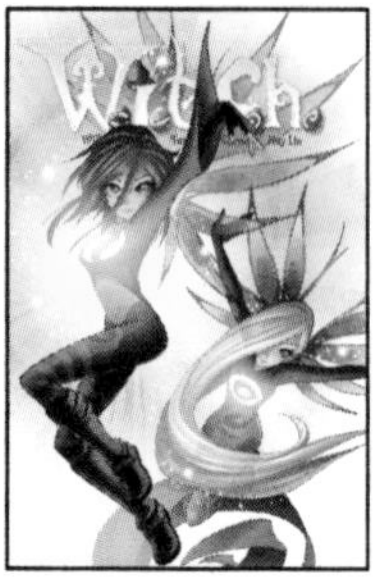
W.i.t.c.h.
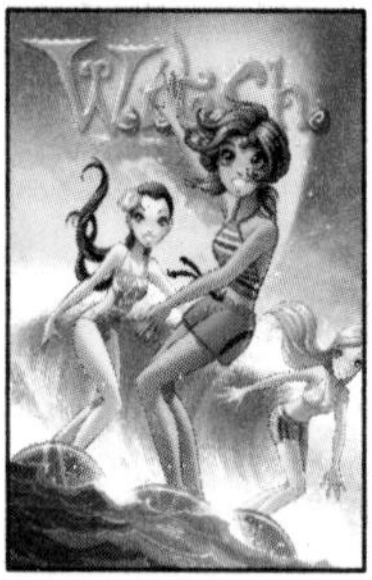
W.i.t.c.h.
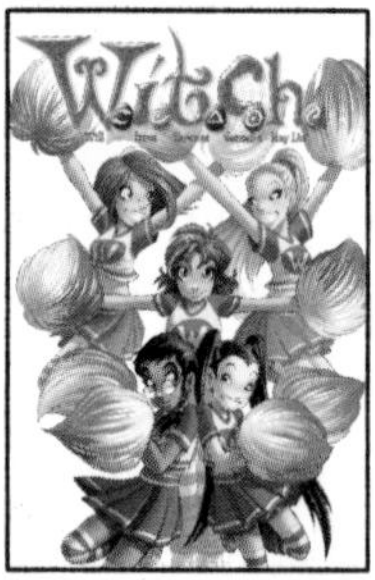
W.i.t.c.h.
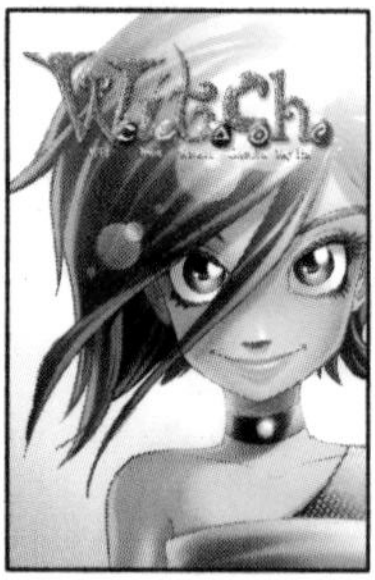
W.i.t.c.h.
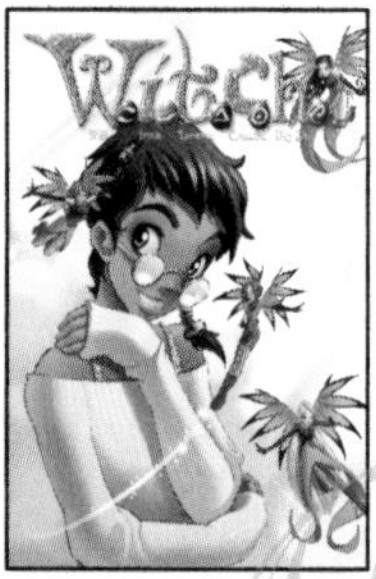
W.i.t.c.h.

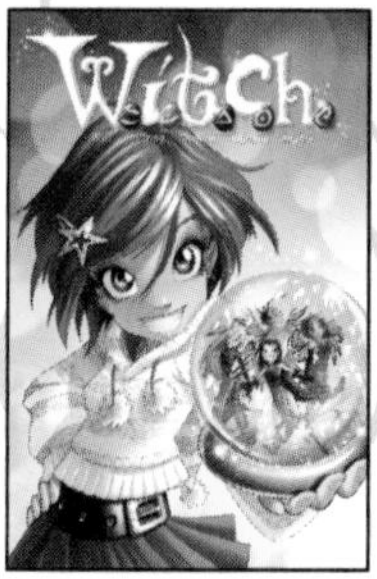
W.i.t.c.h.
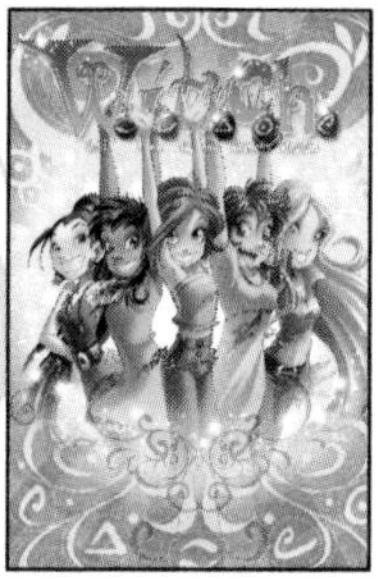
W.i.t.c.h.
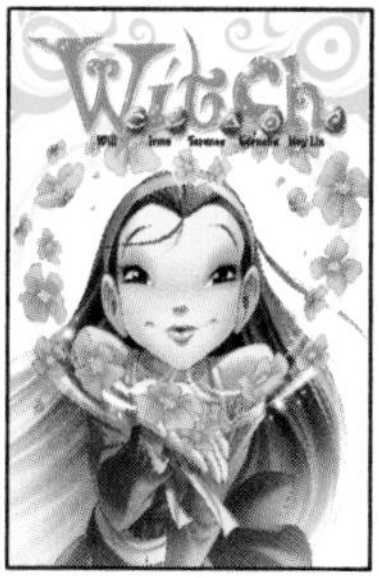
W.i.t.c.h.
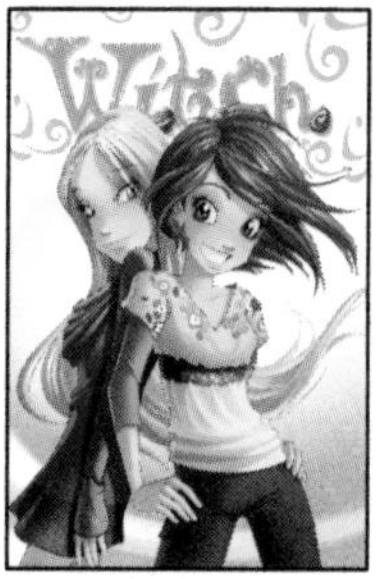
W.i.t.c.h.
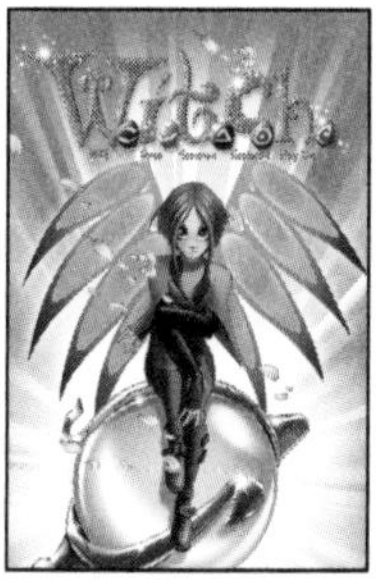
W.i.t.c.h.
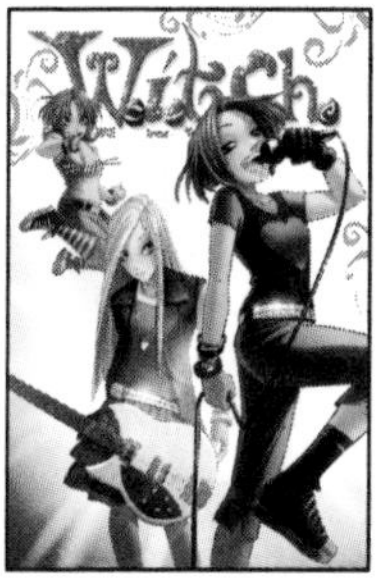
W.i.t.c.h.
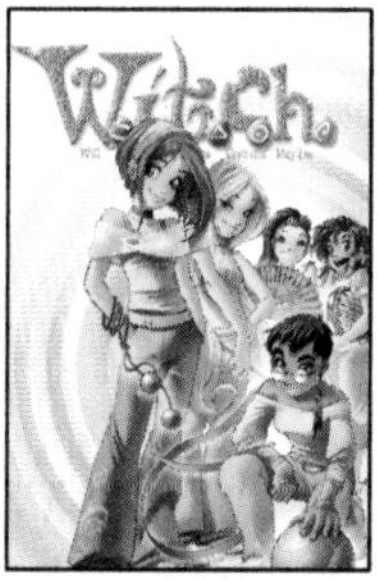
W.i.t.c.h.
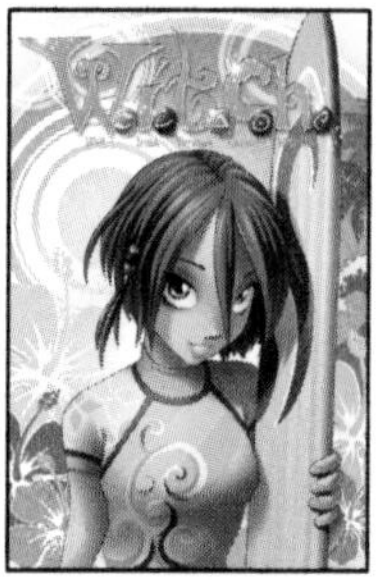
W.i.t.c.h.
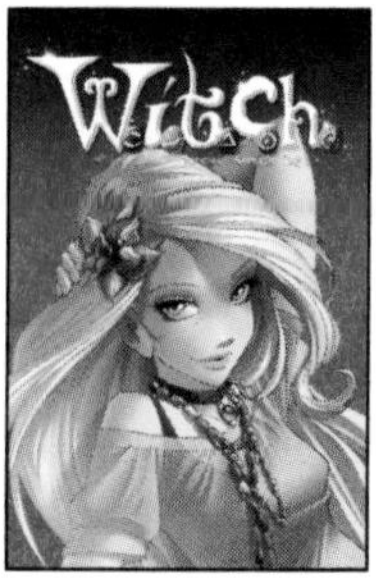
W.i.t.c.h.
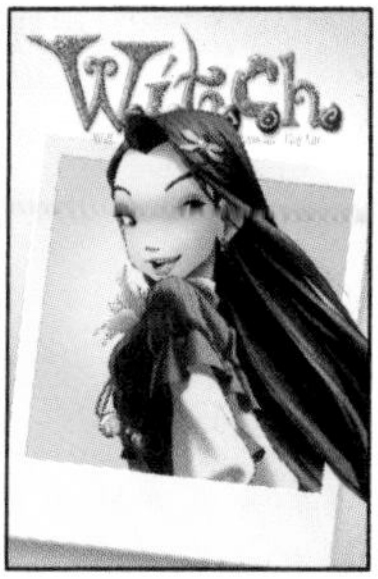
W.i.t.c.h.
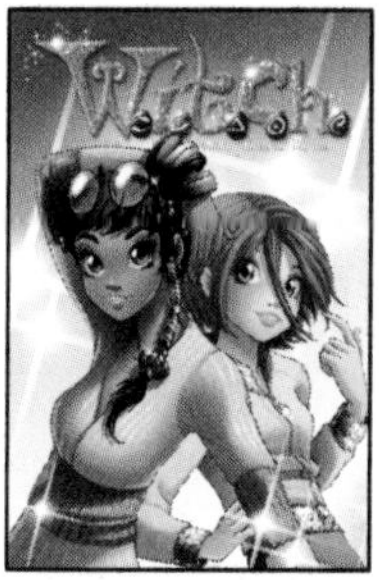
W.i.t.c.h.
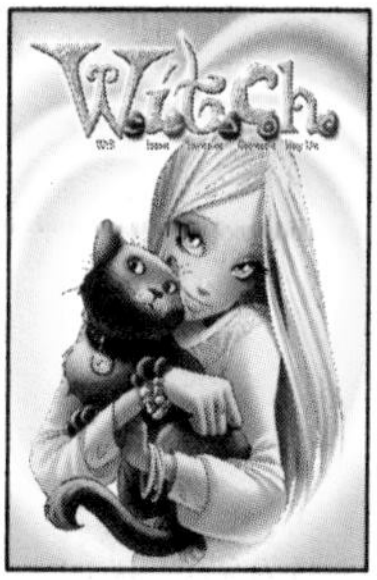
W.i.t.c.h.
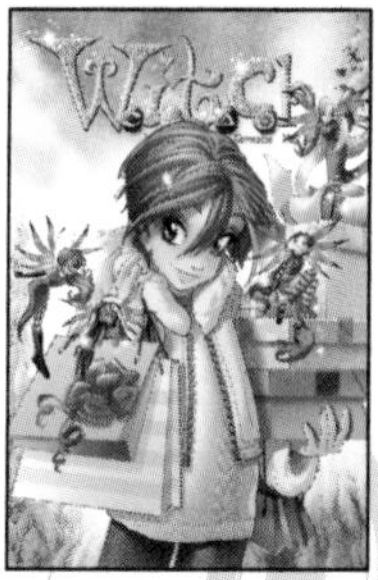
W.i.t.c.h.
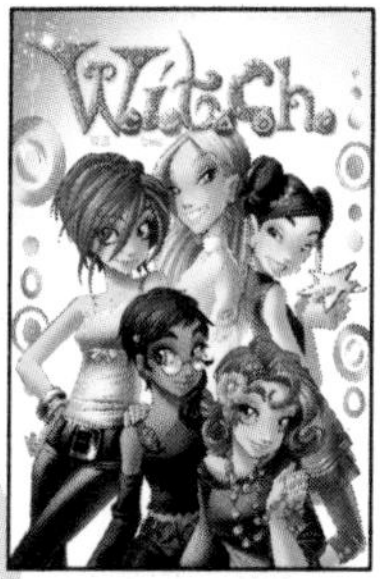
W.i.t.c.h.
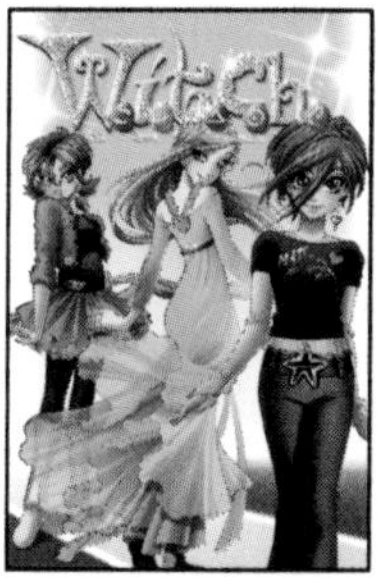
W.i.t.c.h.
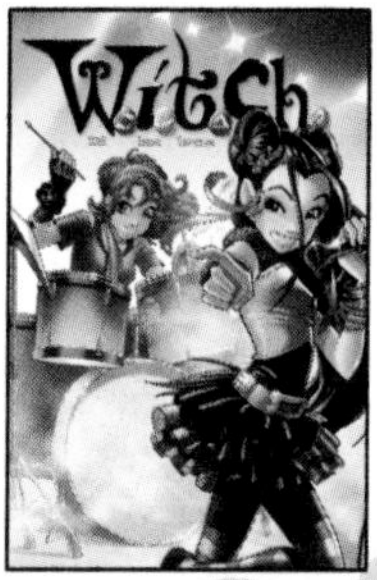
W.i.t.c.h.
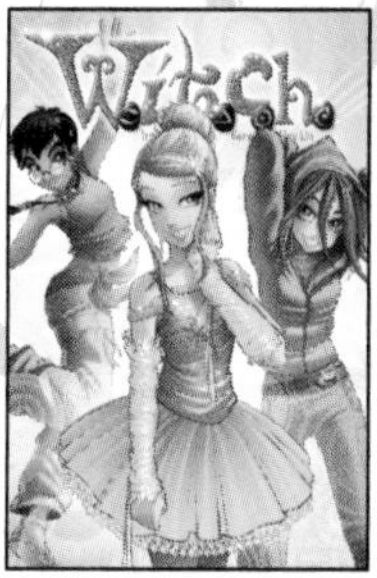
W.i.t.c.h.
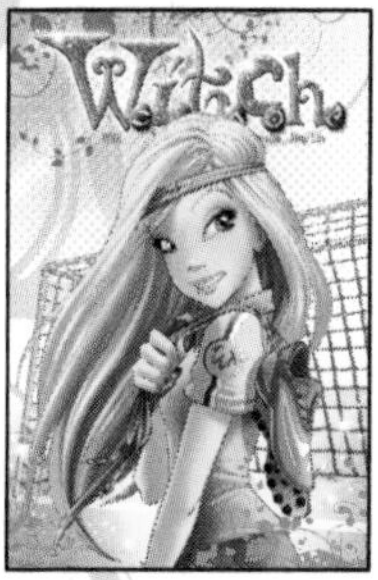
W.i.t.c.h.
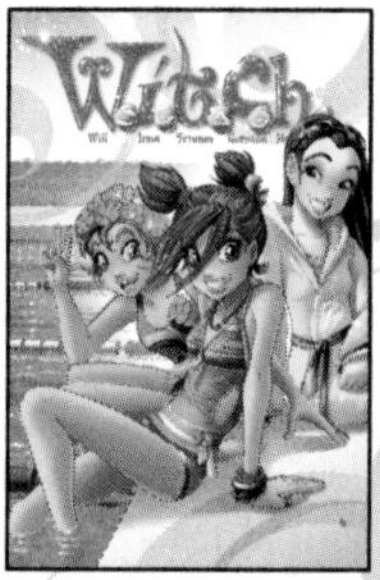
W.i.t.c.h.
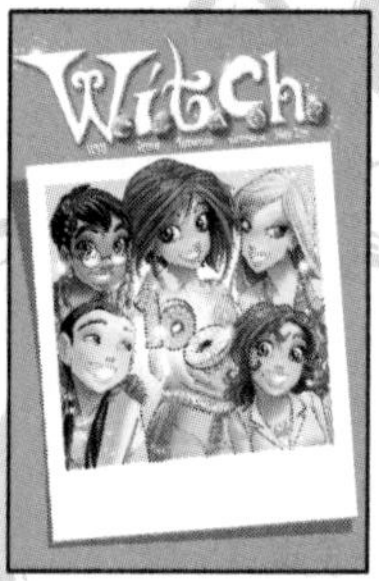
W.i.t.c.h.

W.i.t.c.h

Will Irma Taranee Cornelia Hay Lin

Part IX. 100% W.I.T.C.H. • Volume 1

Series Created by Elisabetta Gnone
Comic Art Direction: Alessandro Barbucci, Barbara Canepa

W.I.T.C.H.: The Graphic Novel,
Part IX: 100% W.I.T.C.H.
© Disney Enterprises, Inc.

English translation © 2021 by Disney Enterprises, Inc.

JY
150 West 30th Street, 19th Floor
New York, NY 10001

Visit us at jyforkids.com
facebook.com/jyforkids
twitter.com/jyforkids
jyforkids.tumblr.com
instagram.com/jyforkids

First JY Edition: October 2021

JY is an imprint of Yen Press, LLC.
The JY name and logo are trademarks of Yen Press, LLC.

The publisher is not responsible for websites (or their content) that are not owned by the publisher.

Library of Congress Control Number: 2017950917

ISBNs:
978-1-9753-2321-9 (paperback)
978-1-9753-2322-6 (ebook)

10 9 8 7 6 5 4 3 2 1

LSC-C

Printed in the United States of America

Cover Art by Giada Perissinotto
Colors by Andrea Cagol

Translation by Linda Ghio and
Stephanie Dagg at Editing Zone
Lettering by Katie Blakeslee

100% W.I.T.C.H.

Concept and Script by Augusto Macchetto
Layout and Pencils by Giada Perissinotto
Inks by Marina Baggio and Roberta Zanotta
Color Direction by Francesco Legramandi

THE NASCENT STAR

Concept and Script by Bruno Enna
Layout by Elisabetta Melaranci
Pencils by Daniela Vetro
Inks by Marina Baggio and Roberta Zanotta
Color Direction by Francesco Legramandi

THE FIRST DAY

Concept and Script by Augusto Macchetto
Layout by Antonello Dalena
Pencils by Manuela Razzi
Inks by Marina Baggio and Roberta Zanotta
Color Direction by Francesco Legramandi

THE ONE YOU'RE NOT

Concept and Script by Alessandro Ferrari
Layout by Paolo Campinoti
Pencils by Frederica Salfo
Inks by Marina Baggio and Roberta Zanotta
Color Direction by Francesco Legramandi

ANOTHER WORLD

Concept and Script by Bruno Enna
Layout by Alberto Zanon
Pencils by Davide Baldoni
Inks by Marina Baggio and Roberta Zanotta
Color Direction by Francesco Legramandi